I0708187

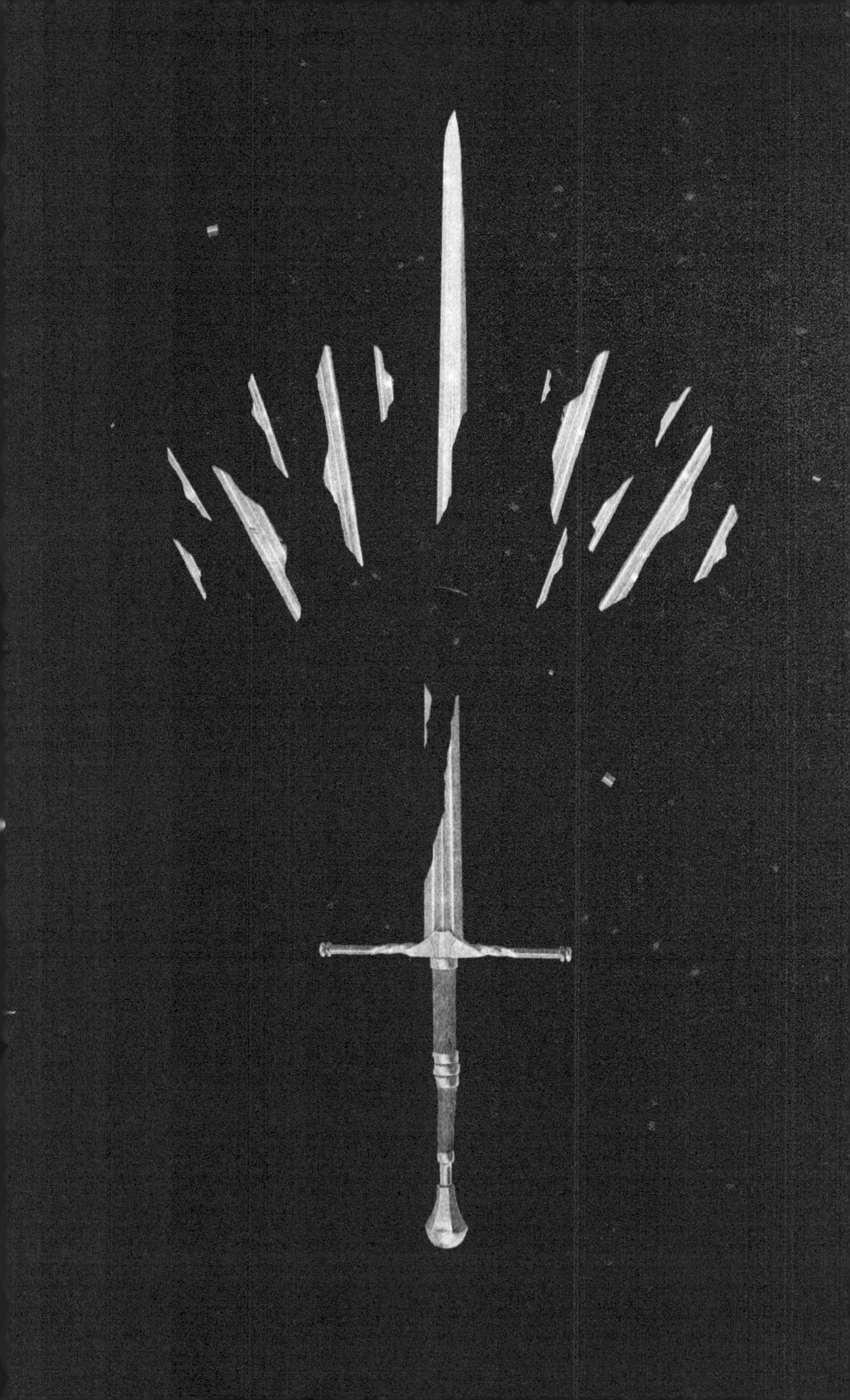

THE BADLANDER

TOM GOLDEN

This is a work of fiction. Names, characters, places, and incidents either are the product of the author's imagination or are used fictitiously. Any resemblance to actual persons, living or dead, events, or locales is entirely coincidental.

Copyright © 2023 by Tom Golden

All rights reserved. No part of this book may be reproduced or used in any manner without written permission of the copyright owner except for the use of quotations in a book review.

First paperback edition 2023

Book design, illustrations, and map by Natalia Junqueira

ISBN: 979-8-9885421-0-0 (paperback)

ISBN: 979-8-9885421-1-7 (ebook)

Library of Congress Control Number: 2023911597

Published by Thomas Golden

Waterford, Michigan

THE
BADLANDER

THE COLLECTED REALMS OF
VINGALLEA
THE GATE OF PARA
THU
MOORS
URGUKORGE
ASHLANDS
NAFFABYIN'S MONASTERY
THE EINMAZ MOUNTAINS
THE EINFALLEN RIVER
THE IMPERIAL HIGHWAY
THE NIGHTLANDS
DA
BARREN VALLEY
N
BLIGHTED FOREST
THE IMPERIAL HIGHWAY
VIN-SADAVAT
CRATER OF THE SOUTH

THE ISLE
OF
CREATION
JRM
THE VIOLET
PALACE
KAFARBJORN
HARBOR
THE
DAYLANDS
THE
STAGNANT SEA
LANDS
GANACHIMS'S
INFLUENCE
DABOR
BADLANDS
THE GATES
OF
PUNISHMENT
THE
STERLING
BRIDGE
MUD
FLATS
DRIED
BASIN
GANACHIM'S
TEMPLE
REALM
BLAST PLAIN
NW
NE
W
E
SW
SE
S

PART I:
SUMMONINGS

CHAPTER 1

The view through the warped ancient glass of the tower window was just as it always was. Gray, pre-dawn light slid off beyond the walls of the last city and into the darkness of the west's perpetual night.

Seated at his weathered wooden desk, Cyprian Fontaine gazed absentmindedly into the gloom. He slowly drummed his fingers on the rough edge of the desktop, across splintering wood as old as the drafty window. His eyes lingered on the horizon, and familiar thoughts began to coalesce.

He enjoyed the relative darkness of his quarters, so different from the Office of the Curator. That chamber, previously held by his father, his father's father, and every Fontaine before that, leading all the way back to the re-founding of the city, was bathed in the constant dawn that kissed the eastern walls. It was too bright for him. Here, he could remain in dark, quiet privacy.

That privacy was soon interrupted by two short raps on the chamber door. Reluctantly, Cyprian turned from the window.

"Enter."

The door creaked open and Cyprian's assistant, white-haired and crooked, poked his head inside. Well-aware of Cyprian's penchant for quiet, Jotun Berg tried to be respectful of Cyprian's moods, even if he did find them tiresome at times.

"My lord," Jotun said, "there's a royal guardsman here to see you."

Jotun raised his eyebrows quizzically, as if expecting an explanation as to what Cyprian could have done to catch the attention of a royal guardsman. Cyprian did not have an answer, and felt a small knot of apprehension move within him.

"That's strange," he responded. "Did they say what they wanted?

"I'm afraid not. I was kind of hoping that you would tell me. Should I be concerned?"

Cyprian bristled slightly at Jotun's paternal tone—one that he'd heard many times throughout his life.

"I'm quite sure that you'll be fine, at any rate. Send them up."

"Yes, my lord."

Jotun shut the heavy door behind him, and Cyprian turned back toward the window. A royal guardsman had no business with him. Unless, of course, they were just being used as a messenger by his esteemed master, the Curator of the Hall of Antiquities.

The thought intensified the knot in his guts. He was satisfied that Phir-Ramarian remained at the Vinecrown Keep, that the curator office he never should have been given, in all its sunlit brilliance, remained vacant. The less contact Cyprian had with his pompous cousin, the better. If he was sending some lackey to relay a message, it certainly would not be a good one.

Possible scenarios turned through Cyprian's mind, finally interrupted by another series of knocks at the door, these ones rapid and harsh.

"Enter," he said again, with some trepidation.

The door swung open and a man in a formal burgundy uniform strode confidently inside. Cyprian spied Jotun looking in apologetically through the doorway. Cyprian nodded at him, and Jotun quietly left the office, shutting the door behind him.

"Officer, please take a seat," Cyprian said, motioning at the creaky wooden chair on the other side of his desk.

The guardsman looked at the chair with some derision. He brushed off the seat. "Captain," he said as he swept his velvet cloak aside and sat down.

"I'm sorry?"

"My rank is captain. I do not fault you for being unaware of the meanings of my insignia, but I would also appreciate being titled properly. I expect that you understand that." He paused for a moment. "My lord."

Cyprian smiled humorlessly. "Of course, Captain …"

"Mather. Captain Gorlin Mather."

"Of course, Captain Mather. Of what service can I be to the Crown?"

Mather leaned back in his chair and inhaled deeply through his nose. He folded his large hands on the rise of his belly and fixed his deep-set eyes on Cyprian. "I've been asked to personally escort you to an audience with the king. His Majesty has an important matter that he believes you to be an essential part of. Beyond that basic explanation, I can provide nothing further. He wants to speak with you now."

Cyprian was shocked and flooded with dread. He had not had a personal meeting with his uncle since his father's symbolic shepherding. Almost ten long-cycles had passed, and in the intervening time, he'd heard increasingly little from the king. His mother, who'd never recovered from his father's disappearance, had remained as the last connection. When she passed, the king had not even attended her shepherding.

Cyprian's only interaction with his esteemed relatives since had been with Phir-Ramarian. Now, suddenly, he was being summoned.

"I imagine that this is less of a request and more of a command?" Cyprian asked with resignation.

"That's correct." Without waiting for an answer, Mather stood up and motioned toward the door, never breaking eye contact with Cyprian.

Cyprian stared back at the impassive face. He rubbed a hand across his stubbled cheek and slowly stood up, scooting his chair in.

"Well, let's go, then."

•   •   •

The two men left the Hall of Antiquities together, with Cyprian feeling like Mather's prisoner. As they passed through the main foyer, Cyprian had observed Jotun peering from a darkened doorway. Faye had been standing behind him, watching Cyprian pass, her eyes squinted in unease. He'd smiled weakly at his wife, hoping that it was some reassurance. Faye was well aware of the tension between Cyprian and his royal kin, and was clearly disturbed by his being summoned.

Stepping out into the permanent dawn, Cyprian was greeted by the familiar light of a sun that had been riveted above the eastern horizon since long before anyone alive was born. Mather led him sunward on the Mercantile Causeway, flanked on all sides by market stalls. The normal bustle of the street was unusually subdued. The most recent harvest had been a weaker one, and many of the stalls were shuttered.

A grimy-looking peddler seemed to consider approaching them but, after receiving a withering gaze from Mather, quickly moved on to a small group of shepherds. The shepherds, clearly disinterested, brushed past the man without uttering a word. Cyprian briefly wondered if they were on their way to a shepherding, or if they had recently dispatched a shade. Either way, he doubted that their grim business would allow much time for idle wandering through the market.

Two city guardsmen on patrol snapped off salutes to Mather as they walked by. Mather only nodded in return, his dark eyes fixed on the four massive spires of the Vinecrown Keep, which stretched above the squat and dull dwellings beyond the market. The heights reached by the spires of the keep were only rivaled by the tremendous size of the gabled roof between them.

Cyprian had to admire the architectural prowess of the old kingdom. The keep, even after many long-cycles of neglect, still mostly retained its original majesty. The vines that crawled up the walls had slowly started to wither, and the polished white gleam had become discolored with grime, but the elegance of the original structure was still very much intact. As with the Hall of Antiquities, the forgotten secrets of the old kingdom's builders had produced a lasting legacy that outlived most of the practical, utilitarian structures built since.

They continued on, weaving their way through the narrow alleys that passed between the bland, stone homes of the lower classes. No doubt, they were traveling a shortcut that Mather's experience as a guardsman had taught him. Cyprian attempted to engage Mather in conversation, but the stoic guardsman would not bite.

When they emerged back onto the main causeway, they had reached the encircling wall that protected the castle grounds. Mather, never breaking stride, led Cyprian to an arched gateway and two bored-looking royal guardsmen. They snapped to attention at Mather's unexpected approach.

"Captain," they said in unison, saluting.

Mather's stony face betrayed just the slightest irritation at his subordinates being caught off guard. He waved them out of his way and they scurried to the gates, each pulling one open. As if chained to him, Cyprian followed the captain inside.

Like the castle itself, the beauty with which the grounds were sculpted was undeniable, if suffering from a lack of upkeep. Opulent fountains languished dryly; brown weeds sprang up through the cobblestone; an enormous marble statue of the city's first sitting Vingallean monarch, Phan-Casmia, the Preserver, had partially sunk into the earth of the courtyard. At some point, the statue's right hand, reaching toward the heavens, (and a glorious future, no doubt) had been broken off and lost. Still, despite the blemishes, Cyprian found himself enchanted by the architecture of the old world.

As the steward of the Hall of Antiquities, entrusted with the city's treasury of precious artifacts, Cyprian had a keen eye for items of the past. In them, he could see what the world had been like before the war—an age when the Fontaine family had been the lords of the city, before they were relegated to being curators.

Now, even that title had been stripped away. Old resentment simmered within Cyprian's veins.

They entered the darkness of the keep, passing through an ornate doorway and into the coolness of the foyer. Several nobles of the royal court milled about inside, their shadows cast on the stone walls by the flickering candlelight as they spoke in hushed tones, then laughed at a mumbled joke. Servants walked silently amongst them, refilling goblets.

Cyprian did not know what function these sycophants performed in a city where every person needed to fulfill a vital role. Somehow, thanks to their ancient lineage, they had secured themselves comfortable positions within the keep. He knew that his lineage had afforded him certain benefits as well, but still considered his own situation to be different. He was still driven by actual purpose, and had not slid into aristocratic obsolescence.

Mather seemed to pay the nobles no mind, and the two men continued up the grand staircase and into the massive throne room, which easily comprised the majority of the castle. The beams of the high ceiling were barely visible in the gloom. Four enormous hearths, one set on each wall, encircled the hall, the fires within smoldering sullenly. There was no one else in the room.

"Wait here. I'll let His Majesty know that you've arrived," Mather said in the direct tone of an order. Cyprian nodded his understanding and watched as Mather stalked away into the shadows on the far side of the room.

He stood in the spot where Mather had left him for only a moment. Being alone now, he began to circle the room slowly, gazing at the countless relics within.

Worn tapestries hung flaccidly from the walls, their images of past glories nearly faded away. Long rows of tables adorned with tarnished dinnerware stretched the length of the room, though the king had not hosted a formal feast in his lifetime. A massive, ornate clock bearing the original markings of the sun-based time system ticked away. The figures etched on the face, the forgotten hours of the former day and night, had long ago been replaced by the terminology of cycles, a basic system to keep time in a world that never changed. The Crown's timekeepers continued to log the passage of time based on the old ways, with clocks such as this one, or using handheld chronometers. The long-term accuracy of these antiques, which required winding and maintenance, was dubious at best. It was impossible to know how inaccurate the counting of the long ages had become, or exactly how long ago the sun had stopped, though the detailed records of the royal genealogies helped form an estimate.

All of these items, these memories of a more glorious age, should have been in the Hall of Antiquities, where they could have been properly cared for. Instead, they remained scattered about the throne; sad, moldering reminders of what had been.

Reaching the far end of the hall, beyond the raised platform of the marble throne, Cyprian stood before the ancient remains of the legendary God of Punishment, Aedesda. Fixed to the stone wall with metal hooks and wires, the immense skeleton was a ghoulish display of the king's triumph.

Truly, the triumph belonged to Cyprian's father, and once again, the skeleton should have been preserved at the Hall of Antiquities. Cyprian remembered when his father had returned from his expedition and presented the desiccated remains to the king. The body had been mummified and was identifiable; tissue had still clung to it.

Now, nineteen long-cycles of being displayed like a hunting trophy had turned the last tissue into dust. The misshapen, brittle bones were all that remained.

Easily twice the height of a normal man, the barbed and jagged skeleton was a horror to behold. The empty eye sockets leered at Cyprian above a mouth of jagged teeth. Curved horns stretched from the temples of the skull. Fixed above it was the ebony halo that had once hung suspended above the god's head. Unlike the body, the halo was as polished as it certainly had been in the age when the gods had walked the earth.

Staring at the halo, Cyprian shuddered. He could not imagine what it must have felt like for his father to discover such a thing. The fear and wonder it must have evoked. The knowledge and glory provided by a find like that was incalculable. It was no wonder that he'd gone out again.

Cyprian considered his own paltry finds in the relatively benign areas surrounding the city and felt embarrassment. His self-pity was interrupted by the sound of footsteps echoing through the hall, and he turned to see several royal guardsmen, including Mather, entering the throne room.

They assembled in an obviously practiced way, and one stepped forward. He was dressed in a shabby red uniform adorned with faded yellow epaulets and carried a tarnished horn. He pressed it to his lips and let loose a long, tone-deaf honk. The musical skill once possessed by the king's heralds was as lost to the ages as the architectural prowess of the old kingdom's builders.

"Announcing! Phar-Mindorius, Lord of the City of Nordabor and High King of the Collected Realms of Vingallea!" the herald shouted unnecessarily to his gathered comrades and Cyprian. He stepped aside flamboyantly, and the rest followed suit, parting for the entrance of their king. Mather looked impatient and irritated by the pointless, but traditional, introduction.

Phar-Mindorius, threadbare royal raiment draped over his thin body, made his way slowly by the guardsmen. He gingerly ascended the marble steps, then lowered himself onto his throne with a sigh.

"Thank you. You are dismissed," he said, not unkindly. "I wish to speak with Lord Fontaine in private."

"Yes, sire, of course," Mather responded. He looked at the other men and gestured swiftly for them to clear the room. The guardsmen filed out efficiently, leaving the king alone with his sister-son.

Cyprian noted with some sadness that the stresses of the crown had made his uncle old before his time. He sat hunched slightly forward, as though an invisible weight rested upon his shoulders. The robes he wore, passed down through generations of monarchs, were frayed and worn, and matched his matted gray beard and the unkempt, black eyebrows that twitched upon his deeply creased forehead. Above that, the Skullcap Crown of Phan-Ellara rested upon his head. The ancient bone fragment, recovered from Vingallea's greatest queen, was encrusted with priceless gems, and was the only part of Phar-Mindorius's appearance that accurately reflected the power he wielded.

The king smiled gently at Cyprian, who gave a small, curt bow in response.

"Cyprian. It's been too long," he said warmly.

"That it has, Your Majesty. How can I be of service to you?"

"There's no need for such formality with me. We are kin. I know that our relation has been a distant one for these past long-cycles, and I take responsibility for that. Rorik, bless him, left me in a very tough position. Left us all, really. And what he put your mother through …" Phar-Mindorius trailed off, seeing Cyprian's hostile gaze looking through him. "I don't mean to be opening any old wounds. I just wish to clear the air."

"My father did not choose to fail you, my mother, or the kingdom. For all we know, he and his men are still out there, completing your orders. We have no proof otherwise. You wouldn't allow any search parties beyond the edge of the forest, even after they found his cache."

Phar-Mindorius looked at him with a mix of sadness and pity that made Cyprian feel like a child again. It infuriated him, but he bit back on his anger.

"It's been nineteen long-cycles. All reports say it is a hostile and unforgiving world out there." The king shook his head sadly. "I am not hopeful. I'm sorry, Cyprian. Your father was dear to me as well."

Cyprian turned away and stared intently into one of the sputtering fires, saying nothing.

"Your father's expedition is part of why I've summoned you here," Phar-Mindorius said. The words caught Cyprian's attention, as he must have known they would.

"I'm listening," Cyprian replied cautiously.

"Rorik's search for a better land, in the traditional sense of such a thing, was misguided. I am as much to blame as anyone for that. We were focusing on finding something akin to Nordabor, while misunderstanding the opportunity before us. Some new information has come to light that has changed that. Knowledge of antiquities—the knowledge held by you—is now of the utmost importance. I need your help."

Cyprian assumed that this last statement was meant to instill awe in him; being needed by the king should seem like a great honor. He said nothing and waited for Phar-Mindorius to continue. A look of frustration passed over the king's face.

"When your father left, many did not understand the full nature of his expedition. That was by design. We've reached a point where I do not feel it's necessary to hold anything back. The city is beginning to fail; do you deny it?"

Sudden urgency had seized Phar-Mindorius's voice, adding an unsettling tremor. It sounded like fear.

Cyprian considered what he said. Things in Nordabor had been declining within recent memory—lower crop yields, more illness, unrest in the lower classes. It was subtle, but undeniable. He'd lived long enough to remember when things had been better.

"No, I don't deny it. I see what you're talking about," Cyprian said slowly. "Nordabor is finally following the rest of the world. It's inexplicable that it's taken this long."

"But it's not. There is a reason that the city has survived. It has thrived for generations. Only now does it begin to fail, and the process is accelerating. Come."

With some effort, the king stood up. "I have something to show you."

He descended the marble steps and walked toward the rear door. Despite his misgivings, Cyprian's curiosity was growing. He followed.

"You know much of the history and lore of our land. I know this," Phar-Mindorius said without looking back. "You know of the war between the old ones that broke this world. That froze the sun in the sky and killed the wind. The traitorous brothers and their disastrous rebellion. The loss of the old ones' true divinity."

"Of course," Cyprian responded. The conversation had turned firmly into his wheelhouse, and he was a bit surprised at the king's knowledge of specifics. It had taken him many readings of archaic tomes to glean details like that. He'd never seen the king in the Hall of Antiquities, and Phar-Mindorius certainly hadn't learned anything from his son.

"Not all of the old ones met the same fate as our friend Aedesda back there. Rather, they all faded into obscurity after the Father-God's murder. Even the false god, the usurper Ulesreto, was able to disappear while his brother lay dead in the sand. They all slid into myth, as you know well."

As Phar-Mindorius spoke, they wound their way through narrow, unfamiliar, soot-walled passages, barely lit by low-burning torches.

"That is, until your father dug out Aedesda's remains. Until he found the Gates of Punishment. Then, old legend became fact." He stopped abruptly and turned around, facing Cyprian. "But the royal lineage of this realm has known for certain the existence of the old ones since antiquity. We've always known they were flesh and blood, just as we are. Let me show you how."

Phar-Mindorius whirled around and continued down the passage, moving faster than Cyprian would have believed was possible. Cyprian remained fixed for a moment, processing what the king had just said. Somehow, he and his predecessors had known more about the old ones than the curators.

"Wait," he said, half jogging to catch up. Before he could continue his line of questioning, Phar-Mindorius stopped in front of a black door. Cold air poured into the passage through the cracks in the damp wood.

"This hold has been able to survive for so long because of a stroke of luck, Cyprian. When even Vin-Sadavat fell, Nordabor survived. Because of that, Vingallea lives on. Phan-Casmia was a refugee from the capital when she arrived here, when your ancestor, Thandale, abdicated the throne for her. Together, our family has kept this city alive."

He was speaking very quickly now, the words cascading out in an anxious monologue. Cyprian only stared back, transfixed.

"We will continue to keep this city alive. Once I show you this, you will know the full truth of our survival. I can then explain to you what we need to do next."

Phar-Mindorius pushed open the door, which opened into darkness. The sound of running water could be heard echoing out of the shadows. He lifted a torch from a sconce on the wall and stepped inside.

"Be careful on the steps; they can be slick."

Cyprian followed him into the darkness, and the two descended a slippery, uneven, stone staircase. Upon reaching the bottom, the sound of the water had grown to a low roar, and was accompanied by a strong, earthy stench of decay. Phar-Mindorius dipped the torch into a large basin, igniting the material within and filling the grotto with flickering firelight. Cyprian gasped.

Suspended from heavy chains, partially submerged in the rushing waters, was a humanoid figure as large, and nearly as thin, as the skeleton of Aedesda. Its head hung down, facing toward the water, and its long arms were pulled up and back by the chains. Fungal growths covered the moldering-bark texture of its skin. Wet black hair, entangled with putrid ivy, hung down in filthy streaks from its head. Beyond some slight swaying due to the pull of the water, it was still. Above the limp head, a simple halo of rotten wood hung unnaturally, perfectly still in the cold air.

Cyprian had studied much of the old world, and had pored over the information available regarding the old ones especially. He knew, based on the recorded testimonials of veterans who had survived the war between the gods, that the Father-God, Alminnian, had been killed by the rebels. He knew that at some point, the rebel god Aedesda had been killed as well, as evidenced by the skeleton displayed upstairs. As for the others, he'd assumed that they'd all met some end at one point or another, as no evidence of them remained. He never imagined that he would come face-to-face with a living specimen. Assuming the still form in front of him was still alive.

"She's still alive. Barely," Phar-Mindorius said, as if he'd been reading Cyprian's thoughts.

"This is an old one," Cyprian said, in awe.

"Indeed. She was known as Ganachim, revered as the God of the Earth. It's because of her that Nordabor has survived while everything else has gone to ruin."

Cyprian looked at the languishing body of the god. The wooden halo. There could be no doubt.

"How did-why-does she speak?" he stammered eagerly, suddenly envisioning this god answering his questions about the past.

"She was found near the Einfallen's northern split not long after the war. She must have been injured in the conflict, and further weakened when the Father-God perished and took the world's divinity with him. The scouts who found her brought her back here in the time of Thandale. He saw to it that she was imprisoned down here. As far as I know, she's always been catatonic. She's never uttered a word."

Cyprian took a few tentative steps forward, crouching slightly to gaze up into the face of the limp head. Discomfort washed over him as he observed that her rheumy eyes were open. They stared into oblivion from her pallid, wet face with milky indifference. He stepped back, grimacing. His initial excitement waning, he now began to feel pity for the hanging body.

"Why is she here? And why the secrecy?" he asked.

"It is her power that fuels the natural world around the city. Her remaining divine influence has kept the surrounding forests lush, the crops growing and the livestock healthy," Phar-Mindorius explained. He gestured toward the running water. "She purifies the waters of the Einfallen that we drink. As for the secrecy, she is the only thing keeping this kingdom alive. It would be far too dangerous if her presence were known to all. It would invite anarchy. One disgruntled commoner, given the chance, could topple the kingdom—not to mention threats from outside the walls should word of her existence somehow pass beyond our realm. No, the fewer people who know the secret of our survival, the better. Thandale knew that, and the secrecy has been sustained ever since."

Considering his position in the royal family, Cyprian felt insulted at his exclusion from this knowledge. Phar-Mindorius seemed to sense it.

"I'm sorry, my boy. This knowledge is held only by the direct line of succession and the shepherds. It was never believed that there would be a need to tell anyone else. Thandale assumed that she would last forever; after all, the gods were believed to be naturally immortal. She required no food, no care—nothing—making her the ideal engine for our survival. I am unfortunate enough that, after the many illustrious lifetimes of my forefathers, it has fallen on me, in my time, to witness her final collapse."

Phar-Mindorius gazed at the captive god with sorrow, lost in thought. He suddenly seemed exhausted.

It occurred to Cyprian that Phar-Mindorius's cold disposition toward him during these past long-cycles had much to do with the heavy burden of this knowledge. He'd had all of his hopes pinned on Rorik Fontaine. Rorik's failure, his young son, and his grieving wife were constant reminders of the king's inability to save his entire realm from impending doom.

"Did my father know about this?" Cyprian asked, stirring the king from his thoughts.

"He knew only what was necessary for his expedition. He knew only what we sought, not why. I want to do things differently with you. I don't want to repeat my mistakes."

Cyprian processed this for a moment. His curiosity forced him to put aside his resentment.

"Why is she suddenly failing now?"

"It could be a number of things. Her captivity, coupled with her old wounds, could have led to a slow decline. She may have been failing for several long-cycles, and we're finally now seeing the effects. The forging of the shepherds' blades has appeared to weaken her as well."

"The shepherds' blades?" Cyprian asked, considering for the first time that the shepherds were also privy to this secret knowledge. He'd known that the elite shepherds, utilizing their hallowed blades, were the only ones capable of destroying a shade, of freeing a soul. He'd assumed that the esoteric order had some mysterious way of doing so, but he'd never imagined that it involved a captive god.

"Yes. Anointed in the blood of Ganachim. As the god of all natural life, whatever power moves through Ganachim's veins, the shades are repulsed by it. My ancestors, desperate to extend their own lives, ordered their private sect of healers to use Ganachim's blood as an elixir, thinking that her power might heal their ailments. It didn't, but though it failed to save them, those healers, who eventually became the shepherds, found that the elixir harmed any shades born from the dying subjects. Through experimentation, it was found that when a newly forged blade was quenched in her blood, the blade could actually destroy the shades. Unfortunately, the many long-cycles of bloodletting have taken a toll on her."

Cyprian struggled to organize his thoughts. He considered everything he'd just learned, and wondered why Phar-Mindorius was telling him now.

He stared again at Ganachim's massive body. From what he'd previously read, she had been a mighty force in the old days. It was hard to fathom that such a being's power could have waned so much. It was haunting to see a mythological figure laid low before him.

He turned away from her and faced the king. "You said you needed my help. You said you'd learned something new that changes things."

"That's right. Come. I tire easily now, and I wish to return to more comfortable chambers. I'll tell you the rest then."

. . .

They had returned through the maze of darkened passages and emerged in a small, warm chamber adjacent to the throne room. There, Phar-Mindorius had reclined on a burgundy couch and taken a moment to compose himself. The hike through the lower passages, and the revealing of Ganachim, had left him physically and mentally exhausted. Cyprian sat in an ornately carved wooden chair near the hearth and waited for the next revelation.

"When your father was sent forth, I knew that Ganachim was winding down," Phar-Mindorius explained finally, as if there had been no pause in the conversation. "I believed that our best chance was to find somewhere that still thrived, despite all evidence to the contrary. Rorik went first into the Daylands, but found them to be dry, inhospitable wastes. While there, of course, he found Aedesda. I should have been more focused on that, but I was too focused on the simple solution of finding a new land. If I had truly considered your father's find, I might not have sent him back out so swiftly, and so recklessly."

He gazed into the fire and shook his head slowly, ruminating on his regret. Cyprian said nothing, knowing that the king was speaking to himself as much as to him.

"You see, the real answer was what Rorik found with the body of Aedesda. I overlooked it at the time, but now I fully understand the significance." He broke his gaze from the fire and looked at Cyprian.

"Embedded in the chest of the corpse was the hilt of a broken sword."

Cyprian sat up in his chair and leaned forward. He'd never heard that a relic had been recovered with the body. It was yet another ancient treasure that had never made its way to the Hall of Antiquities, where it belonged.

"It just seemed like another useless relic. I didn't imagine it had any bearing on our situation. However, I was wrong."

"So what is the significance of this hilt?" Cyprian asked, running through his own knowledge to try and discern an answer.

"I have recently been approached by a wanderer from the outside. A badlander. The knowledge he imparted, combined with that already known to me, has made me realize that this hilt may be the key to our salvation. It may be the handle of the Scale of Judgment."

Cyprian was immediately incredulous. The Scale of Judgment, the rebellious god Ulesreto's fabled key to the Gates of Paradise, was said to have shattered when Alminnian died. Without the Father-God, Ulesreto was stripped of his divine power of judgment, and the gates had been permanently sealed shut.

"The Scale of Judgment? Even if it was, the blade is broken, and the gates are shut. You can't possibly be suggesting that entrance into Paradise is somehow possible. Who is this badlander peddling fairy tales to the king?"

Phar-Mindorius's countenance darkened.

"He is called Duncan Starkad, and what he speaks of is no fairy tale. You, of all people, should understand the accuracy of the recorded legends. Have you not just witnessed a living god with your own eyes? The surviving old ones understood that the blade could be reforged. Perhaps Ulesreto did not, as he left the hilt with the brother he presumably killed after their rebellion failed. But the others knew. Starkad, whom you've spoken ill of so glibly, has travelled farther than any living person in this city. His knowledge of the ancient exceeds your own. He has told me that the living old ones remain hidden in this world, hoarding the broken shards of the blade so that none might ever try to open the gates again. So that Vingallea, who followed the rebels into war, might be punished until we are no more."

"So, this wanderer—this Starkad," Cyprian said cautiously, not wishing to raise the king's ire further, "has somehow made it into the city just to convince you of the value of an artifact that only you knew you had?"

"He encountered your father in his travels. He may have been the last person to see the expedition before their disappearance. Trading goods and knowledge with Rorik, he learned of the purpose of the quest. Rorik was smart; he saw the value in the hilt before I did. I imagine he asked Starkad for any tidings related to the blade shards. Starkad was inspired to seek them out himself. Now he has come bearing knowledge of their locations."

The news of his father had blunted Cyprian's misgivings. If this badlander knew anything of his father's last whereabouts, he needed to speak with him. If he knew enough to seek out Nordabor with that sort of information, perhaps there was some legitimacy to it.

"What's in it for Starkad? Why does he come now bearing this important knowledge?"

"It took him many long-cycles to determine the locations of the old ones. He appears to be an adept explorer, and succeeded where we failed. Once he had the information we sought, he came here to offer it in exchange for title, land, and power. He is no altruistic man of Vingallea. He is of the wastes, but he seeks comfort and security. If he is right, and we're able to enter Paradise, he can have whatever he wants."

Entering Paradise seemed impossible. Myth and history intersected at one important point: the gates were sealed shut. The records of the final conflict, crumbling scrolls supposedly documenting eyewitness accounts, were often muddled and contradictory, but certain consistencies were clear—the final battle had resulted in the death of the Vingallean monarch, Phar-Karrian, the destruction of the blade, and the permanent closure of the gates.

Still, Cyprian allowed himself a slim hope. "So, I have to imagine that you want me to lead an expedition to these locations. You want me to somehow get these blade shards from living old ones."

"I want you as a *part* of this expedition. As the curator, my son will be leading it, but we both know your knowledge is invaluable."

The objection jumped from his mouth before he could stop it.

"You cannot put Phir-Ramarian in charge of an endeavor like this; not if you want my assistance," Cyprian spat. "My father, as curator, was entrusted with leading. It is my rightful place to lead this."

"Your rightful place," Phar-Mindorius said icily, "is to obey your king's orders. We are family, Cyprian, so I will forgive your speaking out of turn. Phir-Ramarian is my son, and I trust him completely. He is also your curator and your prince. You may lack faith in his abilities, but I do not. In an expedition of this magnitude, the steady hand of a sovereign is needed."

Cyprian considered walking away, letting his spite and resentment take the reins. However, the unpleasant prospect of being second to Phir-Ramarian on the expedition was not enough to deter his desire to leave the realm. To see the outside world and encounter the old ones. To seek the glory of obtaining the hidden blade shards and, possibly, bringing salvation to Nordabor. He knew that, resentment or not, he would be unable to resist the call of this journey.

"I understand," he said evenly, "and I accept the honor of joining this expedition."

Phar-Mindorius smiled. "I knew you would, my boy. Captain Mather will gather the other leaders. When we have our full company accounted for, you'll be summoned again. Starkad will outline the expedition's route. He'll be joining you as well, as a guide. You will, of course, be one of the high-ranking officials on the expedition. As such, you can assemble your own team of subordinates."

Faye and Jotun jumped to Cyprian's mind.

"I will await your further orders, then," Cyprian said, rising from his chair. He was now eager to speak with the badlander, to learn all he could of his father and of what awaited him beyond the city walls. He excused himself politely and began a slow walk back to the Hall of Antiquities. He had much to consider.

•   •   •

With Cyprian's involvement secured, Phar-Mindorius retired to his private chambers to await word that the others had been notified. An order from the king would ensure that those he felt were necessary for the completion of this endeavor would comply. Unlike his nephew, they would not all need to know the specifics. Nor would the less-inquiring minds bother asking.

Of course, the king had not been entirely truthful regarding who was aware of Ganachim's presence in the city. As the chief officer of the Royal Guard, Mather knew. Starkad, despite not saying so, appeared to have gleaned the source of Nordabor's survival. And most importantly, unbeknownst to anyone else in the kingdom, the hidden vizier knew.

He knew much.

Beyond the king's own chamber, only accessible to him, was the vizier's chamber. He went there now to update his advisor on the progress of their plan.

Phar-Mindorius had depended on the steadfast guidance of the vizier since he'd inherited the crown from his mother, Phan-Yavurnia. She had brought him to this undisclosed alcove near the end of her time and told him of the vizier's presence and purpose. How he had approached her in her youth, and provided her with a deep well of knowledge over the course of her reign. How the other advisors of the court had feared and distrusted the mysterious outsider. At his own urging, he had been secreted away in a hidden chamber.

In all of the king's long-cycles, he'd never broken bread with the nameless vizier. He'd never even seen him outside of his private residence. The king was no fool, and suspected that there was something unnatural, something divine, about the advisor.

In all of the records of the gods, nothing was said after the war concerning the ancient God of Knowledge, Nuroh. Phar-Mindorius suspected that Nuroh had made his way to Nordabor in order to continue his role of guiding mankind, despite their hatred and fear of the old ones.

He also believed that Nuroh was aware of his unspoken suspicions, but he had grown so dependent on the vizier's counsels that he dared not question him, lest he cease his assistance.

Whatever the source of his divine power, he was no mindless husk to be enslaved, like Ganachim. And it was his suggestion that had launched the first successful expedition. It was he who had determined that the blade could be reforged when Starkad came bearing knowledge of what the old ones were doing.

Phar-Mindorius entered the chamber quietly in order not to disturb the meditations of his oracle. Within the room, a narrow, elevated platform, surrounded by stone steps leading to the top, dominated the space. On top of the platform was a high-backed wooden chair that was invariably occupied by the vizier. Around the circumference of the round platform, a thin blue veil hung, partially concealing the frail, elderly vizier.

"Your Majesty," the vizier rasped in a near-whisper after a few moments of Phar-Mindorius waiting.

"I have spoken with my nephew, and he's agreed to help lead the expedition. He's rash, like his father was, but his knowledge of the old world is unmatched by all. Except, perhaps, for this Starkad."

"Very good, my lord," said the weak voice from the shadowed figure behind the veil. "No doubt, he will be an asset. As for Starkad, he knows much, but he is not of Vingallea. He cannot be relied upon if things become dangerous. He should be relegated to being only a guide. He will go whichever way the wind blows. Either way, I trust that your nephew, and your son, of course, will guide this expedition to completion."

Phar-Mindorius nodded in agreement. "The other leaders will be notified shortly. Very soon, we'll be ready for the expedition's departure. I can only hope it finds success."

"It is the hope for us all," the vizier replied.

The king remained there, standing before his unusual advisor awkwardly, unsure of what else to say. These meetings often left him with a feeling of inferiority, as if he were the servant.

"You are dismissed," Phar-Mindorius finally managed.

"Thank you, sire."

CHAPTER 2

The merchant was held in high esteem. Gathered around his death-bed were family, friends, and business partners who had nothing but the utmost respect for the man. Some of the gathered muttered prayers to the unknowable Void-God, some knelt, and others simply touched the dying man's body, intending to ease his pain. All parted when the shepherds entered the bedchamber.

High Shepherd Eldred Moore approached the dying man, flanked by his two apostles, Leon Galt and Micla Daeg.

"Please, give us some space. Thank you," Moore said in his well-bred baritone, bidding the people to back away further. He knew that it would be better if they were not present at all, but there were benefits to witnessing the birth of a shade, if such were to be the case now. Such trauma could foster a more righteous life, which would please the Void-God.

Moore took his customary place, standing solemnly at the head of the bed, while Galt and Daeg stood on either side, near the foot.

He looked down into the wide face of the dying merchant. The man's brow glistened with cold sweat. His eyes were shut, but appeared to be moving occasionally under the lids, and his breath came in shallow, ragged stutters. His illness had been unaffected by the best efforts of the healers. Whatever it was, Moore hoped it wasn't catching.

The small crowd had filed back as far as they could, with many exiting the room entirely. They had grown utterly silent.

Moore took a deep breath and closed his eyes for a moment, preparing for the ritual ahead. Ever since the rebellious brothers had abandoned their rightful duties of judgment and punishment and murdered the Father-God, the shades of the unworthy dead had been free to walk among the living, spreading disease and mayhem, terror and death. When the dying lacked the necessary piousness in the eyes of the Void-God, and prayers for them were not enough, it was his holy duty to destroy the shades they birthed and to shepherd their souls properly to the Void.

"Dead god, unjustly cast into the Void you now beckon from, we beseech you to guide this soul into your blessed embrace. We seek your favor in guiding"—Moore paused, realizing that he'd forgotten the man's name—"our beloved into your flock. Please spare him from the wretched fate of the unworthy. Please forgive him of his sins and unjust actions, and ensure that his soul is absorbed and absolved in your black nothingness."

Moore pressed his hand against the man's forehead and grimaced slightly at the clamminess there. He forged ahead with the prayer, feeling the eyes of his apostles on him. He knew that Daeg, who'd only recently completed his training at the Ivy Citadel, was enraptured by his oratory skill and devotional power. As for Galt, Moore suspected that he was hoping the fat merchant wouldn't produce a shade, if only for the time it would save them. The surly veteran preferred hastier ceremonies, such as those performed for dying folk of lesser social standing—ceremonies that were largely perfunctory. He failed to grasp that the more-renowned members of the citizenry expected a higher level of service.

The ritual continued, with Galt and Daeg bowing their heads, folding their hands, and repeating the prayers at the proper time. Moore eventually reached the conclusion and announced that they would continue in silent prayer until the suffering man finally succumbed to death. He was pleased that he had made it through the entire ritual. Often, the dying would pass before he was finished, interrupting the entire process. Now, they simply had to wait while the poor wretch choked out his last, jerking and spitting, clutching the sheets with plump, ring-laden fingers.

Moore glanced at Galt. He'd closed his eyes and was standing perfectly still, in what must have seemed like intense prayer to the onlookers. In actuality, he was nearly asleep when the merchant suddenly cried out.

His eyes had fluttered open, and Moore immediately stepped in close to whisper further prayers. The man's eyes jerked around wildly, looking through everyone and everything at some unknowable beyond. Moore revered this moment, but feared it as well. This man was glimpsing the Void, the most holy final destination anyone could hope for since the war between the gods had closed the realms of Paradise and Punishment forever. He was also mere ticks away from the deciding moment.

The merchant clutched wildly at the sweat-soaked bedding spread across his wide girth. He began to kick, prompting Daeg and Galt to grab his legs and hold them down. Moore pressed down on the man's shoulders in an attempt to hold him steady. He sucked in one last wet gasp and collapsed back on the bed, where he remained still. A final death rattle leaked slowly from the body. The three shepherds backed away, the time for prayers finished. Each placed hands on the hilts of their anointed blades. Quiet sobbing was heard from the crowd behind them. They waited.

Violent convulsions began to shake the body. The crowd, now pressed into the doorframe, gasped. Some shrieks and louder cries broke out, and Moore barked at them to be silent.

The shepherds drew their blades and backed away from the body as an unearthly howl began to emit from the body's slack mouth.

The face remained unchanging, eyes half-lidded, yet the disturbing scream grew in intensity. The shaking of the body continued to increase until, suddenly, all movement ceased.

At that moment, a sharp cracking sound filled the small room as the top of the body's head exploded outwards, showering the headboard with blood and brain matter. More screams rose from the crowd.

"Get them out of here!" Moore bellowed. They had seen enough to appease the Void-God; now they were a dangerous distraction.

"Everyone back up! Clear the room!" Daeg shouted, approaching the group and gesturing toward the narrow doorway. They stumbled back in compliance. Once the last mourner had cleared the threshold, Daeg pulled the heavy iron door shut and threw the bolt. Just as he turned back to the deathbed, the shade completed its birth.

From the gaping hole in the top of the head, a contorted, pulpy mass of blood-slick tissue began to wrench itself forth. The shredded scalp, hair now soaked in blood, was peeled back and over the face of the dead man.

"Steady," Moore cautioned. The timing had to be right. Too early, and the shade could re-form from the tissue remaining within the body of the deceased. Too late, and the fully formed shade would become exponentially more mobile and dangerous.

The twisted mass of crimson flesh suddenly erupted from the hole, clambering up the headboard and extending to its full height. As it slithered free, the corpse appeared to deflate. The mass began to take shape—the unmistakable shape of the man it had just desecrated. The contorted, skinless face of the shade, with empty sockets and a wet, open mouth, continued its inhuman howling. A moment longer, and it would be formed enough to begin a violent attack on anyone nearby.

Now that the shade had cleared the body, it was time to strike.

"Now!" Moore hollered.

The three shepherds lunged at the shade, thrusting their blades into the wet, undulating tissue. The wounds immediately began to hiss, and the shade seized violently. Daeg leapt back from the thrashing form and nearly slipped in the blood covering the stone floor.

The shade writhed away from Moore, now on the defensive. Galt was ready. He hacked savagely at the creature, tearing it to shreds and showering the walls and ceiling with more of its corrupt blood. As it weakened, Moore and Daeg pressed on as well, continuing the assault. As the collapsing creature flailed wildly, sending more blood and gore across the room, the shepherds were careful to turn their heads and clench their mouths and eyes shut. Shepherds had been known to grow ill from exposure to a shade's blood, and some had even died.

Finally, it shuddered for the last time and slumped in a heavy pile on the floor. Slowly, the shade began to dissolve into a large, hissing puddle. The shepherds stood by, panting. All things considered, it had been a fairly routine shepherding.

"His soul is free now. He is forgiven. May he enter the sweet silence of the Void," Moore said, almost to himself.

He looked over the extensive cleaning they would now have to undertake. Part of their holy duty was to take the body to the burning fields outside the city walls. They would also need to clear the remains of the shade, lest a citizen become ill from exposure. Behind him, Galt sighed heavily.

"Shall I notify the family?" Daeg asked, gesturing toward the door.

"Yes. You can let them know that their loved one was delivered into the Void successfully. Please do not let anyone in, though; not until we clean some of this. Leon, fetch the bag."

Daeg and Galt both turned to complete their assigned tasks. Galt grabbed the bag and began to clean his blade first. Daeg unbolted the door and opened it.

Instead of weeping family, he was greeted by a captain of the Royal Guard. All of the mourners had been cleared from the hallway.

"I'm sorry, sir—" Daeg began, confused, but assuming the guardsman had some sort of relation to the deceased.

"I'm not here for the dead man," he interrupted, peering around Daeg at the mess inside. "I can see that he's been properly guided to the Void. No, I'm here for your master."

The stranger at the door had caught the attention of Moore and Galt, who approached.

"I'm the high shepherd of this chapter," Moore said, wiping his hands on a rag.

"Captain Gorlin Mather," the guardsman said, introducing himself. He extended his hand, but then, noticing the blood on Moore's hands, lowered it.

"The king wishes to speak with you."

CHAPTER 3

Upon his return to the Hall of Antiquities, Faye and Jotun wasted no time in needling Cyprian for information about his meeting with Phar-Mindorius. Cyprian was cagey with his answers; he wished to speak with his wife regarding the matter in private. Jotun, always a nosey and involved individual, continually stepped around the hints that Cyprian was dropping, finally forcing him to be blunt.

"Jotun," he said, leveling his gaze on the old man, "my conversation with my uncle was very important, and I want to share the details with you. But I need to speak with Faye first. Alone."

Faye looked slightly embarrassed at Cyprian's lack of tact.

Jotun shook his head. "I understand, my lord. We untitled folk can bear to wait. Never mind my long-cycles of loyal service," he said with mock hurt. But Cyprian sensed that, despite being dressed as a joke, Jotun's words were sincere.

"Thank you for your understanding," Cyprian said, ignoring Jotun's attempt to make him feel guilty. He turned to Faye. "What do you say we go for a walk? The hollow?"

"That sounds just fine. We'll be back soon, Jotun, and if he doesn't fill you in, I will."

"I would expect nothing less, my lady," Jotun said with affection.

The two left the hall and walked sunward, toward the Vinecrown Keep. The Mercantile Causeway was as vacant as it had been cycles earlier when Cyprian had passed through with Mather. The emptiness, a mere curiosity before, now seemed to him an ill omen. With the imminent failure of the city now an immutable fact, it was impossible not to see the signs.

"This must be very, *very* important if you seek my counsel above the wisdom of Jotun," Faye said with a smirk.

"I meant what I said; I'll tell Jotun later. This is actually important enough to warrant a private conversation."

The two passed into the shadow of the massive keep, a large darkened area housing what had once been castle gardens. With the perpetual darkness on the shadowed western side of the keep, the royalty of the city had given up on trying to cultivate the area. Now, the shaded hollow was populated by only the hardiest trees, crumbling stone walls, and the occasional firefly.

Cyprian and Faye came to the area often, enjoying the privacy and seclusion of this otherwise-deserted area of the city. They had explored the ruined gardens thoroughly, even unearthing interesting artifacts from the mossy ground. For Cyprian, the hollow was fascinating because it represented a vision of what the entire city would have become if the sun had been frozen only a short time earlier. The city had been spared, not just by Ganachim's hidden presence, but by the precious daylight that still reached it. This hollow, in all its ruin, had to be what Vin-Sadavat, much further to the west and firmly in the Nightlands, had become.

"Okay, I think we're alone," Faye said, casting an exaggerated glance around them.

"What do you see?"

Faye furrowed her brow and looked around again, this time with no hint of sarcasm. "I don't know. Trees? Rocks? The keep? What are you getting at?"

"Look at the trees again," Cyprian said solemnly.

Faye was used to her husband's peculiarities of mood, but this was unusual, even for him. Feeling slightly like he had lost his mind, she looked again, then turned to him with a shrug.

"The trees are dying. Slowly, but certainly, they are dying," Cyprian said.

Now Faye looked yet again, this time seeking evidence of Cyprian's claim. Sure enough, some of the previously hearty old pines were beginning to show signs of rot. Faye was still skeptical.

"Haven't they always suffered here, in the darkness?"

"Not like this; this is different. It's not just the pines here. Now I see evidence of it everywhere. This city is failing."

"This city has outlived every catastrophe that the world has thrown at it," Faye responded. "You and I know that better than anyone. Think of the records. A lot of really terrible things have happened out there, and Nordabor has survived. I don't know what your uncle may have told you, but one bad harvest does not mean the end."

"He told me quite a lot, actually, and there's more happening than one bad harvest," Cyprian said. He gestured toward a partially crumbled wall, the ancient stone shot through with wilted vines. "Let's sit."

They sat in the gloom, and Cyprian relayed the entire conversation he'd had with the king. Faye's incredulity quickly turned to shock.

"So, after all this time saying nothing to you, shunning you, now, he suddenly wants you to go out on an expedition based solely on a hunch and the word of some self-serving drifter? After long-cycles of forbidding any venture beyond the forest? This doesn't seem like a good idea. This seems like madness."

"There is no doubt that this city is dying, that the god under the keep is dying. We can't afford to ignore that. Madness might be what's called for. It might be the only way," Cyprian replied, placing a reassuring hand on Faye's arm. She shrugged it off and stood, brushing her auburn hair out of her face.

"And he's putting that idiot in charge? Phir-Ramarian knows nothing of history, artifact preservation, or leading an expedition. This will not end well," she said, growing heated. "If an expedition led by your father failed, then what hope does this one have?"

Cyprian ignored the reference to his father. "It has a clear direction and a clear purpose. I'm sure that Phir-Ramarian's presence will hardly be noticed. Now, I haven't spoken with this Starkad yet, but from what Phar-Mindorius says, he knows the wastes better than anyone. It would not benefit him at all to lie or lead us to ruin. Not if he wants his reward."

"Maybe he doesn't care about any reward. Maybe he's just a badlander who decided to gut our city from the inside. Maybe soon, we'll have invaders on our doorstep."

"Faye, think for a moment," Cyprian said, a bit more harshly than he'd intended. "How would he know everything he does if he hadn't encountered my father? There's at least truth in that. He'll be surrounded by some of the king's best men. If there's even a whiff of danger, he'll be dead. At any rate, it's trust him or perish."

The reality of the situation seemed to settle over Faye like a veil. She looked down at the mossy ground and said nothing.

"This could be a chance not only to survive, but to restore Vingallea's glory. We could actually accomplish what the old kingdom had sought, but this time without meddling gods pushing their own agendas. It would be on our terms."

Faye scoffed. "You don't buy any of that. That sounds like Phar-Mindorius's words coming out of your mouth."

"Then consider this. We've been sequestered in this city, spending our lives digging through this dirt—dirt that holds no new secrets. The rare chances we've had to explore the forests have yielded almost nothing. This is an opportunity for a fully funded, fully manned expedition into the old kingdom. An expedition that would have us finding perhaps the most precious artifact known to man. Even if the blade can't be reforged, even if the old ones aren't really out there, think of what we could discover. We would be the most renowned explorers in the kingdom. We would prove that the Fontaine name is not synonymous with failure."

The words washed over Faye. She stood still and eyed her husband, his ambitions laid bare. "Is that why you want to do this? Glory? To redeem your father's failure?"

Cyprian realized he may have said too much and decided to rein it in. However, Faye had provided him with fodder for a better explanation.

"I want to find out what happened to my father. This is the only way," he said, shrugging. Despite his using it to soothe Faye's concerns, it was also absolutely true; the mystery of his father's fate was never far from his mind, and he was eager to speak with Starkad about him. His manipulative way of mentioning it to Faye left him feeling sour, but he needed her on this with him. Her knowledge of antiquities and cartography were unmatched, and she was capable of holding her own in the field.

Beyond that, he loved her deeply. The thought of leaving Nordabor, possibly for the last time, without her was untenable. He told her as much.

Faye turned and gazed into the shadowed wood around them. There were fewer fireflies than there used to be. The air somehow tasted staler. She wondered if it was just her imagination, in light of everything Cyprian had told her. She had serious misgivings about this expedition, but understood Cyprian's motivations regarding his father. She loved him, and dreaded the idea of him leaving her there. And, if she was being perfectly honest with herself, what he had said about exploring the outside world did resonate with her. Although naked ambition was ugly on Cyprian, she was not entirely immune from the pull of greatness. Her passion for antiquities, the opportunity to see ancient works that no living person had seen, partially clouded over her apprehensions.

"I'm not exactly sold on this," she said, "but I can see that you're going to do it regardless."

"Yes."

"I guess I'll be joining you, then. For your father. To chase this insane dream of opening Paradise. And to take credit for whatever we find," she said with a roguish grin. Cyprian returned the smile.

Still, her doubts remained.

•   •   •

As the two returned from the hollow, Faye voiced concern that Jotun might be too old for such an undertaking.

"Yes, he's old, but he's determined. And despite his little bit of a hunch, he's still pretty capable as well. I think it haunts him that he didn't go on my father's second expedition. I don't think I could keep him away from this one."

The old man's will was indomitable to the point that it was sometimes irritating. If he hadn't broken his back in a nasty fall during the return trip of the first expedition, he would have gladly set out on the second. Whenever he was feeling wistful about his past exploits, he would lament that he'd let Rorik, his closest friend, down. As he told it, Rorik had had to convince him to stay.

His close tutelage of Cyprian in the subsequent long-cycles was no great mystery. In Rorik's absence, Jotun had essentially become the father Cyprian had lost.

As it was, Cyprian was right. As he explained what had occurred at the Vinecrown Keep, Jotun's deeply lined face slowly lit up. The three of them had gathered in the hall's foyer and sat in saggy leather chairs before a crackling fire. The firelight danced across the faces of the two men as they excitedly discussed the expedition. Faye, hearing the sketchy details again, felt some of her reluctance reigniting.

"I never imagined I would see beyond this realm again," Jotun said dreamily. "And a living old one, within these very walls. I must see her."

His statement shook Faye from her worries. She'd been so taken aback by the magnitude of the proposed expedition that she hadn't really given due consideration to the marvel of having a living god almost under their feet.

"I agree," she said. "I want to see her too."

"I don't know if that will be possible. My uncle was very protective of her presence down there," Cyprian replied. "When I return to the keep for the overview of the expedition route, you two will be with me. Perhaps you can see her then."

At the mention of the expedition route, Jotun appeared almost giddy.

"Oh, there's so much to do. Faye, I'll need your help collecting some of the old maps. Both those retained from the old kingdom and those that Rorik and I worked on. I can't imagine what else we'll be able to add with the information this wanderer has."

Jotun stood up, excitement making him almost spry. He placed a gnarled hand, still full of strength, upon Cyprian's shoulder, and his expression grew somber.

"We will do this, Cyprian. We will complete your father's journey, and we'll find him out there."

He patted Cyprian's shoulder heavily and started for the door. "Come on, Faye, I need your eyes," he called as he left the room, not pausing to wait for her. She looked at Cyprian and raised her eyebrows quizzically.

"You heard him," Cyprian said with a smile.

"Well, I suppose I'll be humoring him for a while. You're welcome." She stood up and stepped over to his chair, where she bent low and kissed him. "I know you're no map expert, but feel free to join us."

"I will in a little bit," he said. He squeezed her arm and smiled again. She left the room feeling a strange mixture of dread and excitement.

Now alone, Cyprian gazed into the fire and let his thoughts unspool. This endeavor would be dangerous, there could be no doubt. Now, Faye and Jotun would be placed in the same danger. Still, there was nobody else he would trust to join him. Perhaps they could actually succeed.

He thought of the wide expanse of unknown waste beyond the small island of protection afforded by Nordabor. Soon, they would be trekking through it. Possibly over the same broken lands that his father had passed through. Once again, he dwelt on what had become of his father and his expedition.

Soon, he hoped, he would find out.

CHAPTER 4

When the summons for the overview of the expedition finally arrived, it was not Mather, but a young courier who delivered the news. She advised Cyprian that the king was requesting formal attire for the meeting, which Cyprian found strange. Nonetheless, at the nineteenth cycle, he, Faye, and Jotun donned the highest-quality garments they owned and headed for the keep under the grey light of the frozen sun.

As they approached the main gate, they saw that it was abuzz with city guardsmen. Ceremonial torch sconces, usually unlit, now crackled with fire. Curious commoners were milling about the outer wall of the keep, talking excitedly amongst themselves. It was clear that something unusual was happening.

The guards seemed to ascertain immediately that the three of them had been invited, simply by the quality of their clothes. They stopped them as a formality.

"Halt," an acne-scarred young guardsman said. "The castle grounds are closed to all but those bearing a personal invitation from the king."

Cyprian produced the formal summons the courier had given him, and the guardsman gave it a cursory glance. "Lord Fontaine," he said respectfully, stepping aside. The two guardsmen flanking the doorway followed his example, and Cyprian, Faye and Jotun walked into the courtyard and toward the keep.

As they approached the entrance, a gaily dressed servant greeted them. "Ah, more of the king's honored guests. Come in, come in," he said eagerly, ushering them toward the door. The three of them exchanged confused looks and followed the servant inside, where once again, royal courtiers and highborn nobles were gathered, now dressed in formal robes.

They were led into the throne room, and Cyprian was immediately struck by the transformation that the formerly gloomy room had undergone. The sooty, low-burning fires were now blazing. The tapestries and treasures spread across the space had been cleaned and polished. The long tables were now formally set with shining dinnerware. All throughout the room, the elite of the realm mingled, sipping wine and mead from jeweled goblets. They laughed heartily and slapped each other on the back, spilling drinks that the multitude of servants weaving through the crowd were quick to clean up. Phar-Mindorius presided over it all, smiling from his throne, nodding and waving at well-wishers.

The macabre display of the dead old one hung in its place of honor behind the throne. It, too, appeared to have been polished.

"Apparently, this 'meeting' is actually a formal feast," Faye said, leaning in close to Cyprian.

"Apparently," he agreed. He peered around the room, looking for a place for the three of them to sit as far from the crowd as possible. Jotun busied himself with looking as well. He appeared to be extremely uncomfortable in the company of the aristocrats. He clumsily shuffled the rolled-up maps he had brought with him from under one arm to the other.

"Lord Fontaine!" a voice boomed heartily from behind the group. Cyprian turned and felt no small measure of disgust rise within him as Phir-Ramarian sauntered toward the group, brimming with self-satisfied importance. He was wearing a full suit of pristine decorative armor with a burgundy cloak clasped about the neck. Under one arm, he carried a gleaming helm that had never seen combat. To Cyprian's eye, it appeared to be an antique, a strictly decorative piece. Phir-Ramarian brushed his long, immaculate locks back from his round, boyish face and stuck out his velvet-gloved hand, seizing Cyprian's in an outsized handshake.

"It's been too long, cousin," he said. "You've been hiding over in that hall. It's good to see you."

Cyprian smiled tightly in return. Before he could respond, Phir-Ramarian had already turned away from him.

"And Lady Fontaine, as beautiful as ever." He bowed dramatically and planted a wet kiss on the back of Faye's hand with his bulbous lips. She grimaced slightly, despising not only the kiss but the formal title. Born a commoner, the title bestowed on her after her marriage to Cyprian had always felt like an ill fit.

The prince looked at Jotun last, nodded at him curtly, and turned back to Cyprian.

"It does my heart good to see such cheer in my father's keep again," he said, gesturing about the room. "It's astounding that such an opportunity has come about in our time."

"Yes, it is," Cyprian answered flatly.

Before Phir-Ramarian could bloviate further, the king's herald blew his horn, and the room grew silent as Phar-Mindorius lifted himself from his throne and gazed with satisfaction at the gathered crowd. The herald opened his mouth to make a formal announcement of the king's presence, but Phar-Mindorius raised a hand to silence the unnecessary declaration. The herald, looking somewhat crestfallen, sat down.

"This cycle is, truly, a time for celebration," the king said, gazing across the room with pride. "I have spoken with many of you individually about the purpose for this gathering. To the others present whom I did not speak with, I believe your masters have instructed you on the specifics. Everyone here has an interest in seeing this quest succeed. Everyone here understands what is at stake."

He paused while a general murmuring passed through the room. Cyprian was unsure of how many present knew the full truth. It occurred to him that he might not even know it.

"We are on the precipice of a greatness that has not been dreamed of in Vingallea since the time of Phan-Ellara."

The crowd briefly bowed their heads in reverence.

"It is within our grasp not only to save the collected realms of Vingallea and ensure the ascendancy of Nordabor, but to seize the glory of Paradise that was promised to our people so many ages ago."

He paused again, letting the excited murmurs of his audience pass through the room.

"This expedition will build on the gathered knowledge and success of our people. This will be a victory for humankind, and humankind alone. The meddling of the old ones doomed our world to a slow death. We will correct that. The very best of us," he said, glancing at his son, "will embark on this undertaking, and prove the might of our Vingallean bloodline. Nordabor will carry the legacy of the old kingdom to its rightful conclusion. I say this with true conviction. We will be delivered. The people of Nordabor will enter Paradise."

A spontaneous roar of excitement burst from the crowd. Nobles who'd never considered the lore of the old kingdom were suddenly certain of their divine right to the spoils promised by legend.

Cyprian looked at their cheering faces with concealed scorn. They had no idea what the king was really saying; they only knew their ruler was guaranteeing their continued prosperity. They had no idea what was really out there. None of them knew how desperate this plan was and how unsure of the outcome the king really was. There was no guarantee that they would find the blade shards, that they could reforge them, or that a reforged blade could even open the Gates of Paradise. They also had to reach the gates themselves, which were believed to be on an isle off of the far northern coast.

In the throng of cheering red faces, Cyprian spied a man sitting on the far side of the room calmly smoking a pipe. He had clearly made no attempt to meet the king's request for formality. He was wearing a woolen cloak over a ragged, worn tunic crisscrossed by belted pouches. Through the pipe smoke, Cyprian could see a jagged, livid scar running down the length of the man's deeply tanned face, puckering the left side of his mouth. He appeared unmoved by the king's rhetoric.

This stranger could be none other than Duncan Starkad. It was clear that this was the badlander who had walked under the endless sun of the Daylands and passed into the blackness of the Nightlands, who had wandered the wide wastes and encountered Cyprian's father. Cyprian wanted to speak with him at once, but he realized that now was not the time.

As the cheers subsided, Phar-Mindorius, beaming, raised his hand for silence.

"The chosen leaders of this endeavor will be meeting with me afterwards to discuss the particulars. But first, we feast." The king clapped his hands, and servants came forth from the rear chambers bearing platters of succulent meats and roasted vegetables, igniting further cheers. The crowd began to shuffle toward the benches and settle in, bowing the old wood.

"Please, you must join me at the expedition leaders' table," Phir-Ramarian said, guiding Cyprian and Faye toward the same far table that the stranger with the pipe occupied. Jotun, though he had not been explicitly invited, trotted after them.

They took seats among the eagerly chattering group already sitting, Jotun cautiously placing the maps at his feet under the bench. Starkad continued puffing on his pipe and silently appraising the others gathered at the table.

Cyprian marveled at the spread before him. Roasted boar, braised hen, stewed hare, sweet potatoes, roasted peppers, corn, beans, warm loaves of bread, and a variety of cheeses. All of the excess seemed very irresponsible, considering the inevitability of the impending famine.

"You'd never think that we'd had a weak harvest or failing livestock looking at this," he said quietly to Faye. She nodded in agreement, her eyes never leaving the platter before her.

Excessive or not, the trio joined the other guests in eating heartily. As they did so, Cyprian looked around the table and found that he recognized few of his fellow diners. Mather, in formal uniform, chewed his food mechanically, nodding at the appropriate places as a stout woman explained something to him. Cyprian only knew one other diner by name.

That man was Fritz Rayburn, who would undoubtedly be the provisioner for the expedition. He had supplied the tinned meats, water casks, preserves, equipment, and livestock for his father's two expeditions, as well as smaller expeditions that Cyprian had been involved with into the areas surrounding the city. He'd never actually travelled outside of the city himself, usually sending representatives to oversee the dispersal of foodstuffs. A plump, cheerful individual with a gin-blossomed nose, he was a reliable source for quality goods.

Idle conversation continued around mouthfuls of food. A tangible energy buzzed between the diners as anticipation for the real discussion to come grew.

"Look at this gathering of minds—the best this kingdom has to offer," Phir-Ramarian boasted, lifting his goblet into the air for a toast.

"Hear, hear," a gaunt, white-haired man in the dark robes of a shepherd said, raising his own drink. The rest of the table followed suit. Cyprian noted with irritation that, as always, Phir-Ramarian was basking in the high esteem of his subjects, who seemed incapable of seeing the prince's obvious faults.

Phir-Ramarian, cheeks flush, downed his entire drink, slammed the goblet to the table, and stifled a belch. "My father and I have crafted the perfect company for this undertaking," he said matter-of-factly. "Where others have failed, we will undoubtedly succeed."

Cyprian bristled at the barbed reference to his father's failure.

"What do you think, Captain?" Phir-Ramarian asked Mather pointedly. Mather, who'd been listening dutifully to the woman beside him, now turned to face Phir-Ramarian.

"The Crown has the utmost confidence in this venture," he answered, as if he were reading his response.

"Well-put!" Phir-Ramarian responded, seemingly oblivious to the fact that Mather's statement had not really answered the question at all. He turned to Rayburn.

"I'm under the assumption that you'll be providing not just donkeys for hauling, but riding horses as well?"

"Well, my lord," Rayburn answered, spooning another heaping helping of stewed hare onto his plate, "we'll have more than enough donkeys. Man-hauling will hopefully be avoided completely. As for the horses, I'll be able to provide a handful. Enough for the titled members of the expedition, certainly."

Purebred, quality horses were not common in the city, and had not been for generations. Attempts at breeding had proven largely unsuccessful. Mostly, smaller donkeys unsuitable for riding were available.

"Excellent," Phir-Ramarian replied. He turned to Cyprian. "I'll ensure that you and your lady are provided with quality steeds."

Jotun, who was bent over his plate, scoffed under his breath.

"And I understand," Phir-Ramarian said loudly, directing his words toward the woman who'd been speaking to Mather, "that our engineers have cooked up something truly incredible to assist us on our journey?"

"That's correct, my lord," she answered.

"Well, I cannot wait to hear the specifics," he said, smiling broadly, leveling his gaze on the engineer.

"It sounds like you've accounted for everything. You are a very wise leader."

Phir-Ramarian turned toward the source of this unexpected commentary. Near the end of the table, Starkad sat stoically, blue pipe smoke swirling around his thinning, dusty blonde hair.

"Why, yes, we have," he said, seeming suddenly flustered. He cleared his throat, quickly regaining his composure. "Everyone, this gentleman is the source of our newfound knowledge, Duncan Starkad. He will be our guide on the expedition."

The others peered with naked curiosity at the strange outsider, as if Phir-Ramarian's acknowledgement of him had finally given them permission to do so.

"My father and I have discussed our plans with him," Phir-Ramarian continued, "and with his assistance, we've developed a plan that is sure to succeed."

"You and your father have certainly discussed many things, but neither of you, nor anyone else at this table or in this hall, have any real understanding of what you are about to embark on," Starkad said, before taking another puff of his pipe.

"I believe you've illustrated things quite clearly," Phir-Ramarian replied. He shifted in his seat, his bulky armor clinking.

"You believe many things that I think will be disproven once we leave the walls of this city. Still, I applaud your efforts to prepare. I'll hopefully be able to correct your failures along the way."

Phir-Ramarian's pink cheeks grew redder. He blinked repeatedly at Starkad in exaggerated disbelief at his words. Cyprian and Faye exchanged a quick look of delight at the prince's frustration. The table had grown quiet, and like a spreading pool, the silence was moving to the surrounding tables.

Phar-Mindorius, who'd remained on his throne greeting an endless slew of fawning nobles, took note of the sudden tension and rose. "I believe the time has come for the principal members of this party to adjourn to private quarters to discuss the specifics of our endeavor," he said with a somewhat forced smile. "I invite all of you to continue to make merry in our absence."

He turned to the table of expedition leaders and gestured for them to follow him. In turn, they looked at Phir-Ramarian and Starkad, whose eyes were locked. Finally, Starkad's gaze flickered to the king, resting for a moment on the crown of bone upon his head.

"We best follow the king," he said, rising. The standoff broken, the others rose as well. The feast slowly resumed as the group shuffled out of the throne room and into a hallway leading to a private chamber.

Somehow, it was clear that Phir-Ramarian had been bested, which pleased Cyprian deeply.

•   •   •

"I hope that you all enjoyed the food," Phar-Mindorius said, ignoring the thread of tension that had been growing between his son and the wanderer. "I imagine that you're eager to hear the specifics of this campaign."

The expedition leaders had once again settled around a table, this one a broad, round slab of dark wood riddled with scratches. Stomachs full and heads buzzing with drink, they looked expectantly at the king, who was standing before them.

"First and foremost, I would like to discuss the organization of the command structure. My son is the overall commander of this expedition. His word is law, and is tantamount to my own. I will not have any questions to his authority."

He spoke without malice, but looked at both Starkad and Cyprian. Neither said a word.

"Under his leadership," he continued, "the company will be divided into two tiers: the Exploratory Contingent and the Sovereign Guard. Lord Fontaine will head the Exploratory Contingent. I see you've assembled your team?"

"Yes, Your Majesty," Cyprian answered, looking to Faye and Jotun seated nearby.

"Jotun, I'm happy to see that you'll be entering the field again. As I remember, you were indispensable on Rorik's first expedition."

"Thank you, sire," Jotun replied, obviously uncomfortable at the praise.

"Lady Fontaine, a pleasure," Phar-Mindorius said, acknowledging her presence.

"Your Majesty," she responded in turn. Her response betrayed none of the emotions that Cyprian knew she was feeling. She'd never embraced her role as a lady of the court, and Phar-Mindorius had never really recognized her as one. His use of her title now seemed patronizing.

"Under the purview of Lord Fontaine will be the other civilian members of the expedition. This includes our guide, Duncan Starkad, whom I believe you've all just met."

Starkad sat impassively. Cyprian was privately elated. Being directly in command of the mysterious badlander would provide him with ample opportunity not only to ask about his father, but to ply his mind for information regarding the old ones and the outside world.

"Also included is Grand Healer Jacqueline Bellamont. You've assembled your team of subordinates?"

"I have some people in mind," a tall, slender woman with bright red hair and ivory skin answered.

"Excellent. Finally, a ten-man team of general laborers will be provided by our provisioner, Fritz Rayburn. Have you finalized your selections?"

"I have," Rayburn said coyly. "However, if it pleases you, sire, I'd like to directly manage the laborers and oversee the provisions, rather than putting a representative in charge."

The request came as a surprise to Cyprian, who'd never known Rayburn to have any desire to get his hands dirty. The man was not in peak health, and certainly had to be underestimating how arduous the journey would be.

"I see." Phar-Mindorius appeared to be as surprised as Cyprian. "Why the sudden interest in joining the company?"

Rayburn blushed. "I've provisioned for several expeditions, but I've never been out of the city myself. Considering the magnitude of what we're discussing, it might be the last expedition there is. I want to be a part of it. A direct part of it."

He paused for a moment and glanced at Cyprian guiltily. "Also, whatever happened to Rorik and his people, I hope it had nothing to do with what I provided. I aim to make sure that's not the case this time."

Cyprian's encounters with Rayburn had always focused on business affairs. He'd never heard the man vocalize any regret or concern regarding the lost expedition. He was taken aback, and despite his doubts about Rayburn's fitness for the journey, his respect for the man grew.

"Well, I caution you that this undertaking will not be an easy one," Phar-Mindorius said, "but if that's what you desire, I will not hinder you."

"Thank you, sire," Rayburn said, clearly relieved to have the matter settled.

Still nursing his pipe, Starkad shook his head slowly.

"Now, as for the Sovereign Guard—that will be under the command of Captain Gorlin Mather, who will lead a detachment of ten royal guardsmen."

Mather, arms folded across his chest, nodded solemnly.

"Also under his authority will be a chapter of shepherds, headed by High Shepherd Eldred Moore, and a team of engineers, led by Chief Engineer Blair Dupree."

The gaunt shepherd and the squat woman who'd been speaking with Mather each nodded in acknowledgement and looked around the table at their peers.

"Phir-Ramarian, Duncan, and I have designed this expedition to be a swift, tightly formed, and well-rounded group. The oversized expeditions of the past were hindered by the amount of supplies that had to be transported across unknown, hostile lands. This slimmed-down roster, coupled with the knowledge and expertise of Duncan, should ensure that the expedition can cover the huge distances required to complete this voyage in the shortest amount of time possible."

What went unsaid, Cyprian thought, was that even if the king had wanted to launch a larger expedition, or even assemble the City Guard into a small army, there just wasn't the means to do so. Despite what the lavish feast they'd just enjoyed might imply, they would be unable to provision for a fully mobilized force, not to mention that doing so would leave the city largely unguarded, open to internal strife, aggressive badlanders, and wandering shades. It just wasn't feasible to mount anything but a small expedition.

"I'll now allow Duncan to further outline your objectives and the route you'll be taking to reach them." Phar-Mindorius stepped aside and took a seat in a high-backed chair near the dim chamber's smoldering fire. He gazed into the flames, lost in thought.

Starkad said nothing for a moment. He slowly stowed his pipe in one of his many pouches and leaned back in his chair, which creaked in protest.

"I have no doubt that the more learned amongst you know much of the war between the gods. I'm sure that the Vingallean spin on what occurred is memorialized in your people's records. I, however, come from a different background, with different traditions. The badlanders were not afforded the opportunity to dwell behind high city walls, safe and comfortable, while the rest of the world bled. We were not given the opportunity to forget the past or reform the specifics to our liking. Generations of badlanders have toiled in the wastes, and we remember the old ways. Our people may not have a written record, but we have a rich oral history that has remained unchanged for as long as the sun has remained static in the sky."

It was quite the monologue for the taciturn outsider. Cyprian wasn't quite sure that he bought the concept of a flawless oral history, and certainly not one established by the savage badlanders. Still, he was intrigued to hear what new details Starkad offered.

"Our legend has it that before the world began its march to slow death, life was governed by the High-God, Alminnian, and his pantheon of servant-gods. He forged each in his likeness to perform a given task, to control the natural world, and to guide his most beloved creation, mankind.

"Despite the guidance they received, mankind still turned to wicked ways. As such, Alminnian created the two brothers, Ulesreto and Aedesda. When a person died, Ulesreto would pass judgment on them. Those deemed worthy would be allowed through the Gates of Paradise, where they would live forever with Alminnian. Those deemed unworthy would be reduced to shades and taken through the Gates of Punishment, where Aedesda would torture them for eternity."

At the mention of shades, Moore perked up.

"These two brothers," Starkad continued, "eventually grew tired of the roles they played. Aedesda, sickened by the constant wickedness of mankind, even when they knew the risk of sin, dreamed of taking Alminnian's place. He sought to seize the throne of Paradise and reshape reality to fit his own will. A will consumed by his desire to dominate. Ulesreto also sought the throne, but to remake the world in a wholly different way. A Vingallean way."

Cyprian, Faye, and Jotun immediately exchanged confused glances. It was known that the brothers, particularly Ulesreto, had manipulated Phan-Ellara into pledging Vingallea's loyalty to their rebellious cause. Later, when her brother Phar-Karrian took the throne, he marched a Vingallean host into open war with Alminnian. Before any of them could articulate their disagreement, Starkad continued.

"You see, your queen, Phan-Ellara, driven by an insatiable obsession with moral perfection, had sought out Ulesreto. The two grew in fanaticism, feeding into one another's egos and absolute surety that they could properly judge what was right and what was wrong. They eventually were wed, and ruled together."

The besmirching of Phan-Ellara sent a stir through the room. Even those who knew next to nothing about history held reverence for the greatest Vingallean monarch.

Phir-Ramarian stood up abruptly. "You speak blasphemy, badlander," he huffed.

"Tell your boy to sit down, my lord," Starkad said with irritation, ignoring Phir-Ramarian, whose face only grew redder.

"Ramarian, please, let him finish," the king said, still facing the fire. The absence of his formal title made Phir-Ramarian's face almost purple with humiliation. He opened his mouth as if he were going to argue further, then promptly dropped his weight back onto his chair. The only way the humbling could have been better in Cyprian's eyes would have been if the chair had then collapsed under the prince's weight.

All the same, he was skeptical of Starkad's tale. It would not be unusual for denizens of areas hostile to Vingallea to paint them as the villain in any story. After all, at the height of Vingallean power, the southern and northern kingdoms had been unified under the Vingallean banner. The legendary northern nations of Aurangzeb and Faedalia had been conquered. The descendants of those peoples would undoubtedly view Vingallea as the great enemy, the source of the world's woes. It was well-documented, however, that Vingallea had been fooled by Ulesreto. Cyprian voiced these concerns.

"Lord Fontaine, is it?" Starkad asked, seemingly amused by Cyprian's line of questioning.

"Yes, that's right."

"You are very well-read. Your father was too, from what I can recall of my meeting him. Unfortunately, not everything is written down as it actually occurred. Again, consider your sources. All the documentation you cite is of Vingallean origin. Whatever scribes created the texts you've pored over obviously would not want the legacy of their greatest ruler, or her brother, marred by the knowledge that she was a despot who loved an even-more-tyrannical god. Or that her brother marched the kingdom to ruin of his own volition."

Despite his disbelief that campfire tales told by barbarians could bear more historical accuracy than Vingallean texts, Cyprian had to admit that Starkad had a point. The sources were all one-sided in their depictions of events. Furthermore, his desire to argue the specifics shriveled at the mention of his father. This wanderer could hold answers that would otherwise be lost forever. It was best to remain cordial with him.

"I don't disagree with you," Cyprian allowed.

"Cousin, please, you can't possibly be buying any of this," Phir-Ramarian said.

"Let the man finish," growled Mather, growing impatient with the interruptions. The captain's unspoken authority cowed Phir-Ramarian, who folded his arms and looked away.

"It wasn't until Phan-Ellara had already passed away that the brothers launched their coup, backed by several of the other gods, as well as Phar-Karrian and the entire Vingallean legion. They marched to the Isle of Creation, where Alminnian and the loyal gods were waiting at the Gates of Paradise. Ulesreto demanded that Alminnian abdicate his throne and allow them to pass into Paradise unimpeded. Unsurprisingly, Alminnian refused. The rebels began to lay siege to the isle, and Alminnian responded by obliterating the southern kingdom. As a warning."

Cyprian was familiar with this aspect of the legend. It had been verified by his father's first expedition that a massive crater stretching to the horizon was all that could be found in the south.

"Well, the brothers then refused to surrender, and a vicious battle ensued, during which Alminnian was struck down. Which, as we all know, is to blame for the ills of the world. Now, what the brothers did not know was that their strength was tied directly to Alminnian's. When he died, the gods lost their true divinity and the majority of their power. The brothers quickly blamed each other for the unforeseen circumstances they found themselves in, and their alliance crumbled. Aedesda fled, and was eventually caught and killed by Ulesreto, who then vanished into history. The evidence of that fratricide is now hanging in your throne room."

Cyprian had always believed that, like the other old ones who purportedly survived the war, Ulesreto had simply faded into a self-imposed exile before meeting some kind of end. Starkad's description seemed to support that, though Cyprian had growing doubts. With the recent revelation that Ganachim still lived, held captive beneath their feet, he found himself wondering what had really become of the usurper.

"And with Ulesreto losing the ability to psychically judge the dying, and Aedesda not taking the wicked to Punishment, the shades were left to roam free. That's why we must pray to the Void-God to pass judgment," Moore interjected, clearly pleased to have something to add.

"More importantly," Starkad said, "with the loss of his power, Ulesreto's key to the Gates of Paradise, the sword known as the Scale of Judgment, shattered, leaving him with just the hilt. As a result of that, the gates themselves were permanently sealed shut. After the brothers fled the battlefield, the God of the Furnace, Veathyadell, examined the broken shards of the blade. He was a master of the forge and metalworking of all kinds, and he surmised that, with the hilt, the blade could be reforged. However, the surviving gods, most of whom had actually sided with the brothers, decided that the idea of a god, or mankind, attempting to access Paradise was the reason for all the misery that had now been brought into the world. The rebels repented and agreed to assist Veathyadell in separating the shards of the blade.

"Now, Ulesreto had no way of knowing any of this, and so, after he killed Aedesda with the jagged bit of blade still attached to the hilt, he left it buried in Aedesda's chest, where Lord Fontaine's father found it. Luckily for the city of Nordabor, and the Vingallean people, I encountered Fontaine senior on his trek. I learned of the interest he had in these blade shards, and I realized that if the hilt had been found, there must be real truth in the old legends. I told Fontaine I'd keep an eye out for the shards in my travels, though by the time I confirmed their locations, I never saw him again.

"Which brings us to the current expedition. I will lead you to these remaining gods and the shards they hoard."

The amount of specific details in Starkad's account lent it an almost fanciful quality. Cyprian simply could not believe that such facts would be clearly known by badlanders. Yet everything Starkad explained seemed to mesh with the witness accounts dating to the war, the discoveries of his father, and the known lore of the gods. He looked to Faye and Jotun; they appeared as awed as he was.

"How is it that one man could succeed where my father failed?" he asked.

"It's as your king said. Your father's expedition was too large, too cumbersome to hastily cover ground. I don't know if they met with any success, but it still took me many years—rather…that's the old term of my people. How do you say it? 'Long-cycles?'"

Cyprian nodded.

"Many long-cycles to determine these locations. I can't imagine how a force as large as your father's could have gotten anywhere."

"So where are these old ones hiding? Where are you going to lead us?" Dupree interjected.

Starkad smiled grimly. "Eager, are we? That tone will change once we leave this city, I'm sure."

"I'm tired of hearing a half-baked history lesson. Whatever truth there is to any of this, it ultimately amounts to orders from my king. So, please, explain where in this wide world we'll be visiting," the engineer retorted irritably. The smallest hint of a smile crossed Mather's face.

"As you wish." Starkad stood up abruptly and pulled a dented metal tube from under his ragged cloak. He unclasped the lid and slid out a yellowed scroll of parchment, which he unraveled and spread out across the table, placing rocks from a belt pouch on the corners to keep it from rolling back up. Seeing that it was a map, the others all got up and circled behind Starkad or craned their necks from their seats. Jotun nearly shoved Starkad aside in his bid to see the unfurled treasure. Only Phir-Ramarian remained where he sat, glaring at the far side of the room in an active bid to avoid looking at the map.

Cyprian gazed at the detailed markings, recent notations that showed things only guessed at by the ancient maps in the Hall of Antiquities. Markings that far exceeded any of the cartographic work completed by his father or Jotun on their first expedition. He felt Faye's hand touch his back, nearly buzzing with excitement despite the serious nature of everything unfolding. They exchanged a look of giddy exhilaration.

"Where we are 'visiting,' as you put it," explained Starkad, gesturing toward Dupree, "is relative to *who* we are visiting. I've discerned that six of the old gods still remain."

"Six?" Rayburn sputtered.

"Yes, six," Starkad replied, as if he were addressing a child. "Of those six, I suspect that only four retain pieces of the blade; how many pieces, I'm unsure. There is, of course, Veathyadell, who, as I said, is believed to have concocted the plan to separate them. He appears to have taken up residence in the cliffs of the crater wall far southeast of here, beyond the sands of Aurangzeb." He indicated on the map the area that he was referring to.

"Rorik and I mapped that area fairly thoroughly," Jotun said. "I can't imagine we would have missed something like a living old one."

"Not thoroughly enough, I'm afraid, although he is well hidden, and certainly would have shied away from a large caravan moving through the area."

Jotun furrowed his brow, considered Starkad's words, and decided that he'd provided a sufficient explanation.

"There is also Tariono, known as the God of Beauty. She appears to have established a fiefdom in the ruins of your old capital, Vin-Sadavat. The remains of the city are nominally controlled by a local chieftain called Heilrune, who fancies himself a collector of crowns. Heilrune has supposedly conquered every neighboring clan, enslaving their people and personally executing each rival warlord. Many badlanders have told tales of others having made pilgrimage to Vin-Sadavat to pledge fealty in order to find refuge from the wastes. In exchange for security, they must adhere to Heilrune's faith, a cult-like worship of physical beauty. He apparently cites the higher power that protects the city as the source of his success. Being deep in the Nightlands, I didn't venture too close, but there seems to be truth to these rumors. All signs point to Tariono."

At the mention of the chieftain, Phir-Ramarian could no longer feign disinterest. He looked across the table at the map and snorted in derision.

"No king of savages, ruling over a filthy warren, should be of any concern to us. We are going to be spearheaded by the best fighting men that the Vingallean bloodline has produced."

"Nevertheless," Starkad said, "I suggest we use caution. A diplomatic solution will most likely be impossible. A stealthy entrance into the city would be best."

"Our men can manage that," Mather said without a hint of bravado. Starkad nodded in response.

The idea of entering Vin-Sadavat, once the crown jewel of Vingallea's power, but now a near-forgotten wreck far in the Nightlands, excited Cyprian. Hearing that it was overrun with badlanders, however, was disheartening. He'd always imagined that if he ever went to Vin-Sadavat, it would be for a lengthy, organized archeological excavation. Not a stealthy raid under the nose of a murderous cult leader.

"The most physically demanding portion of our voyage," Starkad continued, "will undoubtedly be to confront the God of the Wind, Naffabyin. I believe he has retreated to a monastery once used to worship him. It is on the highest slopes of Urgukorge."

From the map, it was clear to all present that Urgukorge, the highest peak of the Einmaz Mountains, was north of Vin-Sadavat, placing it firmly within the Nightlands.

"I'm not sure we have the means to summit any peak in the Einmaz Mountains, much less Urgukorge," Rayburn said, crestfallen. "Nobody in this room, excluding Jotun, has ever been in any elevation higher than the city. And, my apologies, but the eastern badlands are not much higher, are they?"

"No," Jotun admitted, "and they're not trapped in perpetual darkness, either."

"I have traversed through those mountains. Not to the monastery, but close enough to know that Naffabyin broods upon the mountaintop, surrounded by a protective tempest. I believe, Rayburn, that you and I will need to examine what equipment you have available. Dupree, you can join us. We will fashion something equivalent to what we need to scale the mountain. I can provide training and guidance to whoever will be making the climb. I suggest we select the most physically fit and combat-capable from amongst the expedition to make the ascent, for I believe that Naffabyin will fight. I will, of course, guide them."

"I'll commit myself and the best of my detachment," Mather said, apparently undaunted by the task, earning another nod of acknowledgment from Starkad.

"I, too, will be ascending," Phir-Ramarian said. "I will lead by example."

"Of course," Starkad said.

"I'm sorry," Rayburn interjected, "you say you travelled near this old one's mountain retreat, and that it was surrounded by a 'tempest?' What do you mean by that?"

"Naffabyin was said to control the weather, and even with his now-limited power, it seems he has the means to summon and maintain a tremendous storm that encircles the summit."

Cyprian—who, through his studies, had some familiarity with the purported abilities of the old ones and the ancient phenomena of weather—looked around the table. Looks of confusion abounded. No weather, aside from the blanket of gray clouds, had been experienced in Nordabor for many lifetimes, not even rain. Crops had survived through artificial irrigation from the Einfallen, their only source of water.

"He means things we've never experienced in Nordabor," Cyprian clarified. "Rain, snow, lightning, high winds."

Now, looks of concern joined the confusion. Cyprian continued, doing his best to describe the different weather phenomena as they were depicted in the books of yore. If Starkad disagreed with any part of Cyprian's explanation, he didn't say so.

"You experienced these things?" Rayburn asked the badlander.

"I did. And their severity seemed to increase the closer I got. I believe that Naffabyin's tempest is actually the source of the Einfallen. All of that rain and snowmelt comes down the mountains and forms the river, just as, I imagine, it did naturally before Alminnian's death."

They sat in silence for a moment, mulling over what Starkad had suggested. The waters of the Einfallen, a precious source of life for Nordabor, were dependent on Naffabyin's continued power. "So, if we were somehow to destroy Naffabyin, that would also extinguish the river?" Faye asked.

"I would think so, yes."

"That is of no consequence," Phir-Ramarian interjected. "We won't need the Einfallen anymore once we have the blade shards. We'll be abandoning Nordabor altogether."

"Assuming the blade can be reforged, and the Gates of Paradise can actually be opened," Cyprian murmured, his thoughts suddenly shadowed with doubt. This plan was, in fact, a gambit. For the first time, he considered that their actions could actually do more harm than good.

"Of course they'll open," Phir-Ramarian said dismissively. "We're getting off-track. What of the other old ones?"

"The final god we will need to locate and confront will be Chortelak, called the God of the Festival," Starkad continued. "In the old times, he was worshipped by those seeking revelry and hedonistic pleasure, so say the legends. From what I can discern, he is now somewhere deep in the ashes of Faedalia." He motioned to a large swath of the map on the western edge of the Dawnlands, far north of Nordabor. "I know little about the specifics of his whereabouts, just that some badlanders travel into the ashes to seek out the promise of physical pleasure."

Cyprian was still stuck on the possible ramifications of their god-hunting, and it took him a moment to realize that Starkad's summary of what they faced had apparently wound down. The others were murmuring amongst themselves when Phar-Mindorius left the fireside and approached the table.

"So," the the king said, "once you've dispatched these old ones, or acquired the shards however you may, they are to be entrusted to Cyprian and his team. He will ensure that they're protected and restored to whatever state they need to be in to be reforged. Once they've all been obtained, you are to return to the city. With the hilt already in our possession, we'll be able to reforge the blade."

"Your Majesty, if I may," Rayburn said, "the journey described seems almost circuitous. Wouldn't it make more sense to send a small contingent, or even a single courier, back with each shard, rather than carry all of them with us? I'm certain I could outfit smaller splinter groups appropriately."

"And how do you suppose these groups would find their way back to Nordabor?" Starkad asked. "Particularly if they end up taking different, more direct, routes back to save on provisions, which I understand will already be precisely measured."

Rayburn opened his mouth, made a small sound, and closed it again.

"Duncan is correct," Phar-Mindorius said. "We couldn't risk losing a part of our company, or any blade shards, out in the wastes. Without Duncan to guide them, there would be no certainty that anyone could find their way back to Nordabor, and we don't have the time or provisions to halt the entire company in order for Duncan to lead smaller contingents back. It's not ideal to carry the relics throughout the entire journey, given the dangers therein, but we have no other choice."

Once again, Cyprian knew that their plans were being dictated by their limited manpower and supplies. Still, he did like the idea of keeping all of the shards in his possession through the duration.

Phar-Mindorius cleared his throat and continued as if the interruption hadn't occurred. "Once the blade is reforged, I will then lead a vanguard north to the Isle of Creation, where the Gates of Paradise are said to be. Any on this expedition who wishes to join me on that trip will be more than welcome. Once we ensure that the Scale of Judgment can open the gates, a courier will be sent to the city to notify the nobility. I will entrust them to organize an exodus of the citizenry in my absence. We will usher the Vingallean people into Paradise, as they always should have been."

Fears of the monumental task before the group were blunted by the king's hopeful speech. Starkad quickly resharpened them.

"There are just two other concerns regarding the approach to the Gates of Paradise," he explained. "First, the God of the Sea, Opriseur. She still wanders the Isle of Creation, staying close to the body of Alminnian, which remains where he fell on the battlefield."

Cyprian and Faye stared at each other in surprise. It was known that Alminnian had been killed, but none of the writings had ever mentioned what had become of his remains. Cyprian had never put much thought into it, assuming that, like the other old ones, the body of the Father-God had been lost to the sands of time. His father had been given the opportunity to find and study the body of Aedesda; now he would get to pore over the corpse of the Great Creator. Even if the Scale of Judgment failed to open the gates, to study the remains of Alminnian would be reward enough.

Faye squeezed his hand tightly and a broad grin broke across her face. She was clearly as elated as he was. The two were momentarily oblivious to Starkad's continued warning.

"I approached the isle over the dried strait that used to separate the isle from the mainland. I saw Opriseur. I don't believe she has any of the shards, for the simple reason that she appears to have become completely feral in the time since her god's death. She wandered the shoreline of the isle, loudly babbling incessantly and incoherently to herself. When she saw me, I was still far enough away that I could escape. She began to charge toward me, and I'm certain that she would have torn me apart had she caught me. We will need to either navigate around her or deal with her directly."

A hush had fallen over the group again.

"What if she does have part of the blade, and just, over time, became like that?" the Grand Healer, Bellamont, asked cautiously.

"We'll know if there are any unaccounted-for pieces once we can lay out all the ones we have," Faye answered. "Assuming we know how the hilt will fit on."

"I'll provide you with measurements and diagrams of the hilt piece," Phar-Mindorius said.

After waiting a moment to make sure that the issue had been settled, Starkad continued. "Lastly, we need to concern ourselves with Ulesreto."

The revelation that Ulesreto, the bane of Vingallea and the author of their kingdom's downfall, was still out there and could impede their expedition sent a wave of consternation through the group. Cyprian, his recently formed suspicions suddenly confirmed, felt a combination of wonder and dread.

"There is no reason to believe that Ulesreto has learned of the plan of the other gods. After all, he carelessly left the hilt with Aedesda's corpse. That being said, if he were to discern such a thing, I have no doubt that he would stop at nothing to obtain the shards himself. He would find a way to reforge them, and he would follow through on his own designs for entering Paradise. Now, if you believe your own history, then Ulesreto was simply using Vingallea for his own ends. If you consider the history I've provided, maybe it would be to the benefit of your people to seek Ulesreto out. Maybe you could help each other."

"Absolutely not," Phar-Mindorius said emphatically, showing sudden anger. "I understand the alternative history carried by your people, Duncan, but even if it were true, whatever pledge our ancestor supposedly made to Ulesreto is long-since expired. I will not have my people delivered into Paradise simply to be thralls to another fickle god. The war between the gods broke this world; it is up to us to save ourselves now. We will enter Paradise alone."

Starkad seemed to consider this for a moment. "Then Ulesreto is to be avoided. I believe he lingers on the cape of Thunsturm near the old lighthouse there. The only issue I see is that this lighthouse falls along the route that we'll have to take to access the dried strait. The waters of the Stagnant Sea are still too deep to pass in any other area unless you plan on providing ships for your entire people.

"We will sort that out after we've reforged the blade. It is not the priority right now," Phar-Mindorius said, still flustered at the suggestion of cooperating with the usurper.

"Fair enough," Starkad replied, removing his pipe from where it was stowed and relighting it. "So now you know our objectives and the barriers to our success. Let's discuss the route we'll be taking."

•　　•　　•

The discussion went deep into the cycles generally designated for sleep. Once the route had been established, after some disagreement and argument that mostly resulted in adhering to Starkad's original ideas, the team adjourned. A departure date had been set for five full-cycles from then. They had the interim to make their own final preparations.

They shuffled out of the private chamber and dispersed, some a little inebriated, some overwhelmed and anxious, and all of them exhausted. The revelry in the throne room had died out some time ago, the vast space now populated only by servants who scuttled back and forth, clearing the detritus of their masters.

Before the king could disappear into his private rooms, Cyprian called after him.

"Yes?" he said wearily. The preceding discussion had obviously worn him down tremendously. His liver-spotted head sagged beneath his crown.

"I was hoping to have the opportunity to show Faye and Jotun..." He paused, unsure of how to refer to the old one.

Phar-Mindorius picked up on his intention nonetheless. "Of course, I understand their desire to see it. I'm quite tired, though; I'm afraid I can't join you this time, but I'll gladly have Captain Mather escort your there. Just, please—I understand your academic interest, but please do not touch it. It's far too fragile now."

"Of course." Cyprian looked to Faye and Jotun, who were waiting nearby. He nodded to them, and they exchanged excited smiles.

The king tapped one of the young servants on the shoulder as she hustled by, startling her. She stopped abruptly, looked at the floor, and shuffled uncomfortably.

"Your Majesty?" she squeaked.

"Please, fetch Captain Mather for me. I believe he just passed into the foyer."

"Yes, Your Majesty," she said, darting off to fulfill the command. It was probably the first time she'd ever spoken directly with her king.

A moment later, Mather stalked back into the room, clearly irritated to be summoned back after such a long meeting.

"Yes, sire?"

"Lord and Lady Fontaine, as well as Jotun here, would like to see the old one," he said quietly. "I would take them myself, but I'm exhausted after so many cycles."

"Yes, of course, Your Majesty."

Phar-Mindorius smiled weakly and patted Mather on the arm, then turned to Cyprian, Faye, and Jotun. "Captain Mather will take care of you."

The three offered simultaneous thanks as Phar-Mindorius left for his bedchamber, walking gingerly. The group watched him go for a moment, then turned to face one another.

"All right. Let's go, then," Mather said, no longer even attempting to hide his irritation. Without waiting for them to answer, he strode off toward the hallway they'd just exited. Cyprian, Faye, and Jotun followed.

After passing through a winding array of dim stone hallways that appeared to follow a completely different route than Cyprian had been led down before, they arrived before the same nondescript wooden door. Mather pushed it open unceremoniously, snatched a torch from the wall and stepped inside. This time, Cyprian warned the newcomers of the slick steps. They descended into darkness and toward the sound of rushing water until, once again, Cyprian stood before a god.

He looked at Faye, who stood frozen, gazing at the unnaturally large frame suspended before them. Her mouth hung slightly open, and she was wringing her hands at her waist. Jotun was stepping carefully across the filmy rocks below the great hanging head crowned by its withered halo, inspecting the creature and muttering to himself. Mather stood back near the steps, holding the torch and gazing into the darkness disinterestedly.

Faye turned to Cyprian. Her eyes were wet. Over the rush of the water echoing through the grotto, only Cyprian could hear her words.

"I thought I would be thrilled to see her. This is just sad. She's a shadow of what she must've been."

Cyprian thought of the glassy, dead-eyed gaze he'd seen when he looked into Ganachim's sallow face.

"I can't believe she's been down here this whole time," Faye muttered.

"Fascinating, isn't it?" Jotun declared with a broad grin as he approached the two of them. He didn't seem to notice the disturbed look on Faye's face.

"Yes, she is," Faye answered distantly, once again gazing at the shadowed body. Her eyes followed the length of the thin, pallid arms to where the rusted shackles met the bony wrists. Long fingers, tipped with filthy nails, hung limply. Fat drops of brown water, stained from the rust of the chains, dripped from them. Upon a second viewing, Cyprian was struck even further by the unsettling misery of the enslaved, catatonic being.

Faye had seen enough, and she and Cyprian lingered near Mather and his dwindling torch. Jotun buzzed about the old one for a while more, jotting things down on a small notepad and apparently trying to take rudimentary measurements with his own arm span. Twice, he nearly fell into the dark waters of the subterranean Einfallen.

Finally, he caught on to the fact that the rest of the group was eager to leave. He walked away from Ganachim reluctantly, and the group began the trek back to the front of the keep.

Once they'd reached the foyer, where Mather was confident that they could see themselves out without assistance, he broke off from the group almost without acknowledgment, only briefly stating that he'd see them when the expedition departed.

They stepped out into the gray light and trudged back toward the Hall of Antiquities. The overcast dawn that had blanketed the sky when they'd entered the castle remained unchanged. Still, after the darkness of the cave and the keep, the light made them shield their eyes.

CHAPTER 5

"Shovel more of that shit over here."

Leon Galt and Micla Daeg stood in the knee-deep muck of the burning fields, enveloped in the suffocating haze of scorched bodies. Greasy black smoke swirled around them, accompanied by the foul stench of blackened human flesh. They shoveled the wet, ashen slop at their feet, extinguishing the last of the smoldering corpses.

It had been a busy full-cycle. With Moore occupied by preparations for the expedition that he'd graciously volunteered Galt and Daeg for, the two apostles had been left to handle the normal workload alone.

Their chapter alone had responded to three deaths in this tour, only one of which had produced a shade, thankfully. The first, a middle-aged servant who'd acquired some form of pox, had produced a particularly savage shade that was made all the more difficult to dispatch by the lack of manpower. They'd then handled an elderly woman who'd passed peacefully and a young farmhand who'd been kicked in the head by a donkey. That had been a rush job, and could have been disastrous if a shade had been born without them being there. Luck was certainly on their side in that case.

Now that the final clearing of the departed had been completed, they could head back to the Ivy Citadel and get some rest. Fresh chapters of shepherds would soon be walking the city, prepared to guide any unfortunate soul to the Void.

"So," Daeg said, breathing heavily as they trudged through the field and back toward the city walls, "what do you make of this expedition?"

"I haven't really thought about it at all," Galt answered. "We follow our high shepherd. It's unusual and unexpected, but we'll perform the same function out there as we do here."

Daeg seemed to mull this answer over. "I'm kind of excited to be leaving the city, to see what's out there," he said, almost defensively.

"As far as I can tell, what's out there is the same thing that's in here. Dying people and shades. Whatever else they hope to find is a pipe dream," scoffed Galt in return.

"But what of the old ones? They're real; they're out there." Daeg *was* defensive now.

"They're either dead or essentially powerless. And so is this broken sword Moore's been going on about. I don't think that any reforged blade is going to open a door that's permanently shut. If we believe that this world's creator is the Void-God now, then that power he once wielded is gone for good. Otherwise, do you think he'd stay banished to the Void?" He shook his head and snorted in derision. "No work of man can undo what a god cannot. I'm following Moore out there because I'm sworn to him. Unfortunately. And that's it."

Daeg didn't see any need to argue. He certainly couldn't change Galt's mind.

They walked on in silence, passing through the city gates and toward the citadel. As they reached the arched entryway, shot through with withered ivy, they encountered two shepherds heading out for their tour.

"Busy, eh?" one of the shepherds asked, eying their muddied robes. Galt recognized the shepherd as Ophelia Solgard, a veteran known for her reliability and steadfast dedication to their order. Her immaculate robes were as richly black and shining as the impossibly straight hair that framed her pale face. Her partner, a man built like a slab of stone, was called Blackburn, though Galt couldn't remember his first name.

"Aye, that's right. Three this shift. One went shade. Fellow with pox."

Solgard furrowed her brow. "That's awful. Hopefully everyone can remain living for the next twelve cycles."

Galt grunted in agreement and began to walk away, Daeg in tow.

"Hold on, Leon," Solgard said, following behind. "We actually need to talk to you."

Galt turned around, eyebrows raised. "Yes?"

"Your high shepherd spoke to mine. I guess he's looking for two more apostles to join him on some sort of expedition?"

"Did he, now?" Galt answered carefully. He'd assumed that only he and Daeg would be accompanying Moore. Three shepherds for a group of that size seemed like enough. Perhaps they feared that encounters with wandering shades would be a common occurrence and sought extra protection. Either way, he didn't know how much Solgard and Blackburn knew.

"High Shepherd Moore has already been granted our following by High Shepherd Salis," Blackburn said unenthusiastically. "The old git's retiring. I imagine they're going to replace the whole chapter with new initiates."

"So you'll be joining us, then?" Daeg said, privately elated at the thought of having other shepherds to speak with.

"That's correct," Solgard answered. She stuck her hand out in greeting to Daeg. "You're newer, huh? I don't think we've met. Ophelia Solgard."

"Micla Daeg." He shook her hand heartily, pleased by her friendly nature.

"This is Ferro Blackburn," she continued, gesturing toward her sour-faced partner. He nodded in acknowledgement. Daeg returned the nod.

Blackburn looked the way that Galt felt—like he had no interest in taking part in a suicide pilgrimage to nowhere. Galt followed the orders of his high shepherd because, as his sworn acolyte, he had to. It appeared that Blackburn shared a similar outlook.

"So, we'll all be working together on this." Solgard paused. "What, exactly, is 'this?'"

"I think that will be up to High Shepherd Moore to discuss with you," Galt said, turning from his new companions. "In the meantime, I hope you have a pleasant shift."

With Daeg trotting after him, Galt continued into the quiet warmth of the citadel.

•   •   •

In the open-air chapel atop the Ivy Citadel, Moore knelt before the shrine of the Void-God. Previously a temple to Ulesreto, the busts of the failed usurper had long ago been toppled. Now, Moore whispered prayers to the Void-God before a heaped pile of rubble, with numerous candles wedged into the rocks. The flames barely flickered in the cool, stale air.

The impending journey weighed heavily on his mind. He was honored that his long service to the Crown had been noticed and rewarded with his selection to such a prestigious position. However, he was an old man who'd never travelled beyond the sight of the city walls. At times, wading across the burning fields, he'd gazed into the darkness of the surrounding pines and wondered what was out there. Now he would find out, and the truth was, he was frightened.

He concluded his long-form prayer, and, with some effort, rose to his feet and brushed his knees off. He looked out over the stone rampart at the shadowed woodland encircling the city. The gray waters of the Einfallen, a blessing that he'd only recently learned flowed from an old one's mountain fastness, snaked through the forest toward the city from the northwest and away again to the south. In the east, the sun hovered low behind the clouds, as it always had. He pulled up the collar on his robes and walked toward the worn steps leading back inside.

Countless souls, he thought, must be suffering out there in the unknown lands beyond the realm. So many, with no knowledge of the Void-God, no chance of experiencing his sweet grace.

Moore's small chapter had been bolstered with the addition of the two shepherds recommended to him by Salis. Five shepherds protecting a flock against a world's worth of shades. Vin-Sadavat alone would be inundated with them, he was sure. Five shepherds being all the Crown could spare, even for an endeavor as important as this. Nordabor truly was facing desperate times.

The reason why was clear: waning belief in the benevolence of the Void-God had eaten away at the fabric of the city. There was a time, Moore was certain, when faith in the Void-God's power had been universal. In the aftermath of the Father-God's death, the ancestors of Nordabor had known that he still governed from his exile in what came to be known as the Void. They knew that he'd reclaimed his rightful mastery over judgment of the dead, and that the souls of the worthy would join him in his new state of existence. The fact that the shades of those he found unworthy now wandered amongst them instead of being cast into Punishment was simply the penance to be paid by the remnants of the misguided Vingallean people.

Yet, despite the overt evidence of the wages of sin, it seemed the pernicious desires of man not only continued, but grew. The city, more so than ever, was rank with feigned piety and outright disbelievers. Moore had prayed over countless citizens who *appeared* to be virtuous, but the Void-God always knew.

Even the Ivy Citadel's numbers had shrunk appreciably. True devotion within the shepherds had eroded. The sanctity of the founding shepherds, those royal healers once tasked with extending the lives of their sovereigns, the first warrior-priests who'd unlocked the secret of destroying the shades and who'd ended the barbaric practice of expelling the ill and infirm from the city, was but a distant memory. Many of the modern shepherds, in Moore's view, merely paid lip service to the oaths of the order. Even Galt, his own acolyte, slowly seemed to have lost touch with the holy mission that they were sworn to pursue.

Time was running short, there could be no doubt. Moore had much to prepare. Several anointed daggers would need to be assigned to each shepherd in case any of their blades suffered damage along the way.

Not for the first time, Moore found himself wishing that it was possible to produce anointed bolts for crossbows. Despite many long-cycles of tinkering with the process, the intensity of the quenching in the old one's blood always rendered the small bolt heads too fragile to be of any use. Attempts to enlarge the bolts had resulted in crossbows that were too unwieldy to operate as mobile weapons.

So, unfortunately, the deliverance of the accursed dead remained an intimate affair. Of course, the closeness was necessary for another reason: the performance of the rituals for the dying. The most crucial rituals, those most beloved by the Void-God, would have to be honed before their departure. They could not risk disappointing the master of their fate with sloppy prayers, not out in the perilous wastes.

Moore knew the dire cost that mishandled prayers could incur. His own High Shepherd, nearly thirty long-cycles ago, had resided over the unexpected shepherding of the queen. Phan-Nelsinore had been in labor with her and the king's second son. The healers had been unable to stem her bleeding, and, fearing the worst, had summoned High Shepherd Tyburn, who was trusted immensely by the Crown. Tyburn, Moore, and a third shepherd had been presiding over a fisherman who'd fallen and broken his neck. Tyburn, knowing the Crown desired privacy, insisted on going alone.

His hasty invocations had apparently not been enough. Horrifyingly, Phan-Nelsinore had produced a shade. Tyburn, who couldn't believe that the queen could be so wicked as to become a shade, even with the intercession of his prayers, had nearly been overcome by the hideous monster. Only after dispatching the shade did it become clear that the queen's half-born infant son had died as well.

Tyburn, understandably, was quite shaken by the ordeal. Phar-Mindorius and the young Phir-Ramarian could not understand how such a thing could occur. To the king's credit, he did not lash out at Tyburn. The young prince had been calling for his head; Phar-Mindorius simply stripped him of his title and cast him out of the order. He refused to speak with Tyburn, and never recognized the fact that the queen's soul had still been freed from the prison of the shade, or that the infant's death had not produced one.

As for poor Tyburn, he had been exiled from the citadel and left unmoored amongst the commoners, filled with guilt and humiliation at his botched ceremony. Eventually, he approached a chapter of shepherds wandering the Mercantile Causeway and slit his own throat before them. In a final cruelty, he produced a shade that was swiftly destroyed. His desecrated remains were hauled out and burned in the same fields he had once overseen.

Now, fears of a similarly grand failure hung over Moore's head. To have the favor of the Crown was a blessing and a curse. He'd previously earned the king's esteem when he'd shepherded his sister successfully. Now, the pressure never to let that shine dull had pushed him into accepting the assignment to this expedition. An honor, to be sure, but a stressful one for an old man leery of disappointing his king.

Descending the ancient steps, Moore was acutely aware of the dull ache in his arthritic knees. Beyond the stress of his responsibilities on the expedition, he also worried that he was just too old to meet the physical demands of such an undertaking.

But all doubts, he surmised, needed to be put aside. The Void-God had been receptive to his needs throughout his entire life. He needed to have faith that he would not be abandoned now.

Nonetheless, he faltered on the steps and lingered in indecision. Ultimately, he decided to return to the altar and continue his prayers.

CHAPTER 6

Faye awoke to find that she was alone. To begin with, her mind had barely skipped across the surface of sleep, the looming departure forcing her thoughts into a buzzing mixture of excitement and fear. The knowledge that she would be leaving the Hall of Antiquities, possibly for the last time, in only a few cycles made real sleep impossible. Still, she'd failed to notice Cyprian getting up, and was briefly confused when she reached for him and felt only the coolness of the bedding.

She slipped from the bed and padded across the rug, pulling her robe around her as she left the bedchamber. Cyprian, it seemed, must have been struck harder by the inability to sleep than she had, and she expected to find him in his private quarters. Passing through the hallway, she saw that he hadn't pulled back any of the curtains blocking the windows, leaving the corridor in semi-darkness. Apparently, he hadn't been ready to give up on sleep entirely.

Poking her head into Cyprian's chamber, Faye was surprised to find that he wasn't there. She considered that he might be going over their equipment, making final preparations for their departure, or possibly even conferring with Jotun, but something inexplicable told her that he wasn't doing any of those things.

She knew where he was.

In the Office of the Curator, which was incandescent after the dimness of the western passages, Faye found Cyprian standing before the great window, watching the permanent sunrise. The chamber, which had once housed Rorik's greatest treasures, seemed enormous in its emptiness. Like most of the artifacts previously held in the hall, the Crown had assimilated the majority of Rorik's personal trophies into the vaults of the Vinecrown Keep. Phir-Ramarian, though nominally the curator, had never used the space.

In his mourning, then in his resentment, Cyprian had never made any move to make the room his own. Only a plain wooden desk, a single cabinet, and a creaky stool remained. Spread out across the desk, Faye observed several pieces of creased parchment that were all-too-familiar to her.

Among those papers, the assorted cargo manifests, personnel rolls, and projected routes of Rorik's lost expedition, was an inconspicuous note that had nevertheless cast a long shadow over her husband's life. It had been recovered from a stone cairn along the edge of the Imperial Highway, at the northernmost edge of the living wood where the last trees gave way to the blasted wastes. Discovered by one of the few search parties permitted by Phar-Mindorius after it became clear that Rorik, who was long overdue for his return, wasn't coming back, it was the last-known record of the expedition.

That is, until the badlander had arrived. The specifics of his supposed encounter with Rorik were still unknown, and Faye knew that Cyprian was eager to speak with him. Only the numerous preparations they'd all undertaken had prevented Cyprian from seeking him out.

Faye, whose entrance into the chamber had gone unnoticed, or at least unacknowledged, lifted up the weathered sheet and scanned the familiar, faded words.

For any who follow,

Company has made excellent time and had no issues following the projected route. Bridge spanning the Einfallen west of Nordabor in disrepair, but sound enough to cross without incident. Imperial Highway still clear and viable. Reached the northern border of living lands after fifteen full-cycles. No encounters with badlanders. Few shades spotted; only two dispatched. No casualties and no loss of equipment. Some of the men are hesitant to enter the dead lands, but they need not fear. Our company is prepared and will be embarking into the unknown shortly. We will cache further messages along our route.

—Rorik Fontaine, Curator

It was as brief as it was unhelpful. The short missive, the last words imparted by Rorik, painted a rosy picture that was hard to reconcile with the knowledge that he and his expedition had never returned. Not even the slightest hint was made towards what might have later doomed them. Indeed, what that doom was remained unknown, though Faye was certain that they were dead. To hope otherwise was to ignore the obvious willfully.

Of course, Faye would never speak so bluntly with Cyprian, who for a long time had grown doleful and bitter whenever any allusion was made to his father being dead. Rorik's expedition had failed, yes, but in Cyprian's mind, there'd been no proof of his demise. Only in the past few long-cycles had he begun to speak about Rorik in terms that implied he'd accepted his apparent death.

Still, Cyprian's thoughts on the matter were guarded and mercurial, and Faye worried that this new expedition had rekindled false hope within him—and not just a hope of finding and somehow rescuing Rorik, but a hope of redeeming his tarnished family name.

For as long as she'd known Cyprian, he'd had a complicated relationship with power. Outwardly, he eschewed the trappings of his royal lineage, but privately, he'd often simmered with a deep resentment at being passed over as the curator of the Hall of Antiquities, a role he'd believed was guaranteed by his birthright. He linked his father's disappearance to a loss of faith in his bloodline's ability to perform their duties, and often lamented that Phir-Ramarian had been given what was rightfully his. This new expedition was just an extension of that. Cyprian hadn't said as much, but Faye was certain that he coveted Phir-Ramarian's leadership position, and believed, probably rightfully so, that he would be better suited to guide them to the triumph that he craved.

His compulsion for acclaim had once seemed enticing to a young woman who'd come from nothing and who'd been equally enchanted by the wonders of the old world. His position, his knowledge, and his drive had been a potent combination in Faye's eyes. It wasn't that she'd actively sought to marry into the nobility; coming from commoner parents, both simple farmers eking out an existence on the lower rungs of their rigidly divided society, Faye had never dreamed of penetrating the upper echelon. Her relationship with Cyprian had been as unexpected as it was incredible.

Faye had met him while wandering the public area of the Hall of Antiquities, ogling the priceless relics celebrating the city's venerable past and Vingallean heritage. Her own love of history had blossomed when she'd discovered an amulet etched with detailed markings while tilling her family's modest field. She'd reluctantly taken the amulet to the Hall of Antiquities on her parents' orders; they were hoping it could be sold. There, she had been delighted to learn from a clerk that it was a worthless trinket, allowing her to keep it. Whether or not it was of monetary value had meant nothing to Faye. Its mysterious nature, the unknown hands that had handled it, fascinated her. From that point on, she had haunted the Hall of Antiquities almost constantly.

It had been different then. Rorik, whom she occasionally caught a glimpse of as he busied himself throughout the hall, had still been the curator, and he'd commanded many loremasters and servants. Most of them had been lost with him when he and his expedition vanished. The esteem that the Fontaine name had commanded, and their unquestioned mastery of the Hall of Antiquities, had been lost with him as well. But all of that had seemed unimaginable at the time.

When Cyprian approached her, she'd been doubled over a display case containing a detailed map of the northern coastline. She'd been fascinated by the blue denoting open ocean. He shared her fascination, and the two of them had discussed the wonder of a flat, endless expanse of water for some time.

Cyprian had seemed interested in her at once, and later told her that it was not only her beauty, but her frank, unpretentious interest in the map, and the unknown shores it represented, that attracted him. The noble class, so pleased with their positions and themselves, put little thought into what else could be out there unless it was to flaunt their knowledge.

They'd explored all the treasures of the hall together, as well as every hidden area of the city. Cyprian knew things about Nordabor's architecture and history that the fairy stories Faye had grown up listening to had scarcely mentioned. It also helped that, as the curator's son, he had access to almost every restricted area, including the keep and the hollow in which they'd often excavated.

As they grew into adulthood their friendship turned into something more. The two of them became inseparable, their bond growing stronger with each passing long-cycle. They weathered the loss of Faye's parents, the disappearance of Rorik, and the subsequent fall from grace of the Fontaine name together. The loss of Cyprian's mother followed, and though they were not wed, Faye came to live with Cyprian at the hall, which had become strangely empty. There were many hoisted eyebrows amongst the nobility, but they didn't care.

The mood at the hall changed. Cyprian's relationship with his royal kin had grown strained, and he was officially passed over for the role of curator, but was allowed to remain at the hall as a mere steward. Despite the hardship, Cyprian had found solace with Faye, and the two were eventually wed. Phar-Mindorius did not attend; Phir-Ramarian, unfortunately, did.

For some time, things had been good. Cyprian had finally seemed to come to terms with his father being gone and with his place in the kingdom, a place many would have been greatly satisfied with. Yet, here he now stood, surrounded once again by the detritus of a past that Faye had hoped had been settled.

She placed the note back on the desk and considered what to say. Before she could decide, Cyprian turned around, an affable smile on his face. "Trouble sleeping?" he asked.

"Yeah," she said. She gestured toward the strewn papers. "I see you've dug these back out."

"Well, I couldn't sleep either, not when we're so close to leaving. I figured I'd look through his old notes, compare things, and see if there was anything in there that might give us some final insight."

Cyprian may have been acting nonchalant, but Faye knew he was obsessing over the decisions that Rorik had once made. The final note had only ever whetted his appetite for more information. The discovery of the message had prompted many to call for continuing the search, especially Jotun, who'd been part of the initial searches, and Cyprian, who'd been barred from participating in any rescue operation from the start. Phar-Mindorius had not wanted to risk his young nephew being lost beyond their realm, thus denying his sister both her husband and her only child. Cyprian had been apoplectic, but powerless to change his uncle's mind.

This note, read and reread, obviously offered nothing new. "Did you find anything?" she asked anyway.

"No, not really," he admitted.

Faye nodded. "Well, either way, I'm sure we'll be fine, though I'm going to miss this place. Not this room, really, but the rest."

Cyprian pursed his lips and scanned the room. "Yeah. It's odd to think that, whatever happens, this place won't be home anymore."

"It's hard to imagine what could come after. If we succeed, I mean." She chose not to examine what might happen if they failed.

Cyprian must have sensed her unspoken thoughts. Without a word, he wrapped her in an embrace, and she hugged him back tightly.

Together, they stood on the precipice of a journey that they could barely comprehend. The world beyond Nordabor was completely foreign to them, and for Faye, that was as terrifying as it was enticing. She knew that it was too late for doubts; she'd made up her mind, and nothing could halt the plans that were now in motion. Soon, she and Cyprian would be leaving everything they'd ever known in search of something far greater.

As they held each other, Faye looked through the window at the dawn, which, as always, promised a day that would never arrive. When they separated, she saw that Cyprian's gaze had remained on his father's final message.

CHAPTER 7

Nordabor's dockyard had not seen such a commotion in several lifetimes. With trade between Nordabor and the outside world ending long ago, the sleepy, dilapidated docks had become a haunt for commoners seeking to eke out a living by snagging any fish that still resided in the Einfallen. They traveled the river along its path through the realm, trawling the waters. Unbeknownst to them, Ganachim's influence had kept life spawning in the area. At least, until recently.

Now, the bustle of final preparations filled the air. For several cycles, the general laborers recruited by Rayburn had been loading crates, casks, and wagons and herding several donkeys and a few horses into the hold of a repurposed fishing vessel.

As Cyprian watched the workers straining to slide and drag the unwieldy loads into the yawning entrance to the hold, he considered how audacious this part of Starkad's plan truly was. His father's first expedition had set out sunward on foot and had to pass through a massive expanse of woodland before reaching the lands outside of the realm. His second expedition had crossed the Einfallen on the crumbling Imperial Highway bridge spanning the river and headed north. Never had they considered utilizing the river as a means of transport. Even now, Jotun eyed the battered vessel doubtfully. Cyprian really couldn't blame him.

The riverboat, called the *Fortune*, undoubtedly in hopes of bringing some to its captain, had actually been repurposed before. Underneath the long-cycles of wear and alterations to the structure, Cyprian could see the hallmarks of Vingallean military engineering. He'd studied the naval prowess of the old kingdom, and knew that Vingallea had boasted a massive fleet of impressive warships. The *Fortune*, although a smaller vessel designed for transporting cargo and soldiers, was still much larger than any other fishing boat yet afloat. It was clear why it had been pressed into service at the behest of the Crown.

What was less clear was whether or not Phar-Mindorius had been aware of the boat's apparently dilapidated state. The *Fortune* appeared to be barely afloat, despite the refurbishments that Blair Dupree and her team of engineers had overseen. Even now, Dupree stalked across the deck of the boat, barking final orders to her crew, who rushed to complete the tasks. Rough metal plates were patched over warped and grime-encrusted wooden beams. Weighed down by the load of provisions in its hold, the riverboat sagged woefully in the dark waters rushing by its rocking sides. The entire boat groaned and creaked in protest at its new burden. It would be a truly disappointing start to their campaign if the boat holding their supplies sank before they'd even left.

Standing with Rayburn atop the rusted deckhouse, watching the commotion below, was the *Fortune's* captain, Barrett Winslow. Due to the relatively minor part they'd play in the expedition, Winslow and his small crew had not been informed of the true purpose of the journey. Promised hefty pay, Winslow hadn't asked any questions. Rayburn had assured the other expedition leaders that he could be trusted to fulfill his obligation and that the boat would remain afloat.

That obligation consisted of transporting the expedition and its supplies downriver, continuing south through the Dawnlands and into the Daylands as the river bent to the southeast. Where the river turned westward, they would anchor and continue on foot to the southeast, where they would hopefully locate the god Veathyadell along the crater's edge. Assuming they succeeded in obtaining whatever blade shards the old one possessed, they would return to the riverboat and continue west, toward Vin-Sadavat. Once the expedition unloaded near there, Winslow would be free to return to Nordabor. The remainder of their journey would be northward, on foot.

"This boat is a floating piece of shit," Faye announced as if she were reading Cyprian's mind. He chuckled, shaking his head, and she grinned.

Jotun did not share in their amusement. "It is," he said. "This is exactly why your father never considered this. First of all, we were looking to map as much of the territory as possible, not circumvent it. Second of all, we did not want to put our trust, and the trust of the Crown, in some fisherman's floating trash heap."

"Look, if Rayburn says this Winslow and his *Fortune* are trustworthy, then what else can we do? Would you like to march south along the river and try to keep up?" Cyprian asked.

Faye smiled again, this time at the thought of the crooked old man jogging after the riverboat. Jotun sputtered with irritation, but failed to produce a proper response. Cyprian nodded, considering the matter settled.

As the haulers finished loading the last of the equipment, the other expedition leaders began to arrive at the docks. Cyprian observed the high shepherd, Moore, looking at the boat with the same sour grimace that remained on Jotun's face.

Finally, the royal procession arrived in stately splendor. Phar-Mindorius led the way, with Phir-Ramarian and the king's herald flanking him. Captain Mather and his contingent of royal guardsmen, shadowed by courtly retainers and standard bearers, followed. Starkad meandered behind them, clearly separate from the pomp.

As the procession filed onto the docks and settled into formation, he wandered off to the hold, presumably to check on the provisions.

The herald blew his horn, which appeared to have been recently polished. "Announcing! Phar-Mindorius, Lord of the City of Nordabor and High King and Savior of the Collected Realms of Vingallea!"

Phar-Mindorius looked slightly embarrassed at the addition of "savior" to his formal title, and Cyprian wondered if he or the fawning herald had come up with it.

"You all know why we're here," the king said after waiting a moment for the small crowd to grow silent. "You all know what's at stake. All I can do now is give you the cumulative blessing of myself and every Vingallean monarch before me. May the Void-God watch over you all, and may you bring this endeavor to fruition."

A few cheers and claps passed through the group. Cyprian felt the short speech had been the perfect mix of inspiring and vague. Those listening who did not know the full purpose of the expedition would not glean anything from it, and those who did know would be reminded of how important their quest was.

"I leave you now with a heavy heart, lightened only by the knowledge that you are being left in capable hands." Phar-Mindorius smiled tightly and nodded toward his son, who stepped forward. He was once again wearing his impractical formal armor and carrying the resplendent helm under his arm.

"I have the utmost faith in all of you. Together, we will succeed where all others have failed."

Cyprian frowned.

"I expect nothing short of perfection from this crew. Loyalty, bravery, diligence in your duties. This expedition will push us all to our limits, I'm sure. However, Vingallean might can overcome any obstacle. Now, let's finish here and board our vessel," Phir-Ramarian said proudly.

Another, smaller, round of cheers followed, and the formal ranks broke apart as the guardsmen went about their business. The king and his son continued speaking privately, surrounded by their court.

"'Our vessel,'" Jotun said with disgust, still looking at the battered riverboat as if he'd smelled something foul.

•   •   •

The last of the boarding was a process of confusion. With the lower hold packed full of livestock and crates, every person was forced to try and find somewhere to stow their personal gear in the limited space available for crew. Winslow remained in his small private cabin within the deckhouse, but the rest of his crew had been forced from their normal quarters by order of the Crown. They'd been relegated to settling amongst the crates, and they made their displeasure known.

Thankfully for Cyprian, Faye, and Jotun, a private room had been held aside for them by Phir-Ramarian. Really, it had only been for Lord and Lady Fontaine, but they'd been unwilling to cast Jotun out on his own and made room for him. As it was, the cabin, which had belonged to the first mate, had only been meant for one, and made for extremely cramped quarters. The three agreed to spend as little time in the tight, fish-stinking room as possible.

As for Phir-Ramarian, the largest cabin, which had previously housed several of the crew, had been held for himself and his personal scribe, a young, eager chronicler called Bastion Pike. As Phir-Ramarian surveyed the *Fortune*, Pike scuttled after him, jotting down whatever the prince said.

Rumors abounded regarding Phir-Ramarian's closeness with his favorite subject. Publicly, the bachelor prince was known to have brought many women to his bedchamber, from maidens of the nobility who harbored fantasies of becoming queen, to commoner whores. Privately, many whispered amongst themselves that Phir-Ramarian was perhaps *too* interested in having Pike around. Cyprian thought it just as likely that he really was pompous enough to have Pike document his every moment, but either way, he cared not. Any discussion of whom the prince was bedding, like all palace gossip, was the foolish pastime of the worthless aristocracy.

Once it was confirmed that everyone was onboard, the final call was made for departure. The surly crew pulled the ropes from the docks and the *Fortune* cast off into the pull of the river. From his spot on the deck, Cyprian noticed Phar-Mindorius gazing solemnly from the dock, still surrounded by his retainers. He lifted an arm and waved, not to Cyprian, but to Phir-Ramarian, who stood at the bow. The prince, a momentary look of grief passing over his face, waved back.

Cyprian wondered if Phir-Ramarian was at all worried that they wouldn't return. He knew the thought had crossed his own mind. He did not want to share the same fate as his father.

Cyprian squeezed Faye a little closer to him and watched as Nordabor shrank away. Soon, only the four spires and gabled roof of the Vinecrown Keep were visible, barely touched by the light of the perpetual dawn.

•　　•　　•

After so much buildup to such a momentous event, the helpless waiting Phar-Mindorius would now have to endure was going to be excruciating. He had returned to the keep, his servants buzzing about, praising him and promising the success of the expedition. It was exhausting.

Finally, after settling into the comforts of his private chamber, he dismissed the last of them. He now sat alone, listening to the ringing in his ears and staring into the coals of his fireplace.

He had endured this sort of waiting before. First, when Rorik went east. It had been the first expedition of its kind, and so much hung on its success. Of course, Rorik had returned triumphant, which softened the memory of the waiting. Then he'd left again, and the many hopeless long-cycles that followed had taken a toll on the king.

Now, he would have to relive that constant cloud of dread, of not knowing. Compounding that was the fact that this truly was Nordabor's last hope. Previously, there had been time; the decline of Ganachim had not been so severe. Now, all of his best men were gone, including his direct successor, searching for a last-chance solution to their doom. There was no backup plan.

Most of all, he worried for Phir-Ramarian. He knew his son was a capable leader, but he was not blind to his shortcomings. It was good that Cyprian would be there to balance him out. He wished that he were young enough to lead, but even if he were, a king could not leave his people during a time of crisis. He was needed here, upon the throne, to reassure them.

At least, until the crops truly failed, the water became poison, and their society finally followed the rest of the world into collapse. Then, he knew, those same obsequious followers would come for his head.

His thoughts wandered to his hidden vizier. The nameless oracle had proven indispensable, but even he could provide no information regarding Rorik or any guarantee of success for Phir-Ramarian. Phar-Mindorius wondered what would become of the vizier if the city fell. Would he vanish as mysteriously as he had arrived? Move on to some other outpost that might still exist out there?

As he often did when he ruminated on the vizier, he felt uncomfortable. The loyal advisor's boundless depths of knowledge should have been comforting, but only disturbed him. A boon for Nordabor, but one that left him feeling sullied. Still, he needed the vizier, and he felt obligated to advise him of the expedition's departure.

Phar-Mindorius puzzled over his complex feelings at the moment. He unconsciously decided to do what he'd done his entire life: smother his doubts and fears under the veneer of authority. He rationalized that he, as the king, was beholden to no one, least of all his own advisor, so he would speak with the vizier when he felt it necessary to do so. For now, he would rest.

He shuffled to his broad bed and slunk under the heavy blankets. The darkness of the room pressed in on him reassuringly. He could wait. He had guided his kingdom through difficult times before and he would do it again. He closed his eyes and prayed to the Void-God for deliverance until sleep took him.

PART II:
STATIC SUN

CHAPTER 8

Galt, Daeg, and their two new partners had left their crowded cabin and now walked the warped boards of the main deck. Moore had left them to their own devices as he attended a private dinner being held for the leaders of the expedition in the dining cabin belowdecks. After a time of prayer and meditation, the stifling clamminess of the small room had become too much.

Now, the steady forward movement of the boat produced a breeze across their faces. Used to the typical dead stillness of the air, it was a welcome change, even if it was cold. The flowing air also helped to alleviate the nausea caused by the rocking of the boat, a sensation that none of them had felt before.

They'd been cruising down the river for a few cycles now, and the terrain surrounding them remained unchanged. On both sides of the broad water, dark evergreen trees and the occasional hanging willow created a nearly black wall of impenetrable foliage.

"Seems like the sky has lightened a bit. I think we've started bending sunward," Daeg said hopefully.

"I think that's just your imagination. Looks the same to me," Galt said, gazing up into the unchanged gray sky. Solgard and Blackburn exchanged glances, but said nothing.

They lingered near the rear hatch at the stern, watching the white churn of the boat's wake cascade across the water's ebony surface. The speedy current had ensured that the ship's crew had not needed to man the large oars splayed out through portholes on the boat's sides, beyond the occasional corrective push one way or another.

Daeg broke the silence again. "What do you think they're discussing?" he asked.

"I don't think they're discussing anything," Blackburn answered. "I think our titled masters are just enjoying finer food and drink than we'll get whenever they get around to feeding us."

Galt laughed and agreed. It was refreshing to hear another shepherd who seemed to share his outlook, as opposed to the young and naive Daeg.

"Come now, Ferro," Solgard scolded. "No need to put ideas like that in this poor young man's head. I'm sure they're discussing very important matters."

It sounded like she was defending him, but Daeg couldn't help feeling like his intelligence had just been insulted.

As the four shepherds spoke, they wandered from the stern toward the bow. Near the forward hatch, they encountered five of the royal guardsmen, who were sitting on small boxes and coils of rope, passing a bottle around.

Tension between the shepherds and the guardsmen, royal or city, had always existed. Coupled with their faith and devotional lifestyle, the shepherds were often considered the most formidable fighters in the realm. Their duties required a level of skill in combat that not all people could achieve. It was well-known, if unspoken, that many guardsmen were men and women who'd simply failed to achieve selection into the ranks of the Ivy Citadel. As such, in Galt's experience, shepherds were often treated with derision by the guardsmen.

He was surprised when one of the royal guardsmen called out in a friendly, if slightly insulting, greeting. "Hey, herders, come join us," the guardsman said, displaying a smile full of crooked teeth. He held the bottle up in offer.

The other shepherds were also well aware of the normal animosity, and were as surprised and reluctant as Galt. After a pause, Daeg, the most willing to put old hostilities aside, sat, took the bottle, and expressed his thanks. The three others sat as well, with some hesitation.

Daeg took a healthy swig from the bottle, the burning liquor forcing him to stifle a cough. The crooked-toothed guardsman smiled again. Daeg offered the bottle to Galt, who declined. He looked to Solgard and Blackburn and raised his eyebrows. They both shook their heads.

"Some endeavor, huh?" the guardsman said, ignoring the other shepherds' discomfort. "I don't know about you all, but this is the farthest I've ever been from the city."

"Aside from the burning fields, I believe that's the case for us as well," Solgard said politely, deciding to cautiously engage with the friendly guardsman. The other shepherds did not contradict her. Daeg still looked as if he was trying not to cough.

"Well, we're in it for the long haul now. We're going to get quite the tour of our wide world," the guardsman said. "No need to remain strangers. We're going to be working very closely together for quite some time, and out here, guardsman or herder, we're all beholden to our masters."

He gestured vaguely toward the stern of the riverboat, where the gathered expedition leaders were enjoying their private inaugural dinner.

Solgard smiled. "Well-put." She reached out for the bottle and took a drag. Daeg, whose cheeks felt flush, was slightly embarrassed to see that she didn't struggle with the harsh liquor at all.

"Drayton Kovak," the guardsman said, introducing himself. He proceeded to introduce the rest, and Solgard took care of the introductions for the shepherds. Galt and Blackburn were still wary of their new companions, and Daeg felt foolish and out of place, saying nothing.

"So, we're here because we're duty-bound to our high shepherd. Did any of you volunteer?" Solgard asked.

"No, we're Captain Mather's private contingent. The best of the best," another guardsman, a hulking goon called Sarin Gricks, boasted.

Galt smirked slightly at the man's idiot bravado.

"The king knows we'll carve a path through anything out here," Gricks continued. "I faced badlanders when I was a city guardsman; they were no tougher than your average drunken lout on the Mercantile Causeway. Didn't even come close to breaching the walls."

"And what'll you do if you encounter a shade?" Galt asked with feigned innocence.

Gricks's face darkened. "Give me your fancy fucking sword and I'll run through it as easily as anything else."

"Okay, okay," Kovak interjected, "none of that, now; what did I just say? We're all on the same side here."

Solgard glared at Galt, irritated by his instigating.

"Point is, I'm not worried about anything we'll encounter out here. We're Vingallean men. We're world-conquerors. It's in our blood. Badlanders, shades, even the old ones, we'll run them all down," Gricks said, igniting some whoops of agreement from the other guardsmen.

Realizing that he and the other shepherds would be stuck working with blowhards like this for the foreseeable future, Galt held his tongue.

After an awkward lull, the conversation turned to more mundane things, such as family, old stories, and complaints about their growing hunger, a topic they could all agree on. They continued to pass the bottle around until it was empty, all the while glancing toward the rear hatch and waiting for a sign from their leaders that it was their turn to eat.

•　　•　　•

"A toast. Not only to this expedition and its assured success, but to the culinary skills of Horace Barrow."

The cook, one of Rayburn's haulers who was also responsible for food preparations, had been in the ship's galley for some time, and had produced a meal that was remarkably good: fresh salmon from the river, potatoes, biscuits, and asparagus. Now he stood before Phir-Ramarian and the other assembled leaders smiling and blushing furiously.

"Thank you, my lord."

The prince smiled back at him. "No, thank you. You are dismissed. You may return to clear the dishes when we're finished in here."

Barrow's smile faltered slightly at the abrupt dismissal, but he thanked Phir-Ramarian again and left the small dining room.

The room, glamorous by no means, was still sufficient for their needs. The leaders had gathered around a long, narrow table to celebrate the beginning of their voyage and to discuss the trials to come. A feeling of general mirth permeated the room. Even Cyprian and Faye, excited for their sojourn into the outside world, were swept up in it. Only Starkad remained somber and silent, sitting at the end of the table, smoking his pipe and waiting for the casual conversation to wind down.

"So, Lord Fontaine, I understand that you've been able to compile detailed maps of the areas we're going to be visiting first?" the grand healer, Jacqueline Bellamont, asked.

Cyprian wiped his mouth as he finished a final bite of the succulent meal. "Well, no. My father and his partner Jotun did the actual mapping on their first expedition. Jotun is a fantastic cartographer and surveyor. Rivaled only by my wife here."

"I helped Jotun gather what we needed, but I haven't really mapped anything," Faye said with some embarrassment. "Really, I've mostly just studied what we already have. Jotun is the real expert."

Jotun had been unable to join them for the dinner, which avoided the awkwardness of determining whether or not he was actually invited, lacking title or a leadership position. He'd grown ill due to the rocking of the riverboat, causing him to double down on his dislike of their mode of transport. Cyprian personally felt he was being dramatic to prove a point. Either way, he was not present to explain the intricacies of his craft.

"But regardless, you have maps of where we're going, correct? We're not relying completely on Starkad as of yet? No offense," Bellamont said, directing the last toward Starkad, who hardly seemed to notice.

"None taken," he replied around the stem of his pipe.

"Yes," Cyprian said. "The maps we have of the southeast are very detailed. The area in which Veathyadell is supposed to reside has been thoroughly surveyed. Things may have changed in the intervening long-cycles, though, and that's where Starkad's knowledge will come in handy. That, and directing us toward where, exactly, the old one is hiding."

"Which, I believe, brings us to how we intend to best the old one, assuming that he's unwilling to part with what we want," Phir-Ramarian interjected. "As our esteemed guide has made clear, it's much more dangerous out here than we could imagine. As such, I had Chief Engineer Dupree work with Captain Mather on the construction of a solution."

He leaned back in his chair with a look of satisfaction and gestured toward them, indicating that it was now time to begin their impromptu presentation. Starkad sat up with some interest.

Mather and Dupree exchanged a look of mutual discomfort at being put on the spot, and after a pause, Dupree took the lead.

"It's known, based on the compiled lore and the studies of both the skeleton of the recovered old one and the living one beneath the keep, that the old ones are to be considered a formidable threat. Correct?" She directed this toward Cyprian.

"Yes, that's correct." Cyprian was curious. Dupree and Mather had plied him for specifics regarding the purported abilities of the old ones during preparations for the expedition, and now, it seemed that he was going to learn the details of what they'd been working on.

"So, we expect to encounter many threats out here. Shades, badlanders; those are nothing that can't be handled by our shepherds and guardsmen. They're relatively known entities. Obviously, encounters with badlanders have been rare, but they're not unheard of. The old ones are different, though. We assume they'll be a threat, but the extent of their real power is largely unknown."

The group had grown quiet, all eyes fixed on Dupree. The thought of confronting a god was sobering.

"Of the biggest concern, based on the histories provided by the Hall of Antiquities and the information provided by Starkad, are the old ones Veathyadell and Naffabyin. And that's just the two that we know we have to confront. By all accounts, Ulesreto and Opriseur are equally dangerous. Lord Fontaine, you're the authority on the lore. Could you reiterate what we're up against?"

Cyprian cleared his throat. "Well, Starkad previously covered the basics of each of the old ones we'll face. Specifically, threat-wise, Veathyadell will have a command of fire and the implements of warfare, as was his purview in the legends. I would expect that he could, if he still has enough power to do so, burn us all alive."

Sudden looks of concern shot through the group.

"As for Naffabyin, we've previously discussed what to expect. If he still has the power to generate such an intense storm system, we've got to expect that his direct attacks will be ferocious, and of a nature that we're fundamentally unfamiliar with."

The reminder did nothing to tamp down on the unease that had quickly bloomed amongst the leaders.

"So, we understand that those two represent a very real, physical threat. Whereas, the others ...?" Phir-Ramarian looked expectantly at Cyprian.

"Yes, well, the other two, Tariono and Chortelak—they're not believed to wield such obviously dangerous abilities, but they're still thought to have a larger physical stature, and, considering what Starkad said, they may have human followers to worry about. And as for Ulesreto and Opriseur, Ulesreto was capable of killing the

Father-God, so that speaks for itself. Opriseur controlled the ocean, and I would think she could drown anyone she encounters. Hopefully, we won't be anywhere near her until after we've reforged the blade in Nordabor. I suppose we can deal with that problem then." He smiled weakly.

"So, as far as the physical threats posed by Veathyadell and Naffabyin," Dupree said after a moment of silence, "Captain Mather and I have worked together to forge a specialized armor designed to mitigate those threats."

Starkad raised his eyebrows slightly, but said nothing.

"We've modified the design of a typical heavy plated armor, such as that worn by standard guardsmen in full-combat situations."

The guardsmen, Cyprian thought, had never really faced a full-combat situation. It had been several long-cycles since there had been any serious incursions into the realm by badlanders, and even those were merely skirmishes that resulted in the badlanders being essentially picked off by archers before they reached the city walls. Internal strife in Nordabor had never really risen to anything beyond isolated incidents of law-breaking.

"The armor has been forged with amiant, a silicate mineral mined from the grottos beneath the city. Amiant has been found to resist heat."

"Our ceremonial robes are interwoven with amiant fibers. It works; they resist the flames and heat when we're working in the burning fields," Moore added.

"We theorize that its properties may also insulate against any of the phenomena produced by Naffabyin," Dupree continued.

Cyprian was not thrilled about the theoretical nature of the protections provided by the armor, but was comforted by the knowledge that he would not be the one donning it.

"We were able to prepare three sets of this amiant armor, which will be worn by two of my best men and myself," Mather said. If he was at all nervous about confronting a god in untested armor, it didn't show.

"This armor will ensure that our men are able to best any old ones with minimal danger to themselves," Phir-Ramarian announced proudly.

"We'll see," Starkad said. "For the sake of your men, I hope you're right. Otherwise, being cooked alive within your armored suits will be a truly horrendous way to die."

Phir-Ramarian glared down the table at Starkad, his irritation at being continually undermined by the badlander's insinuations painted clearly on his face.

"Thank you for your input," he said icily. The rest of the group remained silent.

He broke his gaze away and addressed the others with a clear shift in tone. "So, we have several full-cycles to go before we reach the westward bend in the river, where we'll anchor. I suggest you all get some rest. Come, Bastion."

Phir-Ramarian stood abruptly and departed the dining cabin. The scribe, who hadn't spoken a word through the entire dinner, followed like a shadow. The remainder of the group, the conversation thoroughly extinguished, began to rise slowly.

Cyprian watched as Starkad exited toward the stairwell leading to the deck. He turned to Faye.

"I'm going to catch up with Starkad. Now's my chance to talk to him about my father," he said quietly to her. She nodded and squeezed his arm.

Faye didn't really trust the badlander, no matter how much he appeared to be helping them. She may have enjoyed his refusal to knuckle under to Phir-Ramarian and his penchant for insulting the prince, but he was still an outsider, and one apparently motivated by greed and power. A title in the court, coupled with a comfortable life of wealth, was hardly a noble pursuit. If things became as dangerous as Starkad said they could, she expected him to abandon them easily to save himself.

Starkad's old encounter with Rorik was also troublesome. She understood Cyprian's desire to discover his father's fate, but she did not want whatever Starkad had to say fueling a misguided belief that Rorik could still be rescued.

She thought all of this, but said nothing as Cyprian left.

• • •

Leery of the uneven wooden planking, Cyprian strode quickly across the deck toward the bow of the boat. He passed a group of royal guardsmen and shepherds sitting in a semicircle.

"Have you all finished, my lord? Is there food for us yet?" called a guardsman with teeth pointing in every direction.

"Yes, see Rayburn's man, Barrow, in the galley," Cyprian answered distractedly. He continued by the group, not waiting to see if they got up. Starkad had just come this way a moment before, (presumably he'd ignored the questions of the hungry guardsman) and Cyprian was intent on catching up to him.

He found Starkad leaning across the rusted railing of the bow, gazing into the dim light of the permanent dawn. Suddenly, Cyprian felt foolishly nervous. He approached Starkad quietly.

"How can I help you, Lord Fontaine?" Starkad asked before Cyprian could announce himself.

"I'm sorry, I don't mean to bother you, but I figured now was as good a time as any to ask you some questions about my father."

Starkad turned around slowly, leaned his back against the railing and shrugged. "Go ahead."

Now that the moment had come, Cyprian felt tongue-tied. He was unsure what to ask first and afraid of what the wanderer might answer. He forged ahead.

"When and where did you encounter my father? Was he in good spirits? Was he okay?"

Starkad nodded along patiently with the questions, then pursed his lips in thought for a moment before answering. "It was long ago. About twelve long-cycles, by your people's reckoning. It was on the northern moors; northwest of the ancient harbor of Kafarbjorn. Still within the Dawnlands. He and his people were a bit haggard, but were doing well."

Cyprian tried to picture his father out there in the wastes, plotting his next move, perhaps standing over a newly detailed mapping of the northern lands in a canvas tent, issuing orders to his men or jotting down his thoughts and plans. He found that he had a hard time picturing his father's face.

"What did he say when you spoke to him?"

"Well, initially, he and his men were hostile. They saw me as just another badlander, a threat. I made it clear that I meant no harm, that I only sought shelter for a while. I'd wandered further than I'd intended, into the darkness, even, and found myself nearly out of food and water. Your father allowed me into his camp and provided me with aid. We then struck up a conversation, and he asked me if I knew anything of the blade shards or the old ones."

"And did you at that point?"

"Not a thing. I knew of the old legends, though, and it all made sense. I may have gleaned more information from your father than he realized. You must understand, his knowledge of the shards was very scant. Not much more than a hunch, really. His primary directive was still to search out a living land. He asked me about that as well, which I also had no helpful information about."

Cyprian frowned. "And you never saw him or any of his men after that?"

"No. After our discussion, and after he provided me with some of his provisions, I continued south. When they broke camp, and where they went after that, I have no idea. I decided to pursue the old ones and their blade shards independently."

"So you could bargain your way into Nordabor," Cyprian said, a bit more harshly than he'd intended. It irked him that his father's expedition had never returned, while this man, who stole his father's idea, had found success.

"Essentially, yes," he replied, surprising Cyprian with his blunt honesty.

His demeanor darkened. "It is harsh in the wastes. Harsher than someone who has been coddled at the nipple of Nordabor his entire life can imagine. Your idiot prince thinks that he can wag his princely finger at *gods* and demand what he wants. He will have a harsh reminder of the power of the old ones, and the vicious, unforgiving nature of the wastes, before this is over. All I want is what you want: deliverance from a dying world. Whether that's slightly longer behind the walls of your city, or for eternity in Paradise, I want it. Sneer if you wish. I do not seek approval, only to fulfill my purpose and secure my survival. I've answered your questions."

Starkad turned away and resumed gazing beyond the bow as if Cyprian had vanished. Cyprian tried to think of something to say to prolong the conversation, but failed. His questions had been answered. The answers were unsatisfying, but he wasn't sure what else he'd been expecting. At least now he had some idea of where his father had been. Even if it was many long-cycles ago.

Feeling somewhat embarrassed and stupid after being lectured, Cyprian walked away without another word.

CHAPTER 9

The mossy forest floor was suffocated by silent shadows. Each snap of a branch or crunch of a heavy footstep on the pine needles echoed thunderously through the stillness of the woods as the hunting party picked their way gingerly through the low growth, aware of how loud their passage through the pine forest was. As they delved deeper into the sylvan unknown, the dim light of the open air around the river and the security of their anchored vessel fell away. They had to stay close to the shoreline lest they become lost in the pressing darkness.

They'd been ordered off of the boat to seek out fresh game. Rayburn had advised Phir-Ramarian that it would be wise to find it while they still could, saving their provisions for when they truly needed them. Soon, they would be leaving the still-living lands of Nordabor, and with them, any chance of finding healthy game or edible plant life.

The hunting parties, each commanded by a guardsman and escorted by a shepherd, were comprised of haulers with hunting or trapping experience. For commoners, it was not unheard-of to search the woodlands around the city for any viable game. Fresh meat was always welcome, and any pelts collected could fetch a hefty price from the nobility, who delighted in the prestige and high fashion represented by the relatively rare animal furs.

Despite their experience, none of the men pressed into the hunt were particularly excited about leaving the safety and familiarity of the boat behind, and some hid their unease behind bluster. "This is idiotic," one of the haulers, a man called Rand Brunson, whispered. It sounded like a shout in the silence. "It's too quiet. We're going to scare away anything that's out here before we can get near it."

"You running your trap is certainly not helping," Drayton Kovak whispered back.

The hauler's face grew crimson and he looked away, an angry retort that he didn't dare fire back at the under-captain simmering behind his lips.

Daeg watched the exchange and wished desperately that he was back on the boat. It occurred to him that if he was feeling this much fear being a short distance from the boat, perhaps he was not cut out for this expedition.

Not that it had been up to him.

He was now responsible for protecting the small hunting party from any shades they may encounter. The other shepherds, save Moore, who had remained on the *Fortune*, were also accompanying hunting parties scattered along the river's edge, though Daeg doubted that any of them felt as out of place as he did. Surrounded by the three surly haulers and Under-Captain Kovak, he felt very inadequate.

Daeg knew these men, particularly the haulers, did not understand what he did, and probably assumed that he was more than capable of handling any shade. They did not see the truth: that he was a young, inexperienced, and, frankly, scared kid. Although he had been an excellent pupil at the Ivy Citadel, was a skilled and loyal follower of his high shepherd, and was a steadfast devotee of the Void-God, he couldn't help feeling that he was out of his depth.

There was nothing routine about what he was doing, and there was no senior shepherd to guide him. Instead, he had only the under-captain to look to for direction.

Kovak had been so friendly and inviting when they'd first met, Daeg had never suspected that the man was Captain Mather's second-in-command. Now, he was all business, barking orders with authority. Daeg was almost more frightened of him than the encroaching darkness surrounding them.

The shepherds were organized in a very different way than the Royal Guard. Moore, while a strict leader, was also a teacher and mentor. Kovak's leadership style seemed a bit harsher. His derision for the haulers was obvious. Daeg assumed that, despite his initial friendliness, Kovak really felt the same way about him.

The group reached a small clearing, where they stopped. The full light at the edge of the tree line was now barely visible.

"We'll wait here. See if anything passes nearby," Kovak said.

Another one of the haulers, Lars Scudamore, glanced nervously in the direction of the remaining light. "We should have tied a rope to us so we could follow it back to the boat," he murmured. Kovak shushed him, but Daeg silently agreed.

Time passed, but in the gloom, it was impossible to tell how much. Daeg was not important enough to have been bequeathed a chronometer by the expedition leaders, but he saw Kovak check his several times. This was probably Kovak's first time inspecting a chronometer, and he seemed to struggle with reading it. The devices, provided by the Crown's timekeepers, were old and unfamiliar to most. The typical citizen of Nordabor needed only to worry themselves with the chiming of the great iron bell of the Vinecrown Keep.

They had been ordered not to spend more than three cycles on this hunt. Daeg wondered how close they were to being able to return. He didn't care if they came back empty-handed; one of the other parties would probably have better luck, anyway.

The sound of rustling leaves reached their ears, and each man froze. Their eyes searched the forest floor, seeking the source of the noise. Brunson, Scudamore, and the third hauler, Lido Hughes, hefted their crossbows in preparation. Daeg wondered how experienced any of them were with the weapons.

The rustling continued, and seemed to be growing closer. Finally, a dry bush parted slightly and a lean wild pig pushed its wet snout through. Daeg was taken aback by the creature as it stepped into the clearing. He could tell it was a pig, but it sported short tusks and black, coarse hair across its body. The pigs in Nordabor were pink, hairless, and bred fat for consumption.

The pig eyed the interlopers with curiosity, but no obvious fear. It occurred to Daeg that it may have never encountered a man before.

Hughes was the closest to the animal, and slowly raised his crossbow, nestling it against his shoulder. The others all held their breath in the complete silence. Hughes's finger slowly depressed the trigger with an almost imperceptible creak of tension. The snap of the bolt firing was quickly followed by an earsplitting shriek of sudden pain and terror from the pig, which nearly tripped over itself in its sudden flight from the clearing.

"Follow it!" Kovak ordered.

Hughes and Brunson trampled into the underbrush to chase down the wounded pig. Scudamore started after them, then stopped, unsure of whether to follow.

"At this point, just stay," Kovak said with disgust. Scudamore returned to Kovak's side obediently.

"Well, Daeg," Kovak beamed, slapping him on the back, "looks like we found some success after all. I was beginning to have my doubts."

Daeg was unsettled by Kovak's sudden change of demeanor and was not sure if the under-captain was somehow mocking him. He offered his best attempt at a pleasant answer brimming with camaraderie.

The sound of the men going after the pig began to grow faint, and a look of concern crossed Kovak's face.

"They're going to get themselves lost chasing that thing," he said. "Fuck. We need to stop them."

The three remaining men jogged off after their crew mates, following the path of pig blood, snapped branches, and disturbed pine needles as best as they could. They could no longer hear Hughes, Brunson, or the pig. The light from the river was now fully extinguished.

They nearly ran into the backs of the two men, who were crouching side-by-side near the base of a massive pine, the gnarled roots of which stretched crookedly into a hollow.

"What are you—" Kovak began before the two men, startled by the arrival of the others, snatched at their cloaks and pulled them downward, shushing them. They pointed, wide-eyed, into the hollow.

In the scant light that filtered in through the forest canopy, Daeg could just make out the crumpled shape of the unusual pig. It appeared to have finally succumbed to its injury, but something had stopped the men. Daeg stared hard into the shadows, following the outstretched fingers of Hughes and Brunson. Then he saw it.

The shade had obviously been wandering the woods for longer than any of the men had been alive. The normally wet, exposed flesh and nerves of the creature had coagulated into a hard, almost black network of cracked and hardened scabs. It trudged without uttering a sound, peering around the hollow with empty eye sockets buried deep in a twisted, disfigured face.

Daeg realized that the others were now looking at him.

"We need that pig. You're up, kid," Kovak whispered. It was an order.

Daeg looked from Kovak to the shade and fear seized him. His heart hammered in his chest, sending vibrations through his eardrums. He'd never handled a shade alone, much less in an uncontrolled environment. Briefly, he considered offering Kovak one of his anointed daggers and asking him for help, but he knew that it was pointless. The under-captain would most likely refuse, and Daeg would come off as weak and incompetent.

No, the destruction of the shade was his responsibility. He just had to figure out how to approach it. The shepherds were trained to time their attacks precisely as the shades were forming post-birth, when they knew that the entire creature was free of the body, but before it could fully take shape. This one was fully formed, and appeared to be ancient. Perhaps its age had led to decrepitude.

Daeg stood slowly amongst the crouched men.

The shade circled the pig as if it were considering its options. Daeg knew that shades did not eat, and though they would maul a person, they wouldn't consume them. Their condition drove them to lash out in violence for no other purpose but to inflict extreme suffering, to mirror their own. The shade seemed almost intrigued by the pig's body, and was certainly distracted by it as Daeg approached stealthily.

He drew his anointed blade from its scabbard as slowly as possible. The sound of metal against metal seemed very loud. His pulse continued to pound; he could feel it squeezing against the back of his eyes. He tried to slow his breathing as he took step after tremulous step toward the abomination. He'd done this before, he thought, he'd done it plenty of times. Still, the bizarre, dried-out husk of the shade was like nothing he'd ever encountered before. Finally, his blade was clear of its sheath and hefted. It was time.

In one swift motion, Daeg lunged forward and swung his blade in a wide, powerful arc toward the shade's midsection. The broadside bounced harmlessly off of the creature's scabbed carapace of solid flesh. Daeg stumbled back in surprise, the vibration of the failed attack shooting through the blade and into his arms. The shade whipped its head around, facing Daeg with its hideous visage.

Wasting no time, Daeg drove the blade up into the gut of the shade as hard as he could. This time, to his relief, the pointed end of the blade pierced a weak, weeping crevice in the shade's flesh and sank deeply into the tissue beneath, causing a hissing, steaming wound.

The shade howled in pain and violently jerked back, ripping the blade from Daeg's hands. He scrambled backward, drawing a short dagger and praying to the Void-God that the creature would succumb quickly. It shambled through the hollow, swinging its long, thin arms wildly. In its flailing stumble, it stomped across the pig, crushing it and sending guts squelching out of the body.

Daeg scuttled across the ground, trying to keep distance between himself and the shade. It swung its head around until it seemed to spot the source of the attack. Once the distorted face settled on Daeg, the shade rushed toward him. Every fiber of his being screamed at him to run, but he knew that he had to best this creature. The other men were watching; he could not fail at his single purpose for being there. He would be ostracized and possibly expelled from the order. He clutched his anointed dagger as tightly as he could and braced himself.

As it closed in on him, it stretched its long, grasping hands out. The sword embedded in its gut bobbed up and down with each step. Just before it could snatch him, he rolled away and drove the dagger into the back of the shade's pockmarked leg. It collapsed to its knees as Daeg wrenched the dagger free and rose. He lifted the dagger above him, preparing to drive it down into the top of the shade's lumpish head.

Before he could finish, the shade spastically thrashed around, smashing the back of a bony hand into the left side of Daeg's head.

A flash of brightness shot through his vision before everything went dark. Daeg lay sprawled across the ground and, stunned, floundered in the dirt.

He couldn't see anything. He gingerly touched the side of his head, and felt that his previously hard skull was now a shattered, pulpy mess. He didn't know what happened. He tried to look at his blood-slick fingers, and couldn't understand why he didn't see them.

More than anything, he was confused.

"What? What?" he asked mindlessly to no one.

Then the shade was on him.

CHAPTER 10

"How could you let this happen?"

Under-Captain Kovak sat at the long table in the dining cabin before Phir-Ramarian, Mather, Cyprian, and Moore, who was trembling with rage. Bastion Pike sat further down the table, feverishly jotting down the transcript of the inquiry.

Kovak and the haulers had fled the wood while Daeg was being torn apart, and, terrified, blundered their way back to the *Fortune*. Now, Kovak, indignant at any suggestion of mismanagement, had just outlined to the expedition commanders what had occurred in the woods.

"It wasn't something I allowed to happen," Kovak answered testily. "Shepherd Daeg was expected to perform his role. It was necessary to complete our hunting excursion. I couldn't help that he failed. It's not like any of us could have stepped in and helped him."

"By your own account," Moore seethed, "you sent him to confront that shade for a pig. *For a pig.* He was there to protect you and your men if it was absolutely necessary. You should have left the pig and returned to the boat as soon as you saw the shade. Or, at the very least, you should have waited to see if it would wander off on its own."

Kovak looked expectedly at Mather, who shifted uncomfortably in his chair.

"And why wasn't there any warning that we would be facing something different out here? This shade's appearance should not have been a surprise. Why didn't the badlander have anything to offer? Or what of your man, Berg?" Moore demanded, directing his ire toward Cyprian. "He's been out here before."

Cyprian, surprised to be put on the spot suddenly, felt his face flush. "I don't think Jotun ever got close enough to a shade to tell what might be different here." He chose not to add that the shepherds who had accompanied his father's first expedition, the ones who might have known those differences and been able to impart that knowledge, had all been lost with his father's second expedition.

Moore scoffed with disgust and folded his arms. "And the badlander?"

"He's advised us that, in his travels, he avoided shades at all costs. He had no way to defend against them, so, beyond knowing the typical dangers they presented, he had nothing to offer," Mather said.

In his agitated state, no answer would placate Moore. He sputtered for a moment, then turned back to Kovak. "Well, whatever the case, you should have known better. You should have led your men to safety, not stood there uselessly while Micla was killed."

"I understand your displeasure, High Shepherd," Mather said diplomatically, "but please refrain from telling my men what their orders are. Under-Captain Kovak was attempting to complete his assignment, and cannot be held responsible for Shepherd Daeg's loss."

"He was responsible for those men," Moore nearly shouted in response. "There would have been no punishment for returning empty-handed. We are not starving; we were just looking to supplement our stores. This is outrageous—the complete lack of regard for my men is monstrous! I want this imbecile demoted! Better yet, in shackles for gross incompetence!"

"Upset or not, I won't abide that tone," Mather growled, scooting his chair back.

Cyprian looked back and forth between the two men, anticipating that they were about to come to blows, then at Phir-Ramarian. The prince, who was responsible for all of them, sat with his eyebrows slightly raised, watching without comment.

"One of my men is dead, and you want to lecture me about orders and tone?"

"You're out of line."

Phir-Ramarian finally realized that Cyprian was staring at him and that it was up to him to restore order to the meeting.

"Silence, both of you," he snapped. Moore and Mather stopped arguing and looked at him. Once he had their attention, he seemed unsure of what to say next. After a pregnant pause, he continued. "What happened to the shepherd was tragic. We will have a shepherding ceremony for him with full honors. And we will make sure that in the future, any separate excursion is accompanied by two shepherds, who will only engage shades when needed. But what occurred was not the fault of the under-captain, or any of the men with him. It was a tragic accident. The matter is settled. You are dismissed, Under-Captain."

Moore sank into his chair and put his head in his hands. Mather's face was a stoic mask. Kovak, who clearly felt vindicated, rose and thanked the prince profusely for his good judgment.

"Just answer me one more thing," Moore said.

Kovak paused.

"Did Micla produce a shade?"

"We didn't wait to see."

Moore nodded to himself and inhaled sharply. Kovak lingered for a moment before looking toward Mather, who gestured for him to go. Once he'd left, Moore turned to Phir-Ramarian.

"I sincerely hope your life is never in that man's hands, my lord." He rose swiftly and stalked out of the cabin, banging the door against the wall on the way out. Phir-Ramarian, who would normally never accept being addressed in such a manner, sat dumbfounded.

"I'm sure the high shepherd just needs some time to think things over. To process his loss." Phir-Ramarian smiled weakly. "Let's hope it's the only loss we suffer."

•   •   •

The symbolic shepherding of Micla Daeg was a grave affair, one attended by every member of the expedition, aside from Daeg himself, whose remains had been left far behind by the steadily cruising riverboat. Moore officiated, and his short speech was punctuated by pleas to the Void-God and barely veiled criticisms of the expedition commanders. The remaining shepherds stood by Moore, looking miserable.

Phir-Ramarian ignored the critique, watching the whole ceremony with a look of detached solemnity. Kovak, recently endorsed by the prince, stood near him. He appeared unmoved. For the rest of the company, the ceremony was an uncomfortable reminder of the very real dangers they faced. In an abstract sense, they'd all acknowledged the possibility of death on the expedition. None had imagined that it would occur so soon.

In the absence of a body to burn, Moore finished by symbolically lighting Daeg's non-essential belongings before casting them overboard. Any useful things he'd owned had been retained by the other shepherds. The small crowd began to disperse, returning belowdecks and back to whatever tasks they needed to complete. Moore, flanked by the other shepherds, remained at the railing, gazing into the black waters below.

•   •   •

Changes to the hunting party excursions were implemented, as Phir-Ramarian had said they would be. Only one party was sent out at a time, reducing their chances of success, but allowing for two shepherds to accompany the hunters, while the other two remained aboard the *Fortune*. Rayburn, who felt immensely guilty for suggesting the hunts that had inadvertently led to Daeg's death, was determined to ensure that they were safer in the future.

He had approached Moore tentatively after the shepherding ceremony and confessed his guilt. Moore had been surprised by the man's earnest nature, and comforted after Kovak's complete denial of culpability. They had sat in the musty darkness of Moore's cabin and discussed what could be changed.

"The Under-Captain," Moore had said with derision, "did impart some useful information. He said that the shade's body had been like a hardened shell. Micla's attempt to slash at it with his blade failed; he only found success when he stabbed it. I'll make sure that my acolytes know this. By the Void-God's blessing, Micla's death has at least granted us some wisdom."

Rayburn had nodded along, unsure of what else to say. In the end, he'd simply vowed to assist Moore in any way he could and pledged that his men would be instructed to help any shepherd in trouble.

Scudamore, Brunson, and Hughes were not selected for the next hunting excursion, and did not complain. As a show of good faith, however, Phir-Ramarian ensured that Kovak still led the party, despite the palpable tension between him and the shepherds. Per the new policy, both Galt and Blackburn escorted the hunters, and the two men, especially Galt, seemed ready to kill Kovak themselves. The hunting party returned empty-handed, but more importantly, with no losses.

All the while, the *Fortune* steadily continued its journey south. The river began to bend slightly to the east, and the sky lightened noticeably. The strangely bright sky, changed for the first time in any of their lives, raised spirits and restored confidence in the expedition.

Concordantly, the third hunting excursion returned triumphant. Under Kovak's leadership, they had netted two large pigs and a small horselike creature. The animals were appropriately butchered and treated for preservation, with some of the meat set aside for a celebratory feast. It restored the spirits of the company further, though some muttered that it was a waste.

The successful outing came at a fortuitous time. Shortly after, they seemed to reach the end of the lands kept alive by Ganachim's influence, and an end to their chances of finding any game.

The sudden change in their surroundings was startling. The previously dense pines that had enclosed either side of the river dwindled, first to skinnier, sparser trees, then to twisted, malnourished ones, sporting only a few brown needles. Scrubby undergrowth seized on the opportunity to receive slightly more sunlight and flourished briefly. Then that, too, shriveled.

The river bent further east and began to grow broader and slower. As the full-cycles passed and they continued east, the sun slowly crept higher in the gray sky, threatening to pierce the clouds at any moment. The temperature began to rise, and the malnourished trunks became sun-bleached husks. The eerie surroundings were soon forgotten as the first real rays of sunlight that most of them had ever felt reached them.

They had entered the Daylands.

CHAPTER 11

Golden light filtered in through the slatted window of the cabin. Cyprian and Faye lay together, crammed into one of the cots, the beam of bright, warm sunshine cascading across them. They were blissfully alone in the room, having sent Jotun off with a thinly veiled excuse that he took at face value.

The natural warmth of the sun breaking through the ceiling of dull clouds that had been the roof of their world for their entire lives had invigorated them like nothing had before. After some time on deck, with an unspoken understanding, they had returned to their cabin and made love in a pool of light. Now, they lay in the aftermath, tangled in the sheets and each other, feeling strangely electric.

The eruption of pure daylight had helped to erase the last of the sour mood that had permeated the company since the shepherd's death. Now, pleasantly exhausted, Cyprian's thoughts wandered far away from death or danger. Faye looked up at him dreamily, the sunlight lighting every ridge and valley within her hazel irises. She smiled.

Behind her smile was a lingering smear of worry for her husband that even the sunlight and intimacy could not erase from her mind. He'd returned from his conversation with Starkad in an irritable and closed-off mood, unwilling to address what had happened. When he was finally ready to talk about it, he'd explained how little Starkad could tell him. He spoke of his father in an unsettling present tense, which Faye chose not to point out.

Since then, she had avoided the topic of Rorik completely. It had been relatively easy, as first they'd been distracted by the loss of the shepherd, then the changing scenery.

Faye was fascinated by the transformation of the shoreline, and despite the inherent risks, had petitioned to be included on a hunting excursion. Phir-Ramarian had not even entertained the idea, and did nothing to hide his amusement at the suggestion. Cyprian had urged him to allow it, though he was also hesitant to see her leave the boat after the previous death. She had reminded him that they'd all be leaving the boat soon enough, and he'd been at a loss for words.

Ultimately, the hunting excursions had ended before she could needle the men further, and she'd missed her opportunity. Now, the barren, rocky shore through which the brown waters of the river meandered captivated her as much as the dense woodlands had.

And the sunlight. It was indescribable, and as comfortable as she was now, the desire to bask in its direct shine was an almost-physical pull. She was about to voice her desire to get up when Cyprian spoke.

"We've stopped moving."

Puzzled, she lifted her head up. He was right—the constant rocking had ceased. She got up with some effort and squinted out the window. Once her eyes adjusted to the light, she could see that they had indeed stopped.

"We have," she confirmed. "Why? There's no way we're at the turn."

"No, definitely not," Cyprian agreed, getting up and dressing hastily. She joined him, suddenly feeling that the cabin air was very stuffy.

A moment later, they were dressed and ascending the bowed steps to the open air of the deck. The previously pleasant sun now felt slightly oppressive in the stagnant air. Without the movement of the boat, the illusion of wind was gone. They looked at each other with concern as they saw the crowd gathering on the deck.

"Watch out, step aside," Cyprian said, forcing a way through the group until he and Faye reached the bow. The reason for their stop was now apparent.

The Einfallen, which had been steadily widening, now resembled a marshland. The muddy waters had enveloped the shore, feeding an otherwise-strangled growth of reedy, brown grasses. The bright sky, a hazy light blue, was still breathtaking. Further along the horizon, the flat land rose dramatically into two ends of a massive ramp. A monolithic stone bridge that had once crossed the Einfallen was now a heaped mountain of rubble, blocking the waterway and forcing it to burst its banks.

"The Sterling Bridge of the Imperial Highway," Starkad said from near Cyprian's elbow. Surprised, he turned toward the badlander.

"When I last passed this way, about six long-cycles ago, the bridge was still standing. It was a marvel of Vingallean engineering. You'd have appreciated it," he said to Cyprian, the animosity of their prior conversation apparently forgotten. "It appears that time has finally caught up with it."

Cyprian squinted back toward the tumbled debris, hazy in the daylight.

"Is there any way around it?" Faye asked, realizing with some excitement that they may be disembarking sooner than expected.

"The crew might be able to manually paddle the boat closer, but soon, we'd run the risk of running aground, I imagine. We need to talk to Phir-Ramarian and Winslow," Cyprian said.

He hesitated for a moment. "Starkad, you should come, too. We'll need your knowledge of the territory to come up with a solution."

Starkad nodded, saying nothing. Cyprian told the small crowd who'd been listening to what they were saying and murmuring amongst themselves to wait. He, Faye, and Starkad then headed for the wheelhouse. Cyprian couldn't help but notice that Phir-Ramarian was nowhere on deck.

As they reached the wheelhouse, Jotun shuffled up to them quickly. "We've stopped!"

"Yes, we know," Cyprian said. "Have you seen Phir-Ramarian?"

"No."

Cyprian snagged the arm of a hauler that was passing. The hauler skidded to a halt and turned. "Yes, m'lord?"

"Go and fetch the prince from his cabin. We need him at the deckhouse."

"Yes, m'lord," the hauler answered obediently, though his displeasure at the task was evident.

Nearly a cycle later, Phir-Ramarian, followed by Pike, finally arrived. A private meeting ensued, attended by them, Cyprian, Mather, Starkad, and Winslow, who hosted them in his small deckhouse. The other leaders waited anxiously outside. Faye, irritated at her exclusion, remained there as well.

"So, how far out are we?" Phir-Ramarian asked, mopping his sweating brow.

"We're much further north than our originally intended drop off point," Starkad answered. The seriousness of the situation had blunted his normally sardonic attitude toward the prince. "If there's no way to navigate around the collapsed bridge, we'll have to go on foot from here. It could add several full-cycles to our trek."

"The current is about nil, but my crew should be able to navigate us closer to the bridge with the oars," Winslow explained. "Not too close, mind you; I won't risk bottoming out on any debris in that shallow water."

"Fair enough," Phir-Ramarian allowed.

"Once we get closer, we can use the skiffs to get your men and equipment on shore. It'll take time, but we'll get it done."

The skiffs had been just large enough to be utilized by the hunting parties. There were only three total, and the thought of loading the donkeys on to them, not to mention the horses, convinced Cyprian that he would be avoiding whatever skiff they occupied.

"Can we haul the skiffs around the collapse? Continue down the river on them?" Mather asked.

"It would be impractical. More impractical than just continuing on foot from here, I mean," Starkad said, removing his pipe from a pouch. "As it is, it will take several trips just to unload everything we need. To take the skiffs, we'd either need to leave the majority of our supplies or our company behind. Or make multiple time-consuming trips, fighting the current half the time."

Mather nodded.

Phir-Ramarian frowned and scratched his dimpled chin. "Can we do this?" he asked with uncharacteristic uncertainty.

"We're not so far out that it's impossible," Starkad answered. "What do you think, Lord Fontaine?"

Based on his recollection of Jotun's maps, Cyprian was inclined to agree with Starkad. Furthermore, he refused even to consider that turning back now was an option. Not when they had basically just started.

"I agree," he said. "It's achievable."

Phir-Ramarian seemed to consider his options for a moment. He looked to Pike, who had been performing his typical hasty scribbling after every spoken word. The scribe seemed to be waiting eagerly for his master's next declaration, his quill hovering over the parchment.

"We'll begin preparations for departure immediately," he said slowly. He appeared to be figuring out his plan as he spoke. "Captain Winslow, please have your crew get us as close as possible to the east coast, near the bridge. Prepare the skiffs. We will deploy the full contingent we'd planned on and leave a token force behind to hold this position, with the *Fortune* serving as our basecamp, just as we'd intended."

"We'll need to bring more provisions if we're leaving with the same amount of men as we'd originally planned for. We have further to go now," Mather interjected.

"Of course."

"Another thing to consider. We won't be able to utilize the river to approach Vin-Sadavat. It's quite a bit further on foot," Starkad said.

Phir-Ramarian began to look slightly overwhelmed. "We'll figure that out when we return to the *Fortune*."

He paused, then added, somewhat unconvincingly, "Triumphant."

．　　．　　．

Their adoration of the sun's newfound strength was quickly replaced by exhaustion as they toiled in the sweltering air. Being unaccustomed to the heat and light only added to the difficulties of unloading. Moving the equipment to the skiffs and ferrying it to the shore fell just short of being a complete debacle.

True to his word, Winslow navigated the *Fortune* as close to the rocky shoreline as he could. Closer to the hulking wreck of the Sterling Bridge, enormous slabs of stone rose from the water, their lower halves obscured by the murkiness. Twice, the riverboat scraped hideously against unseen hazards before Winslow, flushed and sweating, declared that they would go no further.

With no dockyard gangplank to assist with the process this time, the cargo was hauled out through the upper hold doors built into the deck. This proved especially troublesome for the skittish livestock, who were extremely put off by the harness-and-crane system that hoisted them into the air and lowered them to the waiting skiffs below. Two skiffs were loaded successfully, but during the loading of the third, a particularly upset donkey flailed hard enough in its harness that it nearly kicked one of the haulers in the head. When the harness straps were hastily removed, the terrified animal ran at once, plunging headlong into the water and nearly capsizing the skiff in the process. It never resurfaced, having presumably broken its neck against a submerged boulder. After the commotion, Phir-Ramarian sighed with relief and stated that at least it hadn't been a horse.

After over three cycles, the last of the equipment and men had been ferried to the nearest bit of stable shoreline. Phir-Ramarian, Cyprian, and Faye had been on the last skiff, which carried nothing that could risk a capsize. As it was, Phir-Ramarian eyed the water with discomfort. Prior to departure, he had donned his splendid armor with its useless, ceremonial helm. It had apparently not occurred to him how quickly he would sink in the impractical getup until they were already in the wobbling skiff. With much assistance, he scrambled across the broken rocks of the shoreline, soaking only his feet in the process.

Once the last of them were on solid ground, the skiffs returned to the *Fortune*. Staying with Winslow and his crew were three of the royal guardsmen, a healer, and the shepherd, Blackburn. Moore had argued with Phir-Ramarian, demanding that two shepherds remain behind so as to avoid the risk of having another situation similar to Daeg's, but the prince dismissed his concerns, advising him that remaining on the boat would hardly constitute the same risk as venturing into the wilds. Three shepherds would be needed to escort the company; the boat could make do with one. Moore, increasingly despondent about the way things were being handled, hadn't bothered to argue further.

It took another cycle to sort through the equipment and stow it properly into the wagons that had been hitched to the remaining donkeys. The last wagon, which had been meant for the donkey that had been lost, now needed to be man-hauled. Rayburn had initially suggested that it be attached to a horse, but the harnesses used by the donkeys would not fit the much larger animals. In response, Rayburn established a system of rotation to make sure that the haulers had sufficient breaks from pulling the heavily laden cart.

Phir-Ramarian, with further assistance, mounted his horse. Once in the saddle, he seemed practiced enough to control the animal easily. Cyprian and Faye, who'd had limited exposure to riding, had much more difficulty. Realizing her discomfort with the animal, Faye slid off and offered the reins to Jotun, much to Phir-Ramarian's irritation. The crooked old man, sweating profusely without even walking, was very grateful. Having ridden a horse during Rorik's first expedition, he handled the animal with skill.

Faye, who declined Cyprian's subsequent offer to take his horse, thanked Phir-Ramarian, somewhat facetiously, for bringing the steeds. The prince responded absentmindedly, still frowning at the sight of the untitled Jotun sitting upon a royal saddle.

Finally, after everyone had been accounted for and all of the provisions had been properly secured, the company set off on their long march.

CHAPTER 12

"Thanks be to the Void-God for finally putting us on solid ground."

Galt grunted in agreement as he, Moore, and Solgard shook out the bottoms of their mud-caked robes. Moore continued to espouse their good fortunes, but Galt was hardly listening, and he felt that Moore hardly meant it.

The truth was that their spirits had been permanently deflated since Daeg's death. Galt had never felt particularly excited to leave Nordabor to begin with, but Moore had spoken of their journey as a divine pilgrimage. Now, his attempts at praising the good will of the Void-God had an empty quality. As for Solgard and Blackburn, though they'd barely known Daeg, they had been crestfallen to lose one of their order. Blackburn had seemed relieved to be left behind on the *Fortune*.

Their journey on foot had so far done nothing to raise their spirits. The wreckage blocking the Einfallen had forced the water to spread further than they had realized. Though they'd disembarked onto a jumble of stone that constituted solid ground, the surrounding area was a muddy quagmire. The heat of the perpetually shining sun had baked the upper layers, creating a thin crust of earth on top of a thick bog. What appeared to be solid ground quickly yielded underfoot. Plodding through the boot-sucking mud had been a messy, exhausting endeavor.

The royal guardsmen, clad in their heavy armor, had fared even worse. They slipped and stumbled through the mud flat, trying hard to maintain their marching formation. The sun glinted off of their armor, sending winks of blinding brightness into one another's faces. Leading the group, Captain Mather's sweat-drenched face was frozen in a scowl of determination. Galt had noticed with no small pleasure that Under-Captain Kovak seemed to be struggling the most, huffing and groaning with each step.

Now, the company, caked in dried mud, had finally reached a point where the mire had ceded to badlands. Before them, a boundless desert of reddish stone stretched toward the horizon, bereft of a single shred of life. Besides the noise of the laboring company, silence reigned.

Phir-Ramarian, whose struggling horse had managed to keep him above the mess, called for a halt in order for the company to regroup. The last of the wagons, water casks sloshing, were pulled free by the straining donkeys and the miserable haulers, who were gasping in the heat. Phir-Ramarian ordered that a private tent be raised in which the expedition leaders could review the maps and continue to plot their course. Galt suspected that it was also an opportunity for the red-faced prince to enjoy some shade.

"Well, I suppose I should join the others," Moore said, watching the leaders file into the tent.

Galt followed the high shepherd's gaze and longingly stared into the blackness beyond the flaps. He found that his head was throbbing from the combination of heat, exertion, bright light, and constant squinting.

"We'll be here when you get back," Galt croaked, his throat very dry. He'd finished off his canteen nearly a cycle ago.

"Not that we have anywhere else to go," Solgard added, gesturing at the vast expanse of nothing that surrounded them.

Moore smiled feebly at her attempt at humor. With his white hair plastered down by sweat and his thin, pale cheeks marred by ruddy pink blotches, he looked very old. He downed the last of his canteen, which he'd just refilled, and set off toward the tent with a limping gait.

Galt watched him go with pity. He turned to Solgard.

"Let's get some more water."

·   ·   ·

"Obviously, our maps did not reflect the changes to the landscape," Lord Fontaine was saying as Moore parted the flaps and entered the darkness of the tent.

It took his eyes a moment to adjust. The interior of the tent, though a respite from the sun, was hot and stuffy. The leaders stood around a small table mopping their brows, careful not to drip sweat onto the maps spread out across the tabletop.

"Nor did we realize the extent of the flooding," he continued.

"Perhaps our guide could have prepared us for this," Phir-Ramarian said, cradling his flamboyant helm.

"As I said before, the bridge was standing when I passed here last," Starkad responded. "Now that we've cleared the floodplain, I'm certain that the going will be easier. Relatively, anyway."

Phir-Ramarian did not seem satisfied by this answer, and ignored it. "Well, how far out are we?"

"Based on the mapped routes, I would say probably a full-cycle and a half's march," Lord Fontaine said. He looked at Starkad for confirmation. The badlander nodded.

The idea of another full-cycle and a half of trudging through this inhospitable land and its relentless sun crushed Moore. Not for the first time, he wished that this task had never fallen on him or his chapter. His thoughts once again turned to Micla.

"Well, that being the case, we will continue on for another twelve cycles before we set up an encampment and rest," Phir-Ramarian declared.

Moore nearly shouted out in dissent, but caught his tongue. Phir-Ramarian had allowed several outbursts from him since Micla was killed, and he knew that the prince's patience was running out. Thankfully, someone else spoke up.

"My lord, if I may?" Rayburn said timidly. His heavyset face, peppered by gray stubble, was flushed. The prince turned to him with his eyebrows raised.

"This heat is beyond what any of us had expected. My men are exhausted." Rayburn paused, and then, with some embarrassment, added, "I'm exhausted."

"Well, you had to expect that this would be a taxing journey. And we're behind." Considering the matter settled, Phir-Ramarian disregarded Rayburn and turned to the others. "We will continue."

Moore's distaste for the prince simmered. It was easy for him to order a long march from his comfortable perch on horseback. Silently, he nearly begged the Void-God for patience.

Murmurs of dissent passed through the other leaders, but they were, surprisingly, silenced by Starkad.

"It pains me to say so, but I agree with our leader." The last word carried an air of disrespect. "We are behind, and the longer we linger in any given area, the faster our provisions will dwindle needlessly. We need to keep moving."

Being provided with a reasonable explanation, as opposed to a blind order, seemed to satisfy the others. Moore still dreaded the thought of stepping back out into the simmering heat, and the look on Rayburn's face reflected the feeling.

"Well, okay, then. It's settled," Phir-Ramarian said, clearly unsettled by Starkad's ability to take his orders, make them his own, and gain the compliance of the leaders.

"I, I just—" Rayburn stammered, delaying the inevitable.

"You can take my horse," Lord Fontaine said, interrupting him.

"Thank you, my lord!" he said, brightening. A nasty jealousy bloomed within Moore, who now wished he'd spoken up. Not that he knew how to ride a horse, anyway.

"Lord Fontaine," Phir-Ramarian said, "the horses are for the *titled* members of this expedition. It's not your place to gift it beyond that. I've been lenient with Berg."

Lord Fontaine leveled an icy gaze at the prince. "Fritz provided the horses. I think we can make another exception."

Seeing the sweating, miserable faces staring at him, Phir-Ramarian relented. Moore wondered if he'd realized that somebody might suggest he give up his own horse if the conversation continued.

"Before we adjourn," interjected Captain Mather, who was holding his own helmet, "we need to discuss our armor. It's not practical to continue in this heat wearing so much heavy equipment. I suggest we stow it with the amiant armor until such a time as it's needed. We will continue with light gear, but retain our full weaponry."

Phir-Ramarian seemed to consider this for a moment, turning his helm over in his hands. "Yes, that seems appropriate. We can do that."

Moore assumed that the prince had been looking for an excuse to remove his own heavy armor without seeming weak. As for Moore, his robes were sacred. Heat or no heat, he would not be removing them.

"Everyone should keep long-sleeved layers on, despite the heat," Starkad said. "As I told you before we departed Nordabor, the sun will easily burn any exposed skin. For anything that can't be covered, there's the salve I've instructed Bellamont to produce."

"Now that we're clear of the mud flat, I've ordered Healer Hale to distribute it," Bellamont explained. "I'll assist her when we're done here. By the time we're ready to set out, everyone should have been issued a tin."

"Excellent. Well, you all know what you need to do. Prepare to depart," Phir-Ramarian said. The leaders rose and began to shuffle out of the tent.

As he followed the others out, Moore observed Phir-Ramarian thrust his canteen toward Pike, who'd been sitting silently beside him. "Fill this, then get back here and help me get this armor off."

•   •   •

The water, though lukewarm from sitting in the sun, was extremely refreshing, and easily coated Galt's dusty throat. He smacked his lips in satisfaction and went back for another draught from the cask.

"Sorry, boss's orders. Only one fill-up per stop," the hauler in charge of the water distribution said.

"I wish you'd told me that before I'd finished this off," Galt said testily.

The hauler, a younger man called Garat Anders, was clearly uncomfortable. "I'm sorry, sir," he repeated.

"Here, have some of mine," Solgard said, offering her canteen. Galt thanked her and poured a third of what Solgard still had into his own canteen. The two lingered near the wagon, watching the command tent and saying nothing. Anders glanced toward them occasionally, as if anticipating further trouble from Galt.

As they waited, Lady Fontaine and her elderly map keeper, Berg, approached the cart.

"My lady. Sir," Anders said dutifully as he collected their bottles and filled them.

"They're my maps. My writing is upon most of them," Berg was saying. "To be excluded from their meeting is not only insulting, but foolish. Rorik understood my expertise. It never mattered to him that I held no title. Cyprian should push for us to be in there. If anything, you should be; you have a title."

"Yes, Jotun, I agree." Lady Fontaine sighed, nodding thanks to Anders. "But Phir-Ramarian is too stupid to consider things that fall outside of his rigid beliefs. You have no title and no appointed leadership position. I, on the other hand, am a *lady* of the court. My lord takes precedence in a situation like this. Cyprian is just playing the game."

Galt was curious to hear complaints about the prince coming from high-ranking members of the expedition. Solgard appeared to share his interest, and the two exchanged a look.

"Well, it should be Cyprian leading this expedition," Berg said almost too quietly to hear. "Rorik and I completed a lot on our expedition without the Crown breathing down our necks. Cyprian knows what's at stake."

Lady Fontaine said nothing, but took a thoughtful sip from her canteen. Nearby, a group of royal guardsmen guffawed at an unheard joke. On the wagon they stood near, two haulers hefted a large cask and hurled it over the side. The apparently empty cask burst apart as it crashed onto the stony ground. The haulers brushed their hands off on their pants and said something about ditching unnecessary weight. Galt wondered how many extra servings the guardsmen had to have sucked down to have already finished off the cask. To their credit, Lady Fontaine and Berg made no attempt to fill their canteens further.

Lady Fontaine seemed to notice that Galt and Solgard were hovering nearby.

"Hello. I don't believe we've formally met," she said, approaching them with a hand extended. "I'm Faye."

Galt, slightly taken aback by Lady Fontaine's casual use of her first name, faltered. Solgard stepped in and completed the introductions for them.

"I'm sorry that you've already lost one of your own. Our prince may have glossed over it, but your man is not forgotten," Lady Fontaine said.

Galt appreciated the sentiment, but suspected that she did not know Micla's name.

"We appreciate everything you do," Berg added with an awkward smile.

"So, we happened to overhear that you're also excluded from the meeting," Solgard said, hastily changing the subject. The condolences and praise had left an uncomfortable silence in their wake. "Thankfully, High Shepherd Moore is in there, keeping us somewhat in the loop."

Berg glowered, apparently not liking that his exclusion was common knowledge.

"Well, ideally, everyone would be properly represented in there. Whether Phir-Ramarian, in his abundant wisdom, would listen is another thing," Lady Fontaine said, apparently comfortable with speaking ill of her prince. A privilege enjoyed by the nobles that would have a commoner in shackles, or worse.

Despite his initial curiosity, Galt was now eager to leave the conversation. Lady Fontaine's complaints about the prince were not the same as the complaints of the shepherds. Phir-Ramarian's mismanagement had allowed one of their chapter to die needlessly. Lady Fontaine was just personally insulted by her exclusion.

Before the conversation could descend into another awkward lull, the group was approached by Moore, Lord Fontaine, and the prince's scribe.

"Hey," Lord Fontaine said casually to Lady Fontaine and Berg. He nodded in acknowledgment at Galt and Solgard and then continued as if they weren't there. "We're going to continue the march here soon. Bellamont and one of her healers are issuing the salve now."

Galt, who'd already collected his tin and applied the pungent-smelling goop, rubbed the back of his neck, which still felt tender and hot to the touch.

"Oh, and I gave my horse to Fritz," Lord Fontaine added almost as an afterthought.

Lady Fontaine slowly smiled. "How did Phir-Ramarian take it?"

"Not well," Lord Fontaine said, grinning.

While the lord and lady were speaking, Anders, who had politely refrained from speaking to any of them, finished filling a large canteen for Pike, who thanked him and turned to go, before stopping suddenly and turning to Berg. "Excuse me. You worked on our maps with Rorik Fontaine?" he asked.

"Well, yes, I did," Berg answered.

"They're very impressive. Some of the best documentation I've seen."

Berg chuckled with pleasure, and the two began to discuss the cartography process before Pike suddenly remembered that he had to return to the prince.

Moore was standing by with Galt and Solgard while the others spoke, looking exhausted. As the others slowly walked away, Moore turned to his remaining acolytes.

"You heard Lord Fontaine. The march will continue shortly. Void-God be with us." Moore trudged away, his empty canteen banging hollowly against his belt.

Galt looked at his own canteen for only a moment before jogging after Moore and offering it to him.

CHAPTER 13

The caravan's journey from the edge of the mud flats proved to be much less arduous, despite the fact that Cyprian and Faye were now both on foot. Cyprian was struck by the surroundings and reminded of a conversation he'd had long ago with his father.

Rorik had recently returned triumphant from his first expedition, the mummified remains of Aedesda in tow. He and Cyprian had been in the sunlit curator's chamber, as Rorik still retained that title at the time. The walls were lined with dusty tomes and recovered relics, scraps of metal and cloth, rock and parchment, all evidence of the empire that once was. Rorik had been beaming, describing the eastern badlands to his son with near reverence. A teenaged boy at the time, Cyprian had listened to his father recount his feats with a wide-eyed intensity.

Now, all this time later, Cyprian was looking at the same impossibly blue sky and rising walls of crimson stone, boasting bands of multicolored silicate. The flatlands had given way to jutting crags of rock, offering sweet, shadowed darkness in their eaves. No plant life was present, only crumbled gravel settled in the low points between the winding canyon walls.

It was a breathtaking view that was completely removed from anything Cyprian had ever known. His father's descriptions, vivid as they were, had done nothing to illustrate the actual stark beauty of the place.

Faye seemed equally enamored, her head swiveling around constantly, trying to see everything at once. Cyprian watched her and wondered if he'd ever have a child to describe this place to.

He and Faye had been wed six long-cycles ago, and had only ever casually discussed having children. Jotun had brought it up on a few occasions, in his own nosy, pushy way, but generally, they had never seriously addressed it. Cyprian suspected that Faye dreaded the idea of bringing a baby into a broken world.

For his own part, Cyprian was leery of repeating history. There was danger even in his small excursions into the forest outside the city walls, nevermind any journey beyond their realm. He did not want to vanish, leaving a fatherless child behind, and he was relieved that they hadn't had a child before embarking on this expedition.

These thoughts were rolling through Cyprian's mind when a harsh voice called out, ordering a halt. His head snapped up, looking for the source of the order. Mather, now garbed in a light leather cuirass, was stalking down the line toward Phir-Ramarian, who'd brought his horse to a stop. Mather had been leading the vanguard, and had apparently spotted something up ahead.

"We've sighted seven shades in a basin over the ridge line, my lord. They're some ways off, but it would be best if we waited for them to leave the area entirely. We don't want to risk direct confrontation." He stated this last bit as a fact, not a suggestion.

Phir-Ramarian nodded in agreement. "Send the order down the line. We'll continue once the shades are clear. They do appear to be moving, correct?"

"Yes, my lord. They appear to be making their way out of the basin."

"Excellent. A chance to stretch my legs," Phir-Ramarian said, unaware of how irritating the comment was to all who'd been walking. He swung his considerable bulk from the saddle and dropped heavily to the ground. "Captain, I'd like to see the shades, if you don't mind. Can you take me to where you spotted them?"

Mather's face was entirely unreadable. If he thought the prince's request was foolish, he didn't show it. "Yes, my lord."

Phir-Ramarian turned to Cyprian and Faye. "Care to join me? I'd like to see what's so different about these shades that our shepherd couldn't handle one."

Cyprian was glad that Moore, who was furious about the loss of his acolyte, hadn't been within earshot of Phir-Ramarian's callous remark. He looked at Faye, who shrugged noncommittally.

"Sure, we'll check it out," Cyprian said. Truthfully, he was curious about the shades. He'd only ever seen a shepherding a few times, and the shades had always been struck down before they'd fully formed. Jotun and his father, who'd relied on their shepherds to handle any wild, wandering shades, hadn't been able to tell him much about them, and the descriptions provided by Kovak and the haulers had been both frightening and intriguing.

"Bastion, watch Honey for a moment," Phir-Ramarian said, patting the neck of his horse lovingly. Cyprian and Faye exchanged a look of amusement at the name.

"Yes, my lord," Pike answered at once, taking hold of the reins. Cyprian suspected that, had she cared to, Honey could have dragged the diminutive scribe away in an instant.

Mather led the three of them ahead of the caravan, reaching a ridge line where the rust-colored walls of stone receded. He sent another guardsman back to notify the others of the reason for stopping, then indicated to Phir-Ramarian where the shades had been spotted. Phir-Ramarian squinted in that direction for a moment, then lifted his field glass to his eye. Cyprian and Faye, who'd provided him with the glass from the stores of the Hall of Antiquities, lifted their own in the same direction.

It took a moment for Cyprian to spot the creatures, but once his searching eye fell upon them, they were unmistakable. They trudged aimlessly in the wavering heat of the basin, their baked bodies almost completely black. Their long, sinewy limbs dangled listlessly, but Cyprian knew that those arms could tear a man apart in an instant. Their formless heads lolled as they walked. How they came to be grouped together was unknown, and they apparently had no interest in each other beyond generally heading in the same direction. What motivated them to cross the basin was also unknown. They may have been crisscrossing the basin for generations.

"Look at that," Faye gasped next to Cyprian, grabbing his arm and startling him. He lowered his field glass to see where she was indicating, then trained his glass on it. Phir-Ramarian and Mather followed her outstretched hand as well.

On the far side of the simmering basin, opposite the area where the shades were congregating, was a small, crumbling ruin. Nestled amongst the rising bluffs, it was almost completely hidden, but once seen, it was clearly man-made.

"Some sort of ruins," Cyprian said quietly. "Are those on any of the maps?"

"I'd have to consult with Jotun, but I'm pretty sure they're not," Faye said.

Cyprian's heart fluttered. Before them lay ruins of the old Vingallean kingdom, completely unexplored. Unless, of course, Starkad had been to them before. Despite being on a journey to seek out living old ones, the simple, jumbled remains of this building still awoke Cyprian's passion for antiquities. And, unlike the ruins of the Sterling Bridge, these appeared to be intact enough to truly appreciate them.

"Seems like a perfect place to set up our encampment," Mather said, appreciating the ruins not for their historical significance, but for their tactical advantages. He turned to Phir-Ramarian. "Crossing this basin ought to take up the remainder of the time allotted for this march."

"Yes, I suppose," Phir-Ramarian said, still peering through his field glass. He looked back toward the shades. "They still haven't cleared the basin yet. I guess we'll wait, then make our way to the ruins."

With their plan settled, Cyprian, Faye, and Phir-Ramarian returned to the caravan, leaving Mather and the rest of the vanguard to wait out the shades. Upon their return, Cyprian and Faye found Jotun, who'd been chatting amicably with Rayburn, both men settled comfortably into the saddles of their horses.

They told Jotun what they'd seen, and, enticed, he pulled several maps from the leather-bound tubes strapped to his gear. After scouring the maps, they determined that the ruins had not been documented before. Finally, Cyprian spoke with Starkad, who did indeed have some familiarity with the ruins.

He sat upon a boulder, pensively gazing into nothing, the end of his pipe clamped in his teeth. "I passed near this way; heard tales of the ruins, but didn't seek them out. Nothing indicated that a god might still be there. They're a small notation on my map." He patted the dented metal tube that he kept separate from Jotun's maps. "From what the nomads in the area said, the basin ahead used to be a large lake surrounded by thick woodlands before the fall of Alminnian. The ruins were once the temple seat of Ganachim. And we know what became of her."

Cyprian's thoughts flicked uncomfortably to the emaciated wretch shackled in the darkness beneath the Vinecrown Keep. The glazed, white eyes that hadn't seen daylight in ages.

"Phir-Ramarian has decided that we're going to set up our first encampment there," he said, pushing the unpleasant memory aside.

"Then you'll have plenty of time to enjoy the sights. Legend has it that it was quite the temple in its heyday."

Starkad's tone was completely flat and unreadable, but Cyprian sensed some sort of derision. He struggled with what to say next, but was saved by one of the guardsmen loudly announcing that the shades had cleared the basin. Starkad hopped lithely to his feet, patted Cyprian on the shoulder, and started up toward the ridge.

"We ought to get a move on, my lord."

.   .   .

Cyprian was unprepared for the heat of the basin, which made the temperature in the canyon ridges above seem refreshing by comparison. The company slogged through it, trying to move as quickly as possible to escape the pounding, white-hot sun, which sat malevolently in the apex of the sky. Cyprian found himself wishing for the cool darkness of his chamber. It was impossible to believe that the sun's touch had recently felt so pleasant when they'd still been on the Einfallen.

The ruins shimmered in distorted waves at the edge of the basin, seeming to grow no closer as they went. Some of the men excitedly declared that they could see water ahead until Starkad, familiar with the peculiarities of the Daylands, informed them that it was only an illusion created by the heat distorting the air itself.

After nearly two cycles, and several liberal applications of Bellamont's salve, the company finally ascended the opposite rim of the basin and approached the dilapidated temple, eager for an extended rest.

Despite the ravages of time and the ceaseless sun, the temple was still a sight to behold. Stone bleached completely white rose up in a dome, a large piece of which had collapsed into the structure. Petrified remains of what had surely been a verdant garden wrapped around the circumference of the building. Intricately carved reliefs on the outer walls were still visible, despite the details being rounded off by the abrasive sand that had run down from the dried cliffs crumbling above. Whatever colors had adorned the image had flaked away long ago.

"Look at that," Faye said, her voice weak and dry, but still filled with awe. She walked up to one of the immense walls near the main entrance and examined the images carved there. Cyprian and Jotun followed her.

The carving depicted an enormous figure, rays of light extending from a halo above its crowned head. Its arms were extended benevolently, and springing forth from them was another figure, this one obviously female. The female figure, also adorned with a halo, was extending her own arms. From them, a plethora of vegetation and animals, many of them unrecognizable, populated the image. On the other side of the door, a mirror image of the same carving flanked the entrance.

"It's the Father-God's creation of Ganachim," Cyprian said.

"And her creation of the natural world," Faye added reverently.

"I can't believe that we missed this," Jotun said, making Cyprian wonder what his father would have thought of it.

As they gawked, Mather, accompanied by three of the royal guardsmen and the swarthy shepherd whom Faye and Jotun had been speaking to by the water cart, passed through the open entrance. Only brittle iron hinges remained; the door itself appeared to have dry-rotted away long ago. Just beyond the entrance, a tumble of broken stones marked where the entryway ceiling had buckled beneath the weight of the ancient edifice. Mather and the others took a moment to pick their way through, then disappeared into the darkness beyond. A short time later, they returned and announced that the temple was clear and safe for them to enter.

Too exhausted for words, the company slowly filed into the temple, forcing aside just enough of the debris to make a clear, but narrow, path. Cyprian quickly sketched the wall carving, and then he, Faye, and Jotun entered the temple, the last of the party to do so.

Cyprian blinked in the darkness, letting his eyes adjust as the relative coolness inside washed over him.

The inside of the ruin was essentially one massive room. Columns, which Cyprian sincerely hoped were still trustworthy, rose to the dark ceiling. The last remnants of pews, which had collapsed and started to disintegrate, were scattered across the dusty floor. In the center, under the zenith of the dome, was a desiccated wooden throne. Petrified branches entangled around one another, forming the rough shape of a chair. A dried trough passed from one end of the temple, bifurcated around the throne, met on the other side, and continued to the opposite wall. A pile of rubble near the throne marked where the collapsed section of the dome had crashed to the floor. A beam of light shot through the hole, illuminating the area behind the throne, where an altar was placed before a towering marble sculpture.

The sculpture made Cyprian shudder. It clearly depicted Ganachim, and the likeness was eerily accurate. Or, more accurately, what Ganachim had been before her long enslavement. The statue was robust, with a full bosom and large hips. Lifelike carvings of lush foliage sprang from the head and cascaded down the broad shoulders. The face bore an expression of calm benevolence and undeniable power.

When he considered the reality of what Ganachim had become, what mankind had done to her to ensure its own survival, Cyprian felt a deep, indescribable shame. The certainty that, had he known all along of her presence, he would have done nothing about it only increased that shame.

Cyprian looked at Faye, and found that she was making a point not to look at the statue. In contrast, Jotun was excitedly making his way across the room toward it. As Cyprian's gaze followed him, he noticed Starkad standing nearby, looking toward the statue. An odd frown, as if he'd tasted something unpleasant, passed over his face for a brief moment, then he turned away. Phir-Ramarian appeared not to have noticed the surroundings at all, and was fussing over the men hastily assembling his private tent. All around them, the rest of the company had gone about the business of setting up the camp.

Canvas tents were erected, bedrolls were unfurled, and foodstuffs and water were hauled in from the carts, which, with the livestock, had been too large to make it through the rubble-choked entryway, and had remained outside. The sound of small cooking fires, fueled by the abundance of dry wood, crackled throughout the chamber. A general feeling of pleasant relief filled the air as, for at least a little while, they were free of the sun and able to rest.

Once the dining had wrapped up, Mather and Moore divided their men into watches, and the remainder of the company settled in to rest. Despite the incredible surroundings, and the mixed feelings of excitement and guilt they spawned, Cyprian found that he had no problem falling asleep.

CHAPTER 14

Silence permeated the ruins, the snores and occasional coughs of the men inside muffled by the thick temple walls. Moore sat upon a low wall of toppled stone, blessedly within the shadows at the far side of the temple. He found that if he remained very still, the heat wasn't so stifling.

He rested his head against the wall that rose behind him and closed his eyes. His chin began to sink, and he jerked his head up, looking around.

He'd taken the second watch. Galt had thankfully volunteered for the first.

When they'd reached the temple, Moore had been exhausted beyond comprehension. His knees had been screaming, his robes had clung to his sweat-drenched back, and the inside of his skull had felt like it was full of nails. The constant, blinding light had caused a tremendous headache to bloom behind his eyes. The few cycles of sleep he'd been allowed within the temple had felt like salvation. Upon being awoken by Galt, who had stayed on watch longer than he was supposed to in order to allow Moore a little extra sleep, he'd been confused. Only after a bewildering few moments had he realized where he was. With a great effort, he'd shuffled from his tent and out of the temple.

Now, he sat waiting eagerly for his chance to return to his bed-roll. He didn't want to let on how much he was suffering; he didn't want to seem weak or ill-fitted for the expedition. He had been chosen through the will of the Void-God, and no matter how punishing the circumstances were, he had to prevail. He had to be a leader to his acolytes, and he could not let Micla's death be for nothing.

Despite his determination, the coupling of his exhaustion with the dry heat surrounding him conspired to put him to sleep. Moore knew that he should get up, walk around in order to force himself to stay awake, but he simply could not will himself to get to his feet. It felt as if his legs had turned to stone and merged with the wall on which he sat. His slow breath rattled through his dry throat, yet he was unable even to lift his canteen, as his arms were as heavy as his legs. The canteen, half-filled with warm water, hung within easy reach on his belt, but it may as well have been in Nordabor.

As the heat slowly pulled his eyelids shut yet again, a hoarse shout cut through the silence. Immediately, Moore was on his feet with his blade drawn, all of his pains forgotten. He listened intently, seeking the source of the shout. A moment later, several voices rang out from the direction of the temple's front, where the animals were hitched. Moore raced around the rounded circumference of the temple, kicking up plumes of dust.

As he reached the front, he saw three of the guardsmen, swords drawn, hacking savagely at two interlopers, who were stumbling backward, parrying the blows as best as they could. A third was clinging to the back of one of the diminutive donkeys and whipping at its hindquarters, shouting unintelligibly. The confused animal, too small to have ever been ridden, bucked wildly, refusing to carry the man away. One of the wagons had been hastily hitched to the donkey, and rocked violently with its thrashing.

The strange men, clad in billowing white robes with hoods cinched tightly around their heads, had to be badlanders.

One of them fell to the assault of the guardsmen, and the other turned to flee. He only made it a few steps before he was run through from behind, sputtering and spitting blood down the front of his robes. The crimson spatter contrasted starkly with the ivory cloth.

With the two dispatched, one of the guardsmen hoisted his crossbow, taking aim at the badlander clinging to the back of the donkey. A tick later, the bolt cut through the air before plunging into the side of the badlander's head, protruding ghoulishly from the other side. The man immediately went limp and was flung from the back of the donkey before landing heavily in the dirt. Free of its unwanted burden, the donkey began to settle down.

Aside from the panting of the guardsmen and the irritated braying of the donkey, it was silent again. Moore approached the scene, watching the bodies intently. Blood pooled in the dirt under them. He became aware of the sounds of commotion within the temple. The alarm had been raised, and soon others would be joining them. Still, he focused on the bodies.

The second man to die began to twitch and jitter, his hands and feet becoming caked in the blood-soaked dirt underneath him. Moore knew that he should utter some sort of prayer for these faithless men, but the impending conflict with the shade consumed his attention. His eyes flicked to the other corpses, watching for any signs of shade birth.

The telltale pop of the skullcap bursting apart heralded the shade that slithered out of the desecrated head of the dead man, settling into a coiled pile of flesh and gristle. The mass then began to rise, taking shape.

Moore strode forward, no longer feeling his age, no longer feeling the heat. He hefted his anointed blade and, in a concise, powerful strike, cut the rising bulk of flesh in half. The top half plopped wetly to the ground, the new wound hissing and steaming. The loosely formed legs dropped a moment later. Moore stabbed at the remains a few more times, just to be certain. The harmless hunks of tissue hissed weakly, dissolving into a foul-smelling liquid.

Moore once again turned his attention to the other corpses, but they remained still. He slowly became aware that a small crowd had gathered around him.

"Is everyone okay?" It was Lord Fontaine, whose thick, black hair was standing up on one side. He'd dressed hastily, and was holding a short blade. Moore wondered if he'd ever handled a blade that wasn't a relic he was examining. Lady Fontaine stood by him, frowning at the scene.

"We're fine. We caught these badlanders attempting to take off with one of our carts," answered the guardsman who'd felled the last man with his crossbow.

Moore looked at the corpses and truly considered them for the first time. They hadn't been attacking the company; they'd only been trying to steal supplies. Probably to ensure their own survival in an inhospitable waste. And they'd only been after one wagon, just enough to sustain the three of them. Belatedly, Moore softly muttered a prayer to the Void-God.

"Get back," Captain Mather ordered calmly as he stepped away from the group and ushered the others back. He looked to the man with the crossbow. "Gricks, take Rackham and Baylor and get some rest. Your watch is over."

"Yes, sir."

The three guardsmen, who'd finished wiping their blades off on the clean parts of the dead men's robes, walked back toward the darkness of the temple. They nodded at Moore as they passed, briefly acknowledging his assistance.

"Rath, Lowther, Shaw," Captain Mather called, looking toward three other guardsmen standing nearby. "Search the bodies. Take anything of value."

They set to work at once. Near Captain Mather, Kovak surveyed the scene. His eyes met Moore's and the two men stared at each other for a moment. The last of Moore's adrenaline dissipated as Kovak's presence reminded him of Micla. He looked away in disgust, preferring to see the corpses. His fatigue rushed back upon him, and he wavered slightly. Galt and Solgard were suddenly at his side. Galt put a hand to his back, a subtle protection against falling.

"Are you okay?" he said quietly into Moore's ear. "You could have waited for us."

"I'm fine," Moore said, pulling away.

"What's happened?" Phir-Ramarian said, pushing through the crowd. He reached the front and looked from the corpses to the men looting them, then to the donkey and its jumbled cart.

"My men stopped some badlanders who were attempting to steal our wagon," Captain Mather explained, gesturing toward the donkey. "It appears that High Shepherd Moore also eliminated a shade."

"Good show!" Phir-Ramarian said. "Old friends of Starkad's, I assume. Did they get away with anything?"

"No. And we suffered no casualties, either," Captain Mather added pointedly.

Phir-Ramarian took a moment to process Captain Mather's tone. "Oh, excellent," he said, seeming to understand. He checked his chronometer. "Well, there's still several cycles to go before we're set to depart again. Let's get this cleaned up."

The bodies of the badlanders were efficiently stripped. They'd been carrying canteens that were almost empty, a few bits of dried meat, and some unknown herbs, which were turned over to Bellamont. Their bloodied robes and rusted swords were cast into the same pile of refuse as the company's empty food tins. The men's scant belongings further convinced Moore that they'd been desperate, and the theft of the cart had been a final gambit for survival.

The stripped bodies lay stretched upon the dirt, awaiting destruction. They were impossibly thin, and so tan that they appeared to be made of leather. The crossbow bolt, still intact, had been pulled from the head of the one man. The second man's head was strangely deflated, blown apart by the shade it had birthed. The third, aside from the blood on his face, could have been sleeping.

As Moore, Galt, and Solgard prepared to burn them, Starkad wandered over and peered at the bodies with mild interest.

He looked at Moore. "Badlanders, yes. None I ever encountered."

"What brought them out here?" Moore asked, feeling compelled to learn more about the men he'd watched die.

"Who can say? They must have been looking for a way to make it in the wastes." Starkad looked at them with pity. "Obviously, it didn't pan out."

Starkad left them to their work, and they set about dragging the bodies to an appropriate distance, paying special mind to avoid touching any of the noxious blood left by the shade, which had mostly dissolved into the parched dirt. In the dry conditions, the fire ignited easily.

The shepherds, desiring no additional heat, stood far back. The smell of charring flesh still reached their nostrils.

When the fire had dwindled, Moore turned to his acolytes. "Ophelia, I believe it's your watch," he said with a casual air that he did not feel.

"Yes, High Shepherd."

Moore trudged back toward the temple, Galt strolling easily beside him.

"The Void-God was truly with me, Leon. He gave me strength when I needed it. He will see us through."

"Of course, High Shepherd," Galt said.

"I just wish we could have been there for Micla. He passed alone, without a single prayer being uttered for him. I can only beg that the Void-God give us some sign that Micla was accepted into his embrace."

Galt said nothing, which was fine. Moore was speaking to himself more than anything else. The permeating, complete fatigue had returned fully, and only his faith could keep him going. He fumbled onto his bedroll and collapsed, breathing hard. Despite his exhaustion, he was determined to recite a ritual of praise.

He was asleep before he'd finished the first sentence.

• • •

"The old man did not look good."

"No, he didn't," Galt agreed. Despite his weariness, he was unable to sleep. He'd decided he'd rather walk the perimeter with Solgard than listen to Moore's rasping snores.

Solgard bit her dry, cracked lip, lost in thought. They passed near the last smoldering remains of the bodies, where the blood was already baked into the ground.

"Seems to me like Moore's really struggling with the whole thing," Solgard said. "I for one don't think the Void-God would make anything happen that resulted in one of his shepherds dying."

Galt considered his response carefully. Like Moore, Solgard had an abundance of faith. Unlike Moore, she had been able to process the death of Daeg more easily, as she hardly knew him. Her faith was not as rattled; Moore was clearly having trouble reconciling what had happened with the Void-God's supposed will.

"No, I don't think the Void-God willed that. Whatever his will, that was random bad luck. Our God does not guide all things to a neat conclusion. I think Moore has to believe that he does in order to make sense of a senseless tragedy," Galt said, restraining his true thoughts.

In Daeg's death, he saw further evidence that no divine will was at play. No guiding hand had led them anywhere. It was blasphemous to think so, but Galt couldn't help it. Daeg could be wandering that dark wood, suffering in torment as a shade at this very moment, no matter how many prayers were chanted on his behalf. Perhaps the Father-God, in any form, was truly gone.

"And how are you making sense of it?" Solgard asked after some hesitation.

"Micla?"

"Yes. You haven't really talked about it at all. But it seems like you were fairly close with him."

Galt paused, gazing out into the basin. He scratched at his sparse beard and cleared his throat. "Micla was a good lad. Eager, faithful, and hard working. It was a fucking disgrace to us all that he died the way he did. That he was left without a proper shepherding. We should have been there with him. We should never have come on this hopeless endeavor in the first place. I had no hopes for success, and I told Micla the same before we'd even left. Now, more than ever, I know it was folly to embark on this. Our prince is going to lead us all into ruin, mark my words. Micla's blood is on his hands. It's on all our hands."

Blood thumped at Galt's temples, and he realized that he was very angry. Not just at Phir-Ramarian or their circumstances, but at himself, for allowing Daeg to go out there alone. The boy had respected him and looked to him for guidance, and Galt had failed him.

Solgard was watching him with a pained expression on her face, and he felt suddenly embarrassed by his outburst. "You really think it's hopeless? That we're all going to die out here?" Solgard asked.

Galt considered backtracking on what he'd just admitted, but ultimately decided against it. "Yes. That's what I believe."

Solgard's expression hardened. "Then I feel very sorry for you." She turned and strode away, leaving Galt behind.

He closed his eyes tightly, heaved a sigh, and wished yet again that he'd never left Nordabor.

CHAPTER 15

The departure from the dilapidated temple was a bittersweet one. Many of the company, particularly the haulers, who had to take shifts pulling one of the heavy carts, were reluctant to restart the march. As the encampment was packed up, the bags stowed, the tents furled, and the garbage cast aside, the men groaned and stretched, sore from the previous trek.

Despite the bloodshed that had occurred, the company still largely viewed the temple as a place of refuge. Perhaps because of the success of their defense of it, the guardsmen especially looked about the place with affection. The defeat of the badlanders, and the relatively easy destruction of the shade that followed, were a positive contrast to the disastrous result of the last skirmish.

Jotun too, desperately wished to stay at the temple. Facing a treasure of antiquities unlike any he'd seen since, perhaps, the Gates of Punishment, Jotun wished to stay and catalogue every detail. Cyprian, despite the unsettling effect that the statue of Ganachim had on him, shared some of that enthusiasm. More alluring, though, was the desire to move on and locate a living old one. Faye seemed eager to leave, the clash with the badlanders cementing the dislike of the place she'd felt since she first laid eyes on the statue.

After a sluggish start, the company finally departed, only slightly behind schedule. A final consultation of their maps had led Starkad to declare that they had slightly over a full-cycle's worth of travel to go. Phir-Ramarian, who happily stated that he felt rejuvenated after a pleasant sleep, was confident that they'd reach the crater rim before then.

They continued heading southeast, picking their way through low-walled winding canyons, across dried riverbeds, and over tumbled boulders. Sporadic toppled ruins dotted the landscape, but despite Jotun's protestations, the company passed them by without stopping. Eager to make up for any lost time, Phir-Ramarian would not order a halt, telling the men to eat and drink as they walked. This was met with general unhappiness, with many resentful eyes watching the prince, Jotun, and Rayburn perched on their horses.

Six cycles into the trek, the features began to level out. The precious moments of shade ended and an expanse as wide and flat as the basin lay before them. At Starkad's urging, Phir-Ramarian finally called for a halt and for the command tent to be erected. Once the leaders were packed inside with their maps spread out over the thin-legged wooden table, Starkad addressed them.

"We've almost reached the edge of the blast plain, an area once held by the kingdom of Aurangzeb, and believed to have been covered in endless sands. Or so the legends say."

Cyprian was familiar with Aurangzeb and its ancient holdings. Conquered by Phan-Ellara, the kingdom of Aurangzeb had once stretched from Vin-Sadavat in the west, which had been its capital, all the way across the sea of dunes to the eastern shoreline, which had been the kingdom's last holdout.

He craned his neck to get a closer look at Starkad's roughly drawn, but highly detailed map. Compared with the map composed by Jotun and his father, it was clear to Cyprian why so much of the land they'd covered had been unfamiliar to Jotun. His father's expedition had traveled due east much further than they had, and when they'd made the turn to the south, they'd been far east of their current location, missing Ganachim's temple and the other scattered ruins entirely.

Cyprian's pondering of what could have been if they'd traveled south sooner was interrupted by Starkad.

"The southern badlanders believe that the sprawling dunes that once covered this land were completely blown away when Vingallea's old kingdom was annihilated. What remains is a vast expanse of pulverized rock, bits of glass, and the occasional boulder. The remains of everything that was expelled by the explosion, I imagine. It will be taxing to cross, to say the least. Similar to the basin, but a longer haul, with no promise of shelter on the other side."

Moore wiped a quivering hand, reddened by sunburn, across his brow. He looked ill.

"My lord," Bellamont cut in, addressing Phir-Ramarian, "I suggest you order a rationing of the salve. Several of the men have come to me asking for more, and we're already running low on our reserve supply. There's still the return trip to consider."

Phir-Ramarian, whose broad face was bright pink, frowned. "How is that possible? I was under the impression that we had more than enough for our needs."

"Well, we started on foot far sooner than we'd originally planned to," Bellamont explained. "We stocked salve based on our initial estimates of how long we'd be marching. That, and some of the company have been reckless with their usage, despite our warnings."

"Perhaps I should have placed Rayburn in charge of the distribution of the salve," Phir-Ramarian said. "There doesn't seem to be the same issue with the victuals."

Bellamont, her burnt face as red as her hair, looked at the table. "Medicinals are the purview of healers."

"That they are," Phir-Ramarian agreed. "As such, I would think you would know the importance of proper dosage, and wouldn't need an order to make adjustments. Nevertheless, here it is: do not distribute any more of the remaining stock until ordered otherwise, and reiterate to the men the importance of rationing. Any who fail to heed your warnings will find that the sun is punishment enough."

"Yes, my lord," Bellamont said, her voice wavering. Cyprian assumed that, being a master of her field, she was unaccustomed to being criticized.

"What about the herbs that my men recovered from the badlanders?" Mather asked. "Could they be of any use?"

"They're similar to what was used for the salve," Starkad said. "Crushed, the juices within them can work as a protection from the sun, but they won't bolster our supply by much."

An uncomfortable silence followed, during which Bellamont glared at Rayburn. He averted his gaze and nearly jumped when Phir-Ramarian addressed him. "How *are* we faring with the provisions?"

"We're doing excellently, my lord," Rayburn answered, sounding relieved to have good news for the prince. "All of our supplies are at acceptable levels for the anticipated length of the remaining journey."

"Good. And how is our equipment? Is the amiant armor ready for a quick deployment when we need it?"

"Yes, my lord," Dupree answered eagerly. The closer they got to their impending conflict, the more excited she appeared to be. The chance to test the armor she'd designed seemed more exciting to her than the opportunity to encounter a living god. She didn't seem to be worried about the risk of someone being cooked alive within it at all.

"And have you chosen who will accompany you?" Phir-Ramarian asked Mather.

"Yes. Joining me will be Sarin Gricks and Roderick Baylor."

Cyprian recognized them as two of the guardsmen who'd defeated the badlanders.

"Excellent choices," Phir-Ramarian said. Cyprian doubted that the prince would recognize either of the men if they were in the tent with him.

Having covered everything, the leaders began to disperse, heading back to their people to pass on news and get some food and drink.

As Cyprian ducked under the tent flaps, Phir-Ramarian called after him to wait. Now only he, the prince, and Pike remained.

"We're nearly there, cousin," Phir-Ramarian said. "I trust you and Lady Fontaine will be able to take good care of any blade shards we obtain? My father certainly put his trust in you."

"We will be more than up for the task," Cyprian said, slightly irritated. "Is there anything further?"

"I just wanted to make sure that you had no doubts," Phir-Ramarian said, putting his hands up in mock defense. "You were fairly quiet in the meeting, and with all the grumbling and negativity some of the members of our expedition are presenting, I wanted to make sure you were still in the fold."

He laughed casually. "Why, the old shepherd looks like he's apt to drop dead at any moment. There are complaints all around about the sun and the heat, and I have to contend with Starkad's bitchy little comments. At least Mather and his men can be relied upon, and Rayburn said we have plenty of provisions. And Dupree's got the amiant armor set to go; that's good. She's a good one."

Phir-Ramarian trailed off and looked at Cyprian, blinking deliberately with his eyebrows hoisted, clearly waiting for a response. Pike nodded stupidly, as if his agreement with Phir-Ramarian were so automatic that he didn't even realize that the prince had stopped talking.

"I think some of the complaints have some merit. If Moore is suffering, perhaps you could lend him your horse?" Cyprian said.

Phir-Ramarian laughed again, this time with a harsh edge. "It's bad enough I have to see Rayburn and your old fool Berg on a royal horse. I will certainly not be unsaddled by a shepherd. Those horses were meant for us; we are titled men of Vingallean blood. You've insulted me enough, you and your wife. I was being particularly gracious offering her a horse in the first place; she's only titled through marriage, after all."

Cyprian stared at his royal cousin with blossoming hatred. Phir-Ramarian was as talented and intelligent as the shit his precious horse dropped. Yet, due to his lineage, he was the leader of the expedition, the curator of the Hall of Antiquities, which he knew nothing of, and heir to the throne. Phar-Mindorius, blinded by rigid adherence to ancient laws of succession, had put the fate of their entire kingdom, and perhaps mankind, in the pudgy, useless hands of a buffoon so infatuated with himself that he couldn't see the need to give a dying old man a horse. And beyond all of that, he had insulted Jotun and demeaned Faye right to Cyprian's face.

"My commoner wife and I," he said through clenched teeth, doing everything he could to contain his simmering rage, "will do what has been asked of us by our *king*. But do not confuse that with support for you or your decisions."

Before Phir-Ramarian could say anything, Cyprian stalked out of the tent. The sunlight outside hit him like a slap across the face, amplifying his anger. He knew that if Phir-Ramarian followed him out and flapped his fat lips any further, he'd be unable to stop himself. Thankfully, the prince remained in the tent.

"What's wrong? What happened?" Faye asked as she approached, instantly detecting his anger.

Cyprian took a deep breath and shook his head. "Nothing. I need to talk to you and Jotun. Where is he?"

"He's right over there," Faye said, confused. Jotun was nursing his canteen, telling Anders and two other bored-looking haulers about his previous exploits.

Cyprian, with a concerned Faye following, pulled him aside and proceeded to explain to them what he had in mind. The trio then approached Moore, who was leaning against a cart, staring at the ground, his acolytes hovering nearby.

"Absolutely not. I do not need assistance," Moore insisted after hearing Cyprian's offer.

"I think maybe you do," Faye said, trying not to sound insulting.

"There's no shame in it," the dark-skinned shepherd, the one Cyprian had learned was called Galt, said quietly. Based on his features, Cyprian wondered if Galt was a descendent of the original inhabitants of Faedalia, the northern realm conquered by Vingallea, in which Nordabor had been established.

"The Void-God will not let me fall. He sustains me," Moore protested.

"The Void-God works in many ways, and through many people," the female shepherd, Solgard, said. "This is a gift."

"Take it," Galt added forcefully, but kindly.

A short time later, the company started for the blast plain. Cyprian and Faye now carried much of their equipment on their backs. Jotun, careful not to overload his horse, carried only slightly more gear. Sitting squeezed in amongst the provisions in the rear of the cart that had previously held their packs, Moore looked slightly embarrassed, but also relieved to be off of his feet.

Cyprian looked at Phir-Ramarian, expecting the prince to be cowed by his actions, or even ashamed enough to offer his horse to Moore belatedly. He was surprised when Phir-Ramarian guided Honey alongside him and, instead of an apology, quietly offered some advice.

"I suppose you think you've done well. My assessment may have been harsh, I know this, but I wasn't wrong. Everyone on this expedition knew what it would entail, and special considerations cannot be taken every time somebody is suffering. My father understands this, and he knew that you wouldn't. Leadership is not about accommodating; sometimes, you will not be popular. There's a time and a place to indulge your subordinates. Pleasing the old shepherd now will only create resentment amongst the rest. Don't think they won't wonder when it will be their turn to ride, or to take one of the horses, for that matter. We of the titled caste were meant to ride the horses, because the men needed to see that we were their superiors—that our actions, pleasant or not, were unimpeachable. Now, I won't contradict you and order the shepherd on his feet; I don't wish to sow any further discord, but I hope you keep this in mind in the future."

Nonplussed, Cyprian said nothing as Phir-Ramarian steered his horse away. His decision to aid Moore, a choice motivated more by his desire to undermine his cousin than by any altruistic notions toward the shepherd, suddenly felt foolish. His pride dissolved into embarrassment, further stoking his rancor. The fact that Phir-Ramarian would lecture him about leadership was outrageous to the point of being farcical, yet his words rang true.

Cyprian looked at Moore, nestled into a makeshift cocoon of canvas, shielding himself from the oppressive sun, and knew that Phir-Ramarian was right.

·   ·   ·

As the company slogged toward the blast plain, Cyprian found himself unable to shake what Phir-Ramarian had said. His fantasies of seeing the prince unhorsed, tromping along like the rest of them, had clouded his judgement and driven him into essentially taking Moore on as his ward. Faye, who'd been close enough to eavesdrop on their conversation, had been tactful enough not to ask Cyprian about it. He knew that her agreement to help Moore had sprung from a more noble place, and loved her for it. Whatever Phir-Ramarian said, Faye had no issue standing by Cyprian's decision to help the high shepherd.

After only a cycle, the company reached the edge of the plain, and Cyprian's frustrations were driven from his mind. The entire horizon glittered and shimmered, the white light of the sun dancing manically across the countless pieces of glass that coated the scorched earth. Cyprian felt as if his mind itself had dried out at the sight, purging any thought beyond water and shelter.

Descending a very shallow incline, they began their march to the crater's edge, their footsteps crunching upon the myriad fragments of glass. The heat pressed down upon them like a physical weight, as dry and relentless as ever. For those who'd run out of salve and refused to cover themselves with extra layers, the sun wasted no time scorching any exposed flesh.

After twelve cycles, some of the men began to voice the opinion that they would never reach the end of the plain, that there was no crater. Others, as Phir-Ramarian had predicted, pointed out the unfairness of Moore, who was supposed to be protecting them, being carried in a cart while they marched. Phir-Ramarian made it clear that the high shepherd's situation was a unique one, and that no others would be permitted to add their extra weight to the wagons. Grumblings of dissent were not humored. Mather and Kovak walked the line, ordering anyone who voiced doubts to remain silent.

The fact that Phir-Ramarian continued to stand by Cyprian's choice in order to create the illusion of a united leadership somehow annoyed him even more than the dressing-down had.

After fourteen cycles, they finally stopped, but standing still in the flat expanse of sweltering air was almost worse than walking through it. No one wished to linger in that death zone for long, so after the the men filled their canteens with an additional ration, the company moved on quickly.

Finally, after over sixteen cycles of trudging through an expanse of static desolation, the horizon changed.

A jagged row of tumbled rocks rose low in front of them. As they approached it, they could see clearly that it sloped up sharply. What was beyond, none could see. Jotun advised Cyprian that it was undoubtedly the crater rim; it had looked just the same when he and Rorik had reached it so long ago.

Upon reaching the foot of those low, sharp rocks, Phir-Ramarian ordered a full stop. An encampment was established, and the men gratefully slithered into the shadowed interiors of their tents. They would not offer the same relief that the temple had, but any escape from the sun was seen as a blessing.

Cyprian, on the other hand, was eager to see the crater. "Faye and I are going up—you coming?" he asked Jotun, who was gingerly dismounting his horse. Nearby, Moore was being helped out of the cart by Galt and Solgard. Though he'd spent the entire trek resting, he was still ashen-faced except for two bright red blotches on his cheeks.

"Yes, I think I'd be up for it," Jotun said, squinting up at the rocks and rubbing his lower back. Cyprian imagined that the rocks Jotun had broken his back on must have looked very similar.

The three of them scrambled up the short rock face and, reaching the top, marveled at what lay before them. Stretching beyond the horizon, a vast bowl of open earth yawned. The colossal emptiness was impossibly deep, with the bottom lost in shadows. The other side was obscured in haze, and as they looked to the sides, the crater lip continued unbroken in an almost straight line in both directions. Cyprian peered nervously over the edge and saw a steep slope of loose stone that descended in a sheer drop into nothing. He had a difficult time fathoming the amount of power that would be needed to wreak this kind of destruction. The amount of lives lost, the history lost, was impossible to imagine. Faced with such an astounding sight, his squabbles with Phir-Ramarian seemed absurdly petty.

"It's still breathtaking," Jotun murmured.

"How could anything capable of doing this be killed?" Faye asked, her voice trembling. "If the Father-God could annihilate an entire kingdom, how could he ever have been overthrown?"

"He splintered his power," Starkad said unexpectedly from behind them.

Cyprian, who was still near the edge, jumped slightly, and for a panic-inducing moment envisioned himself tumbling down the embankment to his certain death. He took several steps back from the edge.

"Splintered his power?" Faye asked, more intrigued by Starkad's words than his sudden presence beside them.

"According to the lore of my people, Alminnian put too much of his own power into the servant-gods he created. When they decided to usurp him, he no longer had the power to destroy his own creations. He could still do this." He gestured toward the colossal crater. "But he ultimately could not stop Aedesda and Ulesreto."

They stood looking out over the crater in silence, each of them thinking of the titanic conflict that had torn apart their world so long ago. This barren, lifeless crater was a visible scar of the past.

"If that power still existed," Faye said, breaking the silence, "we wouldn't stand a chance against it."

"Thankfully, Alminnian took the majority of it with him," Starkad said. "The gods we'll encounter will be a threat, yes, but not insurmountable."

Cyprian did not feel particularly comforted. If even a fraction of this type of power remained with the old ones they sought, they would almost certainly fail.

"So, where do you suppose this elusive old one is hiding?" Jotun asked, looking up and down the crater rim.

"Veathyadell is not far from here, I estimate. Lord Fontaine, I'll advise you, because our leader is not receptive to ideas that are not his own. I'll take a small party, lightly equipped, along the rim. I know what I'm looking for; others may look directly at Veathyadell and not realize what they're seeing. Once I verify where he is, I will not engage, but will send for Mather and his men. They can confront the god."

"That makes sense," Cyprian said, wondering how anyone could see a god and not recognize it.

They returned to the encampment, and Cyprian, despite being newly hesitant to circumvent Phir-Ramarian, went directly to Mather, who was organizing the watch. Mather had no issue with the plan, and assigned Kovak, Rath, and Shaw to accompany Starkad on his reconnaissance. Solgard joined them as well, leaving Galt and a sleeping Moore behind.

The small crew ate, drank, and rested for a short period before departing. Cyprian, Faye, and Jotun watched them go before crawling into their tent. Excited and nervous about the coming confrontation, the three of them lay awake, discussing what could happen.

They spoke in hushed tones, their murmurs the only sound in the otherwise-silent encampment.

CHAPTER 16

Gorlin Mather had never had any qualms about anything that had been asked of him during the expedition or during any of his service to the Crown. Since his earliest time as an enlisted guardsman, he'd never questioned orders or doubted the holy right of leadership bestowed upon the lords of the city. Though he had little respect for Phir-Ramarian, he never questioned the prince's power or the orders that he issued.

It was a simple fact of life: Phir-Ramarian was the son of his sovereign and heir to the throne. His word was law, and Mather lived to enforce that law.

Still, as he was being fitted with the amiant armor, the knowledge that he would be confronting an old one shortly filled him with a doubt that he had never experienced before. What if the prince, and by extension, his king, were wrong? Perhaps this strategy was unwise to the point of being objectionable.

Mather briefly considered suggesting an alternative before a lifetime spent following a strict code smothered any concerns under a mantle of rigid discipline. Unwise or not, it was the order of the Crown. It was his place to follow it.

Their badlander guide had returned after four cycles with the news that his scouting party had located the old one. Kovak, Rath, and Shaw, who'd had very little rest between the march across the blast plain and their departure on the scouting trip, had nearly collapsed upon their return. Thankfully, Rackham and Lowther had been handling the first watch, so Mather, Gricks, and Baylor had been able to get some rest. Not nearly enough, though.

Mather didn't dare suggest that they wait to confront the old one, exhausted or not. Phir-Ramarian was eager for success. Beyond that, any extra time spent in the inhospitable desert they were now suffering in was borrowed time. The sooner they completed their task and left, the better.

Starkad had led Mather, Gricks, Baylor, and the engineers to a staging area a safe distance from where the god was purported to be. Joining them was also Phir-Ramarian, who would oversee the operation, his scribe, the shepherd Galt, Bellamont, and, for academic purposes, Lord and Lady Fontaine, along with their assistant, Berg. Everyone but Mather and his men would be remaining at the staging area to watch the confrontation from a far enough distance away that they could flee if need be.

Dupree and her three assistants, Kahlam Shagalov, Barton Vane, and Faris Hayves, were now fitting Mather, Gricks, and Baylor into the amiant armor, carefully adjusting the different straps and plates in order for the identical suits to fit each man snugly. It was the first time that Mather was putting it on since he and Dupree had designed the armor, and he'd forgotten how cumbersome it was. They hadn't taken the heat into consideration, and it was stifling inside of the heavy gear. Thankfully, they had decided not to put it on until they were close to the god.

The party was gathered on an outcropping of rock that jutted out perilously over the side of the crater. Starkad had assured them that it was quite stable. From this vantage point, they had a clear view of the surrounding crater wall stretching away to the horizon. Starkad had pointed out where the god was lying, apparently dormant. More imposing than the god itself was the small, rugged pathway he and his men would need to follow down from the staging area to reach it. In the bulky armor, losing his footing on the loose scree would be all too easy.

Actually, the god itself was not really anything to behold, from what Mather could tell. Starkad had apparently spotted it with his naked eye, but Mather needed to use a field glass to see it. What he saw was nearly indistinguishable from the red rock surrounding it. It was a broad, flat, rust-colored lump, slowly rising and lowering. Nestled amongst the rocks on a thin lip below the crater rim, it was hard to imagine that this shape could be a god. Regardless, Mather knew what power these beings had once wielded, and knew not to underestimate it. Its benign appearance almost made it more threatening, its true strength unknown.

"I've just got to secure the helmet and you're all set," Dupree said. She looked at him as though it might be for the last time. She'd been confident in her design; now, that confidence seemed to be wavering.

"Are you ready?" Phir-Ramarian asked him.

He had trouble moving his neck in the armor, and needed to turn his entire body to look at the prince, who was standing to his left. Phir-Ramarian was wringing his hands, apparently nervous.

"Yes, my lord," Mather answered, betraying none of his own nervousness. A captain of the Royal Guard was not to show fear in the sight of his sovereign.

"Excellent. This is it. This is the crucible in which the fate of our kingdom will be decided," Phir-Ramarian said. "We cannot fail. I know you won't."

Mather did not need the reminder of what was at stake. If he were to perish, or if the god refused to admit knowledge of the blade shards and none were recovered no matter what the outcome, the entire expedition would be a failure. The search for these blade shards was a gamble with long odds throughout.

Mather had to remind himself yet again that none of that mattered. It was the order of his king that had brought him here, and it was his noble purpose to fulfill it.

Mather looked to Gricks and Baylor, who were also fully equipped, aside from their helmets. Their faces were set in grim determination. The engineer attendants waited for the final order.

"I'm ready," Mather said.

Dupree fitted the helmet over his head and a claustrophobic stuffiness surrounded him. The world looked dimmer through the tinted glass that covered the narrow eye slits. He knew they were a weak point, and sincerely hoped that a blast of fire from the god did not shatter the glass directly into his eyes.

Dupree tightened the final straps and secured the connections between the helmet and the gorget, and Mather turned toward Gricks and Baylor, who were now indistinguishable in their armor. He made a mental note to have some sort of distinct marks put on the different sets of armor in the future. He signaled to them to fall in, and the three headed for the narrow pathway along the cliff wall.

"Good luck," Phir-Ramarian said with forced cheerfulness as they trudged away. His voice sounded muffled and remote. Lord and Lady Fontaine merely continued to stare at the god through their field glasses, uneasy looks frozen on their faces. Starkad nodded as they passed, his unlit pipe clenched in his teeth.

The descent was a slow, methodical process. Mather touched the rough wall to his left with a heavily gloved hand, knowing that if he slipped, he'd be unable to find any useful grip. It occurred to him that they should have brought the climbing gear they were planning on using in the Einmaz Mountains. Each step was deliberate, Mather watching his footfalls through the narrow eye slits of the helm. The sound of his own breathing filled the hot darkness enclosing his head. He looked up occasionally to check his route and to peer at the rumpled shape of the old one.

The pathway leveled out, but narrowed, and Mather shifted sideways to shuffle across the ledge. He stared out over the open expanse of the crater, making a conscious effort not to look down. To his right, Gricks and Baylor followed his example and scooted sideways along the wall.

Finally, they reached the point where the path widened out onto the lip where the god resided. The three of them gathered round for a moment, relieved to have made it down. Mather peered up at the spur they had come from. He couldn't see the others.

There was now only a short distance between the men and the heaped boulders where the brick-colored form slowly undulated. Mather licked his lips, tasting the salt of his sweat. He blinked away more, wishing he could wipe his face. He turned to look at Gricks and Baylor and motioned them forward. They nodded with their entire bodies and the three of them crept toward the god. Mather drew his sword, his clumsy gloved grip on the hilt making him wish he'd had more practice handling a blade while wearing the cumbersome armor.

As they approached, the stony mass began to shudder. They froze, weapons in hand, waiting. The flesh of the being rippled and wavered, dirt and bits of stone sliding off. Broad, thick arms lifted from beneath the shape and planted heavily on the ground. With a sound of stone grating against stone, the entire bulk of the god lifted, unfolding itself as it rose.

It was as if a living statue stood before them. The old one's thick, bulky body, crisscrossed with scrapes and cracks, was perfectly still. Mather knew that even the fiercest blow would bounce harmlessly off. He may as well try to slay the rock wall behind them. Feeling uncharacteristically unsure of what to do next, and acutely aware of Gricks and Baylor standing behind him, awaiting his order, Mather took a cautious step forward. He didn't know what exactly he'd been imagining the old one to look like, but it hadn't been this.

The cracks spread across the being's body began to glow, as if lit by some internal light. Mather once again froze, bracing for some sort of strike. The misshapen head of the god, with its lumpish, indistinct features, began to shudder and crack. Layers of the plated, stony skin fell away, revealing a wide, red face shimmering with a low light.

The god suddenly lifted its arms faster than Mather would have thought possible, causing him to jump backward. With a booming crack, the outer layers of stone were flung from the heavy, stout arms. The blunt-fingered hands then tore layers of the rocky carapace away from the torso and legs, allowing it to step free of its shell.

The appearance of a statue was now gone. Towering over them at nearly twice Mather's height was a bronzed, rotund body. Barrel-shaped and wrinkled, it still boasted some old muscle definition, hints of a former strength that hadn't completely left. The cracked, hard flesh glowed weakly from within with red light. A simple, ragged robe of brown linen, cinched with a frayed belt, was all the god wore. Above its bald head, a halo of low-burning coals turned slowly.

The god surveyed them with black, beady eyes. Its mouth was pulled down in a scowl, and ragged, whistling breaths could be heard passing in and out of its flat, broad nose. It said nothing.

Mather could hear one of his men breathing hard, possibly panicking. He could feel the eyes of Phir-Ramarian and the others on him, waiting. He needed to do something.

He stepped forward again. "Am I addressing Veathyadell, called the God of the Furnace in the old times?" he called, his voice sounding very loud inside of his helmet.

After a long pause punctuated only by its whistling inhalations, the god opened its mouth and coughed. A small plume of dusty cinders issued forth, and it licked its cracked lips with a black tongue.

"Yes," it said in a deep, sonorous voice. "And you must be men of Vingallea. It has been a long time, but I knew you would come. Your grasping nature has made this inevitable."

Veathyadell sighed heavily, suddenly looking ancient and doleful. "Tell me. Who is your master now? Ulesreto? Aedesda? Are they here?

Mather was surprised by the questioning, expecting nothing but wild hostility from the god. "We are—we have no master," he stammered. "No godly one, that is. We are men of Nordabor. Aedesda is dead. Ulesreto is somewhere in the north. We are here of our own accord."

"Aedesda is dead?" Veathyadell asked, sounding pleased. "I assumed one would kill the other. I'm not certain which I would have preferred."

He trailed off, lost in thought. Mather felt more awkward than ever as he stood, forgotten, before the god.

Veathyadell seemed to remember that the men were there and looked back at Mather. "Then you have sought me out for what purpose?"

Mather braced himself again. "We seek any shards of the Scale of Judgment that you may possess."

Veathyadell did not look surprised. "I thought as much. How you learned of the shards without the influence of the gods, I do not know, but again, I've always known that this moment would come. I see your strange garments, your weapons. Do you plan to take the blade shards by force?"

"If you will not give them freely, yes," Mather answered, forcing himself to sound confident, though he felt small and foolish.

Veathyadell did not seem afraid. He gazed out over the vast expanse of the crater, looking melancholy. "It has been so very long. I have held out here, hidden within this wound in the earth, waiting for you. Living a fruitless life of ruined divinity. Prolonging the inevitable decay of a world that is already in its grave. Preserving Alminnian's vision when it has already been lost."

He turned his strange, glowing face toward Mather, his halo flickering. "I could muster my admittedly limited strength. I could incinerate you and your strangely dressed men. Broil you within your metal shells."

Mather, Gricks, and Baylor stepped back in unison, raising their weapons defensively. Behind Mather, one of the men was practically panting. Mather hoped he wouldn't pass out.

"I could do that," Veathyadell continued, ignoring their defensive postures, "but to what end? More of you would follow, bent not only on taking the shards, but on exacting revenge. They would concoct new ways of confronting me until one succeeded. I could hurl the shards into this abyss, and you would scour the entire breadth of the crater to find what you seek.

"Mankind was always Alminnian's greatest mistake. You could not be stopped; a relentless legion of vermin that, when determined, would carry on to eternity, your ambition never slaked. As I said, it was only a matter of time until, somehow, someway, you came to me seeking the shards. I have grown tired of this waiting, and now that the moment has finally come, I find that I'm too weary to stand in your way. This scheme was concocted out of spite as much as anything. The truth is, all is lost for me. Your arrival is almost a relief."

Veathyadell reached down to the rope cinched around him. He pulled a wrinkled, leather pouch from behind his back and opened it with his thick fingers, then emptied the contents into an upturned palm, revealing three dark-gray lengths of broken steel. Carelessly, he tossed two of them into the dirt at his feet. The third piece looked like a small dagger in his broad hand.

"Whatever you seek to do in Paradise, I suppose it cannot be worse than this corpse of a world. Though decaying with this world is exactly what your kind deserves. Either way, I am finished."

Suddenly, Veathyadell raised the blade piece to his own throat and carved a deep gash across it. Hot black blood spurted down his front, the faint glow leaving his body with it. His halo briefly flickered into a full flame before fizzling out into a brittle, gray crust. The blade shard dropped from Veathyadell's grip and landed in the dirt by the others as he staggered to his left, his small eyes darting about, his mouth moving soundlessly. He lurched toward the edge of the lip, clutching at his throat, the inky blood running between his fingers. The god grew still as he reached the edge. He closed his eyes and a small smile creased his broad face, and then he tumbled backward off of the ledge and was gone.

Mather, Gricks, and Baylor stood frozen in the same defensive position, staring at the spot Veathyadell had just occupied. Mather was absolutely dumbfounded.

Behind him, he heard the panting cease, and the heavy clang of a body collapsing. He turned around to see one of his men sprawled in the dirt. Mather sheathed his sword, unclasped and ripped his gloves off, and fumbled with the buckles at the rear of his helmet. Finally, he freed the helm and pulled it off. The dry heat felt exquisite compared to the inside of the helmet. He blinked in the sudden brightness and set to work stripping the helmet from the collapsed man. Next to him, Gricks had pulled his own helmet off, revealing Baylor to be the man who'd passed out.

With his helmet removed, Baylor slowly came to, blinking in confusion. Mather and Gricks sat on the ground beside him, looking at each other in disbelief. Indistinct shouting could be heard from the spur far above.

Mather's gaze finally turned to the three hunks of unremarkable steel, glistening in a quickly drying pool of black blood.

CHAPTER 17

The entire encampment was raucous with celebration. Even the oppressive heat was forgotten in the jubilation of success. Several tents had been strung up wide into a makeshift canopy, under which the men drank and sang cheerily. Phir-Ramarian had ensured that several casks of mead, hidden behind other casks of water, were brought with them to properly celebrate their success. The men had cheered when they'd returned triumphant, but they'd absolutely howled with joy when Phir-Ramarian announced the presence of the mead. It mattered not that it was piss-warm; the men guzzled it greedily. Even Moore, Galt, and Solgard were drinking, though they stood off from the others, talking quietly to each other and occasionally casting a cautious eye toward the horizon. The watch had been abandoned in the revelry, fears of badlanders and shades forgotten in the aftermath of their defeat of a god.

Phir-Ramarian mingled with the crowd as easily as if he were hosting a feast in the great hall of the Vinecrown Keep, slapping men on the back and laughing heartily with them. The haulers, who'd so recently been cursing their lot, now hailed him as a conquering champion. Quaffing drinks together, he happily toasted them for their tireless work.

The guardsmen, aside from Mather, Gricks, and Baylor, who were being treated for heat exhaustion, had seized a cask to themselves, and were quite drunk. Kovak filled their canteens with glee.

In the darkness of the command tent, Cyprian leaned over the three blade shards spread out across the thin wooden table. The sounds of the celebration echoed unnoticed outside. Faye stood beside him, her fingertips lightly touching his back. In the shadows behind them, Jotun excitedly discussed the shards with Pike, who, interested in lore, had been allowed by Phir-Ramarian to remain in the tent.

"I cannot believe that this is real," Cyprian murmured. The blade shards, wiped clean of the dark, sticky blood of Veathyadell, winked in the light that passed through the gap in the tent flaps. A filthy rag, cast aside, was all that remained of the god.

"Looks like Starkad's people were right," Faye said, her eyes never leaving the table.

Cyprian considered this and realized that perhaps the oral history of the badlanders, the history that painted Vingallea as a corrupt people who gladly marched into disaster behind their god-king, was more accurate than the accounts of the noble-but-misled people that he'd learned about growing up. From what Mather had reported of his conversation with Veathyadell, the recently deceased god's final words supported this negative view.

The entire encounter with Veathyadell, as described by Mather, had been bizarre, and totally different from what Cyprian had been expecting. He and the others gathered at the staging area had been prepared to watch a violent conflict. Cyprian had marveled at Veathyadell, wishing he could get a closer look. When, through his field glass, he watched Veathyadell drop what appeared to be the shards, his heart had hammered against his ribs. The god's subsequent suicide had seemed to come from nowhere.

When Mather and Gricks, helping the half-conscious Baylor, had finally made it back to the staging area, Cyprian and the others had bombarded them with questions. Mather had been combative, demanding that Dupree and her engineers get him and his men out of the unwieldy armor. Phir-Ramarian tried to ask about what Veathyadell had said, but Mather was not listening. The normally stoic captain had been strangely affected by his brush with the divine.

He'd dropped the blade shards unceremoniously onto the ground as Dupree undid his armor's straps, and there, Cyprian had gotten his first look at them. He'd produced a strip of fabric from his pack and hastily wrapped the shards up, intending on thoroughly examining them later. Starkad watched the commotion with mild interest.

Once out of the amiant armor, Mather had been able to explain what happened. Phir-Ramarian was so relieved and satisfied with the outcome that he'd almost tittered with glee. Dupree, on the other hand, had appeared to be quite disturbed by Veathyadell's claim of being able to easily defeat the armor. She and her engineers reluctantly packed up the heavy gear, which remained untested.

"We should send scouts down, see if they can't locate the body," Jotun was saying to Pike, who nodded along.

"As much as I'd love to study it," Cyprian said, turning from the shards with some effort, "that's just not feasible. We don't have the equipment to haul it back out, it would be extremely dangerous to climb down there, and we have no idea how far down it landed."

They'd peered carefully over the ledge of the spur and scoured the visible depths of the crater with their field glasses, but Cyprian and Faye had been unable to spot any sign of Veathyadell's body.

"Yes, that's true," Jotun admitted. Undoubtedly, memories of the glory he'd experienced delivering Aedesda's remains to Phar-Mindorius had passed through his mind.

Cyprian turned back to the shards. Though undoubtedly ancient, they bore no rust or corrosion. Dark gray, and, now that they'd been cleaned, completely smooth and nonporous, the only blemishes on each were the points of breakage, and even those were almost perfectly straight, clean breaks. Of the three pieces, two fit together so nicely that the seams almost vanished when the pieces were pressed against each other. Reforging the blade not only seemed possible, but almost like it would be easy, assuming the other shards were in the same condition.

"Based on the size and the relation of these two," Faye said, indicating the two that Cyprian had fit together, "and the measurements we have of the hilt, I would guess that there are maybe four, five more pieces."

"Dispersed between three old ones," Cyprian added. "Assuming that Starkad's assumptions are right, and Ulesreto and Opriseur don't have any."

"Sometimes it's disconcerting how much of this hinges on assumptions."

"Well, in this particular case, the assumptions appear to have been correct. We now have three pieces of the Scale of Judgment." Cyprian smiled broadly.

Being out in the field, collecting priceless antiquities, filled Cyprian with joy. The wonders that he and Faye had dreamed of seeing, the lofty goals they'd imagined achieving as they dug in the shadowed dirt of the derelict castle gardens, were finally coming to pass. It was a remarkable feeling.

"May I get a closer look?" It was Pike, who had been inching up toward the table, peering inquisitively.

"Of course!" Jotun answered for Cyprian, stepping up alongside him. Cyprian, feeling suddenly possessive of the shards, wanted to tell Phir-Ramarian's greasy-faced pet to go find his master, but Jotun had taken a liking to the young man, and Pike, despite choosing to commit himself to scrawling down Phir-Ramarian's every word and action obsessively, was actually fairly intelligent. He'd spent much of the time they were traveling needling Jotun with questions. Jotun, whose past accomplishments had been nearly forgotten between the disappearance of Rorik and the new expedition, clearly enjoyed the chance to recount his period of celebrity. Cyprian found Pike to be grating, though.

Cyprian stepped back, allowing Jotun to point out the features of the blade shards and to describe some of the lore surrounding them. Pike listened with his eyes wide, hanging on Jotun's every word. Cyprian waited, hiding his impatience, wishing to get back to examining the shards himself. Faye caught his eye and smirked mischievously, amused by his frustration.

From outside of the tent, the sounds of the celebration were cut through by yelling. Cyprian's head snapped up, and he strode toward the entrance while Jotun trailed off in confusion, watching him go. Cyprian opened the flap and, joined by Faye, peered outside to see what was happening.

Mather had parted the small crowd and was shouting at his guardsmen, who stood fixed, canteens half-lifted to their mouths. Bellamont and her subordinate, Nicoletta Hale, stood behind him, looking embarrassed. They'd clearly tried to stop Mather from leaving the medical tent.

"This conduct is unacceptable," Mather growled, the crowd growing silent around him. "I don't care what victory we've claimed—for royal guardsmen to abandon a watch in violation of direct orders is disgraceful."

Kovak moved his mouth, the beginnings of words forming, before he was summarily silenced by Mather.

"Under-Captain, I believe it is you, Rath, and Shaw who should currently be on watch. Get yourselves cleaned up and get out on the perimeter." He scanned the wide-eyed guardsmen. "You should all receive lashes for this."

Kovak made another sound of protestation and looked expectedly at Phir-Ramarian, who had been shunted into the side of the group and was watching impotently.

"And, High Shepherd," Mather said, turning toward Moore, who looked frightened, "I wouldn't dream of telling you how to man your chapter under normal circumstances, but out here, you are under my command. I don't care how hard this journey has been on you—you need to be responsible for your people. The watch is as much your duty as ours."

Before Moore, who looked like he had just been slapped across the face, could say anything, Phir-Ramarian finally interjected.

"Captain!" he shouted. "You are unwell. You're still addled from the heat. I understand your concerns, but we are quite safe here. We could see any threat coming; we are not oblivious. That's the tactical advantage of this spot—you said it yourself."

Mather simply glowered at the prince, saying nothing.

"Come, Gorlin. Let's step into the command tent, discuss the particulars of our situation. After all, *I* ordered the festivities; I think I know what's best." Phir-Ramarian's voice had taken on a tone of authority that Mather could not deny.

"Yes, my lord," he said in a strangled voice.

The two men started toward the tent, Phir-Ramarian placing a guiding hand on Mather's back, the crowd watching them go silently. Phir-Ramarian turned back toward them.

"Please, continue! It's a celebration, after all!" he said, the jovial words carrying a harsh edge.

As they approached the tent, Cyprian and Faye backed away from the entrance and looked at each other, suddenly realizing that they were trapped inside. Cyprian turned toward the table, where Jotun and Pike were standing, also staring toward the commotion outside. His eyes fell on the blade shards.

He envisioned Phir-Ramarian, soaked in mead, deciding to fumble around with the blade shards. Or, worse, making a sudden declaration that he would retain custody of them during the expedition, further negating Cyprian's role. No, Phar-Mindorius had, for once, used his good sense in giving Cyprian that responsibility. He would not let the prince strip him of yet another charge of his birthright.

Cyprian scooped up the fragments of steel carefully but quickly, rewrapped them in a cloth, and slid them back into a leatherbound metal tube. He'd designed the tube prior to their departure for just this purpose, and was pleased to see that the shards fit nicely within. As he screwed on the end of the tube, Phir-Ramarian and Mather entered the tent and an uncertain murmur began to rise outside.

"What is the meaning of this outburst?" Phir-Ramarian hissed quietly, turning on Mather the moment the tent flaps closed.

Cyprian, Faye, and Jotun shrank against the back of the tent. Pike stepped forward, apparently ready to document his master flexing his sovereign power.

"My lord," Mather said, calmer than he'd been outside, but still clearly frustrated, "what happened out there was not a victory. It was luck. That being, whether its true power was neutered or not, was still a god. I believed it when it said it could have easily killed us. It only killed itself instead because it was convinced that we would never stop trying. It said it was too weary to fight us. It had no idea that this is it, that there is no one else coming. The odds that the next ones will just fold upon seeing us are slim. If any of them are as powerful as that one was, then we will not succeed."

"Powerful?" Phir-Ramarian scoffed. "It preferred death at its own hand to fighting us. And Starkad said it was one of the strongest! If I recall, the next old one we're set to confront is the God of Beauty. That doesn't sound very threatening."

"And what of the one after that? The wind-god?"

Phir-Ramarian waved his hand dismissively. "What of it? We will deal with it when the time comes. I still have the utmost faith in the amiant armor."

"My lord, what of the immediate threats of shades or badlanders? Just because we succeeded in obtaining—

"Enough," Phir-Ramarian said. "I will not listen to any more. We have acquired what we sought. We had no loss of life, and we will soon be leaving this wretched desert behind. The men need a celebration, not to hear you fretting about danger. If you want to walk the perimeter, be my guest. There will be no punishment for any of the men. We're done here."

Phir-Ramarian stared at the captain, pointing toward the exit. Cyprian was shocked; he'd never seen Phir-Ramarian speak to Mather, whom he'd always seemed intimidated by, in such a manner. Perhaps the expedition's recent success—or the mead—had gone to his head.

Mather stared down at his prince, his face unreadable. A single bead of sweat descended from the close-cropped gray hair at his temple and ran down his stubbled cheek.

"Yes, my lord," he recited mechanically. With a strange, unfocused look, he turned from Phir-Ramarian and left the tent.

Phir-Ramarian watched him for a moment, then sighed heavily. He turned to the others, acknowledging them for the first time.

"Lord Fontaine, Lady Fontaine," he said with awkward formality. Apparently unsure of what to say next, he flashed a forced smile, nodded at them, and turned to leave. "Bastion, come along."

"Oh. Yes, my lord," Pike answered as if shaken from a stupor. He trotted obediently after the prince.

Cyprian, Faye, and Jotun remained in the tent, listening to the slowly returning, though still subdued, sounds of celebration.

"He must have needed a toady to tell him he was right," Faye said, finally breaking the silence.

"Bastion's not such a bad kid," Jotun replied.

"I don't know," Cyprian said, lost in thought. "I can't believe I'm saying this, but I agree with Phir-Ramarian."

Faye and Jotun looked at him in disbelief.

"Don't get me wrong; I still think he's unfit to lead this expedition, but he's right." Cyprian chose not to add that Phir-Ramarian had recently proven that his understanding of his command position was a bit more nuanced than Cyprian had initially believed. "However we obtained the shards, we got them. It's been a difficult journey, and many doubted that we would be able to achieve anything. The men need this morale boost, especially before heading back the way we came."

The sound of revelry increased, as if in agreement. Faye was watching Cyprian with an appraising look.

"The captain's right about the next old ones, though," Jotun said. "We still have a lot of unknowns to conquer. A long way to go."

"All the more reason to let them celebrate now. It may be their last opportunity."

CHAPTER 18

After the scheduled period of rest that followed the jubilation, the company got off to a slow start. The cycles spent drinking had extinguished the casks of mead entirely and left a majority of the group with sour stomachs and pounding heads. The ever-present sunlight was completely unforgiving and further punished the ill men.

As much of a gracious host as Phir-Ramarian had been during the celebration, he was twice the taskmaster now. Apparently unfazed by the amount of mead he'd consumed, he strutted through the camp, ordering the haulers to collapse and stow the tents and gear faster. Their purpose here complete, the prince no longer wished to dally, and, ill or not, the men mostly agreed. Everyone was tired of the heat, sand, and relentless sun. The last of Bellamont's salve had been issued, and, physically accustomed to the dim coolness of Nordabor, the novelty of the more-powerful sunlight had definitely worn off.

When they finally departed, the company passed through the same miserable plain they'd slogged across before, but this time, they were buoyed by their recent success. Even Moore, riding in a cart once again, appeared to be in better spirits, though he pointedly kept away from Mather.

For the most part, Mather's rebuke of the men was not mentioned. The guardsmen stumped along sweating and grimacing, sick from drink, with Mather striding ahead of them. He said nothing about the previous encounter and acted as though it had never occurred. He spoke little to the men, even Gricks and Baylor, who had been with him, and were innocent of any dereliction of duty. Baylor had mostly recovered from his heat exhaustion, though he still lagged behind the others.

They marched ceaselessly, everyone determined to leave the hated plain behind. After slightly over seventeen monotonous cycles, they reached the end of the plain, where the blessed shade of the canyon walls rose up to greet them. After a short rest and the dispersal of a few provisions, they continued, intent on setting up camp in the temple in which they'd previously sought refuge. Finally, after another five and a half cycles, they trudged wearily toward the temple's promise of shadowed relief.

Even Cyprian and Faye, who had been so unsettled by the lifelike statue of Ganachim inside, were happy to reach the temple. They were too exhausted and too bolstered by their success to be concerned about the morality of Ganachim's enslavement. Cyprian, especially, felt confident with the reassuring weight of the tube containing the shards slung across his back. The doubts that had hovered over him for the majority of the journey had temporarily dissipated. Only the sight of the charred husks of the burned badlanders could dampen his spirits.

The temple was cleared by Mather and his men in the same fashion as before and a camp was quickly established. Compared to their frontier post on the edge of the crater, baking in the direct heat of the sun, the temple was as comfortable as any private chamber in Nordabor.

The men spoke casually and excitedly about the next leg of the journey, feeling that success was close at hand. Nobody felt the need to actually address how much distance still lay before them or the threat of the other gods. As if in unspoken agreement, everyone understood that there would be time enough for that later. Only Mather, and, to a lesser degree, Baylor seemed to be refraining from any confident blustering. Mather did make sure that a proper watch was established, though, and his orders were not questioned.

The period of rest spent within the temple passed without incident. Knowing that this stretch of the journey would be their last before returning to the coolness and comfort of the *Fortune*, and free of any lingering sickness, the entire company was eager to depart, but they were held up for nearly a cycle by a group of roving shades once again crossing the basin. Whether or not it was the same ones as before was unknown. The thought of the miserable creatures stalking back and forth across that sweltering space for eternity made Cyprian truly hope that a shepherd would be nearby when he died. Just in case.

After plodding across the basin, the company found relief again in the same stretch of canyons as before. They made excellent time through the more-pleasant terrain before stopping briefly once more at the edge of the mud flats. The memory of just how treacherous navigating the mire had been was fresh in the minds of everyone, and for the first time, the positive energy permeating the group since the victory over Veathyadell started to wane.

The view of the collapsed bridge, and the end of their journey, on the horizon was the only thing that could motivate them to tromp through the muck again. Once the company set off, Phir-Ramarian, atop his steed, trotted down the line, shouting encouragement to the struggling men. Rayburn, Jotun, and Moore could only look on at their suffering comrades, slightly embarrassed, but thankful to be spared from the struggle.

The first indication that something was wrong came when they'd nearly reached the area of jumbled rocks where they'd initially landed. Phir-Ramarian, elevated above the others, first spied the *Fortune*.

"Something's wrong!" he called. "Captain Mather, get your men up here—we need to secure this area!"

Mather barked at his men to assemble around Phir-Ramarian, then staggered through the muck as quickly as he could toward the prince.

Rayburn and Jotun, who were further back in the line, craned their necks, trying to see what was happening.

"What's going on?" Cyprian panted, catching up to where Jotun had halted his horse.

"It looks like …" Jotun trailed off, squinting into the distance. "It looks like the boat is listing to one side."

Cyprian felt his stomach drop into an impossibly low pit. Nearby, he heard Rayburn muttering furiously.

"What did you say?" Faye asked, stumbling up to them. She had fallen at one point, and her entire front was caked in dried mud.

"The boat's listing to one side," Cyprian answered. He turned back to Jotun. "How bad is it?"

"It looks pretty bad."

They waited for some report from the front of the line, some explanation of what was happening. They could hear confused murmurs and calls for answers coming from behind them. The royal guardsmen were gathered around Phir-Ramarian, who had guided Honey up onto the foot of the tumbled rocks.

Now, one of the guardsmen broke away and clumsily sloshed through the mud toward them. As he grew closer, Cyprian could tell that it was Auden Lowther, recognizing him by his mutton chops; he was the only guardsman who hadn't started the journey clean-shaven.

"High Shepherd," he wheezed.

Moore, who'd been leaning over the edge of the cart next to them, looking forlorn, lifted his head. "Yes?"

"Captain Mather needs you and your shepherds. We need to clear the area. There's been an attack."

PART III:
FALLEN CITY

CHAPTER 19

The muddy, exhausted, and crestfallen leaders of the expedition were gathered in the command tent. The highs of their recent victory had been forgotten, replaced instead with the sobering reality that their situation had irrevocably changed.

"What's the final toll?" Phir-Ramarian asked. Dark circles hung under his eyes, and his thick, chapped lips were pressed together tightly. He looked as if he was expecting a physical blow.

"A total loss, my lord. No survivors," Mather answered. He seemed to be keeping his voice steady with a great effort.

The news solidified what they had already known. Based on what they'd found, there had been no indication of survivors.

A small force comprised of the guardsmen and the shepherds had approached the boat and found a massacre. The *Fortune* had run aground on a piling of rocks near their landing point. The skiffs, which the crew had apparently tried to flee in, were smashed or missing. Several bodies floated listlessly in the water, some with the shattered skulls that clearly indicated the spawning of shades. Detritus from the boat floated all around.

The shepherds and guardsmen had picked their way through the rocks, looking for any survivors with no success. A few shades lingered nearby, fully developed beasts that, upon seeing the men, attacked savagely. With Moore, Galt, and Solgard keeping a tight formation, they were able to dispatch the shades one by one. Due to the chaotic nature of the scene, the bodies had not initially been collected for burning. Now, as the leaders met, Kovak supervised the collection of the dead by Galt, Solgard, and the other guardsmen.

"No survivors?" Phir-Ramarian asked, as if he may have misheard Mather. Beside him, Pike reflexively placed a hand on the prince's arm, and Phir-Ramarian, apparently too devastated to bother with pretense for the moment, let it remain there.

"None. Confirmed amongst the dead are Winslow and five of his crew; our healer, Edith Lowe; and our shepherd, Ferro Blackburn."

At the mention of Blackburn, Moore, who'd been staring blankly at the wall of the tent, clasped his hands together, pressed them to his chin, and began whispering a litany of prayers. Bellamont looked as if she wanted to join him.

"My three men, Tannahill, Devonshire, and Luden, are unaccounted for, as well as three of Winslow's crew." Mather consulted the hastily scribbled notes he held before him. "Falstaff, Marbuck, and Castor."

Phir-Ramarian blinked as if waking from a stupor. "And what of the supplies?"

"We were able to recover quite a bit from the boat's hold," Mather explained, clearly preferring this new topic. "With it listing the way it is, and with the water as shallow as it is, a lot of the supplies were either above the waterline or barely submerged. We were able to retrieve almost all of the canned provisions, very few of which were damaged. The climbing equipment was also salvaged, though I believe one crate was crushed too far down into the riverbed to recover. What we did recover seems to be intact. Dupree?"

"Yes, Captain. I've inventoried it. Everything seems to be in working order," she answered.

"And so the food supply will be unharmed?" Phir-Ramarian asked.

"Not exactly," Rayburn answered timidly. The prince turned to him. "That is to say, the canned provisions will not be affected. However, many of the fruits and vegetables floated away on the current when their crates were smashed. A lot of the dry goods were lost. Some was recovered—my thanks to the guardsmen and haulers who pulled through for us—but much of it was lost. Same with the water casks. We lost several of those as well."

"Can't we refill empty casks from the river?" Phir-Ramarian asked. Behind him, Starkad silently entered the tent.

"There are only a few empty casks, and those are the leaky, damaged ones recovered from the boat. We dumped the other empty casks as we went to reduce weight," Rayburn said, looking ashamed. "Still, the damaged casks could be patched. The river water would have to be boiled before consumption, though."

"That will have to do," Phir-Ramarian said.

Looking at how beleaguered Phir-Ramarian appeared, Cyprian found that the leadership position he'd so coveted had somewhat lost its appeal. But only somewhat.

"I recovered Ferro's anointed blades as well," Moore said, his whispered prayers apparently finished. "His body was intact, thank the Void-God."

Nobody said anything for a moment.

"Captain. Were you able to discern what exactly happened?" Phir-Ramarian asked, breaking the somber silence.

"It appears that the *Fortune* was attacked by badlanders. It must have been a fairly large number of them, I would surmise. I believe that Winslow tried to turn the *Fortune* around to flee, but ran aground. At that point, the boat was overrun. Those left onboard were killed. Others tried to escape in the skiffs, but they didn't make it far."

Cyprian considered Mather's account of what happened, thinking of the wreck of the boat, visible just beyond the tent, the Einfallen lapping at its sides. Something didn't make sense.

"Captain," he said, the thought still forming as he spoke. "The badlanders we encountered before were specifically trying to steal our supplies. And there were only three of them. If there were a force large enough to overtake the *Fortune,* why didn't they loot the dead? Or take all of the provisions and equipment from the hold?"

"Because they weren't badlanders."

Every eye turned toward Starkad. He held something loosely wrapped in a cloth. His hands were filthy, and his thinning, blonde hair hung in his face. "They were Heilrune's men, from Vin-Sada-vat. Worshippers of Tariono. They weren't after provisions; they were after slaves. I imagine the missing were captured. The dead refused to submit."

This revelation was met with confused silence.

"Vin-Sadavat is far from here; why would they venture so far into the Daylands?" Cyprian asked.

"As I told you, Heilrune's fiefdom stretches far. I've heard tales that he sends slavers out to extreme distances to hunt for fresh thralls. They'll be forced to adhere to his twisted faith, used until their bodies give out, and then consumed."

"Consumed?" Rayburn asked, fear in his voice.

"Yes. Eaten. They didn't take a single scrap of food, from what we can tell, yes? Lends credence to the rumors of cannibalism that I've heard."

"How do you know that it wasn't just some bloodthirsty bad-landers killing for sport?" Phir-Ramarian asked.

"Because of this." Starkad opened the wrappings he held, and, with a wet thud, a severed head dropped onto the table. The others recoiled.

"You're as savage as the rest of your kind!" Phir-Ramarian thundered, making Pike flinch. "Get that out of here!"

"*Look* at it," Starkad responded calmly.

Reluctantly, Cyprian obeyed. The head was crowned by an ornate topknot tied with ribbons of gold. Below the hairline, the face was a hideous mask of scarred flesh. The nose had been cut away and the lips sliced in the corners, forming a fiendish grin. All across the face, scars of numerous deep cuts and burns were visible.

"So, you mutilated it as well?" Phir-Ramarian said with disgust.

"No," Bellamont said. "Those injuries are old."

"That's right," Starkad replied. "I removed this head from the corpse of one of our mysterious attackers out there. Heilrune's men all bear extreme facial scarring from self-mutilation. It's how they separate themselves from outsiders. It's said that the more mutilated they are, the more revered they are in the eyes of their god. Apparently, Tariono does not wish to have any rivals to her beauty."

"Fine, we understand. Now get that out of here," Phir-Ramarian said.

"Of course." Starkad lifted the head by its topknot and re-wrapped it in the cloth. He left the tent and returned a few ticks later without his bundle.

"So, you're saying that my men, and the rest of the crew, were taken captive by these mutilated cultists?" Mather asked Starkad as he reentered the tent.

"Yes. They'll be initiated once they're returned to Vin-Sadavat, I imagine."

"We need to leave at once," Mather said to Phir-Ramarian. "That was our next intended destination, anyway. We can save our people, then we can worry about slaying the old one and taking whatever shards it has." Mather's previous doubts seemed to have been erased by his desire to rescue his men.

"We don't know when this attack occurred," Rayburn interjected. "They could be long-gone. Your men could have merely drowned and drifted away. We've lost precious foodstuffs, our transportation, and too many men. With all due respect, my lord, we need to return to Nordabor. We can reconvene and launch another expedition later."

Moore and Bellamont nodded in agreement.

The entire expedition hinged on Phir-Ramarian's next decision. Cyprian thought of the blade shards, safely tucked within their protective casing, and of the other shards out there, waiting to be reunited with their brethren. Finally, his thoughts were pulled inexorably toward the Gates of Paradise and what lay beyond. There would be no later expedition. If they returned only partially successful, it was no success at all. Ganachim was failing; Nordabor was failing. Cyprian knew that this was their last shot. More, it was his last shot to find his father and to finish what he'd started.

He looked at Phir-Ramarian, who looked befuddled. Their eyes met for only a moment. Cyprian shook his head almost imperceptibly.

"Captain Mather is right," Phir-Ramarian said with sudden resolve. "We have experienced too much loss to allow more to occur. If we can save our men, we absolutely must. Beyond that, we have come too far to give up on our noble purpose now. We have enough provisions to continue on. The route may be longer, but we will endure. The fate of the people of Nordabor and the rich bloodline of Vingallea depends on our succeeding. And succeed we will."

Rayburn looked as if he wished to say more, but his servility overtook him. Moore and Bellamont simply looked too haggard to speak.

"We will have a shepherding ceremony for our fallen. Then, once we're ready, we will depart for Vin-Sadavat."

•   •   •

The smell of the burning bodies was repugnant and was made all the viler by the knowledge that some of the dead had been their comrades. The burning heap smoked badly, the waterlogged bodies failing to ignite properly. As Moore spoke from a boulder serving as a makeshift pulpit, Galt and Solgard continuously stoked the flames.

Moore had been the obvious choice to recite the prayer for the fallen, but to Cyprian, he hardly seemed up to the task. His cheeks bore ugly patches of burnt and peeling skin, his hair was filthy and lank, and his eyes had a swimming, unfocused look. His voice cracked as he spoke, and he seemed to be having a difficult time keeping his thoughts in order. The loss of a second acolyte had apparently stolen the last of his resolve.

"We pray, deeply and sincerely, to our benevolent Void-God. We pray that…that the righteous dead before us are ushered into the waiting arms of sweet nothingness. And that..we…" He paused, licking his cracked lips. "May the unclean, the unworthy…may the.. unrighteous be…"

Moore lowered his head and looked at his feet. A pregnant silence lingered, interrupted only by the occasional crackle of the stinking fire.

Cyprian shifted uncomfortably and looked to his side. Faye was staring intently at the wreck of the *Fortune*. Parts of it had been stripped away for the pyre, and the exposed ribs of the boat created the impression of a partially submerged skeleton. The dissonant sunshine, completely indifferent to the morbid undertaking it shone upon, shimmered in Faye's hair. Cyprian remembered when they'd first felt the sun rise, when they'd made love in their cabin. It already seemed like a very long time ago.

"We stand at a crossroads," Moore finally said. He appeared to have composed himself. "In one direction, we have more devastation, more suffering, and, certainly, more death. In the other, we have a chance to escape this unholy place. We were never meant to come here. I believed it was the Void-God's will, and I was wrong."

Galt and Solgard had stopped what they were doing and now watched Moore with looks of surprise. Murmurs passed through the gathered company. Phir-Ramarian, who'd been staring into space, suddenly snapped back and glared at the high shepherd.

"Get him down from there," he said to Mather.

Mather nodded to Kovak, who, with Gricks, approached Moore. He began to speak more quickly, sensing that he was going to be silenced imminently.

"This land of the faithless, filled with savages who've never known the true face of the Void-God and abominations that stalk the wastes; it's already taken so many of us, including two of my flock." Moore backed away from Kovak and Gricks, who were attempting to reach him without making a scene.

"And now, we are to plunge into the darkest corners of this blighted land to seek out further peril. Those taken men are gone! Why lose more? I pray that the Void-God has mercy on them, but there is nothing we can do. Has anyone told you of the dangers we will soon face?" He shouted this last question to the haulers, who looked at each other with confusion.

"We'll be butchered before we set foot in Vin-Sadavat!" Moore nearly shrieked.

"Seize him!" Phir-Ramarian roared. "Take him to his tent. He's not well."

Kovak and Gricks, eschewing any subtlety, launched themselves up the rock and snatched at Moore's robes, pulling the old shepherd down from his boulder.

Galt and Solgard ran toward the commotion, but several of the guardsmen stepped out to block their way. "Easy, now, easy," Rath said, hand on the hilt of his blade.

"Get your hands off of him!" Galt shouted around the guardsmen blocking his way. He tried to push his way through and was forcibly shoved backward.

The company was quickly falling into bedlam. Despite Phir-Ramarian's cries for order, the shepherds and the guardsmen were moments away from coming to blows. Mather had waded into the altercation and was pulling them apart, ordering them to back up. Moore was being dragged away from the crowd, his hoarse shouts nearly lost in the commotion.

Shrinking away from the chaos, Cyprian clutched the tube containing the shards protectively to his chest.

The shards.

Cyprian slipped from the tightening throng of people and toward the nearby horses, which were hitched to a metal spike driven into a crevice between two boulders. The animals, sensing the encroaching chaos, were agitated.

"What are you doing?" Faye asked, jogging behind him. Cyprian, acting almost on instinct, didn't answer, but hoisted himself up onto Honey's saddle and pulled the knot holding the horse to the hitch free. The horse immediately bucked, and, for an instant, Cyprian was certain that he was going to be thrown. Remembering his limited equestrian training, he was able to get the horse under control, and proceeded to guide it toward the crowd.

With one hand on the reins, he wedged the tube containing the shards under his arm and unscrewed the cap, then pulled forth one of the shards and held it aloft as Honey slowly and reluctantly began to walk into the crowd, forcing the men apart and distracting them from the impending brawl.

"Stop! Silence!" he shouted, hoping that the horse wouldn't panic and fling him from the saddle. His attempt at restoring order would certainly be undermined if he were unceremoniously dumped to the ground in front of the entire remaining company.

But, more than his commands and the disruptive presence of the horse, it was the shining remnant of the blade that had felled their creator that caused the men to grow silent and still.

"High Shepherd Moore is right," Cyprian shouted. "We do seek further peril, but not just for our taken comrades. We all know what's at stake here. Certainly, there can be no doubt of what dangers lie ahead now. But you also know *why* we face these dangers. We are talking about the survival of not just Nordabor or the legacy of Vingallea, but of mankind itself. Of this entire dying world. We are only a few more of these shards away from Paradise, from a rebirth of this world without the interference of unjust gods. And maybe the Void-God is with us, maybe not. We will make our own way, as we always have."

The crowd murmured. Phir-Ramarian stood watching with a flummoxed expression. Faye was staring at him as if she didn't know who he was. Starkad caught his eye and simply nodded.

"High Shepherd Moore has experienced more loss than any of us on this trek, and his despair is understandable, but he is a strong man, and he'll come to his senses. There very well may be more loss to come. But we cannot flee now. Otherwise, the deaths that have already occurred will have been for nothing. Together, we will see this through to completion." Cyprian paused, unsure how to finish his speech. "We've all been through a lot. Get some rest."

The crowd slowly began to disperse toward their respective tents.

"We will be departing upon my order before too long, so be prepared," Phir-Ramarian added unnecessarily. He looked as if he just needed to say something.

Galt and Solgard eyed the guardsmen venomously as they walked slowly around them, Mather standing between them still. Galt glanced up toward Cyprian with an unreadable look on his face, and then he and Solgard stalked off after Moore.

"You'd better follow them, just to make sure there's no further trouble," Phir-Ramarian said to Mather. He grunted in assent and walked off.

Cyprian resealed the shards within their tube and slid down from the saddle. Faye and Jotun approached him. "Where did that come from?" Faye asked him.

"I guess I've listened to enough of Phir-Ramarian's bullshit to spin some of my own."

"That was not bullshit," Jotun said, a strange twinkle in his eye. "You meant every word. Reminded me of your father."

Faye gave Jotun a sidelong look, leery of any comparison to Rorik that might go to Cyprian's head. Before the thread could be pulled further, though, Phir-Ramarian approached them. Cyprian prepared himself to face the prince's ire for having the audacity to commandeer his precious steed. "A moment alone with Lord Fontaine, please," he said.

"Of course, my lord," Faye said, somewhat pleased by the prince's miserable expression. She grabbed Jotun's arm, and they stepped away.

"That was quite the entrance," Phir-Ramarian said once he was certain that nobody else was within earshot. "And that speech—my words coming out of your mouth."

The thought of being a mouthpiece for the Crown made Cyprian's skin crawl.

"Not exactly," he corrected. "I just said what the men needed to hear—I told them the truth. I get that silencing Moore was necessary at the moment, but he's got a point. We can't pretend that we don't face dangers moving forward."

"I know, I know," Phir-Ramarian said unexpectedly. "Look, I know that I said you don't understand leadership, but what I just witnessed has shown me otherwise. And, perhaps, I spoke out of turn before, regarding you and your wife. The truth is, in light of recent events, I need another steady hand at the helm. The simple vanquishing of the last old one was a blessing, certainly, but compared to the disaster of finding this boat wrecked and our people dead and missing, it's nothing. The men are demoralized, and Moore's inability to keep it together is only fanning the flames. We cannot allow him to speak like that again; the others are frightened enough. You and Mather are my lieutenants out here, and he may follow orders, but the cracks have started to show for him as well. I need you. You still understand and embrace our purpose out here. Cyprian, this expedition is depending on you. I'm depending on you. I know we've had our differences, but we need to continue to present a united front."

Cyprian was taken aback by Phir-Ramarian's frank and humble tone. Clearly, the mantle of leadership had taken its toll on him.

"I understand," Cyprian said. "I'll do what I can."

"Excellent, cousin." Phir-Ramarian smiled weakly. "After all, we are bearers of royal Vingallean blood. If we can't see this through, nobody can."

CHAPTER 20

After the strain of relentlessly marching across the Daylands, only to return to find their basecamp destroyed and their people slaughtered, the company took nearly four full-cycles to depart again. The entire company was antsy to depart, yet they found themselves lingering. They were too physically and emotionally exhausted to quickly leave, and the air was just cool enough to tolerate, letting them rest longer. Despite the gruesome battle that had taken place there, and though the wreck of the *Fortune* leered over them, creating an unshakeable feeling of dread despite the cheerful sunlight, they bathed in the river. Most of them were just happy to be able to properly bathe and clean their clothes for the first time in several full-cycles.

Only Mather seemed ready right away, and the sluggish attitude of his men toward rescuing their compatriots seemed to fill him with ire.

The technical challenge of transporting their considerable amounts of provisions and gear across the river presented another deterrent to leaving, and for most of them, brought the resting to an end.

Starkad had picked his way across the ruins of the Sterling Bridge and reported that swaths of the ancient cobblestone roadway were still intact. Crossing from one massive piece of intact roadway to another, over steep drop-offs to the rubble-strewn water below, would be the real difficulty. Dupree and her engineers drafted several of the haulers to accompany them to the bridge, where they set to work establishing makeshift gangplanks to cross the gaps. The walkways were fashioned from further pieces of the *Fortune's* hull, and little of the boat was left by the time they were finished.

With everything stowed and settled, the time finally came to depart. Phir-Ramarian gave a short speech meant to inspire, but it simply rehashed what Cyprian had said more effectively at the shepherding.

Since his outburst at the botched ceremony, Moore, who'd stayed sequestered in his tent until they were set to depart, had remained silent. Solgard explained to any curious askers that he'd spent the time fasting and praying for their success. People knew better than to ask Galt.

The shoreline was as rocky, muddy, and uneven as the entire mud flat had been, and by the time the company reached the first passable stretch of bridge rubble, they were already drenched, filthy, and miserable. Once they made their way up the bridge remains, they found the crumbling cobblestone crooked and slanted at impossibly steep angles. Through trial and error, they eased the carts along, the men swarming around them ensuring that the loads did not topple. Forcing the panicked donkeys along required near-constant whipping.

The makeshift walkways sagged disconcertingly under the wagonloads, and the carts had to pass one at a time. Several times, the sound of snapping boards accompanied the passing of particularly heavy carts. After a harrowing five cycles, they reached the other bank of the Einfallen, where an ugly march through an almost-identical mud flat greeted them.

When planning their new route, they'd considered the remnants of the Imperial Highway. The highway had cut directly south toward the old kingdom, and thus been of no use to them when they traveled eastward. On the western side of the Sterling Bridge, however, the highway proceeded due west—directly to Vin-Sadavat.

Starkad had cautioned against using the old road, advising that there was a higher likelihood of being ambushed by Heilrune's men if they were out in the open on a designated route. Thus, it was decided that the expedition would follow a path that ran roughly parallel to the road, though far north of it.

So, their spirits at a nadir, they toiled through yet another treacherous bog. As they went, the sun sank slowly behind them.

·　　·　　·

Galt scratched at the scraggly beard growth on his face and squinted into the dim tree line before him. The air was cool and completely still, and, though as stale as it ever was, it still felt incredible compared to what they'd endured in the Daylands. The surroundings were very similar to Nordabor, though the woodlands were still withered and silent this far south of Ganachim's influence.

The camp slept peacefully now, the semidarkness and lower temperature presenting a normalcy that had raised the spirits of the company, Galt included. Standing on the perimeter, gazing into the shadowed areas between the twisted trunks of the barren pines, Galt fantasized about just walking away from the camp and into the sweet embrace of the darkness. Something about the thought of curling up in a small, cool, dark area just felt comforting.

Of course, it was only an illusion. They were far from the safety of their walled city, and beyond the branches encircling their small clearing, many dangers lurked.

Chiefly, Galt thought of Daeg and the description of the shade that had killed him. Of course, the human threat of the slavers from Vin-Sadavat now hung over them as well.

Galt also thought of Solgard, who had now lost her closest companion. Since he'd confessed to her at the temple that he was certain they were doomed, Solgard had been standoffish—polite, but businesslike in her demeanor. Since Blackburn's death, she'd spoken only of her concern for Moore, but Galt knew from experience that she must be suffering greatly from the loss of her longtime partner.

Coping mechanism or not, Solgard's concern for Moore was quite legitimate. If the high shepherd's faith in their endeavor had been tottering before, it had completely collapsed now. Since they'd left the Daylands, he had remained almost silent, staring catatonically into nothing.

Galt had hoped that as they returned to the Dawnlands and the terrain became more hospitable, Moore would recover from his strange episode. Unfortunately, his mental fog continued. Occasionally, Galt would hear him quickly whispering to himself, though the words were indiscernible.

Lord Fontaine, who had been worming his way into command as Phir-Ramarian's grip on the situation started to slip, had graciously allowed Moore to continue riding in their cart. Over the previous three full-cycles of travel, Lord Fontaine had tried to engage Moore in conversation, to no avail. He, his lady, and Berg tolerated Moore's unusual presence while mostly ignoring him. All the while, Galt and Solgard hovered near their ailing leader.

The silence, and Galt's wandering thoughts, were interrupted by a low whistle. It was Kovak, signaling the changing of the watch. Galt headed back toward the shepherds' tent, determined not to encounter or speak with any of the guardsmen.

Remembering Mather's goons dragging Moore away filled Galt with furious disgust. Standing on the silent perimeter, he'd occasionally found himself fantasizing about creeping up behind Kovak and cutting his throat. Obviously, that would be a direct violation of his shepherd's vows and the laws of Nordabor. However, he did a piss-poor job of following his vows as it was, and they were far from Nordabor...

His idle fantasies of meting out his own form of justice occupied his mind until he reached the tent. Solgard was already waiting outside for him, sitting on an overturned bucket. Her eyes were red.

"Hey," he said awkwardly.

She smiled at him, took a deep, shuddering breath, and stood, dusting her bottom off. "Anything to report?"

"No, it's quiet." He paused and decided to take the plunge. "Are you okay?"

"Honestly, no, I'm not," she said. "He's getting worse."

Galt looked at the entrance to the tent. Moore no longer handled any of the watches. "Yes, he is."

"I suppose he's more on your level now."

Galt frowned. "What makes you say that?"

"Well, his will appears to have been broken. He's lost all hope of survival, much less success. I'm the only one keeping the faith. It's not easy, you know. He's supposed to be our leader."

"Listen, I'm sorry I told you that I doubt our prospects, but it doesn't mean I've given up and become a helpless burden," Galt said a bit more harshly than he'd intended, gesturing toward the tent. "We're in this chapter together, and whatever happens, I'll do everything I can to ensure that we survive. We don't know if he's going to recover, but that doesn't mean that you're the only one holding us together. You're not alone. Whatever you think of my faith, my doubts, it doesn't mean that I've given up."

Solgard looked at him appraisingly. He braced himself for a scathing rebuke.

"Ferro and I entered the order at the same time," she said unexpectedly. "I met him during initiation rites at the Ivy Citadel. We were conscripted into the same chapter and served together for my entire time as a shepherd. Twelve long-cycles. He wasn't just a partner; he was my friend."

She turned away, hands on her hips, and stared up into the gloomy, overcast sky. Galt didn't know what to say, but he understood that this was an important moment—a chance to heal the rift and forge a stronger bond moving forward. He needed Solgard, and understood her pain. Once again, he thought of Daeg.

He said nothing, but placed a hand on her shoulder. She turned around quickly and hugged him. They stood for some time, holding each other. It did not strike Galt as a romantic embrace, but one derived from a simple human need to fight isolation and sorrow. Nonetheless, it felt good to hold her.

Eventually, she broke away and wiped her nose with the back of her hand. "Thank you," she said thickly. "I better go."

She walked away purposefully, headed toward the perimeter. Galt watched her go, feeling a confusing mixture of emotions. Once she left his sight, he wriggled into the tent and settled onto his bedroll, pulling a woolen blanket over himself.

In the dark confines of the tent, Moore's rattling breath filled the silence. Galt looked over at the lumpish shape of the man whom, in his youth, he'd considered his mentor in the order. It was no wonder now that he felt so spiritually bankrupt. Moore's idea of faith had always been a veneer of dramatic recitations of apocryphal scriptures and invocations. It had never been tested beyond routine shepherding ceremonies and the destruction of shades. Now, out in the wild lands, faced with loss and challenge, Moore had seen the divine protections he'd assumed would accompany him stripped away. All that remained was a frightened old man.

Galt pitied Moore, but knew that there was nothing he could do. His own lack of faith was a vacant hole within him. This journey had compounded his doubts, and, having already suspected the futility of the plan, he found that he was no more afraid than he had been at the start.

Still, he would soldier on. He would do what he could to protect his chapter, even if he had to carry Moore himself.

The thought of fleeing, of taking Moore and Solgard and just leaving, once again crossed his mind. He knew that Solgard wouldn't go for it, though. And, as little as he felt the touch of the Void-God, he still believed in his vow to protect and shepherd the innocent people on the expedition—the haulers, healers, engineers, and others who could not defend themselves.

He briefly considered sending a prayer out into the Void on their behalf, but couldn't find the right words.

He rolled over, and the only prayer he spoke was one for a dreamless sleep.

CHAPTER 21

The caravan slowly picked its way through the blighted woodlands over the course of four more full-cycles, steadily crossing the Dawnlands.

The temperature and sunlight had dwindled to more comfortable levels, but the terrain was as challenging as ever. Numerous jagged ruts, the last remnants of dried creek beds, cut across the land, forcing the carts up and down crumbling banks. They weaved around the crooked, white husks of lifeless trees, sometimes being forced to hack down the dead trunks that blocked their way. Roots that had long ago ceased feeding from the sterile ground still threatened to break the wheels of their wagons and the ankles of the unobservant.

As they travelled, they began to encounter signs of habitation—small abandoned campsites that appeared to have been recently deserted. Starkad surmised that they'd been occupied by nomadic badlanders who had moved on.

Starkad had advised the leaders that the company would have to cross the northern arm of the Imperial Highway, the route that used to lead toward Nordabor. He'd indicated on his worn map where the ancient road cut across their projected route. The leaders had been gathered around the map, lantern light flickering across their haggard faces. Moore was noticeably absent.

"Is there a chance we'll be ambushed there?" Mather had asked.

"No greater chance than we already face, I would think. It's possible that the slavers could be in the area, but from what I've heard, they stay mainly to the east-west stretch of the road."

Despite Starkad's cautious reassurance, the fear of ambush began to gnaw at the men as the woods thinned out and they reached the derelict settlements that had once thrived along the sides of the highway. The daylight had dwindled to almost nothing, and darkened windows that could conceal any number of hidden attackers leered down at them from the crumbling, squat buildings.

Cyprian's fear was blunted by his interest in their surroundings. The structures were reminiscent of the market in Nordabor, and he guessed that they had once been taverns and shops that peddled goods to travelers passing along the road.

Jotun, who was now in territory that was wholly unfamiliar to him, shared Cyprian's interest. "Imagine what we could find inside any one of these places," he said eagerly. "We should take a break here. We could go through some of them."

"I'd like to see what's inside of them as well," Faye said, "but I'm also worried that we wouldn't like what we found. Or *who* we found."

Cyprian was inclined to agree with Faye, albeit reluctantly.

"Don't fret, Berg." Starkad had sidled up next to them as they walked. "These ruins have probably been completely picked over by generations of badlanders. Anything of value or interest would almost certainly be gone. You're not missing anything."

Jotun's face sank, and he nodded. Behind him, Cyprian could see Moore rocking along with the movement of the cart he still occupied, bearing the same dazed expression that he'd worn since they'd left the Daylands. Cyprian found it very unsettling, and wished that Moore were not constantly near them. Once again, he regretted offering to help, but he didn't dare try to make him walk now. Certainly not when the two sour-faced shepherds were hovering nearby. He could only imagine how they would react.

"So, how much further until we reach the road itself?" Cyprian asked Starkad.

"It's just beyond this—"

Yelling from the front of the line interrupted them. Honey had reared up, and Phir-Ramarian was shouting in surprise. The guardsmen were rapidly hefting their weapons, leveling crossbows at a pale shape darting by the horse's legs. Several bolts flew at once, striking the ground and the crumbling walls around them. Finally, one found its mark, and the shape crashed to the ground, skidding to a halt.

"What *is* that thing?" Phir-Ramarian asked as he fought to get Honey back under control.

"It's a—it looks like some kind of dog, my lord," Rackham answered, prodding the body with the end of his sword.

Cyprian approached the creature cautiously. Rackham was right; it resembled a dog, but not even the mangiest stray in Nordabor rivaled it. The creature was almost hairless, exposing tight white skin shot through with blue veins. The hair that did cling to its grotesque, malnourished frame was gray and lank. Its face was long and covered in old scratches, with small, pink eyes that had already taken on a glassy sheen. The creature's mouth hung open, and a small trickle of blood was oozing from its lips.

Rayburn navigated his horse up to the body, where others were now gathering as well. "It looks like we've obtained some fresh meat to me. We should consider it good fortune that we encountered it." He peered over the others, and, actually seeing the body for the first time, frowned in disgust.

"I wouldn't plan on eating any part of this," Starkad said. "These mongrels are diseased and not suitable for consumption. A badlander could stomach their meat, if necessary, but your stomachs would be destroyed by any of this tainted flesh. Nothing healthy survives in the wastes."

Nobody seemed prepared to argue further in favor of eating the foul beast.

As they stood around it, the sound of low voices and footsteps scrabbling across rock met their ears. From the direction that the strange dog had come, four individuals stepped out from between two buildings and into the open. They froze the moment they saw the company.

They were clearly badlanders, though garbed in heavier robes colored in earth tones and carrying crude-looking bows. One of them was a woman, and another looked to be barely older than a child.

Nobody moved until Kovak, Gricks, and Rackham decided in unison to take aim at the strangers.

"Stand down!" Mather bellowed. The guardsmen held their fire, and the frightened badlanders turned and fled back into the ruins.

"Those could have been slavers," Kovak said indignantly.

Mather whirled around on him and stepped nose-to-nose with his subordinate. "I gave you an order. Don't ever question my orders. Ever."

Kovak withered before Mather's authority and said nothing. "Do you understand me?" Mather demanded.

"Yes, sir," Kovak said, bitterness tinging his voice. Mather continued to glare at Kovak until the under-captain reaffirmed his loyalty, this time without any attitude.

Phir-Ramarian, sensing that the tense moment had passed, cleared his throat. "Why, exactly, Captain, did you order them to stand down?"

"Those were obviously not slavers," Starkad answered. "Captain Mather could see that. I believe they were just a family of badlanders, probably tracking this very dog. It's unfortunate that we scared them away from their quarry; they're probably starving. Nobody is far from starvation out here."

Cyprian thought of the loads of provisions they had. Even by a conservative estimate, and even after losing some of their stock with the *Fortune*, the expedition was still far from starvation. And never in his entire life had Cyprian lacked for food. He looked at Starkad's thin, weathered face, and for the first time, truly understood his motivation to find deliverance within the walls of Nordabor.

Rattled by the unexpected encounters with the diseased dog and the badlanders, the company took a moment to regather and regroup. Tensions, and the fear of ambush, still ran high.

Once they were underway again, it was only a few short-cycles before they reached the Imperial Highway crossing. The disintegrating buildings fell away, revealing a flat span of cracked cobblestone stretching away to the north and south.

Mather and his guardsmen led a vanguard that fanned out across the roadway, creating a protective line on either side for the column of men to pass through. They strode across quickly, mindful of any possible threats lurking amongst the almost-identical ruins on the other side of the highway.

Cyprian noticed that several people, including Rayburn, Bellamont, and Galt, were gazing longingly to the north. Moore, who was staring at his lap with a dull expression, had previously spoken of being at a crossroads at which return to Nordabor was still possible. At no other moment had this been more true than now. Cyprian ignored the northbound road, which stretched away into the darkness, and set his eyes on the dilapidated buildings before them.

"Imagine the multitudes of people who used to travel this road," Faye said, glancing around. "Phar-Karrian marched his host to the siege of the Father-God along this very route."

"We're treading on history itself," Jotun murmured reverently.

The last of the line filed into a narrow alley, and the guardsmen fell in behind them. They shuffled by the others in the tight space and retook their normal positions in the line. The company then resumed its march, suddenly aware that the last light of the sun they had so recently cursed was now sinking away into inky blackness behind them.

•　　•　　•

With lanterns cautiously lit, the company trekked on into the Night-lands for another six cycles before stopping and setting up camp in a clearing surrounded by the skeletal remnants of trees, their barren branches clawing at the black sky. The tents were erected hastily, and the men quickly harvested dry wood from the surrounding trees to get fires burning. Though the company was happy to indulge in cooked food, the pressing darkness beyond the reach of their meager campfires disturbed them, driving them to eat quickly and retreat to their tents.

The watch was increased, with four guardsmen patrolling at a time, accompanied by one shepherd and three haulers pressed into additional service. Despite it being Mather's idea, he was reluctant to arm the jumpy, nervous haulers with crossbows. Ultimately, though, the need for more watchful eyes superseded any doubts he had about the haulers' abilities.

With the camp established, the leaders were called to gather in the command tent to discuss their pending arrival in Vin-Sadavat, the state of the provisions, and what they would face on the journey ahead.

Cyprian was the first to arrive, and as he approached the tent, he overheard Phir-Ramarian speaking quietly inside. His curiosity overtaking him, he paused beyond the threshold and listened.

"I'm worried about the men."

"They're just rattled, my lord." Cyprian recognized the voice as Pike's, though his tone was softer than his typical servile inflection. "It's understandable, considering what's happened. And this darkness certainly isn't helping. Things will turn around."

The conversation seemed to trail off, and Cyprian, feeling slightly guilty for eavesdropping, peered through the narrow gap in the tent flaps. Inside, Phir-Ramarian and Pike were holding each other beneath the lantern light, their foreheads touching. The prince kissed his scribe gently. "I hope you're right. We need a victory to restore morale, and soon. I'm worried about desertion, especially being so close to the Imperial Highway."

"The guardsmen would catch anyone who tried to sneak out of the camp."

"Yes, that's true, and I trust them," Phir-Ramarian said, pulling away. "Mather's episode at the celebration notwithstanding, I know he'd never entertain the idea of desertion or allow anyone else to. But, still, I'm afraid that I might be losing them. I wasn't prepared for things to go so wrong, and I think they can tell. Maybe this was a mistake."

Pike placed a hand on the prince's cheek and looked up into his face. "You will lead us to victory, my lord. I have no doubt."

Phir-Ramarian reached up and clasped his hand over Pike's. He smiled, squeezed the other man's hand, and pulled it away from his cheek. "They'll be here soon." Pike's look of adoration faded as the prince stepped away and absentmindedly began to smooth the front of his tunic.

To see confirmation of the rumors regarding Phir-Ramarian and Pike was neither surprising nor particularly interesting to Cyprian. He was much more intrigued to see that his cousin's self-assurance had crumbled further than he'd let on. It hadn't been long ago that Phir-Ramarian had been pontificating about what it took to lead. In the aftermath of the attack on the *Fortune,* his confidence had appar-ently been shaken to its foundations.

Cyprian couldn't help but feel a grim sense of satisfaction. If Phir-Ramarian was faltering, Cyprian would need to step in and take on a greater role. After all, the prince had explicitly asked for his help.

From the darkness behind him, Cyprian heard the sounds of others approaching. He cleared his throat and casually entered the tent, where Phir-Ramarian and Pike now stood without a hint of impropriety. The prince, who'd assumed his best approximation of his normal look of regal aplomb, greeted Cyprian stiffly, while Pike said nothing.

A moment later, the other leaders filed inside and gathered around the table. Moore was absent once again; his acolyte Solgard had taken his place.

"By my estimate, we should have about four more full-cycles of travel before we reach the outskirts of Vin-Sadavat proper," Starkad explained from his customary position before his unfurled map. "Now is the time to determine how we'll actually enter the city."

Phir-Ramarian stared at him and blinked several times. "Isn't that something our guide should know?"

The other leaders exchanged glances.

"Well," Starkad said slowly, "as I told you before, I determined that Tariono is most likely the power behind Heilrune and his cult, and I determined that they're in Vin-Sadavat, but getting into the city is another thing. Beyond realizing that simply storming in is not an option, I never told you that I had a solution."

"I see," Phir-Ramarian said. "Does anyone else have any suggestions?"

"If we can scout out the city's defenses, perhaps we can find a weak spot for a small force—just me and a few men—to enter," Mather suggested.

"We would have no way of knowing if you were in trouble," Cyprian said. "You could be captured, and then what would we do? Just send in more men after waiting in vain? Not to mention that you don't know where Tariono is supposed to be or where our companions are being held. You would need someone with knowledge of the city's layout."

Mather grunted in agreement.

"Perhaps," Rayburn ventured, "we send a party to Nordabor for reinforcements. We could amass an actual garrison and besiege the city."

"That wouldn't work," Mather said.

"Why not?" Bellamont asked, the mere mention of returning home making her suddenly invested in Rayburn's plan.

"We would have to send Starkad to guide the party back to Nordabor, and we need him here," Mather explained with some impatience. "It would take too much time—our comrades would almost certainly be dead by the time any force were organized and mobilized. Additionally, there aren't enough fighting men of merit to mount a siege of Vin-Sadavat. We have no idea what their numbers are, and if they *are* cannibals, as has been suggested, they won't be lacking for food anytime soon. Our men would starve out here in the dark long before they did. Lastly, taking any more men from Nordabor would leave the city completely defenseless."

Rayburn and Bellamont both looked cowed by Mather's long list of reasons why the plan would fail.

"So, we've established that it's just us out here," Phir-Ramarian clarified. "Any other suggestions?"

Cyprian was just opening his mouth to reply, hoping that whatever he said would be a viable answer, when Faye called out from behind him.

"I might have a solution," she said, letting the tent flaps fall closed behind her as she entered.

"Lady Fontaine," Phir-Ramarian said, looking flustered, "I appreciate your eagerness to help, but this is a meeting of the leaders."

He looked at Solgard, who had said nothing during the meeting. "And their representatives, I suppose."

"Well, I couldn't help but overhear from outside that you're all out of ideas," Faye said pleasantly, ignoring the prince's dismissive attitude. "I felt that I could help. Surely any suggestion is a welcome one?"

Cyprian cut in before Phir-Ramarian could answer. "What do you got?"

"When I was a child, my father would tell me stories of the rulers of Vingallea, of the great feats they accomplished. Fairly standard stuff for bedtime stories."

The others nodded, unsure of where she was going, but curious nonetheless.

"Well, many stories, of course, focused on Phan-Casmia, the Preserver. I mean, her adventures were some of the greatest ever, rivaled only by Phan-Ellara's, really. As an adult, I assumed most of them were exaggerated, growing bigger and more dramatic over time."

"How are children's stories supposed to—"

"Be quiet; let her finish," Cyprian said, cutting Phir-Ramarian off. The prince looked surprised, but said nothing. His sudden subservience to Cyprian did not go unnoticed by the others.

"Well," Faye continued, "as I think we've confirmed with the recovery of some of the blade shards, every legend has a basis in truth.

In this particular case, I'm thinking of the tale of how Phan-Casmia escaped the fall of Vin-Sadavat."

Cyprian, who was familiar with the old tales as well, realized what Faye was thinking, and couldn't believe that he hadn't had the same idea.

After the fall of the Father-God, when the sun froze and the capital was trapped in darkness, civil war erupted in Vin-Sadavat. Led by an ambitious demagogue called Nazhan Nazradir, the descendants of Aurangzeb rebelled against the Crown, and Phan-Casmia had been forced to flee to Nordabor, taking the skullcap of Phan-Ellara with her. Her method of escape was where the documented history gave way to sensationalized legend.

"The sewers," he said.

"Exactly," Faye said with satisfaction. "Phan-Casmia and her trusted retinue escaped into the labyrinth of sewers under the city and found a way out."

"And she single-handedly fought off a hundred shades and scaled an underground waterfall that fell into the depths of Punishment," Dupree said skeptically. "I remember the tale."

"Well, some of it may be embellishment, but there's no doubt that the city has a large sewer system. Whether she used it or not, we can," Faye argued.

"That makes sense. We could infiltrate the city from underneath," Mather said, ignoring the history and legends and cutting straight to the tactical considerations. "From there, we could figure out where our men are being held, as well as where the old one is. Lord Fontaine, you mentioned that we'd need someone with knowledge of the city's layout with us. I assume you meant yourself."

"Yes," Cyprian answered. "We have maps of the city's layout, or at least how it was before the fall. I plan on accompanying you into the city."

"*We* plan on accompanying you into the city," Faye said. Her tone permitted no questioning. Cyprian knew that there would be no dissuading her; she would not let him go alone. And he felt better knowing that she would be there with him.

"After you get us close enough," Cyprian continued, addressing Starkad, "can you lead a smaller group out to find an entrance to the sewers? There has to be some sort of drainage-pipe system that empties outside of the city walls."

"Of course," Starkad said. He appeared to have no qualms with the plan.

"Dupree, we'll need you and your engineers, as well, in case we need to force a way into the sewers. The pipes may be covered with grates or sealed somehow."

"Yes, my lord," she answered, still sounding unsure.

"Okay, so it's settled," Cyprian said. "We all know what we need to do."

Phir-Ramarian, who was watching him closely, suddenly realized that the meeting was coming to a close. "This plan sounds sufficient to me. Everybody get some rest," he added.

The group was already dispersing by the time he spoke.

CHAPTER 22

As they travelled through a seemingly endless forest of blighted husks, the constant darkness that surrounded them began to instill more frustration than fear. The terrain was as difficult and unforgiving as it had been in the Dawnlands, but now, in the total darkness, the march had become a slow, tedious process.

The temperature continued to drop, driving the company to put on extra layers of woolen underclothing, leather gear, cloaks, and even armor. The heavier clothing, left behind since they wouldn't need it in the heat of the Daylands, had thankfully been among the provisions recovered from the wreck of the *Fortune*.

To their amazement, as the temperatures dropped further, the company became able to see their breath. Starkad explained that it was a totally normal occurrence in colder temperatures, soothing the fears of some who were worried they'd contracted an exotic illness.

Finally, after over five full-cycles, they came within view of Vin-Sadavat. Starkad had led them up onto a bluff that rose high enough to see the city, which was illuminated by hundreds of bonfires. The accumulated light reflected off the low ceiling of black clouds, casting a dim, eerie glow over the city.

Cyprian let his eyes adjust to the faint light, then hefted his field glass. The city, easily four times the size of Nordabor, was a breathtaking, terrifying hulk unlike anything he could have imagined. He could only marvel at its colossal, ugly heights.

Built upon an island delta of the lower Einfallen, which snaked toward the city far south of their vantage point, Vin-Sadavat was an oval of towering spires surrounded by cracked ramparts. The mighty Einfallen, possibly due to the damming caused by the collapse of the Sterling Bridge, had been reduced to an inky line within a deep, muddy trough running around the city on both sides.

Evidence of the ancient civil war, as well as the many long-cycles of strife that had followed, were visible across the city. Few of the towers were free of the scars of war, and many had partially collapsed. The walls, which had surely been white marble at one point, were stained black with the soot and grime of endless fires. Despite the damage, the architectural influence of the original Aurangzeb builders of the city was undeniable. Their artistic flourishes, domed parapets, and massive columns were still visible.

In the center of the city, one tower rose above all the others. Open terraces that appeared to have once contained opulent gardens dotted the rectangular structure, which was adorned on multiple, narrowing levels with spires and parapets. The monolithic keep rose to dizzying heights until it culminated in a flat rooftop square hemmed in on all sides by rows of columns. In the center of the square rose a citadel that, had it been on the ground, would have been enormous in its own right. Roaring bonfires burned on either side of the citadel's entrance, and the small dots of revelers moving around the fire were just barely visible.

Cyprian did not need to consult the maps to know that this structure was the Opal Tower, the former royal keep, and seat of Vingallean power. Built by the people of Aurangzeb, the Opal Tower had housed their rulers for ages. When their civilization fell to Vingallea, and Phan-Ellara rechristened the city Vin-Sadavat, she'd taken her place upon the throne and made the Opal Tower her own palace.

"There," Cyprian said, pointing to the impossibly tall keep. "That has to be where Tariono is. If they worship her as their god, there's no way she would be anywhere but the Opal Tower."

Faye nodded in agreement. Unspoken between them was the satisfaction that this dangerous endeavor would at least give them the opportunity to see a historical wonder beyond anything they'd ever encountered.

Vin-Sadavat, and the Opal Tower specifically, cast a long shadow over Vingallean history. The desire to someday retake the city and reestablish Vingallean supremacy had haunted many of the lords of Nordabor. Just to see the legendary lost city and to walk the halls of the Opal Tower seemed like a dream.

"I have to say, that seems like a fair assessment," Starkad said, studying the city through his own field glass. "This is the closest I dared to venture before. I was thinking the same thing, but I had no way of being certain. As for where your men are being held ..." He trailed off.

"If we find Tariono, we find our men," Cyprian said. Deep in the blackest recesses of his mind, a nasty thought whispered that finding the men was vastly secondary to finding the blade shards. He ignored the true impulse. "She'll know where they are, and she'll tell us one way or another."

Faye and Jotun exchanged a look of concern.

"Well-said," Phir-Ramarian chimed in. He was not looking at the city, instead looking nervously back into the darkness of the forest behind them.

"We should begin our search down there," Starkad said, pointing southwest toward the scant waters of the Einfallen. "I'm sure that the city would have expelled its sewage directly into the Einfallen, which would carry it to the sea west of here. We'll have to be wary of the last leg of the Imperial Highway, though. Where it approaches the city, it runs nearly parallel to the river until the river splits under the bridge, there."

Cyprian looked where Starkad was indicating and observed a bridge illuminated by the dim glow of the fires. It spanned the area where the river split around the island delta, connecting the highway to the city. The northern reach of the riverbed could be checked without ever having to cross the Imperial Highway.

A team was assembled to seek out an entrance into the sewers while the remainder of the company established a camp. Cyprian and Faye were part of the search party and, bearing the maps of the old city's infrastructure, they hoped that the rudimentary notations regarding the city's plumbing would mesh with Starkad's theory. Cyprian had no illusions about the dangers of approaching the city, but he was eager to depart, nonetheless.

The team, which consisted of Cyprian, Faye, Starkad, Mather, Lowther, Shaw, Galt, Dupree, and two of her engineers, Shagalov and Hayves, had packed light, carrying only essential gear and provisions in their personal bags. Uncharacteristically, Phir-Ramarian made no attempt to join them or assert control over the team.

As they were making their final preparations, he approached Cyprian gingerly. "A word, Lord Fontaine?"

They stepped aside, out of earshot of the others.

"Might it be best," Phir-Ramarian said in an unusually delicate tone, "if the blade shards were left with me? If something were to happen to you out there, I would hate to have gained three blade shards, only to deliver them to another old one."

Cyprian pretended to consider the suggestion. "It's a good thought, but I think they would be safer with me. Your father entrusted me with them, and they would be just as vulnerable to being lost here as they would be out there with me. I'll keep them."

Frustration bloomed on Phir-Ramarian's face for a moment, a strange look of jealousy that had never disturbed his features before. For a moment, he appeared ready to resume his normal blustering, but the look passed, replaced by one of uncertainty and resignation.

Perhaps it had been the invoking of Phar-Mindorius's will or the resolute finality with which Cyprian had answered no. Whatever it was, he did not push the issue any further.

• • •

The party picked their way down a crumbling slope where the parched earth had eroded away from the bluff. At the bottom, they found themselves on the plain they'd previously been overlooking, with the vast bulk of Vin-Sadavat, wreathed in its sinister glow, dominating the horizon.

They carried no light, hoping to stay hidden from any sentinels on the city walls. Huddled close, they moved as swiftly as possible, staying low to the ground. The footing was treacherous, with numerous splintered tree trunks spread across the otherwise-barren field. Cyprian surmised that the slavers had been clear-cutting around the city, moving further and further out, in order to fuel their fires.

As they slowly grew closer to the city, changes in the terrain swam into view through the murk. Deep trenches had been carved out across the plain, and all around them, scattered human remains and the detritus of war had been cast across the ground.

Disquiet rippled through the group.

"What is all this? What happened here?" Faye asked.

"It must be remnants of the civil war," Cyprian said.

"I'm not so sure. Wouldn't that have occurred primarily *within* the city walls? Why would there be trenches dug on the outside?"

Faye was right. It didn't really make sense.

The team climbed down into a trench, then scrambled up the opposite side, pieces of the trench wall collapsing under them. They passed through three more of the trenches before Faye stooped to examine an intact metal shield partially wedged into the ground. She scowled in concentration, then wrenched the shield free.

The group gathered around her. "We don't have time for this," Dupree said, looking into the darkness around them.

Faye shot her an irritated glance and continued to look at the shield. She brushed some encrusted dirt off of the front and squinted at the faint remnants of the insignia emblazoned across the shield.

"This is the coat of arms of Nordabor," she said, confused.

Cyprian gazed over her shoulder in disbelief. "That's impossible."

"No, look here." She indicated the telltale markings still visible on the dented shield. Cyprian looked closely, squinting in the dim light. He could just make out the four spires of the Vinecrown Keep encircled by a wreath of greenery. Within a stylized heart in the center, the closed fist and halo of Vingallea was also visible.

"Have you read anything that implies that Nordabor was involved in the civil war here?" Faye asked him.

"No. As far as I know, no other holds were able to assist Vin-Sadavat."

"But the records show absolutely nothing about any attempt to retake the city."

"That's because your records are incomplete," Starkad said. "Look here."

He was standing over the lip of the next trench. Cyprian, Faye and the others joined him and gazed into a mass grave. At least thirty skeletal bodies were piled within, dressed in scant remnants of rusted armor. Still, clearly visible emblazoned on some of the breastplates was the same coat of arms.

"It looks like at some point after the fall of the city, Vingallean forces from Nordabor tried to retake it," Starkad said.

"It looks like their siege failed," Mather observed. "Just like I said any attempt at a siege would fail for us."

"I know that retaking Vin-Sadavat was the dream of many of the exiled Vingallean monarchs, but there is absolutely no evidence that any of them ever attempted it," Cyprian said doubtfully.

Yet the evidence was right in front of him.

"The masters of your city probably wanted to erase all evidence and memory of their failed attempt," Starkad said. "It doesn't exactly fit the narrative of Vingallean superiority."

"This is all very fascinating, but it's really neither here nor there," Dupree said, her voice strained.

Before anyone could respond, Galt spoke. "Be quiet," he ordered, urgency in his voice. Everyone froze and began peering into the gloom surrounding them. "Shades."

Following his gaze, Cyprian was just able to make out a group of five or six lank black shapes trudging along. He'd never been this close to a shade before, and the hair on his neck rose instantly. With some surprise, he found that he was trembling slightly.

"Get down into the trench, slowly," Galt whispered. The team crept as silently as possible, sliding down the wall of the trench and into the mass of dusty bones and pitted armor. Galt slid down last, drawing his blade. "Spread out, burrow down."

Everyone obeyed, no one questioning Galt's sudden authority.

Cyprian squeezed down against the wall of the trench, trying to get as low as possible, and suddenly found himself face to face with a moldering skull. It grinned wickedly, its black, impossibly deep sockets promising him a similar fate. Cyprian looked away and searched for Faye. He could see no one else amongst the dead. He tried to slow his breathing, each breath sounding explosively loud to him. Unconsciously, he clutched the tube containing the shards.

The sound of dragging footsteps reached his ears. Cyprian gazed up toward the faintly glowing darkness of the sky and saw a vaguely man-shaped blackness silhouetted against it. He clenched his jaw to keep from screaming. He could not see the shade's face, but knew that it bore the grotesque features of a damned soul.

It turned its lumpish head slowly, apparently surveying the trench. Cyprian did not know if shades were intelligent, or if they acted on anything beyond hateful instinct, and he was too petrified to consider it. There was nothing in his mind but overwhelming terror.

After what felt like an eternity, the abomination turned and plodded away. Cyprian remained frozen, his pulse pounding wildly in his ears, sending rhythmic flashes of white across the edges of his vision. He wasn't sure how much time passed, but eventually, as he regained his composure, Galt quietly called out an all-clear.

Hesitantly, the team crawled out of the trench. Cyprian quickly found Faye.

"Are you okay?" he asked her.

"Yes," she said, brushing herself off. "Shit, that was close. Are you okay?"

"Yes," he said, though he wasn't entirely certain that he was. He was unnerved by how frightened he'd been. He turned to Galt, who was still watching the opposite side of the trench. "Good eye."

"Of course, my lord," Galt answered. He appeared unimpressed with the praise.

Not knowing what else to say, Cyprian turned back toward the others. "Is everyone here?"

The team regrouped, determined they were all present, and set off again toward the northern arm of the river. Vin-Sadavat grew larger until it consumed their view, making them strain their necks to see the highest spires. After crossing several more trenches, they finally reached the meager trickle of the Einfallen.

On the bank of the half-dried river, Cyprian, Faye, and Starkad huddled together with a cloak pulled over their heads. Starkad lit a match and let it slowly burn, lighting the tiny space under the cloak, illuminating their map. Outside the small, hidden dome of light, the others stood guard. After consulting the map and comparing it to their relative position, they decided to continue northwest along the riverbank.

With the hope of coming across a drainage pipe large enough for them to pass through, they waded across the shallow, fetid water and continued their search.

CHAPTER 23

The first thing that Moore heard was the frantic shouting of the watch. He opened his eyes, but remained perfectly still as the shouting intensified into screams of terror, then shrieks of pain. The horrific chorus was joined by mad hooting and cheering.

They had ignored his warnings, ignored his pleas to return to Nordabor. Now, they had plopped their camp down right on the doorstep of the faithless, heathen savages who had butchered and enslaved their companions. Daeg was dead. Blackburn was dead. Based on the commotion outside, Solgard was most likely dead. And Galt had left with the doomed search party, which had almost certainly been intercepted.

There was nothing left; no hope, no salvation. The Void-God had turned his back on them. What they had done to displease him so, Moore was unsure. Perhaps their vain grasping for his holy realm, his Paradise lost even to him, had sealed their fate. Whatever the reason, they were entirely, utterly alone.

The sounds of violence grew closer. Moore knew that his time as a high shepherd had ended. He had failed not only his flock, but his entire people. He had joined his mistaken leaders in their hubris, in believing that Paradise was theirs by right. He had willfully misinterpreted the Void-God's will, all while ignoring his gnawing doubts.

Now, innocent lives had been lost, caught in the folly of their masters. People were dying without any shepherding, their souls forfeit to the Void-God's whims with nobody to intercede on their behalf. Moore knew that even if he could pray over each one, his empty words would fall on deaf ears. There was nothing left for him to do but flee this place of death. He couldn't return to Nordabor—the kingdom had no use for a disgraced old fool—but he would not meet his end here.

Moving with a vigor he hadn't felt since before Daeg's death, Moore snatched up his blade and his pack, which was filled with enough meager provisions to see him through for a short time. He felt shame hefting the anointed blade, but realized its necessity. It would cut through the flesh of any man as easily as it cut through a shade.

Moore took a deep breath, steadied himself, and thrust open the tent flaps.

He was met with a scene of chaos. In every direction, strangely clad men with torches were running through the camp, tearing down and burning the tents and dragging people out of them. Some were fighting back, and were being savagely assaulted for it. Moore watched as one of the haulers kicked spastically at his attackers and was rewarded by a heavy blow to the skull from a hammer.

Moore did not wait to see if a shade was produced. He turned and fled toward the tree line, intent on nothing but escape. As he ran, he tripped on a hidden root and plowed face-first into the ground. He whirled over, certain that one of the slavers was going to be above him, but for now, he was safe.

The sound of clashing metal caught Moore's ears, and he looked toward it. Three guardsmen had gathered around Phir-Ramarian's tent and were fighting back against the invaders, several of whom fell dead at the guardsmen's feet, their spilled blood looking black in the firelight.

Phir-Ramarian emerged from the tent, clad in his formal golden armor, his splendid helm upon his head, brandishing a gleaming broadsword, and formed a small phalanx with the guardsmen, forcing back the slavers. Though the prince had almost certainly never faced a situation where his life was in his own hands, Moore was surprised to see that he rose to the occasion. Undoubtedly, he'd received extensive training in swordplay. As the leading point of the wedge, Phir-Ramarian thrust his sword deftly into any slaver that drew near, felling three of them while shouting orders over the din, desperate to prevent the rout that Moore knew was already happening.

As Phir-Ramarian slammed his sword through the collarbone of a slaver, cleaving the man crookedly down the middle, one of the new corpses upon the ground began to convulse. Apparently realizing what was happening, the guardsmen circled around the prince and began quickly shuffling him away from the body. As they did so, a group of slavers charged them from behind. Their attention turned toward the developing shade, the guardsmen didn't see the slavers coming until it was too late.

A hulking brute clad in a black leather cuirass, his exposed flesh a patchwork of scar tissue, smashed his hammer down directly onto the head of a guardsman, dropping him instantly, then swung the hammer around toward Phir-Ramarian, who raised his sword to parry the blow. The hammer shattered his blade and struck him heavily in the breastplate, knocking him to the ground.

One of the guardsmen turned and fled as the other was subdued and restrained with ropes. The slavers gathered around Phir-Ramarian and began dragging him away, tying him up as they did. He shrieked, kicking wildly at his captors, who were only amused by his struggles.

To Moore, it seemed a fitting and logical end to the arrogant prince's campaign.

The shade born of the dead slaver was now fully formed, and, enticed by the chaos, it began to flail wildly, flattening Phir-Ramarian's tent.

Moore finally willed himself back to his feet and limped quickly toward the tree line. As he did, the thundering of a horse's hooves rose behind him. He looked over his shoulder and saw Rayburn, a look of dire panic on his face, riding hard toward the wood.

"Help me! Take me!" Moore called out, realizing that Rayburn had come to the same conclusion about their chances he had. He stood directly in the horse's path, waving his arms, certain that Rayburn would stop for him.

The merchant paid him no mind and failed to slow. As the horse approached, Moore realized that Rayburn was not going to stop, or make any attempt to move around him. Belatedly, he tried to lunge out of the way, but it was too late. The horse barreled into him, tangling him beneath its legs as it trampled over him. Moore tumbled across the ground and came to rest on his back, staring upside down at the horse as Rayburn regained control and plunged into the forest, disappearing with the sound of snapping branches.

It took only a moment for his adrenaline to give way to pain, and he struggled to lift his head, knowing that something was seriously wrong. He looked down at his immobile lower half and saw the gleaming white of a jagged piece of bone rising from the blood-soaked robes around his left thigh. His head swam instantly, and he nearly passed out. He flopped back and stared at the bizarrely glowing sky, the realization that he could not move without excruciating pain filling him with despair. He wasn't fleeing anywhere now.

Moore wished desperately, and fruitlessly, that he hadn't tried to stop the horse. He could have already been in the woods, hunkered down, intact, alive. It seemed unreal that he was here now. Mere moments before, his bone had been undamaged, safely within the meat of his thigh, where it had been from the moment he'd been born. Now, it was thrust out into the world, and with its broken edge exposed, Moore's fate was sealed.

As he lay, mind reeling, the sounds of the battle began to subside, though in the woods beyond the clearing, he could hear screaming. It seemed Rayburn hadn't made it much farther.

He was vaguely aware that the slavers were driving several shades away with torches. He had to admire their primitive, but effective, method. It wouldn't destroy the shades, which could burn endlessly and never be consumed by the flames, but it would keep them away for the time being.

Unmanned by pain and the sudden realization that nobody would be there to shepherd him, Moore began to weep. Almost certainly, the Void-God would not meet his cowardice and collapse of faith with mercy. The pain he felt now would be like a pleasurable dream compared to the torment that awaited.

His sobbing apparently caught the attention of some of the slavers, who sauntered over to him, laughing merrily. One of the hideous men crouched low, looking at Moore's leg. He shook his scarred, earless head and stood. "This one's still alive, but not for long. It's no use to us with that leg. We can take the meat, though."

Terror dulled Moore's pain and unmercifully brought him back from the brink of losing consciousness.

"Maokreev!" the slaver shouted, turning toward the others still milling about. The massive fiend who'd felled Phir-Ramarian stomped over. "Kill it."

The one called Maokreev smiled, exposing crooked black teeth, and hefted his tremendous, gore-smeared hammer over his mutilated head. Moore trembled violently, trying with all his might to drag himself away. He squeezed his eyes shut, desperate to make the horror disappear. He tried to picture the peaceful altar atop the Ivy Citadel, groped within his mind for some sort of prayer, something to stir the Void-God from his indifference. He couldn't find the words.

Despite his best efforts, Moore couldn't help but open his eyes just in time to watch the hammer fall.

CHAPTER 24

After two cycles of walking along the riverbank, Cyprian and his team found a pipe large enough for a person to enter. Beneath its opening, an odious pile of filth had collected. It was clear that the occupants of the city still utilized the ancient sewer system to dispose of their waste.

A metal grate had been hammered over the grimy, foul-smelling opening. Shagalov and Hayves initially balked at the order to examine the repulsive mouth of the pipe and determine if they could force entry, but Cyprian reminded them that it was not a request, but an order, and reluctantly, they obeyed, eventually determining that the rusted, deteriorating grate could be cut through. Utilizing their saws, they set to work, grimacing at the stench. After half a cycle of work, the grate was pulled away.

Mather, Galt, Lowther, and Shaw climbed up into the pipe, lit a lantern, and travelled ahead far enough to ensure that the pipe did not rapidly narrow. They determined that the route appeared viable, if maze-like; the pipe they'd entered branched off in numerous directions. Cyprian hoped that their maps would assist with that particular problem.

After a fruitless attempt to clean their hands in the equally filthy water of the Einfallen, the team headed back to the encampment, eager to share the news of their success.

•   •   •

By the time they scrambled back up the eroded hillside and hiked to the top of the bluff, the fires had dwindled to almost nothing. The only indication that something was wrong was the sound of wet sobbing cutting through the darkness as they approached the camp.

They exchanged worried glances and clumped together defensively as Mather, Galt, Lowther, and Shaw drew their weapons and took point. Cyprian drew his own short blade, trying to ready himself for anything. He watched the others do the same and wondered how much experience each of them had.

At the outset of the expedition, every member of the company had been assigned a blade, just as a matter of basic safety. Cyprian was lucky enough to have done some basic weapons training in his youth, being afforded the opportunity due to his lineage, but for many of the others, it may have been their first time handling a blade.

They cautiously skirted the perimeter of the camp, watching for any sort of movement. As they grew closer, it became clear that there had been an attack. Cyprian felt a cold sweat break across his back as fear for Jotun gripped him.

"What happened?" Hayves whispered, sounding panicky. Mather hushed him as they continued their slow check.

Finally, when they had cleared the perimeter, Mather addressed them quietly. "Whoever did this appears to have left, but that's not to say that they couldn't be hiding within the woods or even amongst the tents. Let's fan out into two groups. Half of you, come with Galt and me, the other half, go with Lowther and Shaw. Check for survivors, clear the tents. Stay vigilant."

They quickly divided themselves and set to work. Mather made it his first priority to approach the source of the crying. Cyprian joined him, and with Faye, Starkad, and Galt, they approached the collapsed wreck of Phir-Ramarian's tent. As they did so, the sobs grew quieter, and were then stifled completely with some apparent effort.

"Is someone there?" a voice called timidly from within the flattened folds of the tent.

"It's Captain Mather. You're okay. Come on out."

A shape began to wiggle under the canvas. Pike stuck his head out, saw Mather and the others, and crawled out. Faye helped him to his feet.

"What happened here? Where's the prince?" Mather asked.

This apparently upset Pike again; fat teardrops spilled from his eyes, and his body was racked by hitching sobs. "They took him. They took everybody."

"The slavers?" Mather asked.

"Yes," Pike managed, the word morphing into a wail.

"You need to be silent," Starkad interjected, looking at Pike with a mixture of pity and disgust. "We're here now. We don't need any noise that might entice the slavers into coming back."

Pike stared back at the badlander and regained his shaky composure, looking angry to have been silenced so unkindly.

"What about Jotun?" Cyprian demanded.

"I don't know," Pike said.

They searched the remainder of the camp, Cyprian and Faye desperate to find Jotun and filled with dread at the prospect of discovering his body. Ultimately, there was no sign of him, but plenty of others were located.

The toll inflicted upon the company was horrendous. Five haulers lay dead. Cyprian was ashamed to realize that he didn't even know all of their names. For certain, two of them were Scudamore and Brunson. One was too mangled to identify. The almost-unrecognizable corpse of a guardsman was found as well. Only by the tattered remains of the body's gear was Mather able to identify it as Rath. All of the bodies had large hunks of meat cut from them—choice parts of thigh, buttocks, bicep, and other bits of muscle. It reminded Cyprian of the two boars Kovak had netted on one of the earlier hunting excursions. The sight was repulsive. Scattered about were also the hideous remains of several slavers, who had been butchered just as casually.

Near the outer edge of the camp, Cyprian and Faye encountered Galt standing above another body. Like the others, it had been butchered. Unlike most of the others, it also bore the telltale signs of birthing a shade. Though the face had been smashed in by some sort of blunt weapon, the top of the skull had exploded outward with the violent force created only by a shade. Faye looked away, trying not to be sick and gripping Cyprian's arm like a vise as he stared into the grotesquely crushed face of Moore.

"He's gone," Galt stated blankly. He turned toward Cyprian with an indescribably pained expression. "The old man's gone."

"I'm sorry," Cyprian said, not knowing what else to say. Galt didn't seem to hear him. The shepherd looked back at the body and sighed heavily.

"He's probably wandering the woods around here now, suffering. I truly hope that he has no understanding of what he used to be or of what happened to him. If only I'd been here." He put his head in his hands.

Cyprian hesitated, then reached out to put a hand on Galt's shoulder. Faye caught his arm in midair and shook her head silently. Her features grimly set, she led Cyprian away.

Only three other survivors were located. Vane, the engineer who'd stayed behind, and Anders, a hauler, had been hiding in the wreckage of a tent. The relief of the reunited engineers was obvious, though tempered by the depth of the loss around them. Baylor, the only remaining guardsman, wandered back into the camp looking shamefaced. They each clarified what had happened. Baylor trembled as he spoke, admitting that he'd fled when the prince fell. Mather stalked away, saying nothing, leaving the man to quaver and sputter the remainder of his tale to Cyprian.

In addition to Phir-Ramarian, many others were missing and assumed captured, including Jotun, Rayburn, Bellamont, Solgard, and Kovak. At the realization that Solgard was not among the dead, Galt seemed to regain some of his stoic demeanor.

They gathered the remains of the dead in the center of the camp. Galt wished to burn them properly, particularly the desiccated remains of his former master, but Mather decided that it was too risky—the fire would be large enough for the slavers to see, and he'd rather they be under the impression that everyone in the camp was either dead or captured. Galt begrudgingly agreed.

Once the gruesome task of inventorying the dead had been completed, they turned their numb, exhausted attentions to what remained of their provisions. The outlook was similarly grim. Every horse and donkey was missing. The carts were overturned, some of them burned. Almost every tent was unsalvageable. They picked through the wreckage and assembled what they could.

Finally, in a loose circle, they sat on the ground on the outskirts of the camp to discuss what came next. Unlike the private meetings before, nobody was excluded.

"First and foremost, where are we with food and water?" Cyprian asked Anders, who, with Rayburn gone, had inherited the role of provisioner.

The young man looked dazed and befuddled, but when he spoke, he at least made sense. "We have one wagon that the engineers were able to cobble together out of the remains of all of them. Two water casks survived, though one was already damaged in the *Fortune*. It's leaking badly. Many of the dry goods were burned. Canned goods fared decently. Aside from being dented, most of them are still intact. They didn't seem interested in our food at all, aside from destroying it."

"They have their own food sources," Starkad said, putting into words what everyone was thinking. "I doubt they even recognized the cans as food. It looks like everything they destroyed was just collateral damage."

"We were also able to salvage enough canvas and poles to have three full tents," Dupree added.

"What of the climbing gear or the amiant armor?" Cyprian asked.

"Some of the climbing gear was scattered, but we were able to gather it up," Dupree said. "I don't think they realized what any of it was. Same for the crates containing the amiant armor. They set fire to the wagon that carried them, and though the crates burned somewhat, the armor was mostly undamaged. It appears to be fireproof after all." She smiled weakly.

Cyprian nodded, considering everything. It was time to address the real issue.

"All of you understand that things have fundamentally changed. This expedition has been severely injured. But our goals remain the same—chief among them being to rescue our companions. We already needed to do so, and now, the need is only more dire. I assume nobody wishes to abandon our purpose now?"

The remaining company stared at him, fell expressions on their thin, haggard faces. Nobody spoke.

"Then it's decided. We'll carry on as planned. With the pipe we found, we can enter the city. We'll load our packs up with some basic supplies and cache the rest with our remaining wagon somewhere near here. When we've rescued our companions and gotten whatever shards Tariono has, we'll return here, get the rest of our supplies, and leave this hateful place for good."

He did not mention that if they managed to rescue the others, food and water would suddenly be in extremely short supply.

The group nodded in assent and slowly rose to gather their remaining gear. As they did, Mather pulled Cyprian aside.

"I suppose you're in command now, then?" he asked, his tone unreadable.

"As the second-in-command, yes," Cyprian answered carefully. "At least until Phir-Ramarian can resume control."

"We are both second-in-command," Mather said. "I am in charge of the Crown's interests here; I lead the Sovereign Guard.

As this is now primarily a combat-based endeavor, it makes sense for me to command."

Cyprian stared at the captain, who stared back expressionlessly.

"Combat or not, the true purpose of this expedition remains the same," Cyprian said slowly. "And though you may lead the guard, as you said, you are beholden to the Crown. Without the prince here, I believe I'm the highest-titled person. As a lord, I'm in the line of succession. Captain, I respect your input, and will rely on it heavily in the coming conflict, but I am in command here."

The words felt strange, but in that moment, he spoke with true conviction. With the prince gone, he'd simply assumed that the mantle of leadership would fall on him. After all, he'd been taking on Phir-Ramarian's responsibilities for some time already, and, really, he should have been leading the expedition from the start. Now that he had authority, he would not let anyone question it.

He decided right then that even after they rescued Phir-Ramarian, he would not be relinquishing command. His cousin would certainly be so grateful just to be alive that he would accept Cyprian's ascendancy without protest.

Mather watched Cyprian closely, considering everything he said. Finally, he spoke.

"I suppose you're correct," he answered in the same maddening monotone as before. "I will do whatever I can to support you. My lord."

CHAPTER 25

The first thing that Solgard became aware of was a rough, jostling movement, bouncing her limp head against something hard. It didn't hurt so much as it slowly returned her to consciousness. She opened her eyes slowly, and like a landslide, the terrible memory of what had occurred returned to her.

Reflexively, she attempted to grab her blade and found that she was bound tightly, her hands tied behind her back and lashed by a short rope to her feet, which were also roped together. Even if she weren't tied, she'd been stripped of her weapons, her arms were numb from lying on top of them, and any movement took a great deal of effort.

She rolled clumsily onto her side and raised her head as best as she could to look around. She was in the back of some sort of cart, trundling along what must have been the last leg of the Imperial Highway. In front of her, the massive gates of Vin-Sadavat rose. Pulling her cart, and other carts nearby, were about two dozen of the slavers, all bearing varying amounts of appalling scarification. They murmured amongst themselves, occasionally letting out barking laughs or whooping cheers. Several of them were shouting in frustration at three of the donkeys and a horse that Solgard recognized as Phir-Ramarian's, trying to force them forward with whips and ropes. They did not appear to be trying to ride the animals, nor did they try to use them for the laborious pulling of the carts. Solgard assumed that they were being driven to slaughter.

In her dazed state of shock, she found herself wondering what would become of the other animals, who'd almost certainly fled into the darkness of the forest during the attack—most likely, pointless wandering, followed by starvation and death.

She looked at the slavers and wondered if her fate would be any better.

Solgard peered around the cart at the other prostrate forms in the semidarkness. She was shocked to see that Phir-Ramarian was among her fellow captives. He met her gaze and stared wide-eyed, seized by fear. It was not reassuring to see that the leader of their expedition was as hopelessly trapped as she was. She doubted there was anyone left to mount a rescue now. She let her head drop back onto the bench and winced as the muscles in her tightly lashed arms screamed in protest.

A shout rose from one of the slavers, hailing someone watching the gate. A muffled voice called back, and the gate began to slowly rise. As soon as the slavers could clear the entrance, they continued inside.

Watching the spiked teeth on the bottom of the gate pass over them, Solgard couldn't help but feel that she was entering the maw of some horrid behemoth. She tried to formulate some kind of prayer to the Void-God, but couldn't find the words. Any last vestige of hope she'd been clinging to slipped away as the gate rumbled shut behind them.

The cart rolled on, and Solgard peered with equal parts dread and curiosity at her new surroundings. All along the pitted thoroughfare, people came out from darkened doorways to watch the grim procession. Obviously of a lower caste than the conquering slavers, these lowly thralls were emaciated and dressed in rags. They still bore facial mutilations, but nothing close to the extent of their severely disfigured masters. Solgard was horrified to see women amongst the crowd, and even more disturbing, children. Her stomach threatened to leap out of her throat when she saw a child no older than four long-cycles whose face was a smooth knot of burn scarring, the nose a black hole in the center of the carnage. Numerous other children, each bearing some kind of mutilation, lingered about, limply holding the hands of their disfigured mothers.

Presently, one of the slavers addressed the crowd with a bellowing shout. "Look upon the newest flesh! Fresh meat for the Empress! They will join our ranks, devote themselves to the glory of the Empress, and carry Her beautiful kiss upon their virgin skin, or they will be the foundation we walk upon, the meat in our bellies, the blood in our veins!"

The crowd murmured in assent, but their reaction was apparently too lackluster for the slaver.

"Maokreev! Teach them the adulations!"

A towering monster of a man stepped forward and savagely whipped the nearest thralls, sending up frightened shrieks from the scattering victims. The rest cheered in forced praise, as had been expected of them.

"Our master, Heilrune, Harbinger of the Empress, will be pleased with this fresh harvest! He will beseech Her on our behalf, earning us Her divine kiss!"

The crowd cheered again. Solgard almost couldn't fathom the desperation for survival that had driven generations of people into this madness. She trembled at the thought of what was to come.

The procession continued, with the outspoken slaver crying out praises to his empress and rousing the crowd to action. All along, the brute called Maokreev whipped any he believed to be lacking the proper spirit.

After almost a cycle, they finally came to a stop, having apparently reached their destination. "Cut em' loose," the slaver who'd been shouting rasped.

The gate of the cart was dropped, and several slavers crawled up into it. They seized Solgard and the others roughly, cut the short ropes tying their hands to their feet, and forced them to stand. Before Solgard's muscles could properly unfold, she was shoved harshly. "Move," the slaver who'd cut her free ordered.

With her feet still bound loosely together and her hands tied behind her back, climbing down from the cart was an arduous task, but she managed. Behind her, she watched Kovak, Gricks, and a hauler, Barrow, fumble down after her. A voice cried out in pain, and Solgard turned to see Berg, who was similarly tied, collapse to the ground behind a cart. A slaver kicked him savagely in the gut and screamed at him to get up.

"Stop it!" It was Bellamont, standing behind the slaver. Without a pause, the slaver backhanded her so hard it sent her sprawling. Three more slavers laughed heartily and yanked her back to her feet, running their filthy hands up and down her body. She fought against them, earning a gut punch that doubled her over. The slavers took the opportunity to grab her backside.

Solgard wished desperately that she had her blade. As she imagined driving it through the skulls of every slaver around her, Phir-Ramarian fell heavily from the back of the cart and crashed to the ground. A pauldron broke off of his gaudy armor and rolled away, eliciting further laughter from the crowd.

"On your feet, initiate," the lead slaver crowed. "The Master will be most pleased to make your acquaintance. You are a king, no? Your armor certainly suggests you are."

Phir-Ramarian looked down at his armor as if he were seeing it for the first time. "No, no, I'm not, I'm just a-a soldier; it's just armor," he stammered.

"I'm not so sure." The slaver smiled, stretching his scar tissue hideously. "I don't think a lowly soldier would have a retinue defending him. Heilrune and the Empress will be pleased to know another marauding invader has been defeated. Our realm remains peaceful and safe."

Once the prisoners were all on their feet and the more aggressive captors had been ordered to calm themselves, the prisoners were herded under another gate and into a black chamber, scarcely lit by weakly flickering torches. Solgard could barely see, but the slavers appeared to be totally content, navigating their chattel through the darkness easily.

After much uncomfortable shuffling surrounded by the reeking, sweaty bodies of the slavers, the prisoners were escorted onto a wooden platform. In the center of the platform was a metal bowl containing low-burning cinders. Chains attached all around the platform rose up into the blackness of a shaft above them. Solgard noticed that many of the slavers had left them at some point as they wandered through the dark halls. Six remained, including Maokreev and the leader.

Maokreev seized a handle attached to a large, grimy metal gear built into the floor and started rotating it with heaving grunts. The chains began to lift the platform shakily up through the shaft. Nobody spoke; the only sounds were the rotating of the winch, the labored breathing of Maokreev, and some quiet sobbing.

It seemed to go on forever, and Solgard's dread increased with each turn of the handle. Her mouth was impossibly dry, and her mind kept rejecting the evidence that her senses were feeding it. This terror could not actually be happening.

Finally, the platform rattled to a stop, and the slavers resumed prodding them toward their final destination. They passed through a doorway and exited out onto an open rooftop terrace. Lines of columns ran the length of the roof, terminating before an immense marble cathedral. Flanking the soot-stained cathedral were tremendous bonfires, their heat and light buffeting the captors as they filed toward the cathedral's entrance. Several heavily scarred, completely nude worshippers were dancing around the fires, chanting strange, guttural prayers to the rising cinders. Several of them appeared to have been castrated.

Solgard's horror, which she'd assumed had reached its pinnacle, continued to grow.

Two robed beings so scarred that they seemed scarcely human opened the massive, iron doors of the cathedral. The slavers and their prizes entered the interior. The doors shut behind them, and the revelry outside was immediately silenced.

Their footsteps echoed as they stepped further into a vast, marble-floored room with a vaulted ceiling. The back half of the room was shrouded in total darkness. The half they occupied was only slightly brighter, lit by two of the metal bowls filled with flickering coals. A nondescript marble throne occupied the space within the circle of light they cast.

"Master, we come bearing initiates, captured before they could attack the city," the leader said, suddenly nervous. "Interlopers from a foreign land. I believe their king was among them. We have him now."

He pulled a rucksack he'd been carrying from his shoulder and tossed it into the shadows, where it clanged across the floor. "Tribute for the Master." His nervousness was now obvious as he waited for some sort of response.

"Ahh," a smooth, deep voice finally said. "Davhal, you have done well."

"Thank you, Master," Davhal said.

From across the room, whispers could be heard, voices conferring in the darkness. Then heavy footsteps echoed toward them and a figure stepped into the circle of light.

Nearly the same height as Maokreev, and adorned in a patchwork armor assembled from numerous pieces, presumably collected from his fallen foes, Heilrune took his seat upon the marble throne. Strung across his chest was a sash upon which hung several crowns. Some were glittering artifacts of the glory of Vingallea's past. Others were little more than circlets of wood, undoubtedly worn by badlander chieftains he'd conquered. Upon Heilrune's head, partially obscuring his mutilated features, was Phir-Ramarian's tufted helm. The prince stifled a cry as he saw it.

"This crown is a beautiful piece, unlike anything I've seen in a long time," Heilrune cooed, running a hand softly over the helm. "Certainly work of the ancients. The Empress was even impressed."

"Thank you, Master," Davhal said again, his tone descending toward groveling.

"So, who are these interlopers sneaking about in the realm of my Empress?" Heilrune reclined lazily, his gaze passing over the miserable captives before him. "Who among you is the king?"

Phir-Ramarian remained pointedly silent, staring at the floor. He gasped as Davhal snatched him by the shoulders and thrust him forward, causing him to fall face-first on the ground. Solgard and the others remained silent, knowing there was nothing they could do to help.

"This one, Master. He denies it, but he was in possession of the helm. He was guarded by this one," Davhal said, gesturing toward Kovak, "and several others who would not submit."

"Indeed," Heilrune said quietly, apparently considering the crumpled form before him.

"We think this might be the rest of the group that we encountered at the bridge. They're dressed in the same armor, and similar weapons were recovered," Davhal explained, seeming proud of his deduction.

"Yes, I think you're on to something," Heilrune agreed, making Davhal beam. He then addressed Phir-Ramarian. "You, there. King. Who are you, and what business do you have in the realm of the Empress?"

Phir-Ramarian's mouth moved, but he seemed to be incapable of forming words. Heilrune simply watched, absentmindedly digging out gunk from beneath one of the iron gauntlets encasing his wrists. After a moment, he rose and strode toward Phir-Ramarian, making the prince scream and scramble backward. Heilrune seized him by his ragged armor and lifted him from the ground. Phir-Ramarian panted with terror.

"Are you a king or not?" Heilrune demanded, his sonorous voice booming through the cathedral.

"No!" Phir-Ramarian exclaimed. "I'm only a prince!"

Heilrune froze with surprise, then dropped Phir-Ramarian, who crashed heavily back to the floor. Davhal stepped back, clearly concerned that he'd made a fatal miscalculation.

"So, this helm is not from a king, but a prince?" Heilrune asked Davhal, who seemed unable to conjure an answer. Heilrune stroked the helm again, deep in thought. "No matter. It's still a beautiful piece, and a prince is simply a king who has yet to reach his full potential."

Davhal sighed with relief as Heilrune continued. "So, I ask you again, *prince*, what are you doing in these lands?"

Phir-Ramarian was still breathing hard, but he finally seemed to have regained some composure. He raised his head. "We're a survey team. We come from the badlands in the east, from the land of the eternal sun. We were just looking for resources."

Solgard held her breath. In a moment of guile and bravery, Phir-Ramarian had conceived of an appropriate lie to disguise the true purpose of their expedition. For the first time, she felt her esteem for the prince rise.

He must have already realized what Solgard was now considering for the first time: Lord Fontaine's team may not have been captured.

"A prince searching for resources?" Heilrune asked.

"We are desperate. It's our realm's last hope. I was entrusted with it," Phir-Ramarian said. He was not lying.

"Ah, I see," Heilrune sniffed. "Not all realms are as fortunate as our own. A true pity. By the blessings of our Empress, we alone carry the torch of civilization. We alone prosper. But the Empress is benevolent, as am I. We are always willing to welcome the desperate, the refugees, of this broken world. Those who have fled the hateful light of the unmoving sun. And that is why, no matter what your original purpose was, here, you are greeted as initiates."

He smiled broadly, exposing teeth that had been filed to points. There was nothing remotely comforting about his monstrous grin.

From beyond Heilrune, still veiled in the shadows, a soft, melodic voice called. "Heilrune, my sweet darling, you speak my words delightfully. But please rest, my beloved champion. I wish to speak with these newcomers myself."

Everyone in the vaulted chamber froze, enthralled by the hypnotic voice. Heilrune bowed low, catching his new helm before it slid off of his hairless head. "Yes, Empress."

He turned to Solgard and the others. "You are truly among the blessed, to have a direct audience with such ineffable grace."

He returned to his throne and motioned to Davhal. "Light the Empress's fires, please."

"Yes, Master."

Davhal and another slaver removed two unlit torches from their wall sconces, dipped them into the simmering coals and, once they were ignited, walked off into the dark. Within a short-cycle, previously unseen fire pits heaped with dry kindling roared to life, filling the ancient throne room with light, exposing soot-covered walls and blackened tapestries.

Solgard's eyes were immediately drawn to the Empress, the god of this nightmarish fiefdom—Tariono.

She sat upon an ornate throne, carved to resemble a massive oyster opening to reveal its pearl, that easily dwarfed Heilrune's simple perch. She appeared to be roughly the same height as him, but she exuded a magnificent aura that made her seem to fill the space around her completely. The voluminous, baroque robes she wore spilled down the steps around her throne, their intricate beadwork and stitching beautiful but for the filthy stains of soot and grime across the entire raiment. A flawless silver halo hovered perfectly still above her white hair, which was tinged slightly yellow and piled high upon her head in opulent curls. They framed her most striking feature, her face, which wasn't a face at all. Staring blankly, but bewitchingly, was a sculpted mask of smooth porcelain with delicate, mesmerizing features painted upon it.

Above the ruby, heart-shaped lips, the lightly blushed cheeks, and the petite nose, her otherworldly eyes watched from behind the mask. The irises, which constantly shifted between several dazzling hues that Solgard had never seen, radiated a strange feeling of peace. Any thought of the distant and unknowable Void-God was swept away as Solgard beheld the undoubtedly divine presence before her. The longer she gazed at Tariono, the less she noticed the filth on her robes, the dinginess of her hair, or the unsettling quality of the mask. Despite all of her fear and horror, she found herself drawn to the goddess, a bizarre desire to earn favor dancing across her mind.

Tariono sat up a little straighter and breathed in slowly and deeply. "I care not who you were or what your aims were when you entered my realm. My heart weeps for all orphans wandering such an inhospitable world, for we are all victims of our wretched circumstances."

She lowered her static face, emoting sorrow, then lifted her head hopefully. "Now, I offer you a chance at salvation under my watchful protection. All I ask in return is for you to pledge your fealty."

Held by that captivating gaze, Solgard felt her doubts slipping away. Here was a safe haven—eccentric, yes, but a respite from the relentless hardships she'd endured on their pointless quest. What was a vague possibility of Paradise compared to the beauty and wonder before her now?

"All sins of the past will be forgiven as you are reborn as my chosen." Tariono rose slowly from her throne. "I know what it is to be led astray, to be lost and seeking deliverance, only to find ruin. I offer redemption, freedom, love. Who among you wishes to be welcomed into my embrace?"

Overcome by relief, Solgard felt like weeping with joy at Tariono's benevolence. As she inhaled to cry out her elation and acceptance, a voice rang out, interrupting her.

"I want to be saved!" It was Phir-Ramarian, tears of gratitude streaming down his face. "I can't handle this pressure—this failure. I don't want the responsibility. I just want to be saved, please!"

Tariono watched Phir-Ramarian with those impossible eyes, her head slightly cocked, as she walked toward him. "Rise, my sweet prince." Her porcelain lips remained frozen in their coquettish smile.

Heilrune clapped with pleasure as Davhal lifted Phir-Ramarian to his feet and cut his bindings. The slaver smiled approvingly as he urged the prince forward with a gentle push. Tariono opened her arms lovingly, and Phir-Ramarian staggered toward her.

As he reached her, she placed her long-fingered hands upon his shoulders and turned her serene mask toward his face. Solgard stared jealously, wishing she'd spoken sooner.

Her eyes settled for a moment upon Tariono's fingers, and she noticed that the goddess's fingernails were long, broken, and encrusted with dirt. In the far recesses of her mind, disquiet stirred, fracturing her infatuation. Suddenly, she did not envy Phir-Ramarian; she feared for him. The entire scene, which had seemed so pleasant, now slid back toward horrifying.

Phir-Ramarian stared at the floor, his entire body trembling visibly. Tariono lifted his chin. "Such beautiful, succulent lips," she said, running a finger across his mouth. His trembling increased.

"By the edge of my own sin, receive my blessed kiss upon your pristine flesh and be changed. Be saved."

From within the folds of her gown, she withdrew a short ivory-handled dagger and lifted it high above her head. Phir-Ramarian watched it rise. The blade was dark gray and irregularly shaped, but without a single blemish.

Solgard knew at once that it was a shard of the Scale of Judgment.

Tariono suddenly seized Phir-Ramarian by his hair, yanking his head back. With her other hand, she brought the blade down. He shrieked as the blade shard carved into his face.

The stupor that had seized the other prisoners was snapped completely, and they cried out in terror. Kovak, Gricks, and Rackham renewed their struggles, trying to get to their prince, and were shoved down violently by the slavers.

"Silence!" Heilrune ordered. "The Empress requires *silence* from the audience!"

Phir-Ramarian slapped feebly at Tariono's arms, continuing his horrendous screams all the while. When she'd finished, Tariono pulled the blade away and appraised her ghoulish work. Hanging from the blade's edge was a chunk of bloody flesh.

"Take our new brother to rest," she said calmly. Two slavers rushed over, took hold of Phir-Ramarian, and carried him toward the doors they'd entered through. With his head hung low, blood coursed freely down his front, dropping heavily onto the marble floor. He was sobbing in wet, guttural coughs. Solgard looked away as he was carried by, his feet dragging through his own blood.

Once Phir-Ramarian had been removed, Tariono tossed the hunk of bloody meat to Heilrune and wiped the blade clean on a cloth presented to her by Davhal.

"Thank you, Empress," Heilrune purred. He bit into the bloody tissue and chewed noisily until it was devoured, then sucked the last of the blood from his dirty fingertips, making Solgard dry heave. Tariono noticed her reaction with mild interest.

"I know it's an unusual custom to many, but my beloved children need sustenance. They need other rewards as well. Davhal?"

"Yes, Empress?"

"Don't think for a moment that I've forgotten your heroic deeds that brought these initiates to me. You and your men will be reward-ed handsomely." She ran her fingers along the dagger's edge.

"Oh, thank you, Empress. We await the kiss of your blade." Davhal caressed his scarred face eagerly.

Tariono turned her attention back to the prisoners. "Who else among you wishes to receive my blessing? To join our kingdom?"

The enchantment had been totally dispelled. Solgard and the others shrank away from the mad god and the offer to join her hid-eous collection.

"I understand that witnessing an initiation can be unsettling. Why, almost all of the previous initiates from your realm refused when they learned what was being asked of them," she said dreamily. "Few have changed their minds."

Solgard realized with dismay that Tariono was referring to the men who'd been captured when the *Fortune* was attacked.

"And others have refused my blessings before, in much harsher ways." Her hand rose toward her masked face briefly. She paused for a moment, but then continued, the sleepy, soft lull of her voice now a foul hiss. "I will give you some time to consider. Do remember the finality of the alternative. As with the false king I found upon this throne many ages ago, and every soul who's denied me since, I will have you gutted and thrown from the pinnacle of this tower."

Tariono turned and strode back toward her throne.

"Snuff out the fires," Heilrune ordered, sending two slavers scurrying over to the flames, which they hastened to extinguish with buckets of black water. Columns of acrid smoke rose, and the chamber was plunged back into darkness.

"Take the prisoners to the dungeon."

CHAPTER 26

They crossed the trench field as quickly and quietly as possible, the specter of attack hanging heavily over them now. With marked relief, they arrived at the gaping pipe, each of them feeling a weight lift as they filed in.

It was short-lived. They had not traveled far before it became clear that the sewer, on top of being vile, was also a dangerous labyrinth, more vexing than their initial estimates.

Lord and Lady Fontaine had their heads pressed together over their apocryphal map, trying to suss out a route through the bowels of the city. Galt stood by, eyeing the darkness of the pipework on either side of their small circle of light. The ankle-deep filth was cold; he hoped that it hadn't managed to seep through the seams of his boots. He was growing impatient and anxious.

It was still difficult for him to reckon with the fact that he was now utterly alone. Moore was dead. The thought still seemed to ring false, and he had to keep reminding himself painfully that it was true.

His relationship with Moore had been complicated. He'd often thought of the old man as overbearing and grandiose, with a penchant for melodrama. Nonetheless, having been Moore's acolyte since he'd entered the order, he'd spent the majority of his life with him and learned much from the man. Moore was the closest thing to a father Galt had ever had; his actual father had abandoned him before he was even born.

And now, of all people, Moore was damned to wander as a shade. Galt felt an awful mixture of guilt, sadness, and confusion at the fact that Moore had spawned a shade and that he hadn't been there to shepherd his mentor. Troubled or not, if one as pious as Moore could end up as a shade, what hope did any of them have? What hand did the supposed Void-God have in any of it?

Not for the first time, Galt felt his already-tenuous grip on his faith slipping further.

In what seemed like both a very short and a very long period of time, Galt had lost Moore, Daeg, and Blackburn, whom he admittedly had not known well, but who had certainly seemed like a good man. And now, he stood on the precipice of losing Solgard, too. His mere acquaintanceship with her had been forged through shared pain into something unique and incredibly important. He would do everything he could to rescue her.

Until then, he'd need to rely on others, and, as distasteful as it was, he'd need to rely on those who could wield a blade. With some hesitation, he approached Mather. "Captain."

"What is it, Galt?" Mather answered, his eyes never leaving the darkness of the tunnel ahead of them.

"Due to recent events, I find myself as the only shepherd on this expedition."

Mather looked at him with a small look of pity.

"If something were to happen to me," Galt continued, "or if we were to be overwhelmed by shades, it might behoove us to have a few extra hands with anointed blades."

He opened his rucksack and removed a sheathed sword, which he held toward Mather. "It was Moore's. Generally, receiving an anointed blade comes part and parcel with a ceremony where the vows of the shepherds are taken. Considering the circumstances, I think we can skip that."

Mather looked at the sword for a moment, a perplexed expression on his face, then took it. He unsheathed the blade and hefted it, testing its weight.

"Seems like a normal sword," he said, apparently unimpressed.

Galt felt a twinge of annoyance. Despite all of his experience with guardsmen, he'd somehow expected that being presented with the dead high shepherd's sword would have carried a little more emotional weight for Mather.

"The blood of the old one changes the blade in ways beyond its weight and feel," he explained. "More so, it's how one uses it, if one has the fortitude to face down the terror of a shade, that makes the real difference. In a coward's hand, the sword is useless."

"And you think me worthy of this honor?" Mather asked, a small hint of humor in his voice.

Galt began to regret his decision. "Yes—of your group, you seem to be the most competent, I suppose. At any rate, I'd rather have an untested hand holding the blade than none at all."

Mather grunted in agreement. "Well, thank you. I appreciate you placing your trust in me." His tone was unreadable.

Galt forged ahead. "I've also got Blackburn's blade, if there's one of your men here you can trust with it. They have to understand that it would put them on the front line against any shade we encounter."

"I'll find someone to take it. I'll make sure they understand." Mather was now deadly serious.

Galt removed Blackburn's blade from his rucksack and handed it to Mather, privately pleased that Kovak was not there and could not possibly receive the blade. A small, ugly part of him actually hoped that Kovak was dead.

Mather thanked him again and hitched Moore's scabbard to his own belt, then approached Lowther, leaving Galt standing alone. As the two of them spoke quietly, undoubtedly about the blade, Galt was seized by an even greater sense of sadness. The dead shepherds' blades, so sacred to them, were now average weapons in the hands of men they'd had nothing but ill will toward.

Still, Galt understood the necessity. He was happy that he'd at least retained their daggers, which hung from his own belt.

After another half-cycle, Lord Fontaine finally announced that they'd determined which way to go, and the group continued to slog through the muck.

"It looks like the smaller individual sewer lines all converge at a number of different points," he explained. "The outer rings of the city, where I assume the commoners lived, shared several points for waste disposal that are spread throughout the city. When you move further inward, the individual homes of the nobility had individual systems for waste disposal that fed into these hubs. We need to follow the lines inward toward the center of the city as much as possible. When we reach a hub, we can try to find an exit there. There has to be a larger access point where a lot of people could dispose of accumulated waste easily."

Galt was not so sure. If they never found an exit larger than the mouth of a commode, they would be forced to backtrack all the way out to the trench field. They'd be back to having no plan for entering the city, and that was if they could even find their way out. They'd already passed several smaller interchanges where three or four tunnels came together into a larger one, then inexplicably split again. The ancient sewer had clearly been built and altered in a patchwork manner over many long-cycles, and as far as Galt knew, nobody had thought to keep track of which way they'd gone.

After several more random interchanges and two more stops to consult the map, they finally emerged into an open vault of total blackness.

"I think we've reached a hub," Lord Fontaine said quietly.

"Excellent. How do we get out now?" Mather asked.

Beyond the island of light formed by their dim lanterns, they could see nothing.

"We could walk along the outer wall here, look for a way up," Dupree suggested.

"Yes, that's a start," Starkad agreed, "but dim your lanterns, I've got an idea."

The group exchanged confused looks, with Shaw in particular looking to Mather for guidance.

"Do it," Mather said.

The lanterns were snuffed out, and darkness engulfed the group. They waited without saying anything, only occasional echoing drips disturbing the silence.

"What are we waiting for?" a voice finally whispered. Galt was fairly certain it was one of the engineers, maybe Hayves.

"That," Starkad said, but of course, Galt couldn't see what he was referring to.

"I see it," Lady Fontaine said. "Cyprian, look there." In the darkness, Galt could hear her physically moving Lord Fontaine toward whatever she and Starkad had seen.

"Ah," Lord Fontaine said.

"Light," Lady Fontaine said. "It must be coming from the surface."

Galt peered into the darkness, the lack of stimuli causing kaleidoscopic images to sway within his vision. Finally, his eyes adjusted enough to settle on something real. An extremely faint glow of light from the fires in the city above, just enough to be visible in the total darkness of the sewer, was passing into the chamber through some hole in the ceiling.

"So, how do we get up there?" Mather asked.

"Dupree said it. We stick to the outer wall and find a way up. People had to have been able to get in here to service these tunnels. There's got to be a way up and out," Lady Fontaine said.

"We just need to remember where the light seems to be coming from and aim for that," Starkad added.

The lanterns were relit, and Galt immediately lost where the light had been. He hoped someone else had a better eye for this sort of navigation than he did.

The group started along the platform, which ran along a curved outer wall in what was apparently a round chamber. Toward the inside of the chamber, a grime-encrusted railing separated the platform from an indeterminately deep drop-off.

Galt felt like they'd already circled the room three times when they finally encountered a slime-coated ladder. Mather took Shaw's lantern and ascended first, followed by Galt, who grimaced at the sludge covering each rung. Mather's fingers and boots had left deep grooves in the filth.

Upon reaching the top, Galt heard a wet slithering sound. Something was wrong. "Stop," he said, grabbing Mather and pulling him back. He took the lantern and lifted it cautiously toward the ominous sound.

From the layers of foul-smelling gunk that coated the nearby wall, a humanoid shape suddenly unfolded itself. Without hesitation, Galt thrust the lantern back into Mather's arms and unsheathed his blade, then launched himself forward and drove the blade directly into the sternum of the shade while it was still extricating itself from the wall it had been almost cocooned against. It screamed in pain and thrashed wildly. Galt kicked against it and pulled his blade free, then swung with all his might. The blade bounced off of the shade's thick hide, and Galt immediately remembered what Moore had told him about Daeg's disastrous encounter.

The shade clutched at Galt as he leapt backward, tearing through the sleeve of his robes and barely missing the skin beneath. As he turned, bringing his sword around for another thrust, Mather crashed into the shade's side, driving Moore's blade in to the hilt. The shade seized it, yanking the blood-slick blade from Mather's hands and sending him stumbling back with a look of surprise on his face.

With a gasp of exertion, Galt ran his blade up through the shade's throat and into its head. He pulled the blade free, and the shade collapsed in a steaming heap, already beginning to dissolve. He retrieved Moore's blade from the remains and handed it back to Mather, who was panting.

"Thanks," Galt said as Mather took the blade. The captain nodded his own thanks back. As Mather collected the lantern, which he'd set aside, Lord Fontaine scrambled to the top of the ladder with Lady Fontaine and Starkad directly behind him.

"What happened?" he asked.

Before they could answer, a strangled scream rang out from below. Galt and Mather ran to the ladder's edge, pulled the others away, and looked over the side. In the light of the lanterns, Galt saw Pike, Anders, Lowther, and Shaw ascending the ladder. Below Shaw, Hayves clung to one side of the ladder while the slick black arm of a second shade, which had emerged from the accumulated filth coating the wall, clutched at him. Shaw was hacking away uselessly at the arm with his sword, while the others screamed from the platform below.

"Move!" Galt shouted, knowing that Shaw would not hear him, and that even if he did, he wouldn't understand where he was supposed to move to.

Galt unhooked one of the anointed daggers from his belt, took aim for only a tick, and threw it toward the darkness where he believed the shade's body was. The dagger sailed through the air, striking nothing but the wall beyond with a clang. A moment later, Hayves lost his grip on the ladder and was pulled into the blackness. His screams were quickly muffled, leaving only the slopping sounds of the shade as it clambered down the wall.

"Lowther! Get him! Use your blade, dammit!" Mather boomed.

Lowther, looking scared and confused, fumbled down the ladder until he was just above Shaw, then jumped onto the platform. He ran into the darkness and vanished, foolishly neglecting to take a lantern.

"Hurry up! Either get up or down!" Galt shouted, pulling Pike over the edge. Anders followed, then Shaw a moment later, and then Galt jumped on the ladder with Mather right behind him.

"Stay up here," Galt told him. "In case there are any more shades."

Mather simply nodded, clearly understanding that, when it came to shades, Galt was the authority.

Galt scrambled back down the ladder as quickly as he could, simply sliding the last few feet. His boots hit the stone floor, and he whipped around, blade drawn.

"Give me the lantern," he demanded. Baylor, who was clutching the lantern, didn't move.

"Give it to me!" Galt snatched the lantern from the guardsman's hands and shoved him toward the ladder. "Get up there, all of you!"

"Was that Hayves?" Dupree asked desperately.

"Yes, I think so. But we can still get him. Just get up the ladder."

In the glow of the lantern, Dupree looked haunted. She clearly did not believe that Hayves was coming back. In truth, neither did Galt, but he had to try. At any rate, he had to find Lowther now, too.

Dupree marshaled Shagalov and Vane and they ascended the ladder hastily. Galt charged off after Lowther, continuing back along the wet, curved wall. He nearly collided with him as Lowther groped through the darkness back toward the ladder.

"Where's Hayves?"

"He's gone. Let's get out of here," Lowther said, a distinct note of panic in his voice.

Galt frowned, dissatisfied that Lowther, who was clearly frightened, had been entrusted with Blackburn's blade. "You go back and get up the ladder, then. I'm going to look for him."

Lowther peered up toward the lantern light of the others, then down at the expanse of darkness that separated him from it. "I'll come with you," he said.

They continued further along the walkway, searching for some sign of Hayves or the shade who'd taken him. In Galt's experience, a shade would attack relentlessly wherever it encountered its prey, and wouldn't generally take them very far. He guessed that the shade had gone over the edge of the drop off, perhaps to some network of pipes or tunnels it was familiar with, tearing Hayves apart as it fled from its attackers. Despite the fact that their destruction would end their suffering, shades had an innate desire for self-preservation. Galt supposed that it had been built into them when they were first conceived as a form of punishment by the Father-God. Suicide to escape their eternal torment would not be an option.

Frustrated and disheartened, Galt finally gave up. After several short-cycles of searching, they'd found no sign of Hayves, and the chamber had grown deathly silent again. He risked shouting out for Hayves only once, and there was no return answer.

After following the glow of the others' lanterns to find the ladder again, Galt and Lowther cautiously and quickly scaled it. Dupree, Shagalov, and Vane approached Galt as soon as he reached the top.

"Is he … ?" Dupree started, her face grimly set.

"Yeah," Galt answered wearily. "I'm afraid so."

She nodded. Shagalov placed a hand on Dupree's shoulder. Vane stared off into the darkness with a look of disbelief. There had been so much loss already, but until then, it had not struck the close-knit group of engineers.

"We need to keep moving," Lord Fontaine said gently but firmly. Behind him, barely visible in the lantern light, Starkad stood impatiently.

It was peculiar and disturbing to Galt that, as the expedition dragged on, more lives were being lost and less time was spent mourning them. Daeg had had an entire service dedicated just to him. The deaths since had resulted in mass burnings and just a few words. Now, Hayves had vanished, and they couldn't afford to spend more than a moment even considering it. Galt knew that other people's lives hung by a thread, but the cheapening of Hayves's life was terrible. Even a short prayer would seem appropriate if he could summon the words. As it was, nobody asked him to.

With renewed caution, they continued along the walkway, occasionally snuffing out the lanterns to reacquaint themselves with where the dim light of the surface was filtering in. Eventually, they reached another ladder, and the layout of the chamber as a series of circular walkways overhanging the main cistern became clear. With each ladder they climbed, they braced themselves for attack, but none ever came.

At what appeared to be the uppermost walkway, the light from the surface was now undeniable. They found themselves at the final ladder, which ascended toward another grate, the last obstacle between them and the surface. In the center of the chamber's ceiling, an even dimmer vein of light was visible. Galt assumed that it was the trapdoor that would open in order for accumulated waste to be dropped into the cistern.

"Can you get us through it?" Lord Fontaine asked Dupree. The hint of empathy his voice had carried before was already gone.

"Yeah," she said, her voice quavering. "We should be able to."

"Let me clear the ladder first, my lord," Galt interjected.

"Of course," Lord Fontaine answered. "And, considering the circumstances, I think we can drop the formalities. Please, call me Cyprian."

Galt nodded in acknowledgment and started up the ladder. He was sure that *Cyprian* had meant it to be a gesture of solidarity, showing that he was in the same position as his subordinates, but coming from the ambitious lord, whose dislike of Phir-Ramarian and desire to lead the expedition had been obvious, it just seemed like another calculating move to cement the support of his underlings. Perhaps then nobody would object when he declined to hand the reins of leadership back to the prince, should they even succeed in rescuing him.

But for the moment, the political maneuvering of Lord Fontaine would have to be ignored. They faced more immediate problems. It wouldn't matter who was in charge if they were all dead.

Galt reached the grate and listened. The surface seemed to be silent. He studied the grate for a moment.

"It's all quiet," he called down. "The grate looks like it's just held with a latch. I can open it."

The others filed up after him as he popped the latch and flipped the grate up and open as quietly as he could. He peered over the edge and looked around. It appeared to be some sort of square, surrounded on all sides by dilapidated buildings with broken windows and crooked doorways. Nobody was around.

Quickly and quietly, the party clambered out of the sewer and headed for the cover of a nearby alley.

They were inside the walls of Vin-Sadavat.

CHAPTER 27

All fears aside, Cyprian was entranced by the winding streets, sweeping architecture, and historical weight of Vin-Sadavat. From the moment they'd left the sewer, an architectural marvel in its own right, he'd been assaulted with a veritable barrage of archaeological wonders.

Creeping through the ruins, slowly making their way toward the Opal Tower, every landmark they passed beckoned to Cyprian. Despite the scars left behind by civil war and time, the beauty beneath was undeniable. Under different circumstances, he could have spent the remainder of his life cataloging every treasure within the city. The spell was only broken by occasional wandering groups of slavers or their thralls, which sent the party scurrying into hiding. In those moments, fear replaced his fascination.

After passing through a dilapidated atrium, the exotic trees formerly flourishing within now dried husks, they came across a ruin so incredible that almost the entire party was as interested as Cyprian. Even Starkad seemed strangely enthralled by what they'd stumbled upon.

Beyond a few tottering walls, the majority of the structure had collapsed in on itself, the clay tiles of the roof peppering the scattered rubble. Still intact, however, were the two gargantuan statues that dominated the courtyard in front of the wreck. Holding scepters aloft, their other hands clasped together, there could be no doubt who the statues depicted.

"Phan-Ellara," Faye said, gazing up at the crowned head of one of the statues. "And that must mean that the other statue is … "

"Ulesreto, the God-King of Vingallea," Starkad answered.

Cyprian stared at the statues in amazement. They seemed to confirm Starkad and his people's version of historical events. It appeared that before the fall, Ulesreto and Phan-Ellara had been worshipped together as king and queen of the empire. "So, it looks like your legends are true," Cyprian admitted, now doubting the veracity of everything he'd ever learned from Vingallean sources.

"Yes, I know. The badlanders may not write their past down, but they are fastidious with their oral history."

Cyprian looked at the statues again, and a question gnawed at him. "Our sources are in agreement that Phar-Karrian, Phan-Ellara's brother, was the monarch when the rebellion was launched against the Father-God, correct?"

"Yes, that's right."

"Because," Cyprian continued, "Phan-Ellara had already passed. Do your legends account for why Ulesreto didn't retain the throne after she passed? Or, if they were wed, why they hadn't produced an heir?"

Starkad smiled humorlessly, a distant expression in his eyes. "Your records don't seem so complete anymore, do they?"

Cyprian said nothing.

"As I've always heard the tale," Starkad said, "Ulesreto had originally set his sights on Paradise not to reshape the world under Vingallean rule, but to be with Phan-Ellara again. After she passed, he obviously judged her worthy and sent her soul to Paradise, intending to join her there. You see, his love for his human queen was so great that he was willing to walk away from his role in Alminnian's pantheon, from his nearly limitless power, in exchange for simply entering Paradise with the one he loved."

Pausing, Starkad removed his pipe from a pouch, seemed to consider it for a moment, and then stowed it. He cleared his throat and continued. "The problem was that Alminnian wouldn't let him abdicate his duty and join her. Apparently, the High-God did not wish to see his delicately balanced system altered in any way that he had not conceived of. When Ulesreto was denied the chance to be with Phan-Ellara, his resentment festered into a desire to overthrow Alminnian, and his ambitions only grew, as he eventually resolved to usurp his creator. Ulesreto planned on not only reuniting with Phan-Ellara, but giving her all of creation to rule over from Paradise—a new Vingallean kingdom that would last for all time. Aedesda, with his own motivations, was happy to capitalize on Ulesreto's aspirations. While the brothers were off scheming, Phar-Karrian inherited the throne. As I said before, he was fully in support of the plan to seize Paradise."

Cyprian considered Starkad's words, wishing that he could speak in depth with whatever tribal elders had passed this knowledge on to the badlander.

"As for an heir," Starkad said, gazing off into the shadows around them, "legend has it that they couldn't conceive. Perhaps gods and humans are just not compatible in that way."

As Cyprian considered the logistics of god and human relations, Faye, who'd briefly wandered off, approached them. "I think I know what this place is. From the tale of Phan-Casmia's escape. Based on the architecture and some of the inscriptions that are still readable, it has to be the Sepulcher of Phan-Ellara."

Cyprian looked at the ruin with renewed interest. Phan-Casmia was said to have escaped into the sewers while besieged by Nazradir's forces, who'd surrounded her while she prayed inside of the monument to Phan-Ellara. The same monument was said to have housed Phan-Ellara's tomb, and it was from there that Phan-Casmia had taken the skullcap—before the entire sepulcher was demolished.

"So the rest of Phan-Ellara's remains are buried under all of that rubble?" Cyprian said, fantasizing about an excavation to recover them.

"I would think so, yeah," Faye answered, eyeing the ruin. She must have been thinking the same thing.

Starkad stared into the jumble of stone, dimly visible in the murk. He looked up at the statues again for a moment, then turned to Cyprian. "We need to go."

"Yes, I know," Cyprian said reluctantly. He knew that an excavation of the tomb would never take place. At any rate, he needed to focus on their actual objective.

He turned back toward the others and saw that their interest had already waned. They waited with expressions running the gamut from impatient to nervous.

Without further delay, the party continued picking their way through the tortured interior of the city, taking special care to avoid any areas that seemed to be occupied. Undoubtedly, the glory and splendor of Vin-Sadavat was long gone. The slavers now coursed over the fallen city like flies on a corpse. The group passed along the outskirts of a square where dozens of them appeared to be celebrating around a bonfire, feasting and drinking. Among them, skittish slave women were being passed around, their cries eliciting laughs from the men. In the light of the dancing flames, Cyprian could see that the women were as mutilated as the hideous men who enslaved them.

"I think we're nearly there," Starkad whispered as they passed through the shell of a derelict bathhouse.

Ducking under a splintered doorway, they stepped back onto the street. The Opal Tower now loomed over them. Their proximity to the base made it impossible to see the rooftop terrace and the cathedral. Only the glow of the bonfires separated the top of the tower from the sky beyond.

Cyprian was about to ask how they were supposed to infiltrate the tower when Starkad spoke. "This way. I think I know how we can get in."

• • •

They followed Starkad down a scree of collapsed stone and toward the base of the tower. From their angle of approach, the vast wall of marble, coated in an age's worth of soot and grime, was a windowless monolith stretching to infinity. Through a collapsed portion of a wall, they entered what appeared to have once been castle gardens that encircled the base of the tower. Cyprian was reminded instantly of the hollow he and Faye had spent so much time digging through.

Around the remnants of fountains and across dusty tracts of dead earth, Starkad led them toward the western flank of the tower, seeming certain of their path.

"Where are we going?" Cyprian finally asked.

"Your own maps gave me the answer," he said, keeping his head on a swivel, looking for any sign of the slavers as they walked. "I've noticed that a canal runs from the western edge of the island directly to the Opal Tower. I assume that it was used by the monarchs to board ships without ever having to leave the security of the palace."

"So you think we'll be able to get in through whatever entrance is at the canal?" Faye asked, fumbling to remove a map from its protective tube.

"Yes, and don't worry about looking at the map right now. We don't have time. I know where we're going."

Faye slid the map back into the tube and screwed it shut. "What makes you think there will be any less security at the back entrance?"

"Because I don't think the city has ever been infiltrated. It doesn't look like there's much security anywhere. But as soon as we encounter even one slaver who can raise an alarm, we'll be surrounded and won't stand a chance."

"And you think there will naturally be more of them milling about the main gate than at an unused canal entrance," Mather said.

"Exactly."

"Why didn't we just enter the city through this canal?" Dupree interjected, a hint of hostility in her voice. "Sounds like we could have avoided the sewers completely."

She didn't mention that Hayves could have been spared.

"The entrance from the canal to the tower may be laxly defended, but I can guarantee you that where the canal meets the city walls is as fortified as the front gates," Starkad explained in a lecturing tone. "The interior of the city is not particularly guarded because there's nothing to guard against. They're under the impression that the entrances are patrolled heavily enough to guarantee that nobody can get in. The sewers were the only option."

Dupree didn't seem particularly satisfied, but said nothing.

They continued in silence until they'd reached the end of the gardens. Starkad pushed aside a corroded metal gate and ushered them through. On the other side was a series of steps carved into the stone wall, leading down to an easement. Below that was the canal itself, which had dried out long ago. The massive, dry-rotted shell of a sailing ship languished in the dirt.

Starkad motioned for them all to get down behind a short wall that separated the top of the walkway from the descending steps. "Do you see them?" he asked Mather.

Mather peered toward the darkened overhang where the dried canal ran into the base of the tower. Within, a small fire was burning. He held his field glass up for a moment. "Yes. I count four. Maybe five."

Cyprian followed Mather's gaze and looked through his own glass. He could barely make out the shapes of maybe two men sitting around the fire.

"My men and I can crawl down there, hopefully take them out with the crossbows. It will have to be precise." Mather sounded doubtful.

"I don't think we have another option," Cyprian said, running through scenarios about how they could proceed in his head. He came up with nothing.

A moment later, Mather, Lowther, Shaw and Baylor readied their crossbows and, accompanied by Galt, shuffled in a low crouch down the length of the short wall until they'd reached the steps. They descended a few, then slithered over the edge of the stairs and dropped out of sight.

"I don't like this," Pike said almost directly into Cyprian's ear.

He reflexively shrank away and turned toward Pike, annoyed. "Do you have a better idea?" Pike gazed into the shadowed overhang and said nothing.

Cyprian leveled his field glass again and tried to spot the men. As far as he could tell, they'd vanished. His mouth felt very dry, and fatigue swam over him. A sudden, overwhelming urge to be done with Vin-Sadavat forever hit him, and he hoped desperately that Mather and his men would succeed.

The sound of bolts flying cut through the air, followed immediately by strangled yelps. Cyprian stared manically through the glass, trying to see what was happening. One confused shout rang out before it was silenced with a muffled cry. A short-cycle passed, and a baleful moaning emanated from the darkness, followed by two popping sounds in close succession. Another shout rang out, then inhuman screeching, then silence.

The party remained riveted in place, waiting to see if a band of slavers would come seeking the source of the cries. Cyprian tried to convince himself that the violent nature of the marauders meant that random cries of pain probably occurred there all the time, and that nobody would be stirred to come and investigate. Ultimately, it seemed that he might be right.

After a few more short-cycles, Mather poked his head up over the stairs and ushered the others forward. They followed him down the stairs and across a walkway that led to the campfire the slavers had been sitting around. Galt, Lowther, Shaw, and Baylor were there waiting. Galt was cleaning blood off of his sword. The remains of the slavers and the shades that two of them had spawned were cast about the ground. Cyprian did not pretend to know much about the ways of the Void-God, but it seemed impossible that any of these horrible men could die without producing a shade.

"We cleared the rest of the hangar," Lowther reported. "These were the only men here."

Mather nodded in acknowledgment.

"This way." Starkad motioned toward a ramp leading up to an archway. One metal door hung languidly from a broken hinge. Detritus and garbage littered the open doorway. Cyprian felt yet another tinge of sadness at what the squatters occupying the city had reduced it to.

Without a second glance behind them, the party filed inside.

CHAPTER 28

The maze of tight, damp stone corridors they passed through was reminiscent of the hallways that Phar-Mindorius had led Cyprian through to bring him to Ganachim. The most telling difference was that, although the halls of the Vinecrown Keep had been dim, there was still some light. The Opal Tower's hallways were, so far, blacker than the Nightlands outside. Risking detection, they had lit a lantern. Starkad led the way.

As they crept along, unexpected serendipity arrived in the form of voices echoing down the hallways toward them. Starkad immediately snuffed out the lantern, and they stopped. Cyprian tried to hold his breath, feeling as if any sound would give them away.

"Have any of the newest initiates taken the kiss?" a voice asked.

A bark of laughter followed. "Only one so far. They're a weak litter, that's for sure. It's surprising—the way they were armed, I would have expected a little more fortitude out of them. Four have already been scraped up and brought to the scullery. At least the one the Empress *did* claim is a fine prize. She rewarded me tremendously for him. The Master was pleased as well, took a real shine to him. I've heard the Empress gave him the initiate as a personal servant."

"That's quite an honor, to be Heilrune's chosen," the first voice said with awe. "Many of our ilk have risen to greatness from there."

"Indeed," the second voice said. "Weak or not, this catch has been a tremendous boon for us. Look at poor Bolenz scouting up and down the coast." He laughed again. "His fruitless endeavors have cost him the favor of the Empress, whereas we have been lauded for our efforts. The other scouts languish in the wilds, hunting, while we grow fat and satisfied here, reveling in the sweet embrace of the Empress. Truly, we are blessed—to be given the opportunity to personally present the initiates that we, ourselves discovered! Come, let's get the next batch."

A third voice, guttural and deep, grunted excitedly.

"Yes, Maokreev, my pet, the Empress wishes us to make haste," the second voice said. "She craves fresh adulation."

In the dark, Faye clutched Cyprian's arm tightly. He had no doubt that the slavers were discussing their companions. Some of them were certainly dead. At least one had been taken for some foul purpose. They listened as the footsteps receded away from them.

Without relighting the lantern, they continued down the corridor, hands placed on one another's shoulders to ensure they stayed together. They rounded a bend and found a bowl of dimly smoldering coals lighting a T-junction. They paused, unsure which way the slavers had gone. From the passage to their left, voices rose again.

"Uncuts, leave." It was the second voice, the one that sounded so pleased with itself. The command was met by the sound of bodies shuffling out of whatever chamber the slavers had entered. Someone grumbled indiscernibly.

"Shut your trap!" the second voice snapped. "You may talk to me when you earn a few more marks, you babe-smooth little shit." The twisted hierarchy of scarification must have been clear to whoever had grumbled, because they said nothing more.

Before Cyprian had time to consider what would happen if the ejected slavers proceeded toward them, three shapes passed through the T-junction and disappeared down the opposite corridor.

"Maokreev, you may open the cell. I wish to extend the Empress's offer again."

The brutish voice grunted in response. As the scream of metal dragging against metal filled the space, Starkad motioned for them to move. The entire party hurried after him until the noise ground to a halt, and he abruptly stopped, causing them to pile up behind him. For a heart-stopping moment, Cyprian was afraid that the slavers would notice the sound of them shuffling to a stop. Thankfully, they didn't.

The party was now close enough to see the glow of torches lighting the hallway just ahead. The slavers' voices were very close now. "Davhal," the first voice said, "may I make the selection?"

"No," the second voice, Davhal, said with finality. Apparently, no further explanation was needed. "You and you."

Anguished cries of fear and the sounds of scuffling were heard.

Mather squeezed up next to Cyprian, Faye, and Starkad. "If those are our people, we need to act now."

Cyprian agreed. He hadn't thought that they would find the prisoners, and he had doubted that Tariono would free them when confronted—if there were even any left to free. He'd already started to mourn Jotun, though he knew that Faye held out hope. Now, they suddenly had an opportunity to actually rescue their companions. They had to seize it.

"It may raise an alarm," Starkad warned.

"We can risk that," Cyprian said, though a small part of him privately worried that it would jeopardize their main purpose. He shunted it aside. "We have to attack."

Without further hesitation, and considering the matter settled, Mather started ahead, moving swiftly but lightly. The other guardsmen bumped past Cyprian with Galt in the rear.

Cyprian knew that this conflict was different. Before, the guardsmen and shepherds had been tapped specifically to confront threats;

he could always afford to remain behind in safety. Not now. This would be bloody, close-quarters combat with a vicious foe in desperate circumstances. If he was going to truly lead this expedition, assuming they survived at all, he would have to prove that he was actually a leader. He not only needed to be in this foray, he needed to be in the front of it. The prisoners had to see that it was him rescuing them.

Before he had time to doubt his reasoning, and before Faye could stop him, Cyprian started off after the others. He overtook Galt, who shot him a confused look, and was midway in the line when the slavers finally detected the noise of their approach.

"Who's there?" Davhal called with irritation. It didn't sound like the threat of intruders had crossed his mind.

The hall dead-ended, with torchlight spilling out of a doorway on the right. Sparing no time at the chokepoint, Mather drew his blade and launched into the room with a tremendous roar. The other guardsmen, Cyprian, and Galt charged in after.

Mather directed his attack at the largest target in the room, a giant brute gripping an iron wheel attached to the wall. Whirling toward the unexpected threat, the slaver released the wheel, and the cell door screamed shut, violently pinning another slaver's arm against the wall. He bellowed in agony, releasing the hair of Bellamont, whom he'd been trying to drag out of the cell.

"Maokreev! No!" the trapped slaver screamed. Cyprian recognized the petulant voice as belonging to Davhal, and made for him at once.

To his left, Baylor and Shaw were hacking away at the third slaver, and Lowther and Galt had jumped in to assist Mather. Blade drawn, Cyprian descended on Davhal, who was trying to draw his sword awkwardly with his left hand. He clearly favored his incapacitated right. Cyprian, who had never killed another person, was mildly surprised to find that he faced it now with an icy resolve. In his eyes, any slaver was less than human.

With an animalistic growl, Davhal finally wrenched his sword free and swung once ineffectually. Cyprian easily parried the strike and drove his own blade deep into the slaver's throat. Hot blood spurted out, and Davhal made a high keening sound. He slapped weakly at the blade, having already dropped his own. Cyprian pulled his sword free and turned toward the others, not bothering to watch as Davhal wound down.

The third slaver was dead. Now, the men surrounded Maokreev and lunged at him from different angles as he tried his best to deflect the blows with a massive hammer. Despite his overwhelming strength, the hulking slaver could not stave off so many attackers. As Maokreev swung at Lowther with a tremendous blow, Shaw slashed at the back of his left knee, and he collapsed to the ground. Mather delivered the killing strike, driving his sword straight down into the back of Maokreev's head.

There was no time to celebrate their success. They all backed away from the bodies, waiting to see what would happen. One after another, in the order of their deaths, the bodies seized and their skulls burst. Galt, assisted by Mather and a nervous Lowther, calmly and quietly dispatched the shades as they were born.

The remainder of the party filed into the tight space, eager to see what had happened. Cries of jubilation rang out from within the cell.

A strange, euphoric sensation pulsed through Cyprian. He'd never been in a real battle before, and the effect it had on him was complicated. At the most basic level, he was grateful to be alive, but he was also filled with a giddy feeling of elation.

The skirmish was over; the slavers were dead, and they had won.

And he had led them to victory.

•　　•　　•

"You must be invincible," Cyprian beamed, clapping Jotun on the shoulder. He couldn't believe that the old man was standing before him.

"No, I don't think so," Jotun said wearily, "just very lucky."

Faye hugged him tightly, squeezing him hard enough to elicit a surprised gasp. "I'm so happy you're alive."

"Me too, me too." He patted her on the back and smiled warmly.

Cyprian watched as Galt and Solgard embraced nearby. They separated after a moment with a tinge of embarrassment.

For all of them, the reunion was both joyous and somber. The surviving prisoners were grateful to have been rescued, but the additional loss of life was hard to grasp. Confirmed dead were Rackham and three of the haulers, Raynard, Haskell, and Hughes. Rayburn was unaccounted-for, and there had been no sign of those taken from the *Fortune*. It seemed that by then, they'd either submitted to the depraved desires of their captors or been killed.

Cyprian had quickly learned that Phir-Ramarian was the one who'd been taken as Heilrune's personal slave and that he'd been maimed somehow by Tariono in the process. The revelation shook him deeply. Though he thought little of his cousin, and his resentment even approached hate at times, he knew that Phir-Ramarian did not deserve to be brutalized by monsters.

The party lingered in the dungeon chamber only long enough to regroup and prepare for the coming conflict. They redistributed gear and provisions, including food and water for the hungry captives. So far, the violent encounter had not drawn any attention, but Cyprian worried that Tariono might send others when Davhal failed to return soon with a supply of new victims.

"Undoubtedly, we have to rescue Phir-Ramarian," Cyprian said to the gathered company, a look of determination on his face. "We cannot leave him behind. Furthermore, we have not come this far, and endured so much, to give up now. You all know this. So, how do we get to Tariono?"

"The platform," Kovak said. "When they brought us in here, they took us to some kind of platform that they raised up with chains. That big one hoisted it up." He gestured toward the body of Maokreev. The shepherds had made no attempt to clean up the corpses.

"Do you think you could take us to it?"

"I-I'm not sure."

"I can get us to it," Solgard said. "I can remember the way. I tried to memorize every turn we took in case we escaped and needed to backtrack."

"Excellent," Cyprian replied. "Now we—"

"There's another thing you need to know, Lord Fontaine," Solgard interjected.

"What's that?"

"The weapon that Tariono used to cut Phir-Ramarian—I'm almost certain it was a piece of the blade. She revered it enough to make a dagger out of it, and she called it her 'sin.' I think it might be the only piece she has."

The promise of another blade shard had just come closer to fruition. Cyprian hadn't doubted that she'd have one, not after recovering the first three from Veathyadell, but to hear confirmation was satisfying.

"Okay, good," he said, realizing with some guilt that he was concealing his excitement. "Now we just have to decide who's going to go. There's no need to jeopardize everyone. Many of you are unskilled in combat, and would be better suited in a support position. I suggest we form two teams—one that will retreat to a position of relative safety within the sewers, and one that will confront Tariono. We'll regroup after and leave this place behind forever."

"I'm going with you," Solgard said without hesitation. "I just need a blade. They took mine."

Galt held his hand out to Lowther, who looked down in confusion for only a moment. Realization dawned on his face, and with a look bordering on relief, he unhooked a scabbard from his belt and gave it to Galt.

"Here," Galt said, handing the sheathed sword to Solgard. "It was Blackburn's."

Solgard accepted the blade with a sad smile. "Thank you."

Ultimately, they decided that Cyprian would spearhead the assault team, accompanied by Solgard, Mather, Lowther, Shaw, and Baylor.

Kovak, Gricks, and Galt would accompany the other team, navigated by Faye and Starkad, back to the sewer entrance and into the cistern chamber below, where they would await the others and hopefully avoid any shades. They agreed on a time limit of three cycles. If the assault team hadn't returned to the sewer by then, it would be up to the remaining company either to mount another rescue operation or to flee the city for good.

Galt had wanted to accompany the assault team, but had been overruled by Mather. Mather had also questioned Cyprian's decision to go, but yielded to his authority, begrudgingly admitting that Cyprian had held his own against the slavers.

There was one last thing to do. As final preparations wrapped up, Cyprian pulled Faye aside.

"Take this," he said quietly, gently pushing the tube containing the shards into her arms. "I know you'll still be in danger, but we can't risk bringing these directly to Tariono."

He thought of his last conversation with Phir-Ramarian. In the end, he'd been right to retain the shards. Now, however, the circumstances had changed, and he trusted Faye to protect the relics.

"I understand," she said. An uncomfortable silence lingered until she suddenly spoke again. "Why are you going with the assault team? You are the head of the Exploratory Contingent, last I checked. I get that you wanted to run the whole expedition from the start, but look where that got Phir-Ramarian. You need to let Mather handle this. That's exactly why he and his men are here."

Cyprian was surprised by her unexpected rebuke. Nearby, Jotun watched them with a look of discomfort. He obviously knew what they were discussing.

"Jotun agrees; you're being reckless. What was with you charging in with the guardsmen?" Her voice was rising, and she sounded incredulous. "You are not a soldier."

Cyprian felt his hackles rise. Until now, he had enjoyed Faye's universal support. She'd commiserated with him often about how he should have been tapped for command of the expedition. Beyond that, she was now implying that he couldn't defend himself. The blood on his sword said otherwise.

"More than ever," he said slowly, containing his frustration, "this expedition needs a leader."

"Don't give me one of your rousing speeches," she retorted. "I don't know if this is about saving the kingdom, or finishing what your father started, or your own damn ego, but your ambitions are going to get you killed."

She turned and stalked away. Cyprian nearly followed, but decided he'd only end up saying something he'd regret. He didn't want his potential last words with her to be worse than they already had been.

Cyprian looked to Jotun, who shrugged sadly and followed Faye toward the gathering group, where Starkad and Galt waited. Feeling an uncomfortable mixture of anger and guilt, Cyprian turned and walked over to Mather and his men.

Without the blade shards slung across his back, he felt naked.

CHAPTER 29

"Here it is," Solgard whispered, peering around a corner.

They'd followed her lead through the labyrinthine hallways, and despite backtracking once, it had not taken them long to arrive at the platform. Cyprian was pleased that they'd gotten there without any further altercations. He was still flustered from his conversation with Faye, and was eager to confront Tariono without any further delay.

"I don't see anyone," Solgard said.

"Let's move," Mather responded.

The small unit fanned out into the room and quickly determined that it was empty. Cyprian had never received any of the tactical training that Solgard or the guardsmen had, and he found himself simply aping their motions, but it seemed to be working fine.

"Lowther, Baylor, watch the entrance," Mather ordered. He turned to Solgard. "How does it work?"

"This handle, here. It just has to be cranked, and the entire plat-form lifts up. As far as I could tell, it goes straight to the top without any other access points. We should be good to reach the roof. Once we're up there, though, there will be a lot more of them."

Cyprian examined the splintered wooden platform. It was yet another example of the marvelous engineering of their forebears. The design was simple, but impressive. He assumed that it had once shuttled the ruling monarchs directly from their throne room to the private dock below. Now, it only transported human chattel for ritual suffering.

With the mechanism figured out, they all gathered on the platform. Lowther took the handle first, but was unable to make it budge, so Baylor and Shaw gripped it as well, and with a heaving motion, they were finally able to get it to start lifting. It was a slow process, and clearly exhausting work. Cyprian offered to help, but the men refused.

"Before we get up there, there's something I need to explain," Solgard announced. "Tariono has a strange sort of allure. When she was speaking to us, everything she said made sense. I think that's why Phir-Ramarian joined her, why he pledged himself to her. I even felt the urge to, and I'm sure others did as well."

It made sense to Cyprian. Tariono was, after all, the God of Beauty. Though her true divinity had been lost, he was certain that she still possessed enough power to sway hearts. After all, she'd built an entire fiefdom on the backs of cultists who worshipped her.

"Once we saw what she did to Phir-Ramarian, the illusion was gone. She wasn't beautiful at all; she was horrible." Solgard paused. "And she wore this unsettling mask."

"A mask?" Cyprian asked, intrigued.

"Yes. She made some vague reference to someone 'refusing her blessing.' I think maybe she was attacked."

Cyprian considered this, wondering if her own hidden face was the reason for her servants' disfigurement. More than ever, he found himself eager to leave Vin-Sadavat and its horrors behind.

They continued to rise steadily until the light of the low-burning fire in the center of the platform reached the ceiling of the shaft.

With their weapons drawn, Cyprian, Mather, and Solgard peered over the lip of the ledge where they would soon be disembarking. It was deserted. The platform rattled to a stop, and they stepped off onto solid stone.

"The open rooftop is just through that doorway," Solgard said with some trepidation. Ahead of them was a set of double doors, slightly warped with age. Flickering light slipped through the gaps between the doors and their frame. "Once we cross that, we'll be at her throne room."

They took one last moment to prepare their weapons while Solgard further explained what to expect on the terrace. From her description, it sounded like unarmed, naked degenerates were all they would have to contend with. Still, Cyprian suspected that, even unarmed, Tariono's followers would fight fiercely to defend their goddess.

As before, they planned on maintaining stealth and utilizing their crossbows as long as possible. Mather led the way through the doors and out into the glow of the tremendous pyres, with Lowther, Baylor, and Shaw following closely behind. Cyprian and Solgard, who did not have crossbows, could only trot after them.

It was a surreal feeling for Cyprian to be walking upon the terrace he'd previously viewed through his field glass from so far away. It had seemed nearly unachievable that they would ever get this far. Yet, despite everything that had gone wrong, they were finally about to come face-to-face with Tariono.

In the shadows of the mostly intact rows of ornate columns, they snaked their way toward the cathedral that dominated the center of the promenade. The fires burning on either side of the edifice crackled giddily, sending showers of sparks toward the sky. The revelers described by Solgard were there, as were several hulking slavers who appeared to be enjoying the erotic dancing of their thralls. Two robed figures lingered by the cathedral doors.

"Lord Fontaine, Solgard, stay close to me," Mather whispered. He turned to the others. "Backtrack until you're certain they can't see you. Cross to the other row of columns and proceed until you're parallel with us. We'll fire at them from the cover of both sides. Aim for the slavers first, then we can hopefully mop up any of the slaves who figure out where the bolts are coming from and charge us. Then we'll deal with any shades."

Lowther, Baylor, and Shaw nodded in acknowledgment and crept back the way they came, disappearing completely into the shadows. A few short-cycles later, they reappeared amongst the opposite row of columns and settled into position to await Mather's signal. Cyprian's pulse accelerated in anticipation of the call that would unleash violence upon the unsuspecting slavers.

Mather shouldered his crossbow and took aim. He lifted his left hand with his index and middle finger extended. It hovered in the air for only a moment before he let it drop. From the opposite row of columns, the *thwack* of bolts flying snapped through the air.

The results were immediate. Three slavers dropped heavily, sending a ripple of confusion through the crowd. Mather's shot joined the others as he fired into the stunned slavers, felling another man. As the captain reloaded with mechanical precision, Cyprian could only marvel at the speed with which he handled the weapon.

As a second volley hit, three more slavers collapsed, and the crowd scattered, including the robed sentinels, who retreated within the cathedral. The rooftop was now deserted.

Ominously, a horn blew from somewhere in the darkness.

"We need to advance before they can mount a real defense," Mather said quickly.

They all rushed forward, Cyprian instinctively making himself as small as possible. They'd nearly reached the fires when the slavers re-emerged from the side of the cathedral and charged toward them. The guardsmen fired into the attackers, dropping a couple, then drew their blades, and the slavers crashed into them a moment later.

Cyprian, his vision narrowing and his heart pounding, lifted his sword just in time to deflect a savage swing from a wild-eyed brute coated in scar tissue. Though he'd received some classical training in swordplay, real combat was very different. His merciless execution of Davhal had not been a fair fight, and hadn't really prepared him for what he now faced.

He leapt back to avoid a swing from the slaver and, before he could counterattack, Solgard plunged her blade into the slaver's back. He cried out feebly and fell. Cyprian forced himself to look away, trying to spot the next threat.

Another slaver materialized behind him, bellowing as he raised an axe high above his head. Without thinking, Cyprian launched forward, the ingrained lessons of his training finally kicking in. His tutor, a crusty old guardsman named Bullock, had taught him to close the gap when an enemy combatant overswung. He did just that.

Before the slaver could bring the axe down, Cyprian had driven his blade up into the man's sternum. The axe flew from his hands as he cried out. Cyprian wrenched his blade free and delivered a second blow to the slaver's neck, finishing him. He spun around and found his companions bloodied and panting, surrounded by bodies.

On the far side of the terrace, additional slavers began to rush out of darkened doorways, apparently drawn by the horn. The party was immediately outnumbered. Fortuitously, as the slavers approached, shades from the first to fall began to form in between the advancing attackers and the party.

Cyprian and the others ran for the cathedral doors just as several of the newly dead began their telltale seizing. The slavers began to panic and tried to beat back the shades, shouting for someone to bring torches. As more fell, a deadly cascade started with additional shades joining the fray, sowing chaos amongst the diminishing ranks of the slavers.

As Cyprian and the others reached the doors, they unexpectedly flew open. The robed figures exited first and dropped to their knees in supplication as their master strode out. A collection of crowns hanging from a blood red sash bounced against his armored torso as he walked. Upon his disfigured head was Phir-Ramarian's helm. Cyprian immediately knew that the monster before him was Heilrune.

He assessed them with his arms crossed, ignoring the screams of discord wafting across the terrace. It wouldn't be long before the shades finished off the last slavers and came searching for new victims.

"So, you are the interlopers who have disrupted the Empress's peace," he said, surveying the group. "Absolutely vile."

"We seek an audience with Tariono," Cyprian said, sounding bolder than he actually felt.

"Tariono? How dare you speak the Empress's secret name with your blasphemous lips," Heilrune responded harshly. His tone turned diplomatic. "If an audience was all you sought, you could have simply requested it. We are a peaceful realm. There was no need for senseless bloodshed."

"This entire place is built on senseless bloodshed," Solgard spat. "There would be no parlay. You would do the same to any ambassador as you did to us."

Heilrune eyed her with mild surprise. "If I remember correctly, you were already collected for initiation. If you're here, with these … unexpected guests, then I suppose Davhal is dead?"

"Yes," Cyprian answered.

"He was a sweet soul. The Empress will be distressed to learn of his passing." Heilrune stepped aside and held an arm out toward the open door in invitation. "Well, you seek an audience with the Empress, and I grant it. You've proven yourselves stalwart; she may see fit to offer you clemency and a spot within her domain. Come."

Cyprian looked at Mather, who gave a small shrug. The silent blackness of the cathedral's open doorway promised a trap. However, the alternative was to remain on the rooftop, where the shades would soon close in on them.

Heilrune seemed to read Cyprian's mind. "You'll be quite safe inside if you behave yourselves. Of course, if you prefer to remain out here and deal with the results of your mess-making, that is your prerogative."

"Alright. We'll come," Cyprian said, seeing no other choice. Nobody else in the party objected.

"Of course," Heilrune said pleasantly. He backed into the doorway and gestured for them to follow. Packed together, weapons still drawn, they followed him into the cathedral. The robed servants scuttled in after, shutting and audibly bolting the doors behind them. Cyprian's eyes fought to adjust to the near-darkness.

"Light the fires," Heilrune ordered. The servants hustled away to do their master's bidding, igniting torches from the only visible fire in the room, a barely smoldering metal bowl. From somewhere in the dark, a whimpering moan echoed.

"Here she comes," Solgard said.

A moment later, the throne room was suddenly bathed in firelight, and Cyprian saw Tariono for the first time. Reclining upon her throne, she was just as Solgard had described. Despite knowing better, he still felt a strange tug of hypnotic desire.

It ended abruptly when Mather drew his attention to the other figure in the room.

"Oh, my lord," Mather said in a tone of horror and pity that Cyprian had never heard from him. Cyprian followed his gaze and, after taking a moment to recognize who he was looking at, recoiled. He'd known that something terrible had happened to Phir-Ramarian, but the sight of what the once-proud prince had been reduced to still shocked him.

He sat on the floor, dressed in filthy rags. An iron collar was around his neck, chaining him to a smaller throne near the center of the room. His head had been shaved haphazardly, with the few remaining strands of hair hanging languidly. His eyes seemed vacant and distant, as if he had retreated deep within himself. Below them, where his lips had once been, there was now a weeping gash. The circular hole had been clumsily stitched, leaving his white teeth on display in the center. He seemed to realize that they were staring at him, and he averted his gaze, humiliated. Some bloody drool seeped out of his now permanently open mouth.

"I see you are admiring my newest initiate," Tariono said silkily from behind her porcelain mask. Its approximation of beauty was disconcerting. "He begged for my blessing, and I happily gave it. The transition can be a difficult one, but he is growing into his new role within my dominion."

Heilrune smiled and patted Phir-Ramarian on the head affectionately, causing him to flinch away.

"Heilrune, my sweet, what has happened outside?"

"These interlopers have killed many good men, including Davhal."

Tariono heaved a heavy sigh.

"They've also stolen the other initiates, I assume, as one is here with them."

Tariono turned her disturbing visage toward Solgard, and her head tilted slightly in recognition. "Yes, I remember this one. Well, whatever you have done, I am always willing to forgive. There is always a place in my realm for worthy champions of distinction. Your presence here proves that you are certainly worthy," she purred.

Cyprian found his eyes drawn again to Phir-Ramarian, who cowered at Heilrune's knee. He forced himself to look away and stepped forward. "We haven't come here to be any part of your twisted cult. We've come for your blade shard."

Tariono's hands involuntarily shot to the plumage of robes gathered about her chest, where the dagger must have been safely tucked away. "My shard?"

"Yes, your shard. Turn it over to us and we will happily leave you to your business. We'll take the rest of our companions and leave here forever. If you refuse, however, we'll take it by force."

Mather glanced doubtfully at Cyprian, apparently skeptical they were in a position to be offering ultimatums.

Tariono chuckled softly. "So, Ulesreto has finally learned of Veathyadell's little plan. And now he's sent his Vingallean lapdogs to do his dirty work. I should have known you were Vingallean stock from the start. So proud and boastful."

Heilrune looked back and forth between Tariono and the invaders in confusion.

"I made the mistake of bending to Ulesreto's whims. He and his murderous brother, who I have to believe got what was coming to him. Aedesda didn't send you, did he?"

Cyprian said nothing.

"Of course not. Only Ulesreto could inspire this sort of blind loyalty. I fell for it once, and I bear the weight of that sin every moment of my life," Tariono said with maudlin flare. "Paradise is not for us. Any of us. I have my own paradise here; I seek no other. And I will not let Ulesreto and his minions repeat the sins of the past. You are still welcome to cast aside these foolish aspirations and join me, but I will not give you what you seek."

"We are not minions of the usurper," Cyprian said. "We are our own masters, and we seek Paradise to save mankind."

Tariono assessed him silently for a moment. "That changes nothing. Whatever you think you're doing, I will not give you my piece of the blade. You may choose to submit to me, or you may choose death."

Heilrune understood that plainly enough. He stepped between Tariono and Cyprian, who reflexively backed up. "Kneel before the Empress. Pledge your fealty. Now."

Cyprian and the others stood their ground.

"So be it," Tariono said.

At her words, Heilrune stalked forward, flexing his hands. Cyprian suddenly realized that he carried no weapon, which was somehow more frightening.

"Hold," Mather commanded, pulling Cyprian back and stepping forward to meet the impending threat head-on. "On my mark."

Before he could give the command for the party to attack, a strangled cry rang out behind them. Cyprian turned in time to see one of the robed servants pulling a knife across Shaw's throat. The other was grabbing at Solgard, trying to do the same. They'd been so focused on Tariono and Heilrune, they hadn't noticed the servants creeping back behind them.

Without thinking, Cyprian lunged at the nearest servant, who abandoned his attempt to cut Solgard's throat and tried to defend himself. There was nothing he could do with only a knife, though, and Cyprian ran him through easily. Mather struck down the other servant, but it was too late to save Shaw, whose open throat was spouting blood.

In the confusion, Heilrune had closed the distance. Baylor turned back from the melee with the servants in time to raise his blade, but Heilrune snatched it from his hands easily. Baylor was still gaping at his empty hands when Heilrune slammed the hilt of the blade down into his skull, killing him instantly.

Mather and Lowther launched themselves at Heilrune, who deflected the deadliest blows with his gauntleted wrists, all while gleefully allowing the lesser strikes to cut his skin. Nearby, Solgard hovered over the four bodies, waiting anxiously for any shade to be born.

Cyprian stood between them, torn. Finally, he sprinted around the fighting and directly toward Tariono. Phir-Ramarian watched pitifully from his place on the floor.

"Give me the shard," Cyprian demanded as he ascended the few small steps before Tariono's throne. She stood up, startling Cyprian with her height, which equaled Heilrune's, then reached into her robes and withdrew the ivory-handled dagger Solgard had described.

"You foul little man of Vingallea. You disrupt the peace of my realm for your own selfish gains. How dare you address a *god* with such petulance? You'll get this shard when I run its edge against your fine flesh."

She lunged forward with a speed that Cyprian had not expected. He stumbled back, lost his footing on the steps, and fell. He immediately started to scramble backward, but Tariono seized one of his booted feet and dragged him across the dirty marble floor toward her. Panicking, he kicked wildly with the other foot and connected directly with Tariono's face. She fell backward clutching at her mask and howling with rage. The sound was otherworldly.

Cyprian leapt to his feet, panting, his eyes on the dagger still held tightly in her right hand. Behind him, he heard Heilrune cry out in distress. "Empress!"

The momentary distraction was all it took. Mather smashed his sword into the side of Heilrune's head, buckling the ornamental helm into the skull beneath. Heilrune spasmed violently and fell to his knees. "Empress?" he sputtered again, sounding like a lost child. He wavered for a moment, then collapsed.

"No, no, no, no," Tariono muttered furiously, oblivious to Heilrune as she traced her dirty fingers across her mask, inspecting it. The force of the kick had fractured it; a long crack ran down the center, splitting the rosy cheeks and pouted lips. Her eyes darted desperately within the holes of the mask.

"You struck me," she said fussily. "My face...*my face!*"

She lunged toward Cyprian again, but this time, he was ready. He leapt out of the way as she swung wildly, still clutching her face with the other hand. In her flailing, she lost her balance and stumbled forward, falling to her knees. Her hair, piled high in intricate curls, slipped off of her head and fell to the floor, revealing a hideously scarred bald head. She clapped a hand to the top of her head in an almost-comedic fashion.

Mather, Lowther, and Solgard, who'd finished off the shades born from the two servants, approached them. Lowther kicked the wig away, then jumped back as Tariono blindly slashed at him. She was surrounded.

"*Get away, all of you—get away!*" she shrieked, pointing the dagger at them. "*Just give me a moment!*"

Cyprian stepped forward, and she stabbed at him uselessly. As she did, Mather brought his blade down on her arm, nearly cutting it off. The dagger flew free of her hand, which bounced grotesquely, the forearm still held together only by some tissue. Involuntarily, she grabbed her arm, releasing her grip on the mask. The two pieces slipped from her face and struck the floor, shattering completely.

The face beneath was a true horror to behold. It looked to Cyprian like she'd been struck with acid. The skin was a bubbled, tortured mess of burn scarring, webbed rivulets of patched flesh that had been stitched and mended in countless failed attempts to mitigate the damage. Her nose was gone, revealing a bony hole only partly covered by crooked cartilage. Her lips were just extensions of the same twisted flesh that coated the rest of her face. They barely covered her mouth, where several teeth were missing. The remaining ones clung tenuously to blackened gums. From out of the wreck, her flawless eyes stared manically.

Tariono's destroyed features pulled back in horrid sobs. The near-severance of her arm apparently forgotten, she tried to collect the broken pieces of the mask. Blubbering incoherently, she pressed the pieces against her ruined face. Her dangling arm dragged around uselessly through the porcelain shards, smearing black blood across the floor.

The party stood around her, watching the last of her life drain from the gushing wound. Her halo slowly lost its luster, revealing itself to be tarnished and bespeckled with small dots of corrosion. The toppled god looked up at her attackers, her eyes swimming within the mangled flesh of her face. A deathly pallor had descended over the twisted knot of tissue, and the anguished hole of her mouth moved soundlessly.

Though Cyprian doubted that Tariono could hurt anyone now, he prudently remained beyond her reach as he picked up the dagger and examined it briefly. It was, in fact, a blade shard; there was no doubt.

"Why did you have to come here? Why couldn't you just leave me be?" Tariono finally managed to say with a wet croak. "You people and your traitor god took everything from me. I once gazed upon vistas of waving grass beneath a boundless blue sky. The light... the colors...I can still see them. They were mine; I painted the world with them."

As she spoke, the halo above her head flickered, casting a kaleidoscopic shine across the dim misery of the chamber. Her voice fell away, replaced by a low rattle, and her halo dimmed to nothing.

As Cyprian watched her filthy, crumpled form and listened to her increasingly shallow breaths, he was struck with a sense of guilt. As wicked as she had become, she'd once been equally radiant. The Father-God had crafted her in the forge of Paradise to deliver the beauty of his finest creations into the lesser world of man. Vingallea, with Ulesreto, had irrevocably dimmed that splendor; now, he and his men had snuffed it out for good.

Cyprian looked at the shard in his hand, and his guilt was eclipsed by pride. There was no question this time—they'd defeated a god and taken their prize by force.

Finally, with several of the jagged pieces of the mask driven into her scarred flesh, Tariono slumped over for good. Mercifully, she was face-down.

They continued to linger around her corpse until Cyprian spoke. "We've got what we came here for."

"Yes, I suppose you're right," Mather said, looking ruefully toward the bodies of Shaw and Baylor.

"They went in peace," Solgard said, touching Mather's arm tentatively. Cyprian assumed that she was referring to the fact that they hadn't produced shades. He was glad of it, but couldn't help noticing that, somehow, Heilrune's body had also remained intact.

"Thank you," Mather said. "Now we need to get out of here. With the prince."

They all turned, Cyprian felt sure, with the same knot of dread in their stomachs. Phir-Ramarian was lying on the floor, facing away from them, curled in the fetal position. He seemed oblivious to the fact that he was being rescued. Perhaps, after sustaining that sort of injury, there was no rescue.

Perhaps, Cyprian considered, it would have been better if Phir-Ramarian hadn't been found at all.

CHAPTER 30

After a few decisive blows from Mather's sword, the chain tethering Phir-Ramarian's collar to the throne gave way. Mather and Lowther hoisted the prince up between them, the short length of chain still attached to the collar swinging as they moved. Cyprian attempted to speak with Phir-Ramarian, but aside from actively avoiding eye contact, he appeared to be catatonic.

There was now nothing they could do but cross the rooftop back toward the platform. They'd been unable to find another way out of the cathedral, and to randomly attempt a different passage from the terrace could result in them becoming lost or trapped in a position where they were outnumbered. Certainly, the entire tower had to be in an uproar now, and other slavers would be roaming the grounds. So, their options limited, they'd resigned themselves to crossing the rooftop, which was presumably crawling with shades.

"I'll take point," Solgard said, preparing to unbolt the door. "Lord Fontaine, do you think you could help Lowther so that Captain Mather can help fend off any shades?"

"Sure," Cyprian said with some reluctance that he hoped hadn't been audible. He noticed that Solgard hadn't specifically referred to Phir-Ramarian. Undoubtedly, his presence disturbed her.

Mather lifted the prince's right arm off of his shoulder and held it up for Cyprian, who draped it over his own. Immediately, Cyprian was struck with the stench of body odor, and Phir-Ramarian's fetid breath, passing through his exposed teeth, brushed hotly against Cyprian's cheek, causing him to recoil. He felt a mix of disgust and defenselessness. Phir-Ramarian weighed so much that he knew he'd be unable to protect himself without dropping the prince completely.

Solgard threw back the bolt and cracked open the door. "It's clear from here to the platform. It looks like some of the slavers are still alive; they're trying to drive the shades back. They've got torches."

She opened the door wider, and the sounds of the continuing battle echoed from the far side of the terrace. Cyprian could see the blazing forms of several shades, fully engulfed in flames, being forced back by the slavers until they slipped over the ramparts and vanished, plummeting into the darkness below. The shouts and inhuman screams were joined by the explosive pops that preceded the birth of new shades.

"We might be able to get to the lift without anyone—or anything—seeing us," Solgard said. Mather nodded, and they began to cross the rooftop without further discussion.

Hearing the infernal screeching of the shades, and seeing their distorted forms writhing, wreathed in flames, Cyprian felt the same fear that had seized him in the trench. He did his best to ignore it, though every fiber of his being wanted to drop Phir-Ramarian and draw his sword, even knowing that his weapon would be useless against the shades. He glanced at Lowther, who looked like he felt.

Cyprian wondered which of them would abandon the prince first.

Staying low, they continued toward the platform that promised them deliverance. The rooftop seemed impossibly large now, their steps taking them no closer to escape. Cyprian began to strain under the weight of Phir-Ramarian, and he couldn't stop himself from glancing toward the violence on the far side of the terrace.

From behind them, a blaring horn cut through the air. Instinctively, Cyprian whirled around, nearly tripping over Phir-Ramarian's dragging feet, and forcing Lowther to a stumbling stop.

The reason why Heilrune had not produced a shade was now obvious. The slaver chieftain stood swaying in the doorway of the cathedral, blood streaming down his face, the dented helm crookedly wedged into the left side of his head. With one arm, he was bracing himself against the doorframe; in the other, he clutched a horn.

"The Empress has fallen!" he thundered. *"Stop the assassins! Get them! Tear them apart!"*

He pointed wildly at Cyprian and the others, shaking the horn toward them. *"Spill their blood! Spill it!"*

Heilrune's blowing of the horn had gotten the attention of the remaining slavers; his revelation of their goddess's death and his pointing out of those responsible made them forget the shades entirely. In a shrieking frenzy, the slavers rushed toward the party; the freshly hatched shades, indifferent to the news of Tariono's death, slashed at them as they passed, and the burning shades that hadn't yet been forced over the edge lumbered after their erstwhile attackers.

"Move!" Mather ordered.

Before turning to flee the impending wave of brutality, Cyprian witnessed Heilrune slouching back into the cathedral, slamming the doors shut as he went. Tariono's champion had been loudly wailing.

As Cyprian started toward the platform, it took every ounce of will that he possessed to cling onto Phir-Ramarian. He squinted hard, trying to focus only on the backs of Mather and Solgard in front of him. More horns blared as calls of the Empress's death rang out, fueling the hysteria of the slavers. Next to him, Lowther screamed in terror, but held on, and they ran with Phir-Ramarian dragging heavily between them.

They approached the entrance to the platform, where the doors were still hanging ajar, and Solgard and Mather began to pivot around them, no longer guarding their pathway forward, but now protecting their retreat. The fastest slavers reached them, and Mather and Solgard cut down two scrawny men brandishing clubs as Cyprian and Lowther crossed the threshold and floundered onto the platform, dropping Phir-Ramarian and immediately setting to work on the crank.

The platform shuddered to life and began to drop, causing Cyprian's stomach to lurch. Mather and Solgard entered the chamber a moment later, hacking at the grasping arms of the slavers as they forced the doors shut behind them. The two of them leapt onto the descending platform, making it wobble drunkenly on its chains.

As they descended, Cyprian could hear the doors being forced aside, but it wasn't slavers that appeared at the rapidly disappearing top of the shaft. Several shades slithered into view, and the sounds of screams and renewed fighting echoed down past them. Cyprian hoped that whatever innate drive prevented them from killing themselves to end their suffering would also stop them from hurling themselves down the shaft after their prey.

For two of the shades, their bloodlust overtook their self-preservation. They flung themselves down the shaft, crashing into the platform almost simultaneously. It tilted violently with the force and the new weight, dipping down where they'd landed. Cyprian was bucked into the air, then hit the floor of the platform and slid a short distance toward the shades. The bowl of cinders tumbled past him and collided with one of them, sending it toppling over the edge before the rocking lift could right itself.

As the platform beneath him grew steadier, Cyprian clambered backward. The second shade had found its footing, but before it could descend on him, Mather and Solgard were there, savagely plunging their blades into the creature. It writhed and swiped at them, but outnumbered and freshly born, it was quickly beaten into a gore-slick mass. It wasn't long before they stood over its steaming remains, panting. Nearby, Lowther was sprawled across Phir-Ramarian, wild-eyed. The prince had slid dangerously close to the edge of the platform.

Watching the light of the rooftop recede away, Cyprian nearly laughed with relief.

With the metal bowl of cinders gone, they were once again in almost-complete darkness. They had no idea when they'd reach the bottom of the shaft, and it happened sooner than expected. The platform landed crookedly with a shuddering jolt, nearly sending them sprawling again. A squelching sound came up from between the boards as the shade that had fallen was crushed beneath the platform.

Cyprian knew that the monster was still alive and would continue to be, even if it remained smashed under there forever. He almost felt pity.

Still breathing heavily, Cyprian and Lowther once again shouldered their load, and the party ventured back into the dismal murk of the corridors.

·　　·　　·

If any other slavers had been wandering the hallways, word of the commotion on the rooftop must have drawn them away; the passages were deserted. Solgard led them back to the cell she and the others had been held in, and from there, Cyprian, Mather, and Lowther were able to remember their route well enough to guide them back to the canal exit.

Mather and Solgard had been carrying Phir-Ramarian, as Cyprian and Lowther were physically spent. Reaching the exit, they lowered Phir-Ramarian to the ground and leaned him against a wall. His chin sagged against his chest and, in the gloom, it was difficult to make out his face. Cyprian considered it a blessing.

"It's clear," Mather said, peering out into the open air of the canal. As eager as Cyprian was to leave the cramped, squalid corridors of the Opal Tower, they had at least offered some sense of security. What awaited them beyond the Tower's confines might look clear at first glance, but Cyprian doubted that it would last.

Mather shared the sentiment. "We need to move fast. Word will spread soon. This entire city is going to be looking for us."

As if in response, a horn blew from somewhere in the distance. Cyprian couldn't be sure, but it did not sound like it came from the rooftop above them. Several other horns sounded, the eerie calls seeming to come from every direction.

"Lowther, you're up again," Mather said, gesturing toward the prince. "Lord Fontaine?"

"Yes, of course," Cyprian said, wishing ardently that he could refuse. He could, but he knew that it would destroy their opinion of him as their leader. He hoisted up the stinking bulk of Phir-Ramarian, intent on showing nothing but fortitude, as the party crept out of the shadowed doorway and started toward the steps that would take them away from the canal.

As they crossed the easement, a flaming mass crashed to the ground directly behind them. Shocked, Cyprian whipped around, and this time, he did trip over Phir-Ramarian's feet. They toppled to the ground, dragging Lowther with them. Cyprian wasted no time in extricating himself from the jumble and rising, his eyes locked on the burning pile.

"It's a shade," Solgard said, helping Lowther to his feet. She looked up toward the distant heights they'd just come from. "The slavers are still driving them off the roof."

"Is it dead?" Lowther asked.

The fiery lump shuddered, groaned balefully, and began to rise.

"No. Fire, falls—nothing ends their suffering but this." Solgard lifted her blade.

"It's not our problem. No need to stay here and let it be," Mather said.

Cyprian was reminded of Moore's long-ago declaration that the hunting party that had gotten his acolyte killed should have just walked away. It seemed like the right course of action here. "Let's go," he said, stooping to lift Phir-Ramarian again. They hurried up the steps and away from the re-forming shade, then slipped back through the metal gate that led away from the canal.

As they started to backtrack through the ruins, they were met with a scene of bedlam. All around the base of the Opal Tower, burning shades continued to crash to the ground, smashing through rooftops and sending up plumes of fire. What desiccated wooden structures remained ignited easily and burned voraciously, belching black smoke into the sky. Other shades, having already risen from the dirt, had proceeded to attack anyone nearby ferociously. Screams of terror tore through the permanent night as helpless thralls who'd sacrificed their humanity in exchange for some modicum of protection watched their world collapse around them. The slavers, who'd enjoyed a comfortable existence of barbarous pleasures, a status quo of untouchable power, were now fighting desperately to keep order and to stem the tide of shades.

All the while, the horns continued to blow. Soon, desperate and miserable cries joined them, howling lamentations for the fallen Empress. It seemed that word had spread; the slavers knew that no help was coming from on high.

Creeping along the outskirts of this spreading horror, Cyprian felt himself growing numb to the sounds of the slaughter. His entire existence had been whittled down to the weight of the catatonic prince on his shoulder and to placing one foot in front of the other. He was no longer paying any mind to the remnants of beauty still visible in the structures around him. He'd gotten the blade shard, which was safely tucked into his bag, and he was ready to leave Vin-Sadavat forever. The city was a tomb, its previous magnificence lost completely, and the physical and emotional toll that it had taken on the expedition was incalculable.

Still, with the shard in hand, they could claim victory. As long as they made it out alive.

They weaved their way through alleys, derelict shells of buildings, and filth-strewn courtyards, avoiding the growing chaos. In a small copse of petrified trees that encircled a shattered fountain, Cyprian and Lowther began to lag behind. Lowther sagged under the weight of the prince. "I need to stop," he gasped, lowering Phir-Ramarian. Cyprian, though he wouldn't admit it, needed the reprieve too.

Mather noticed them and snagged Solgard by the sleeve. The two of them trotted back, their heads swiveling as they came. Mather looked at Lowther, who was trying very hard to compose himself. "Alright, let's—"

"Keep searching!" a rasping voice called from somewhere beyond their derelict oasis. They froze, and Cyprian felt his breath stop in his throat. He squinted into the darkness around them and watched as a contingent of slavers wandered into view, bearing torches.

"Searching for what?" a slaver hissed. "What proof of invaders has there been? The Empress has not spoken. We should be at the tower, where the—"

"Have you not heard the calls?" another slaver shouted. "The Empress has been murdered!"

"That's impossible."

"Silence!" the slaver with the rasping voice ordered. "The initiates are fleeing!"

As he watched the argument ensue, Cyprian had failed to notice that several members of the group had started to slip away. He assumed that they were the slaves, pressed into escorting their overseers in a hunt for an unknown threat. Knowledge that their leader was dead had apparently sapped their desire to serve. The slavers pursued the defectors, managing to snag one woman by her hair, wrenching her backward and slamming her to the ground.

As the rest of the slavers caught up and converged on their victim, enthusiastically scourging her, Cyprian was surprised to see a larger group of thin, malnourished forms materialize out of nearby doorways and windows and close in on the slavers, beating them savagely with bricks, stones, and metal pipes. The crowd roared with an animalistic fury as they tore apart their masters.

"It looks like Tariono's realm isn't quite as stable and peaceful as she thought," Solgard observed.

"These people must have been waiting for an opportunity," Cyprian said.

"Well, there's no reason to risk them doing the same thing to us," Mather said. He turned to Solgard. "It's our turn. Let's go."

With Mather and Solgard now carrying Phir-Ramarian, they continued on, passing more scenes of pandemonium. The slave uprising they had witnessed was not an isolated incident. Cyprian didn't know if there had been any great scheme to revolt, or if many of the long-suffering slaves had simply come to the same conclusion, but the results were the same. All throughout the blasted remains of the ruined city, warfare had erupted once again. Cyprian witnessed the thralls attacking with anything they could get their hands on, and the slavers responding in kind, mercilessly butchering anyone who failed to obey. Punctuating the madness, there was a nearly continuous chorus of screams, the cries of countless shades being born.

And still, the horns blared, and the sounds of devastated wailing filled the air.

Fumbling through the dark, desperate and terrified of being found when they were so close to escaping with their prize, Cyprian could hardly believe it when they finally reached the square where the sewer grate, and a welcome reunion with their companions, beckoned.

Yet, between them and their subterranean refuge, another clash had broken out, spanning the square. Nearly two dozen slaves, clad in ill-fitting armor they'd clearly pilfered from their dead captors, were attempting to form ranks against a fresh onslaught of slavers. The element of surprise had apparently expired, and the slavers now had the upper hand, despite being outnumbered. A mantle of fear had settled over the slaves, who were backing into a tighter and tighter circle, quickly glancing at one another.

One of the slavers hooted wildly, and they all pounced, tearing into the slaves and sending them scattering. Some fought back, and the assault devolved into a bloody quagmire. The party stood just beyond the clash, an audience to the carnage.

"We need to get into the sewer before the shades come," Cyprian said. Nearby, the skullcap of a corpse exploded in agreement.

"Definitely," Mather said. "You two take Phir-Ramarian; Solgard and I will take point. We'll make sure you get inside."

Without a word, Cyprian and Lowther hefted Phir-Ramarian, whose head lolled sickeningly. Cyprian grimaced, adjusted the prince's arm around his neck, and nodded to Mather. The party headed toward the sewer grate, skirting the edges of the melee as much as possible. Cyprian clutched his sword, readying himself to drop Phir-Ramarian and fight if necessary.

It wasn't long before they caught the eye of a slaver. The debased creature paused in his bloodletting and gaped at them, seeming to realize what he was looking at. *"I have them! I have—"*

Before the slaver could complete his announcement, a bolt plunged into his sternum with enough force to topple him immediately. Mather expertly slung his crossbow over his shoulder and transitioned back to his blade without missing a step.

The grate was mere feet away when Cyprian was struck stiffly in the back. Panic surged through him, as death seemed imminent. Out of the corner of his eye, he saw a dark shape bounce away, and realized that he'd only been struck glancingly by a hurled stone. He was flooded by relief.

The feeling evaporated as three slavers rushed toward them. Mather and Solgard met them head-on, deflecting their brutal blows. Mather managed to disarm one of them, deftly twisting the man's wrist with a flick of his blade and sending the slaver's mace sailing into the air. Before the slaver could react, he was cut down. Another slaver attempted to decapitate Mather from behind, but Solgard was there, gutting him before he could complete his attack.

It felt wrong for Cyprian to keep going while Mather and Solgard were bogged-down with attackers, but he and Lowther continued on, reaching the grate. They dropped Phir-Ramarian unceremoniously, and Lowther turned back toward the battle, his sword ready, while Cyprian wrenched the grate open.

Below him, a lantern ignited. Awash in its light, Faye looked up at him.

Cyprian heaved Phir-Ramarian to the edge. "Somebody take him now!" Before anyone could respond, he slid Phir-Ramarian into the hole, holding on to the prince's legs for as long as his arms would allow. He finally let go as he felt Phir-Ramarian's weight pass into other hands.

He briefly considered leaping down into the sewer, but knew that he couldn't abandon the others. As it turned out, he needn't have worried. Mather and Solgard reached the sewer entrance, nearly knocking Cyprian in as they skidded to a halt. Behind them, several bodies were jerking spastically. Cyprian ushered them down the ladder, with Lowther following, then swung over the lip, grabbed the grate, and prepared to shut it behind him as he descended.

For one last moment, he saw the interior of Vin-Sadavat. All around the square, bodies littered the bloodsoaked ground, framed by the light of the burning buildings. Their escape into the sewer appeared to have gone unnoticed by those who remained fighting; the first batch of shades had interrupted the combatants, leaving their personal war, and the assassins in their midst, forgotten in the face of the undying horrors.

Tariono's depraved empire, delicately balanced on a knife-edge, had collapsed.

CHAPTER 31

As before, it was a bittersweet reunion. Any celebratory feelings regarding their defeat of Tariono and subsequent recovery of the shard were tempered by the further loss of life.

Additionally, the return of Phir-Ramarian in his violated state brought only discomfort. After moving some distance from the surface, struggling to lower Phir-Ramarian down each slippery ladder as they went, Bellamont and Hale set to work on him. Without their normal supplies, there was little they could do. Ultimately, they made a makeshift bandage out of some torn cloth in order to cover the wound. More importantly, it prevented anyone else from having to see it.

Still wary of any shades that might be lurking in the sewers, they advanced cautiously but eagerly toward the exit. During Cyprian's absence, Faye and Starkad had reviewed the map and confirmed their return route, following the same passages they'd taken on the way in.

As they walked, Cyprian quietly explained to Faye what had occurred when they'd reached the top of the Opal Tower. Self-conscious of others listening, particularly Mather, Lowther, or Solgard, he was careful not to embellish his own role in things. Faye listened intently, all of her prior anger toward him momentarily lost in the relief of his return.

Several times, she nervously glanced back toward Phir-Ramari-an, who was now being carried by the last remaining haulers, Anders and Barrow. "Do you think he'll recover at all?" she asked.

"It's hard to say. What they did to him seemed to damage his mind even more than his face."

"Well," she said slowly, choosing her words carefully, "we've got four of the shards now. Two of the old ones are dead. Considering Phir-Ramarian and the other losses, maybe now would be the smart time to return to Nordabor and regroup. I'm sure Phar-Mindorius would want a chance to help his son."

Cyprian kept his face blank, not wishing to betray his true thoughts. He was about to attempt a nonchalant answer when Stark-ad interrupted.

"I'm sure that *all* of the families of those who've perished would've wanted the chance to help their loved ones, but it's too late. Make no mistake, the prince will soon be joining the perished. That wound is undoubtedly tainted. It would be pointless to return now. We would squander the progress we've already made going west toward the Einmaz Mountains, and we would use up all of our resources in a time-consuming march back just to tell the king his son is dead and we only half-succeeded. Our agreement was not that I would lead you to *half* of the shards, and your king knows it. He would owe me nothing. I know it isn't my place to say it, but I think we need to continue."

Cyprian agreed completely with Starkad, but sensed that his re-established peace with Faye was a thin one. "Those are valid points," he said diplomatically. "When we get back to the cache, we'll reassess Phir-Ramarian's condition and discuss with everyone what our next move should be."

Faye wasn't satisfied with that answer. "Your motivations are quite clear, Duncan. I, however, am less concerned with your reward and more so with the life of everyone else in this company."

"Fair enough," Starkad said.

Cyprian was once again acutely aware of the others listening. He wondered how many of them had heard Faye's desire to return or Starkad's naked self-interest. He needed to keep morale firmly on the side of continuing, and he needed to cement his control. After all, Phir-Ramarian was in no condition to lead.

If too many desired to turn back, especially Mather or the shepherds, all of the titled authority in the world couldn't stop them. He needed Faye on his side, and he needed everyone to understand that continuing on was the right thing to do. It would certainly be difficult, what with the specter of Phir-Ramarian being dragged along every step of the way.

At least they could take solace in the fact that Tariono and her hive of lunatics would surely be the worst that they would face.

•   •   •

"So those are our choices. It's not really a choice at all," Cyprian finished.

They'd finally returned to the cache, which they'd subsequently moved some distance away in case any remaining slavers were to return to the area surrounding the old camp. After a reassessment of what gear and provisions were left, and allowing some time for further tending to Phir-Ramarian's injuries, Cyprian had addressed the weary group. As before, the company was no longer divided between leaders and subordinates, but all were present under Cyprian's egalitarian leadership. His assessment of their current situation had been tinged heavily with his own desire to continue, and the implication that his say was absolute. It was a gamble, and now he would see if it paid off.

Kovak was the first to voice doubts. "Half of our company is dead. The rest of us are exhausted. Most of all, our leader is gravely injured. We need to go back."

Cyprian bristled at the reference to Phir-Ramarian as their leader. Kovak clearly did not recognize Cyprian's command.

"We can't drag a dying man into the unknown. He needs real aid. There's only so much we can do with what we have now," Bellamont added. She looked haunted. The slavers of Vin-Sadavat still clearly occupied her mind.

Cyprian looked at the sagging tent behind her. Beyond its canvas flaps, Phir-Ramarian was lying in the dark wrapped in woolen blankets, fresh bandages on his disfigured face. Thankfully, Dupree had been able to force the lock and remove his collar.

Cyprian felt a tug of guilt and sorrow for his cousin. He'd been a brash fool, but he didn't deserve to be in that condition, undoubtedly listening as they discussed his fate. Assuming he still understood what was going on.

"You said it yourself, Jacqueline. He's dying. Even if we turn back now, he's liable to pass before we've even reached the Dawnlands." Cyprian paused, debating whether he should invoke the unknowable will of the injured prince. He forged ahead. "This expedition was Phir-Ramarian's dream. Every step of the way, he pushed us to continue. He wanted more than anything to deliver the people of Nordabor to Paradise. He would want us to continue now."

Out of the corner of his eye, he saw a look of disquiet pass over Faye's face. Thankfully, she said nothing.

"What are the chances that he'll recover his faculties?" Mather asked Bellamont.

"I have no idea. My chief concern right now is the wound. Whatever monster stitched it up did a hack job; it's corrupted, and it's getting worse. It's a wonder that all of them haven't died of corruption."

"So, the outlook, in general, is grim?" Mather asked.

"Yes."

"Like it or not," Mather said with a sigh, addressing the remaining guardsmen more than anyone, "our prince is most likely going to die. Even if he continues to hold on, in this state, he's incapable of leading us. This expedition may have suffered tremendous loss, but we retain the rule of law. We are not to be broken by this world; we enforce our own order upon it. That means Lord Fontaine is our commander now. As the highest authority of the Crown present, we will follow his orders."

Mather's eyes were dim, the stirring reverence for authority not making it beyond his lips. He didn't seem to like it, but he still clearly felt beholden to his oaths to the Crown. Cyprian breathed a small sigh of relief.

"He is only a lord, and of nothing but moldering garbage," Kovak said angrily.

Without a moment's hesitation, Mather backhanded Kovak, sending him reeling into Gricks and Lowther, a look of shock on his red face. "I have tolerated too much insubordination out of you. You are supposed to be my second-in-command, yet you continually question my orders. You're demoted. Any further word of defiance from you, and I'll have you stripped of your gear and sent into the wilds on your own. You'll be free to walk back to Nordabor as you please. Lowther, you're my under-captain now."

Kovak wrested free from Gricks and Lowther, who looked surprised and somewhat embarrassed. Kovak seethed, but seemed to know that Mather was not bluffing.

"We need to remember that we are royal guardsmen. Our oaths still ring true. I need to know that I can rely on you all," Mather said, staring at Kovak.

"Yes, sir," he answered.

Cyprian stood by, watching with amazement. He was incredibly grateful that Mather, whose position of power was unimpeachable, had chastised Kovak. Cyprian might not have succeeded, and could have ended up looking weaker as a result. "Thank you, Captain," he said briskly, wishing to move on.

He assessed the rest of the small crowd. Faye continued to stare at him with an unpleasant frown. Galt and Solgard both looked miserable, but neither questioned him. Dupree, Shagalov, and Vane stood silently, utterly defeated. Jotun retained a quiet optimism, though it seemed to be marred by a growing cloud of concern. Pike stood by Phir-Ramarian's tent, looking lost. Starkad simply smoked his pipe and watched, keeping his selfish opinion to himself.

Cyprian wondered how it looked to have his desires fall in lockstep with Starkad's. At least he had a noble purpose for pushing on.

"Is everything but the tents stowed and ready for departure?" Cyprian asked Anders and Barrow, who'd been lingering near the wagon, looking like they'd rather be anywhere else in the world.

"Yes, my lord," Anders answered, clearly uncomfortable with his new position of responsibility.

"And we made room for Phir-Ramarian," Barrow added.

"Okay, thank you," Cyprian said, cringing. Every time the prince's name was spoken, a small piece of the company's morale eroded away. "Everyone get some rest. We'll depart in eight cycles. Captain, set a watch. I'll volunteer for the first half."

"That won't be necessary," Mather said. "We can handle it."

"All right," Cyprian said as the group slowly dispersed either to walk the perimeter or crowd into the three remaining tents. He drummed his fingers absentmindedly on the tube he once again carried. Inside, the newest shard, its gaudy handle still attached, for now, had joined the others.

Cyprian looked at what now passed as the command tent with a sense of trepidation. He would be sharing it with, among others, Phir-Ramarian. He dreaded lying in the dark enduring the continuous whistling breaths coming from Phir-Ramarian's ravaged mouth, but he had to be there for his injured cousin. It was the right thing to do, and the company had to see him doing it.

Now that he was in control of the expedition, Cyprian knew that he needed to continue to inspire the others, to show them what true leadership was. He needed to ensure that they would remain loyal and follow him, no matter what.

Triumph was so close. He would deliver his people to Paradise; he would finish the journey his father had set out on so long ago.

He would not stop now.

PART IV:
HEIGHTS OF
DARKNESS

CHAPTER 32

It was impossible to know if the slave-god could hear him, but he spoke nonetheless. Phar-Mindorius found that with her, catatonic as she seemed, he could speak freely, eschewing the vague pretenses of the royal court and embracing a frankness that would have been impossible with his courtiers. The elderly king spoke to her of his fears and hopes, his aches and doubts, the son he missed and the nephew he'd regrettably shunned. Knowing that his own time was growing short, hastened by a life spent under the weight of his crown, the king felt no need to mince words with the being who had been the sole source of his survival, and whose pending demise guaranteed his own.

Phar-Mindorius still struggled to accept that, should his son fail in his quest, he would be the final Vingallean monarch, the last ruler of what had once been the greatest kingdom ever known. His progenitors had enjoyed a global dominion, but the war between the gods, and the steady march of time, had reduced that power to one city. Nordabor was a moldering holdout compared to the glories of the past. Where his ancestors had walked alongside their creator, Phar-Mindorius now stood in the damp darkness of the hidden grotto beneath his keep, confessing his failures to the only god he'd ever truly known, a silent, shackled wretch.

Ganachim had once spawned the entire natural world. Now, her splendor gone, her presence barely managed to keep their final measly crops from withering on the vine. Each time Phar-Mindorius came to the failing god's miserable cell, he fully expected to find her dead.

His little visits had grown in frequency ever since Phir-Ramarian had departed. Phar-Mindorius, oscillating between two certainties, would sometimes tell his captive audience how certain he was that his son had found success, and at other times, he would lament that his son had perished, taking any chance of their kingdom's survival with him.

On this occasion, Phar-Mindorius was feeling cautiously optimistic. "Many full-cycles have passed, yes," he said, as if Ganachim had suggested it, "but, realistically, I would not expect them to be returning any time soon. They have a long way to go, though I think it likely that Phir-Ramarian has collected at least a few of the shards by now."

Ganachim, suspended by her grime-slick chains, remained silent. As she rocked gently in the pull of the subterranean waters of the Einfallen, Phar-Mindorius imagined that he could see her nod in agreement. His eyes settled on the unnatural halo of rotten wood that hovered above her head. It was a peculiar reminder that, despite their humanoid features, the gods were vastly different.

And, somewhere beyond their realm, either beneath the relentless burning of the unmoving sun in the east, or in the blackness of the endless night of the west, Phir-Ramarian would be facing these monsters, demanding that they turn over the shards of the sundered blade they hoarded.

At least Phir-Ramarian was not alone. Cyprian was with him, and despite his sister-son's tendency toward being argumentative and opinionated, Phar-Mindorius knew that he was loyal to his kin, though it was a loyalty that perhaps had more to do with their shared history and what they sought to save than with any goodwill that Phar-Mindorius had fostered.

The king felt a sting of remorse as he once again considered his frigid treatment of Cyprian in the wake of Rorik's failed expedition. After all, it wasn't Cyprian's fault that his father had never returned. Yet Phar-Mindorius couldn't look at his nephew and not see Rorik, whose disappearance had robbed him of hope and driven his sister to dwell obsessively on her husband's fate until her own death. Similarly, he knew that Rorik had not vanished on purpose, but given his difficult position as the sovereign of a collapsing kingdom, Phar-Mindorius couldn't help but resent him for his failure. Perhaps, if they succeeded in recovering the shards, their triumph would mend his rift with Cyprian. Regardless, he was grateful that his nephew was a part of the expedition. He was certain that Cyprian's expansive knowledge of antiquities was proving invaluable to Phir-Ramarian.

Of equal importance, he was sure, was Starkad's guidance. The badlander had undoubtedly spoken truth in regards to his many travels throughout the wastes, and while he may have shown a sneering disdain for Phir-Ramarian, his allegiance was assured. Starkad could be trusted to lead Phir-Ramarian and his men to the hidden gods for a simple reason: he craved a life of comfort and pleasure, of deliverance from the ruined world, something that only the king of Vingallea could provide. Phar-Mindorius would have no issue granting Starkad a titled position of leisure once he set foot in Paradise and the new Vingallean kingdom was born.

Thoughts of that eternal kingdom were both comforting and disheartening. Phar-Mindorius's fantasies contrasted sharply with the reality around him. He looked at Ganachim and felt a bitter, self-pitying anger rise within him. "Why did you have to do this in my lifetime?" he asked the mute, living corpse. "You've existed for an eternity, yet now you fail. It's not fair."

He bowed his head and looked at his gnarled hands. The sound of the rushing water filled his ears. Without another word, he turned from the imprisoned god and tottered back up the slick steps, cognizant of the fact that an untimely slip would leave the kingdom without a ruler. He assumed that the lesser branches of the royal bloodline would begin squabbling immediately over who was the rightful heir, a circumstance as dangerous to the continuity of the kingdom as any other. Despite this possibility, he could not bring himself to name another successor. To do so would feel like he was confirming Phir-Ramarian's demise.

This time, his worries were for naught. He reached the top of the steps and exited back into the corridor, where Captain Vitus was waiting for him. The captain had offered to accompany him down the steps, but Phar-Mindorius, protective of his private musings with the old one, had waved him off.

"My lord," Vitus said, peering into the darkened doorway as Phar-Mindorius closed the nondescript wooden door behind him. Vitus, who'd taken over as the chief officer of the Royal Guard while Captain Mather accompanied Phir-Ramarian, had only been told the bare minimum regarding the god's presence, and hadn't been allowed to see her. Despite his best efforts to act otherwise, he was clearly curious.

"I'm finished," Phar-Mindorius said. No other instruction was necessary.

They headed back toward the king's private chambers, Vitus hovering shortly behind as they walked. The escort was probably not necessary, but Phar-Mindorius liked to keep a personal guard with him. If anything, it was just to have someone to fetch him whatever he might need. Vitus was certainly good for that; the captain, elated at his recent promotion, was eager to please. In that sense, he too-closely resembled the fawning nobles of the court. Phar-Mindorius found himself missing the taciturn efficiency of Mather. At the same time, he was glad that his most trusted guardsman was supporting Phir-Ramarian.

As they reached the king's chamber, Phar-Mindorius paused at the door, and Vitus stopped obediently a few paces behind him. "You are dismissed, Captain. Thank you for your assistance."

"Of course, Your Majesty. Thank you." As he spoke, Vitus hurriedly knelt in acknowledgment and rose. He marched away stiffly as Phar-Mindorius entered his chamber.

The worst thing about the cycles of useless waiting was the tedious boredom. Beyond his private discussions with the unresponsive Ganachim, Phar-Mindorius had little to do. The basic functions of the kingdom were consistently addressed by his underlings, leaving very little to occupy his time. The expedition was gone; there was nothing left to plan or prepare. Attempts at leisure or sport left him restless and anxious. In the vacuum of his mind, unfettered as it was by any pressing action, insidious doubts were free to take root. It was easy to slip into despair. It seemed there was nothing left for the old king to do but putter around his dilapidated keep and fret.

But that wasn't entirely true.

Phar-Mindorius stood before the heavy tapestry that he'd swept aside many times before. Concealed behind the faded, dusty depiction of a bygone lord of Nordabor leading a hunt through a sun-dappled glade was the door that would lead him to the hidden vizier. Like an invisible beacon, the promise of esoteric knowledge, of whispered secrets divined by the vizier, called to him. If anyone could supply Phar-Mindorius with comforting news, it would be his mysterious advisor.

Since the expedition had departed, the vizier had been able to tell him little, but the knowledge he had been able to impart had been encouraging. He reported vague hints of progress and success, and no clear signs of disaster. The strange, inhuman presence of the vizier made him uncomfortable, but the chance to hear anything regarding his son had proven impossible to resist. He'd visited the vizier a number of times since the expedition had left, always with a mixture of fear and yearning, and he'd invariably departed with a faint sense of relief that had quickly given way to an even greater sense of dread.

Standing before the tapestry, his heart thumping steadily against the inside of his ribs, Phar-Mindorius decided that his one-sided discussion with Ganachim had not been enough. He shoved the tapestry aside and pushed open the narrow door.

Beyond the threshold, he entered the small, windowless room. The few stubby candles that lit the space guttered briefly with the influx of new air. Atop the thin platform surrounded by a veil, the vizier would be where he always was: sitting upon his wooden chair, waiting.

As unsettling as it was to speak with the creature beyond the veil, the silence beforehand was somehow worse. Phar-Mindorius was always leery of interrupting the vizier's meditations, and truthfully, felt awkward anytime he was forced to address the vizier directly. Even after so many long-cycles, he was still uncertain of what to call him. He would certainly never dare to call the being by what he believed to be his true name. To reveal his suspicions, to make plain his belief that Nuroh had survived the war and had come to aid his people, would be to risk upsetting their arrangement. If the vizier wished to remain anonymous, Phar-Mindorius would not impede that.

After the time spent in the cold, damp grotto, Phar-Mindorius's joints ached, and he began to grow impatient. He cleared his throat pointedly, yet the vizier remained silent. He considered leaving, but the thought of slinking out of the chamber was demeaning enough to override his trepidation. The vizier, whatever his origin, was a servant of the king.

"Have you any news of my son?" Phar-Mindorious asked, dispensing with any formalities. Still, no answer came. He approached the platform, feeling—absurdly—like he was trespassing.

"Hello?" he called, squinting into the shadowed folds of the veil. His voice echoed meekly through the space, its pathetic sound filling him with indignation.

He stumped up the narrow steps of the platform and yanked the veil back. Panic engulfed him; icy sweat broke out across his clammy skin.

The vizier was gone.

CHAPTER 33

Starkad led them north.

Though it was a great relief to leave the horrors of Vin-Sadavat behind, their journey toward the mountain fastness of the God of the Wind was by no means a joyous one. Obligations and orders drove most of them on, coupled with the knowledge that striking out on their own meant almost certain death.

The fact that two gods had already fallen provided little comfort; untold dangers still awaited them. In the lands north of Vin-Sadavat, they were just as liable to encounter roving bands of slavers or the shades of the dead as before, and the ever-present darkness, which had been blunted by the eerie glow of Vin-Sadavat's many fires, now fully engulfed them. Without lanterns, it was impossible to see. And all the while, the air remained cold, sapping their already-dwindling energy.

There was little they could do to regain it. The re-evaluation of their provisions had revealed that they were now woefully short. As such, a system of rationing had been enacted. The meals enjoyed by the company on the first legs of the journey seemed like banquets in comparison to the meager portions they now shared. The lack of water was an even more dire situation. The damaged cask had leaked further while the rescue operation was conducted, and refilling their canteens had become a rare luxury.

Starkad assured them that when they reached the Einmaz Mountains, there would be rain to collect and snow to melt, generated by Naffabyin's great storm system. Nonetheless, dry mouths and empty stomachs were still the constant companions of the struggling company, and there was little hope for a change soon.

Through the inky murk, they struggled over terrain as unforgiving as anything that had come before. The rickety wagon, which had to be hastily repaired by Dupree, Shagalov, and Vane on two occasions, was continually battered by thick roots, rocky outcroppings, and sudden shifts of the loose dirt underneath it. Hauling it was now everyone's responsibility, and they all took turns at the backbreaking task. All the while, Phir-Ramarian, bundled, silent, and haunted, bounced along inside of the wagon, squeezed in amongst the foodstuffs, amiant armor, and climbing gear, all of which were packed as well as they could be into whatever materials had been recovered at the destroyed encampment.

After nearly three full-cycles of morale-crushing hiking through a monotonous slew of harsh terrain, they seemed to emerge from the last of the blighted woodland. The twisted trees thinned out, and the ground smoothed into a flat, hard-packed earth. It was a welcome change.

Starkad explained that they'd moved into an area that was believed to have once served as pastoral farmlands and prairies, growing the crops needed to sustain the people of the capital, as well as providing plentiful fields for the grazing of livestock. There was now nothing to indicate any of that beyond the area's flatness.

Their small island of light continued through the night-locked land unimpeded. It took another two full-cycles of marching deeper into that flat nothing before they detected the first indication that something was changing.

They had stopped to establish camp. The three ramshackle tents had been put up, accompanied by three meek fires fed by dry branches collected from the dead trees they'd left behind. Galt and Solgard sat on the hard ground, eating scraps of salted pork, tepid cans of lukewarm beans, and some extremely old hardtack. With only a minuscule ration of water to wash the meal down, Galt found that his mouth was almost too dry to chew the salty foods. Based on the look of displeasure on Solgard's face, she was having a similar experience.

Further complicating the process, the tough bread and meat were severely irritating a sore molar that Galt had been trying to ignore. At the outset of the expedition, every member had been assigned basic utensils for cleanliness; included had been toothbrushes and dental paste from Bellamont's stores. Unfortunately, almost all of her extra medical supplies had been destroyed, and Galt now found himself with nothing but a dry brush. His teeth felt scummy, and the molar in question, which had already been suspect, now seemed doomed.

As Galt gingerly tongued his dying tooth, Anders, who was sitting on the other side of the fire, sat up straighter and stopped his own labored chewing. "Did you feel that?" the hauler said, awestruck. Galt, Solgard, and Barrow all looked up and stopped eating.

A moment passed, and Galt was about to resume his careful chewing when he did feel something.

It was subtle, a barely detectable tickle of movement in the stagnant air. It felt like a breath passing over his face, and reminded him of standing on the deck of the *Fortune*, the movement of the boat creating the illusion of moving air.

But this was no illusion. This was real, natural airflow.

"That must be wind," Solgard said, a small smile creasing her face. Galt noticed that her cheeks had almost shed the last of the peeling sunburn she'd earned under the blazing sun of the Daylands.

"There it is again!" Anders said. He was standing now, his meager rations temporarily forgotten.

Galt closed his eyes and let the gentle movement of the air wash over him. Almost as soon as it started, it was gone.

"We must be headed in the right direction," he said to Solgard. "I imagine that the wind is going to pick up quite a bit the closer we get to Naffabyin and his mountain."

"Hopefully Starkad is right about the, uh, rain and snow," Solgard said, fiddling with her stone-like hardtack. "We need the water."

"If Starkad's right about Naffabyin's power, I suspect we'll have plenty of both," Galt said. A new feeling of dread was blooming within him. The dangers posed by deranged slavers or shades suddenly seemed quaint compared to climbing a mountain in the dark while being assailed by brutal weather wielded by a hateful god.

"I, for one, don't think it can come soon enough," Solgard said around a chewy bite of dried pork.

Galt suspected that she'd be changing her mind about that before too long.

•   •   •

The sleep cycles passed uneventfully. Galt and Solgard took their turns on the watch, wearily gazing into the darkness around them, waiting for any sign of pursuit from Vin-Sadavat. Still, none came. Perhaps, Galt considered, the slavers had been destroyed, vanquished by the thralls who'd risen in revolt. More likely, it'd taken time for the slavers to put down the rebellion and now, with Tariono dead, they'd fallen into infighting over succession. Whatever the cause, they didn't seem to have pursued the interlopers who'd felled their god.

After the designated eight cycles, they stowed the tents, Anders distributed the rations under Mather's supervision, and the company prepared for departure. Lord Fontaine, with Starkad standing at his elbow, addressed the group about what lay ahead and how much further they had to go.

Galt listened with growing distrust. Fontaine had been too eager to lead, too eager to shoulder the burden of command. He tried mightily to disguise it under a mask of casual interaction with the men and reluctant responsibility, but Galt knew that he relished his new role. He wondered what would happen if Phir-Ramarian came to his senses, particularly if the injured prince wished to return to Nordabor.

All in all, his recovery seemed unlikely. He remained silent, and according to Bellamont, the bandages she replaced carried the foul odor of growing corruption. Despite the chill air, a slick sheen of sweat clung to Phir-Ramarian's brow, plastering down the few strands of hair the slavers had missed. Death seemed to be taking him by degrees.

The march continued further north through the sterile valley. As they grew ever closer to the still-unseen mountains, the strange phenomenon of moving air increased. No longer was it a small exhalation; now, it was an undeniable breeze from the north. Though it chilled them further, it carried a refreshing quality very different from the listless air that had hovered around them all their lives. Even the wind on the *Fortune* had seemed fetid in comparison. Galt drank the air in deep gulps and felt it revitalizing him in a way that their pitiful foodstuffs did not.

Another identically bleak encampment was established, and Galt found himself trudging toward the perimeter to relieve Solgard of the watch. She was to come and wake him for his turn, but being unable to sleep, he decided to preemptively start his shift.

He found her on the northern edge of the camp, barely illuminated by a campfire, gazing sleepily into the darkness. The memory of the embrace they'd shared after leaving the wreck of the *Fortune* briefly flashed through his mind. "Hey," he said quietly, hoping not to startle her.

She turned toward him, whatever reverie she'd been lost in fading slowly. "They haven't signaled yet."

"I know. I couldn't sleep. Figured I'd take over early."

A gust of wind, slightly stronger than the now constant breeze, rustled their robes. Solgard resumed looking toward the north for a moment, then turned back to Galt. "Thank you."

"It's no problem. Like I said, I couldn't sleep anyway."

"Not for that," she said shaking her head with a hint of a smile. "For sticking with Fontaine and coming after me and the others.

You could have assumed I was dead and taken off on your own. You didn't. You said we're a chapter still, and you obviously meant it."

Since their reunion, they had initially been consumed by the need to simply survive. Once the march began and Vin-Sadavat receded in the distance, things had returned to a simple, pragmatic relationship between them, the sort of relationship Galt was quite accustomed to maintaining with all of his fellow shepherds. This was the first time that Solgard had addressed her rescue.

Galt had never expected thanks; he'd just done what came naturally. In his mind, deserting her while there was even a chance that she was still alive would have been unconscionable. "You would have done the same for me," he replied.

She nodded. "So, now that we're together, and momentarily safe, why haven't you tried to convince me to leave with you? You must've considered it."

In truth, Galt had. It would not have been too difficult for them to steal enough provisions to get by in the short term, and with both of them being capable warriors, they could fend for themselves in the wastes. Furthermore, his conscience would be clear in knowing that Mather had an anointed blade and was competent enough to defend the remaining company.

"Yes, it's crossed my mind," he admitted. "We could make a go of it. I don't care if we've left two dead gods in our wake; this expedition has lost half its men, and our leader is about to join them. Only greater challenges lie ahead. And I don't trust Fontaine. I think we're just a means to an end for him, no matter how affable he pretends to be. I certainly don't adore Phir-Ramarian, but at least you know where you stand with him."

Solgard nodded again. "So, again, why haven't you suggested that we leave? I know you aren't planning to leave without me."

"Absolutely not," he said without hesitation. Then, with some reluctance, he said, "You're the reason I haven't suggested it. I know the faith you have in this; I assume it's still strong. I may not agree, but we both took the same vows. I'm beholden to support you. Truth be told, I want you to be right."

Solgard watched him with a curious expression that made her look suddenly beautiful. Despite everything that had happened, her faith remained strong, while Galt had slipped easily into cynicism, his faith crumpling at the slightest introduction of doubt. She stood before him unbowed, a well of strength. It was that aspect of her character that made Galt unwilling to consider leaving her or trying to bend her from her devotion to their task.

"Thank you," she said again. "I'm glad I've got you here with me. I do still believe that the Void-God's will is for us to see this through, but I know I couldn't do it without you."

Her sincere belief in the Void-God made Galt feel like an imposter dressed in stolen robes. He was spared having to formulate a proper response by Solgard's face suddenly being lit in a splash of ethereal, bluish light. Her eyes widened intensely, and she clutched his sleeve.

"Leon, look," she said, her voice almost trembling.

He followed her gaze up and gasped. The winds from the north, which must have been stronger higher up, had pushed aside the dense cloud ceiling that had been hovering solidly in place since they'd reentered the Dawnlands. Only now, instead of the relentless glare that had dominated the Daylands, thousands of bright pinpoints of light shone down upon them from a dark tapestry, bathing them in cold, distant light.

"Are those..." he said.

"Stars," she murmured. "Windows into the light of Paradise, punched through the sky by the Father-God for our pleasure. So that people everywhere could enjoy some light in the darkness. He has always loved us, and he continues to do so, even from the Void."

Galt was not so certain that this was a sign of divine love. He'd read about the stars in the scriptures he'd studied during his training at the Ivy Citadel, and, when he'd been a younger man, he'd imagined them to be warm and brilliant, nearly close enough to touch. As the long-cycles had passed, though, he'd forgotten about them entirely.

Now, bathed in their cool whiteness, he was struck by how remote they seemed. He stared up at them, wondering at the yawning distance they appeared to shine from, until the passing clouds began to hide them again. Across the valley, he could see other patches of light piercing the dark cloud cover.

Far away on the horizon, a shadowy bulk rose directly into the clouds. The Einmaz Mountains.

If Naffabyin's mountaintop tempest was moving the clouds this far away, what sort of power could he wield up close?

Galt's nagging doubts were interrupted by Solgard's fingers intertwining with his own. She rested her head on his shoulder, and they gazed into the sky.

CHAPTER 34

For two full-cycles, the winds continued to declutter the sky and the stars shone down upon the travelers. Cyprian was grateful for the light. They were able to save fuel for the lanterns, which, like everything else, had been running out.

Cyprian knew what the pinpoints of light were, or at least their origin. Undoubtedly, they were stars; relics of the Father-God's creation, riveted to the sky for no greater purpose than to demonstrate his mighty powers of creation. The recorded histories of Nordabor and the myths of Starkad's people seemed to be in agreement over this. Apocryphal writings revered by the shepherds claimed that they were the light of Paradise itself.

Cyprian had perused these works in the past, appreciating them for their historical significance, but he'd remained unconvinced. If the war between the gods had proven anything, it was that the Father-God had been jealously protective of his Paradise. Cyprian doubted that he would want to share its light with any unworthy soul or lesser god who would be denied entrance.

Whatever their purpose, they were a sight to behold. Cyprian knew that Faye must have been enraptured, but his wife remained distant, barely speaking to him. Jotun was acting as a sort of intermediary, but all he would say was that Faye wouldn't talk to him about what her problem was. Cyprian suspected that she had, and that Jotun shared her opinion. He, too, had been somewhat distant since they'd left Vin-Sadavat.

Cyprian did not need Faye to tell him why she was upset. It was clear that she disagreed with how he had handled the transition of power and the fact that he had refused to seriously entertain the notion of returning to Nordabor. But he knew that she would eventually come around. She always did.

As for Jotun, he must already agree with Cyprian, but his soft spot for Faye made him paternally defensive of her. It had been that way since Cyprian had first introduced them. Where the old man had been a stern, lecturing father figure to Cyprian, he was loving and tender to Faye.

Two things would incline Faye to see it his way. The first would be when they successfully obtained whatever shards Naffabyin held. Cyprian knew it wouldn't be easy, but no part of what had come before was easy, either. With nearly all of the pieces in hand, nobody could consider giving up.

Secondly, and more immediately, Phir-Ramarian. As soon as he succumbed to his injury, any last discussion of returning to Nordabor for his sake would be finished.

But he wasn't succumbing. By Bellamont's account, he should have perished from the corruption running rampant in his wound, yet he tenaciously held on to his ruined life, slowing their every step.

Cyprian sat on the hard dirt, warming himself by a small fire, staring into the darkened opening of the command tent. Phir-Ramarian stubbornly remained within, undermining his still-fragile grip on authority. In his hands, he turned the shard recovered from Tariono over and over. He'd carefully removed the handle and stowed it separately. It was a relic in its own right. Across the fire, Starkad sat silently, his pipe clenched, unlit, in his teeth. He'd apparently run out of whatever he'd been smoking.

He hoped that Starkad was right about the rain and snow. For now, the sky was clear, and though beautiful, it offered no water. He wasn't sure if they could make it to the Einfallen's northern arm, wherever it cascaded down from the mountains. Soon, they would have no fire either. They'd nearly used up the last of the firewood hewn from the dead woodlands.

They needed to get to the mountains as quickly as possible. There, certainly, they would find water and wood. They might even find some fresh game living on the shores of the Einfallen's headwaters.

It was just a matter of getting there.

•　•　•

Slowly, the rising heights of the Einmaz Mountains loomed larger on the horizon, taking up more and more of their view. The steady wind, always in their faces, had lost some of its charm. Their skin, previously red from sunburn, was now chapped by the constant gusts of cold air.

The company had stopped for yet another repair of the cobbled-together wagon, and Cyprian did his best to disguise his frustration. Though he didn't dare say it, he was certain that they could divide their meager provisions amongst themselves and abandon the burdensome cart. Unfortunately, there would be no control over the rationing, and some of the more shortsighted among them would probably consume the remainder of their food and water in short order.

The real issue, however, was that there would be no way to carry Phir-Ramarian. Cyprian watched him wriggle slightly in the bed of the wagon as Gricks and Kovak strained to lift it high enough for Dupree and Shagalov to reset the wheel. He let a slow sigh out between his teeth.

"Weather's about to turn," Starkad said next to him. He pointed at a roiling wall of black clouds that was slowly gobbling up the stars.

"Do you think it will finally rain?"

"Yes."

Cyprian nodded and walked to where the last repairs were being completed. "Starkad believes that the clouds moving in will bring rain. He's given me an idea of what to expect. I think it would be best if we established camp now and got some rest."

Murmurs of agreement passed through the group, and Cyprian paused to enjoy them.

"Anders, Barrow," he continued, "get the casks opened, and set them up to catch as much rain as possible. Dupree, Shagalov, Vane, try to rig some of the extra canvas to work as a catch, to funnel the water in. Everyone else who isn't on the watch, get the tents established and bed down. We don't need everyone getting soaked by this."

He didn't add that they were to skip making fires. He didn't need to; they'd used up the last of the firewood at the previous encampment. There would be no more fires until they either found more wood or started burning equipment in desperation.

With everyone hustling to get things in order before the rain arrived, Cyprian went to help erect the command tent. Faye and Jotun were already fussing with the bent poles.

"Need help?" Cyprian asked with forced nonchalance.

"Help, my lord? No need; we'll have your tent up in just a moment," Faye said. Jotun frowned apologetically.

"Funny," Cyprian said, failing to find any humor in it. "Faye, if you have an issue—"

"I had an issue. I made that abundantly clear," she said, suddenly unloading. "I said we needed to go back."

She was speaking loudly now, and before Cyprian could urge her to be quiet, lest anyone else hear, she railed on. "Listen, I wanted to do this just as badly as you. I still want to do it. We can still succeed, but we need to do it right. To march ahead blindly, to ignore every sign that we need to back off, is just sheer hubris. This can wait; we can regroup; we can get Phir-Ramarian help. I can't stand him either, but it's our duty to do what we can to save him. I told you all of this before, but you'd rather listen to Starkad, who is *absolutely* only looking out for himself."

Cyprian was surprised by her broadside. He knew, as did Starkad, that if they retreated now, only partially successful, and returned to Nordabor with Phir-Ramarian and half their company dead and the remainder exhausted and disheartened, there would never be another expedition. Phar-Mindorius would be crushed by the loss of his son, and Ganachim would probably perish before the king even had time to process his grief, much less to allow for the organization of another expedition—one that would be severely lacking in provisions, equipment, and men.

If they turned back now, their kingdom was doomed.

These thoughts chased themselves through Cyprian's mind, and he struggled to condense them into an easy answer that would appease, and silence, Faye.

"I'm not just listening to Starkad; I'm doing what's right for our people," Cyprian managed to retort. The answer sounded weak even to him.

"You're doing what you think is right for your fucking *legacy*. You say you don't care about your title, but here you are, doing everything you can to restore glory to your precious name. I'm sorry your father never returned—I'm sorry that he *failed*. Marching into oblivion after him will not fix that."

Cyprian was dumbstruck. Faye had never spoken to him like that, and certainly not about his father. Before he could even begin to formulate a response, she shoved the canvas she was holding into his arms and stalked off.

Cyprian looked at Jotun.

"I'm sorry, Cyprian. We all want to bring this to completion, but I think she's right," he said. "I see so much of your father in you. He had the same determination, the same drive. Unfortunately, I think it led to his demise. I don't want the same thing for you. Think about what we're doing here."

He held Cyprian's gaze for a moment, then started after Faye. "I'm not sure where she's going, but I'll make sure she's out of the rain."

Cyprian watched him go. The wind heaved, and the starlight illuminating Jotun disappeared behind the clouds. Cyprian stood very still, holding the canvas, listening to the wind. He knew he should get the tent up, but he remained there unmoving, thoughts rolling through his mind.

"Let me help you with that before we all get drenched."

Starkad took the canvas from Cyprian's arms and went to work immediately. Cyprian's strange dissociation started to fade, and he joined him. The badlander was driving the last stakes into the dirt when Anders and Barrow arrived, hauling Phir-Ramarian between them. He'd lost weight. Bellamont and Hale followed shortly behind.

"Here, get him inside," Cyprian said, pulling aside the flaps.

"I've got his bedroll," Hale said, scooting by them and entering the tent first. She laid it out and arranged some blankets before the haulers lowered Phir-Ramarian onto the bedding.

"How is he?" Cyprian asked.

"Same as ever," Bellamont said, her already-sharp features now bordering on emaciated. "Lowther insists that he made sustained eye contact with him during his last turn hauling. I'm not so sure; he's still averting, as far as I can tell. He hasn't made a sound, and the corrupted tissue must be very painful. His fever has spiked and broken a few times. To be honest, I can't believe he's still alive."

"It's remarkable," Cyprian agreed.

"Based on his current condition, it's possible we could have gotten him to Nordabor in time to be properly treated," Bellamont added with a small hint of derision.

Cyprian chose to ignore the remark completely. "Is there anything else?"

"I just changed his bandage, as well as his undergarments. I suspect he should be fine for the duration. Let me know if anything changes or if I'm needed."

"Will do, thank you."

The thought that Phir-Ramarian needed to have his undergarments changed like a baby filled Cyprian with pity. The healers had been unable to force the prince to consume anything but some heated water and soft canned goods, and that was even with massaging his throat to help him swallow, so he couldn't be producing that much waste. Still, Cyprian wondered what was happening to the soiled undergarments. None of them had properly cleaned themselves or their clothing since they'd left the Einfallen behind. Cyprian hoped that Bellamont hadn't been wasting their water to clean Phir-Ramarian's makeshift diapers.

"He's all set," Hale said, exiting the tent with Anders and Barrow behind her.

"Thank you." He turned to the haulers. "Did the casks get set up?"

"Yes, my lord. Dupree is finishing securing the catch tarps now," Barrow answered.

"Excellent. Thanks."

Cyprian and Starkad entered the tent and prepared their own bedrolls in silence. It was almost spacious. Faye and Jotun were apparently finding somewhere else to bunk, and Cyprian had exiled the irritating Pike to a different tent one full-cycle after leaving the outskirts of Vin-Sadavat. The scribe had wished to remain by Phir-Ramarian's side, where he'd cried and begged for him to recover. Knowing the discreet relationship the two had shared, Cyprian understood Pike's pain, but still, it was too much.

Now, only he and Starkad remained with the prince. Cyprian could not understand how he had lingered between life and death for so long. If he were healthy enough to continue living, Cyprian thought, he should have been able to communicate, or feed himself, or wipe his own ass. Cyprian had to keep reminding himself that the man had been through a traumatic event, and that the wounds Tariono had inflicted upon him obviously went much deeper than just those that were visible.

The feeling of pity continued as he gazed at Phir-Ramarian's bandaged face. Even if he somehow did survive, what sort of existence awaited him?

Cyprian resolved to put Phir-Ramarian out of his mind. Faye and Jotun, too, for that matter. He pulled his bedding tightly around himself and began to slide toward sleep.

•　　•　　•

The arrival of the rain woke him. He suspected that he hadn't been asleep for long. A check of his chronometer would have confirmed it, but in the blackness of the tent, he couldn't see anything.

Cyprian raised his head groggily and listened to the falling water lash the wavering sides of the tent. As he listened, he became aware of the distinct pattering of droplets falling onto his bedding, and he reached out. Sure enough, a steady stream of drops was coming through a leak in the canvas ceiling. Cyprian pulled his bedding aside and leaned forward to let the drops run into his parched mouth. It was the most refreshing drink he'd ever had. After gulping down as much as he could stomach, he fumbled in the dark for his canteen. A moment later, he was filling it to the brim from the same leak, feeling quite pleased with himself.

As he secured the lid to his canteen, a ragged cough came from the darkness where Phir-Ramarian was lying. Cyprian jumped slightly, spilling some of the precious rainwater. A moment later, he heard a low moan over the pouring rain. Cyprian stared into the darkness with growing horror as the moan became a word.

"Si-rian…"

He knew at once that Phir-Ramarian was trying to say his name, unable to form the consonants properly without his lips. He was considering lying back down and pretending that he hadn't heard when the muffled voice came again.

"Si-rian … hlease …"

As far as he knew, this was Phir-Ramarian's first time speaking since he'd been mutilated. Cyprian shuffled across the floor of the tent and toward his cousin.

"I'm here," he whispered, his voice trembling slightly.

"I can't see yuh."

Before Cyprian could reply, a match was struck and a lantern lit. It was turned low, barely lighting the space. Starkad held it aloft. "He's awake," he said with some wonderment.

Cyprian nodded and turned back to Phir-Ramarian. "I'm here," he repeated.

Phir-Ramarian gestured weakly toward his bandages, which were wrapped tightly over his mouth and pressing against the bottom of his nose. "It's hard to hreathe."

Cyprian looked to Starkad, who frowned slightly. He then reached out and unclasped the small metal pin that secured the bandages against Phir-Ramarian's face. Cyprian lifted them off slowly, grimacing. The smell of decay was immediate. Cyprian turned away, stifling a dry heave. The same frown remained etched on Starkad's face.

Phir-Ramarian's eyes swam from pain and humiliation. His labored breaths passed through the gaping hole of his mouth, pushing forth hot wisps of rotten air. The tissue surrounding the wound was green and milky, the gums black and inflamed. One of his large, white teeth had fallen out at some point; the others hideously contrasted with the putrefaction that surrounded them. The entire effect of his exposed teeth, corrupted flesh, and swollen pink cheeks was that of a fat skull.

"Hlease, don't look at hee," the prince wheezed. "Is 'astion here? Has he seen hee?"

It took Cyprian a moment to realize that he was referring to Pike. "No—not without the bandage. And he's not here. He's staying in a different tent." Cyprian was sure that Pike had, at some point, seen the severity of the wound, but he decided to spare Phir-Ramarian the pain of knowing that his lover had seen him in his ruined state.

Phir-Ramarian closed his eyes and nodded almost imperceptibly. A single tear escaped his right eye and slid down the side of his face. He took a shuddering breath and opened his eyes. "Are we alnost nack to Nordador?"

Cyprian and Starkad exchanged a glance. "No," Cyprian ventured. "We're nearly to the Einmaz Mountains."

Phir-Ramarian blinked several times, as if he was processing this new information only through great effort.

"We got the shard from Tariono when we rescued you. I decided to keep going," Cyprian explained. "We can still succeed."

"No, no," Phir-Ramarian nearly cried. "I don't care adout that. I need helt. Take ne to Nordador. Take ne to ny dather."

Worry began to gnaw at Cyprian. Suddenly, Phir-Ramarian's comatose state had seemed to pass, and he was clearly demanding that they return to Nordabor, to Phar-Mindorius.

But, surely, he was delirious and didn't know what he was saying. Possibly, he'd slip back into being unconscious again. Cyprian attempted a diplomatic approach.

"You're receiving the best possible treatment here," he lied. "Bellamont knows what she's doing. And I know what I'm doing. I've led the company on in your absence, guided by what I believed you would want. You do want to bring this expedition to completion, right? To be the one who delivers your people to Paradise?"

Phir-Ramarian lurched upward, and his terrible face, coated in a sheen of sickly sweat, was further illuminated by the lantern. Drool ran freely down his chin. "*Si-rian, hlease, I need helt.* Look what they did to ne." He fell back, his pleas tapering off into a series of wet coughs.

Somehow, against all odds, Phir-Ramarian had woken up, and was now doing exactly what Cyprian feared. He would have very little ground to stand on if anyone else spoke with the prince and determined that he was cognizant enough to make the call to turn back—especially considering Bellamont, who obviously wished to return, would be the one making that call. Injured or not, Phir-Ramarian could still retain command. His awakening would be the death knell for the expedition. Even if the corruption took him while returning to Nordabor, nobody would follow Cyprian's command to resume the quest.

Outside, the rain and wind continued their discordant symphony. Cyprian stared hard at Phir-Ramarian, who wept and begged for them to turn back. He clutched weakly at Cyprian, who backed away slightly. It was over. Their one true shot was finished. They'd be too weakened and demoralized to ever launch another expedition. There would be nothing left but to slide slowly into extinction. And it wasn't like he could just march out into the wastes alone. The moment Phir-Ramarian ordered them to return, it would be finished. He'd never learn what became of his father, and he'd never open the Gates of Paradise. He would perish in obscurity and failure with the rest of the kingdom.

"We need to talk," Starkad whispered in his ear. He looked toward the badlander, who nodded away from Phir-Ramarian. They rose and stepped to the other side of the tent, leaving the prince to his quiet blubbering.

"This seriously changes things," Starkad said.

"I know that," Cyprian snapped. "If he wants to go back to Nordabor, and I can't convince him otherwise, there's nothing I can do."

"We can't let that happen, Lord Fontaine. You know as well as I do that he's inept—or he was before he was tortured. Now, he's inept *and* unbalanced. The rabble out there might be eager to listen to him again if he offers them an easy way out, but you can't let them. There's too much at stake. They need a leader who will push them to see this through, not give up and turn tail. You are that leader."

Starkad held his gaze in the dimly flickering light. The canvas snapped in the wind.

"You have my support, no matter what. I could tell from the start that if anyone could deliver on this, it was you. I understand if you have to take certain … measures to ensure the salvation of your kingdom. Nordabor is the last hope for humanity, not just for me. And you're the last hope for Nordabor. Do what you need to do."

Cyprian eyed Starkad suspiciously. "What are you suggesting?"

"Only that you're capable of finishing this. Provided that any complication in your way is dealt with." His eyes flicked to Phir-Ramarian.

"You are speaking of murder," Cyprian said in a barely audible whisper. "It's akin to regicide. He is the prince."

"He *was* the prince. And even then, he wasn't much of one. The man he was died in the Opal Tower. That weeping shell is a burden, the chaff of a dead man's soul that stands to do nothing but weigh you down. To snuff out your chance of delivering your people to Paradise. I know you're thinking the same thing. We cannot let this stop us."

Starkad's weathered face, still tan despite the darkness they'd toiled in for so many full-cycles, bore an expression of desperate resolution. The white line of scar tissue running across it held stories Cyprian couldn't begin to guess at. His desire to escape the endless struggle of his own existence was clear. Life in the wastes was no life at all.

And if Cyprian failed, if they returned to Nordabor, it, too, would become a waste, and soon. How long before it fell to madness and cannibalism, before it turned into another Vin-Sadavat?

And once it was gone, there would be nothing. Starkad was right—Nordabor was not just the last hope for the Vingallean people, but for all of humanity.

And it all rested on his shoulders.

He turned toward Phir-Ramarian. His heart thudded dully in his chest as he approached the prince's crumpled form. The rain continued to pound outside, but he no longer heard it. His movements felt sluggish, as if there was a lag between his brain's signal to move and his muscles' response. After what felt simultaneously like a lifetime and the blink of an eye, he was standing over Phir-Ramarian's awful, ruined face, reaching out for the bandage.

"Cousin, hlease," he pleaded. Somehow, he seemed to sense that something had changed. "We can go ack. I need to go ack."

Cyprian pinched the bandage and began to pull it back over Phir-Ramarian's mouth.

"Si-rian, listen to ne," the prince said, the ghost of his former authority seeping into his voice. "I'n ordering you to *take ne ack.*"

The bandage eclipsed the wound, blessedly removing it from Cyprian's sight. He re-clasped the pin, and before he could think about anything further, he seized Phir-Ramarian's pillow from beneath his head, which thudded onto the bedroll beneath.

Cyprian had only a moment to see Phir-Ramarian's eyes go wide before he pressed the pillow over his face. The pressure on his injury made the prince scream, but between the muffling of the bandage and the pillow and the relentless rain, there was no chance that anyone could hear it. He slapped at Cyprian ineffectually before

Starkad seized his arms and pinned them down. He continued to kick feebly, knocking his blankets off.

All the while, Cyprian squeezed his eyes shut and tried to be anywhere else in his mind. He had killed before, and only recently, when fighting through Vin-Sadavat. But this was something wholly different. This, truly, was a point of no return.

He hoped that the end would justify the means. It had to.

"It's done," Starkad said.

Cyprian opened his eyes, hoping that somehow it had all been a dream. It wasn't. A bolt of guilt tore through him violently, and he wished he'd never left Nordabor or that he'd heeded Faye's advice and returned when they'd had the chance. If she ever learned of what he'd just done, she would despise him. Nothing would erase that stain, not even Paradise.

He stood up quickly, his head swimming. He felt like he was going to be sick.

"Get ahold of yourself," Starkad said, grasping Cyprian's shoulders. "We need to back up in case he produces a shade."

Cyprian nodded dumbly and let Starkad guide him away. It occurred to him that his fate was now permanently tied to that of this badlander, his co-conspirator.

They waited in anticipation. To their surprise, nothing happened. Cyprian realized that he would have felt better if a shade had been produced.

Starkad walked back to the body. He pulled the pillow off of its face and placed it back under the head, then pulled the blankets back over the body in a ghoulish mockery of tucking someone in and returned to Cyprian.

"Listen to me. We're going to go back to sleep. Or at least try to. When we get up at the scheduled time, we will discover that Phir-Ramarian passed in his sleep. He finally succumbed to the corruption in his wound after a brave fight. Everyone, even Bellamont, has been anticipating it. No one will question it. We'll count ourselves lucky that he didn't produce a shade. We'll say a few words, particularly about his desire to save the kingdom, and we will have the shepherds dispose of the body. Then we will move on."

Cyprian nodded, a bizarre numb feeling spreading throughout his body.

Starkad snuffed the barely smoldering lantern out, and could be heard crawling back into his own bedding. Cyprian remained standing, frozen in place.

"You did what had to be done," Starkad said quietly from somewhere in the dark. The same dark now occupied by the body of the murdered prince. "You know history. It's populated by many people who had to make the tough decisions, who got their hands dirty for the greater good. I know it was unpleasant, but it was necessary. Time will show that."

Cyprian hoped he was right. He had to be right.

CHAPTER 35

"We didn't always see eye to eye, but on one thing, we were in total agreement. And that was the necessity of seeing this through, of bringing deliverance to our people. I only wish that he could be there with us when we reach the gates."

The vigil was, in many eyes, the inevitable conclusion to what had become of Phir-Ramarian. Faye stood in the dense fog, hauntingly illuminated by several lanterns, wondering if things could have been different. She watched as her husband eulogized a man that she knew he'd never cared for.

Still, he did seem rather shaken. Awakening to find his cousin dead had disturbed him more than Faye would have thought. His eyes were red-rimmed, and dark circles hung from them. His wiry beard growth and ration-induced weight loss added to the hollow look of his face. Faye wondered if he was feeling guilt for not trying to get Phir-Ramarian to Nordabor, where he might have been saved. It was clear that he was pushing through the eulogy with great effort.

"He was a complicated, difficult man. But he was noble, and he had the best intentions. I think our shepherds can attest to how meaningful it is that he passed peacefully."

Galt and Solgard stood over the shrouded body, waiting to do their duty. Phir-Ramarian's blanket had been tied tightly around his body. The shape of the intact skull was clear.

"I know it's mere coincidence," Cyprian said with a sad smile, "but I can't help but feel that this rain was somehow a final gift from him."

The rain had been a tremendous bounty. The catches put together by Dupree and her team had worked flawlessly, nearly filling the two casks, although the damaged one still leaked profusely. Additionally, pools of water had settled on the tops of the tents, creating perfect reservoirs. Faye and Jotun had shared a cramped tent with the haulers, healers, engineers and Pike, and everyone had been able to refill their canteens from the tent's sagging roof.

The sleeping arrangements had certainly raised some eyebrows, and though Faye was furious with Cyprian, she still understood the need for discretion, so she told the others that she couldn't bear to be near the injured prince, and Jotun, ever the loyal friend, had accompanied her. As for Cyprian, he'd insisted on remaining by Phir-Ramarian's side. It was at least partially true. Faye really had wanted to avoid Phir-Ramarian as much as possible. His desecrated state had filled her with unease.

"A final toast to our prince." Cyprian hoisted his canteen and stared at the body, ensconced in its dirty blankets. He took a small sip, and the rest of the company, save Kovak, followed suit. The demoted guardsman simply watched Cyprian, his face unreadable. Cyprian didn't seem to notice. He nodded to the shepherds and turned away.

Despite her anger, Faye still felt a powerful tug of sadness for her husband, who was obviously hurting. His actions had certainly been questionable of late, but he was still the man she loved.

Galt poured a small amount of lantern fuel across the body. There was little to spare. Solgard struck a match and, cupping a hand around it, lowered it to the shroud. The fuel ignited, and she stepped back. For a moment, it looked as if it would fizzle out, but eventually the flames stretched across the blanket and began to gnaw at the body beneath. The dampness of the air made it a slow, smoky affair. The smell and sight were equally unpleasant.

Pike openly wept for his master, and Jotun placed a comforting hand on his shoulder. Faye watched the bundled corpse burn with mixed feelings. She had strongly disliked Phir-Ramarian, even hated him at times, but she'd never wished for his death. Still, now that he was gone, she didn't feel immensely sorrowful, either. She'd wanted to get him help, but more so, she'd felt the turn in their fortunes. His injury had been a clear signifier that they needed to retreat. Not to give up, but simply to regroup.

Now, his death seemed like a guarantee that they'd never return. She wondered if they'd be burning her body before they were finished.

Perhaps there would be nobody left to burn it.

•　　•　　•

It did not take long for the smoldering remains of Phir-Ramarian to become lost in the foggy landscape behind them. For many, a sense of relief was coupled with the general feeling of mourning. His suffering had been a constant reminder of the perils that they faced. Additionally, the prince had been heavy, and there was now that much less weight to pull in the cart.

As they continued north, the fog dissipated, and the clouds overhead cleared yet again. Now the celestial smear across the sky was reflected with equal intensity in the thousands of small pools left on the plain by the deluge. The sight was staggering in its beauty.

Faye wished she could share the moment with Cyprian, but things were still tense between them. He remained as resolute as ever in his determination to continue, and though upset about his cousin's death, clearly felt emboldened by the lack of anything holding them back now. With Starkad at his side, he continued to lead without hesitation. No questions about his legitimacy as their leader remained. At least, none were spoken aloud.

All the while, the Einmaz Mountains grew until they dominated the horizon. Distinct features became clear in the starlight—dotted areas that looked like woodlands, glistening snow, and black crags of rock jutting forth from the upper slopes. Nothing was clearer than the lofty peak of Urgukorge, which loomed highest of all. It was encircled by a slowly turning gyre of clouds, spinning off into storm fronts headed in various directions. There was no doubt that the unfathomable power on display was the tempest of Naffabyin.

Gazing up into the swirling mass of clouds, Faye doubted that any of them would ever reach the top. It just seemed impossible. Yet the march north continued.

•   •   •

"The fires are burning," Mather reported, a hint of a smile actually creasing his face.

"That's wonderful news, thank you."

Cyprian was gazing up at the tremendous flank of Urgukorge through his field glass as Starkad showed him what he believed to be the best route up the face. Faye and Jotun stood nearby. Though the estrangement between them remained, Faye was unwilling to deprive herself of knowing exactly what Cyprian was planning, even if that meant passing up on huddling by a fire.

They'd reached the end of the valley, and the land suddenly sloped upward into harsh, rocky terrain. The wagon had been beaten to pieces and patched back together twice before they'd finally reached the tree line. Settled amongst the feet of the mountains were numerous dried trunks—all that remained of what had surely been a lush evergreen forest before the sun permanently departed. An encampment had been quickly established, and the men had set to work at once on harvesting wood for fires, which would be the first since Phir-Ramarian's shepherding ceremony four full-cycles before.

"If you don't mind, I'm going to head down. My bones need to be warmed," Jotun said.

"Of course," Faye replied. Jotun looked quite worn. There was no horse for him to ride anymore, and he was much too proud to ask for a spot on the wagon—not that anyone would have been willing to take on the extra weight at this point anyway. Everyone was exhausted, hungry, damp, and cold. At least they had water. And, hopefully, the fires would do much to improve their spirits. Heated rations sounded slightly more appealing than cold ones. Jotun gingerly followed Mather back down toward the camp, which was spread across a spit of gravel surrounded by the remnants of trees.

From the outcropping of stone serving as their overlook, Faye could clearly see the licking flames of the bonfires. Her body physically ached for the heat. The temperature had started to drop as soon as they'd entered the foothills, and it was now distinctly uncomfortable. She dreaded the thought of it getting colder. Living in one temperature for her entire life had left her body unequipped for extremes, as she was sure was the case for everyone else, aside from Starkad.

The badlander seemed to be as comfortable in the cold as he'd been in the heat. Faye listened to him explaining their route and found that she increasingly disliked him. She'd always known, academically, that his only motivation was his own well-being, but there had been something fascinating about him. Perhaps it'd been his expansive knowledge of the terrain and of history, colored by his people's legends, or it may have been the way he refused to kowtow to Phir-Ramarian, but whatever it was, the mystique had now completely dissipated. What remained was a clear picture of a mercenary who would only help them so long as it was convenient for him. His self-interest had been made clear when he'd balked at the idea of returning to Nordabor. The fact that Cyprian had become increasingly reliant on him after assuming command did not go unnoticed, either.

Since taking command, Cyprian had changed. Faye questioned if she was, in fact, seeing his true inner workings. Standing before Urgukorge, watching as the obsessive drive to recover the shards consumed her husband, she realized that he'd never really reckoned with any of the old, resentful notions he carried. The failure of his father, being passed over for the title of curator when he'd believed it to be his birthright, the exclusion he'd experienced at the hands of Phar-Mindorius, his perennial desire to achieve something of acclaim—these ghosts had haunted Cyprian for a long time, and now the bitter desires that he'd never conquered, the cravings that had only lain dormant, were being fully unleashed. His will was now bent entirely toward fulfilling his quest, and no amount of reasoning could dissuade him. He'd already proven that the bond the two of them shared held no weight in comparison to the beckoning call of glory.

"Faye?"

It was Cyprian. He'd apparently finished plotting their route with Starkad and realized that she was still standing there with them. She'd been so lost in her ruminations that she hadn't noticed them wrapping up.

"Yes? Are you finished?" she asked.

"Yeah. We're heading down."

"Can you hold up? I'd like to talk," Faye asked, feeling stupid for having to ask for a private moment with him.

He turned to Starkad, who was a few steps ahead of him, and shrugged apologetically. Starkad smiled slightly and continued on.

The small moment between them spoke volumes, and Faye found her irritation growing. The fact that her husband was now casually implying that she was some kind of interruption, a nagging nuisance, made her want to smack him. She tamped her anger down, determined to have a conversation with him that did not end with one of them storming off.

"So, what would you like to discuss?" he asked impatiently. Her pity for his recent suffering and her desire to comfort him were evaporating quickly.

"Something's bothering me," she said. She'd dreaded confronting him about this, but knew it had to be done.

"What's that?" he asked calmly, but Faye noticed the mask of self-assurance slip. Her question had struck a chord, and the haggard, miserable look he'd worn at Phir-Ramarian's shepherding was briefly visible.

"Jotun told me what happened in the dungeon of the Opal Tower," she said. "He told me about how you killed that slaver stuck in the door."

Faye was confused to see an unusual expression flit across Cyprian's face, something akin to relief. "Yes, I killed him. I did what had to be done to rescue the others."

She'd been just outside of the chamber when he'd charged in with Mather. At the time, she'd been terrified that he would be killed. She hadn't considered how she would feel about him doing the killing. When Jotun confided in her that he was concerned about Cyprian, and told her about the ruthless way Cyprian had killed the slaver, Faye had been unable to reconcile the man she knew with killing of any kind. To hear his flippant explanation now was chilling, even if it made sense at face value. Killing the slavers had been necessary, she supposed. But how could he be so casual about it?

"I know that," she said gently, trying to keep things calm. "Jotun said that you just did it ... very naturally."

"Yeah, I suppose so," he said, softening. "I was kind of surprised by that too. I guess that, in the moment, knowing that Jotun and the others could have been ticks from death, and knowing what the slavers had already done, I didn't even think of it as killing another person."

For a moment, she wanted to reach out to him.

"I killed others too, on the rooftop. They weren't trapped; they were trying to kill us. There's no question there. Again, I killed because I had to. For our survival. For the expedition."

The expedition. Cyprian had been willing to kill, not just to save himself or others, but to continue the expedition. On some level, that meant he was doing it to save their kingdom, and ultimately humanity, as that was really the point of the expedition, after all.

But, somehow, to subscribe that sort of grand intention to it seemed disingenuous. Faye could sense the unspoken reasons for his actions, the reasons that she feared now dictated all of his decisions. She resolved to try to appeal to his better judgment one final time.

"Do you think there's any chance that your reach is exceeding your grasp? Please, consider history. The last time that humans tried to force their way into Paradise, it ended in disaster. The entire southern realm, and all the lives there, wiped out. The Father-God killed; the remaining gods fallen. Shades loosed on the world. The Vingallean kingdom devastated, reduced to one hold clinging on to existence while the rest of the world collapsed into ruin. Now look at what's already happened to our company. Think of the lives lost. Is it worth it to keep going now? When the only guarantee is further misery?"

Cyprian listened silently.

"If we succeed here," she continued, "if we defeat Naffabyin, we'll simply be hastening Nordabor's collapse. Without him, the Einfallen will dry up. And suppose we still fail to open the gates. What if the reforged blade doesn't work? What if we encounter Ulesreto before we make it to the Isle of Creation? He's still out there. He was willing to kill his creator for Paradise. What do you think he would do to us? There are so many unknowns. If we return to Nordabor, we might be able to live out the rest of our lives in peace. The Einfallen is still flowing. Ganachim could last longer than we think; it's possible. We can return to our life. It's not too late."

Cyprian said nothing for some time. He stared out toward Urkugorge, lost in his own thoughts. Faye started to think he was refusing to acknowledge her, and was preparing to walk away when he finally spoke.

"You were in this," he said quietly. "We were in it together. We shared the same hope. What happened? I understand that you wanted to return to Nordabor to regroup, but now you're telling me that you want to return and simply give up?"

"'What happened' is that people have died," she said, trying hard to keep her voice even. "And I've realized that there's truly no turning back if we kill Naffabyin. We'll be snuffing out Nordabor's only source of water, and that's if we can even get to him. Climbing that mountain is suicide."

"I think you've just lost your nerve," Cyprian said. "And there is no life to return to. Things are in motion that can't be stopped now. Even if they could, our life in Nordabor is over. That city is doomed.

Ganachim could already be dead—you saw her. This is it, the only option, and I've come too far to go back. I can't go back."

He stared at Faye, and she understood completely that Cyprian would either succeed or he would die, just as his father had—lost in the wastes, chasing a dream. She could either stand by him and share his fate, or she could leave this place without him. She knew that she'd never make it back to Nordabor alone. More so, she still loved Cyprian deeply, and would never really consider leaving his side. For better or worse, their fates were intertwined.

"Fine," she said. "I'm done trying to dissuade you. You've made up your mind, and there's obviously nothing I can do to change it. I hope you're right. That's all I can say—I hope you're right."

"We can do this," Cyprian said. "Together. I need you, Faye. I can't do it without you. I promise you, in the end, you'll see that everything was worth it. Just, please, don't lose faith now."

He held his arms open, a pleading look of love and need in his eyes. She let him envelop her, and she hugged him back woodenly. The embrace felt like a formality. But the issue was settled, she supposed. They would continue, the promise of Paradise leading them on.

As he held her, she wished again that they could return to their old life. She'd carried high hopes for the expedition, but found only doubt and sorrow. She wondered what kind of life awaited them on the other side.

Assuming, of course, that they survived at all.

CHAPTER 36

From the copse of dead trees that surrounded their camp, Solgard gazed intently over the slope of jumbled stone that marked the beginning of the foothills, looking across the great plain they'd finally left behind. She'd been sleepily manning the watch, thinking fondly of the heat of the fires and of the feeling of having warm food in her stomach. Her choice to look out over the plain had been both practical and spiritual; the starlit valley, still glimmering with thousands of puddles reflecting the beauty of the Father-God's lights, was preferable to the vast bulk of Urgukorge, which rose threateningly over them, dwarfing its neighboring peaks.

As for practicality, Solgard had surmised that any threat was more likely to materialize from the plain than the rocky heights beyond their camp.

And now, it appeared that her theory had been correct.

What she'd initially hoped was a trick of the light had coalesced undeniably into moving forms. They marched not with the shiftless wandering of shades, but with the purposeful movements of living men.

Solgard's breath caught in her throat as a miserable certainty stole over her. The slavers were coming.

The terror she'd felt as a captive, the suffocating horror of being trapped within the walls of Vin-Sadavat, came crashing into her mind. She tore her eyes from the advancing force and rushed back toward the interior of the camp. Once she'd reached the center of the clearing, the three sagging tents surrounding her, she stopped, took a deep breath, and prepared herself for the bedlam she was about to unleash. "The slavers are coming!" she shouted. "Wake up! They're coming! From the plain!"

Almost immediately, Mather was scrambling out of the tent he shared with his fellow guardsmen and the shepherds. He looked as if he'd been awake, simply waiting for his turn on the watch. "Where are they? Show me," he said as Lowther and Galt emerged from the tent behind him.

Solgard's eyes met Galt's, and the look they shared said it all. This time, the slavers would not separate them.

Mather turned to his under-captain. "Make sure everyone is armed and ready."

"Yes, Captain," Lowther said. One of his unruly mutton chops was standing straight out, while the other was flattened to his cheek. He looked equal parts frightened and asleep.

Solgard quickly led Mather back toward the spot where she'd observed the slavers. Behind them, she could hear voices rising as the others awakened. "Down there," she said as soon as they'd reached the edge of the slope. Mather immediately pulled out his field glass and aimed it where she'd pointed. His face was a stoic mask as he scanned the plain below.

"Is there any chance that it's just some badlanders?" Solgard asked as a hopeful notion occurred to her. Just as quickly, it was extinguished.

"No, I'm afraid not," Mather said, still focusing through the glass. "They're wearing armor and carrying weapons. I think they're hauling a cart of some kind."

Solgard squinted into the dark and saw a larger shape moving at the center of the loose formation of bodies. Without another word, Mather turned and strode back toward the camp, leaving Solgard jogging slightly to keep up.

As they reached the others, Lord Fontaine and Starkad approached them. "How many are there?" Lord Fontaine asked.

"I counted twenty-six, but that's not to say there aren't more. We need to be wary of a vanguard that might already be encircling the camp."

"Kovak, Anders, and Barrow were ordered to remain on the perimeter," Lowther reported. "They'll hopefully be able to detect anyone coming from the ridge or the passes above us."

The small crowd—all that remained of their company—gravitated toward them, listening intently.

"What's the likelihood that they know we're here?" Lord Fontaine asked.

"I would say high," Mather said. "If they've been trying to track us, then the rain would have helped them. We've left footprints in the mud, and the cart has left tracks. And we weren't exactly shy with the fires." The captain frowned, and Solgard knew that he was privately furious with himself for allowing such complacency.

"Could they be badlanders?" Bellamont asked, echoing Solgard's hopes.

"No," Mather said, eliciting a chorus of groans. "We need to fan out along the ridgeline with the crossbows and prepare to pick them off as they climb up. Lowther, get Kovak back here. Have someone else take his place on the perimeter."

"I'll do it," Pike said. He seemed to shrink as everyone turned to look at him. "I'll take the perimeter spot." Solgard wondered if Pike had volunteered out of bravery or a belief that a perimeter spot would be somehow safer.

Mather said nothing for a moment, and Solgard could almost see the gears turning in his head. "Yes, fine," he said as he turned to Lowther. "Take him to Kovak's spot, brief him on the signal, and get back here."

With a nod, Lowther grabbed Pike by the arm, and the two men trotted toward the western arm of the ridge, slipping into the cover of the petrified trees and vanishing. A few short-cycles later, Lowther returned with Kovak, who wore the perpetual scowl he'd borne ever since Lowther had replaced him as the under-captain.

"The four of us," Mather said the moment they returned, eschewing preamble, "will take up spots on the top of the ridgeline. Lowther and I will hold the center. Kovak, take a spot west of us here. Gricks, take a spot east. You have free rein to fire whenever you can make your shots count. Chances are they know our camp's up here, so I'm not concerned about giving away our position. That being said, once you start firing, move. We don't want them zeroing in on where exactly we're firing from. Understood?"

Lowther, Gricks, and even the normally outspoken Kovak assented without question.

"Galt, Solgard, I want you two to split up and hunker down in the tree line near the slope. Galt, take east of us, and Solgard, west. If any of them make it up the ridge, obviously engage. If any who fall produce shades, I want you to try to drive them back down toward the slavers. I've got a blade as well; I'll do the same if needed." Mather patted the anointed blade hanging from his belt—Moore's blade. Solgard felt a twinge of sadness for the dead high shepherd, but her fear of meeting a similar fate at the hands of the slavers quickly overtook it.

"If any of the slavers break through our line, fall back to the camp immediately." Mather turned to Lord Fontaine. "If we determine that anyone or anything has outflanked us while we're down there, we'll all return at once."

Lord Fontaine nodded, though he seemed to be somewhere else in his thoughts. He blinked several times and turned toward the others. "Everyone be ready. I don't expect they'll be taking prisoners this time. If they reach the camp, each and every one of us will have to fight. We've defeated them before; we struck down Tariono. I have no doubt that we can conquer them again."

His words seemed to bolster the others, though Lady Fontaine bore a sour expression. She turned to Berg and muttered something as Solgard and Galt followed the guardsmen toward the slope.

As they approached the tree line, they crouched low, moving as quietly as they could toward the edge, where Mather risked a quick look over the side. "They've started up," he whispered. "Take your positions. Close ranks on my signal."

Solgard slunk along through the trees toward a spot west of where Mather and Lowther had hidden. She looked back once and saw that Galt, following Gricks in the opposite direction, had already disappeared into the shadows. As she settled behind a broad trunk, Kovak passed her without a word, trudging further along until he, too, was lost in the darkness.

Feeling suddenly isolated, Solgard turned her nervous attention to the forms slowly picking their way up the slope. From her position, she had a clear view of them approaching. Despite the steady wind at her back, she felt certain that she could smell the rank odor of their filthy bodies.

Above them, the stars were suddenly smothered behind a black cloud. Absolute darkness fell across the tumbled rocks of the slope, and the slavers vanished. Solgard, staring into the darkness, strained her ears, listening for the sounds of footsteps or the movement of disturbed stones.

Her thoughts jumped to the Void-God, who she knew was watching from beyond their world. Gripping her blade tightly, she prayed silently, but fervently, for the clouds to clear. Her prayers were answered; the clouds split, splashing milky brilliance across the entire vista.

The hideous, leering face of a slaver rose over the edge directly in front of her.

Solgard whipped out from behind the tree and slammed her blade into the top of the man's head before his scarred face could even show surprise. With a savage kick to the slaver's chest, she yanked her blade free and sent his body tumbling back down the slope. Almost simultaneously, she heard the *thwack* of fired bolts, followed by several screams of pain and rage.

"Forward!" a voice bellowed from below. Solgard could see several slavers now clambering upwards, as well as at least two bodies flopping back down. A second volley of crossbow shots began, each of the guardsmen firing in close succession. More shouts followed.

"*Forward!*" the voice thundered again. The slavers redoubled their efforts and, realizing the nature of the attacks against them, began to hurl stones up the hillside, attempting to strike the unseen defenders.

Solgard was once again behind the cover of the trunk, waiting. Several stones bounced harmlessly into the trees around her. A hatchet soared through the air and clattered against the rocks a short distance away.

Then she heard it. A sharp cracking sound rang across the slope, and Solgard, staying low, rushed to the edge. Halfway down, she could see the form of a shade slithering free from the shattered skullcap of a dead slaver, the corpse deflating sickly as the mass of wet tissue began to solidify. The slavers below the creature immediately fled back down the slope, and those few above scrambled upward, heedless of the bolts. The sounds of two more shades being born echoed through the darkness as the final few slavers approaching the top were shot, sending their bodies toppling down the embankment.

"*Fall back!*" the voice commanded, its frustration apparent. Solgard watched the rapidly descending slavers and saw the source of their orders: a strangely shaped wagon at the bottom of the slope. A few more bolts were fired toward the retreating slavers, but they appeared to be out of range, and the bolts ricocheted off of the rocks and spun away.

Three shades now flopped across the stones below, apparently unsure of what to do. A fourth crack sounded.

At the bottom of the embankment, the regrouped slavers were hastily moving further west. A whistle sounded in the darkness—the signal to regroup.

For now, they'd won.

•　　•　　•

"I estimate that nineteen of them remain."

Mather had just finished briefing Lord Fontaine. As soon as they'd returned to the camp with news of the skirmish, Lord Fontaine had ordered the tents to be stowed and for everyone to prepare for immediate departure. They'd nearly finished their frantic breakdown of the site by the time Mather completed his report. Solgard and Galt remained nearby, watching, in case the shades loosed below managed to reach the top of the ridgeline.

"Thank you, Captain," Lord Fontaine said. "You've bought us some time. Duncan, the passes ahead of us—will we be protected on them?"

"Protected?" Starkad asked.

"Yes. Will they offer us an advantage? Tactically, I mean. If they continue to pursue us?"

"Yes and no," Starkad said. "The passes are steep, narrow, and winding. It could force them into a funnel, but it could also do the same to us. We could even get caught in a bottleneck where we're dealing with attackers from behind and dangerous terrain ahead."

Mather looked across the spit of gravel where the tents had been. "This spot isn't exactly a dream either. We got lucky before. They'll be expecting a similar defense wherever they choose to ascend again, and we're running low on bolts. We should take advantage of the fact that they'll be far west of here when they try again. We should move on from this place and lose them in the mountains."

"Not to mention, those shades could still reach us here," Solgard interjected.

Lord Fontaine nodded, but said nothing to acknowledge her input. "I don't want to keep fleeing from these savages. They've done enough damage to this expedition. Captain, is there any chance we could put them down once and for all?"

"Here?" Mather said, his tone unreadable.

"Yes. We don't need to be looking over our shoulders constantly anymore. It's time to put this behind us for good."

Mather had opened his mouth to answer when a shout rang out. At once, they turned toward the sound. On the edge of the tree line, Pike and Anders were standing with their swords drawn. Between them, a robed figure, his entire face yanked tightly back by a series of metal hooks embedded in his scarred flesh, stood with his hands raised in submission. "I caught this one approaching from the west," Pike said shakily. "He surrendered."

"I heard Pike shouting," Anders explained. "Barrow is still holding the perimeter," he added quickly, as if fearing a reprimand for leaving his post.

"This brutish escort is not necessary," the slaver said, his voice high and lilting. "I wouldn't have harmed anyone. I am merely an emissary, a majordomo to the Master. He wishes to parlay."

CHAPTER 37

"You cannot seriously be entertaining this *thing's* offer. It is a trap, plain and simple."

Faye stood defiantly before Cyprian, her hands planted on her hips. Before the expedition, Cyprian had found her obstinance charming, almost cute. Now, it was simply exhausting, and something he did not have time for.

Here was an opportunity to see them delivered from the constant fear of pursuit. The slavers had tried to take them by surprise and had failed; they now had the upper hand. The sending of an emissary was proof that, whatever they wanted, they knew they couldn't take it by force. It was also strange. Cyprian had imagined that they were interested in nothing but unrestrained slaughter; he couldn't fathom what they would hope to gain through negotiation.

"Yes, I agree," he admitted. "A trap seems likely, but I think it's one born of desperation. If they had the numbers to do it, they would have already surrounded us and attacked. After all, *he* snuck up on us." Cyprian gestured toward the emissary, who was sitting upon the ground nearby, his distorted eyelids closed as if in quiet meditation. Kovak and Gricks stood over him. Pike, relieved of his prisoner, lingered nearby. He still looked shaken by his close encounter with the slaver.

"If he'd wanted to attack us, he could have. No, I think they've got something else in mind. Either way, we don't have another option; Starkad believes the passes ahead might be too treacherous to defend ourselves, and Mather doesn't think we can defend our position here now that they know our strategy. And, quite frankly, we can't afford to sit here and wait to see what they do. We need to keep moving, and we need them gone."

What Cyprian didn't say was that he knew the continued presence of the slavers conjured thoughts of Phir-Ramarian, his brutal disfigurement, and his death. Cyprian wished ardently for the dead prince to vanish from everyone's thoughts as quickly as possible, and a decisive victory against the creatures responsible for so much of their fear and misery would hopefully do just that.

"Desperation could make them more dangerous," Faye said. "This could be some wild gambit that you're about to walk right into. We should all head up into the passes and take our chances there."

"Like I just said, Starkad thinks—"

"I don't care what Starkad thinks."

"My lord," Mather said, as though he were oblivious to the developing argument. At the captain's sudden presence, Faye's rising anger seemed to deflate. She looked at Mather, then back at Cyprian, her lips pressed into a thin line. Whatever else she thought, she seemed to realize the time for argument had passed.

Cyprian was grateful; he did not want the barely reestablished peace with his wife toppled. He was happy to let her vent her frustrations to Jotun, as he knew she would. "Yes, Captain?" he said, still watching Faye.

"We're ready."

Cyprian glanced toward the emissary. He was certain that he was out of earshot, but he lowered his voice anyway. "And everyone is clear on the plan?"

"Yes, my lord."

Cyprian expected treachery from the slavers. He wondered if they would be expecting the same from him. He nodded and cleared his throat. "Alright, let's go."

The plan was elegant in its simplicity. A small group would follow the emissary to the parlay, while Starkad would guide the remainder of the company up onto the first pass, where they would wait. The badlander, who'd already proven his desire to avoid putting himself in any direct danger, had readily agreed.

Cyprian, as the leader of the company, would represent them at the parlay. It was a move that, should things go well, would further cement his position of control. They would remember that he was the one who'd finally put down the slaver threat.

He and Mather had formulated their plan so hastily that there had been little time to consider where the shards would be safest. As he had in Vin-Sadavat, Cyprian decided to hand off the tube containing them to Faye, though he'd found himself increasingly reluctant to do so. Unfortunately, things were moving too quickly to have lengthy discussions—or, as he was certain the case would be with Faye, further arguments.

Cyprian, flanked not by guardsmen, but by Anders and Vane, approached the emissary. "Stand him up."

Kovak and Gricks, doing nothing to hide their revulsion, seized the slaver by the arms and hoisted him up, stepping away quickly. The emissary smoothed his robe fussily, then smiled at Cyprian, his already-stretched features widening further, the scar tissue shining slickly in the starlight. "You've been selected as the representative of your people?"

Cyprian bristled slightly at this. "I'm the leader of my people."

"Oh?" The emissary blinked eagerly at this, and Cyprian regretted his admission. "Well, this will please the Master."

The Master. Cyprian had little doubt that the emissary was referring to Heilrune. Though Cyprian had known he'd survived their clash in the Opal Tower, he'd hoped that the injured slaver had been killed in the chaotic aftermath. Perhaps he had been, and some other heathen had inherited his title. After all, Cyprian knew little of whatever strange hierarchy might exist in Vin-Sadavat.

"I'm ready for you to lead us to him," Cyprian said.

""Us?'"

"Yes. My personal guard will be accompanying me." Cyprian gestured toward Anders and Vane. He had no illusions about the hauler or the engineer providing any meaningful defense, but it was important that the slavers thought they were his sole protection. For what it was worth, both Anders and Vane had volunteered for their impromptu roles. "I would not be foolish enough to go alone."

The emissary nodded in understanding. "Of course, of course. Very prudent." He clasped his dirty hands together. "Shall we?"

"Show us the way."

The emissary nodded again and turned back toward the shadowed boughs where he'd been captured. Cyprian, Anders, and Vane followed, and as they slipped into the trees, Cyprian spared a glance backward. The bulk of the company was already beginning to move toward the pass, with only Galt and Solgard remaining as a rearguard. Mather, Lowther, Kovak, and Gricks would be fanning out into the treeline shortly. It was a division of their forces that favored Cyprian's theory that the slavers were not prepared to encircle and attack them, and certainly not after their recent defeat. Initially, Mather had been extremely reluctant, but after having taken a moment to weigh their options, had agreed.

Now that their plan was in motion, it was easy to see its flaws. Cyprian felt absurdly exposed walking through the darkened wood. The bone-white trunks, with their brittle limbs rattling softly in the wind, could have concealed any number of threats. A petrified branch snapped under Anders's foot, and he jumped.

Cyprian thought of the suggestion the hauler had made only a few short-cycles before—that they should use the amiant armor. Cyprian had considered it, but Dupree and Mather had been quick to dissuade him, explaining that the guardsmen needed to remain nimble and unseen, and the bulky armor would probably be more of a hindrance. As for Cyprian, Anders, or Vane donning the armor, it was designed for protection against heat and the elements more than the weapons of multiple, quickly moving assailants. They might be dragged down and hacked apart while they struggled to move, and should they even survive, they might find the armor they needed to face Naffabyin damaged beyond repair before they could even reach him. Still, being encased within a suit of armor sounded appealing now that he was plunging deeper into the unknown.

At least the fear was temporarily purging him of the hideous thoughts that otherwise relentlessly traipsed through his mind. In that sense, it was a welcome reprieve.

They continued west along the wooded ridgeline, each step taking them closer to the gathered warband of slavers and further from the relative safety of the company. Cyprian's head swiveled as he simultaneously tried to watch for threats, to seek out any sign that Mather and the guardsmen were shadowing them, and to take note of their surroundings in case they had to retreat back to the clearing.

After almost half a cycle, the emissary suddenly veered left and continued toward the edge of the ridge. Cyprian, leery of being led out into the open, stopped amongst the last of the dwindling trees, causing Anders and Vane to halt behind him. The emissary, realizing they'd stopped, turned to face them. "The Master is waiting just beyond this point."

Cyprian edged around the emissary and looked down. Just slightly further west, he spied the slaver camp on the valley floor beyond the foot of the slope. A gossamer veil of clouds had scuttered across the sky, muting the starlight. Only a single fire glowed weakly in the dark, illuminating a circle of hunched forms. At the edge of the light, other shapes were visible sitting slumped amongst the rocks. It was a far cry from the tremendous bonfires and wild revelry of the Opal Tower. "Go. Fetch your master," Cyprian said.

"The Master would prefer if you were our guest."

"Absolutely not. We'll wait here," Cyprian said, trying to count the number of men he could see around the fire. It was impossible to know if any other slavers had infiltrated the woods. He wished that he could take a moment to use his field glass, but he didn't dare divert his attention from the unpredictable emissary.

"Well, considering the reception our ambassadors received the last time we approached you, I think we are at an impasse. Perhaps I could persuade you to come halfway down? I'm sure the Master could speak to you from the bottom if you came a little closer."

The first unexpected wrinkle had developed in their scheme. Cyprian, who wished that he could somehow confer with Mather, repressed the urge to look for the captain. They'd planned on having the advantage of the high ground and the cover of the trees. If he, Anders, and Vane were to venture down the slope, they'd be stranded and exposed on the uneven ground, and the slavers could potentially remain out of range of the crossbows unless Mather and his men revealed themselves and ventured down the slope as well. Yet, if they didn't go, they'd be in the same situation they were in before: left either waiting for another attack or trying to escape one in the mountain passes.

Despite his trepidation, Cyprian knew there was only one path forward. "Fine. Go on," he said, wondering if Mather could hear them.

The emissary bowed slightly and started picking his way down the slope. As Cyprian followed, he glanced back at Anders and Vane. Vane, blinking sweat from his eyes, nodded, and they started moving haltingly. Cyprian hoped they would remain steadfast.

They followed the emissary down the slope until Cyprian reckoned they'd reached the halfway point. The emissary tried to cajole him into continuing on, but sensing that the slaver was simply trying to see how much he could get, Cyprian refused. Accepting this, the emissary continued on toward the camp.

As they waited, the smear of clouds above them passed toward the horizon, clearing the sky. The unfettered starlight allowed Cyprian to see more than the measly fire had illuminated. He watched as the emissary approached the others, who leapt to their feet, and then continued toward the bulk of a wagon.

"Arise!" a voice commanded moments later. Several of the slavers gathered around the wagon and began hauling it toward the foot of the slope.

As it grew closer, Cyprian lifted his field glass and peered at the approaching convoy. The wagon was actually an ornate, though moldering, chariot, undoubtedly a relic pillaged from the private collections of the Vingallean monarchs. It was not difficult to imagine that Phan-Ellara or Phar-Karrian had once stood within, waving at their subjects over the filigreed rail, their entire royal procession pulled by handsome steeds through the sunlit streets of Vin-Sadavat. Now, hulking armorclad bodies heaved the rusted chariot over the broken ground, its tarnished bronzen sides shuddering as it lurched along on its spoked wheels.

Cyprian's eye fell on the shape that now stood crookedly within the chariot, and his breath caught in his throat. The porcelain mask of Tariono stared back at him.

Confusion crashed through his mind for only an instant before he realized that it wasn't the dead god who now bore the mask, but her champion. The broken mask appeared to have been mostly pieced back together and clumsily grafted to the front of Phir-Ramarian's tufted helm, which Heilrune still wore. Cyprian wondered if he could remove it even if he wanted to; the blow that Mather had delivered to his head had left the helmet dented so intensely that it seemed to have been driven permanently into the side of his skull.

As the slavers reached the bottom of the slope and came to a stop, Cyprian stowed his field glass and watched as Heilrune, gripping the rail with his left hand, hoisted himself up further, but remained slumping heavily to his right side. The collector of crowns had changed appreciably since their last meeting. His muscled bulk had withered, and his right arm hung languidly by his side. He seemed to have suffered some sort of apoplexy, and Cyprian wondered how much the hard crossing of the barren plain had exacerbated the lingering effects of his head injury.

"My servant has advised me that you are the leader of your people," Heilrune called up to them. Despite his physical decline, his voice carried the same booming strength as before. "You are the one who assassinated the Empress?"

Cyprian considered how to answer this. Though he had not delivered the killing blow, he was certainly responsible for orchestrating her demise, so he decided to keep things as simple as possible. "Yes, I am," he announced.

Heilrune's mutilated features, hidden behind the splintered face of Tariono, were unknowable. "I had hoped to meet you again. From nowhere, you and your barbaric followers came. You murdered our Empress and left her realm in ruin. Her beautiful haven has been lost forever. Those few of us who survived were left hopeless, robbed of our great joy. The weak fled. Only we standing before you remain to carry out the holy mission of bringing to justice those responsible."

"Is that why you pursued us? 'Justice?'" Cyprian asked, his own questionable actions forgotten in the face of Heilrune's warped perspective. Looking at the chieftain's weakened state, he felt suddenly emboldened. "What do you and your butchers know of justice?"

"We are no butchers. We only ever wished to spread knowledge of the Empress, to teach more wayward souls of her benevolence, her purity—that which *you* snuffed out. For that, we pursued you through this unforgiving world. Many innocent souls were lost along the way, their bodies sustaining us, their blood a final gift." Heilrune paused, his sorrowful body language much like his dead god's. "I mourn for them still, just as I mourn for that sweet initiate that you stole from me. We found his desecrated body—the body you so callously wasted. We salvaged what we could, and his meat sustained us. Bless him."

The thought of Heilrune and his men picking Phir-Ramarian's bones clean sent a cold shudder down Cyprian's spine. Still, to see the warlord reduced to a scavenging ghoul brought him a strange sense of satisfaction. He wondered if the loyalty of Heilrune's followers had been dampened at all by the the fall of their city, their arduous trek, and their recent defeat, but the fact that Heilrune still ruled, despite his failings, physical and otherwise, seemed a testament to the fanaticism of the slavers.

"Well, now you've found us, and your attack has failed," Cyprian said, choosing not to acknowledge that Phir-Ramarian's body had been cannibalized. "What could you possibly wish to gain from this meeting?"

"Only you. I understand that your misguided people acted upon your orders. I am willing to extend them forgiveness. Mercy. If you agree to turn yourself over to me, the rest of your people can walk away."

Behind him, Cyprian heard either Vane or Anders move slightly, and renewed fear blossomed within him. He knew there was still a specter of dissent within the company—those who had wished to return to Nordabor, those who doubted his ability to lead them to Paradise. He dared not appear weak by glancing back at the men, instead reassuring himself that, having volunteered to defend him, they could be trusted. He was grateful that the entire company was not present to hear Heilrune's offer, not that there could be any truth in it. Given the right opportunity, the slaver would certainly spare no one. Still, the weakest and most desperate might have chosen to believe him.

"I do not agree to your terms, nor do I believe them," Cyprian said. "And I doubt that you're really in any position to make such demands."

"Pay for your atrocities and spare your people," Heilrune said, rage creeping into his voice. "This is my final offer."

"Leave us and flee back to your ruined city," Cyprian said, hoping they'd actually storm up the slope and into the range of the crossbows. He did not want them slinking off to regroup.

Heilrune remained completely still, his head tilted to the right. Several of the slavers glanced at him, and the emissary shifted nervously.

Cyprian sensed that, although Heilrune was using the pieces of Tariono's mask to evoke her power, he might not command the same blind obedience that she had. With his patroness gone, perhaps his position was not quite as secure as it had initially seemed.

"Take him!" Heilrune suddenly bellowed.

From the jumbled rocks just below them, six slavers rose from the shadows, shedding dark cloaks as they lunged up toward them.

Cyprian, seeing now why the emissary had wished to lure him further down the slope, ripped his sword from its scabbard and stumbled back into Anders and Vane. "Move!" he ordered, shoving them upward. "Get to the top!" The three men clumsily scrambled up the slope, the slavers just behind them. They were no longer whooping with the pleasures of the hunt, as they had before, and their fell silence spoke of a desperate hunger.

Something thumped heavily against Cyprian's back and he staggered forward, nearly losing his footing. He risked a quick glance backward and saw a slaver stooping to snatch up a stone just as two more of them also hurled stones at him. One thudded harmlessly nearby; the other struck him in the back of his left thigh. He ignored the pain, instead focusing entirely on the tree line above him. A knife sailed past his head and clanged off of a rock, bouncing out of sight.

"*Seize him!*" Heilrune roared from below. "*Bring him to me! I will tear him apart! I will spill his blood for the Empress!*"

Heilrune's shouts were abruptly drowned out by a wet scream. Cyprian whirled around and saw a slaver clutching at his throat, from which the back end of a bolt protruded. Blood coursed from between his fingers, and Cyprian could see the starlight reflected in its crimson darkness. Two more slavers, bolts protruding from their heads, were already tumbling back down the slope, and a third had fallen to his knees, gasping as he tried to pull a bolt free from his belly.

The last two slavers had stopped, and were gaping at their fallen comrades. Almost in unison, they both turned and started to leap back down to safety. Heilrune had grown silent, and this time, Cyprian heard the bolts fire. The last two slavers plunged forward and rolled some distance before they slid to a stop. It would not be long before the shades emerged.

"Advance!" Cyprian shouted, knowing that the guardsmen could hear him. He looked at Anders and Vane, who stood further up the slope, looking shaken. "Let's finish this."

Cyprian trudged back down the slope, feeling untouchable. He passed the slaver who'd been struck in the throat just as the man collapsed. As he reached the kneeling man with the gut shot, he hoisted his sword above his head. The slaver's scarred face turned up toward him, and the subhuman creature raised a hand in a feeble show of surrender.

Cyprian ignored it.

The guardsmen emerged from their cover, and Cyprian led his small force down toward the slaver camp, his gaze fixed on Heilrune. The chieftain remained frozen in place, while his retainers, weapons drawn, looked toward him expectantly. Cyprian could hear their hissing voices rise as he drew closer, passing the halfway point.

"Hold and prepare to fire," Mather ordered. The guardsmen stopped and shouldered their crossbows.

Before they could fire again, the *crack* of a shade's birth echoed across the slope. Almost in response, a mutinous slaver leapt onto the side of the chariot and swung his axe at Heilrune, who caught the slaver's arm in midair with his functioning left hand and savagely head-butted the man, who crumpled immediately. Heilrune, no longer holding the rail, lost his balance and tottered over, spilling over the back of the chariot and landing in the dirt.

All around him, the last of his true believers imploded.

Cyprian watched, transfixed, as the starving slavers, bereft of their god and the holy order she'd created, turned their brutality on each other. They hacked and clubbed at one another until their bloodslick weapons slid from their hands and the entire warband dissolved into a pile of carnage. The emissary shrieked for order and a slaver bit him in the throat and dragged him to the ground. With violent abandon, the remaining slavers began to devour each other alive, slipping and wrestling in their own gore. Heilrune tried to drag himself away, and three slavers descended on him, ripping him apart. The fallen champion cried out incoherently before disappearing into the grisly spectacle.

Cyprian heard another skullcap explode behind him, but still, he did not move. "We need to go," Mather said, touching Cyprian on the arm. Behind them, a third crack could be heard over the chorus of screams and gurgles issuing from the dying mass below. Cyprian looked around at the others and saw his feeling of horror and relief reflected on their faces.

They headed further west along the slope, putting distance between themselves and the growing number of shades. When they reached what seemed like a safe distance, they began to make their way back up toward the dead wood.

Cyprian looked toward the bloody morass one last time. Only shades remained, lurching about amongst the shredded corpses.

The slavers had consumed themselves, and would haunt them no longer.

CHAPTER 38

This time, Cyprian's triumph had been complete. No loss of life had marred his victory; no mutilated survivor remained to taint his success. They had returned with glad tidings that Cyprian felt were unimpeachable. The threat of pursuit by the slavers had wholly evaporated, and, since Phir-Ramarian had passed, no burdensome proof of the horrors they'd inflicted remained. Passed was perhaps a sanitized description, but it was the term that Cyprian was the most comfortable with. Whatever the case, he was eager to lead the expedition on, happily leaving all of that behind.

The company seemed to share this feeling. The meandering monotony of the valley, coupled with the long lack of water and fire, had been disheartening nearly to the point of collapse. He'd felt their morale steadily fraying as the mountains hung on the horizon, seeming to grow no closer as they relentlessly trudged on. But now, things had changed. With the defeat of the slavers, there had been a general uptick in the outlook of the company.

Most of the company, anyway. Despite his recent victory, and his prior attempts to clear the air, Cyprian still sensed tension with Faye. At least she was sleeping in his tent again. It was painful to see what their relationship had devolved into, but he knew that she would eventually understand, and that things would be righted between them. After all, as troubling as his recent actions were to his own conscience, it was impossible to ignore the good that had come of them. They were now very close to capturing another blade shard and being one step closer to fulfilling the grand purpose of their voyage.

So, it was with renewed vigor that the company hiked into the mountain passes, where their cautious optimism only grew. Firewood was once again plentiful, and, though the terrain was difficult, it offered a welcome change of scenery from the dreary nothingness of the valley.

And, of course, there was the water, though it was something of a double-edged sword. As they approached Urgukorge, the dropping temperatures and sudden downpours that left them completely sodden had coalesced into a new, insidious threat. Their canteens were never lacking, but the frigid sheets of rain now came in unpredictable squalls that whipped against them before they could even consider setting up shelter. There was nothing to do but soldier through. If it were not for the regular fires, dying of exposure would have been inevitable.

Starkad was not troubled by the rain. He assured them that, firstly, the rain did not mean that Naffabyin knew they were there, for the breaks in the cloud cover showed each front was only a random offshoot of his swirling tempest. Secondly, it would soon be transitioning into snow, which would be cold enough to not soak them, but rather settle on them, where it could be easily brushed off. The concept of rain had been strange; the concept of snow was completely alien to the company.

Throughout the trek, Starkad continued to be inexhaustible. He didn't seem bothered by Phir-Ramarian's passing in the least, and his indefatigable spirit kept Cyprian focused on the task at hand—reaching a suitable location for their basecamp. From there, the climbing team would launch their bid to reach Naffabyin's monastery below the summit, hoping that he didn't somehow detect their presence before they reached him. It would be an extremely tricky operation.

After two full-cycles of travel, they established an encampment in the eaves of a windswept ridge line that served as the summit of one of Urgukorge's lesser sisters. The full breadth of Urgukorge now leered over them, its storm-crowned summit blotting out the stars beyond.

Gathered around the comfort and light of a fire, Cyprian listened as Starkad, Mather, and Dupree outlined the particulars of the impending climb. Faye and Jotun remained at his side, though they said little.

"Logistically, the biggest problem we're going to face will be getting the amiant armor up there with us," Mather was explaining.

"I assume we can't just wear them up there?" Cyprian asked.

"No, for the same reason we didn't wear them into battle with the slavers—they're far too cumbersome," Mather said. "Even walking along the edge of the crater when we confronted Veathyadell was extremely difficult. For a climb like this, it would be impossible."

"There would have to be a pulley system for anytime the climb became too vertical to simply haul them up," Dupree interjected.

"Is that something you can construct?"

"Not with what we have, no."

Cyprian mulled things over for a moment, trying to figure out a way to proceed. Starkad provided the answer. "We'll be the pulleys."

Everyone looked at him, awaiting an explanation.

"The climbing technique that we're going to be using relies on a rope system. I understand that none of you have any experience climbing mountains; to send you up there alone would be to send you to certain death. So, I will make the dangerous ascents and fasten ropes that you can follow me up on. I have a number of iron spikes that I can drive into the stone to secure the lines. You'll be outfitted in the basic climbing gear fashioned under my direction by Dupree and Rayburn, and that will be enough to get you up the routes I lay out for you. The armor can then be pulled up with the ropes behind us."

The others sat in silence, contemplating how it would work. Cyprian wondered what it would feel like to have his life depend on the security of a fixed rope. He'd know soon enough.

"There is an existing route that, from what I could tell, has not fallen completely into ruin. I believe it was used by worshippers making pilgrimage to the monastery," Starkad continued. "We will follow it as much as we can, but our journey will require some vertical climbing of sheer rock faces. Especially if we wish to maintain the element of surprise."

"That's a necessity," Mather said. "We'll need time to put on the armor. If Naffabyin gets the upper hand from the start, we won't stand a chance. He'll blow us off the mountain before we're within striking distance."

They had already decided that Naffabyin would be treated as hostile. No attempt to initially speak or negotiate with him would occur. The risk was too high, and if Tariono was any indication, he would be unwilling to part with any shards he possessed. The odds of him having a similar reaction to their arrival as Veathyadell were slim.

"You plan on utilizing your crossbow?" Cyprian asked Mather.

"As much as I can, yes. We'll have exactly seven chances, as you know."

One unfortunate byproduct of their recent victory was that their supply of bolts had been nearly wiped out. The few that remained had initially been dispersed amongst the guardsmen, but now, the plan was to take the entire inventory with them. Every bolt would be needed in their bid to conquer Naffabyin.

"Remember," Cyprian cautioned, "we don't wish to kill him outright, only incapacitate. We need to know how many shards he has, and where they are."

"I hope to wound him enough that we can make a quick approach and speak to him," Mather said. "And then finish him, if necessary."

Cyprian nodded, hoping that it would go as cleanly as Mather described.

"Once we've decided on a team," Starkad said, "I'll run them through some basic climbing techniques and make sure we all understand what our roles will be up there."

"Understood," Mather said. "So, you'll be accompanying us all the way to the top, then?"

"Yes," Starkad confirmed.

"I, too, will be ascending," Cyprian added. He'd already discussed it with Starkad, who had no objections.

Faye glared at him, but remained silent. He had not advised her of what he intended, as he'd known exactly what her reaction would be. In another time, she would have been eager to make the ascent with him, to glimpse an unknown world far removed from their own, to explore a forgotten monastery, encounter an old one, and collect a priceless relic. Now, she simply glowered at him, doubting every decision he made. It grew tiresome, and he longed for the moment when Faye would witness his perseverance pay off.

"As you wish, my lord," Mather said. "As for the remainder of my guardsmen, our numbers have dwindled too far. I commit only myself to this. Lowther will remain in command here. Under your direction, of course, Lady Fontaine."

Faye blinked in surprise, realizing that she would be the highest-titled person remaining at basecamp. "Yes, of course."

If they failed to return, she would retain full command, with Under-Captain Lowther as her second. Cyprian had no doubt that if that were the case, she would abandon the quest without hesitation. The thought disturbed him, but there was no alternative. He could not remain in the camp and allow others to do his bidding; he wasn't Phir-Ramarian. He needed to see this through by his own hand.

"Beyond that, I've advised Dupree and Vane that they'll be needed to ensure that the climbing gear can be maintained and that I can be fitted properly into the amiant armor."

Dupree nodded solemnly. She obviously did not relish the fact that she would be part of the climbing team.

"The healers will remain at camp," Mather continued. "With the majority of the company there, Bellamont and Hale will have their hands full dealing with any issues that might arise from the cold or hunger. Should any of us be injured, I know enough to provide emergency ministrations, as, I believe, do you." He directed this at Starkad, who nodded in agreement. "The shepherds will stay behind as well. I have the high shepherd's blade; I'm confident I can handle any shades we encounter. I doubt there will be many that high up. Better to have the two shepherds down here, where there's apt to be more."

Cyprian had no issue with that. As it was, they hadn't encountered a shade beyond those produced by the battle for some time. The wandering shades hadn't seemed to have penetrated this far into the mountainous wilds. Still, the lack of guardsmen and shepherds begged a question. "If none of your men are accompanying us, who else will be wearing the amiant armor?" Cyprian asked.

"Well, you've proven yourself capable in combat, my lord."

"No," Faye interjected. "It's bad enough that you're going with them; you cannot possibly be thinking of putting that on. It's not your job to fight."

"I know," Cyprian said. Her objection irritated him. "But things have changed. If there's nobody else to wear it, I will. Otherwise, we've hauled it all this way for nothing. And, like Captain Mather said, he'll be ambushing Naffabyin from some distance. Putting the armor on will just be a precaution."

He was not excited about donning the cumbersome armor, but, like ascending at all, he saw no choice. If he was going to lead, he had to lead.

Faye looked like she wanted to say more, but Jotun put a restraining hand on her arm and shook his head. The disappointment on his face was clear, and Cyprian found himself irritated by that as well. Like Faye, Jotun would eventually come around.

"As for the last set," Mather said, "Duncan, you're certainly able to handle yourself."

"I'm your guide, not a soldier for the Crown. I can handle myself fine, sure, but this wasn't part of the deal," Starkad objected.

Cyprian grew nervous. Starkad was too important to the expedition for there to be any strife. And he could not risk Starkad being at odds with him. Not when they shared certain knowledge. Still, he needed to rein him in. He couldn't afford to look weak in front of the others, and Starkad had to know that he was beholden to Cyprian.

"We need you, Duncan," Cyprian said. "It's just a precaution; we're not expecting you to take on Naffabyin. But our success depends on all of us working together. All of us."

Starkad thought for a moment. "I understand. I'll do it," he finally answered begrudgingly. He turned to Mather.

"You better make those shots count."

•　　•　　•

The first snow began to fall as they reached the plateau that would serve as their basecamp. Small speckles danced before them, twisting gently through unseen currents of air. Despite their exhaustion, many stood still, watching the falling flakes with wonder.

The trees had thinned out to almost nothing, and the plateau was quite barren. Across its rocky expanse, a rising slope dotted with massive boulders rose toward a sheer rock face that eventually disappeared into shadow. Here and there, broken hunks of ice, fallen pieces from the frozen heights above, were scattered amongst the boulders.

The climbing team was gathered near the foot of the slope, gazing up at the tremendous expanse of rock and ice. Behind them, the remainder of the company busied themselves with setting up the semipermanent camp that they'd be living at until the climbers returned. Fires were already blazing, illuminating the thin curtain of falling snow.

"We're supposed to climb this?" Vane asked doubtfully.

"Not here, no. This is just the most logical place for a camp. Beyond here, there's not enough flat, open land," Starkad explained.

Vane nodded, still peering up at the impossible heights.

"We'll hike slightly east of here, cross the Einfallen's source, and then start our assent along the remains of the old route."

"How long can we expect to utilize that?" Cyprian asked.

"For probably two-thirds of the climb, I would think," Starkad said. "The old route is still dangerous, though, particularly once we pass the Einfallen. It was in shambles when I last took it. It will serve as a fine lesson in climbing before we reach the true challenge."

"How high did you actually go on your previous excursion?" Mather asked.

"To the point where we'll have to leave the route. I didn't feel comfortable climbing any higher. I don't know the limits of Naffabyin's remaining power, and I felt that the longer I lingered on his pathway, the more likely it was that he would sense me there. I was satisfied with my conclusion that he was up there."

Nobody said anything for a while, lost in their own ruminations. Cyprian wondered how devoted Naffabyin's followers must have been to climb all that way just to supplicate themselves at his feet. Even when the route was clear and well established, it certainly must have still been a dangerous trek. His stomach, which had, for the most part, been in a miserable knot since Phir-Ramarian's passing, cinched tighter at the thought of what lay ahead. He tamped his fear down.

When they grew tired of gazing upward, straining their necks and their imaginations, they returned to the inviting light of the camp they'd soon be leaving.

CHAPTER 39

The majority of the men were clearly content to remain at the stability of the basecamp for some time. The respite from the seemingly endless marching and hauling of the burdensome cart was welcome.

For the climbing team, there was no such relief. What little spare time they had for rest was consumed by thoughts of the impending climb, and the majority of their time was spent preparing their limited gear and provisions, practicing the techniques Starkad instructed them on, and familiarizing themselves with the climbing gear. Dupree and Vane, who had helped to design and construct the gear, seemed quite comfortable with it, but Cyprian found it all slightly overwhelming, and was somewhat pleased to see that the typically unflappable Mather was also frustrated.

The gear, which had been based on Starkad's own equipment, consisted of a harness system that wrapped around their torsos and thighs. The harnesses were adorned with metal hooks, designed to open and latch shut by simply pressing a hinged side. According to

Starkad, they would be used by the climbers to fasten on to the ropes. The hope was, if someone lost their grip on a rope, the hook would catch them by locking tight when the weight of their body pulled down on the lock. Cyprian was skeptical. He'd rather not find out if they worked.

Connected to the other metal hooks were two short axes, the blades of which narrowed into sharp points. Starkad explained that the axes would be used by driving them, one after another, into rock or ice in order for them to pull themselves up a sheer face. For their feet, he'd devised leather soles with nails driven through them, which were to be strapped onto their boots. Though the nails made normal walking difficult, they would apparently help them find their footing on any of the vertical stretches of the climb. Again, Cyprian was skeptical, but had no choice but to defer to Starkad's judgment and hope that the work of the engineers was dependable.

After two full-cycles of rest and preparation, the climbing party was set to depart. Cyprian would have preferred a little more practice, but knew that they had no time to spare. As comfortable as basecamp was for the remainder of the company, it would not last. He knew that when the enjoyment of their newfound rest wore off, they would soon feel antsy, cold, and, worst of all, hungry. Cyprian chose not to think about what could happen if and when the food ran out. Instead, he set his focus on finishing their business at the desolate mountain as quickly as possible and moving on. He'd lately grown quite capable of ignoring intrusive thoughts and focusing on the endgame.

There was a gathering of the company, during which Cyprian delivered a short address regarding their purpose, what was at stake, and how their stature as chosen men and women of Vingallean heritage would surely see them through. It was fairly standard fare; Cyprian had already drawn from that well many times, and even to him, the speech seemed perfunctory. Still, as their commander, he knew he had to say something.

For what it was worth, the group seemed to nod along. At the very least, Pike listened with shimmering eyes. Cyprian felt a small shudder of disgust at how much his words mirrored Phir-Ramarian's. Still, the rousing nature of the old platitudes had a useful function. They reinforced who was in charge and reminded the men of a higher purpose that would supplant their own fear and suffering. For a little while.

After the speech, Faye, Jotun, and Lowther saw off the climbing party. There were few words exchanged, but a massive weight passed between the two groups. Faye and Lowther were now in temporary control of the expedition.

Cyprian was only too aware that his command had started in the same manner. He wondered at how quickly Faye might assume the worst and order a return to Nordabor. Unlike the parlay with Heilrune, when things had happened too rapidly for there to be any real transition of power, he now expected to be gone for some time, leaving Faye squarely in control. He'd told her to wait at least ten full-cycles for them to come back—far more than enough time, according to Starkad—and as an extra precaution, this time, he'd decided to retain the collected shards. If Faye had any remaining desire to fulfill their duty, then she would be unwilling to return to Nordabor empty-handed. If she held the proof of their success so far, it would be all too easy to decide that the climbing team wasn't coming back, and the remainder of the company needed to flee to Nordabor. Furthermore, she lacked his level of expertise, and couldn't be trusted to properly handle the relics. Cyprian no longer trusted anyone with the blade shards but himself; they were far too important for unskilled hands.

When Cyprian told Faye his intention to hold on to the blade shards, he'd expected to have to defend his decision. Surprisingly, Faye didn't ask him for any explanation, though he'd had several ready. She'd accepted his decision with a quiet resignation that Cyprian found equal parts refreshing and troubling.

Now, as he left her, perhaps for the last time, she offered little in the way of well-wishes. They hugged, though it lacked conviction.

"Come back to me," she whispered in his ear. There was a multitude of unspoken feelings woven into that simple sentence, and Cyprian felt the fist seizing his insides tighten like a vice. In that moment, he wished more than anything that he could go back with her, back to how things had been. He felt wretched and permanently tarnished.

He could never go back. The only way now was forward.

"I will," he said.

She stepped back, looking suddenly old. The thin line of her mouth showed that his answer had not satisfied her.

Cyprian was still reeling from the emotional gut punch he'd just experienced when Jotun stepped up to him. "Good luck, my boy," he said with a tinge of sadness in his voice. "I trust you're making the right decision here, and I hope to see you soon."

"You will," Cyprian said, unsure of what else to say.

Jotun gazed up toward the hidden heights of Urgukorge's summit and whistled. "This is so far beyond what your father and I accomplished, so far beyond what we could have even imagined. I wonder what he'd think of all this. He was an ambitious man, your father. It didn't always serve him well."

Cyprian easily picked up on the lesson slipped into the words. He found Jotun's barely subtle nudging, despite the good intentions, irritating. He didn't have time for the old man's implications. Jotun didn't know what had happened to his father or what his motivations had been; if he hadn't hurt himself, the lecturing hypocrite would have happily marched into oblivion along with Rorik, as he insisted whenever the subject arose.

"As always, I appreciate your concern, Jotun," Cyprian said evenly, despite his annoyance. "But I am not my father. Take care of Faye for me."

He cast one last look at his wife and smiled wanly. She remained expressionless.

It was not the send-off that he had hoped for. It did not feel like a hero's departure, but rather, it carried a funereal air. Torn between his desire to prove to her that his actions were justified and right and his sudden desire to confess his offense and try to salvage their relationship, he settled on saying nothing.

The climbers departed the camp as they'd arrived, immersed in the slow dance of the falling snow. As they trudged away, Cyprian glanced back, trying to catch one last glimpse of Faye.

She was already gone.

·　　·　　·

The beginning of their journey was indistinguishable from the previous mountain passes they'd traversed, but without the entire company or the cart, they were able to move slightly faster, even with each person bearing a heavy load. Beyond their personal gear, pieces of canvas had been rigged into makeshift sacks to carry the amiant armor. The burdens of the armor, and the tent, had been divided between them, as were the lengths of coiled rope. Still, they were incredibly heavy, and Cyprian wondered how he would be able to climb even simple slopes with so much weight on his back.

He decided without hesitation that when they were finished with Naffabyin, they would leave the amiant armor behind at the monastery. With the old ones it had been forged to deal with behind them, there would be no further use in hauling the heavy gear. Similarly, the climbing gear would be dumped at basecamp upon their return, and they would hike out of the mountains with their remaining provisions on their backs. The ramshackle cart could be left behind too.

Thoughts of what would come after the climb were comforting to Cyprian, but he knew they were only a fleeting fancy. Urgukorge loomed menacingly over them, blotting out any consideration of what could follow.

"We're nearing the headwaters," Starkad advised. "There, we'll meet up with the old route and start our ascent in earnest."

As they grew nearer, they heard a low hum that eventually grew into a steady roar. Starkad assured everyone that it was only the sound of the rushing water. Cyprian hadn't been sure of what to expect from the headwaters, and when they reached them, he found himself awestruck.

Tremendous pillars of water cascaded down the jagged cliff face, roiling through troughs carved over epochs. The dark, churning waters reflected the swathes of starlight cutting through the clouds above in a shimmering, swirling imitation of their brilliance. A heavy mist rose lazily from the depths far below, where the walls of plummeting water were crashing into an unseen pool. Above, the tumbling falls issued forth from a colossal mass of ice that clung to the black rock of the mountain and ascended into the clouds skirting the upper slopes. Like the waters it fed, the ice reflected the stars, making it glow with an internal turquoise light of indescribable beauty.

"Right this way!" Starkad shouted over the din of the falls.

Cyprian had a difficult time focusing on the trail and the placement of his feet with the pounding intensity of the captivating falls so nearby. He noticed that Mather, Dupree, and Vane were also moving slowly, their gazes fixed on the elemental wonder. Only Starkad, who continued to urge them forward, remained unmoved. He'd apparently seen this before, and was no longer impressed, if he'd ever been at all.

They picked their way up the sharply inclining slope that ran parallel to the falls. Cyprian's amazement soon gave way to exhaustion as the slope grew increasingly steep, the surface an unstable scree of loose rocks. He huffed and panted, planting his feet deliberately. Starkad reached the apparent pinnacle of the slope first and turned to watch and await the others. As Cyprian reached him, the badlander extended a hand and helped hoist him to the top.

As the others filed up, Cyprian caught his breath and assessed where they were. It was a thin, relatively flat ridgeline that snaked away to the east, crossing onto the frozen mass that fed the Einfallen's waterfalls, which were now below them.

"We've reached the old pilgrim's route," Starkad explained as he helped Dupree up. "The pathway continues east over the Urguein Glacier and switches back west, gradually rising all the way. It follows that pattern of switchbacks for most of the ascent."

It seemed to Cyprian like a fairly simple route as he followed the path with his eyes. Of course, at such an immense scale, it was hard to really tell. The bulk of ice that Starkad had labeled the Urguein

Glacier appeared to be close enough to touch. The tricks played on the eyes by size and light were disorienting.

The party remained there for a moment, catching their breath. Vane in particular, the last to make it up the slope, seemed to be struggling the most. He was breathing heavily and sitting upon a low boulder. Starkad, who hadn't broken a sweat, watched him with barely disguised impatience.

"Are you going to be okay?" Dupree asked, genuine concern in her voice.

"Yeah," Vane gasped, nodding. "I just need a tick."

Cyprian felt for the man, but shared Starkad's impatience. If Vane was struggling this much already, it seemed doubtful that he'd be able to handle the more difficult sections of the climb. Standing there idly, Cyprian could feel his cooling sweat sapping his body temperature further.

"We need to keep moving," he urged after waiting a polite moment. Vane nodded in agreement and stood up, some of his composure regained. Cyprian was grateful that the immediate route ahead of them was a more gradual climb.

The party continued onward along the narrow ridge. On their left, the black rock of the mountain stretched to infinity. To their right was the open air of a drop-off that made Cyprian's fingertips tingle if he gazed at it too long. If he were to fall, he wondered, how long would it take before he hit something? He decided not to think about it.

As they approached the glacier, the true scope of the ice shelf became clearer. It seemed as if some giant hand had pressed the ice into the mountainside, where it now blotted out the route. The side of the glacier rose sharply before them, creating a cliff all its own.

"So this is all from Naffabyin?" Cyprian asked with wonder.

"Yes," Starkad said. "His tempest seems to deposit tremendous amounts of snow atop the mountain, which compresses into this ice."

"And the ice sort of slides down the mountain until the temperature rises enough for it to melt?"

"Exactly. That's where the Einfallen comes from. My people's legends regarding the mountain say the Einfallen always flowed from here. I imagine that when there were normal weather patterns, there was still a glacier. It was, perhaps, smaller then."

"Makes sense. With sunlight, the ice would have melted sooner."

"That explains why it's now cutting right through our route," Mather added. He didn't seem particularly interested in the history of the glacier, which, to his pragmatic mind, must have been just another obstacle.

Upon reaching the glacial wall, it became clear that they would need to utilize their climbing gear. Dupree and Vane helped Cyprian and Mather put on their equipment, while Starkad, who had quickly donned his own gear, chewed his pipe restlessly. Once they were all ready, Starkad unspooled a length of rope.

"Tie on to one another with this. Dupree, help them with the knots, like I showed you. This way, as you climb, you won't only be secured to the ropes I'm going to lay; you'll be secured to each other. If one of you falls, the others can hopefully catch you. When we're all up there, I'll tie on as well. It's going to be slick."

Cyprian looked down at the unusual nail-soles strapped to his boots and hoped that they would work.

Once the four of them were tied together to Starkad's satisfaction, the badlander dropped his portion of the amiant armor and began his own climb. With a short axe in each hand, he started to scamper expertly up the wall. He drove an axe in, then kicked a nail-studded boot into the ice. Over and over, he continued the pattern until he disappeared over the top of the glacier. A metallic pounding followed shortly after, and then a fat rope uncoiled down the side of the cliff. Starkad's head peeked out over the edge.

"I've secured the rope up here. It's your turn!" he shouted down.

Cyprian unshouldered his bulky, makeshift sack carrying the pieces of armor and dropped it near the end of the rope. The others lowered their burdens nearby, and Dupree set to work tying the sacks on to the rope in short intervals. Cyprian hoped that the sacks would hold. If they failed, they weren't only losing the armor, but the canvas for their tent.

With the armor sacks as secured as they could be, Cyprian approached the wall with apprehension. Mather was tied on behind him, then Dupree, and finally Vane. He would have to start. He attached his locking hook to the rope and gave it some test pulls. It slid up and down easily. He hoped that it would lock tightly if it needed to. He pulled the two axes free from their loops, tested their weight in his hands, and looked up. It was time.

With a *thwack*, he sunk an axe into the ice. He pulled at it, seeing how easily it would come free. It took a significant amount of wiggling before he could wrench it loose. Feeling somewhat more confident, and self-conscious of the others waiting behind him, Cyprian once again drove the axe into the wall, followed shortly after by the other one, then pulled himself up and kicked his feet into the ice. Sure enough, the nail-soles dug in, securing him in place. He was now latched to the side of the wall as securely as if he were standing on flat land. Assuming he didn't lean back enough to lose his purchase.

Slowly, he followed the cracks and gouges left by Starkad up, utilizing the same technique of axe, step, axe, step. Behind him, he could hear the sound of the others beginning their own ascents. As he haltingly crept higher, the world began to narrow until its entire breadth had been reduced to whether or not his next axe swing or step would keep him attached to the wall of ice.

Before he realized it, he had reached the top. Starkad grabbed the back of his cloak and helped pull him up over the last lip of the ice, where he unhooked from the rope.

Cyprian sprawled at the top, breathing hard and feeling exhilarated. The simple focus of mastering oneself enough to take each step higher had momentarily cleared his mind of everything else. While he'd climbed, he'd been free of the haunting vision of Phir-Ramarian's widening eyes, of the scolding words of Faye and Jotun that brought his guilt bubbling to the surface, of the pressure of command and the fear of failure. Sprawled across flat ground once again, the thrill of being alive eclipsed those concerns.

He could only revel in the feeling for a moment, as Mather and Dupree soon arrived at the top, panting. Cyprian got to his feet, stepping gingerly on the ice, and helped to unhook them from the rope.

They stood in a semicircle, slowly catching their breath and awaiting Vane. Starkad, Cyprian observed, was standing with the rope wrapped around his waist and held tightly in his hands. Behind him, the rope was tied around an iron stake driven deep into the ice.

After waiting a few more short-cycles, the relative quiet interrupted only by the hum of the falls far below and the occasional sound of Vane's axe bouncing against the ice, Dupree ventured to the edge and called down to him.

"Do you need help?"

"I, uh … I can't get the axe to stick anymore. I'm too … I'm just too exhausted," Vane wheezed.

"We'll pull you up," Starkad yelled, "but you need to fall in order for the hook to catch you."

"What?" came the bewildered cry from below.

"If you let the hook catch you, we can pull you up just like the equipment," Starkad shouted. "You can try to hold on to the rope, I suppose, if you have the strength."

Vane said nothing for some time. Cyprian and Mather joined Dupree at the edge and looked down cautiously. Vane was fumbling with an axe while holding on to the rope. He abandoned his attempt to resecure the axes, letting them dangle from their hooks at his sides.

"Okay," his tremulous voice finally called. "I'm holding on to the rope. I'm gonna … kick off."

"We'll pull you up; just hold on," Dupree assured him.

Vane was breathing hard, and Cyprian detected obvious notes of panic. He, Mather, and Dupree all grabbed ahold of the rope behind Starkad. A moment later, Cyprian felt the rope go taut with weight.

"Okay, let's start pulling him up," Starkad directed.

They heaved the rope upward three times before Vane let out a choked scream. Dupree ran from her spot, leaving the others to strain against the added weight. She dropped to her hands and knees and scrambled to the edge, where she let out a sharp laugh of relief.

"It caught him," she beamed. "The hook caught him."

She rejoined the others, and they hauled Vane to the top. Dupree left the rope again to pull him over the edge and tend to him, while

Cyprian, Mather, and Starkad finished hauling up the sacks of armor, which, blessedly, did not break.

The stars vanished behind a passing flotilla of clouds. The glacier lost much of its glow, and a frigid wind whipped against them. Standing upon the ice, once again cooling off from his exertion, Cyprian could feel the glacier leaching his body heat away quickly.

"We need to get off of this glacier before we even consider setting up a camp," he said.

Mather and Starkad nodded. Dupree looked from them to Vane, obviously torn between her compassion for her friend and her knowledge that he was becoming a burden. Cyprian started to wonder if Shagalov might have been a better choice to accompany them. Vane, who'd shown bravery and competence when he'd accompanied Cyprian to the parlay, had seemed like the natural choice. Now, seeing the man sputter and gasp, Cyprian began to regret his decision. Based on the look on Mather's face, he seemed to be feeling the same way.

Unfortunately, it was too late to turn back. Beyond losing nearly a full-cycle to backtracking, they would lose even more time training a replacement.

As he had several times before, Cyprian decided that the only way to move was forward.

Eventually, they were able to get Vane moving again, and they all hefted their portions of the amiant armor. Starkad re-coiled the rope, extracted the stake, and bade them to follow him across the glacier. In a slow procession, they followed, making sure the nails strapped to each boot bit into the ice securely before taking the next step.

All the while, the wind buffeted them. Cyprian yearned to reach the end of the glacier and establish a camp in some protected cove. His brief feelings of elation and thrill had evaporated so thoroughly that it was hard to believe they had ever existed.

He chose not to look to his left, where the heights of Urgukorge stood as a stark reminder of how far they still had to go.

CHAPTER 40

"Next."

Galt stepped up to the side of the wagon and Anders handed him a can of stew and a crumbling bit of stale hardtack with an apologetic look. The young hauler had not quite taken to his role as head provisioner, and must have been relieved that Lowther, in Mather's absence, was the one actually enforcing the rationing.

"Next," Lowther called out.

Solgard followed Galt and received the same dismal portion. The two of them headed back to their fire to warm the stew as best as they could. Barrow was already sitting by the fire, eating his ration with a despondent look. Galt wondered if he was remembering the sumptuous meals he'd once cooked for the expedition leaders.

They opened the cans and placed them on a small metal grate at the edge of the fire. While they waited for the heat to work its way through the nearly frozen slop, Galt did his best to eat the biscuit. He found that a large gulp of water with each crumbled morsel helped to make it chewable. Thankfully, water was still abundant.

While he struggled, Solgard nudged him, then directed his gaze with a nod back toward the ration line. Kovak was now receiving his portion. Galt couldn't help but smile. The demoted guardsman clearly bristled at answering to Lowther. Kovak's feelings prior to the change were largely unknown, but he clearly hated Lowther now. For Galt and Solgard, it was a pleasure to see the formerly arrogant and outspoken Kovak humbled.

He received his ration and stalked back toward a different fire, where Gricks waited.

"Does my heart good," Galt said.

Solgard smiled, but feigning piety, said nothing.

Galt's eyes lingered on her for a moment as she nibbled at her hardtack. He had known Solgard, at least in passing, for several long-cycles before the expedition, and he'd never really given her a second thought. By all accounts, she was a capable shepherd, but obviously of no interest to him. Per their vows, any shepherds consorting with one another were immediately expelled from the order, and marriage of any kind was completely forbidden. Of course, Galt, like many shepherds, had found that there were broad loopholes in those vows, as a trip to a brothel certainly didn't constitute a marriage.

Still, as a fellow shepherd, Solgard had never even been a consideration. Now, perhaps because of their shared circumstances, something had definitely changed. It was unspoken between them, and had not advanced beyond private, simple signs of comfort and affection, but it invigorated Galt. Her furtive glances reminded him of the simple time of his bygone youth, before his vows, before the slow death of their realm had become apparent. Certainly before he'd ever dreamed of embarking on something like this.

Their growing connection was the only thing that helped to pass the doldrums at the bleak basecamp. Lord Fontaine and his cohort had left only two full-cycles ago, but idly waiting for their return had already brought time to a near-standstill. The novelty of rest from the constant marching had worn off quickly. Now, they lived in a monotonous cycle of sleeping and watching, punctuated only by the two feedings of rations they received each full-cycle.

But the person who was suffering the most was perhaps Lady Fontaine. Galt often saw her pacing along the edge of the camp, peering up toward the hauntingly lit mountain through her field glass. He supposed she was hoping to catch a glimpse of her husband and the others toiling up the slopes. If she had, she never said so, at least not to him. Galt and Solgard, among others, were now sharing cramped quarters with her in one of the two remaining tents, but even still, they exchanged few words.

A fact that made it all the stranger when Lady Fontaine, followed by Berg, joined them at their fireside. "May we join you?" she asked with absurd politeness.

"Of course," Solgard answered while Galt was still processing what was happening. Lady Fontaine had always been friendly, if slightly aloof, but it still struck him as unusual whenever she initiated any casual contact with them.

She and Berg sat on the ground, the old man having to be helped somewhat. When they got settled, Solgard plucked her and Galt's cans off the grate and offered it to Lady Fontaine.

"Thank you," she said, arranging their cans and sliding the grate toward the flames.

Barrow, who had apparently finished eating, abruptly stood up and walked away without a word. Lady Fontaine watched him go with a look of concern. Like the clouds that blotted out the Father-God's lights above, it passed, and she turned to them with a comforting smile. "How are you holding up?"

Galt and Solgard exchanged a quick look that was equal parts surprised and pleased with their secret.

"Fairly well, I suppose," Solgard answered, blowing on a spoonful of stew. The congealed hunk of food was at best lukewarm, making her gesture wholly unnecessary. "And you?"

"Just marvelous," Berg answered grumpily. "Though I truly wish we could have kept the chairs."

Like much of their equipment, the chairs had been either destroyed during the slavers' attack outside of Vin-Sadavat, or burned after they'd run out of wood during the last leg of their trek through the barren valley. The barrels and crates utilized by the low-ranking members of the expedition were also gone now.

"Other than that," Lady Fontaine said, "we're doing the best we can, considering the circumstances."

The group lapsed into silence. After a moment, Galt could tell that Solgard was going to plunge in.

"I'm sure Lord Fontaine and Captain Mather have things handled up there," she said. "I have faith that they'll return soon, and with good news."

"Thank you," Lady Fontaine said with a smile that didn't reach her eyes. "I'm sure you're right."

Berg nodded, removing the cans from the fire. Part of the metal burned him, and he pulled back his hand with a curse. "Yes, Cyprian is very capable," he added distractedly, nursing his burnt thumb.

Galt sensed an unresolved tension in the way that Lady Fontaine and Berg had responded. Neither of them seemed particularly hopeful about or supportive of Lord Fontaine's venture. He remembered that the lord and lady had spent several sleep-cycles apart around the time that Phir-Ramarian had died, and that several hushed arguments had occurred between them, during which Lady Fontaine had been overheard disagreeing with her husband's decision to continue.

Galt felt a transient pity for her. He wondered if her husband was as phony and manipulative with her as he was with his subordinates. Perhaps she was realizing it now, and it was straining their marriage.

As they ate in renewed silence, Galt tried to pinpoint exactly what had given him such a negative impression of Lord Fontaine. No egregious examples came to mind, but more of a general impression of his overall character. He did things that, by all accounts, seemed good, but he did them in a conspicuous manner so that all would see how good he was. It was an act, in Galt's opinion. Every good deed had the ulterior motive of bolstering his own standing. And now, through happenstance, he had found himself in command.

Galt wondered what Phir-Ramarian would have ordered had he ever awoken. Maybe the prince would have continued their suicidal venture, or, considering his injuries, maybe he would have had them return to Nordabor. Either way, they'd never know now, which was very convenient for Lord Fontaine. Despite his protestations, he clearly enjoyed his position, and was dead set on continuing the expedition.

The shepherds had finished eating, and Galt made the uncharacteristic decision to ask Lady Fontaine her opinion on continuing the expedition, though he suspected he already knew the answer. Before he could, he was interrupted by Lowther trotting up to them. "Everyone's been fed, my lady," he reported. "The remainder's locked up."

"Thank you, Under-Captain," Lady Fontaine said. Once again, Galt thought pleasantly of how that title had belonged to Kovak. "Get some rest."

"Of course, thank you."

Lowther headed for the measly wreck that constituted the command tent—the same tent Galt and Solgard had been shuffled to. Galt was suddenly relieved that his question had been interrupted. To ask her so bluntly now seemed intrusive and inappropriate.

The conclusion of the second meal meant the beginning of the cycles designated for sleep. It also provided the perfect opportunity for Galt to extricate Solgard and himself from the increasingly awkward silence. He mumbled some nicety and stood. Solgard, undoubtedly hoping to revive the conversation with Lady Fontaine, opted to remain by the fire. She had a knack for speaking with others that Galt did not share, an ability that was as admirable as it could be frustrating.

Feeling restless, Galt volunteered to take the first watch. Solgard shot him a wink as he left the fireside.

It warmed him more than the flames had.

· · ·

The crunching of his boots on the loose, brittle rock was the only sound. Around him, the snow had started to fall in a light, powdery haze, blown about by the wind. Visibility had dropped to almost nothing, and the last firelight of the encampment had almost disappeared behind him. Galt made his way toward the light, his footfalls oddly muffled. He passed a large boulder that he recognized, which helped him gain his bearings, and there he stopped, intent on keeping the watch as long as he could still tell where the camp was.

It was a disconcerting feeling. Anything could be approaching through the silent wall of falling snow. His mind started to conjure creeping shades or barbaric slavers intent on exacting vengeance. He knew either scenario was unlikely. The power of the slavers finally seemed to have been broken, and the shades produced by the last of those dying men were the only ones the company had encountered since leaving Vin-Sadavat. It seemed as if every wild shade in the area must have been drawn to the city. Surely there wouldn't be any in the mountains, where no men had ever lived, and only transient pilgrims had ever visited.

Of course, there were always threats from within as well. Lord Fontaine and Starkad had been extremely lucky that Phir-Ramarian hadn't gone shade when he died as they slept nearby. Anything could happen, and Galt fought to avoid complacency as the watch began to feel more and more like a formality.

Weariness finally came over him as he stood in the midst of the silent snow. His feet felt numb inside his worn leather boots, and he pulled his robe tightly around himself, cinching the hood down as best as he could. He let himself lean back against the boulder, but before he could start to close his eyes, he began tonguing his aching tooth, letting the discomfort force him to stay awake. He wasn't sure when the signal would sound to change the guard, but it had to be soon. He felt bad about having to rouse Solgard, but he needed to rest. He knew she wouldn't mind.

As his thoughts turned to the woman who'd increasingly occupied them, he was disturbed to hear a hushed murmuring. He recalled who else would be out with him on the scant patrol. It should have been only Gricks and Barrow; the hauler had been pressed into service assisting with the watch while his younger counterpart had become responsible for the provisions. But as Galt listened intently, willing the words to take form, he detected the unmistakable timbre of a third voice.

Despite not knowing what they were saying, their tones carried a conspiratorial air that Galt did not like. Taking care to move as quietly as possible, he crept slowly around the boulder. As he rounded the base, his eyes fell on three darkened forms huddled together on the other side.

Startled by their closeness, he backed up and waited, holding his breath. They hadn't noticed him. Gathered surreptitiously in this secretive spot, they must have been wholly unaware that Galt was just on the other side of the boulder. Perhaps the snow had muffled him more than he'd thought. Now, having almost reached them, he could just make out what they were saying.

"…it's ridiculous. He's got no idea what he's doing," one voice said. Galt was fairly certain that it was Barrow.

"And we're all just supposed to sit here, freezing our asses off, waiting to starve to death," a second voice said. It sounded like Gricks. "They're probably already dead up there. Only the badlander had any idea what he was doing; even the captain was clueless."

"The captain follows orders like an obedient dog." It was Kovak. "Whatever idiot has the highest title out here could order him to slit his own throat, and he'd do it. I think we should be beyond following titles now."

The others murmured in assent. Galt felt gooseflesh break out across his body. One of these men had obviously organized this meeting for a conversation they didn't feel comfortable having in the open. He would have bet it was Kovak.

"What can we do about it? The captain doesn't listen," Gricks lamented.

"Like you said, they're probably all dead already. We don't need to worry about what the captain would say."

"So should we talk to Lowther?"

"Fuck Lowther," Kovak spat. "I wouldn't trust him to lace up his own boots, much less think for himself. If Mather told him to stay, the loyal pet will stay."

"So what are you suggesting?" Barrow asked cautiously.

"I'm suggesting a change in direction. We'll speak with the esteemed lady reasonably and convince her that staying here is pointless. We barely have enough provisions to get us back to Nordabor. If Fontaine somehow survives—and that's a pretty big if—he's going to want to continue. We'll starve. We need to convince her to leave now."

As much as Galt detested Kovak, he found himself agreeing. Fontaine didn't care what happened to the rank-and-file as long as they helped him achieve his goal. Galt had never thought much of the expedition, and it seemed others were catching on.

Yet Solgard still had hope. She still believed it could be done. Galt knew he couldn't turn his back on his promise to her. Still, if Lady Fontaine were to change her mind…

"What if they're not dead? What if they succeed and come back, and we're gone?" Barrow asked, his voice barely audible. "We'd be guaranteeing that they would die."

"Well, I'd say that'd be a fitting end for Lord Fontaine. A pity for the others, yes, but fitting for him. He forced us all on; he essentially guaranteed that Phir-Ramarian would die. We could have gotten him help in Nordabor, but instead, we kept going. Fontaine knew what would happen. In fact, I wouldn't be surprised if Fontaine nudged him along. It was just him and his badlander shadow in there with the prince, after all."

Galt recoiled at the thought. Could Fontaine's desire to command really have pushed him to murder? He doubted it. As conniving as the lord was, Galt felt that deep down, he was a coward who was unwilling to get his hands dirty. Maybe Starkad, who'd been openly hostile toward the prince, but not Fontaine. Either way, though, the thought was troubling.

Gricks and Barrow seemed disturbed too, but neither argued for Fontaine's innocence.

"I've spoken with a few others who agree with me, but they still have doubts. They want to give Fontaine a few more full-cycles. Personally, I'd rather not, but then, I'd have given the son of a bitch to the slaver chief if I could have—if I'd believed for a moment that the sick fuck would actually keep his word. At any rate, we need more support. Those I've spoken to have assured me that, if it comes to it, they'll back us," Kovak explained. "I know we can convince the lady to do what's right. We can all get out of this alive."

"I hope you're right," Gricks said. Barrow simply nodded.

Their business settled, the three walked off in different directions, leaving Galt alone beside the boulder.

What he'd just heard was nothing short of the first stirrings of a mutiny. He knew he should report it at once to Lady Fontaine. However, they hadn't said anything about using force, and though Galt knew nothing of the offer the slavers had made, he felt that Kovak's talk of turning Fontaine over to them had sounded like hollow blustering. Yes, the secrecy of the meeting, as well as the others Kovak purported to have had, certainly made it suspicious, but he'd still spoken only of convincing Lady Fontaine. Galt wondered if they might succeed; after all, she was unhappy with the actions of her husband. Perhaps not enough that she would abandon him after such a short time, though.

And, of course, there was Solgard to consider. He supposed that she'd follow any order to return to Nordabor, though it may disappoint her.

Unsure of what exactly he wanted the outcome to be, and of what Kovak and the others were truly planning, Galt decided to sit on the information. Exposing them could escalate things dangerously if all they really wished to do was talk. Maybe they would convince Lady Fontaine, and maybe not. Galt still doubted their chances and wished to return, but he also wanted Solgard to be able to see this through.

And what if she was right? What if it was possible?

He decided to leave it up to fate.

Chapter 41

"Line's secure!"

Mather squinted up into the dark, following the echo of Stark-ad's voice. It was impossible to see him. Thick clouds had rolled down upon them, reducing visibility and turning the mountainside as black as pitch.

A moment later, Mather could hear a rope unfurl down the rock face. "I've got it," Fontaine said after groping in the darkness for a moment. "I'm on the line. Ready?"

"My lord," Mather said, "perhaps we should wait for the clouds to break. We could bivouac here."

"No. We haven't made enough progress yet."

Fontaine rebuffed him with no further explanation. None was needed. Mather understood his place, and knew that, beyond urging Fontaine to do something, he could not waste time trying to change his mind. Like it or not, Fontaine was in command.

Despite the suicidal nature of the climb they were about to embark on, it was understandable that Fontaine wanted to prolong the time between camps. It was their third full-cycle on the mountain, and they'd already had two miserable bivouacs on the cliffside, establishing their tent on craggy bits of land barely flat or wide enough to hold it. The wind had savagely snapped at the canvas, threatening to tear it away completely, and fires were impossible; no flicker of flame could survive the wind long enough to grow into a proper blaze. As such, their canned rations had been almost frozen, warmed by nothing but their body heat until they were at least edible.

In the brutal conditions, the best watch they could establish was one person standing just outside of the tent's vestibule. Remaining static in the frigid, whipping air, each sentry could only last a cycle out there before needing relief. The result was poor, patchwork sleep for everyone. Not that sleep came easily, anyway. Despite their exhaustion, the strange, thin mountain air made sleep difficult. Mather had started awake several times feeling as if he were suffocating.

The thin air also sapped their strength further. They'd now made countless short ascents that required Starkad's method, and it should have been growing easier. Instead, each one was a morale-crushing slog that made Mather feel like his lungs were being torn asunder. He had no idea how Vane had managed any of it.

Tapping him for the climb had been a miscalculation. The engineer had been faltering since the climb began, and he was growing increasingly disoriented. Though he could go through the motions, he did so with a groggy, sleepwalking quality that made Mather leery to trust him on the ropes.

Unfortunately, there was no other choice. Fontaine would never permit them to turn back, which would be an unnecessary waste of time and supplies, and they couldn't leave Vane behind. In his state, he'd be liable to walk off the mountain while trying to take a piss.

"Come on, Barton. There you go," Dupree said, coaxing Vane into hooking onto the line. Mather had climbed up behind Fontaine, and watched over his shoulder with dread as Dupree started up. Vane stood below her, swaying drunkenly in the buffeting wind. He was beginning to feel that each climb would be Vane's last. So far, he'd been proven wrong, but he didn't know how much longer Vane could continue.

He turned his attention toward focusing on the climb. He drove an axe into the rock and gave a test pull. It slid out easily. The rock was much more difficult to secure the axes into than the ice was, and Mather had resorted to feeling around for handholds on several occasions. It was all the more difficult in the dark. He bitterly wished that a lantern could be lit, but the unrelenting wind was as prohibitive of lighting lanterns as it was campfires.

Already, Fontaine had vanished into the murk. Over the sound of the wind, Mather could just make out the steady thunk of his axes carrying him upward. He hoped that Fontaine was being as cautious with the axes as he was. Mather gave his another mighty swing, and this time, it seated in tightly. The second followed suit, and after a few kicks, he was slightly higher.

It was a tedious and taxing process, and in his exhausted state, Mather had to remind himself of the danger. His own thinking had been dulled by the thin air, and the risk of sloppy errors had grown.

The wind shoved against his back, pressing him against the rock. As it relented, Mather was suddenly seized around the middle. He shouted out in confusion, his first thought being, nonsensically, that someone was attacking him.

His axes snapped free, and he peeled off of the wall, the hook catching him with a violent jerk. He swung back toward the wall and bounced off, kicking and swinging his hands in an attempt to find his bearings. Finally, he steadied himself and tried to regain purchase on the wall, his axes clanging against his harness.

He'd been pulled from the wall by the rope tying him to the others. Someone had fallen.

"What's happened?" he shouted, fumbling to grab one of the axes while also holding the rope and scraping his nail-soles against the rock.

"Is everyone okay?" Fontaine shouted from above.

From below, Dupree called out in a strained voice. "I fell ... the hook caught me ... I'm trying to—"

Before she could finish, Mather was jerked away from the cliff face by a second, more powerful pull. Almost immediately, he realized that the hook hadn't caught him; he was in a free fall. He flailed wildly in the open air, seeking any grip.

Abruptly, he slammed to a stop, gasping as the sudden force of the arrest and the cinching of the rope around his waist knocked the breath out of him. Dazedly, he hung face down, staring into the abyss from which he'd been temporarily spared.

He twisted around, trying to understand where he was and what had happened. "Dupree," he wheezed, "are you there?"

A cough came from below. "Yes," she croaked.

Mather needed to get back on the wall, but fear left him frozen. If he started to swing, his momentum might trigger another fall. He had no idea what was still holding him aloft.

"Get back on the wall!" a voice gasped from above him. It was Vane.

"We've got you!" Fontaine called.

Mather started to swing back and forth until he felt his gloved fingertips graze the rock. Grasping his axes, he waited until his momentum brought him back toward the cliff. Mustering as much strength as he could, he drove the axes into the rock. Within moments, he was reattached to the mountain, though Dupree's weight on the rope threatened to pull him off again.

Presently, Dupree called out that she had made it back on as well, and Mather felt the rope slacken. He pressed his cheek against the cold rock and panted with relief.

Around him, the indifferent wind blew on.

•   •   •

Starkad lowered a second rope, but none of the climbers found themselves able to trust it. With shaking hands, Dupree tied the remnant of the old rope still attached to her hook to the new one so they could haul up the amiant armor waiting below.

Once they were settled at the top, they tried to figure out what had happened. Without seeing what had occurred, they deduced that after Dupree had fallen and been caught by her hook, the secured line had frayed and broken from the pressure of the sudden weight, combined with the harsh conditions. The force of her falling again had pulled Mather and Fontaine from the wall. Fontaine had managed to self-arrest, and he and Vane had been able to hold the other two up via the rope tying them all together.

Mather was thunderstruck. Fontaine had come through when he was truly needed, and had not only saved himself, but Mather and Dupree as well. He could not have done it alone, though, and the lifesaving strength of Vane, whom Mather had written off as being dead weight, was nothing short of incredible.

Grateful to be alive, Mather had gained a newfound respect for both men. Dupree, who'd hugged both of them upon reaching the top of the cliff, appeared equally grateful.

Vane, embarrassed by the praise, brushed it off. Fontaine seemed to enjoy it slightly more, but remained focused on continuing. To the relief of them all, the stretch ahead of them turned out to be a more gradual slope of tumbled ice and loose gravel that offered some respite from the wind.

"I expect that we've got one more climb like that before we reach the top," Starkad told them as they trudged along the scant path. "We'll be leaving the last remnant of the pilgrimage route. It will be the longest and probably the most arduous climb yet, just so you're aware."

It was not what any of them wished to hear.

With the slight abatement of the wind, Mather was finally able to light a lantern. The faces that swam out of the darkness startled him and made him wonder what he must look like.

Fontaine's face was ghoulishly thin, his sparse stubble thickening into a patchwork beard shot through with gray. Starkad's deep tan had finally started to fade, leaving behind a pale mask of deep wrinkles. The cold air had turned his puckered scar tissue purple. Dupree's face was white except for her cheeks, which were chapped bright red from the ceaseless wind. But Vane looked the worst by far. His skin had a sickly sheen on top of a corpse-like pallor and his eyes were swimming, unfocused, and half-lidded. Mather had no idea how the man was still standing, much less how he could have held them on the rope.

Guided by the lantern's light, they plodded on. It began to snow again.

·   ·   ·

By the time they reached the next, and hopefully last, vertical section of the climb, the snowfall had increased into a whiteout. With the lantern's limited light, they only knew they'd reached the sheer cliff when they almost walked directly into it.

Fontaine announced that they would rest there before they made the final ascent, and they set to work on the tent at once. The wind may have died down, but the blizzard conditions still made a campfire impossible. As such, they wasted no time crowding into the tent, where their combined body heat made the air temperature bearable.

They struggled through another cold meal, made all the more difficult to choke down by their waning appetites as the thin air not only robbed them of their strength and sleep, but their desire for food. Mather knew that he was beginning to suffer from malnourishment, but the simple act of swallowing even a small morsel made him want to retch.

The smell alone of the canned meats was enough to drive Mather from the tent, prompting him to volunteer for the first watch. As the others finished eating and settled in, he braced himself for the cold and stepped outside.

The snow was still falling heavily, blanketing the ground around them and coating the canvas of the tent, which glowed dimly from the lantern within. The wind had died down, leaving only an eerie, silent stillness. He couldn't see anything, effectively rendering a watch pointless.

Still, Mather was a man of duty and habit. He remained just beyond the vestibule, occasionally brushing the accumulating snow off himself. In his exhaustion, his mind settled into a static blankness that mirrored the world outside.

After nearly a cycle, his mental torpor was interrupted by Fontaine. "You need relief?" he asked, sticking his head out of the tent's entrance.

"No, my lord. I'm actually enjoying the silence."

"I can't sleep," Fontaine sighed, either oblivious to Mather's desire to be alone or actively choosing to ignore it. "I'll join you for a bit."

If Fontaine hadn't recently played such an integral role in saving his life, Mather may have told him more bluntly that he wished to be left alone. Instead, he decided to let Fontaine speak at him while his thoughts slid back toward nothingness.

"We're almost there," Fontaine said optimistically. After a pause, he continued. "I wanted to thank you for your support. I know that things were a bit tense at the start, but since I assumed command, I've been able to rely on you completely. I appreciate it."

"I'm just doing my duty; what I'm sworn to do," Mather answered, his sluggish mind reawakening at the thought of where his loyalty to the Crown had led him.

He looked at Fontaine as if considering him for the first time. This man, whom he'd originally taken for an inexperienced intellectual who only fancied himself an explorer like his formerly renowned father had been, had proven himself to be a real leader worthy of his royal title. He knew that Phir-Ramarian would never have followed through with his intention to climb with them, and he certainly wouldn't have had the fortitude to hold the line.

"It bothers me tremendously that I couldn't save Phir-Ramarian," Mather continued, "but we both know he was out of his depth. I had my doubts, I'll admit, but you do seem to be leading us well."

Fontaine smiled sadly. "Thank you."

"And I want to thank you properly for saving my life," Mather added.

"You would have done the same for me, I'm sure," Fontaine said, the same strained smile creasing his features. His earlier enjoyment of the praise seemed to have withered.

Since their encounter with Veathyadell, Mather had harbored serious doubts about their chances of success. The power still simmering within that old one had been unlike anything he'd ever experienced. Even their later defeat of Tariono, who had supposedly been weaker, had come at a terrible cost. He still doubted that they could best Naffabyin, no matter how clever their strategy.

Nonetheless, he had kept going because he'd been ordered to. Fontaine had indeed proven capable, yes, but he'd also proven to be unrelenting and inflexible. Mather knew that if they succeeded on the mountain, Fontaine would order them to go on, no matter what state they were in.

He wondered at what point he would say no, or if such a point even existed.

His entire life had been spent in blind service to the Crown. His family line had served as royal guardsmen for generations. He'd revered his father and grandsire and followed them into the service without ever questioning if there was any other option, and over his many long-cycles of duty, Mather had proven himself as reliable and devoted to the monarchs of the kingdom as anyone could be. Lines of succession were clear, unalterable, and sacred. Royal title meant everything, and sustaining the peace of the realm in the name of the sovereign was a holy mission.

He had exercised draconian enforcement measures on any voices of dissent that rose from the slums without a second thought. He'd overseen executions of supposed criminals, tried and convicted in royal courts run by decadent, morally bankrupt sycophants, all doing their best to suckle at the teat of power. Mather had never questioned orders or the authority of those who gave them. Now, as he reflected on his near-death, and the certain mortal peril that lay ahead, he wondered if he could ever refuse.

It occurred to him that Fontaine might have been as compelled by familial tradition as he'd been. The trappings of his title may have forced him into following in his father's footsteps. Fontaine seemed to have a real passion for the historical significance of their journey, but all the while, he was operating in the shadow of his father.

Mather wondered how much Rorik's failure influenced his son's decisions. The lives of many were balanced against the legacy of the past.

From the start, inherited roles had been behind every facet of the expedition. Phir-Ramarian had been chosen by his father to lead simply because he was the prince. Phar-Mindorius had been so entrenched in the old ways that he'd never even considered that his son might be unfit for the position.

But the solid city walls of Nordabor, and all of the little dramas within, seemed very remote now. The more Mather considered it, the more foolish the entire system seemed. Sovereignty and titles were inherited from a distant past with no thought beyond the acknowledgment that it had always been so. Their society, limping along for ages on the back of an enslaved god, was as stagnant as the outside world they'd insulated themselves from.

Despite this newfound understanding, or maybe because of it, Mather knew that he would continue on. The old ways had to survive a bit longer; they had to serve their purpose. Ugly or not, sustaining them was the last hope for humanity. Perhaps whatever rose from the ashes after they entered Paradise would forgo the trappings of the past and establish a new, better order. It seemed unlikely, but anything was possible.

The two men had lapsed into a thoughtful silence when a startling crack sounded from within the tent. They looked at each other, eyes wide, then looked back into the tent as an otherworldly scream rolled out toward them, accompanied by the sounds of panicked shouting and scrambling.

Mather reflexively drew his blade and pulled the tent flaps aside. Dupree clawed past him, followed by Starkad, who had his sword drawn and was backing away from the convulsing form of Vane.

Mather sheathed his normal sword and drew the anointed blade he'd been entrusted with. He'd dispatched shades before, but never from one of his companions. Watching Vane's body shake and contort, Mather was horrified. The man whom he'd just spoken with a short time ago, the man who'd saved his life, was now a mindless terror, eyes bulging, tongue flapping uselessly, shrieking out piercing, guttural screams.

Slowly, the torn scalp flesh folded down over Vane's agonized face, and all at once, the black mass of the shade spilled forth from the shattered skullcap, filling the small space with its foul, oily bulk.

Mather knew he had to strike. It took everything he had to force himself to confront the monster as it rose up and took shape, leaving Vane's body behind like a deflated, shed skin.

He lunged forward and swung broadly. Unexpectedly, the shade writhed out of the way and slammed him in the back with one of its malleable, partly formed arms, and he crashed onto the floor of the tent, gasping at the thin air. Fear propelled him, and he rolled over quickly, bringing the sword to bear just in time to cut deeply into the shade's arm as it swung at him again. It howled viciously and reared back, giving Mather time to scramble to his feet and plunge the blade into its chest. It emitted a piercing wail and staggered backward, the wound hissing loudly. Mather hacked at it several times, cutting into the head-like protrusion that had begun to form from the torso. The shade began to flail wildly, kicking the lantern over and tearing at the canvas walls of the tent. Finally, it succumbed to its injuries and began to dissolve sickeningly onto the floor, soaking the tarpaulin with its foul ichor.

Fontaine, Starkad, and Dupree crowded back into the tent. Mather took little notice as he gasped for air and stared at the desecrated remains of Vane.

"What happened?" Fontaine asked.

"I was half-asleep and I heard Vane start to cough, like he was choking on something," Dupree said, a frantic note in her voice. "He stopped and sighed, so I assumed he was fine. Then he started trembling some, and then …."

She trailed off, following Mather's gaze. "Oh, no. No, no," she muttered, sliding down onto the floor.

Mather shared her feelings. Vane had been physically struggling during the entire climb, and then he'd given everything he had to save them on the rope. He must have had some sort of catastrophic heart failure in his sleep.

"We need to cut away any of the canvas that was exposed to the shade's fluids. We can't risk catching anything it might have carried," Starkad said, offering nothing in the way of condolences. Mather wasn't surprised; he imagined brutal death was common among the badlanders, and in fact, it had grown disturbingly common on the expedition, too.

Fontaine helped Dupree outside as Mather and Starkad set to work. They cut a ragged, gaping hole on the side and floor of the tent, then dragged away the soiled canvas, wrapping the remains of Vane up within the sopping shreds. When it was a safe distance away, they returned to the battered tent and did their best to wash themselves off in the snow.

"Can he be burned?" Dupree asked, not sounding hopeful.

"I don't think so," Mather said sadly. "It's snowing too hard. Everything's too wet."

Dupree nodded and took a deep, rattling breath. "I need to seal up that hole." She dug through her gear and found some basic mending supplies. Mather could tell that it was a simple coping mechanism, but saw no better way for her to process her grief at the moment.

The result was an ugly, pinched mess that barely held the tent together. The space inside was reduced, but, of course, there was one fewer of them now. It would do.

Though the tent was now passably fixed, no one felt like trying to rest anymore. Certainly not with the black stains of the shade's bile cast across the snow and the knowledge that Vane's ruined corpse remained nearby. Although the snow was still falling thickly, the lantern and the stillness of the air made climbing possible. Without much discussion, they agreed to embark.

They stowed the gear and enfolded the amiant armor in their makeshift sacks, and Starkad ascended ahead of the others. While they waited, Vane's absence hung in the air between them. From a strictly practical viewpoint, it meant they now had one fewer person to haul the cumbersome armor.

Mather looked back toward Vane's body and was pleased to see that the snow had already covered much of it. Despite destroying the shade, Mather was not a proper shepherd, and didn't know any of their sacred rites. All the same, he whispered a short, ineloquent prayer to whatever was listening.

CHAPTER 42

Two more full-cycles had passed since Galt discovered the plotting of Kovak and the others, and since then, he'd heard no other rumblings of sedition. It was possible, he admitted to himself, that what he'd overheard had been idle chatter; that Kovak didn't actually have the constitution to confront Lady Fontaine. Though part of him hoped that was the case, he still felt as though many of the remaining company were behaving furtively. Perhaps it was his imagination.

He struggled the most with not telling Solgard, but he knew she would go straight to Lady Fontaine and Lowther. All of his reasons for keeping the information to himself remained valid in his mind, but as time crept on, he grew more antsy. There was something vaguely hostile in the air.

"What's on your mind?" Solgard asked, interrupting Galt's gnawing thoughts.

"Nothing," he lied. "Just letting my mind wander."

Solgard eyed him for a moment. "Okay. It looked like it was wandering to some dark places." She looked up toward the summit of Urgukorge, which was enveloped in an impenetrable blanket of clouds that were illuminated by the open sky around them. "They must be close by now. If they succeed, I imagine we'll know. The weather will stop."

That was an unsettling thought. Their success meant the end of the Einfallen, and certainly the end of life in Nordabor. If they bested the old one up there, but failed to reach Paradise, they'd be directly responsible for their own extinction.

Galt realized that a small part of him was hoping that they'd already failed and that Kovak would convince Lady Fontaine to return to Nordabor. The city might survive for the remainder of his lifetime.

Galt knew that line of thought was doing a great disservice to Solgard, who believed wholeheartedly that they could bring deliverance to their people. Not to mention everyone who'd sacrificed their lives to bring them there. He thought of Daeg and Blackburn and Moore. To walk away now would be to strip away any meaning from their deaths. His waxing and waning doubts and hopes spun in a frustrating circle as constant as the tempest above them.

They were slowly walking the perimeter of the camp, not to serve as a watch, but to find some privacy. It was the middle of the waking cycles, and most of the company were huddled about the fires near the center of camp. Their blossoming intimacy was still a secret, though they hadn't discussed keeping it that way on purpose. It seemed like something fragile and precious that existed just between them, and to speak of it or to let others witness it would perhaps tarnish it.

As they neared the boulder where Galt had witnessed the clandestine meeting, Solgard suddenly seized him by the arm and pulled him behind the rock, then pressed her body against his and kissed him deeply. His mind reeled momentarily, as if doubting the reality of what was happening, but then he kissed her back. When she finally pulled away, her eyes were downcast, and there was a small smile on her lips. Galt found himself transfixed.

"Leon," she whispered, "that was a direct violation of our vows. Don't do that again." Her smirk broke into a grin.

Galt's heart was pounding hard, and he found himself unable to order his thoughts. His desire for her had reached its pinnacle; he longed to seize her by the waist and pull her into an embrace. At the same time, he felt an overwhelming urgency to confess to her what he'd overheard in the very spot they now occupied.

He decided that he had to tell her. She was the only thing left on the expedition that he truly cared about. She needed to know.

"I have to tell you something."

"What is it?" she said, a playful note still in her voice.

Galt was furious with himself for having to extinguish her banter with the grim reality, but he forced himself to continue.

"Two full-cycles ago, I overheard Kovak, Gricks, and Barrow discussing how they were going to confront Lady Fontaine about returning to Nordabor. It sounded like they might not take no for an answer."

Solgard's face dropped into a mixture of alarm and anger. "Why didn't you tell me this sooner? Why haven't you told Lady Fontaine?"

"Because I wasn't certain that they were truly serious," Galt explained, eager to resolve this issue before it damaged his standing with Solgard. "Kovak is a talker, you know that. Everyone's miserable; I thought they may have just been bitching together. To tell Lady Fontaine was to risk escalating things over what might be nothing. We need to keep things calm."

Galt chose not to admit his own partial hope that they would return to Nordabor. It was a hidden shame that he would never tell her about—not when he'd sworn to support her. He also chose to omit the fact that Kovak had been courting others.

The disgraced guardsman's actions suddenly seemed much more serious in Galt's mind. His doubt-and fear-driven justifications for keeping silent had almost made him a co-conspirator. It was time to make things right.

"I wanted to see if I could gather more information, try to determine if there was any legitimate threat. I haven't heard anything else, but I should have told you sooner. If you think we should, we can talk to Lady Fontaine now."

"Yes, I think we should," she said somewhat reproachfully. "You should have told me, Leon. We're supposed to be in this together."

She looked hurt now, and Galt couldn't stand it. "I know. I'm sorry."

Solgard said nothing for a moment, then looked back into Galt's eyes. They were still standing very close. "It might be nothing, but it might be something. We can let Lady Fontaine decide."

"I agree."

"Don't do something like this again," she said.

"I won't." And he meant it.

She leaned in and kissed him briefly, but softly.

"Let's go."

•   •   •

Lady Fontaine sat back and ran her hands through her hair, which was matted after such a long time without bathing.

"You're certain of what you heard?"

"Yes," Galt answered, though he still failed to mention the unknown others with whom Kovak claimed to have spoken.

"You're talking about mutiny," Berg said.

They had taken great pains to ensure that nobody outside of the tent could hear them. Solgard remained outside, ostensibly lounging near the fire. Inside the tent, Galt had told everything to Lady Fontaine, Berg, and Lowther, the only ones he was certain Kovak would not have spoken with.

"You should have come forward with this at once," Berg continued in a scolding tone.

"Jotun, it's fine," Lady Fontaine interrupted. "I understand his reasoning. It's a serious accusation. We need to address it, but carefully. The company needs to know that dissenting opinions can be voiced."

"As long as they know that you have the final say and they'll abide by it," Lowther advised. "I know Kovak, and he's not typically one just to talk things over. You need to be leery of him. We both do."

It was no secret that Kovak deeply resented Lowther for supplanting him. It was not a stretch to imagine that Kovak had ill intentions when it came to his new under-captain.

"So we'll make the first move," Lady Fontaine said. "I'll summon the three of them and tell them it's come to my attention that they have a plan for a retreat. I'll give them the opportunity to voice their ideas, and then I'll tell them no. We'll see what happens after that."

Her meaning was clear. They would suss out Kovak's true intentions, and if necessary, deal with him and his followers as they would any mutineer.

Galt began to worry about what would happen if Kovak's unknown supporters outnumbered them. Couching his concern in hypotheticals, he asked Lady Fontaine what they would do.

"We will do what we have to do. I'm not leaving while Cyprian and the others are on that mountain," she said, frustration and desperation bleeding into her voice. "Believe me, I wanted to go back to Nordabor after Vin-Sadavat. I tried to convince him. But this is the situation we're in, and we just have to deal with it. I'm not leaving them. And I won't allow anyone to take our last provisions and leave them for dead. It's not happening."

Galt knew it was a gamble. He hoped that more of the company were still loyal to Fontaine than he imagined, and hoped doubly that the coming confrontation wouldn't end in bloodshed.

He could feel their already-remote chances slipping further away.

•　　•　　•

Lady Fontaine and Berg waited on the outskirts of the camp, where the conversation could remain private. On Lowther's advice, they'd eschewed having Kovak and the others brought into the tent. If the meeting did somehow devolve into a physical confrontation, the cramped quarters could become a dangerous hindrance.

They had just finished the second disbursement of rations, and much of the company was settling in to sleep. Lowther, Galt, and Solgard were tasked with fetching the three conspirators. It would be a disruption of the normal watch, but Lady Fontaine had felt that confronting them was more important than maintaining a vigil that hadn't encountered a single threat since they'd arrived.

They found them easily enough. Kovak and Gricks were stretched out languidly by the fire nearest their tent. Barrow stuck his head out of the vestibule as soon as Lowther started to speak. "Kovak, Gricks, Barrow. Lady Fontaine wishes to speak to you."

A small hint of alarm passed over Kovak's features, and he sat up. "And what does the lady wish to speak to us about, *sir*?" he sneered.

"That's her business. We've just been sent to get you," Lowther said evenly.

Kovak looked at Galt and Solgard as if noticing their presence for the first time. "Are these herders here to assist in collecting us? Seems outside their purview."

"Drayton, it's an order. Get up." Lowther's demand carried a small note of pleading in it, which must have amused Kovak, because he suddenly stood with a nasty chuckle.

"I can tell how important this is to you," he said with mock compassion. "I've been meaning to have a talk with the lady, anyway. Come on, then."

The last comment was directed at Gricks and Barrow, who'd been watching the discourse with mounting looks of concern. Both of them reluctantly joined Kovak, and the group headed toward the meeting spot.

Galt noticed that several curious onlookers had witnessed them. In their relatively small camp, it would have been impossible for them not to. It made him uncomfortable to know that possible supporters of these men were watching what was happening and perhaps waiting to act.

The sky cast its otherworldly illumination down onto the snow, lighting the way to Lady Fontaine and Berg. Behind them, mighty Urgukorge and its tempest crown appeared to be presiding over the provisional court.

"I'm sorry to drag you out here like this," Lady Fontaine said as they arrived before her. Her voice carried a casual air that masked her concern. "Some strange rumblings have reached my ears, and I just wanted to get everything out in the open. I've heard you men have a plan for a retreat."

Gricks and Barrow looked nervously toward Kovak, who retained his defiant attitude.

"I wouldn't call it a retreat, my lady. More like a correction. Our plan would have us doing what we should have done when we left Vin-Sadavat."

"And what's that?" Lady Fontaine asked lightly.

"Return to Nordabor. Immediately. Cut our losses and save the rest of us."

"And what, exactly, do you consider a loss?" Her tone had grown icy.

"We can't assume that they're coming back," Kovak said. "That climb is impossible, and they had no idea what they were doing. If we continue to wait with no guarantee of their return, then we risk reaching a point where we couldn't return even if we wanted to. We're running out of food."

Galt's old doubts drifted to the surface of his mind, finding no fault with Kovak's reasoning. However, the guardsman was acting under the assumption that the climbers had failed. There was no proof of that, and they hadn't yet been gone long enough to assume the worst. He knew what Lady Fontaine's reaction would be; now, it was just a matter of what Kovak did next.

"I understand the position we're in, but we cannot simply leave," Lady Fontaine replied, keeping her voice even with obvious effort. Authority did not come naturally to her. "There are five of our company up there, including my husband. If we have to ration further, we will, but we are not leaving while they are still alive. We can discuss returning to Nordabor to regroup when they return. You're also forgetting that they have the blade shards we've collected so far. If we leave them, we lose every bit of progress we've made."

"I'm sorry, my lady, but that's just not good enough," Kovak said, darkness creeping into his voice.

Galt instinctively gripped the hilt of his blade. He could feel a palpable menace emanating from Kovak. He glanced at Solgard and Lowther and saw that they had also reached for their weapons. Gricks and Barrow noticed as well, and their hands went to their own belts.

Lady Fontaine remained rigid. "It's just going to have to be."

"I think it would be beneficial," Kovak said, "for the entire company, that is, if we had a change in leadership."

At that, Galt, Solgard, and Lowther drew their blades in quick succession and stepped between Lady Fontaine and Kovak, who leapt back and drew his own sword. Gricks and Barrow followed suit, the latter looking extremely frightened, as though he could scarcely believe what he was doing.

"Mutiny!" Berg shouted in disgust from behind Galt.

"Your husband is leading us all to our deaths," Kovak spat, "and you're perfectly content to follow his course. You have no idea what you're doing. A common bitch who married a lord of nothing. You're not going to order me to wait here and die!"

Kovak was shouting now, and Galt noticed with dread that the rest of the company was approaching, drawn by the commotion.

"Stand down!" Lowther bellowed.

"Oh, fuck off, you piece of shit," Kovak shot back.

"Drop your weapons and stand down now," Lady Fontaine demanded. "All of you. Or it's treason."

Barrow looked terrified, but held fast with the others. Kovak was not deterred, and in fact, appeared to be emboldened by the gathering group.

"You want to talk about treason? Let's talk about how convenient it was that Phir-Ramarian died while under the tender care of your husband and his pet badlander, shall we?"

Lady Fontaine reeled as if she'd been smacked in the face.

"I think Lord Fontaine decided he wanted to run the show permanently. Couldn't have the prince waking up and demoting him back to the nothing he truly is, now, could he?"

"You have no idea what you're talking about," Berg seethed, his face purple with rage. "How dare you?"

"Our leader is an unfit usurper, and I'm relinquishing him and his lady of command," Kovak announced to the crowd. He turned back toward Lady Fontaine. "I'll ensure you're treated fairly and provided with the same provisions and safe transport back to Nordabor as anyone else."

"I think you've done the math wrong," Solgard said.

Kovak looked toward his two supporters, then back at the crowd. Bellamont and Hale stepped forward. "Perhaps not," Kovak crowed.

"Lady Fontaine, Kovak is right. It's time to leave," Bellamont said. Reluctantly, she drew her blade. Hale followed suit.

Galt was shocked, but also relieved. The other conspirators had been revealed and, though it was disheartening, they were at least fairly non-threatening, despite their weapons.

Anders, Shagalov, and Pike remained where they stood, bewildered. Pike finally stepped forward and clumsily drew his own sword. The nebbish chronicler was now seething.

"Delivering the people of Nordabor to Paradise was Phir-Ramarian's greatest desire," he said, voice shaking. "Lord and Lady Fontaine are doing everything in their power to keep that dream alive. I stand with them. You will not ruin this."

Apparently unsure of what to do, but realizing that things were about to turn deadly, Anders and Shagalov drew their weapons and stood alongside Pike.

Though surrounded, Kovak did not seem concerned. With a look of pity and resignation, he turned once again to Lady Fontaine. "You would rather spill the blood of your own people than listen to reason?"

"You are the one who is instigating this," Lady Fontaine said bitterly. "The blood will be on your hands."

Kovak seemed to consider that for a moment. Then he looked at his band of followers and nodded.

"So be it."

CHAPTER 43

With numb hands, Cyprian pulled as hard as he could on the rope, and to his relief, the last lumpish bundle of armor finally crested over the lip of the cliff. One more pull slid it securely onto the hardpack ice on which they now stood, gasping in the razor thin air.

Starkad, who was by far the least affected, set to work reeling in the rope. "When we're finished up here, we can take the pilgrim's route back down. It should be much easier. Naffabyin will either be dead or uninterested in hindering us, although I expect the former is more likely. Either way, we won't need to be stealthy," he said between breaths.

Cyprian had to appreciate his confidence. Their success was by no means guaranteed, and, at the moment, the thought of confronting a god seemed preposterous. It was difficult just getting enough of the weak air into his lungs to remain standing, much less fighting. The euphoric feeling he'd experienced while climbing was now completely smothered by exhaustion.

Their final climb had been as physically and mentally taxing as those that came before, but the knowledge that it was the last push before the monastery had helped them to endure. Vane's death still hung over them, but the demands of the climb had largely kept their minds busy. Occasionally, though, Cyprian had felt a tug at his harness as someone below slipped momentarily or lagged behind, and in those moments, the memory of his near-fall had come back with shocking clarity.

Mather and Dupree had lauded him for his efforts, and part of him had accepted the praise. A smaller, more honest part of him knew that Vane deserved all of the credit.

He'd barely managed to stop his own fall, scrambling wildly to gain some purchase. When he'd managed to wedge one of his axes into a crevice through blind luck, the weight of Mather and Dupree had been pulling at him tremendously, and he had been certain that he would snap free from the wall at any moment. Consumed by fear, he'd resolved to cut the line tethering him to the others. He'd been reaching for his dagger when he heard Vane call out to them. Knowing that Vane held the line as well was the only thing that'd stayed his hand.

If their lives had depended solely on Cyprian, they'd both be dead.

He had a difficult time reconciling that with the praise bestowed upon him by the others and with his own perception of himself. He was barely able to hammer it away with the same series of justifications he used to absolve himself of his gnawing guilt over Phir-Ramarian's death. The important thing was that he hadn't been forced to cut them loose, and now they'd all successfully reached their goal. Except, of course, for Vane.

Now that they'd hauled up the last of the equipment and could finally stand still and try to breathe, Cyprian turned to survey the derelict monastery that they'd fought so hard to reach. They were within the eye of the tempest, having passed out of the cloud cover and into the dazzling starlight as they climbed. The air of the plateau where they stood was almost completely still, but concourses of roiling clouds streaked through with jagged, cobalt fingertips of lightning encircled it, hiding the world below. The atmospheric phenomena, previously known to Cyprian only through ancient texts, was mesmerizing, as were the ominous peals of thunder that followed.

The massive storm system seemed to be fed by a thin, undulating column of black vapor that rose in regular plumes from the heaped ruins of the titanic monastery. The dark fog twisted in the air before flattening and rolling down into the bank of clouds below. It gave the unsettling impression that the monastery was breathing.

The tumbled wreck of cyclopean stones lay only a short distance away—close enough for Cyprian to see tremendous bas-reliefs carved upon the still-standing outer walls. They reminded him instantly of those he'd seen at the entrance to Ganachim's temple. A figure representing the Father-God, adorned in the same rays of benevolent light, was depicted creating another figure, which Cyprian took to be Naffabyin. Much of the detail had been worn away, and only his familiarity with the previous sculpture let him discern the meaning behind this one.

Beyond the ponderous front gate, much of the structure had completely collapsed, making it difficult for Cyprian to determine the original design. Still discernible were the remnants of a colonnade that had probably once supported a roof, suggesting the presence of a great hall. Perhaps it was where Naffabyin had once received the pilgrims who managed to reach him. Cyprian suspected that he might reside there still, based on the apparent source of the encircling tempest that streamed from the structure in strange intervals.

"Well," Mather said, still breathing hard, but with a semblance of control that Cyprian envied, "shall we?"

He gestured toward the bundled amiant armor. Dupree had just started pulling open the ties and laying out the gear, trying to organize it. It seemed to be taking a great deal of effort.

"Yes," Cyprian managed, trying his best not to wheeze.

Starkad finished stowing the ropes and joined them before the laid-out suits of armor. He looked down at them with naked contempt.

Cyprian knew that he'd never put much stock into the armor. Now that he was expected to wear it, he made no effort to hide his displeasure.

"Okay," Dupree huffed after a few short-cycles, "they're ready. Who wants to go first?"

It took a distressingly long time to get all three of them into the armor. Mather was fitted first, and as Cyprian waited, he grew colder and colder, stamping his feet and pacing about, willing himself to stay warm. Starkad merely chewed his pipe and looked thoughtfully toward the monastery, the rough-hewn stones of which were bathed in the ethereal blue starlight.

Cyprian followed his gaze, then looked beyond it to the even further heights of Urgukorge's summit. The glistening, snow-capped peak reared up behind the monastery, which was built into the side of the final slope before the summit. A small part of Cyprian wanted to push on and reach the top, which, from his vantage point, looked like a short stroll away. Of course, like the Urguein Glacier before, the distance was misleading. It would probably take another full-cycle of hard climbing to reach the summit, and, unfortunately, they had no time to spare.

When Dupree had finished with Mather, it was Cyprian's turn. He was pleasantly surprised by how warm the insulated interior of the armor was, each adjustable, interlocking piece offering him greater comfort as Dupree fastened them on. Though he would have enjoyed having the extra warmth the whole time, it quickly became obvious why Mather had said climbing in the armor would be impossible. It was just too bulky and cumbersome, restricting normal movement and depriving the wearer of any real dexterity.

As Dupree was preparing to fit Cyprian's helmet on, Mather's insistence that she remove the tinted glass from the eyeholes of all three helmets held the process up. A short argument ensued. Mather insisted that the glass had been there mostly to protect from the heat of any fire summoned by Veathyadell. Its functionality against lightning was unclear at best, and the dark tint made seeing in the already-dim light nearly impossible. Dupree acquiesced, and after a few more short-cycles, the glass was removed.

Cyprian was distinctly reminded of the discussion they'd had on the *Fortune* regarding the armor's potential effectiveness. At the time, he'd been privately relieved that he wouldn't be wearing it.

Things had obviously not gone as planned.

Finally, Dupree lowered the helmet down over Cyprian's head and fastened it tightly. The warmth was almost complete save for the cold air seeping in through the eyeholes. Still, Cyprian was happy that his vision was not obstructed.

Starkad was fitted last, and Cyprian found that he and Mather were nearly identical in their armor. The only obvious difference was the handwritten number scrawled on each breastplate. Based on the lack of precision, Cyprian surmised that they were later additions.

"You all better come back. You're not leaving me alone up here," Dupree said with forced humor. She was remaining behind with their provisions, the climbing gear, and the ragged tent.

"We'll be back," Mather answered, his voice muffled by the helmet. "I'll need you to get me out of this suit."

She smiled weakly and nodded. Cyprian considered saying something to her, some words of reassurance, but came up empty. She and Mather had always been closer; he decided to leave their farewell as the final word.

Their destination clear, the three of them crossed the icy expanse. As they trudged along, Cyprian's own breath seemed very loud within his helmet. They bypassed the front entrance, where the last stretch of the pilgrim's route reached the monastery, and opted instead to enter through a section of collapsed wall to the south. They struggled over the colossal jumble of rubble and clumsily slid down into the monastery's interior.

The hulking columns and sections of wall that remained standing inside were a tableau of milky starlight and stark shadows. They moved as silently as they could in the bulky armor, trying to avoid the light as they headed for the center of the ruins, where the great hall had presumably stood. As they crept along, Cyprian couldn't help but cast a curious eye toward several cracked and faded frescos that had somehow survived on the stone cartouches adorning some of the pillars. The details still visible depicted scenes of severe weather, with minuscule humans powerless to stand against it. It seemed like an ill omen.

"Stop," Mather ordered, interrupting Cyprian's observations. He and Starkad stood behind Mather and listened.

A low, unnatural groan emanated from a frost-rimed pile of debris nearby. Mather began to slowly unsheathe his anointed blade. The encounter with Vane's shade was still fresh in Cyprian's mind, and though he knew his blade would be useless, he reached for it nonetheless. His gauntleted hand felt too large for the hilt.

The sound rose again, and they followed it to its source. It did, in fact, come from a shade, but one unlike any Cyprian had seen before. In a pool of blue light, the twisted form of the creature was barely distinguishable from the toppled stones around it. The shade was lying against the rubble, seemingly encased within varying layers of ice and crumbled stone. Its sinewy, ebon flesh was coated in hoarfrost, some of which crumbled away as it struggled to raise its deformed head. Whether it could somehow see them with the fleshy, bulbous patches that vaguely and horribly suggested eyes was irrelevant. It knew they were there, and its gaping, suckling mouth gnashed slowly.

"It's probably been here for ages," Cyprian observed. He tried to fathom the suffering endured by a person debased into such a being and left to freeze to the ground in such a hostile, alien place.

"There are more of them," Mather said.

After seeing the first one, the others were easier to notice, and were made all the clearer by the increasing chorus of moans. Thankfully, the other shades appeared to be equally incapacitated.

"They see us," Starkad said as quietly as he could from within the muffling helmet. "We must be the first living beings they've seen in a long time. I don't think it's dulled their instincts."

"I don't think so either," Cyprian agreed, listening to the rising crescendo of ghoulish sounds. "How did they all get up here?"

"Perhaps they were worshippers who sought refuge here after the death of Alminnian. Maybe they thought Naffabyin would protect them in the aftermath. He must have grown tired of them."

"We need to keep moving before they give us away," Mather advised.

Taking care to step beyond the possible reach of the frozen shades, they continued toward the center of the complex. They soon left the last of the decaying hallways behind and reached the crooked remains of the colonnade, which was completely open to the sky.

There, upon a slightly elevated platform comprised of crumbling marble, they found the source of the rising stream of fog. Cyprian's original assessment that the monastery appeared to be breathing had turned out to be fairly accurate—the vapor that fed the tempest came from the slow breaths of Naffabyin.

Even sitting, Naffabyin, who was roughly twice the size Veathyadell had been, easily dwarfed the men. He was naked and hideously thin, with flabby white flesh hanging from his long limbs and a stringy, matted beard that nearly reached his knees. His hair hung similarly, though the crown of his head was bald. Like a miniature version of the tempest, a halo of clouds rolled in black waves around his head.

Crouched behind a collapsed slab of stone that concealed them within the last stretch of shadows before the open floor of the hall, Cyprian hesitated to order an attack. He glanced at Mather, who was looking dubiously at his crossbow, as if doubting its ability to do any harm to the colossal god.

Before Cyprian could suggest a different course of action, Starkad motioned for them to come in closer. With their helmets pressed together, he was able to speak in a low murmur that Cyprian hoped wouldn't carry. "Look at his hands. I think he's holding what we're looking for."

Cyprian and Mather lurched to their feet and peered around the stone. Cyprian could just make out that Naffabyin's massive hands were clenched tightly into fists, but he failed to see what the relevance was until he noticed rivulets of frozen black blood running through Naffabyin's thin fingers and down the ice-coated sides of his marble throne.

"I think he's clutching a shard in each hand," Starkad said, their helmets pressed together once more. "Hard enough to make him bleed. Perhaps it's some form of penance."

"It seems like he's dormant," Mather observed. "There's ice practically riveting him to that seat."

Mather was right. Like the shades, it appeared that Naffabyin hadn't moved in a long time. It was possible that he'd been sitting upon his mountaintop throne since his return after the fall of the Father-God.

"I agree," Starkad said. "I think we risk awakening him if we attack directly."

"So what do you suggest?" Cyprian asked, somewhat afraid to hear the answer.

"Someone climbs up there and pries the shards out of his hands. Gently."

Cyprian and Mather looked at each other. "Someone?" Cyprian asked.

"I'll take the crossbow," Starkad explained. "I'm more than capable of handling it. You two can each take a hand, and I'll cover you. If he begins to stir, I'll aim for his eyes."

Cyprian had no desire to approach the slumbering god, and could tell that Mather felt the same.

"You're a good climber and a capable fighter," Mather said to Starkad, "but I'm not willing to bet my life on your skill with a crossbow. Why don't you accompany Lord Fontaine?"

"No," Starkad said. "I'm your guide. Even donning this armor is going beyond my purpose. Your king guaranteed that I would not be confronting these gods directly. I'll do what I can from a distance, but I will do nothing further."

It was a blunt reminder of Starkad's unlimited devotion to himself, which Cyprian often failed to grasp. An uneasy feeling passed over him. As seemingly dedicated to the expedition's progress as Starkad was, he would remain loyal only so long as it served him, and his support was absolutely essential for their success.

Cyprian was also now in a position where he needed Starkad's loyalty above anything else, especially considering what he knew. Once again, he found himself unwilling to argue with Starkad lest anything unravel their partnership.

"Fair enough," he said resignedly. "Captain, give him the crossbow."

Mather started to object, but stopped. Without a word, he thrust his crossbow and small quiver into Starkad's arms.

"I don't see a better way," Cyprian said, embarrassed by his inability to check Starkad. "The plan makes sense."

"It's the only plan we have," Mather said, not quite agreeing.

Starkad positioned himself upon the slab, the crossbow aimed steadily at Naffabyin, as Cyprian and Mather began their approach, taking slow, deliberate steps, all the while watching Naffabyin for any sign of movement. Despite his fear, Cyprian plodded on, consumed by the knowledge that two more shards were almost within his grasp.

As they reached the foot of the throne, Cyprian couldn't help but marvel at the size of the old one before him. By the accounts of Starkad's people, as well as the existing records in the Hall of Antiquities, Naffabyin had been one of the most powerful of the gods. Even now, with his power diminished, his unconscious brooding alone had still been enough to conjure the tempest that surrounded Urgukorge. Cyprian did not want to see what he could do when he was awake.

Near the opposite side of the throne, Mather waited for a signal to start up. Unfortunately, they'd left the climbing gear with Dupree, including their axes. They'd be forced to scramble the short distance up to the arms of the throne by hand—no easy task in the unwieldy armor. Examining the icy face, Cyprian found that it was pitted with numerous small cracks and fissures. He was able to wedge his bulky gauntlets into the numerous cracks and use them as makeshift handholds. As he started up, Mather mirrored him on the opposite side.

Cyprian reached the top, his heavy breathing thunderous within his helmet. Awkwardly, he pulled himself onto the armrest, trying not to touch Naffabyin's flaccid arm. He looked across the god's lap and saw Mather reach the top as well. Unable to help himself, Cyprian gazed up into Naffabyin's long, weathered face.

His deep-set eyes were closed, his purple lips pinched tightly shut. About twice a short-cycle, a black plume poured slowly forth from the ponderous nostrils of his large, crooked nose and rose silently into the still air.

Wrenching his eyes from Naffabyin's otherworldly features, Cyprian turned his attention to the clenched fist only a few steps away. Balancing on the sliver of armrest available for him to walk on, he made his way to it. As he reached the fist, he looked up to check if Mather had reached the other hand. He had.

Cyprian's heart pounded. If Starkad was wrong, and there were no blade shards in Naffabyin's hands, then he would be taking a tremendous risk for nothing. He couldn't help but imagine the giant's hand seizing him and crushing him within his armor.

Slowly, he reached his right hand down into the furled skin where the thumb and index finger came together. The soft, malleable flesh moved easily. Despite the frozen blood, Naffabyin's skin had a nauseating suppleness.

He slowly forced his arm further into the god's hand until he was elbow deep. Finally, his searching fingers grazed something hard and unyielding. His fear of having his arm torn off was suddenly tempered by his eagerness. With his hand wrapped around the object, he began to wiggle it loose, and was able to twist it sideways and pull it up. A moment later, his arm slid free, and he felt a surge of jubilation. Clutched in his gloved hand was a jagged piece of dark-gray steel. Another blade shard.

Cyprian turned with excitement toward Mather, who appeared to be in the process of pulling the other shard free. Mather stopped briefly, the shard having apparently snagged on some loose fold of flesh. He worked at it for a moment, then slid it out quickly.

As the shard pulled free, the hand suddenly opened spasmodically.

Cyprian's joy was immediately replaced with terror. He scrambled down the side of the throne, losing sight of Mather. Dropping off far too soon, he crashed heavily onto the marble floor below and landed on his back. From there, he had a clear view of Naffabyin's ancient, terrible face.

His eyes were open.

CHAPTER 44

On the crimson snow, Galt and Kovak circled each other. Risking a moment of vulnerability, Galt wiped blood from his right eye with the back of his sleeve. Kovak took a step forward, then seemed to second-guess himself.

"I got you good, eh, herder?" he taunted.

"Aye," Galt panted, "you did."

The skirmish had erupted with spontaneous ferocity. Kovak had lunged forward, apparently heedless of Galt, Solgard, and Lowther, in an attempt to drive his sword directly into Lady Fontaine. The three of them had been taken aback by the sudden, explosive nature of the attack, and while they'd been able to simultaneously deflect it, Kovak had moved back to safety before they could punish him for his gall.

Within moments, Kovak and Gricks had closed in again. Galt had shouted at Lowther to lead Lady Fontaine and Berg away, and the guardsman snatched them both by the arm and fled toward a heap of jumbled boulders some distance from the camp as Galt and Solgard met the mutineers head-on.

In Galt's case, it had been quite literal. In the ensuing melee, Kovak had struck him in the forehead with the hilt of his sword, splitting the skin and sending blood cascading down his face. Amid the turmoil, he'd lost sight of Solgard and Gricks, as well as the rest of the company. From the camp, shouting and the sound of clashing steel now echoed.

"Come on, then. Sooner I finish you, the sooner I can chase down that craven bitch."

Galt was not especially fond of Lady Fontaine, but there was no way he was going to let Kovak succeed. Every life spent in service to the expedition, from Daeg on, had not been lost so that Kovak could feast on the remaining canned goods and saunter back to Nordabor, free to spin any tale he wished. Galt doubted he would let any who could tell of his treachery live.

"What are you waiting for?" Kovak demanded, shaking his sword.

His breathing slowing down, Galt continued to stall. He was trying to hold a still posture, projecting an aura of calm and control, in order to imply that he had some sort of esoteric knowledge of deeper strength. It seemed to be working. With his initial adrenaline fading, Kovak now seemed reluctant to attack again, as if leery of an unforeseen counter.

In truth, Galt was just physically spent and trying to slow the fight down. Kovak had been almost relentless before, fighting with a brutal efficiency. It had taken everything Galt had just to mount a defense.

Now, an appreciable distance had formed between them, allowing Galt to consider offensive options. Blading his body so as to hide his left side, Galt slowly unsheathed one of his short daggers and held it low, keeping his sword leveled at Kovak.

The guardsman's patience seemed to fade as his frustration ratcheted up. Apparently unwilling to continue the fruitless standoff, he suddenly raced toward Galt, howling wordlessly.

Knowing he'd only have one shot, Galt waited until the absolute last moment. As Kovak raised his sword for a killing blow, Galt dropped to one knee, leaned his blade against his leg, and seized the dagger with his dominant right hand, then flung it toward Kovak's gut.

It seemed to soar through the air as if passing through molasses.

Galt held his breath, waiting for the satisfying thunk of the dagger sinking into its intended target. Kovak's eyes widened and he skidded to a stop, twisting his body backward and swinging his sword down awkwardly. Against all odds, it connected with the dagger, emitting a hollow clang, and Galt watched as the dagger ricocheted harmlessly away, spinning end over end. Kovak's look of fear and surprise quickly morphed into triumph as he closed the gap between them.

Galt had just enough time to snatch his blade and stand before Kovak began raining blows down on him. He used no strategy, no form; he simply swung at Galt's head over and over with animalistic fury. Galt stumbled backward, driven by the onslaught, doing everything he could to block the attacks.

After a particularly savage swing, he lost his footing and floundered onto his back in the filthy, trampled snow. Kovak lunged for the kill, but Galt rolled aside just in time. As he regained his feet, he drove his blade toward Kovak's ribs. Kovak leapt back quickly enough to only receive a glancing blow, the sword just barely cutting his flesh after tearing through his furs and leather armor.

Kovak slammed his sword down onto Galt's, wrenching it out of his grasp. Galt responded by punching Kovak in the mouth as hard as he could in hopes of distracting him long enough to put some distance between them. Kovak's free hand went to his face, and he swung his sword blindly. As Galt leapt back, he could feel the cold steel cut the air directly in front of him.

Galt fumbled for another dagger, but Kovak was too fast. Before he could complete the arc of his next swing, Galt changed tactics and rushed toward him, tackling him. He tried to pin Kovak's sword arm down, but the shifting of his weight allowed Kovak to roll them over. Now underneath the guardsman, Galt snatched desperately at his belt for another dagger, but once again, Kovak was too fast. He reared up and flipped his blade upside down, preparing to drive it directly into Galt's chest.

"No!" Galt screamed instinctively, though the small part of his rational mind that was still functioning knew it was useless.

Unexpectedly, Kovak's head snapped to one side to the point that it was almost sideways. His hands shot open, and the sword dropped harmlessly, though the blade still thumped rather hard against the leather chestpiece beneath Galt's robes. It tumbled away just as Kovak's arms flopped down.

Certain of his own death, it took Galt a moment of confusion to process what he was looking at. A blade had been driven broadside into Kovak's neck so deeply that it had nearly decapitated him. Hideously, he was still blinking, and his mouth opened and closed uselessly, blood pouring forth with each opening.

The blade pulled free, the force of it flipping Kovak's head over. It dangled upside down grotesquely, attached by only a sliver of intact flesh. The displaced head blinked once more before the eyelids settled on half-open. The body began to slump, and before the butchered mess could fall on top of Galt, his rescuer booted it onto its back.

Galt's eyes moved from the bloodied heap to the person who had saved him. He was flooded with relief to see that it was Solgard. She looked exhausted, but otherwise unscathed.

"Praise the Void-God, you're okay," she said, seizing him by the arm and helping him to his feet. He stood dazedly, unsure of his footing, with blood in his eyes and ringing in his ears.

Still uncertain if he was alive or not, Galt didn't know what to say. He grabbed Solgard and pulled her close. She hugged him back tightly.

"You saved my life," he finally managed.

She looked at him, and with a tender hand, caressed his forehead near the wound he'd received. "Yeah, I guess I did. This looks bad."

"Well, I'll just have Bellamont and Hale look at it," he said sarcastically. "Any idea where they are?"

"I think maybe at the camp. I lost sight of them when Gricks broke from us. He ran after Lady Fontaine and them, and I chased him into the rocks over there. The idiot didn't really consider how outnumbered he would be. He surrendered, and Lowther's holding him now; they're still there, waiting for an all-clear."

"Well, I'm glad you came back when you did," Galt said, still in disbelief.

"You'll have plenty of time to thank me later," Solgard said with a hint of playfulness. "For now, let's get your blade."

Galt scouted around for his blade, as well as the dagger that had failed him, wiping more blood from his face. He looked back toward the crumpled form of Kovak, which remained still.

"I've got it here," Solgard said, fetching his blade from the snow. She trotted up to him and placed it in his hands while he stared at the corpse.

"Why didn't he go shade?" Galt asked, absentmindedly wiping the sword off on his robes.

Solgard, her brow furrowed, seemed to be considering this unhappily. "I can't believe he didn't, but I also can't pretend to know the Void-God's will."

The answer was not good enough for Galt. He felt strangely cheated that Kovak hadn't produced a shade—not that he was eager to deal with one at the moment. It just seemed unfair. As he'd thought many times before, there seemed to be no discernible reason behind the Void-God's blessings. It was maddeningly random and nonsensical, no matter what sins a person may have committed or what prayers the shepherds did or did not chant. But he was too exhausted and grateful to be alive to launch into a theological debate with Solgard, and he decided to keep his doubts to himself.

They headed back to the camp to see what had become of the others, leaving the fallen body of the mutinous would-be commander behind.

•　　•　　•

The short-lived insurrection had failed. Gricks, Bellamont, Hale, and Barrow were now lined up on their knees in the center of the camp with their hands crudely lashed behind their backs. Galt, Solgard, and Lowther stood behind them, awaiting Lady Fontaine. She spoke privately but animatedly with Berg. Galt couldn't hear what they were saying, but he assumed that she had no idea what to do with the four prisoners she was suddenly responsible for.

He looked over the sorry lot of them. Gricks was glowering at Lady Fontaine, his left eye swollen almost completely shut. Galt wondered if he was replaying the events in his head and wishing he'd stayed with Kovak. Bellamont looked miserable, but defiant, and Hale looked numb, as if she'd mentally checked out. Barrow, with tears streaming down his face, was quietly babbling to himself about how he never should have listened to Kovak. Galt didn't disagree with him. He'd thrown his fortunes in with a poorly planned, and even more poorly executed, power grab.

Far worse, however, was what he had done in service of that mistake.

When Galt and Solgard had returned to the camp, they'd found a scene of disarray. Shagalov had been sprawled across a blood-caked patch of slush, mindlessly trying to pile his own intestines back into his cleaved-open gut. In a panic, Bellamont and Hale had been kneeling next to him, trying to do something to aid him. Nearby, Pike and Anders had been holding Barrow down, though he wasn't fighting, but staring in horrified fascination at Shagalov's last moments.

Apparently, nervous and eager to succeed, Barrow had attacked Pike when Kovak launched his own attack. If he'd chosen the diminutive scribe in hopes of finding an easy victory, he'd chosen poorly. By all accounts, Pike had proven himself a surprisingly agile fighter, and he'd avoided the larger man's attacks deftly, which Galt found hard to believe.

Bellamont and Hale, having no combat experience, had apparently done what they could to intervene, trying to muscle Anders and Shagalov back. About the same time that Gricks made his dash after Lady Fontaine, Barrow and Pike had ended up fighting amongst the tents. Forcing his way past Bellamont and Hale, who were reluctant to actually attack anyone, Shagalov had apparently meant to intervene and assist Pike.

He'd received a sword to the belly for his efforts.

When Barrow saw what he'd done, he dropped his blade and submitted to Pike and Anders, while the erstwhile healers had tried to aid a man whose death they were partly responsible for. They'd failed, and to Galt's dismay, he and Solgard had to shepherd the shade that was born shortly after.

Now, despite their contrition, the mutineers kneeled miserably in the muck as prisoners, awaiting the judgment of the leader they had sought to topple.

Lady Fontaine finally approached them with Berg following closely behind. She looked down at each with a look of pity and scorn. She was no haughty lady of the court, and her address to them was frank and unfettered by the delicate speech of the aristocrats who shared her title.

"What you've all done was as stupid as it was vile. You're all responsible for Shagalov's death. All of you." She turned to Barrow, who winced as if he'd been physically struck. "Especially you."

"We tried to help him," Bellamont shot back.

"Please." Lady Fontaine scoffed. "Only after it was too late. Did you not seriously consider that a mutiny could lead to death? Did you think we'd all just bow to Kovak because he said we should? No. You are just as responsible. You knew what could happen."

"We didn't think it would go like this! We just wanted to leave!" Hale shouted.

"Stop. I don't want to hear it. You could have left at any time and taken your chances out there. What you wanted was to maroon five of your companions out here alone with nothing. You would have snatched the provisions and left us all for dead if Lowther or one of the shepherds hadn't always been around. I bet your original plan was to slit a few throats and take what you wanted. You're shit, and I don't want to hear your excuses."

"Fuck you," Gricks snarled. "Ask your husband about slitting throats. I bet he could tell you all about it."

Lady Fontaine stared at him. "You will all be held as prisoners. You'll remain bound at the wrists and ankles, you'll be guarded at all times by two men, and you'll be given one-third of the rations that you were willing to kill for."

The prisoners looked horrified. They were already malnourished; now they would starve.

"And, as for my husband," Lady Fontaine continued, "he has done no such thing. He is the commander of this expedition through unfortunate chance, and as the commander, and the one you were most eager to betray, I'll leave your fate up to him when he returns. He'll decide what your sentences will be."

"He's not coming back," Bellamont grumbled.

"We'll see about that," Lady Fontaine answered. She turned to Lowther.

"Get them out of my sight."

CHAPTER 45

Petrified, Cyprian remained sprawled on his back, hoping that somehow, he would remain unseen. He knew that getting up in the amiant armor would be a struggle, and there was no way he could do it without being detected. Fixated, he continued to stare at Naffabyin's ancient eyes. They were reminiscent of Ganachim's—rheumy, clouded, and sickly, but with a clear spark of life that the enslaved god's lacked. They moved slowly, as if he were surveying his surroundings for the first time. Cyprian watched as he slowly opened his gnarled right hand and looked down toward it, then toward his left side, presumably at the other hand.

He had noticed the absence of the blade shards. A look of intense displeasure grew on the god's enormous features, and Cyprian noticed with increasing fright that the surrounding bank of roiling clouds, hitherto unseen from the interior of the monastery, was now rising ominously above them.

A crackling branch of lightning spread across the enclosing walls of the tempest, bathing the entire platform in a bright, harsh light long enough for Naffabyin to see the intruder at his feet. As a tremendous peal of thunder tore through the sky, seeming to shake the very foundation of the mountain, Naffabyin stared directly at Cyprian. He leaned forward, peering down curiously.

"Ahhh, one of Alminnian's favored children," he rasped in a voice that was strangely weak and booming at the same time. "I never thought I'd have to suffer the presence of one of you again. Not after the last ones. Most of them are Aedesda's children now, though he never came to claim them!"

He laughed hideously, black fog rolling out of his mouth with every chuckle.

"Not that I'm surprised," he continued, "the way Ulesreto chased him off … you have something that belongs to me." The mirth in his voice had vanished.

Certain of his imminent death, Cyprian found himself unable to speak.

"Veathyadell said it would be so. Your master has finally sent you here. A pity that he didn't come himself. I'll have to settle for killing you."

His long-fingered hand reached for Cyprian, blotting out what little light remained. Cyprian tried to scramble backward, but knew that it would make no difference.

Suddenly, the hand jerked back as Naffabyin let loose an ear-splitting shriek. A bolt was sticking out of his left eye, and black blood and milky fluid ran down his pallid cheek. He started to rise from his seat, shattering the ice that had gathered around his legs and midsection and sending splintered pieces raining down around the throne. As he broke free, another bolt suddenly planted itself in the back of his left hand, which had been groping at his injured eye. This time, his howl was one of rage.

Cyprian finally got to his feet and began to run toward the slab where he knew Starkad was waiting. From the corner of his eye, he saw Mather run from behind the throne, where he'd apparently sought cover.

An invisible force suddenly slammed into Cyprian, knocking him onto his back again. It continued to pull at him, dragging him back toward Naffabyin. In the increasing darkness, Cyprian was certain that he'd been seized by the irate god. Then, in a flash of lightning, he saw that Naffabyin was still pulling himself loose, bellowing in pain and frustration, two more bolts sticking out of his chest, and he realized that he was being dragged by the sudden onset of a gale-force wind. Craning his neck, he could see that Mather was also being flung across the floor.

He tried his best to roll himself over and find something to grab on to, feeling as if he were falling down the cliff side again. All sound was drowned out by the whipping wind save for the pounding thunder and the metallic pinging of ice chunks raining down from the tempest and striking against his armor. All the while, he clung psychotically to the shard, knowing that if it left his hand, it would be gone forever.

Still sliding, he blew past Naffabyin and careened into a tumble of loose stone near a toppled column. Skirting against the column, he jammed his arm between it and the floor, barely managing to hold himself steady. The other shards, in their protective tube, were sealed into the armor with him, crammed into the small storage compartment built into the back of the chestplate. There was no way to secure the new shard with them, so he settled for wedging it as deeply as he could underneath the column, hoping that it wouldn't be lost.

An explosion rang out behind him, and he awkwardly twisted his whole body around to look. Immediately, a second explosion followed, caused by a tremendous bolt of lightning driving directly into the spot where Starkad had been. He looked back toward Naffabyin and saw that he was waving his arms wildly, summoning lightning from the vortex above them. His halo was now crisscrossed with blue electricity, casting a ghostly illumination on his malevolent face as he stalked about the platform, firing bolts off randomly, vexed by his unseen attacker.

"Come out and face me, you filthy, sneaking cur!" he seethed. "Come out and stand tall! Show yourself! This coward's game will not win you Paradise. You'll never get all of the shards! You'll never open the gates!"

A small feeling of smug self-satisfaction rose within Cyprian, despite his immediate peril. If only this raging idiot god had any idea of how far they'd already come.

Before Naffabyin could rant further, another bolt struck him in his right eye. This time, his scream carried distinct notes of fear within the rage. For an immortal being once capable of unimaginable power, who had lived in solitude for unnumbered long-cycles, the unfamiliar sensation must have been quite strange.

As the god's screams eclipsed even the deafening thunder, Cyprian felt the wind slacken. He struggled to his feet, just barely able to withstand the buffeting gusts. Small bits of ice continued to ping off of him, accompanied now by driving, wet snow. Naffabyin was quickly disappearing in the haze of the blizzard, his shouts subsiding. He was trying to hide.

Now would be the time to flee. Naffabyin, in his blinded state, surely wouldn't follow. They had the shards, assuming Mather was still alive and had held onto the other one. They could leave.

But what would stop Naffabyin from directing every bit of strength he had into pummeling the mountain with a relentless storm? They'd barely made the climb up with Naffabyin's power unfocused. Even blinded, he could simply pound the entire mountain until he was certain that he'd scoured any living thing from it. And that was assuming he was truly blind. Cyprian didn't know how the physiology of the gods differed from his own. Perhaps Naffabyin would heal from his injuries rapidly. Perhaps he didn't need sight.

Either way, at the moment, he seemed desperate. Finishing him now would leave no question of future risks.

Emboldened by the apparent signs of weakness, Cyprian drew his blade and marched forward. He could only hope that Mather was doing the same.

As he grew closer to where he believed Naffabyin to be, the wind grew stronger, seeming to rise like a wall. Within the swirling shield of air, he could just barely make out the glow of the god's halo. Steadying himself, he drove his blade into the unknown space with all his might. The wind threatened to tear it from his grasp, but ultimately, it connected with something solid on the other side.

The wall of air ripped apart, sending snow and ice blowing in every direction. Suddenly, Naffabyin towered directly over him. Cyprian had just a moment to see that he'd stabbed the god in his shin, drawing another stream of black blood. Naffabyin, both eyes bloodied, the stalks of the bolts still jutting from them, raised his arms, and the clouds above parted. Cyprian's eyes widened as a static buzz and a blue glow blossomed above him.

Before Naffabyin could finish his attack, he cried out and whipped around. Mather stood on his other side, hacking at his exposed calves and the backs of his knees. Now undirected, the bolt of lightning smashed into the ground wide of its mark, sparing Cyprian a direct hit, but the explosive force was still enough to send him flying, ringing the entire suit of armor like a bell. He crashed into the ground some distance away and rolled violently to a stop, certain that he was dead.

The brightness of the flash had left him temporarily blinded, his vision consumed by a white afterimage. His ears rang intensely, he could smell burnt hair, and the interior of the armor now felt unbearably hot. Gingerly, he moved his hands and feet, making sure that they were still there.

Every fiber of his being wanted to remain on the ground, but he knew that he couldn't leave Mather to face Naffabyin alone. He willed himself to stand and found that his sword was missing. He limped through the swirling ice, hoping to stumble upon it.

As his vision slowly returned to some semblance of normal, he once again spotted the glow of Naffabyin's halo. Knowing how close he'd just come to death, he hesitated, and then, mustering the last of his courage, he drew his dagger and waded through the churning snow.

Naffabyin was now on his knees, bloody wounds crisscrossing his legs. He was reaching behind his back, savagely clawing at something, and Cyprian saw with amazement that Mather had attached himself to the giant's back. He'd driven his sword deeply into the flabby skin, and now clung to it while he stabbed Naffabyin again and again with his dagger. Consumed by pain, Naffabyin had apparently been unable to focus enough to call down another bolt. Above them, the tempest still convulsed wildly, but with no one holding the reins.

Cyprian circled the thrashing god, searching for an opening. He found it facing Naffabyin head-on. With his arms searching for Mather on his back, his front was completely exposed. Cyprian seized the opening.

He charged forward and leapt as high as he could, sinking his dagger into the loose flesh of Naffabyin's belly, then slid down, bringing the dagger with him, leaving a massive gash behind. Tar-like blood gushed forth, splattering across Cyprian and pouring into the open eyeholes of his helmet.

As his boots hit the ground, he slipped in the freshly spilled blood and fell, saving his life. Sprawled on his back, Cyprian watched as Naffabyin's hands cut through the air directly above his face as the god tried in vain to crush his attacker. Swinging his arms wildly, Naffabyin lost his balance and tipped forward, catching himself on his right elbow and planting his left hand almost on top of Cyprian.

As Naffabyin leaned forward, Mather, his sword pulling free, slid up the god's bony back. Suddenly astride the back of the god's head, Mather seized a handful of filthy, lank hair for purchase. Still on his knees, Naffabyin reared up and began to reach toward Mather, who had a knot of matted hair wrapped around one arm and his feet planted against the base of Naffabyin's skull.

Cyprian clambered away and rolled over just in time to watch as Mather, using the hair like a rope, swung to Naffabyin's right and plunged his sword into the god's temple.

Instantaneously, Naffabyin ceased all movement. His hideously long, slender arms collapsed to his sides, his face slackened, and he began to totter drunkenly. Mather leapt away, tumbling to the ground not far from Cyprian. The force of him kicking off was enough to send Naffabyin slumping onto his side with a heavy thud, his halo disappearing into a puff of vapor as he landed.

A final wisp of fog drifted slowly from his open mouth, and then he was no more.

•　　•　　•

It took some time before Cyprian could really understand and accept that they had succeeded.

Utterly spent, he flopped onto his back and nearly passed out. Gazing at the sky, he noticed that the lightning had ceased. In a few short-cycles more, the snow thinned to nothing and the center of the clouds began to open, once again allowing the starlight to illuminate them.

He wasn't sure how long he'd been there when Starkad appeared above him. He'd taken his helmet off.

"Nice work. Looks like you two pulled it off," he said as he eyed the massive body. "Need help?"

"Yes," Cyprian croaked. "I need out of this armor. Where's Mather?"

"He's right here. He's walking up now."

Starkad helped lift Cyprian to a sitting position, and after struggling with the buckles to the helmet for a moment, pulled it free. "I believe you dropped this," he said, handing Cyprian his sword.

Cyprian thanked him as Mather staggered up to them, tugging his own helmet off.

"We're even now," Cyprian said.

"Even?"

"You saved my life."

"No," Mather said with a rare smile. "The armor saved your life. Dupree will be happy to learn that it worked." He casually cast his helmet aside.

"I didn't get hit directly. You distracted him."

Mather shrugged. "Close enough."

They helped Cyprian to his feet, and, without his helmet, he was now able to look down at his armor. The entire right side was blackened and still smoking slightly, and like Mather's, it was dented, scratched, and small pieces had broken loose. Starkad's remained relatively unscathed. In his arms, he still held the crossbow.

"I've got to say, you proved yourself an excellent shot," Mather admitted. "If you hadn't taken out his eyes, we wouldn't have been able to get close to him."

Starkad shrugged. "A couple of shots went wide. I used all of your bolts." He handed the crossbow back. Mather took it, seemed to consider it for a moment, then tossed it aside with his helmet.

As Cyprian struggled to stand, unable to truly catch his breath in the thin air, he stared at Naffabyin's body. Formed nearly at the beginning of time, he'd commanded the winds of the earth before the fall of the Father-God, then waited ages just to be struck down. Like the others before him, it was a shame that his wealth of knowledge, the living history he had comprised, needed to be destroyed in order to obtain their vision. In order to obtain Paradise.

He reminded himself once again that everything would be worth it in the end.

"Do you have the shard?" he asked Mather.

Mather nodded and reached down to his left boot, unclasped the buckles, and slid out an almost-rectangular piece of steel. It was a clever spot to put the shard. Cyprian wished he'd thought of it.

"I wedged mine under that column," he said, hoping it was still there. It would be a particularly crushing failure if they'd managed to slay Naffabyin and he'd simply lost the blade shard.

He limped across the platform to the toppled column and reached beneath. To his great relief, the shard was where he'd left it. He pulled it free and held it tightly in his hand, then returned to the others. "We'll hike a little way down the pilgrim's route before we bivouac," he said. "I don't like the idea of all of those shades so close by, and I don't think it's safe to breathe this thin air for too long."

"No objections from me," Mather said. Starkad said nothing, still thoughtfully considering the monstrous corpse.

The three men trudged toward the main gate of the monastery, forgoing all stealth now. Though exhausted, they were still buoyed by their tremendous victory.

All the same, Cyprian's thoughts were shadowed by the grueling descent that awaited them.

He peered up at the dissipating clouds overhead. At least the weather would be clear.

CHAPTER 46

The first sign that Cyprian and the others had succeeded came in the form of a preternatural stillness in the air that Faye knew all too well. It now carried the stagnant character so typical of Nordabor and everywhere else they'd been. She had come to think of it as dead air.

Within a full-cycle of the air becoming flat and listless, they saw a marked change in the tempest. It had spun out, flattening and thinning. Whatever force had fueled it and propelled it outward had obviously been snuffed out, leaving it to wind down. Proof of Naffabyin's defeat, perhaps, but not proof of Cyprian's survival.

Still, it was cause for hope, which had been in short supply. In the aftermath of the failed mutiny, a dour mood hung over everyone. The prisoners, their rations severely reduced and the majority of their time spent in bindings, were suffering greatly. Lumped all together in a single tent and trotted out one at a time for their measly foodstuffs, they no longer spoke of returning to Nordabor. They didn't really speak at all.

Some of those who'd remained loyal seemed to be equally miserable, both because of their own suffering and desire to leave and the plight of their former companions. As time crept on, Faye began to worry that pity and sentiment would drive the captors to release their captives, for even she had moments in which she remembered that, until very recently, they'd been her comrades. She felt it necessary to mention Shagalov's pointless death more than a few times, partly to remind herself of their crimes.

Command had worn on her. She'd never had any interest in accumulating power, and had never anticipated that she'd ever be the highest-ranking individual on the expedition. For her, the historical and archaeological significance of what they were doing had surpassed all other interests, even the potential to bring salvation to their people. That far-off possibility had always been of secondary concern to Faye, and she'd certainly never desired to be in charge of the effort. She looked forward to Cyprian's return not only because she loved him, as complicated as things had become, but because she was eager to relinquish her unwanted authority.

Thankfully, she had Jotun to confer with. Though he had scant experience with leadership, he was familiar with the stresses of an expedition, and was a wise and measured advisor. Lowther had also proven indispensable, and his protection during the uprising had cemented Faye's confidence in his abilities. For the same reason, she'd grown to trust the shepherds, though they still remained somewhat aloof.

Perhaps the most difficult thing she'd had to deal with was the unspoken suspicion that now seemed to permeate the camp, even among her trusted advisors. Nobody had said anything regarding Kovak's accusations, and that was what bothered her the most. Maybe the unsettling notion only lingered in her mind; perhaps the others had dismissed it quickly, and she was only projecting her own nagging fears. Whatever the case, Faye could not shake the idea that something sinister had occurred with Phir-Ramarian's death, and the more her thoughts circled the cinder of doubt, the more the flame grew.

As she examined it again and again, she began to feel that, if there had been any foul play, it would have been perpetrated by Starkad. The badlander had made his self-serving desires clear, and knowing that he'd survived for many long-cycles in the wastes, Faye had little doubt that he was capable of many heinous acts.

She resolved to approach Cyprian about what had occurred. Carefully. The problem would be prying Starkad from his side long enough to raise the issue in private. Once again, she was distinctly troubled by the sway that Starkad seemed to have over Cyprian.

It was while she was languishing in her tent, unable to sleep, her mind stuck in a maddening perpetual loop of worries, that she heard an excited cry from outside. She sat bolt-upright and listened intently, fearing that the prisoners had somehow broken free.

The cry came again, and the jubilation in the voice was clear. Faye hastily pulled on her furs and stumbled out of the tent. The source of the shouting turned out to be Anders, who was running toward her, waving his arms. "They're back! Lady Fontaine, they're back!"

Relief swept through her, purging her mind of all worries. Jotun clambered out of the tent after her, roused by the shouting.

"They're back?" he asked, a delirious tone of disbelief in his voice.

Faye didn't answer him, consumed by her own emotions. She began to run toward Anders, who stopped. Galt and Solgard, who were standing by the prisoner tent, took notice of the excitement and looked as if they wished to follow.

"Stay with the prisoners," Faye ordered, racing past them.

"This way, my lady," Anders said excitedly as she reached him. They jogged over a crest of rock, passing near where the frozen corpse of Kovak remained, partly buried by a snowdrift.

As they reached the top, Faye spied four disheveled forms stumbling toward the camp a short distance away. "Cyprian!" she shouted, her voice echoing in the still and silent air.

One of the forms raised a hand and waved weakly.

Faye rushed down the other side of the embankment and toward the returning climbers. As she reached them, she lunged into

Cyprian's arms. He seemed surprised by the gesture, but quickly reciprocated the hug.

"You did it," she nearly laughed in relief, her face buried in his neck. "I can't believe it. You did it."

"Just barely," he said with some of his old self-effacing charm.

She looked at him, really seeing him. He looked like he'd lost even more weight, and his cheeks had developed blackened patches. She glanced at the others and saw that Mather, Dupree, and, to a lesser extent, Starkad all bore similar marks. She then noticed that Vane was missing.

"What happened?" she asked, dread leaking back into her thoughts.

"I'll tell you everything soon, but first, we need to rest." He coughed dryly. "And I need someone to fetch Bellamont; we're all suffering from exposure. I think my skin has actually frozen somewhat." He gestured toward his cheeks and smiled weakly, wincing.

The memory of everything that had occurred at the camp came surging back to Faye.

"Well, there may be a problem with that."

•　　•　　•

She told Cyprian and the others the basics of what had occurred as they returned to the camp. Dupree had not taken the news of Shagalov's death well. Rather than sorrow, as Faye learned she'd felt deeply at Vane's death, Dupree was consumed with rage. Cyprian and Mather had to convince her not to proceed directly to the prisoner tent to kill Barrow immediately, assuring her that justice would be served. By the time they gathered around a roaring fire, with Anders fetching food for the returning climbers, she had settled into a fell silence.

At the fire, the entire series of events was laid out. Galt, looking somewhat uncomfortable, explained what he'd overheard. Faye and Jotun described the confrontation with Kovak and how Lowther had led them to safety. As disgusted as Mather was with the betrayal committed by two of his men, he was equally proud of Lowther's actions.

He placed a hand on the younger man's shoulder and told him as much. Lowther, apparently unacquainted with praise, blushed furiously.

Solgard finished the tale by describing the capture of Gricks and the death of Shagalov. All the while, at least two of them had split off from the gathered group to stand by the tent containing the unseen prisoners.

Upon learning of everything that had happened in his absence, Cyprian sat wearily, his head hanging between his knees. Faye wondered what he was thinking, still wishing to know what had occurred with Naffabyin. Aside from saying that they'd succeeded, collecting two more blade shards in the process, he'd told her nothing. There were currently more pressing matters at hand, she supposed.

After some time, Cyprian raised his head. "We need to deal with this now."

Mather nodded.

Struggling to his feet, Cyprian started toward the prisoner tent. The others followed suit, and within a few short-cycles, the prisoners had been brought forth from the tent and gathered before Cyprian, their legs unbound. Bellamont and Hale had looks of shock etched on their faces, Barrow openly wept with remorse, and Gricks stared straight ahead, refusing to look at Cyprian and Mather.

"It is with a heavy heart that I return here to find that members of this expedition saw fit to overthrow their leaders and betray their companions," Cyprian said quietly, looking at each of them in turn. Everything from his words to his disdainful glare made Faye shudder. Her husband had once again slipped behind the mask of authority.

"It seems that justice has already found your leader. I passed his body on my way back. You will notice that, despite what you were all so certain of, I am not dead. And I did not fail." He held aloft the two blade shards, letting the prisoners see the fruits of his labor.

Faye watched their faces with mounting dread. She knew what the punishment was for treason, and somehow doubted that Cyprian would have any mercy. She'd known the outcome the moment she'd left their fate in his hands, but a small part of her was still relieved that it would be him that passed the sentence. Despite what they'd done, and what they'd intended to do, she knew that she would have been unable to follow through with the punishment.

"You are all charged with mutiny, treason"—he paused for a moment—"and murder."

At the mention of the last, Dupree spat in Barrow's face. "I'm sorry, I'm sorry," he bleated.

Cyprian ignored him. "The sentence will be death. Without shepherding."

Barrow cried out. The other prisoners remained silent, but even Gricks now looked dismayed. To sentence them to death was one thing, but to refuse them the mercy of being released from damnation should they become shades was a punishment beyond what Faye had expected. Nobody contradicted Cyprian, though Faye noticed brief looks of surprise on several faces, including Mather, Galt, and Solgard. She also noticed Starkad lingering nearby, his face blank. She tried to decipher some darker meaning in his expression, to figure out how he had somehow influenced this, but as far as she could tell, this was all Cyprian's idea.

"There will be one exception," Cyprian announced. "Bellamont. We need a healer, and you are obviously the most skilled. You will remain a prisoner. If you serve loyally until the completion of our business, then I will see to it that your life is spared by the king."

Bellamont was shaking violently, and could only manage a nod.

"Lowther, bring her forward."

As the guardsman shuffled her away from the others and into the group watching the events unfold, Hale cried out. "Take me instead! I never would have done anything if she hadn't ordered me to follow her!" Please!"

Bellamont watched with a tortured expression as her subordinate blamed her and desperately tried to take her place. Faye suspected that Hale was not far off the mark.

"My verdict has been rendered," Cyprian said flatly. "Captain. Escort them to the edge."

Mather herded them from the camp and toward the nearest drop-off. Hale had joined Barrow in sobbing. Facing his imminent death, Gricks grew belligerent.

"You fucking hypocrite, you're going to sentence us to death? How did you end up in charge? You killed him, didn't you? You fucking killed the prince!" Gricks shouted as Mather and Lowther seized him by the arms and dragged him forward.

At the accusation, Faye watched Cyprian's face intently. His eyes widened slightly, but otherwise, he remained stoic. Afterward, she wished that she'd watched Starkad's face instead.

"I don't know where you got an idea like that," Cyprian said with disgust, "but if that's what led you all to follow Kovak, then you made an even-more-foolish mistake than I thought. Phir-Ramarian died from his injuries. His death was inevitable."

Mather and Lowther shoved Gricks to the ground just before the edge. "As tradition dictates, you will be beheaded. Your bodies will then be cast over the edge," Cyprian explained.

Faye had to marvel at the cold calculation in it. The gathered remainder of the company would be forced to witness the bloody punishment for treason, and the bodies of the executed, disposed of over the edge, would be far below the camp by the time any shades were born.

"Fuck you!" Gricks screamed.

"Captain, execute him first."

"Get up," Mather ordered.

"Fuck you!" Gricks repeated, this time at Mather.

Mather seized him by the collar and hoisted him up, his blackened face twisted in sudden rage. "You've forsaken every oath you swore to uphold. I'm done with you. Now stand!"

Gricks refused to lock his knees, and crumpled to the ground as Mather released him. Undeterred, Mather drew his sword.

"In the name of the Crown," he droned over Gricks's shouts, reciting the traditional execution verbiage, "you have been sentenced to death. May the Void-God offer you his mercy."

Gricks struggled to worm away, but his bound arms prevented him from moving. He screeched madly one final time before Mather delivered the killing blow.

Faye looked away, unable to bear the brutal senselessness of it all, as Lowther assisted Mather in dumping the man's body and severed head over the side. Instantly, they were gone. All that remained of Gricks now was a bloody smear reflecting the starlight.

"You," Cyprian said, pointing to Barrow.

"No, my lord, please," Barrow begged as Mather and Lowther led him to the edge. He fell to his knees, continuing his litany of pleas.

"Let me do it," Dupree said loudly, stepping forward, her eyes fixed eagerly on Mather's crimson blade. "Let me kill him."

"You don't really want that," Mather said, shaking his head.

Kneeling beside him, Barrow had grown silent, watching the two of them discuss his fate.

"I do," Dupree said slowly. "When Hayves was taken, I was powerless to stop it. When Vane's health failed, I couldn't do anything. But this—this, I can do something about. Here is this cowardly, worthless fuck, pissing himself in front of me. This murderous traitor. You did Gricks. Let me avenge my friend. Please."

"I trusted Gricks with my life. I hate him even more for making me kill him. Execution does not bring catharsis. It is about upholding the law, not getting revenge. To carry out such a sentence is a terrible burden, no matter what the crime. If I let you do this, the memory will hang on you forever. I'm sorry," Mather said, then turned back toward Barrow who, as if on cue, resumed his babbling.

Mather ignored him. "In the name of the Crown, you have been sentenced to death. May the Void-God offer you his mercy."

Dupree said nothing, nor tried to intervene. She simply watched intently, her hands balled into fists, hate etched on her face. Mather spared her a final sorrowful look and swung his blade, silencing Barrow forever.

As his body was dumped over the edge, Faye stared out toward the horizon, wishing desperately, and not for the first time, that they'd never come to Urgukorge.

Without another word, Mather and Lowther came for Hale. She began to shriek and flail, cursing Bellamont for leading her to her death. Bellamont remained silent and stared at the ground, trembling. Hale fell to her knees, racked by sobs that were so intense she'd grown silent. A long strand of snot and drool hung from her face.

Faye looked away again. She didn't need to see that final indignity.

"In the name of the Crown, you have been sentenced to death. May the Void-God offer you his mercy." With a wet thunk, Mather finished fulfilling his duty, and Hale's body joined the others.

The remainder of the expedition stood solemnly, the hot, coppery smell of spilled blood filling the air. Faye's mind was blank. It was preferable to thinking about what she'd just witnessed.

Cyprian cleared his throat and turned to Bellamont. "I need you to look at the other climbers and myself. Can you do that?" His voice was raspy and spent.

She nodded, still looking toward the bloodstained spot that Hale had just occupied.

"We will take some time to recover our strength," he said, now addressing the group. "And then we're going to finish this."

PART V: LANDS OF ASH AND FOG

CHAPTER 47

The twelve remaining members of what had been Phir-Ramarian's expedition began their hike out of the lower Einmaz foothills and headed east along the plunging torrent of the upper Einfallen. They carried much lighter loads, if not lighter spirits. The abandoned cart, piles of empty cans, two empty casks, a damaged tent, the now-useless crossbows, and a jumbled pile of climbing gear were all that remained of their time at the basecamp, and all that stood as a memorial to the lives lost and taken on the mountain.

They carried the last of their scant provisions divided amongst themselves. The river provided ample water, and they filled their stomachs with prodigious amounts of it to make up for their lack of food. Though the climbers had taken several full-cycles to recover, and the others had remained idle at the camp for even longer, an all-encompassing exhaustion still permeated the company as they stumbled their way eastward, many driven only by the promise of reaching the sunlight again.

Cyprian thought little of the sun. His thoughts were consumed by weightier matters. During his time recovering, he had laid out each of the shards, arranged by their broken borders. Based on that, and the diagram of the sword's hilt provided by Phar-Mindorius, there appeared to be only one piece missing. One blade shard stood between him and triumph, between him and absolution.

And it appeared that the worst was behind them. Naffabyin, who had undoubtedly constituted their greatest physical threat, had been vanquished and his mountain conquered, and the cancer growing within their ranks had been excised.

Initially, Cyprian had been devastated to learn of the insurrection. He'd acutely felt the fragility of his position, and his thoughts had turned to Heilrune's final moments. The slaver chieftain's followers had been fanatical in their devotion, yet in the end, they had still turned on him. Cyprian knew that he should have been more vigilant in rooting out the dissenters in his own ranks. Despite his accomplishments, they had remained, and in his absence, they'd been emboldened.

But the more he considered the insurrection, the more it pleased him. It had exposed completely those who'd questioned him and left no doubt about the loyalty of those who remained.

Aside from Bellamont, of course. Her obedience had been gained by force, and Cyprian knew that she could never be trusted. He had accepted basic care from her, taking no risks and refusing to imbibe any tonic she offered. Still subsisting on reduced rations, she now lagged behind the others. Only the rope tied to her bindings like a leash kept her moving. Lowther, assigned to be her personal jailer, gave it a healthy tug anytime she started to fall too far behind.

The prisoner was, regrettably, a continuing source of distress for Faye. Seeing Bellamont's anguished shambling obviously reminded her of what had befallen the other conspirators. Cyprian could easily sense that the ground he'd gained with Faye by returning alive and triumphant from the monastery had been quickly lost by his ordering of the executions.

Unfortunately, he'd had no other choice. To allow any of the others to live would have been to forfeit his authority. He'd have condemned Bellamont too, if it weren't for his need for a healer. Now, he'd cemented his command beyond all reproach. He was confident that those remaining, whether they really wanted to or not, would follow him to the end.

And, walking along the rushing waters, a weak, purple glow beginning to bloom in the east, it was easy to believe that the end was very close indeed.

Starkad reminded him that it was not. They were kneeling on the bank of the river, refilling their canteens, when he advised Cyprian of the impending crossing.

"We're not far now from the Einfallen's split. We'll have to cross at some point before then so we can follow the northern arm of the river. It will lead us directly into Faedalia."

Cyprian knew that, but he'd assumed there would be a bridge that crossed over the broad expanse of water. "Doesn't the Imperial Highway run as far north as Kafarbjorn Harbor?" he asked.

"Yes, but north of Nordabor, it becomes much more provincial. And that's not even taking into consideration that it's fallen into ruin. When I traveled through these lands before, I found that every bridge had collapsed. They appeared to have been minor—mostly wooden structures—and only their stone abutments remained. We'll have to ford the river."

They'd left the largest of the waterfalls behind, yet the river still ran rapidly, with no indication of growing calm or shallow. Fording seemed unlikely.

"Well, where did you cross before?"

"I didn't. After I found Naffabyin, I traveled along the southern arm of the river, toward Nordabor. I'd discerned that Chortelak resided somewhere in Faedalia earlier, when I was traveling south far east of here."

Cyprian considered this, irritated by the new wrinkle. Then another thought occurred to him. "With Naffabyin gone, shouldn't the river be drying up?"

"It will, in time. For now, the Urguein Glacier will still produce large quantities of water. It could last another lifetime before the glacier's depleted and the river runs totally dry."

Comforting news for the people of Nordabor, but not for Cyprian. He gazed across the broad water at the distant northern shore. It was as bleak as the southern shore they occupied, dotted with gnarled, bare trees and the occasional decaying homestead. It seemed absurd that after ascending the highest peak in the known world, they should be thwarted by something as simple as a wide river.

"We'll just have to hope that we come across an area that's shallow enough to cross."

·   ·   ·

They continued east. Cyprian watched the unchanging waters with growing apprehension. The rest of the party remained unaware that their fortunes were dependent on the river, and Cyprian worried that they would reach its bifurcation before they'd found a crossing.

He called for them to halt marching and establish a camp, partly to offer the company a rest and partly to stall, then pulled Starkad aside and privately asked him to scout ahead, knowing the badlander's uncanny knack for moving quickly and finding routes through seemingly impassable terrain. Without question, Starkad departed into the dim wastes.

Cyprian stood on the shore, hatefully glaring at the dark, quietly rushing water that blocked his way, willing the northern shore to grow closer. Lost in sulking, he failed to hear Faye approach him, and her greeting startled his frayed nerves.

"Sorry," she said. A strange silence lingered between them until she spoke again. "How are you doing?"

"I'm fine," he said distractedly. "How are you?"

"I'm fine," she echoed. Another silence was threatening to engulf their fledgling conversation when Faye took a deep breath and blindsided him.

"I wanted to talk to you about Phir-Ramarian's death."

It took everything Cyprian had to keep his composure as dread flooded his heart, making him feel as if he'd just plunged into the black water he'd been staring at. He had considered this matter settled with the execution of the mutineers, and certainly hadn't expected Faye, of all people, to question him about it.

A sense of unreality washed over him, threatening to shake loose a confession. Clutching the tube containing the shards tightly enough to make his knuckles grow white, he ran through his mantra of justifications in his mind. He was so close. Everything he'd done would be worth it in the end. He was doing what had to be done to save his people.

With great effort, he mastered himself. "Are you talking about that baseless accusation made by Gricks?" he said, trying for nonchalance.

"Gricks and Kovak, yes."

"What about it?" he prodded carefully, terrified of her answer.

"I want to be clear," she stated, "I don't believe that you had anything to do with his death. I know how you felt about him—I felt the same way—but I also know you'd never be capable of something like that."

A tentative relief passed through Cyprian, but he was still acutely aware that the topic at hand was a labyrinth of possible missteps. He needed to guard his words carefully.

"You said that you were sleeping when it happened," Faye continued, "and that you awoke to find him dead. How do you know that Starkad was asleep the whole time?"

Faye was closer to the truth than she realized, and Cyprian absolutely needed to steer her away from this train of thought. If any open accusations were made against Starkad, and he sensed for even a moment that he was threatened, Cyprian had no doubt that he would reveal the truth to deflect blame and save himself. He might even tell an altered version that conveniently omitted the fact that it was his idea in the first place.

Cyprian wasn't sure that his credibility could withstand another accusation, especially from the only other person who had been in the tent. He could deny it, yes, but then what would become of Starkad if they believed him? Cyprian needed him. Starkad was a dangerous ally, but a necessary one. In order to secure his help and keep him in line, the status quo had to be maintained.

"Well, I suppose I don't, but I'm certain that I would have awoken if there'd been a commotion. I've barely been sleeping for some time. I'm sure that if he'd even gotten up, I would have heard it."

Plausible enough. Now it was time to discredit the notion as foolish and inspired by those willing to claim anything if it meant overthrowing him.

"What makes you even ask? You can't think that Duncan had anything to do with it." He assumed his best approximation of a bemused look. "I know he's rough around the edges, but he wouldn't do that. He only acts in his best interest, and that certainly wouldn't have been in it. Nobody wanted to press on more than Phir-Ramarian; they wanted the same thing. Plus, he wouldn't do anything that might jeopardize his arrangement with Phar-Mindorius. You can't possibly be giving any credence to the nonsense that traitor was spouting."

He placed his hands reassuringly onto her shoulders, but she pulled away. "Why are you so quick to defend him?"

"Faye, I trust him." That was partially true. "We all wanted the same thing, Phir-Ramarian most of all. The mutineers just painted it as some kind of cover-up, some conspiracy against the prince, because they wanted to cut and run. If they'd tried that with Phir-Ramarian alive, who knows what other lies they would have come up with?"

"Well, it just seems suspicious," she said, unconvinced of Starkad's innocence. "He hated Phir-Ramarian. I don't know—maybe he thought Phir-Ramarian would get in the way once he was injured. I wouldn't put it past him to finish off someone who was injured and slowing him down."

"We *all* hated Phir-Ramarian; you just said that yourself."

"I didn't say we 'hated' him," she interjected.

"At any rate, however Duncan felt, it doesn't mean he would kill Phir-Ramarian. As for the injury, even if he were inclined to do something like that, he's smart enough to know that Phir-Ramarian was nearly dead anyway. You're forgetting what condition he was in."

"I'm not. I think you're forgetting that Starkad is an outsider whose only concern is himself. You put too much trust in him. I'm worried about how much sway he has over you."

Cyprian could feel his frustration growing. He needed to stamp this out, and Faye just wouldn't let it go. He had to remain calm and close this on a positive note.

"If I appear to be overreliant on him, it's because he is the only way we can do this. Do you think we could have scaled Urgukorge without him? You didn't see him on the mountain or with Naffabyin. He risked his life to help me up there. And Mather. He can be trusted, I promise you. Please trust me on this."

He still hadn't told Faye everything that had occurred during his confrontation with Naffabyin, as they had spoken little since leaving the Einmaz Mountains. Now, he was using that cryptic encounter to paint Starkad as perhaps a bit more heroic than the reluctant badlander had actually been. It seemed to work.

Faye massaged her temples for a moment, collecting her thoughts, then shrugged and dropped her arms to her sides. "Okay. If you're telling me to trust him, then what other choice do I have? Just please be careful, Cyprian. I hope Starkad's loyalty is never tested by one of us being in Phir-Ramarian's position."

It was certainly an unsettling thought. His grip on the blade shards tightened again. "It won't be," he said.

She smiled weakly. "I really hope you're right."

Cyprian was unsure of what else to add, and was grateful when Faye changed the subject. "You know, I'd still like to hear exactly what happened up there."

For a little while, the two of them slipped into an old, comfortable rhythm, and it was easy to forget the tension and lies that hung thickly between them as Cyprian animatedly told the tale. Faye was clearly captivated by the entire affair, and her fascination with the mysteries of the past was on full display. In that moment, it was truly possible to believe that their relationship would survive this, and that everything would be all right.

Then, as the conversation naturally evolved into other pleasant topics, she suddenly looked past him, her face dropping. "He's back."

Cyprian turned to see Starkad approaching them. By the time he turned back to Faye, she'd already resumed her bleak expression. A wave of sadness washed over Cyprian. He couldn't help but think of what he'd lost in pursuit of the things he'd gained.

"Lady Fontaine," Starkad said politely as he reached them. He turned to Cyprian. "I've found a way across."

• • •

Despite his eagerness to reach the crossing, Cyprian did not wake the camp. They would need their strength. By Starkad's reckoning, the area he'd found was passable, but just barely.

After the company rose and the scheduled time for departure arrived, it took only a cycle of hiking before they reached the location Starkad had found. It hardly appeared different from any other point they had passed, but upon closer inspection, Cyprian descried the hump of a thin shoal rising just above the waterline in the center of the river.

"It's marginally shallower on either side of the shoal, but it's still probably chest-high. Those who are shorter might struggle more, but they'll make it," Starkad explained. "The shoal will offer us a chance for a brief rest. We'll need it; the current is pretty strong."

Cyprian looked back at the haggard company waiting behind them and wished that they'd been able to salvage more of the rope, the bulk of which had been so worn and frayed after their climb that the ruined coils had been left behind in a loose heap with the rest of the abandoned refuse. If they'd had more, they could have possibly had the strongest among them carry it across and fix a line to the opposite shore, but at least enough remained that they could tie themselves together. If someone were swept off their feet and pulled away by the current, their companions would hopefully be able to reel them back in.

"All right," Cyprian said resignedly. "It looks like this is the best chance we'll have."

"Do you mean to have us cross here?" Jotun, who'd clearly been eavesdropping, asked as he nosed up behind them. "To wade across? Is there really no bridge?"

"I told you that," Faye sighed. Cyprian had told her the situation they faced after Starkad returned to the camp.

"Well, I thought that we'd be crossing somewhere a little more— well, I don't know, crossable," Jotun stammered.

"I need to address the rest of the company," Cyprian said, choosing not to engage. He turned around and faced the group. "Everyone, gather round."

Dutifully, they gathered before him, except for Bellamont, who stood as far away as her rope would allow. She refused to look at him, and Cyprian felt a tinge of annoyance at her impudence. He'd spared her life, but her submissiveness had been increasingly giving way to open hatred.

He chose to ignore her for now. Perhaps when they returned to Nordabor, he would see to it that she received a proper execution. Phar-Mindorius certainly would not suffer a traitor.

Cyprian was not so lacking in self-awareness that he couldn't immediately see the hypocrisy in his thoughts. He shuddered to think of how the king would feel about certain actions he had taken, but shunted those intrusive thoughts away.

"We are going to have to cross the Einfallen here. Starkad has scouted ahead and determined that this is the best spot to ford the river. Unfortunately, any bridge that used to span it has long-since collapsed.

There were a few surprised murmurs, but nobody seemed to question him. That was good.

"Starkad believes the water will be up to about our chests, give or take. I suggest that the strongest among us tie themselves together and act as porters. They can carry the gear of the weaker across. Then, the rest of us will tie together in groups and cross single-file, being sure to take advantage of the shoal in the middle of the river to rest. Any questions?"

There were none, and in short time, Mather, Galt, and Anders were selected to ferry the gear across. Cyprian felt comfortable enough in his leadership role that he thought it unnecessary to put himself at risk this time. They knew that he was a competent leader; there was no need to demonstrate it at every opportunity anymore.

He would, however, carry his own gear. He didn't trust anyone else with his things, particularly the cylinder containing the shards.

Prior to making the crossing, Mather pulled Cyprian aside. "How long have you known this was the plan?" he asked quietly.

"That what was the plan?"

"To ford the river. How long have you known that there was no bridge?"

Cyprian did not like the slightly scolding tone in Mather's voice. "I've known for a little while. It wasn't always the plan, but Starkad and I realized we'd have no other option," he said.

"I know there's been somewhat of a breakdown of order on this expedition," Mather replied evenly, "but I would appreciate, my lord, if you kept me in the loop. If anything, so that I might advise you. There may have been a better way."

Apparently, Mather resented learning of this plan at the same time as everyone else. Cyprian realized that he would need to make sure the guardsman was not excluded in the future; his support was essential.

He thought of what Faye had said about him putting too much trust in Starkad. He hadn't even considered consulting Mather, who had proven time and again to be an intelligent, capable, and loyal man. Maybe Faye had a point. Still, he had his reasons for keeping Starkad close.

"You're right," Cyprian said. "I will consult with you in the future. I trust your judgment."

Mather nodded. "Good. Thank you, my lord." Without another word, he went about his work, helping to gather equipment from those who felt they were incapable of carrying it across the river themselves.

As Cyprian watched, he overheard Jotun complaining to Faye nearby. "I hope one of them are prepared to carry *me* across; I can't swim. At no point did I agree to swim."

"If you have to swim at all, then you've already messed up," Faye said with exasperation. "The point is to wade across."

"Wade? This is a bit more than wading. My head will almost be in the water," Jotun huffed.

"I'll help you," Pike offered.

"Oh, thank you. You're a good lad."

Cyprian listened to Jotun's praise with mixed feelings. He'd heard that Pike had fought with unexpected valor to defend Faye during the mutiny, and he appreciated that, but he still found him grating. He was also surprised by Pike's survival. By all accounts, he should have perished a long time ago. Stronger, more competent men had already fallen. The scribe was immensely lucky.

As Cyprian's thoughts wandered, Mather, Galt, and Anders finished collecting the gear. Aside from himself, only Starkad, who never let anyone touch his gear, and Lowther had retained their own equipment.

It was time to begin the crossing.

CHAPTER 48

With the awkward bulk of a pack held over his head, Galt took his first slow steps into the dark current of the Einfallen. No slave to dogmatic practices, he'd removed his robes and bunched them up with his own gear, which was currently resting on the shore. He was certain that if Moore had still been with them, he would have stridden into the water, insistent on wearing his robes even then. The old man would have probably been bogged down and dragged away by his own sodden clothing. Galt wasn't sure if that would have been better or worse than what had actually befallen him.

He slipped further into the icy water, feeling gingerly with his quickly numbing feet for the next stable place to step. The riverbed was a slick mess of jumbled, slime-coated rocks. Further hindering him, the pull of the water, though almost silent, was immense.

He may have been tethered to Mather and Anders, but it offered little comfort. He did not want to lose his footing and test their ability to save him. Should the current take him, he considered it just as likely that he would drag them away with him. Galt leaned into the current as best he could and, cursing to himself that Fontaine had tapped him for this role, set his sights on the crest of the shoal.

Ahead of him, Mather was rising out of the water. The captain turned back to check on the progress of Galt and Anders, watching them as he caught his breath. After a moment, he descended over the other side.

With some relief, Galt felt that the riverbed was beginning to rise. His boots sank a little deeper into sand, and in another moment, he was trudging onto the shoal, cold water streaming off of him. He lowered the pack to rest his arms and looked back just as Mather had. Anders, who was slightly shorter, was now almost up to his neck in the water. Galt could see that his teeth were chattering slightly.

"Are you okay?" he called.

"Aye," Anders answered in a strained voice.

"You're almost there," Galt said, unsure of what else to say to help the hauler. He took a deep breath and realized that he was beginning to shiver. The temperature had risen since they'd left the Einmaz Mountains, but was still colder than what he'd been used to in Nordabor. They had yet to reach the Dawnlands proper, despite the tantalizing hint of a purplish glow in the eastern sky, and the cold air was punishing after being submerged. He needed to keep moving. The sooner he was finished, the sooner he could dry off. As he hoisted the pack and descended back into the river, Galt found himself longing for the relentless heat of the Daylands. He'd not seen the sun in a long time.

He was pleasantly surprised to find that the northern half of the river was slightly shallower than what he'd already passed through. Careful not to let eagerness to reach the shore or confidence in the shallower water make him clumsy, Galt plodded along deliberately. Eventually, he arrived at the shoreline, and Mather, who'd already reached the dry land and dropped the pack he'd been carrying, helped him tromp out of the water. Anders, whose face had become disconcertingly bluish, arrived shortly after. With their three loads deposited, there was only one more trip before they would shoulder their own gear, and everyone would make the crossing.

As he slid back into the water, Galt fixated on the fact that he'd only have to complete two more round trips. At least heading back, there wasn't the strain and burden of carrying a pack over his head, but he was careful that this, too, would not cause him to become overconfident.

In the same order that they'd departed, they arrived back at the southern shore to collect their next loads. Solgard had removed her robes just as Galt had, and it was strange to see her in the simple leather tunic she wore underneath. She stared apologetically at him as he took her pack.

"It's okay," Galt said quietly. "I understand, and I insist."

"I'm sure I could manage it."

"It's not worth the risk," he said firmly. He realized that his feelings for her were probably driving his sudden chivalry, but he really didn't care. He'd rather slip up and go floundering into the water than let her chance it, even if she would probably be fine.

Next to him, Mather was lifting the bag Bellamont had been being forced to carry. It had been laden with provisions that she was not allowed to have more than a bare morsel of. Having the emaciated prisoner haul a heavy load of food that she was largely denied was an especially cruel punishment that Galt was certain Fontaine took pleasure in. He probably would have forced her to carry it across herself if her bound hands wouldn't have prevented her from lifting it over her head properly. That, and she would almost certainly slip and drop it in her weakened state. They could not afford to lose the provisions.

With the last three extra loads, Mather, Galt, and Anders began their procession. To Galt's relief, all three of them made the crossing without incident. Once again, they dumped their loads, took a brief moment to rest, and then started back across. Within a few short-cycles, they had rejoined the others on the southern bank. Galt was beginning to feel that he'd gotten the hang of it and that the crossing was not as hazardous as they'd initially thought. He tried mightily to check that dangerous thinking.

"Since you three have made the crossing already, why don't you lead the way?" Fontaine said.

"Yes, my lord," Mather answered.

Galt would happily lead the way, chiefly because he was eager to be done with it. He was beginning to shake more intensely and actually felt strangely warmer when he was in the water. He did not, however, want Solgard to have to cross without him.

"If it's fine with you, my lord, I'll take up the rear to make sure any stragglers can be helped," he said.

"That's fine," Fontaine said. He was barely paying attention. He hoisted his pack and followed Starkad toward the water.

Galt shrugged and fell in with Solgard. As they knotted a stretch of rope around their waists, she smiled at him. "I'm glad you'll be joining me."

"You're the only one I trust to drag my ass out of there if I fall."

"With the strength you just demonstrated in carrying those packs, I assumed you'd be carrying me as well."

"You two are adorable," Lowther, who was also tying onto their rope, chimed in from behind them. They turned to see that he was smiling broadly. "Come on, you'd have to be blind not to see what's going on. It's really very sweet," he teased.

Galt realized he was blushing and turned away.

"Well, I'm glad that we have your blessing," Solgard said with a laugh. She squeezed Galt's arm affectionately. "Come on. I'd say it's almost our turn."

It was a welcome moment of levity that was all too short. Galt was quickly reminded of their grim situation when his eyes fell upon Bellamont standing sullenly behind Lowther, as far away as the rope would allow. The man who had been joking with them was also holding the leash of a prisoner. A prisoner who had taken part in a failed coup that had cost five people their lives. A coup that had occurred because of the many other lives already lost in pursuit of Paradise, including those of Moore and Daeg.

Galt was grateful for the little moments of escape that his relationship with Solgard allowed. They did not erase the pain, but they certainly helped him to bear it.

As they approached the water's edge, he could see that the first roped-together group, Mather, Anders, and Dupree, had nearly reached the shoal. Being relatively short, Dupree seemed barely able to keep her mouth and nose above the water, tilting her head back as far as she could just to breathe. With her fellow engineers gone, she'd unsurprisingly gravitated toward Mather for the crossing. If she resented him at all for denying her the chance to execute Barrow, she certainly hadn't said so.

Behind them, Starkad led the second group, in which Lord and Lady Fontaine, as well as Pike, appeared to be coaxing Berg along, almost carrying the old man. All the while, Fontaine was trying very hard to keep his pack above the water.

Galt winced, just waiting for one of them to slip and drag all five of them in. A callous part of him wondered what orders Mather would issue if the lord and lady were swept away.

"Ready?" Solgard asked.

"Yeah. I'll lead the way." Galt hefted his pack and stepped into the water for what he sincerely hoped would be the last time. Solgard, Lowther, and Bellamont followed, and together, they began to plod along the riverbed. With Bellamont weakened by starvation, their already-slow movement became painfully sluggish, and Galt found himself wishing that he was only tied to Solgard.

Ahead of them, Mather, Anders, and Dupree had passed the shoal, and Fontaine's group was descending back into the water. Berg splashed noisily for a moment, but kept his footing.

Galt risked a glance back at Solgard several times, and each time, she nodded in reassurance that she was okay. Her face, pinched in concentration, had turned almost white from the frigid water. Further behind her, Lowther and Bellamont had fallen far enough behind that the rope connecting them was nearly taut.

As Galt began to crest the shoal, he observed that the other two groups were now closing in on the opposite shore. It was with marked relief that he took Solgard's hand and helped her up and out of the water. He'd felt confident in his own ability to make the crossing again, but his own fears had been compounded by his concern for Solgard's safety. Now, they shivered together, waiting for Lowther and Bellamont and watching as Mather, Anders, and Dupree clambered onto the northern shore. Fontaine and the others followed just behind.

Galt turned to ask Lowther what was taking so long just in time to witness Bellamont's attack. She'd been surreptitiously closing the distance between herself and her captor, all while forcing him to fall behind. With the others now too far away to interfere, she shoved Lowther in the back, causing him to slip and drop his pack into the current. Using the very rope that bound them together, Bellamont looped a coil around Lowther's throat, cinching it tightly. He clawed at the rope and started to thrash. Somehow, they kept their footing.

"Stop!" Bellamont shouted, loosening the grip slightly. "Cut my bindings, and I'll free you."

The commotion had attracted the attention of everyone. Fontaine, who'd just reached the northern shore, now paced furiously along the water's edge. "Release him!" he shouted.

"Tell him to cut my bindings, or I'll strangle him," she declared loudly. "If he wants to fight, we can both drown. I don't care."

Finding himself unable to force Bellamont to do anything must have been torturous to Fontaine. Galt looked back and forth between the two, unsure of who would break. He briefly considered trying to drag Lowther and Bellamont to the shoal by the rope, but stopped, knowing that she could probably strangle him before they were pulled in, and even that was if they didn't both drown first. Beside him, Solgard clutched the rope tightly, but, seeming to have come to the same conclusion, remained still.

"What's your plan here? Where will you go? You have nothing. You're as good as dead on your own," Fontaine called across the water.

"I'll take my chances," Bellamont said.

Fontaine was now standing completely still, and Galt couldn't tell if he'd even heard her response. "Lowther, release her," he shouted after a pregnant pause.

Lowther slowly lowered a hand from the binding around his neck and reached down into the water. A moment later, his hand reemerged holding a dagger.

"Cut the rope at your waist first," Bellamont said.

The dagger descended back into the water for a moment, then rose again. The rope that had tied them to each other, and to Galt and Solgard, drifted to the surface and was pulled away by the current.

"Now cut the bindings at my wrists. Carefully."

Awkwardly, Lowther reached behind him and held the dagger out. Bellamont navigated her wrist bindings onto the blade.

"Pull up."

He did as he was told and pulled the blade upward, wiggling it back and forth. The ropes binding her wrists snapped apart.

"Now turn the dagger around and hand it to me handle-first. Then I'll release you."

"You won't cut my throat, will you?" Lowther asked shakily.

"No. I don't want to hurt anyone. I want to be free. You have my word."

He lowered his other hand from the rope around his neck and turned the dagger around. The rest of the company, even Fontaine, had grown silent. Standing on the slime-coated rocks, one misstep could send the two of them tumbling away with the river's inexorable pull. There was nothing anyone could do to intervene; they were on a miniature world alone, their fates intertwined.

With her right hand, Bellamont released her grip on the rope around Lowther's neck to reach for the dagger.

That was all it took. Lowther dropped the dagger and seized her arm with one hand while wrenching the now-loose rope free with the other. Bellamont yelped as he heaved her forward and slammed the back of his head into her face. In the flurry of motion, they both slipped from their tenuous perches and slid into the water.

A moment later, Lowther bobbed up flailing wildly and screaming for help. Further downstream, Bellamont surfaced as well, clawing at the water desperately. Galt watched helplessly until Solgard snatched the bundled robes from his pack and waded into the water, shouting at him to follow her. Before he even realized that he was doing it, he was splashing into the water behind her.

"Hold the rope," she ordered. Without question, he did as she said, and she strode as far into the water as the line would allow, nearly plunging under the surface. Galt's heels dug into the sandy riverbed, and he sank deeper, feeling the rope biting into his palms.

"Grab on!" she screamed. Forgoing the thin length of rope drifting from her waist, she instead cast her robe out ahead of her toward Lowther. Panicking, Lowther clutched wildly at the flat span of robe floating across the water's surface.

He was just barely able to cling onto the end, and the added weight threatened to carry all three of them from the edge of the shoal. Galt felt his boots sinking deeper into the muck, and he began to pull with all his might. No matter what, he would not fail Solgard. With every muscle in his body screaming, he heaved and trudged backward until he felt the weight slacken as Solgard reached safety. She then pulled Lowther in, and he flopped down onto the sand, coughing. As they huddled around him, Galt heard manic laughter echoing from the southern shore.

Bellamont had somehow managed to drag herself out of the water. She was facing the rest of the company, the blood streaming from her broken nose coloring her toothy smile crimson. She continued to laugh hysterically as she pulled herself to her feet. Galt looked back toward Fontaine, who remained silent and still, watching as his prisoner slipped through his fingers.

Lowther struggled to his feet and started to tromp back into the water. "Hold on," Galt said, snagging his arm, shocked that Lowther was ready to head right back in.

"She's my responsibility," he said, trying to pull away.

"Let her go," Fontaine called from behind them.

Lowther stopped pulling and looked back with surprise.

"There's no need to go after her. She's not worth the risk or the time. There's nothing she can do to hinder us now, and we'll get by without her skills. At this point, she's far more of a hindrance than a help. She can't be trusted. At any rate, I'm certain that she'll be dead shortly. No weapons, no food, no shelter." He paused, then addressed Bellamont. "Good luck."

She was no longer laughing, and her miserable face looked like a blood-smeared skull with wet hair pasted to it. Her escape complete, she faced the reality of being alone in the wastes.

It was Fontaine's turn to laugh. It was a joyless, hollow sound. "Go on. You're free. I release you. Go before I change my mind."

Bellamont wavered, as if she wanted to say something else. She took a few tentative steps backward, lingered for another moment, then turned and clumsily ran off into the shadows, the rope that had bound her to Lowther snaking through the dirt behind her.

Galt watched her disappear amongst the twisted, barren trees. With the adrenaline from the confrontation fading, he began to shiver again. He looked at Solgard and marveled at the valor she'd just exhibited.

"You saved my life," Lowther said with a tinge of embarrassment, finally wrenching his eyes away from where Bellamont had vanished into the trees. "Thank you."

Cold, wet, and numb, they simply nodded.

They tied Lowther back onto the rope, and, as they slid into the water for the final crossing to the north bank, Galt looked at Fontaine, who had apparently already forgotten about Bellamont.

His eyes were fixed firmly on the eastern horizon.

CHAPTER 49

Though he was bothered tremendously by Bellamont's escape, Cyprian was determined to let it go and focus on the task at hand. By all accounts, he'd made the right decision. Faye seemed pleased with his choice not to pursue her, though she remained standoffish. Starkad also approved, noting that pursuing her would have been a pointless distraction.

Cyprian had tried to adopt a casual indifference to her departure, and knew from a logical standpoint that his earlier statements had been true. She was nothing to him or the expedition, and would not impede their progress.

Nevertheless, the gall of her actions, and the fact that she'd somehow managed to overcome the current and make it to shore, irritated him immensely. Her success had struck a blow to his pride, and he often wished that they'd still had a crossbow and some bolts to put her down with. He couldn't help but feel that the remainder of the company were whispering behind his back about his failure to stop her. To soothe his bruised ego, he would often picture her succumbing to starvation somewhere in the wastes.

Cyprian had been tempted to take out his frustration on the one actually responsible for letting her get away. Lowther would have been an easy scapegoat. The problem was that Lowther was generally well-liked, and, considering their dwindling numbers and the close-knit camaraderie of the survivors, Cyprian knew it would be a misstep to punish him harshly. He had publicly assured Lowther that what had occurred was inevitable, and there was nothing else he could have done, as well as commending him for his attempt to stop her.

Privately, he thought that the guardsman had been negligent in letting his prisoner walk behind him. She'd nearly killed him, and furthermore, she'd made him lose his pack and all of its provisions in the river. He'd now inherited Bellamont's overloaded pack, and despite Cyprian's reassurances, he carried it like a mark of shame.

Cyprian had plenty of time to ruminate on Bellamont's escape as they followed the meandering course of the river further into the Dawnlands and the heart of Faedalia. To his relief, they had not encountered any area that would have been easier to ford prior to the bifurcation of the river.

When they reached the broad split, he'd taken a moment to look at the collapsed remnant of whatever scant bridges had once spanned the waters. Very little was left. The far northern reaches of the Vingallean kingdom had obviously not reached the same dizzying heights as Vin-Sadavat. At the ancient crossings, they re-united with the faint remains of the Imperial Highway, which now ran northeasterly along the bank of the river. The road wasn't much different from the parched earth they'd walked since leaving the foothills of the Einmaz.

Their route now followed that old road, headed toward what Starkad believed was the most logical place to seek Chortelak: the elder seat of Faedalia's power, the Violet Palace. Cyprian was some-what familiar with the palace, as it figured into the known history of Vingallea's bygone domination of the north.

After the people of Aurangzeb had been conquered, their capital city sacked and eventually rechristened as Vin-Sadavat, Phan-Ellara had set her sights on extending her dominion all the way to the northern coast. All that remained was to conquer Faedalia, a mostly rural principality that had been a province of Aurangzeb. It had already sent its best men to aid Aurangzeb in the siege of the capital, and subsequently offered almost no resistance as Phan-Ellara completed the northern march of her legions and consolidated her new kingdom.

The Violet Palace, a splendid, sprawling estate that had served as the royal mansion of Faedalia's masters, was seized, and became the home to a long line of regional governors who oversaw the territory. Of what occurred at the palace after the fall of the Father-God, nothing was known. No messengers or refugees from Faedalia had ever arrived in Nordabor.

According to the few maps from the Hall of Antiquities that had survived the slavers' attack, as well as Starkad's own weathered map, the Einfallen's northern arm led directly to the palace, which had been erected on its shore near the center of Faedalia. From what Cyprian could remember reading about Faedalia, much of the territory had been devoted to farmsteads, woodlands, and a tremendous vineyard surrounding the grounds of the palace. It sounded like it had been a beautiful place.

The teachings of Starkad's people painted a bleak picture of what it was now. After the fall of the Father-God, drought and the dim light of the static dawn had withered the previously verdant lands. Starkad explained that his elders spoke of a roaring inferno, a wall of fire that had devoured the land, leaving nothing but ash in its wake. It was unknown what caused the fire, whether it was a careless traveler, armed conflict, or lightning produced by the last of Naffabyin's natural power. Whatever the source, Faedalia burned. All that remained of the sylvan glens and rolling meadows was ash as thick as the snow upon the slopes of Urgukorge.

As they continued to travel toward the palace, Cyprian saw increasing evidence in support of the tales. The dried husks of trees, previously so prevalent throughout the wastes, had tapered off. Dustings of ash across the sterile, hard-packed dirt grew more common.

Seven full-cycles of travel since departing the basecamp had delivered them firmly within the Dawnlands, but as in Nordabor, the sky was smothered in a low blanket of clouds, here streaked through with purple light by the perpetually rising sun.

Tempered or not, the sunlight was a welcome change. The temperature continued to rise, and was now akin to that found in Nordabor. Those standing watch no longer felt a helpless fear of the unknown. Wandering shades could be spotted easily from afar, and with proper precautions, unnecessary danger had been avoided. Fires were no longer a necessity for survival, and the wood they'd collected along their way could now be meted out more conservatively. The fires were now primarily used to heat what little food remained, which had dwindled dangerously low. A grinding hunger now constantly dogged them. Despite the relief of leaving the frigid darkness behind, and the limitless supply of water from the river, the company was still suffering greatly.

"We need to address the provisions," Mather said as the leaders gathered for a private meeting.

It was an understatement. The greatest threat to their success had become something as simple as food. Cyprian, who'd been trying to will the problem away and focus on his grandiose designs, found this issue supremely annoying. His own hunger was easily overshadowed by his ambition, and he struggled to understand how others could not feel the same.

Gathered some distance from the rest of the camp, Cyprian, Mather, and Starkad had met to discuss what lay ahead. Cyprian's view of what constituted leadership had narrowed appreciably, and he no longer wished to discuss everything openly with the company. While he still created the illusion of an open forum, the real business was now only discussed among the three of them. Not even Faye was privy to these discussions, as he didn't wish to hear her questioning, and couldn't bear to see her troubled glances.

Further discussions of a more secretive nature excluded even Mather, as certain matters could only be discussed with Starkad. Of his truest thoughts, Cyprian kept his own counsel.

"I know," he said to Mather. "We're running out. But we're almost there, are we not, Duncan?"

"We are," he answered.

Mather looked at him. "How far?"

Starkad looked eastward and pursed his lips. "I would estimate that we have about two full-cycles of travel left at the pace we're moving."

"Surely the provisions will last through that," Cyprian said.

"They should, yes," Mather agreed, "but the problem will be what comes after. If and when we conclude our business at this palace, we'll still have a long march back to Nordabor. We'll also have to cross the river again, going south. We'll need our strength. We'll need food. I don't think our provisions will last us that long, no matter how small the rations."

"I'm sure there will be a bridge or two at the palace," Cyprian said flippantly. "Something of a higher-quality construction befitting a royal estate, something that will still be standing."

"Assuming there is, it's still a long march back. We'll run out of food."

Mather was right, but Cyprian refused to accept the possibility of capturing every piece of the Scale of Judgment, only to starve to death on the trip back to Nordabor. There had to be an alternative.

"What about fish?" he asked, turning to Starkad. "Could we catch any fish in the river?"

"I'm afraid not. They may still spawn in the waters near Nordabor, where your slave-god's influence has kept life afloat, but they would not be this far north. At least, I've seen no evidence of them."

Cyprian folded his arms and slowly exhaled. "Any chance of there being food at the Violet Palace?"

Starkad shrugged noncommittally. It was a rare move for a man who seemed to have an answer to everything.

Cyprian tried to work through the issue in his head, where a torrent of conflicting thoughts spiraled through every crevice of his mind. Like an audible hum, his murderous actions ran as a constant undercurrent to everything, promising to poison every choice. His thoughts slid together, funneling into his unquenched desire for the glory of success. A vile, black realization rose over the din. He wished he'd thought to strip the meat from the bones of the executed.

As soon as the odious thought occurred, he violently rebuked it. Mather was staring at him expectantly. He had no answer.

"We could go to Kafarbjorn Harbor," Starkad said.

"What?" Mather asked with equal parts impatience and confusion.

"When we leave the Violet Citadel," Starkad said thoughtfully, as if exploring the idea as he spoke, "instead of marching for Nordabor, we could instead go the relatively short distance to Kafarbjorn."

"Why would we do that?"

"Well, there's a possibility that we could find a boat that's still intact enough for us to row down the coast."

Mather scoffed derisively. "You can't be serious. The chance of us finding any boat still capable of carrying us is minuscule. We'd go out of our way just to end up with an even-longer march back to the city. We can't gamble with our lives like that."

"It's not that unlikely," Starkad replied. "I've travelled through the harbor before. I saw many boats that could still function, certainly with some repairs by Dupree. We could travel down the coast and make a much shorter trek west, back to Nordabor."

"How long ago were you there?" Mather asked. "Whatever you saw could be rotted away by now. And what do you know of traveling by boat? How would you know if the boats were still seaworthy?"

"I know enough," Starkad said.

"As you know of everything," Mather sniped.

"Enough," Cyprian interrupted. "I understand your concerns, Captain, but this idea certainly has merit."

It clearly took a great deal of effort for Mather to maintain his composure. He bore the same rigid expression that he'd had during his public confrontation with Phir-Ramarian when he'd interrupted the celebration at the crater's edge. "As you wish, my lord," he said through gritted teeth.

Cyprian eyed him for a moment, then turned back to Starkad. "You would be able to navigate the coast? You'd know where to land to begin our westward march?"

"Yes, I would."

"Okay," Cyprian said. "It would be faster than marching south, and we wouldn't have to stop for camps. We could sleep in shifts on the boat, take turns rowing. If only we had a boat now."

"My lord, if we travel to this harbor and there's no boat, we are doomed," Mather said.

"I know, but by your own account, we don't have enough food to make it south on foot, anyway. The way I see it, this is our only chance."

Mather heaved a sigh. "Yes, my lord."

With the matter settled, Cyprian felt a small amount of relief. He pictured himself on a boat, the sunlight of the Daylands shining upon him, the strife and fear and danger over. Well, mostly over.

A relatively short march back to Nordabor, and he would be hailed as a conquering hero. Everything his father had failed to accomplish in his disappearance, everything that had been trusted to Phir-Ramarian while he'd been shunted aside, he would deliver on. They would sing his name in the tales of the new Vingallea. He would be held in the same esteem as Phan-Ellara and Phan-Casmia; a hero of mythical proportions. His actions would bring salvation, and the means he'd taken to get there, if they were ever even discovered, would not only be understood, but celebrated.

Perhaps when they took Paradise, when his legacy was cemented, then he could finally confess to Faye. At that time, she would surely be unable to do anything but understand.

All he had to do was conquer one more of the old ones and his triumph would be assured.

· · ·

As they journeyed, the Imperial Highway eventually became identifiable only by its proximity to the Einfallen and as a slight depression in the dunes of ash. They staggered under a hazy, violet sky through ash that was knee-deep in some areas. Passing over rolling hills with bare tops, they trudged into shallow gullies choked with the spent cinders of an ancient fire. The air, as flat and stagnant as anywhere else, carried countless tiny fragments of swirling soot disturbed by their footfalls. Ever-present was the dark, murmuring water of the Einfallen cutting through the gray land to their right.

It was a monotonous, sterile place, and Cyprian was eager to be done with it, as was the rest of the remaining company. He'd informed them of the new plan for their return to Nordabor, and there had been no dissent. When he had presented the journey to Kafarbjorn, the procurement of a vessel, and the journey down the coast as a simple alternative to yet another relentless march, during which they would certainly run out of food, the group had been enthusiastic.

Of course, he'd failed to mention the risks, and if any aside from Mather considered them, they did not speak their mind. Even Faye seemed supportive of the idea. Cyprian did not feel it necessary to explain that it had originated with Starkad, which would have certainly soured her toward it, no matter what merits the plan had.

So, with a hope of swiftly obtaining the last shard and beginning the journey back to Nordabor, they continued their march.

Eventually, after cresting a hill that was identical to every one that had come before, they spotted it. On a curve of the river, rising from the sea of ash, was a squat, terraced structure, capped by crumbling parapets. The palace, surrounded by several smaller buildings and the vague outlines of former walls and hedges, was heavily sagging and partially sunk into the river. Like so many of the other ancient structures they'd encountered, the beauty and grace that it had once boasted was still apparent under the decrepitude.

With their goal finally in sight, Cyprian called for a brief halt. "What's our best approach here?" he asked Starkad, peering through his field glass at the decaying palace.

"I think we should stick close to the riverbank. Make entry through one of the exposed chambers where the structure is sinking into the river."

"You've said previously that others of your kind have been known to seek out Chortelak," Mather interjected. "Are we risking another ambush by human followers?"

Starkad scanned the ruins with his own field glass. "I don't see any signs of habitation. No fires, no tracks in the ash. If there are any followers, they're inside. That's not to say that they wouldn't be watching the outside, but that's a risk we'll have to take. There are no options for cover or concealment out here." He gestured toward the barren open space around them.

Mather was clearly not pleased by the uncertainty in their plan. "And what if we *are* being watched and they loose arrows from the windows while we're approaching?"

"Then we hope they have poor aim."

Cyprian ended the discussion before it could devolve into an argument and attract the attention of the others, who were resting on the side of the hill a little way behind them.

Their conversation finished, Cyprian roused the group and they descended toward the palace. It took almost two cycles to reach the grid-like remnants of the fallow vineyards that encircled the palace grounds. Cautiously, they trudged through the ash drifts, watching the windows of the palace. Cyprian was amazed to see that some of them still boasted intricate stained glass that must have already been ancient by the time Vingallea had seized Faedalia.

Approaching the southern side of the structure, Cyprian saw that the upper floors had pancaked down almost to the waterline, pinching the entire structure into a jagged slope that terminated in the river. Broken pillars jutting out of the water like crooked teeth were all that remained of three toppled bridges that appeared to have once attached to a grand balcony and spanned the Einfallen. The balcony itself was now a twisted stretch of wrought iron and scattered bricks, draped across the pile of partially sunken ruins. Visible in the collapsed heap were a few dark gaps—the severed ends of hallways that would provide them with a way inside.

As they grew closer, Cyprian was relieved to find that no attack came. Bolstered by their unimpeded progress, they reached the collapsed southern wall in a short time. Wading into the water and scrambling over some of the wreckage, they soon found themselves standing before one of the gaping thresholds.

The old excitement he'd always harbored for antiquities still stirred, though it had certainly been stifled somewhat. His many concerns had ascended beyond the simple explorations of the past he'd previously found joy in. He glanced at Faye, who was quietly marveling at the imposing facade, and felt suddenly and intensely alone, excised from Faye completely; cast out into another world, separate and removed.

The feeling grappled with his new purpose and fell before its total domination of his will. Every thought bent back toward his desire to gain the final shard, and the coming exaltation that it would herald. Once that was done, and his position secure, there would be time enough for everything else.

Without further hesitation, Cyprian descended into the darkness.

CHAPTER 50

Sloshing through the partially submerged passage, Solgard considered how lucky they were that it was so well-lit. Massive cracks in the walls and ceiling allowed the gray-and-purple daylight to reach the water, and the reflected light shimmered in wavering bands across the walls.

When they first entered, it had been dark and foreboding, and their three battered lanterns had offered little assistance. One wouldn't light, and the other two sputtered weakly as they used the last of their fuel. They'd functioned just long enough to reach the daylight. Like so much of the equipment they'd departed Nordabor with, the now-useless lanterns had been carelessly tossed aside.

The water filling the passage was up to their knees, and as cold as it had been when they'd made the crossing. Solgard's feet were growing numb, and she prayed that it didn't get any deeper. She'd nearly drowned jumping in after Lowther, and she had no desire ever to be fully submerged in the Einfallen again.

The party said little as they went, though she could hear the hushed voices of Fontaine and Starkad discussing which way to go. They'd passed several doorways either choked with debris or opening into dimmer, narrower passages. From what she could glean, it sounded like they were looking for a way up.

The only other voices belonged to Lady Fontaine and Berg, who were discussing the palace itself. "The amount that we could learn, not just about Vingallea, but about the people of Faedalia who came before. It's staggering," Berg murmured. "Imagine if this place has a hall of records."

"I don't think that we'll have much time to waste here," Lady Fontaine said quietly, "but perhaps when we're heading to the Isle of Creation with the reforged blade, we can stop by here for a more thorough examination."

It pleased Solgard to hear a positive outlook like that—unless, of course, Lady Fontaine was being facetious. She seemed genuinely intrigued by the ruin, but also weary. Which seemed perfectly reasonable, given their circumstances.

Solgard would have certainly felt wearier were it not for Galt. He walked beside her now, his mouth a thin line, his brow furrowed. She knew that he was on edge, that he was anticipating shades lurching out of every vacant doorway.

Solgard was aware of her surroundings too, but her faith in the Void-God manifested itself in a constant feeling of preparedness. Her faith had carried her through every hardship they had endured, be it her capture at the hands of the slavers or the bloody insurrection. She knew that Galt's faith was weak; he'd been frank about it before they'd become romantically entangled. He only bit his tongue now to spare her feelings, but she knew that his thoughts had not changed.

Solgard felt sorry for him and wished that he could experience the same connection with the Void-God that she did. If it weren't for the incredible circumstances that had brought them together, she suspected that their theological differences, even more than their vows, would have prevented any bond from developing.

Nonetheless, she found herself feeling what could only be love for the difficult man beside her.

"Look at the wainscoting in this room. I can't believe it's still intact," Berg said, peering into a side chamber.

"Stay with the group," Galt advised. "We don't know who's down here. Living or otherwise."

Berg looked slightly taken aback, but allowed Lady Fontaine to lead him away after the others.

"It truly is a marvel, isn't it?" Pike commented to the old man, stepping clumsily as he looked around the vaulted passage. "A history that predates Vingallea."

"Absolutely," Berg agreed. "Essentially untouched by their architectural or artistic influence. Unlike Vin-Sadavat, where the hallmarks of Vingallean design were everywhere, over top all of the original work."

How Berg had taken the time to admire the architecture of that nightmare city was beyond Solgard. She'd been much more focused on staying alive.

"Not to mention what the slavers did to the place," Lady Fontaine added. "It doesn't look like anyone's been here in an eternity, though. If Chortelak is here, I don't think he's got quite the following that Tariono had."

"That's a blessing," Solgard said, remembering the terror of being held captive by Tariono's legion—the mutilated children, the wanton violence, the grotesque way the slavers had fondled Bellamont. The memory quickly slid into the more recent image of Bellamont's bloody, crazed face. It was hard to reconcile the two images and think of them as the same person. She'd felt pity and fear for Bellamont during their captivity. Now, to feel a sense of frustration at her escape, and to consider her an enemy, was sad and strange.

Nobody had taken her escape worse than Lowther. He'd been spared any sort of reprimand by Fontaine, though Galt suspected that Fontaine was secretly furious with him. Regardless of the public pardon, Lowther was still miserable about his failure. Mather, of all people, had reassured him that he'd done all he could, but Lowther remained sullen and defeated. He was a good man, and it pained Solgard to see him suffer.

"This way," Starkad's hushed voice said from ahead, interrupting Solgard's thoughts.

One by one, the line ascended through a threshold sagging uneasily under the weight of a vaulted passage that threatened to collapse at any moment. Solgard stepped through as quickly as she could. She was relieved to find that they'd reached a balustrade-lined staircase leading up and out of the waterlogged lower level. Carefully, they ascended the lopsided stairs, the stones of which had started to buckle inward.

Reaching the top, they emerged into a more stable section of the palace. A large open-roofed plaza stretched before them. Solgard saw finely carved pillars and empty pools with decorative tiles in their dry bottoms. Intricate chandeliers hung drunkenly along the perimeter of the open roof, most of their crystals having long since fallen to the stones below. The central portion of the plaza was a jumble of different dried ponds and enclosures, some of which were littered with unusual bones.

"Look at that!" Berg gushed with excitement, ignoring Lady Fontaine's pull and trotting off toward the bizarre enclosures.

"What was this place?" Solgard asked, though she was unsure of whether anyone could provide an answer.

"I believe it was a menagerie," Lady Fontaine said. "I remember reading about this. The lords of Faedalia were said to have kept the most expansive collection of exotic animals known to man. After Vingallea seized the palace, they continued that tradition."

Solgard reassessed her surroundings with new interest and tried to picture what it had looked like before the fall. "It must have been remarkable. This whole place, I mean."

"Yes," Lady Fontaine said, running her hand through the coating of ash atop a bust of some forgotten lord. "I'm sure it was."

"It could be again. When we enter Paradise, everything could be as it once was. From Paradise, we could heal this world. We could even restore the Void-God."

Lady Fontaine, who'd been watching Berg and Pike wander across the plaza, raised her eyebrows. "This world could be healed, but I'm not sure anyone is interested in restoring any of the old ones to power, be that your god or otherwise."

"The Void-God loves us still, no matter what our ancestors did," Solgard said with a touch of defensiveness. "We were led astray."

"Yes, but convinced to or not, we wanted what we couldn't have, and that was control of Paradise. I don't think your god would be willing to let us have it now, even if we were responsible for his restoration. That was the cause of all of this in the first place, as I recall."

For the first time, Solgard grew worried not that they would fail, but that they might succeed. There would be many worshippers of the Void-God who would wish to see their creator restored, but there would be many others, certainly among the ruling elites, who would want the power of Paradise to be solely under the dominion of mankind. Beyond those chief philosophical differences, there would be countless other disagreements on how to use their new-found mastery of life itself. Traditionally, mankind did not handle disagreements well.

There would be an obvious struggle over who would really be in control and what they would choose to do with that power. Undoubtedly, Phar-Mindorius would believe it resided with him. She suspected that Fontaine could also make a claim to it, being responsible for their deliverance should they succeed. She remembered the accusations made by Kovak and Gricks and shuddered at the possibility. Whoever ended up in control, Solgard prayed they wouldn't repeat the sins of the past.

"This time," she said slowly, unsure if she even believed what she was saying, "things would be different."

Lady Fontaine looked at her steadily, her face unreadable. "I hope you're right."

She looked away, and Solgard followed her gaze to Fontaine. He was pacing the edge of the plaza, gazing about, speaking quietly with Starkad. She assumed they were discussing where to find the old one.

The others lingered about, waiting for direction. She noticed Galt following Berg and Pike at a distance, clearly irked by their careless wandering. His resemblance to an impatient parent watching reckless children was uncanny, and Solgard couldn't help but smile.

"Come see these bones," Berg called to Pike. "And you two, get over here!" he shouted, gesturing at Lord and Lady Fontaine. "This looks just like the sketches of the elepha—"

He suddenly dropped out of sight with a clipped shout.

Everyone rushed toward him, with Pike and Galt arriving first.

"Hold on, stop!" Galt shouted as the others reached them. "He's fallen through the floor. It's not stable; it'll collapse completely if we all stand on it."

Solgard shuffled back with the others, pulling Lady Fontaine with her. She could see Berg barely holding on to the crumbling edge of a low wall of the enclosure he'd been exploring. His lower half had disappeared into the floor.

"Get me out of here," he wheezed. "I can't hold on."

"I'm coming," Galt said as he stepped carefully onto the low wall. Solgard's heart leapt into her throat as he approached Berg slowly but steadily. "Grab my arms and I'll pull you up."

"If I let go, I'll fall," Berg hissed, his fear turning into frustration with his would-be rescuer.

"Now!" Galt ordered.

Slipping, Berg lunged for Galt's arms. They managed to cling to each other's wrists, and with a mighty heave, Galt hauled the old man out of the hole. As Berg's boots landed on the wall, the floor underneath it buckled further. Galt grabbed Berg by the collar and hurled them both into the enclosure just as the wall they'd been standing on disappeared into the now-gaping hole. They landed heavily and scrambled backward as the hole consumed more of the floor around them, sending chunks of stone thundering into the darkness of whatever halls lay below.

As they reached the opposite wall of the circular enclosure, the erosion stopped. Everyone remained still. The only sounds were Berg's raspy panting and the last tumbles of the falling stones.

"You just almost broke your back for a second time," Fontaine said, carefully helping Berg to his feet. Pike tried to assist, and Fontaine shooed him away.

Berg had just opened his mouth, presumably to thank Galt, when he was interrupted by a chilling sound.

From the darkness of the newly opened chasm, the telltale moaning of countless shades rose to meet their ears. Solgard and Galt locked eyes. Being careful to stay as far away from the hole as she could, she rushed to his side. The others suddenly looked frightened and lost, aside from Mather, who had drawn Moore's blade and was striding to meet them.

"We need to move," Solgard said as the three of them converged. "Now."

•   •   •

As the sound of the shades grew closer, swelling up from the stairwell they'd come from, as well as other unknown passages leading to the plaza, Solgard, Galt, and Mather swiftly assumed command. To Fontaine's credit, he did not try to reassert his dominance, though Solgard suspected that it had more to do with his mounting terror than any tacit understanding that they knew what was best.

"This way—it's clear," Solgard called after listening intently down one of the adjacent corridors to make sure the shades were coming from elsewhere.

The group rushed into the corridor behind Solgard with Galt and Mather following behind, serving as a rearguard. Solgard suddenly realized that she was leading them, but she had no idea where she was leading them to. She darted down the hallway, vaulting over collapsed pillars and heaps of fallen stone from the floors above. The company followed, kicking up plumes of ash and dust that swirled through the beams of sunlight sneaking in through the damaged walls and ceiling.

She could see that the corridor ahead terminated in an impassable heap of rubble, and she started to look desperately into each doorway they passed, seeking an alternative route. Almost every threshold was choked with debris. The moaning had grown into a veritable roar, and she risked a glance back just in time to see shades flooding the corridor behind them, blotting out the light from the open plaza.

A few horrified cries broke out from the group as they reached the end of the passage, and found no way out. Solgard pushed through the crowd as they clumped together against the rubble, finding her way to Galt and Mather.

"So what's the plan? Is there any way out?" Mather asked.

Solgard shook her head.

"We'll hold them off as long as we can," Galt said.

"Move the rocks!" Solgard heard Fontaine call out behind them.

She looked back and saw Fontaine, Starkad, Dupree, Anders, and Lowther scrambling up the rubble slope and pulling stones free. At the top, a tantalizing beam of light was visible, teasing escape.

Silently praying for their survival, she faced the impending wall of shades slithering monstrously down the corridor toward them.

"Brace yourselves," Galt growled.

Death seemed imminent, but Solgard refused to accept it. She held her blade tightly, steadied her breathing, and tried to focus her mind on the call of the Void-God, shielding herself within his divine protection.

As the shades closed in on them, her prayers were answered.

"It's clear! Move!" Fontaine shouted over the increasing din of the shades.

Solgard whipped around and saw that they'd clawed loose a small gap in the rubble. Lady Fontaine was clambering through onto the floor above, with Lowther and Pike pushing Berg up behind her. Renewed hope bloomed within Solgard. She knew that she could hold off the shades.

At least long enough for the others to make it through the gap.

Enough of the company had squeezed through that Solgard, Galt, and Mather could climb up the slope, offering them the limited protection of higher ground. It was just in time.

The slavering horrors reached the base of the rubble and, howling with nightmarish fury, clawed toward them. They hacked at the groping, long-fingered hands, tearing into the shriveled, ash-streaked limbs and twisted visages before them.

"Come on!" Fontaine screamed behind them.

Solgard continued to back up the slope slowly, swinging wildly at the distorted black mass of flesh. The tight space proved to be a boon; the shades were crammed together, desperately snapping and ripping at one another as each sought to be the first to set upon their prey. Solgard, Galt, and Mather stabbed blindly into whatever thrashing shapes seemed to be emerging to the front, and the shades that fell before them only tightened the space, forming a bulwark of hissing, dissolving piles of wet meat.

"Go!" Galt yelled, black blood flinging from the edge of his blade.

He pushed in front of her, and before she could do anything, she was being seized from behind and pulled through the gap by Fontaine and Lowther. To her relief, Galt was pulled through directly after her. He immediately turned around and helped Mather, who was smeared with the black blood of the shades, through as well.

Solgard stumbled to her feet and grabbed Galt. "Are you okay?"

"Yes," he gasped.

"Captain?"

"Yes, I'm fine," Mather panted, wiping his face.

Behind him, the long, sinewy arms of a shade shot through the gap. Solgard yanked Mather away as the creature planted its skeletal hands on the stone floor and began to hoist itself through the breach. As its shriveled head rose into view, the wet hole that constituted its mouth sucking eagerly, Solgard slashed at its right arm, failing to pierce the ancient tissue, but knocking the arm out from under it. The shade dropped, and its head struck the floor. Before it could rear up again, she plunged her blade into the back of its head. It shrieked balefully and started to shake.

As its blood spewed forth, a second shade tried to climb over it, but Galt and Mather set upon the monster before it could gain any purchase, stabbing relentlessly until it collapsed.

The two dissolving shades clogged the gap, but the rest were still very close. Within moments, they would claw through their own dead and clear the breach. The company had to keep moving.

"This way," Starkad said, sounding unexpectedly calm. "Through these doors. I believe we've found what we were looking for."

He gestured toward two massive, ornate wooden doors at the end of the large foyer they'd climbed into. Solgard didn't know if there would be an old one behind those doors, but she thought they looked strong enough to hold against the shades.

Fontaine strode confidently toward the doors, the shades apparently forgotten. The others followed behind, looking nervously back toward the hole in the floor. As Fontaine and Starkad seized the brass handles and pulled the doors open, Solgard watched as the leathery arm of a shade rose through the breach. The group shuffled inside, slamming the doors shut behind them. Without a word, Lowther seized an iron candelabrum and jammed it through the handles. It would have to hold.

Solgard stood panting in the dim light. Slowly, she became aware of a low murmur. It sounded like the pleasant chatter of a relaxed crowd. Her mind was almost unable to process the sound, and she looked at Galt with confusion. Equally flummoxed, he shrugged. Peering into the faint light of the hall, she couldn't see anything that would account for the noise.

"It appears we've been joined by some new guests," a jovial voice called merrily from the darkness. "Weary travelers from the outside lands, no doubt. Come. Rest before my hearth."

The hall was suddenly filled with a rich golden light, illuminating a scene Solgard could have scarcely imagined.

Well-tended fires roared in multiple immense fireplaces. Shining candelabras and chandeliers added to the glow, casting their warm light upon richly woven tapestries that adorned every wall of the immaculate chamber. Most striking of all were the gleaming tables of polished wood that stretched across the room, upon which a feast of unimaginable proportions was laid out—roasted boars, chickens, and meats more exotic than Solgard knew, as well as piles of strange fruits, baked vegetables of a dizzying variety, delicate desserts unheard of, and overflowing goblets of wine and mead. Solgard's desire to dive onto one of the tables and gorge herself was so overwhelming that she almost didn't notice the guests of the feast. Nearly two dozen friendly, well-fed faces gazed at the group with serene benevolence.

"I apologize for the darkness; we've let the fires burn low for some time now. It has been too long since we've had any newcomers. Welcome," their host said magnanimously.

Her attention pulled from the food, Solgard noticed the speaker for the first time. She knew immediately that the being, who'd just risen from his seat at the center of the head table, was Chortelak.

He was tremendous, not in height but in girth, and clad in velvet robes fringed by the pelt of an exotic animal that Solgard had never seen. She assumed that it'd once belonged to one of the bygone creatures of the menagerie. Every finger of his plump hands was adorned in a gaudy ring, and he clutched a massive, shining goblet. He took a long draught from it, spilling wine down his portly, bearded chin. Above his head, which was crowned by a curled tuft of red hair, hovered a halo of interwoven bands of silver, flourished with small golden leaves and berries.

"From whence do you come, travelers?" he asked with genuine interest. He approached them slowly as he spoke, the eyes of his celebrants locked on him fawningly.

The entire company seemed to be as dumbstruck as Solgard. Those who weren't eyeing the feast greedily were gazing about in confusion and wonder. Only Starkad remained unimpressed. He urged Fontaine forward. As if waking from a stupor, Fontaine shook his head and addressed Chortelak.

"We hail from Nordabor, the last city of Vingallea," he said importantly.

Chortelak squealed with delight, clapping his porcine hands. "Well met! I don't think we've ever received a guest from such a distant land, nor one of such prestige! Few were my followers in that serious place. You are not as stodgy as your ancestors, I think—otherwise, you wouldn't be here with me!" He laughed heartily, his corpulent belly waggling beneath his robes.

"We are not here to make merry with you," Fontaine said with a look of mild distaste. "We come seeking your shard of the Scale of Judgment."

Chortelak froze, and the eyes of his guests turned in unison upon Fontaine. It was silent for a moment, then the god emitted another booming laugh. The guests returned to their feasting, drinking, and vacuous, pleasant smiles.

Solgard felt a chill run up her spine. She was suddenly reminded intensely of the strange allure that had emanated from Tariono. A false sheen of delight gilding a foul horror. She looked around the room, feeling as if she were very close to seeing through some sort of illusion.

"Men of Vingallea never understood the simple things," Chortelak said with a whimsical melancholy, as if drawing memories from a deep well of time. "Always so focused on progress. There was a time that I thought their path may lead me to greater pleasures, but alas, I was wrong. And now you wish to discuss something as dull as my little souvenir of that failure? There will be time enough for that. For now, as my noble guests, I invite you to feast."

Fontaine was nonplussed. It was clear that he had expected to demand the shard and be met with force, not an invitation to feast. Clearing his throat, he started to readdress Chortelak, but the corpulent god had already turned back toward the head table. As the chatter of the celebrants returned, he looked at Starkad with his eyebrows raised.

"If he says to eat, then let's eat," Anders interjected. "He even said we could discuss the shard later. He's willing to treat with us, I bet."

Several others murmured in agreement.

"Nobody should eat any of that food," Starkad warned.

Solgard agreed with him completely. She looked at Galt, who looked like he was in physical pain as he gazed longingly at the succulent roasts.

"Just because we've been met with hostility before doesn't mean that he's a threat. Do they look like they're afraid of him?" Berg asked, pointing toward the celebrants. "We should match his courtesy with courtesy. Then we can try to persuade him to give us the shard."

"Are you blind?" Starkad asked. "Have you already forgotten that we're in a ruin? That shades lurk just outside that door? This isn't real."

"It certainly looks real to me. And smells real," Berg shot back.

"Maybe the old one conjured the food," Dupree suggested, eyeing the feast. "Maybe he has the power to do so. And maybe he protects his followers."

"I don't trust him," Fontaine said, "and, regardless, we don't have time for a lengthy parlay."

Solgard's eyes were drifting from the conversation, inexorably drawn back toward the food. Her mind knew not to trust it, but her empty stomach gurgled pitiably.

Suddenly, she realized that Anders had joined Chortelak's other guests at the nearest table. Before she could call out to him, Chortelak's voice boomed jubilantly from the head table.

"Splendid! Enjoy the bounty I offer you," he cheered, his small eyes glinting brightly. "You'll find that I provide generously for those who seek me."

Anders was tearing into a roasted chicken with his bare hands, biting savagely into the meat, juice running down his face. Chortelak's followers watched him with the same unchanging expressions of pleasure, totally unaffected by his sloppy grasping at every food within reach.

Berg began to walk toward the table, but Lady Fontaine seized his arm. "Jotun, stop."

"We're starving. We need this food," he argued, pulling away.

She looked at Fontaine. "What are we going to do?"

"I don't—" He watched Berg trot away. "Stop him."

"I'm trying," Lady Fontaine said with irritation, snatching at Berg's arm while Pike followed behind, pleading with him to stop.

"Stand down," Mather ordered as Dupree and Lowther suddenly started toward the tables, where Anders had moved on to a platter of small cakes.

The temptation of the food was proving to be too much. Solgard looked at the splintering group desperately, knowing that something terrible was going to happen. The feeling of almost seeing beneath the facade was growing, just as the overpowering scent of the food was growing. She clutched Galt close, intent on keeping him from the tables. He hadn't moved yet, but continued to stare in that direction.

"Enough of this," Fontaine seethed, stalking down the center aisle. One of the celebrants offered him a tray of assorted cheeses, and he smacked it aside. He arrived before Chortelak, who was clapping lightly as he watched Anders tear his way through the spread.

"We will discuss the shard *now*," Fontaine demanded. "Give it to me."

All at once, the general sound of festivity ceased. Every one of the strangely similar followers now stared intently at Fontaine, their faces blank.

Chortelak's broad grin faltered. "You speak out of turn, traveller. I open my home to you, and you forsake my bounty and demand something no human hand should ever touch. Those of your party who wish to taste of my benevolence may remain. You are banished."

Fontaine stood defiantly before the god. The only sounds now were the wet smacking of Anders's lips and a rattling at the barred door. The shades were just outside.

"No."

"'No?'" Chortelak repeated. "What do you mean, 'no?'"

"I'm not leaving without that shard," Fontaine said, and there was steel in his voice. As if to punctuate his statement, he drew his sword and leveled it at Chortelak.

"Truly a man of Vingallea. Your forefathers would be proud, not only of your single-mindedness, but of your warmongering. Well, you will not get—" Chortelak stopped, interrupted by the sound of dry, wracking coughs. "Oh, dear. There seems to be something wrong with your man, there."

Fontaine spared a quick glance back toward the source of the coughs, and Solgard followed his gaze. Anders was clutching at his throat, purple blooming across his face.

"He's choking!" Dupree called out, rushing over to him, followed by Solgard and the others. Only Starkad remained where he stood, looking completely unsurprised.

As Solgard reached them, Dupree was already thumping Anders on the back violently. With every cough, ash spewed forth from his mouth and, mixed with snot, ran from his nose. He began to claw at his throat, tearing at the skin. His eyes bulged wildly, and he began to seize, emitting panicked, muffled cries. They tried to hold him still while Dupree uselessly pounded his back and Mather attempted to clear the ash from his mouth with his bare hands. It was no use. Within moments, Anders slumped lifelessly, the ash still spilling slowly from his gaping mouth.

Solgard had known something horrific was going to happen, and now that it had come to pass, she found that the illusion had been stripped away completely. She looked up slowly from Anders's body and was greeted with a scene of ghoulish terror.

The brilliant light had been replaced with a miasmic gloom from the filthy, barely lit fireplaces. The tables were now dry-rotted, collapsed wrecks with scattered drifts of ash upon them. Solgard could clearly see where Anders had been digging through the ash, his bewitched mind believing it to be food. Seated around the tables were numerous corpses. Chortelak had created the illusion of life, false phantoms on strings only he could see, and now, they had been revealed for what they were: the dried husks of those who had previously sought him and had ended up entombed in his charnel house.

"It has been so long since anyone darkened my doorstep," Chortelak said, his voice no longer hearty and robust, but now a wet croak. His appearance had changed as well, and his new aspect was grotesque proof of his debasement. His girth was gone, his body now withered and skeletal. His rings now dangled from bony fingers that caressed his sparse, filthy beard and fingered the swollen, open sores of a hideous pox that coated his lips. The halo above his head was now as filthy and tarnished as he was. The brittle and brown leaves had curled into themselves; the berries had turned putrid and were coated in a pale green carpet of mold.

"I would have gladly allowed you all to join me in pursuit of the limits of the old pleasures, but you came here barking out demands for something you shouldn't even know of. And now, your boorish behavior has driven my guests away, and I'm *alone*," he said with maudlin sorrow.

Clearly taken aback by the sudden, disgusting change in the god, Fontaine had backed away in repulsion. "Give me what I seek, and you'll be free to return to whatever foul festivities you wish to pursue here in the dark," he said with disgust.

"I will not tolerate any more of this in my court!" Chortelak shrieked with a sudden petulant fury, slamming his fist on the dusty table before him. "Get out! Get out! Get—"

Fontaine lunged forward and slammed his blade down upon Chortelak's bony wrist, severing the hand and cleaving the rotten table in two. Chortelak squealed in agony and tried to lurch away just as Fontaine booted him in his concave chest. He was rocked back in his rickety chair, which tipped over and unceremoniously dumped him onto the floor. Fontaine brought his blade to rest on Chortelak's throat.

"Mercy, mercy," the fallen god begged, breathing hard. "I care not so much for Veathyadell's plan as I care for my own life."

"Where is it?" Fontaine demanded.

"Within my robe."

"Get it."

"I can't," he cried. "My arm." He was clutching the ragged stump of his wrist with his left hand, doing little to stem the oozing blood.

"Someone come over here and search him," Fontaine called, his eyes never leaving Chortelak's pockmarked face.

Solgard had absolutely no interest in reaching within the folds of the vile god's robes, and was pleased to see Starkad approach instead. Without hesitation, he flung open Chortelak's fetid, stained robes and reached within, expertly snaking his hands through every fold.

"I have it," he stated. As Starkad announced his success and held the shard aloft, Chortelak's eyes widened.

"Wait!" he shouted.

His prize in hand, Fontaine apparently had no further use for the god. He jammed his blade deep into Chortelak's throat, sending a fountain of milky, rancid blood cascading down the god's chest. Multiple fissures suddenly shot through his halo, spilling feculent juice across his head. His wrist forgotten, Chortelak groped weakly at his neck for only a moment before he grew still. A final wet, rattling breath passed through his diseased lips.

It was silent. Even the sound of the shades rattling at the door had ceased. Solgard stood with Galt, both breathing through their mouths due to the wretched stench of the place. They'd been standing above Anders's prone form, awaiting the birth of a shade that, thankfully, never came.

Now, she watched as Fontaine pulled a rag from his pack and wiped his blade clean before he sheathed it. He tossed the rag to the floor and, with a second one, cleaned the shard, which Starkad had handed him, then wrapped the shard within the rag and slid it into the same metal tube that housed the others.

They'd done it. Every shard of the Scale of Judgment was now theirs. All that remained was to return to Nordabor, where the sword would be reforged, and then one final march to the Isle of Creation, where their entrance to Paradise awaited them.

Solgard was filled with a strange mixture of hope, relief, and dread as she watched Fontaine seal the cylinder shut, a look of complete satisfaction on his face.

CHAPTER 51

His success now assured, Cyprian felt as if everything else was aligning itself neatly to his will. Their departure from the Violet Palace had been far easier than he would have thought possible, as if fate itself were clearing the way for him.

Once the dust had settled after Chortelak's defeat, he'd ordered Galt and Solgard to check the foyer for any sign of the shades, which had either grown silent or departed. The shepherds had nervously slid the candelabrum from the handles and cracked the door open. After a moment of tense anticipation, they'd announced that the room was clear. The shades, denied their quarry, must have wandered back to whatever black hole they'd issued forth from.

Just as they'd been preparing to depart, Solgard had stated her intention to take Anders's body with them in order to dispose of it properly. Cyprian had looked at the crumpled form of the foolish hauler and felt nothing. The man had been loyal enough, but he should have heeded Starkad's warning. His death had been completely avoidable, and Cyprian hadn't been interested in prolonging their time at the palace by carrying out his body. Couching his denial in kind words, he'd told Solgard as much.

She had objected and, at the very least, wanted to burn Anders's body inside, but Cyprian had bluntly vetoed her. A fire would have only increased their odds of attracting the shades again.

As they'd shuffled out, Jotun, Lowther, and Dupree, who'd been eager to join Anders in the feast, had gazed sheepishly at his body and the piles of ash that surrounded it.

With no need to fear human followers, Cyprian had determined that they would seek the main entrance rather than retrace their steps. It proved to be a simple, direct path from the hall to the front gate, and, with little trouble, they'd forced the gate open and departed back into the wastes.

They had left the house of Chortelak, who had been reunited with his followers in death.

·   ·   ·

"Not much farther now. Perhaps four or five cycles," Starkad said, lowering his field glass. "The harbor is just beyond those bluffs."

They were gathered atop a scrubby hill, surveying their route. Only Starkad and Cyprian spoke, the others too exhausted and hungry to do much beyond standing and listening. Mather gazed intently toward the southwest, as if picturing himself walking off toward Nordabor.

Cyprian eyed the distant coastline through his own glass. He could make out a spot where the hills rose and then seemed to drop off into nothing, the Imperial Highway apparently terminating into thin air. Slightly further south, the span of the Einfallen grew wider, and it, too, disappeared over the bluffs. Beyond that, he supposed, was the sea, which remained hidden.

"You weren't wrong; this was a much-shorter trek," he said, feeling again that his destiny was plowing ahead, pushing aside any obstacle.

They'd only been hiking for two full-cycles, and had already left the ashes of Faedalia behind. They were now within the Daylands, moving through a melancholy land of gray sunlight and rolling moors. A mild dampness in the air heralded the sea they would soon reach.

Cyprian inhaled deeply, detecting a faint hint of brine. "I think I can smell the sea," he said to Faye. He exhaled with a smile.

He'd never seen the ocean before, nor had any living citizen of Nordabor. Even his father had never ventured as far as any coast. Their limited knowledge of the great salt seas came from maps and records compiled during the height of Vingallea's dominion. Buoyed by the completion of their quest, Cyprian found that he could once again enjoy the simple act of adventuring.

"I don't smell anything," Faye said, distracted.

Irritation shot through Cyprian. Faye had always shared his desire to travel to the sea, yet she remained dour. More so, she was apathetic about their recovery of the final shard. She voiced little beyond empty platitudes that imitated celebration and her ever-present desire to return to Nordabor.

Cyprian suspected that he knew why. Despite his best attempts to dissuade her, it was clear that Faye still harbored a deep distrust of Starkad. Whenever he was near, Faye chose to lag behind with Jotun, who'd also drifted from Cyprian. In the rare moments where he could speak to Faye with any privacy, Starkad's shadow seemed to hang over them still, poisoning every interaction with unspoken suspicions.

In truth, he really couldn't blame her for distrusting the unscrupulous badlander. As they hiked the final stretch of the derelict Imperial Highway, Cyprian spent considerable time envisioning the world after their successful return. He'd long had dreams of glory and acclaim, but now the problem of Starkad, and what he knew, was attached to them.

Perhaps, Cyprian thought, he would never tell Faye what he'd done. It was his choice, ultimately, and he would never feel safe or secure in the secrecy of that knowledge while another remained who knew the truth. Cyprian grew more concerned, and more certain, that as his power increased within the kingdom, Starkad's power over him would grow with it. Desiring a position of the highest order in their new world, Starkad could easily extort Cyprian into granting him whatever he wished or pressure him into convincing Phar-Mindorius to do so, assuming the king still reigned once they took Paradise. He was old, and now lacked a direct heir. Perhaps Nordabor would soon be ruled by a Fontaine again. Starkad would certainly benefit from that, since he could hold Cyprian under his thumb.

There were just too many unknowns. Cyprian wasn't even sure if their realm, as it stood now, would still exist once they entered Paradise. He was certain, however, that he did not want Starkad's knowledge of his wicked actions hanging on him like chains. He could feel the burden of his guilt, coupled with Faye's continued coldness, robbing him of the joy he deserved to feel.

An idle thought flitted dangerously through his mind—one that had perhaps whispered to him before. They had the shards. They'd nearly reached the coast. Surely, with their maps, they could navigate their way back to Nordabor. Perhaps Starkad had outlived his usefulness.

It was certainly a delicate situation, one that would require the utmost deftness to sort out. When the time was right.

•   •   •

True to Starkad's estimate, it took just under five cycles to reach Ka-farbjorn Harbor. Their journey down the weathered bluffs, which offered tantalizing glimpses of the fog-shrouded sea, was a relatively simple one. The old pathway, the final leg of the Imperial Highway, meandered down the slopes and led to a broad cove in which the harbor was nestled. To the south, the Einfallen fell in a series of squat falls before it broadened out into a wide estuary.

Cyprian doubted that the somewhat-obscure harbor, little more than a fishing village in its heyday, had ever boasted much. Now, however, it had been reduced to a series of decaying, crooked buildings with slanting, sunken roofs. It was unclear if anything remained living in the town, but it seemed unlikely. At any rate, Starkad was confident they were alone.

Passing through alleyways of crumbled cobblestone, they headed directly for the wharves, or what was left of them. There, beyond a partially toppled warehouse, Cyprian got his first real view of the Stagnant Sea.

It had clearly receded somewhat in the age following the fall of the Father-God. The rotted wharves, with derelict boats leaning against them, were half-sunken into the dried, litter-strewn muck. Beyond that, the brackish water stretched away to infinity, listless and flat. Hanging sullenly behind a gossamer veil of clouds, the sun cast its stale light upon the murky and dull surface. Only the incoming current of the Einfallen disturbed the mirror-like stillness, casting the weakest of ripples that lapped sadly at the filthy shoreline. Despite its degradation, the hints of lost beauty, coupled with its fathomless size, still fascinated Cyprian.

"I'm supposed to repair one of these?" Dupree asked, gesturing toward the wrecks scattered along the waterfront.

"Perhaps not one of these," Cyprian explained. "Maybe there's a smaller vessel stored in one of these old warehouses. Something we can easily row."

Dupree looked at the slumping ruins doubtfully. "I have faith in your abilities," Cyprian said.

It was a positive remark that concealed an order. Dupree, Lowther, and Galt went out to search for a boat and any materials they could scrounge that might be used to make any needed repairs. The others set to work on erecting their two sagging tents, establishing their meager camp under a stone walkway that used to straddle the water, but now hung over a dried bed from which the water had long ago receded.

Excusing himself from the work, Starkad advised Cyprian that he was going to search out a possible source of food. He remained characteristically cryptic about the source, but assured Cyprian that it was promising. As he slunk off, Cyprian found himself feeling unsettled. To be outside of Starkad's presence felt strangely relieving, yet not knowing where he was or what he was doing seemed dangerous.

"Where's he off to?" Faye asked, wandering over from the tents, where Mather was getting a fire started.

"He said he might know of a food source somewhere near here."

"More knowledge passed down from his tribal elders?" she asked sarcastically.

"I don't know," Cyprian said. "Why do you say it like that?"

"Well, if he hasn't been somewhere or done something, then his people have the answer in their lore." She looked out over the water, squinting in the glare of sunlight reflected on its dark surface. "For being so learned and wise, his people sure are scarce."

"Well, consider the world they inhabit. They're nomads. They don't have a city propped up by a god," Cyprian said. "I mean, I, for one, would like a chance to speak with his elders, to learn what else they know."

"Yeah, I suppose I wouldn't mind that either," Faye admitted. "Though soon, history won't matter anymore, will it?" She pointed toward the metal cylinder that, as always, Cyprian had slung over his back.

"No," he agreed, "nothing that came before will matter." He liked the sound of that.

"Cyprian, I—" Faye stopped as Dupree approached them, dirty and exhausted.

"I think we've found something passable," she announced without preamble.

"Excellent," Cyprian said, his drive to depart overriding his curiosity at what Faye had been about to say. "Let's see it."

They followed Dupree up and away from the beach, where the others had started to gather by a small boat scarcely different from the scattered rubbish around it. Cyprian eyed it skeptically.

"It's the best thing we could find," Dupree said quickly, as if she could sense Cyprian's doubts. "I think I'll be able to get the leaking down to a minimum."

"Okay, this will do. How long?"

Dupree looked the ugly rowboat up and down for a moment, running her hands over the splintered gunwales and mumbling to herself. "Probably a couple full-cycles of repairs and tests. Once I patch it back up, we'll want to do some shorter test runs to make sure it can sustain our weight for an extended time."

With food dwindling, Cyprian was not keen on lingering so long at the harbor. However, it would still deliver them to Nordabor faster than marching south would have, and they could rest while Dupree completed her work. He would probably need to give her some extra rations to keep her productive, he decided.

"Okay," he repeated. "Why don't we eat and get some rest? You can start the repairs after."

The promise of food pulled the group back toward the fire, though there was little to fulfill that promise. Under Mather's direction, acting upon Cyprian's orders, each of them received half a can of stewed meat. With their grimy utensils, they served themselves the tepid broth and soggy gray chunks of meat.

They savored their rations in their own ways. Mather ate with a mechanical, deliberate slowness. Jotun nibbled little bits at a time, chewing each morsel endlessly. Faye, like most of the others, attempted to eat slowly, but monumental hunger resulted in a quick binge. Ironically, the hasty addition of food into their atrophied stomachs often resulted in cramping and pain. Their brief moments of relief from starvation were also causes for further suffering.

As was often the case, Cyprian ate distractedly, thinking instead of his lofty ambitions, tempered by the fear and guilt that wormed constantly through his mind. Only a couple more full-cycles and they would be leaving this place. It was a slowly closing window.

Perhaps he should have left with Starkad to scout for his mysterious food source. Would anyone have questioned if Starkad had met an unexpected end out there? Would anyone really have cared? Starkad was an outsider, and as Faye had made abundantly clear, an untrustworthy one. He could no longer rely on Starkad's loyalty once they returned to Nordabor, and he worried that if he couldn't control Starkad, then Starkad would try to control him. And, really, Cyprian thought, there would be no place for a runagate like him in Vingallea's new future.

Gazing into the fire, eating his ration without even tasting it, Cyprian contemplated Starkad's demise.

CHAPTER 52

Outside of his time with Solgard, the expedition had been a completely mirthless affair for Galt. Every apparent success had been marred by senseless tragedy. He'd lost both Daeg and Moore, who had been the closest thing to a family he'd ever really known. He'd watched countless others perish in pursuit of something that had seemed unattainable. They'd been commanded by leaders both feckless and vainglorious and had been led to places unfit for sane men and women.

Yet here they were, evidently triumphant. It was a surreal feeling. Sometimes, he wondered if it were all some kind of starvation-driven hallucination. They'd actually obtained the blade shards, and now only a relatively simple return trip stood between them and Nordabor. He gazed around their simple fire, looking at hollow faces that yearned for a safe return. Yet many of them carried the same stunned expression of guarded optimism that he did. Verily, the end was in sight.

Sitting beside him, Solgard gazed sleepily into the fire. Her head drooped until it was resting upon Galt's shoulder. Any pretense of keeping their relationship hidden had fallen away, and nobody really seemed to care, anyway. Galt did, though—he cared deeply, and her head on his shoulder provided more comfort and nourishment than their meager provisions ever could. Across the flames, Lowther caught his eye and, smiling, nodded. Galt, who'd never expected to feel anything but hostility toward a guardsman, returned the gesture.

Surviving everything they'd been through had forged the remaining members of the expedition into close companions. Even Lady Fontaine had found a level of acceptance and camaraderie among the company. Only Lord Fontaine, despite his earlier efforts to appear accessible to the rabble, remained apart. Well, he and Starkad, who always seemed to be at his side. Fontaine's mood had grown increasingly sullen and aloof, and his attempts to foster goodwill with his men had slipped away as he got closer to his goal. Now, he spoke little beyond issuing orders.

Shortly after eating, Fontaine excused himself and retired to the command tent, which was now indistinguishable from its battered counterpart. Lady Fontaine watched him go with a pained look on her face, but said nothing. For the others, his absence was a source of relief. A feeling of being able to speak more freely prevailed, though Lady Fontaine's continued presence ensured that they still guarded their tongues to some extent.

"I feel like we should be celebrating," Lowther said after some time. "Who's got something to drink?"

The remark was met with some small chuckles. Galt was reminded of the jubilation that had followed the capture of the first shards. It seemed like a very long time ago. There had been a lot more of them then. Too many people had died for Galt to seriously consider any celebrating.

"There will be celebrations beyond any we've ever known when we get back, I'm sure," Berg said with a whimsical smile, as though picturing a feast in Phar-Mindorius's hall.

"I don't care if there's a celebration," Dupree said, picking at her grimy fingernails with a knife. "I just want a bath. A real one. No more of this dirty river water shit."

"There's plenty of non-river water right there," Lowther said with a smirk, pointing a thumb behind him toward the flat, glassy expanse of the sea.

Dupree sniffed at the briny air and frowned. "Yeah, I don't think so."

"I'm excited for what comes after Nordabor," Solgard said quietly, sitting up. "For Paradise." Her words were met with a contemplative silence.

"Me too," Pike finally murmured. "I just wish Phir-Ramarian could be there when we reach the gates. This is his victory as much as anyone's. He should be here." He took a shuddering breath and cleared his throat. "I wonder if I could somehow bring him back from the Void once we control the powers of creation. Perhaps I could be reunited with him in Paradise."

Galt hadn't known the extent of the relationship between Phir-Ramarian and Pike, but in the scribe's musings, he saw unmistakably the pain of a man who'd lost somebody he loved. Whatever secrets they'd harbored to avoid the scrutiny of the royal court apparently didn't matter now. Despite his own opinion of the deceased prince, Galt wished that Pike could see the man he loved again, and that, if Paradise was ever reached, they could be free together.

"Maybe we could bring back *everyone* we've lost," Dupree said, seized by a sudden eagerness.

"This is all assuming that the blade will even work," Lady Fontaine sighed.

Berg started. "Of course it will work; its sole purpose is to open the Gates of Paradise."

"We may be able to reforge it, but suppose it held some power bestowed upon it by the Father-God?" Lady Fontaine argued. "When he perished, the blade was sundered. What if the power that opened the gates was lost forever? What if we can physically rebuild it, but it still doesn't work?"

Galt would have been lying if he said he hadn't considered that possibility, though he never would have mentioned it in front of Solgard. He looked toward her for a rebuttal.

"It will work," she said simply. "I know it will."

"Based on what?" Lady Fontaine asked politely, but with an unmistakable edge. Despite her differences from others of her social standing, she was still unused to being contradicted.

"Because I believe that this was our people's destiny. To bring a rebirth to our world and to our creator. To right the wrongs of the past and to create a brighter future."

Galt felt some secondhand embarrassment for Solgard and her earnest assessment of their situation, but also admired her boundless faith.

"Forgive me," Lady Fontaine said, the same stiff politeness in her voice, "but you are not a student of history. You don't know the lore and legends behind all of this. The Father-God's power is gone. Believe me, I hope that you're right and that the blade works. I'm just worried about what will happen if it doesn't. We shouldn't ignore that possibility."

"And you are not a shepherd," Solgard said evenly. "You don't understand our faith or our knowledge of the Void-God. I believe wholeheartedly that the blade will deliver us."

Lady Fontaine blinked several times, apparently at a loss for words, then smiled. "You're right. I don't understand your faith. Ultimately, there will be nothing we can do if it doesn't work. I get your desire to believe it will."

It was a backhanded way to concede the point, but Solgard seemed content to let it be.

"Well, a key is a key is what I think," Berg said. "It will work. Cyprian certainly seems to think so." He suddenly looked uncomfortable.

"Yes, that he does," Lady Fontaine said with a tinge of sadness.

The small measure of cheer they'd been feeling seemed to have been deflated by Lady Fontaine's unexpected doubts. They lingered silently about the flames, watching them die down. Finally, Mather, who had not offered his thoughts, weighty or otherwise, spoke.

"We should get some rest. Galt, Lowther, take the first watch."

·　　·　　·

Finding the open water unsettling and strange, Galt had volunteered to watch the perimeter on the harbor side of the camp. He felt more comfortable among the remains of the ancient shanties than walking the beach along the boundless tract of timeless ocean. Chances were it was as sterile and lifeless as the rest of the world, but its unknown depths disturbed him.

Furthermore, Lowther's confidence was still shaken after Bellamont's escape. Galt hadn't wanted to leave him in charge of watching the harbor, knowing that any danger would almost certainly originate from there. An ambush from the beach seemed unlikely, as one could easily spot any threat from the open coastline. Without explaining his reasoning, Galt had casually suggested that Lowther take the beach, and the guardsman, who seemed to enjoy gazing out across the water, didn't object.

By all accounts, Kafarbjorn was truly deserted. Galt saw no indication that anyone had been there within his lifetime. Layers of dust remained untouched aside from where the group had shuffled through the ruins earlier, seeking a viable boat. There were no signs that any shades had passed through, nor did they come across any bodies. Galt surmised that the residents of the harbor had migrated away after the fall of the Father-God, perhaps when the supply of fish had dried up. Apparently, nobody had remained behind to die.

Galt was following the same path along the edge of the buildings that he'd patrolled for the last cycle when he suddenly heard the sound of footsteps behind him. He whirled around, his hand automatically reaching for his blade. He was relieved and surprised to find that it was only Solgard.

"Hey, sorry," she said. "I didn't mean to startle you."

"No worries. Why aren't you sleeping?"

"Believe it or not, I'm not tired." She shrugged. "I'm exhausted, but not sleepy. I just can't stop thinking."

"About what?"

Solgard laughed and threw her hands in the air. "Everything."

"Aye," Galt agreed, "I get that."

Solgard walked alongside him as he continued his patrol, her hand slipping into his. He couldn't help but smile as he considered that, despite their intimacy, he still thought of her by her surname. It would take some time before they'd be able to fully abandon the ingrained formalities of their order.

They said nothing for a while, and Galt enjoyed the quiet comfort of her presence. He was growing lax in his duties, but he really didn't care. The watch was a formality at this point; they were alone.

"What do you think of what Lady Fontaine said?" Solgard asked after some time.

He weighed how much he wanted to reveal his actual thoughts, and decided to err on the side of caution. "I think her concerns have some merit," he said diplomatically.

"That's a safe answer," Solgard said, seeing directly through his efforts.

"I'm not going to lie; I'm still concerned about whether or not this plan will work," Galt admitted. "There are just so many unknowns."

She smiled at him. "That's where faith comes in. I don't know exactly what's going to happen, but I believe that everything will unfold as it should. It is scary, though, I get it. We really don't know what's going to happen to us. That's why I *have* to believe."

Galt stopped walking and turned toward her. "You mean what will become of this?" he asked, gesturing vaguely between them.

"You think rather highly of our little tryst," Solgard said with a playful laugh. "I think there will be bigger issues at hand, such as who will be making the decisions regarding the new world. Lady Fontaine suggested that there'll be little desire to revive the Void-God. If humans take the reins of creation alone, I fear that it could be disastrous. I pray that it won't be."

"Well, the gods were in charge before, and it was disastrous," Galt pointed out.

"Yes, but that was because of the lesser gods, not the Father-God. He wouldn't make the same mistakes if he were reborn."

"Either way," Galt mused, "our order will be obsolete."

Solgard looked surprised, as if she had never really considered that. Then she smiled broadly and mischievously. "Which means certain antiquated rules will definitely be cast aside."

"Yes, I suppose that would be the case," Galt agreed.

His heart started to beat faster as Solgard took his hand again and led him toward a darkened doorway. "So I don't think there could be any harm in ignoring restrictions that will soon be irrelevant."

They were now inside a small room, its original purpose long since forgotten. Without another word, Solgard removed her robes and dropped them onto the dusty floor. Galt followed suit, and within moments they were lying upon their splayed robes, passionately entwined, pulling their remaining clothing free.

The entire world faded into background noise. All of the suffering, hunger, fear, and uncertainty vanished. Galt had never been with a woman he'd actually cared for, and in Solgard's arms, he found bliss. In the aftermath of their passion, they remained together upon their makeshift bed, Solgard's head resting upon his chest. For a short time, everything was perfect.

A whistle sounded shrilly nearby. Solgard lifted her head sleepily. "That's Mather with the changing of the guard. I've gotta go."

She sat up, and in the dim light of their private room, Galt marveled at her nakedness. She smiled at him as she collected her garments. Reluctantly, he began to dress as well.

As they slipped through the doorway, Solgard turned back and kissed him deeply. When their lips parted, she looked up at him.

"I think I love you."

It was his turn to smile.

"I think I love you too."

CHAPTER 53

Since they'd awoken and puttered through their first rations, Dupree had been toiling ceaselessly with her limited tools and even more limited resources, working to patch and reinforce the derelict boat.

Despite her best efforts, little progress had been made. For now, that suited Cyprian just fine. He needed the extra time to think. He knew that, like every problem he'd been faced with before, he would eventually conceive of a solution. Long he pondered the issue, but when the possible answer came, it was in a form he would have hardly imagined.

As if he had materialized out of thin air, Starkad returned to the camp. He strode swiftly toward the command tent, outside of which Cyprian sat, sipping his canteen. He noticed that Starkad wasn't carrying any new provisions. He'd apparently had no luck in locating his clandestine food source.

"We need to speak at once," Starkad announced as he approached.

Cyprian, who'd been increasingly fearing a turn from the badlander, felt his breath catch in his throat. Surely this would be the moment when his erstwhile loyal guide would begin to insinuate what might occur unless Cyprian were to accommodate whatever whim he could conceive.

"What is it?" Cyprian asked, struggling to keep his voice even.

Starkad looked around, apparently checking to see who else might be within earshot. "Let's walk."

"Sure," Cyprian said with a casualness that he did not feel. The inside of his mouth had turned coppery and dry, and he took another swig from his canteen before he trotted after Starkad, who'd headed toward the water.

When they were a short distance away from the camp, Cyprian could no longer take the anticipation. "Well, what is it?"

Starkad turned and appraised him solemnly. "You asked me once about your father. About what had become of him. I think I now know."

Having feared the worst, Cyprian's emotions were now violently wrenched across a spectrum of surprise, confusion, curiosity, and hope. His machinations were entirely forgotten, as were the blade shards at his side.

"What? How?" he managed to stutter out.

"The source of food that I had in mind was the old encampment where I had encountered your father. I thought that he might have left a cache of provisions behind, but when I reached the camp, I found that he'd never left."

Cyprian's mind was reeling. After so many long-cycles of not knowing, of holding onto a tiny flicker of hope, here was the truth. The blunt, depressing truth.

"So, he's dead, then?" he asked, knowing the answer.

"Yes," Starkad said softly.

Cyprian stared out over the water, processing the information that he'd always known. He'd come so far, crossing vistas undreamt of by most, seeking a prize that his father had only just started to understand. He'd succeeded where his father had found only failure, ending up lost and nearly forgotten.

"I have to see him. Can you lead me to his encampment?"

"Yes. It's about a seven-cycle hike from here."

"I'd like to go now," Cyprian said as if he were in a dream. "I need to grab my pack. Do you need anything before we depart?"

"No, I'm fine. I'll wait here."

Cyprian walked briskly back to the command tent, the heavy burden of his guilt relieved for the moment. The only thing in his mind now was the desire to look upon his father's remains, to learn of what had led to his demise, and to finally have closure.

As he hastily gathered his gear, another thought occurred to him. He and Starkad would be alone upon the moors. Perhaps after he finally put this mystery to bed, he could deal with his other major issue.

Truly, everything was aligning for him, as he knew it would.

"What are you doing?" Faye asked from behind him, interrupting his murderous thoughts.

"Starkad found the remains of my father's expedition," he said, stowing the last of his gear and turning around. "He's going to lead me to it at once."

Faye blinked in disbelief. "What? What are you talking about?"

"He went out looking for a cache that my father may have left behind, and found the remains of the whole damn expedition," he explained impatiently.

Faye followed Cyprian's gaze and spied Starkad waiting near the weakly lapping water. "Hold on a—"

"What, Faye? What?" he said, exasperated by her constant questions. "Are you going to tell me that you don't believe him? Why would he lie about something like that?"

"I don't know," she said, flustered and taken aback. "It's just strange, this happening all of a sudden, and him of all people stumbling upon it. Something's not right. What if he has some other purpose in luring you out there?"

Cyprian could have laughed if his nerves weren't so shot. Here Faye was accusing Starkad of having some dark intentions when Cyprian was actually the one with the ulterior motive. She had no idea how close to the mark she was, and how far away.

"He was the only one outside of the camp. Nobody else *could* have found it. And I don't see how any delay could benefit him. He's as eager to return as we are." Cyprian looked toward the sound of hammering coming from the ongoing repairs. "And we'll be back long before Dupree is finished, anyway."

"Please," Faye said, "you don't need to do this. We're so close to being home. You have your prize, it's over. Do not go back out there with him. I'm sorry, but your father is dead, and you knew that already. Seeing it won't change anything. Leave the past in the past. Stay here with me."

He almost did, but in the end, the pull of knowing his father's fate, of learning the cause behind his family's fall from grace, was too much. And really, just moving ahead with Faye was not a possibility. Not while Starkad remained, ready to spill black secrets whenever it might benefit him the most.

"I can't do that. I have to go." He kissed her lightly and brushed by her. "I'll be careful."

"Well, if you insist on going, then let me go with you."

He would never be able to do what he needed to do if she was with him. "I'm sorry, but no. I need you here to lead."

"Mather is more than capable of keeping things under control."

"Faye, you're the only one I really trust to take command," he lied. Her last turn at leadership had resulted in a mutiny. Still, he expected nothing of the sort from those who remained, and he had to keep her at the camp. "I need you here."

She considered him for a long moment, and Cyprian shriveled under her gaze, as though she were peering beneath his facade and seeing the hideousness squirming beneath.

He just needed to get rid of Starkad and everything would be okay. He would be a hero, winning renown and glory that would outshine everything else. And soon, he'd know, and be able to relate to the people, how his father had passed in service of the same noble quest, thereby restoring honor to his name.

And then everything with Faye would be normal again. Better than normal, in fact. They could reign together in Paradise when the throne inevitably came to the rightful heir and savior of mankind. Upon the seat of creation, perhaps even eternal life could be theirs.

Cyprian just had to do one more ugly thing.

"Okay," Faye finally answered. "I'll stay behind. But I think you should leave the shards with me. It makes no sense to take them back out into the unknown. Not when we're so close to leaving."

"You know I can't do that," he said, shaking his head.

"Why?"

"They're too important."

"So you trust me to lead, but not to protect some relics—something I've essentially done my entire life." Her voice had grown frigid.

"I'm sorry," he said. He had sacrificed too much to let the blade shards leave his sight, whether it was Faye taking them or anyone else. They were everything, and he would not be parted from them.

"Fine. Do as you wish," Faye said. "As you always do."

Cyprian lingered, trying to find the right thing to say. Nothing came, and perhaps there was nothing he could say. He looked at her wearily, everything left unsaid weighing upon him.

Then, without another word, he turned and strode away, leaving her alone upon the shore.

·　　·　　·

They picked their way up the bluffs, the harbor receding into the mists behind them. At the top, they veered northward and away from the familiar view of the Imperial Highway. For some time, they said nothing, trudging up and down the barren hills, crossing through shallow peat bogs that had formed in the troughs between.

As they passed back into the Dawnlands, Starkad finally spoke. "Look there, to the north."

Cyprian followed his outstretched hand toward the horizon, squinting into the distance. There, he spied a dark line cutting vertically into the gray sky. He pulled out his field glass and leveled it on the shape.

It was a tower standing upon a seaside cliff. "The lighthouse at Thunsturm," Starkad stated.

Lowering his field glass, Cyprian turned toward Starkad with surprise. "Where Ulesreto is said to be? We shouldn't be here," he said, thinking of the shards he carried. They were within view of the one being left who posed a threat to them—one who could take the Scale of Judgment back by force.

"Relax," Starkad said nonchalantly. "You would eventually have to go that way anyway to reach the dried strait, if you aim to get to the Isle of Creation."

"Yes, but we'll have the full strength of Nordabor marching with us then. Even Ulesreto will be powerless against so many. Now, we're alone."

"This is true," Starkad agreed, "but I believe there is little to fear. None of my people have ever seen Ulesreto abroad. He's only *believed* to reside there. We should be fine provided we keep our distance. I just wanted you to be aware of it so as to avoid any unexpected surprises."

Cyprian licked his dry, cracked lips and raised his field glass. Through its magnification, he could once again see the lighthouse in detail.

Broad, cyclopean blocks of black stone formed its tremendous base. Rising steeply, the tower narrowed into an iron-crowned point. A tremendous lens of strangely cut, opaque glass, coated in brine, gazed out from the top like a corpse's eye. A platform, girded by a wrought iron rail, encircled the lens. He could imagine Ulesreto as a dark shape walking along that platform, leering out at the island where his attempt to seize Paradise had failed, forever within view of the prize that was eternally denied to him.

And now, Cyprian held the key to that prize. He shuddered at the thought.

"Come," Starkad beckoned, having already lost interest. It was difficult to wrench his gaze away from the hateful tower, which seemed to emanate a hypnotic malice, but Cyprian managed to do so.

As they continued on, he could not shake the feeling that they were being watched. More than likely, they were too far away ever to be seen. And that was if Ulesreto was even there to look.

The rational part of Cyprian's mind knew that the disquiet he felt about the lighthouse was just a manifestation of his knowledge of the usurper god. Really, the ancient beacon, beyond its historical significance, was not significant at all.

All the same, he was happy when they descended a hill and it slipped out of view.

•　　•　　•

The sky grew more sullen and steely as they ventured further onto the moors and further back into the Dawnlands. Cyprian began to feel antsy and nervous, the weight of what he intended to do intermingling with the pending revelation of his father's final resting place. He wondered if his father had produced a shade, but found that he was too afraid to ask Starkad.

His thoughts then turned to whether or not the morally ambiguous badlander would produce one. He supposed he would know soon enough.

Almost four cycles had passed since they had seen the lighthouse. They had once again traveled in silence, and Cyprian began to feel paranoid that Starkad somehow knew his intentions. He began to consider reckless options, tempted to forsake his father's remains in favor of doing the foul deed now.

As his mind warred in internal debate, they ascended a rolling hill identical to many they'd already crossed, and at the apex, Cyprian saw the encampment.

Or, rather, what remained of it.

A rough circle of six drooping tents stood crookedly on a flat stretch of land between the convergence of two hills. Spread amongst them were the collapsed remains of other tents and the scattered detritus of ruined supplies. In the center of the desolate camp stood a large, partially-toppled cairn.

"This is the same spot where you encountered my father? And everything was fine?" Cyprian asked in bewilderment.

"Yes."

"What happened?"

"Let's get a closer look."

Black dread swelled within Cyprian as he followed Starkad down into the mass grave.

A closer look at the scattered rubbish revealed the grisly truth. Piles of ash marked where fires had once burned, inside of which broken human bones were visible. Nearby, grime-encrusted kettles contained the sickening calcified remnants of boiled human flesh and tissue. A toothless skull gazed ghoulishly from within an overturned pot. Skeletal remains clad in torn and filthy garments that still bore the clearly identifiable coat of arms of Nordabor stretched across the ground near the kettles. Within the gaping, mildewed tents, more corpses were visible, swaddled within dirty blankets.

"How did this happen?" Cyprian asked, overcome with revulsion.

"Come here. This will explain everything."

Starkad was pointing toward the cairn, from which he'd removed a sizable stone from the front. A vacant black opening now beckoned to Cyprian.

He staggered forward, stepping gingerly over yet another skeleton, which bore the shattered skull indicative of a shade's birth. Suddenly, he was acutely aware that they did not have a shepherd with them. They would have no recourse but to flee should they be attacked by a shade. Thankfully, it appeared any that had been there had long since departed.

He crouched before the opening and warily peered inside. He didn't like the idea of turning his back on Starkad, but he reasoned that it was in the badlander's best interest to keep him alive. Who else could he extort into granting him access to true power?

His eyes adjusted to the gloom within the cairn, and he observed a corpse slumped against the opposite wall, partially buried by the collapsed section. Though blackened somewhat by decomposition, the body's clothing was slightly more intact than that of the other corpses.

Cyprian gasped and fell backward. The corpse was clad in the formal uniform of the curator.

He'd finally found his father.

"It appears that when all hope was lost, he sealed himself inside this cairn with a written record of what happened," Starkad said solemnly. He pointed at a dented metal tube near the body. "There."

Cyprian found it difficult to reach inside and take the small cylinder. Despite all of the death and ruin he'd encountered, the knowledge that this shriveled wreck had been his father was almost too much. It was as if every memory of him had now been annexed by this new, hideous visage. From outside of the cairn, it was impossible to tell if the skull was intact, and he couldn't bring himself to crawl inside and check.

He reached in, snatched the tube quickly, and shuffled backward. Still on his knees, he uncapped the tube and slid out a weathered strip of rolled parchment. He unfurled it and, his dread inflating, read the yellowed page.

If someone is reading this, it means that the worst has come to pass. I wish it to be known that I am sorry for our failure. I can only hope that those who follow find the success that eluded me.

Firstly, there is no living land beyond Nordabor. Phar-Mindorius hopes otherwise, but he is wrong. This errand that he has sent me on would have been utterly hopeless were it not for its true purpose. The hilt I recovered from Aedesda's remains—I know what it is. It belongs to the Scale of Judgment. Phar-Mindorius bade me to seek any further pieces of the blade, as well as knowledge of any living old ones, though he implied that this was all secondary to my main purpose. There is something more to this desire, and I believe that I have determined what it is.

I believe that if the other pieces could be found, the blade could be reforged. Entry into Paradise might still be possible. Through the written histories, I know that the blade was sundered on the Isle of Creation after Ulesreto murdered the Father-God. I set my sights on the isle, for I believe that the other shards are there. And if not there, then perhaps with the surviving old ones, who left the isle after the war. For why else would Phar-Mindorius want me to seek out living old ones?

Unfortunately, our expedition has experienced several complications. The road north seemed simple, but when we reached the crossings of the Einfallen, things became perilous. We lost some of my best men, and much of our provisions, in the fording of the river.

Shortly after, we were waylaid by badlanders. I fear we moved too large of a force and transported too much unnecessary equipment. I'd hoped to construct a vessel when we reached the northern straits, but now, we've lost most of the supplies and burned what remained. I should have had my engineers make smaller boats to cross the Einfallen, but I was eager to cross and foolhardy in my designs to waste no time. Now, even if we were to reach the shore, we'd most likely go no further.

We are too low on provisions to do anything; too weak from hunger and thirst. I had hoped to cross these moors directly north, but by doing so, we left the river, and our only source of water, behind. Again, my haste has made a fool of me.

Now, we are unable to proceed and unable to return. We have wasted time fruitlessly waiting while the men have grown too ill even to mutiny, though I know they rightly blame me for their misfortune. Please forgive us, for in our desperation, we have turned to despicable acts, although I fear it is now too late for even these blasphemous desecrations of our fellow men to make any difference. For a small few, it has given them the strength to try to return to Nordabor to seek help. I doubt they will make it, and even if they did, I believe we will be long gone before they return. For those who remain here, the sustenance derived from the dead has been just enough to keep us alive, though to what end, beyond fear of death, I no longer know.

The dead will soon outnumber the living, and I fear that the shade of a comrade will eventually overcome my few remaining shepherds. When that happens, our doom will be complete. Undoubtedly, my time is short.

Lastly, I wish to tell my wife and son that I love them. I pray that my actions have somehow helped to rescue them from our kingdom's collapse.

I hope that our situation improves, but I am doubtful. For now, we are holding our own.

The message ended there, and Cyprian let the withered parchment drop.

"I'm afraid I haven't been totally honest with you, Lord Fontaine."

Cyprian started. He'd nearly forgotten that Starkad was there. Certain inconsistencies began to coalesce in his mind, and he rose to his feet.

"You said that when you spoke with my father here, everything was fine. How would he and his men be fine if they were starving and dying here? You were with the badlanders that attacked him, weren't you?"

Starkad shook his head sadly. "As you have all along, you're only grasping a part of what you're looking at. Your father was long-dead when I first came upon this camp in my wanderings."

"W-what?" Cyprian sputtered. Nothing was happening as he'd anticipated. "Why did you tell me that you spoke to him?"

"I needed you to have that motivation. I had no idea that you were going to pursue the shards so doggedly," Starkad explained. "I had expected that the hope to find your father would urge you on when nothing else would. But now, I need you to see the truth."

"The truth? You lied about my father in order to lead me here. Why?" Cyprian demanded, growing angry.

"The truth," Starkad said, seeming suddenly different in an undefinable way, "is complicated."

Fear bloomed from the blackest pit of Cyprian's mind, mingling hatefully with his befuddlement. His schemes had come to naught; something beyond his control, and beyond his understanding, was now unfolding.

Starkad's rumpled shape shimmered strangely, emanating an otherworldly glow. The air itself seemed to suction inward around his frame, which seemed to grow in contrast, and suddenly, Starkad towered over Cyprian, who trembled before him. His filthy leather gear rippled and mutated, reforming into golden pauldrons and a shining breastplate. His previously haggard visage beamed with renewed vigor, and his thinning blonde hair was now full and flowing.

Starkad would now have been unrecognizable were it not for the hideous, jagged scar running down the left side of his face. Above his head, a halo of white light shimmered and flickered. Its beauty was marred by a broken section, the shattered pieces of which levitated above the scar on his face.

"I am Ulesreto, God of Judgment."

Petrified, Cyprian cowered before the god who had walked hidden alongside him for so long. His grand designs had slipped away completely. All that remained was a feeling of betrayal, regret, and failure so absolute that he almost couldn't fathom it. Rendered speechless, he gaped at the terrible majesty of the god.

"For a thousand years, I wandered this dead world, purposeless and adrift, my remaining power shrouded and dormant. I'd killed my insidious brother, who'd convinced me to rebel. I left my hilt buried in his chest, but not before he gave me this." He pointed at his livid scar and broken halo and smiled ruefully. "I'd thought that I'd made my bid for Paradise, and that the gates were closed to me forever. I was without hope. Until I stumbled upon this camp and your father's note."

The voice of the being that had been Starkad carried a deep, melodic resonance that made Cyprian want to clamp his hands over his ears and will it all away, yet he stood transfixed, unable to do anything but listen.

"I read your father's last words. I saw that they were men of Nordabor, of Vingallea. What were once my people," he added mournfully, looking toward the horrific kettles.

"I surmised that if they were this far out in the wastes, seeking the pieces of my blade and the other remaining gods, they had a good reason to do so. I decided to finish what your father had planned to do, and I travelled back to the Isle of Creation to collect the pieces left there. When I arrived, I found that they were gone. Opriseur alone remained by Alminnian's corpse, and in her insane babbling, I discerned a name: Nuroh."

This information finally forced Cyprian's mind to shudder back to life. "The God of Knowledge? There's no record of him after the war. I thought you killed him."

"If only. Didn't I tell you that your records are not as infallible as you think? Nuroh the Craven was nowhere to be found when we finally invaded the isle. He abandoned Alminnian and fled before the battle."

Hearing of ancient events firsthand was overwhelming. Cyprian wavered on his feet.

"Knowing that Nuroh was somehow involved, and that the shards were now gone, I decided to seek out the other gods. That much of my tale was always true. I couldn't risk facing them alone, though—not with my reduced strength. Not if there was even the slightest chance of being overpowered by one of them. Once I learned where they hid, I decided to approach your king under the guise of a wandering badlander. I also intended to collect my hilt. Of course, when I arrived, I finally learned what Nuroh's role in everything was.

"He had long ago returned to the Isle of Creation, where he found Opriseur. She had not yet gone mad. From her, he learned the basics of Veathyadell's plan, which she had refused to take part in, since she hated the rebel gods who had joined me. Despite his prying, she wouldn't tell him anything further. Actually, she attempted to kill him for deserting Alminnian." Ulesreto smiled as if it were a humorous anecdote.

"Well, he escaped, and armed with his limited knowledge, he spawned a plan similar to my own. In the age that followed, he slowly wormed his way to power in Nordabor, the only place that still thrived, thanks to Ganachim's enslavement. Nuroh was the one who initially advised Phar-Mindorius to seek out the shards, though your king was not fully committed until I arrived. I offered him my assistance, and given Ganachim's recent decline, he was more than willing to listen. Once I finished with him, I spoke to the real power behind the throne. I had certain information and skills that Nuroh desperately needed. We came to terms."

"To take Paradise together?" Cyprian asked, feeling numb.

"Absolutely not. I don't know what Nuroh would do if he ever took the power of Paradise, but it will never happen. The throne of Paradise will be mine. Within that boundless realm, I will be reunited with Ellara. There will be no more conquest, no more strife. Alminnian's broken world will be erased. I will restart creation, and only our love and silent peace will remain. My alliance with Nuroh is a means to an end. When he is no longer needed, I will dispose of him. Of course, you know all about that sort of thing, don't you, Lord Fontaine?"

This startled Cyprian, reminding him of his previous intentions. They seemed like thoughts from another life.

"What...what are you...what do you mean?" he stammered weakly.

"Please. Do you really think that I would not have considered treachery from you? You've already proven faithless to your own kin."

Now shame joined Cyprian's plethora of wretched emotions. Shame and denial. "No, you urged me to do it. It was your idea," he insisted. It sounded petulant and false, even to his own ears.

"I spoke aloud what you were already thinking. Phir-Ramarian was going to cost you everything. You wanted him gone. You were already there; you just needed a nudge."

To hear his sins announced so brazenly cowed Cyprian, and his defiance withered. Starkad was right.

Rather, Starkad did not exist. *Ulesreto* was right.

"Yet, in those actions, you proved your dedication to a higher cause," Ulesreto continued. "You proved that you were willing to do what had to be done. You still have the fire of old Vingallea. That is why we are standing here. You see, Kafarbjorn Harbor is not as deserted as you might think."

Cyprian tried to swallow, but his throat was too dry. "Who?" he managed to croak.

"Nuroh, of course. Your king's loyal vizier slipped away and crept north, concealed by his sorcery. Why, when I went on my little errand, I was really fetching him from the lighthouse. He's lurking at the camp now, awaiting my return."

Cyprian's thoughts jumped to Faye, who was suddenly in mortal peril. From the very beginning, the two gods had ensured that everything would pass as they had planned. Their human pawns, who had taken all of the risks, were expendable now that they could reap their reward.

"What are you going to do? Kill everyone at the camp? Kill me and take the shards?" Cyprian asked, holding the cylinder so tightly that he was shaking.

"Not at all," Ulesreto said lightly. "I have a proposition for you. You see, to seize the shards from you was the original plan—Nuroh's plan. You and the rest of your comrades would be killed, yes, so as to prevent any pursuit as we headed directly to the Isle of Creation. After all, Nuroh assumed that humans would never part with the shards willingly or accept becoming vassals to the gods again. He's not wrong there, I think. After all, Phar-Mindorius vehemently insisted that it was out of the question. But, with you, I see a possible exception. After all, you wish to save your people, no?"

"Yes, of course," Cyprian said cautiously.

"Well, I have no interest in any further bloodshed, and certainly not from men of Vingallea. I could ensure that your people survive in my new world."

After so many startling revelations, Cyprian was loathe to trust anything that the usurper said. Unfortunately, he had no other recourse but to listen and hope for survival.

"What is your proposal?"

"That you give me the shards, and I let Nuroh reforge them. He was teaching mankind the art of metalworking before the Great Culling, before Veathyadell even existed. He's the only one left who can reforge the blade. Your blacksmiths would fail; mortal hands could never restore the blade's divinity. Once he's fulfilled his purpose, we'll betray him before he has the chance to betray me. I anticipate that he'll try to kill me and seize Paradise once he's got all of the shards and reforged them before the gates. It's why I refused to help him until he gave me this as collateral."

Ulesreto unsheathed the broken hilt of the Scale of Judgment and held it before Cyprian.

The final piece had been with them all along. Cyprian wondered if Phar-Mindorius knew that it had been stolen from his vaults.

"With you and your men's assistance, even one so cunning as Nuroh will be helpless. Once he's gone, I will be free to take the reins of Paradise, and I will see to it that your people not only survive, but thrive. You are Ellara's people, and therefore, you will always be mine as well. And you *need* me. Look at what's become of those who sought to supplant me," he said, gesturing toward the scattered bones of the dead.

"The throne of Paradise cannot be tamed by a mortal—not even one as ambitious as you, my friend. But if you swear fealty to me, Lord Fontaine, you will be rewarded with a position as my most trusted and renowned thane. And you could be the leader of the people whom you saved. You could be Phar-Cyprian."

Here now was a path to power that Cyprian had never considered. He could align himself with Ulesreto and all but guarantee that they would succeed.

But triumph bought by a pledge to the duplicitous god could never be trusted. Ulesreto had already proven his capacity to deceive, and Cyprian had no guarantee that he wouldn't be eliminated as well once Nuroh was gone. Ulesreto had no qualms about seeing his fellow gods, even those who had once been loyal to him, destroyed one by one. What would a few more human lives be to him?

Above all other considerations, Cyprian would never bow to this creature and commit himself to thralldom's chain, no matter what was promised. *He* had sought out the shards. *He* had faced down the gods. *His* indomitable will, strength, and determination had brought the expedition this far, despite misfortune, mutiny, and manipulation from within. Control of Paradise was his by right as the heir to Vingallea's throne and the deliverer of his people. This was *his* victory, and he would not trade it for a collar in the form of a false crown. He would not be forced into worship of a master that still held his murderous secret. He'd sought to free himself from Starkad, not bind himself to Ulesreto as an eternal slave.

"No."

Ulesreto leveled his ancient eyes upon Cyprian. "What?" he asked flatly.

"My answer is no. The shards are mine. I didn't come this far, forsake those dear to me, and murder my own kin so that I could deliver the shards to you. Vingallea does not answer to you anymore. We are not your people. We have no master. I will not only deliver my people to Paradise, but I will deliver them from the endless oppression and destruction of the gods. *I* will have the throne of Paradise."

An aura of raw power rolled off of Ulesreto, causing Cyprian to stagger backward.

"You have quite the savior complex, my lord," Ulesreto said. "Delusions of being some holy warrior-king, revered through the ages. You don't fool me. You care not for your people beyond their adulation. Do not preach to me about what you have forsaken. I sacrificed *everything* for the woman I loved, her people, and for what I believed was right. I thought a more enlightened man such as yourself might truly appreciate the greater good, but you are merely another vain fool chasing power. You seek to replace Alminnian himself at the pinnacle of reality, so that all might see your glory.

"Now give me the shards, or your forgotten bones will molder here with your father's."

Cyprian's heart hammered in his chest. He drew his blade. He would not be denied his destiny.

"You raise your weapon to me?" Ulesreto asked incredulously. "I have lived for thousands of years. I've seen generations pass, kingdoms rise and fall. I have marked the slow changes of the world itself. I have walked the forgotten lands beyond the southern crater. Your life is but a mote of *dust* upon the tapestry of my being."

"Nevertheless, others like you have fallen in my wake," Cyprian said. "I'm going to—"

Ulesreto lunged forward, snatched Cyprian's sword from his hand, and savagely backhanded him, sending him tumbling to the ground.

"*What* are you going to do?" Ulesreto said, standing over him. "What *can* you do?"

Dazed and bloodied, Cyprian stared at the sky. His two front teeth were missing.

He suddenly realized with swelling terror that he had miscalculated. Mindlessly, he tried to scramble away, but Ulesreto snatched one of his legs and pulled him back, then planted a large hand around Cyprian's throat and lifted him off the ground.

"No god fell to you alone. By my hand were you directed. By my actions did you succeed. Do not confuse my success for your own. I am the master of the Scale of Judgment. I always have been."

Searing pain tore through Cyprian's abdomen, forcing a scream to rise through his tightly clenched throat. His eyes bulged wildly, staring through Ulesreto and into the gray sky beyond. Carelessly, Ulesreto cast him back to the ground, where he landed heavily in a crumpled heap.

He panted, clutching his gut. Blood cascaded through his fingers.

"A pity," Ulesreto muttered. In his hand was the hilt of the Scale of Judgment, the jagged bit of remaining blade smeared with Cyprian's blood. He knelt over Cyprian and unceremoniously cut the metal tube containing the shards from its leather strap. Cyprian was powerless to stop him.

"You're going to die, Lord Fontaine. For that, I'm sorry. I had hoped for something different for you, but your pride has led to folly," the god said, shaking his head. "I could judge you. It's still within my limited power to do so, when I'm present at the moment of death, but I don't wish to judge you. There is still some light within so much darkness. I think I'll leave it up to chance."

He stood, rolled the cylinder over in his hands thoughtfully, and sighed. "Goodbye, Lord Fontaine."

His vision fading, Cyprian watched as Ulesreto, whom he'd known as Duncan Starkad, disappeared into the murk closing in around him.

Cyprian refused to believe that his life was ending. Events had been unfolding in his favor, forced into compliance by his will. He'd done everything he could to succeed, and he had been so close.

Now, his life pooling around him, Cyprian felt only a boundless emptiness. All the horrors he'd endured, including the constant burden of his own atrocity, had been for nothing. There would be no glorious future, no Paradise, no singing of songs or telling of tales.

In that moment, he would have given anything to be back in his dim chamber within the Hall of Antiquities. To see Faye smiling at him again. To listen to Jotun tell a long-winded tale of his past glories.

He had given everything away, had debased himself completely, and now, he'd doomed the ones he loved to unexpected death at the hands of Ulesreto. And all just to guarantee the utter annihilation of the entire world. All to die pointlessly.

He had learned his father's fate, only to join him in it.

As Cyprian's dying mind roiled with fear and remorse, he began to drag himself across the ground. The effort loosed his bowels, but he didn't notice. He needed to warn Faye; she had to know what was coming. And she was so close, almost within reach. Beyond the cairn, he could see her standing upon a hillock, watching him. He tried to call out to her, but only bubbling blood issued forth from his mouth.

He raised a crimson hand feebly, trying to touch her, seeing her in the light of the Daylands, the fireflies in the hollow, her eyes on the maps, everything.

He sucked in sharply, mustering everything he could to call out to her. She would hear him, and he would be saved.

With nothing more than a soft whimper, his head dropped back to the ground. His final breath whistled wetly through his dead lips.

PART VI:
BEYOND THE
GATES

CHAPTER 54

The smell of smoke dragged Galt up from the depths of a dreamless sleep. He blinked away his grogginess, confused by the sudden heat and stifling air within the tent.

Abruptly, a harsh realization struck him: the tent was on fire.

He threw back his cover, which had just ignited near his feet. Backing away from the flames, which had stretched across the front flaps, blocking his exit, he scooted into Lowther and Pike. The scribe awoke with a start and, seeing the fire, began to shout hysterically. Lowther remained still.

"Wake up!" Galt screamed into Lowther's face. Smoke was quickly filling the small, enclosed space, and Lowther appeared to have lost consciousness. Galt shook him violently and smacked him across the face.

"Is he dead?" Pike cried.

"Wake up!" Galt screamed again, ignoring the question.

At the back of the tent, Dupree lifted her head and coughed harshly. Her eyes widened in shock and confusion. "What the fuck?"

"Cut the back of the tent, open it up!" Galt ordered.

Dupree seemed unable to grasp what was happening and remained on her bedroll, staring fixedly at the licking flames.

"Move!" Galt shouted.

As she started to get up, a blade sliced through the back of the tent, narrowly missing her head. It tore straight up the canvas and receded. The slash was pulled open, and the flames greedily leapt up at the influx of new air, singeing Galt's back. In the new opening, Solgard's face appeared. Galt was extremely grateful that she had been on watch.

"Come on!" she shouted.

Dupree scrambled by her as Galt seized Pike and shoved him toward the new exit, then grabbed Lowther under his arms and dragged him toward the opening. Galt stumbled over the bottom of the canvas and tumbled onto his back, leaving Lowther straddling the torn wall. Solgard helped hoist Galt up, and the two of them dragged Lowther clear. Panting and bewildered, they watched as the tent became fully engulfed.

"What the *fuck?*" Dupree repeated.

Galt rubbed his eyes, which felt withered and dry after being trapped in the acrid smoke. Beyond the burning tent, he could see that the command tent was engulfed as well. Something was seriously wrong.

"Is everyone okay?" Mather called, approaching them from around the tent, giving the leaping flames a wide berth.

"Lowther's out," Galt wheezed, his throat feeling like it was filled with broken glass.

Mather quickly knelt next to his last remaining man. "He's breathing, but it's shallow."

"What's going on?" Solgard asked. "I didn't see anybody, then all of a sudden, the tents were burning."

"I didn't see anyone, either," Mather said.

Pike started to tremble as he gazed into the smoky haze around them. "Where are the others?"

As if in answer, a horrifying wail rose from the command tent. Galt knew the sound at once.

The flailing, burning form of a shade emerged from the flames, flinging aside fiery shreds of canvas. Galt and Solgard shared a quick glance and advanced toward it, blades drawn. The twisted shape staggered horribly, emitting a piercing shriek. The shepherds broke from one another, each taking a side to flank the creature.

Solgard moved in first, feigning a jab at the shade's midsection. As it contorted away from her blade, Galt stabbed at its other side. It howled in pain and swung a flaming arm toward him. He ducked the blow, but burning bits of dripping, viscous tissue flew from the swinging arm and struck him across his chest, neck, and face.

The searing pain took him by surprise, and he stumbled over his own feet and collapsed to the ground. Frantically brushing the gunk from his face, he had just enough time to see the shade advancing on him. It raised both of its arms and swung them down in a crushing blow. Galt rolled away, and though he successfully avoided the attack, he was showered in more of the burning tissue that was now continually sloughing off the shade.

It lunged toward him again, but this time, it was interrupted by Solgard hacking away at its back. Distracted, it turned back toward her and heaved its bulk in her direction. Deftly, she sprung backward before it or any of the flaming chunks could strike her.

Galt struggled to get up, and with Solgard out of reach, the shade turned its attention back on him. With a blazing hand, it snatched at him, snagging his robes as he tried to lurch away. The shade yanked him off of his feet and pulled him toward a crushing, fiery embrace. The blistering heat rolling off of it was unbearable, and Galt twisted around, plunging his blade into the creature's chest.

It screeched and flung him away with all its might. Before he could even process what was happening, he was sailing backward through the flames of the burning command tent. He crashed into a pile of rubbish under the stone overhang and rolled to a stop, unable to breathe.

Gasping, he patted feebly at his robes, where a foul slick of burning tissue clung to him. Unable to extinguish the flames, he tore free of the robes and rolled across the damp earth, snuffing out the last of the fire. He tried to force himself to rise, but his battered body wouldn't comply.

He peered helplessly around the side of the command tent, which had collapsed in a shower of sparks. From his spot in the dirt, Galt watched as Solgard beat the shade down. After it threw him, she'd apparently struck it again, decisively enough to bring it to its knees. She was now lopping its head from its shoulders, sending it into a spasmodic fit.

Bathed in the light of the flames, black smoke swirling around her, standing triumphant over the writhing corpse, Solgard was a vision to behold. Enamored as Galt was, he did not notice the form advancing toward her from behind the other burning tent. Before he could call out to her, it was too late.

Illuminated from above by an ethereal light, the form seized Solgard swiftly by the hair. With a short, jagged blade, it cut her throat from ear to ear. Her eyes widened in surprise as blood gushed from the opening wound and poured down her front. The form cast her aside, casually turning away before she'd even hit the ground. Landing face-down in the muck, she came to rest beside the shade she'd just felled.

Galt screamed silently, his ravaged throat emitting no sound. As the smoke billowed by the unknown threat, he caught a clear glimpse of it. Though he could not really understand what was happening, the halo of the god was unmistakable, even with a shattered section ruining its otherwise-pristine beauty.

The god strode toward Mather, who was still kneeling over Lowther, staring in disbelief. Behind him, Dupree and Pike turned and fled. Bypassing Mather, the god quickly pursued them.

Mather started to rise, but the air around him began to shimmer strangely. The pocket of moving air suddenly seized him, and with a series of bizarre ripples, coalesced into a humanoid shape crowned by a luminescent halo of smooth, clear glass. The shape solidified into a small, wrinkled man with a hairless head and a short, gray beard, bundled in voluminous blue robes. He had one bony arm wrapped around Mather's head; the other hoisted a knife.

Before this new god could complete his murderous action, he cried out in surprise. Lowther had awoken and, seeing what was happening, had driven a dagger into the back of the god's calf. In the momentary reprieve, Mather tried to pull away, but the god still managed to drag his knife across the captain's throat. Mather stumbled free and, clutching his neck, collapsed to the ground.

Lowther shouted in surprise and rage and yanked his dagger free before plunging it into the back of the god's thigh. The god squealed and swung his knife wildly toward Lowther, who caught the smaller being's arm.

As they struggled, the god with the broken halo snatched Dupree by the collar of her tunic and yanked her back, slamming her to the ground. She yelped in a strangled voice before being silenced forever as the jagged blade was driven straight down into her neck, severing her head completely.

Overcome with terror, Pike stumbled and fell to his hands and knees. He continued to scramble away, making it barely further than Dupree had before he was dragged backward and brutally gutted. Left in the blood-soaked sand, Pike screamed for some time before his life ran out.

All the while, Galt struggled to rise, his consciousness swimming as the pain, shock, and horror began to overwhelm him. With every attempt to crawl forward, his eyes darted back to the crumpled form of Solgard, sapping him of all resolve.

Lowther was now on top of the second god, each clutching a knife in one hand and the wrist of their opponent in the other. Finished with Dupree and Pike, the god with the broken halo meandered over to them and kicked Lowther savagely in the temple. His head snapped loosely to the side and his entire body went limp.

"Get this thing off of me," the second god spat, struggling under the weight of Lowther's body.

"If I felt so inclined, I might even judge this one worthy," the god with the broken halo said with a chuckle as he pushed Lowther's body aside with his foot.

"And what would you have done if this brute had killed me? Hmm? Now, help me up."

The god with the broken halo seized the other god and pulled him to his feet. The back of the smaller god's robe was torn and bloody where Lowther had stabbed him, and he winced as he put weight on his injured leg. "You're late."

"You were preemptive and overeager. I told you exactly how long I would be gone. For one so wise, I would think that you would be capable of being more prudent."

The pedestrian bickering of the two gods was so beyond anything Galt could have imagined that he simply let it wash over him. His mind had shut down, grief beyond measure rendering him incapable of processing anything. Injured, and with no one left for him to try to help, he had resigned himself simply to lying there, feigning death.

The smaller god glared at his rescuer as if he wished to say something venomous. "Did you get them?"

"Yes." The god with the broken halo held up a metal tube that Galt recognized as Fontaine's. "Let's go."

"You don't wish to judge your subjects worthy first? They've been such loyal pets."

"No. I'm indifferent to them. They've done their part, but they failed to live up to the loyalty of their ancestors."

"Probably because you marched their ancestors to their doom. It's no wonder they despise you."

"They think *nothing* of you, coward. Now move."

Together, the two gods left the burning remains of the camp. The smaller one moved haltingly on his injured leg, leading the other to bark at him to speed up. Before long, they were gone.

Galt remained on his belly in the dirt. The sound of the crackling flames and the coppery stench of blood filled the air, but he hardly noticed.

Some analytical part of his overwrought mind made the connection without him consciously choosing to ponder it. The god who had appeared from nowhere to murder the woman he loved had declined to pass some sort of *judgment*. There was only one answer. Somehow, Ulesreto had learned of their expedition and gotten the blade shards from Fontaine, which almost certainly meant that he and Starkad were dead. Ulesreto had also apparently been helped by another god, though which one, Galt did not know.

And now, everyone was dead and gone but him. He was alone.

An unsettling moan soon robbed him of that notion. He lifted his head gingerly and peered around the scene of the massacre. His eyes once again settled on Solgard's body, which had begun to shake violently, her boots kicking in the bloody muck.

"No … no," Galt whimpered. "Not her … no."

Despite his protestation, Solgard's body continued to seize until it reached the inevitable conclusion. A wretched pop echoed across the water, and Galt watched as the newborn shade slithered clear of the defiled corpse.

Rage flooded through him, momentarily purging him of his anguish. Of every person lost on their ill-fated expedition, somehow, Solgard had produced a shade. It was impossible; it was unacceptable. It wasn't just that an idiot god was careless in its judgments; there could not be any divine hand in the sorting of the dead if she was cast among the unworthy. The only god actually capable of any judgment had left her ultimate fate up to chance.

His fury driving his battered body, Galt struggled to his feet, stepping free of the last smoldering shreds of his robes, and shuffled toward the barely formed shade. If no divine power saw fit to deliver her, he would have to do it himself. Then, his time as a shepherd, a devotee of a false faith, would be over.

He gained speed as he staggered forward, hoisting his blade above his head. Bellowing in primal ferocity, he fell on the shade. It writhed and clawed at him, but he hardly felt it. Fueled by blind hatred, he battered the distorted flesh with blow after vicious blow until there was nothing left but sizzling chunks of dissolving tissue fanned out around him. He was slick with the monster's putrid blood, but it didn't matter. Nothing mattered anymore.

Utterly spent, Galt collapsed to his knees, soaking them in the slop of foul gore that had accumulated at his feet. Bitterly, he wept for Solgard, for the others, for himself.

As his racking sobs subsided, sinking back beneath the numbness, a new sound reached his ears. He turned slowly to see Mather propped against Lowther's body, pressing a hand to his neck. He was breathing heavily, each breath rasping wetly.

"You made it too," he managed.

"Aye. I did."

Mather nodded and leaned back, closing his eyes.

CHAPTER 55

Faye's lungs felt as if they were going to burst. She stumbled to a stop, and with her hands on her knees, gulped down as much of the stale air as she could.

She hoped she was going in the right direction, but in her frantic flight, she'd become disoriented. She'd passed the only landmark, the lighthouse, some time ago, and now, the low, foggy hills all looked the same. Somewhere eastward lay the doomed camp, unwittingly awaiting their own destruction. Behind her lay another doomed camp, where the body of her husband, a murderer, now resided.

It wasn't suspicion of Cyprian that had led Faye to follow him onto the moors. Rather, it had been her growing distrust of Starkad. She'd apparently been right not to trust him, though for reasons she could never have imagined.

She'd followed them from Kafarbjorn after hastily placing Mather in charge. He'd urged her not to go and voiced his concern that they were all taking an unnecessary risk. Going to Kafarbjorn had never sat well with him, and he'd made it clear that the latest wrinkle in their plans had done nothing to improve his disposition. Faye had agreed with him, but she'd still insisted on going, though she'd implored him to keep her absence a secret so as not to alarm the others. As far as they knew, Cyprian and Starkad had gone to search for a cache, and she was in the command tent.

Beyond Mather, she'd only told Jotun of her plan. His reaction had been expected.

"Rorik?" he'd nearly gasped. "I have to go. I have to see him."

"Absolutely not," Faye had said emphatically. "I don't even know if Starkad is telling the truth about that. I'm not risking your life on this too. And I'm sorry, but if I don't leave now, I'll lose them completely. You'll slow me down."

He'd looked hurt and crestfallen at the blunt assessment of his abilities, but he'd known she was right. "It's just—I was supposed to be with him. I need to know if things could have gone differently," he'd said.

"I know, and if there's any truth to this, I'll find out what happened. And perhaps you can visit the site when our people head north," Faye had said with a hopefulness she hadn't felt.

Now, she was certain that exodus would never occur, and worse yet, leaving Jotun behind had left him in imminent danger.

She'd espied Cyprian and Starkad from afar shortly after following the path they'd taken toward the bluffs. Careful to remain unobserved, she had stayed far behind them until they'd reached the old encampment. Then, curiosity and suspicion had driven her to get as close as she could, and she'd crawled across the ground on her belly, skirting the edge of the clearing, until she'd been able to peer down on them from a nearby hillock.

Faye had initially felt a grim sense of vindication when it became clear that Starkad had deceived Cyprian, but when he'd revealed why he had done so, and what he truly was, Faye had been astonished and terrified. Her bewilderment had only grown when the newly revealed Ulesreto had explained that Nuroh lived and that he'd infiltrated their kingdom.

Still, the true horror had come when she learned the truth of what Cyprian had done to Phir-Ramarian. He'd been revealed as a duplicitous killer who'd betrayed his own kin and jeopardized the lives of his people for his own gain. He had let others sacrifice themselves in defense of his honor and in pursuit of his aims. The blood of every person lost since they'd left Vin-Sadavat was on his hands.

And Faye's. In service of his lies, she'd imprisoned others who had suspected the truth. She'd stood by and allowed Cyprian to condemn them to death. Learning this, hearing it from his own lips, she had felt an overwhelming urge to vomit.

The revelation that Nuroh had not only reached Phar-Mindorius's ear, but that he was now lying in wait at the harbor, had almost been lost in the dizzying, nightmarish truth of what Cyprian had done. Ulesreto's promises, and Cyprian's refusal, barely registered as Faye reeled.

It wasn't until Cyprian drew his blade that things snapped back into focus. Suddenly, the blood in her veins had turned to ice, and her breath had caught in her throat. She'd been unable to move, torn between fear of Ulesreto, a desire to help her husband, and a feeling of nauseating disgust at what he'd been revealed to be.

Frozen in that state, internally warring with herself, she'd watched as Cyprian was struck down. When Ulesreto had snatched the shards, the thought to attack him had flickered through her mind, but she'd known that it would have only resulted in her joining Cyprian, and she'd watched impotently as Ulesreto left, passing over a hill and disappearing from view.

When she was certain that he was gone, she'd risen slowly and gazed down at the bloodied form of Cyprian. He'd still been alive, but only barely. By the time she'd rushed down to his side, it'd been too late.

All at once, every repressed emotion had exploded forth. Faye had fallen atop his body, clutching at him, babbling incoherently for him to come back, her words punctuated by shrill, lunatic sobs. All the while, Cyprian's glazed eyes had stared ahead, half-lidded.

The mouth that had kissed hers, that had spoken countless words of affection, had remained silent, a broken hole in a dead face.

Her desperate anguish had morphed into hatred toward him—hatred for deceiving her, hatred for paving the way to his own downfall through his misguided, wicked actions, and hatred for dragging her and everyone else with him. She'd pounded her fists against his chest then, willing him to return so that she might unleash her fury upon him.

Finally, her rage had ebbed, and she'd been left with nothing but a profound and immeasurable sorrow. Whatever he'd become, she loved him still. With his death, her life had also ended. Everything she'd believed, and everything she'd hoped for, was now gone.

Sitting on her knees beside his body, it occurred to her that he hadn't produced a shade. Some time had passed, and his body had remained still. It didn't make her feel better. Instead, she felt herself emptied of all feeling and all thought, save one.

She needed to warn the others.

After rising shakily to her feet and taking one last long look at her husband, Faye had turned from that sepulchral place and run. Somehow, she needed to reach the camp before Ulesreto returned and enacted the plan that he and Nuroh had in place. The others needed to be warned.

Now, as she stood upon the moors, panting and nearly delirious, she realized the hopelessness of her situation. There was no way she was going to be able to pass widely enough around Ulesreto to remain unseen and still beat him there. At this point, he and Nuroh could have already finished butchering the others and left for the Isle of Creation.

Still, there was nothing left for her to do but try. Muscles screaming, lungs aching, Faye forced herself on.

It wasn't long before she realized exactly which way to go. The smoke of the burning camp could be seen rising lazily above the horizon.

• • •

Heedless of the possibility that Ulesreto or Nuroh might still linger about the wreckage, Faye rushed toward the camp with no attempt at stealth. Her footfalls sent plumes of sand up behind her as she raced down the beach. She could clearly see the twin fires smoldering low now, but still belching black smoke toward the sky.

Sitting some distance away, she saw two human forms. Either someone had survived, or the gods had once again masked their power and were waiting for her. She found she was too exhausted to truly consider the second option, and she approached the two boldly.

As she grew closer, she could tell that it was Mather and Galt. They appeared to have been badly beaten, but they were alive.

"Lady Fontaine," Mather said with surprise and relief, rising to his feet as she approached them.

As he did, her legs began to buckle beneath her. Mather grabbed her arm and helped lower her to the ground. Utterly spent, she remained there, looking despondently at the two of them.

Coated in blood, soot, and grime, their eyes stared hauntingly out of their weathered faces. Mather had a blood-soaked scrap of cloth tied around his neck; Galt had blistered burns across his face. His robes were missing, and his leather tunic was burnt and torn. There was nobody else nearby.

With a nauseating lurch in her stomach, Faye noticed the blackened human forms within the smoldering remnants of a large fire. "Are you two … is it … where is Jotun?"

Mather shook his head miserably.

Faye buried her face in her hands, pressing her palms into her eyes hard enough to send phantom spots of light dancing behind her eyelids. She took a deep, shuddering breath and forced her welling emotions down. The relentless bludgeoning of tragedy would not break her, not while there was still so much at stake.

She'd known this was going to happen; the fact that anyone had survived at all was miraculous. She needed to focus on moving forward.

And Mather and Galt needed to know the truth.

Without warning, she unleashed a deluge of information, trying to describe everything that had occurred at Rorik's camp. The words came spilling out of her in rapid bursts, interrupted only by gasps for air. Eventually, her panic passed and, as she told the tale, she regained her composure. By the time she finished, she was speaking in a detached, monotonous tone. The two men stared at her in disbelief.

"So, all along, Starkad was Ulesreto, and he was in league with this other god, Nuroh, and they were manipulating us into getting the shards for them?" Mather said.

"Yes," Faye confirmed.

The three of them sat in silence.

"And Lord Fontaine *did* kill Phir-Ramarian," Galt said. "Kovak was right."

"Yes," Faye repeated. She'd hoped that part of the story would have been lost amid the rest. Though it was not her fault, she felt a deep sense of responsibility and shame for his actions and her part in them. Absorbed as she had been in her own private tragedy, it now occurred to her that Galt had also lost someone he cared for, all as a result of the machinations of the gods and the lies of her husband.

"I'm sorry," she said to Galt, "for Solgard."

He nodded absentmindedly.

"I'm certain that the Void-God is watching over her," she added weakly. She didn't really understand the nature of their beliefs, and was unsure of what else to say.

"No, he's not," Galt said matter-of-factly. "Nobody is. There is no Void-God; there was only the Father-God and his little system that died with him. The faith is a lie. Solgard went shade. Your man, Berg—he went shade too. Burst out of the burning tent. I thought it might have been you, honestly, before Mather told me you snuck off after them. But, no, there's no real god, only these mockeries with their failed power. In death, there's only dumb chance. Shade or nothing. Good or bad, it's meaningless."

Thinking of what had become of Jotun, of everyone, in her absence nearly broke her. She felt hate emanating from Galt, and though she could justify her part in everything to herself, she still felt that some of his ire was directed toward her. But it was pointless to argue with him, and at any rate, she did not begrudge him his hate.

Once again, they lapsed into an awkward silence.

"Well," Mather said thoughtfully after some time, "I suppose command now falls to you, Lady Fontaine."

Faye scoffed. "I think we can do away with titles now. I'm not in command of either of you—you're free now to do as you wish. I know what I'm going to do, though. I'm going after them."

"He wouldn't even deign to judge her worthy," Galt said almost to himself. Then, decisively, he said, "I'm coming with you. If it means that I get a chance to spill their blood, I'm coming with you."

Mather rubbed his neck and winced. "I'm not sure we're in a condition to spill anyone's blood."

"Well, again, you're free to do as you wish," Faye said, "but the way I see it, we have no other option. Ulesreto stated plainly that our entire *reality* will be wiped out if he gets into Paradise. So, you can try to go back to Nordabor, but everything will be erased before you ever set foot there again. Our only hope lies in the fact that they'll inevitably try to betray each other. They both want Paradise for themselves. If we can make it to the Isle of Creation and somehow ambush them in a moment of weakness, before Nuroh has finished reforging the blade, or at least before they can open the gates, then we'll have a chance."

Mather said nothing, clearly thinking intently about what he should do.

"I can order you to come with us, if that would make you feel better."

He smiled slowly, and Faye, despite everything, grinned as well. Galt's scowl remained unchanged.

"I see your point, Lady-er, Faye," Mather said, correcting himself. "But we don't have any idea how to follow them, beyond knowing that they went north. And we don't know how quickly they'll get there or how long it will take to reforge the blade."

"Yes, there are a lot of unknowns," she said with a shrug, "but it's the only option we have. And, actually, I do know the way somewhat. The lighthouse at Thunsturm—we passed it on the way to Rorik's camp. It's near the dried strait, the spot where we can cross. Remember Starkad telling us that at the first meeting? I can get us back there. If we head north then, I don't see how we can miss the isle."

Mather nodded. "Starkad also said that when we eventually crossed that way, we would need to be watchful for the God of the Sea."

"*Ulesreto* said many things. Who knows what was truth and what was a lie?" Galt said bitterly.

"Well, either way, we'll be careful," Faye said. "If Opriseur is out there, maybe we'll get lucky, and they'll be delayed by her. Maybe she'll kill them, or maybe they'll kill her."

"We can hope," Mather said.

"So you're in, then?" Faye asked.

Mather rubbed his neck again and looked toward the fire. "Nuroh almost killed me. Tried to cut my throat—did cut my throat, just not quite as deeply as he'd intended. Lowther got him in the leg and distracted him just enough that it saved me. I owe my life to Lowther."

He turned toward Faye and held her in his gaze. "All this time, I've just been following orders. I executed people based on your husband's lie. I let us be led here when I knew it was wrong because it was my place to obey. I'm done following orders. I'll go with you, not because it's my duty, but because it's what's right. Good men and women have died in service of this quest. Their blood is on my hands too. I won't besmirch their sacrifice by walking away now, even if I could escape what you say is coming. I won't let the deaths of Lowther and Dupree and all the others be in vain. We cannot let Ulesreto and Nuroh succeed. We have to stop them."

Faye was astonished to see that the unflappable captain's eyes were shimmering. She clasped his hand. "We will," she promised.

She hoped she was right.

•　　•　　•

Despite her aching body's protestations, Faye joined Mather and Galt in making the preparations for what would almost certainly be their final journey. Between the three of them, there was a tacit understanding that, should they even succeed, they would still most likely never return to Nordabor. They no longer had any tents, bedrolls, or other basic supplies beyond what each of them had carried before the razing of the camp. From the wreckage, they managed to scavenge four dented cans of stewed meat that had survived the attack. It was the very last of their food. Barring the chance that they miraculously won and gained access to Paradise themselves, they would never make it beyond this one-way suicide mission.

Only water remained plentiful, requiring just a short hike south to reach the Einfallen. Faye and Mather had been carrying their canteens, and though Galt's had burned, he'd collected Solgard's. He'd also retrieved her blade from where she'd fallen.

As they prepared to leave the river for the last time, Galt unhooked his own sheathed blade from his belt and held it out to Faye. "You should take this. At this point, we're all responsible for any shade we encounter."

Faye, who had very little experience with weaponry of any kind, looked at the blade with hesitation. He pushed it into her hands, and the weight surprised her. The short sword she'd been assigned at the beginning of the expedition seemed flimsy by comparison.

"I couldn't. It's yours," she said, not wanting the responsibility.

"I'll be carrying this one," he said, patting the other sword hanging from his belt. "It was Solgard's, and Blackburn's before her. She would want me to carry it. As for that one, I care not for it. It's yours."

"Okay," she said. "Thank you."

Galt grunted in response and turned, leaving her to struggle with attaching the scabbard to her belt. She figured it out just as Mather approached them, finished filling his canteen. He eyed the sword hanging heavily from her belt and raised his eyebrows, but said nothing.

With their canteens filled, the three weary travelers, the last survivors of the expedition, set out once more. Before long, Kafarbjorn Harbor receded into the mists behind them.

There were no backward glances.

• • •

As they trudged up the bluff, Faye was struck by how different her circumstances were compared to the last time she'd passed this way. Following Cyprian, she'd been fixated on pedestrian concerns regarding the intentions of the devious badlander. She'd been incapable of conceiving anything even close to the truth.

Now, her situation had altered so much that the recent past had become insubstantial. Her previous existence had been wrenched away so thoroughly that it was almost difficult to accept those things had ever been real. If it were not for the screaming muscles of her legs, Faye would have readily believed that the entire affair had been some hideous fever dream.

Yet the truth of it all, the image of Cyprian's lifeless body, the knowledge of his guilt, would be branded on her mind until she followed him into death. It was a prospect that no longer seemed very far off.

The three of them reached the moorland, pausing only to catch their breath before beginning the journey across. As the Imperial Highway began to fade from view to their left, the stillness of the air was split by a sudden, desperate cry. They froze, and Faye felt her heart banging against the inside of her chest. Mather and Galt had drawn their weapons, and Faye belatedly fumbled with the blade she'd reluctantly taken.

Before she could even clear it from the scabbard, the voice, which was distinctly female, called out again. "Please, help me."

It was coming from nearby, and Faye's first thought was that it was a trap. It didn't make any sense, considering that Ulesreto and Nuroh believed them all to be dead, but the catastrophic events of late had colored her thinking with dark portents.

"It's coming from over there," Mather whispered, pointing toward a small gully in the shadow of an unusually pointed hillock south of them. Without further discussion, he proceeded toward the source of the voice.

"Please!" it cried again. Faye and Galt exchanged a hesitant look, then plodded after Mather.

The three of them reached the edge of the gully and peered down. The hillock beyond had eroded from the very top, creating a steep slope of loose dirt, stones, and chunks of desiccated moss. At the bottom, amidst the tumbled remnants of the collapsed hillside, was the skeletal form of Bellamont, her right leg twisted unnaturally.

Any lingering animosity that Faye had felt toward Bellamont had certainly evaporated the moment she'd learned that the healer—and the other mutineers—had been right all along. In its place, a deep shame had bloomed. A sudden, compulsive need to confess everything, more than a desire to provide any care, brought Faye to Bellamont's side. "We're here," she said, grasping Bellamont's hand.

The woman's fingers were black with filth and impossibly thin. There was almost nothing to her now. Her eyes had receded into her skull, and her lips had pulled back from her yellowed teeth. Her hair, previously rich and vibrant, had faded and thinned. She seemed to have accelerated into the decrepitude of old age. Faye tried to calculate how long Bellamont had gone without food, but found that her mind was too taxed to sort it out.

"Lady Fontaine, please, show me mercy," Bellamont begged.

"Oh, yes, of course. We have food," Faye said, unshouldering her bag. Behind Faye, Mather and Galt now leaned over them. Bellamont's glazed eyes seemed to focus and grow more alert as she looked at them.

"What's happened to you all? You don't appear to be much better off than me." She gestured weakly toward her leg. Faye was now close enough to see that the bone of her shin had risen jaggedly from the ragged pant leg around it, and her foot was twisted at a nauseating angle. "I was desperate. I crossed the river and followed you all. Thought I might steal some food. This fucking hill collapsed right under me and dumped me down here."

"How long have you been here?" Mather asked.

"I'm not sure. I passed out from the pain for some time. I saw you three and decided I had nothing left to lose. Where are the others? What's happened?" she asked again.

"You were right. You, Kovak, Gricks—all of you." Faye could no longer bring herself to say aloud what Cyprian had done, but Bellamont seemed to understand all the same.

She closed her sunken eyes and chuckled mirthlessly. "And look what it has earned me."

Faye, swamped by humiliation, thrust a can of meat toward Bellamont. "Here, take this. Please. There's so much more to tell you, and we'll need you strong."

This elicited another nasty laugh, and Bellamont nudged the can away. "I was a grand healer, my lady. I know a lost cause when I see one. Whatever else has happened, whatever you need help with, I'm done. I am now beyond starvation. I couldn't eat that, even if I wanted to. My stomach is already dead. And I'm not walking anywhere, not anymore. No, the help I seek is for a deliverance from my suffering."

The three of them watched her, saying nothing. "You all took my weapons away," Bellamont added, as if they had failed to grasp what she was asking for.

Galt nodded, unsheathed a dagger, and offered it to her handle-first. As she reached for it, Faye instinctively backed away.

"You have nothing to fear from me, I'm sure."

Faye flushed, embarrassed and miserable. She realized that she'd been seeking some sort of absolution, and Bellamont had none to offer. She had to remind herself that, considering the circumstances, condescending spite was about all they really deserved. "No, I don't fear you," Faye said. "I wish to help you. We can bind your leg. You could show us how to—"

Mather grasped her arm, and she turned to him. He shook his head. The simple motion said everything that Faye already knew. Bellamont, if she had even desired to come along with them, would be a burden.

Faye was reminded of how the last injured burden among them had been dispatched, and all of the horror that had followed. She was relieved that Bellamont was taking the decision out of their hands.

"Do you wish us to remain by your side? In case ..." Galt said.

Bellamont seemed to consider this, staring fixedly at the knife in her hand. "No. Now that the means to escape is within my grasp, I find that I'd like to wait. I need some time to ready myself, and I wish to be alone. I have no need for useless words of comfort offered by those who imprisoned me, or for the rituals of a shepherd. I know my prayers, and I believe the Void-God will show me mercy."

Galt said nothing, though Faye was certain that she knew what he was thinking.

"So be it. We will leave you to do what you wish," Mather said, gently pulling Faye to her feet. She was still holding the can of meat, and absentmindedly returned it to her bag as Mather led her away. Galt nodded to Bellamont before turning to go.

As they stepped clear of the gully, Faye stole one last glance at Bellamont, but she wasn't looking at them. She was still gazing at the knife, running a finger down the edge of the blade.

If she'd wondered where they were going, or why, she had ceased to care the moment her fingers had wrapped around the hilt.

CHAPTER 56

Though Galt pitied Bellamont, both for her situation and for her continuing belief in a god that he now knew didn't exist, he was grateful that she would not be accompanying them. Any vain attempt to aid her in order to atone for their previous follies would have availed them nothing. Rather, her presence would have only slowed them down, and they could ill afford any more delays or distractions. Not when every passing moment took their murderous enemies further away.

With each plodding step, Galt felt his thirst for vengeance grow. He knew there was no coming back from this journey, and he didn't care. There was nothing left for him now. Solgard was dead. Moore and Daeg were dead. His faith was shattered completely. The only thing that mattered now was revenge.

As they walked, Lady Fontaine and Mather discussed the possibility, however remote, that they could somehow survive this ordeal by defeating the gods after Nuroh had reforged the blade, but before the gods had entered the gates. If they could do that, they could enter Paradise themselves.

Galt wouldn't permit himself any such hope. He fully expected that death awaited him upon the Isle of Creation, but he was determined to take Ulesreto and Nuroh with him. The gods had caught him unawares before, it wouldn't happen again. Things would be different this time.

For now, he focused his mind on the task of putting one foot in front of the other. Hunger and exhaustion strove to drag him to a stop, but his will marshaled against them. At the very least, he was thankful that he'd been sleeping with his boots on when the tent burned. It had saved him the trouble of pilfering ill-fitting boots from one of the dead.

Retracing the path that she'd followed behind her late husband and Ulesreto, Lady Fontaine led them northwest through the moors. The dreary surroundings befitted Galt's thoughts, haunted as they were by grief and hate. Over the blasted heath they wandered until, far off in the distance, Galt saw the black fastness of the lighthouse.

"Do you think they could be there?" Mather asked. "That they might have stopped for any reason? By his own admission, that was supposedly where Ulesreto dwelt."

"If he did ever dwell there, he certainly vacated it once he learned of the shards and started his search," Lady Fontaine said. "I can't imagine they would have stopped now. They think we're all dead. There's no reason for them to plan an ambush."

"We could still encounter badlanders."

"Or shades," Galt added.

Lady Fontaine shrugged. "Those are possibilities. We'll just have to be careful. We'll give the lighthouse a wide berth and hope that we can figure out where the dried strait is."

It turned out that they had no difficulty finding it at all. After proceeding far west of the lighthouse and then resuming their way north, they reached the crest of a lofty hill. From atop the rounded pinnacle, they were able to survey the northern coast for the first time.

Spread out before them, beyond the eroded slopes of the upper moors, was a flat expanse of beach marred by the remnants of ancient fortifications and the tremendous, rusted hulks of ancient siege engines jutting out crookedly from the dark sand. Partially collapsed trenches, bunkers, and scattered refuse littered the ground, and lording over the vista was the lighthouse, which rose dizzyingly from a jagged cape to the east. Its great lens, brine-coated and dark, watched indifferently over the empty lands beneath it.

Stretching away from the shoreline was a broad salt flat where the waters of the Stagnant Sea had receded on either side. Ethereal beams of sunlight broke through the clouds, dappling the exposed seabed with the white light of dawn. If there was any doubt that they'd found the dried strait, the horizon beyond the open tract dispelled it.

Directly north, the sky and land puckered inward bizarrely, creating a shimmering, fractured image of insanely bent and reflected light. The effect seemed to pull the normal light in with it, exposing lines of flickering brightness in the dark sky above. The transient cracks in the sky were shot through with bands of multicolored, wavering luminosity of colors Galt couldn't even begin to identify. Within the distorted image, he could just make out the rising height of a landmass.

"That must be the Isle of Creation," Lady Fontaine murmured, clearly awestruck.

"Yes, but what's happening? Why does it look like that?" Mather asked uneasily.

"I don't know."

"Is it possible they've already opened the gates?"

"I think we'd be dead already if they'd opened the gates," Galt said.

"Probably, yes," Lady Fontaine agreed. "I don't know what's causing that phenomenon, but I imagine we'll find out soon enough. Let's keep moving."

They descended the crumbling northern side of the hill, cutting diagonally back and forth. Although they were now beyond the moors that Lady Fontaine had already passed through, she was still leading the way. Despite initially eschewing the role, she had become their de facto leader.

As they walked, Galt watched his old blade dangle clumsily at her side, hung there by a clear amateur. He'd been hesitant to give her the blade, doing so only out of necessity. Approaching the sand filled trenches and the abandoned barracks, Galt had become increasingly certain that shades lurked amid the rubble. He would not put himself at further risk defending someone defenseless, not now.

"This must be what the Vingallean legion left behind when they were routed," Lady Fontaine said. "After the Father-God annihilated the southern kingdom. I can only imagine what Jotun would have made of this. Or Cyprian."

She stated the last bit in such a flat, listless tone that Galt felt a stirring of pity. Lady Fontaine, like him, must have been mastering her pain in service of the more-pressing matters at hand. It was easy, in his general dislike, to forget that she had endured the loss of a close friend in addition to her husband. And Lord Fontaine, despite his treachery, had still been someone she'd loved for many long-cycles. A lifetime together could not be easily swept away, no matter the circumstance.

Mather seemed to detect her buried misery, and he placed a hand on her shoulder. She smiled wanly, sniffed, and cleared her throat. "Come on," she said, her voice thick.

The three of them picked their way across the beach, and despite Galt's premonition, there were neither shades nor anything else waiting for them. As they went, they passed through the shadows cast by the colossal juggernauts, and Galt marveled at the wrecks, which were completely alien to anything he'd seen before, featuring massive cogs and wheels and an array of pipes and strange ballistae. He imagined that these machines of war must have been the most powerful weapons that mankind, at its pinnacle, could produce. It was frightening to consider that these were playthings compared to the old power of the gods, and that, without Ulesreto, the people of Vingallea would have been completely wiped out.

Now, the three of them, battered and malnourished, were all that Vingallea could muster to oppose the gods again. And this time, Ulesreto would not save them from their annihilation, but instead sought it. Galt hoped that the usurper's power really had been greatly reduced. Otherwise, their plan was utterly hopeless.

The dark sand of the beach slowly gave way to a white, calcified plane of salt-encrusted flatness that shined dazzlingly wherever the beams of sunlight struck it. The reflected light helped to raise the temperature somewhat, though the air was still cooler than Nordabor's and saddled with an unpleasant dampness.

As they proceeded across the flat expanse, Galt was reminded of the valley surrounding the Einmaz Mountains, in which he'd first seen the lights upon the firmament with Solgard. She'd described them as a gift from the Father-God, and had believed that his love lived on.

Galt was certain now that she had been mistaken, and that was truly heartbreaking.

· · ·

They hiked nonstop for a cycle, yet the distorted shape of the Isle of Creation seemed to grow no closer. The only proof that they'd travelled any distance at all was that the shoreline behind them had receded to a series of crooked bluffs in the distance. The lighthouse, grim and foreboding, still leered at them over the salt flat.

After another two cycles, the lighthouse had become a black line behind them, and the undulating warp of the Isle of Creation had consumed much of the northern horizon. The shape of the isle, despite being cloaked in bending light, was now plainly visible. Two ridges rose from each side, but both abruptly ended near the middle, forming a central cleft. Some kind of tower rose between and above the opposing cliff faces. Galt assumed that it was a part of the Gates of Paradise.

"I need to rest," Lady Fontaine declared suddenly. She dropped her pack to the ground and sat on it, resting her head in her hands.

Whether exhaustion or fear had overtaken her, Galt was unsure. His own trepidation was beginning to dull his rancor.

"We should eat before we confront them," Mather said. "We'll need whatever energy we can muster. We'll eat half a can each now, and finish the other halves when we reach the shore."

"What about the fourth can?" Lady Fontaine asked without looking up.

"We'll split it on the way back."

Whether or not Mather actually believed any or all of them would be making a return trip was impossible to read on his lined face. Jest or not, it was enough to make Lady Fontaine look up with a weary smile.

As each of them dug out the can they carried—the final one was in Lady Fontaine's pack—Galt began to grow nervous. He did not like being so exposed, but saw no other alternative. At least they could see any threat approaching, and Mather, who considered everything from a tactical standpoint, didn't seem concerned. At any rate, starvation had dulled his thoughts, and the impending food drove away all other concerns.

He sawed the lid free with a knife and greedily began to eat the congealed lumps cold, scooping them out with his dirty fingers and shoveling them into his mouth, pausing only to gulp from his canteen. The sudden influx of food was so pleasurable that Galt didn't even feel the boils and sores on his face being pulled apart as he chewed. He scarcely noticed when his decayed molar finally came free, spitting it out upon the ground without a second thought.

Lady Fontaine and Mather, equally consumed, paid no mind. Forcing himself to stop as the can neared the halfway point was going to be impossible.

As he chewed blissfully, intoxicated by the stew, a distant thumping sound reached his ears. The small, rational part of his mind shuddered back to life, and he paused between bites and looked up, setting his can down.

A dark shape, distorted by distance, was moving across the flat from the west. He stood up for a better view, squinting toward it. "What's that?" he asked.

Lady Fontaine, finally noticing that something was amiss, reluctantly set her can aside and rose, pulling out her field glass. Mather joined her a moment later.

Panic suddenly washed over her face, and she nearly dropped the glass. "We need to move *now*." She stooped down and, after hastily wrapping a cloth about the open top of her can and jamming it into a side pocket, snatched her pack from the ground. Wordlessly, Mather followed suit.

"What is it?" Galt asked, failing to grasp what was happening. His mind was still sluggish and fogged by the brief tease of the food.

"It's Opriseur," Lady Fontaine gasped.

Galt wheeled around and beheld the advancing form again. It had picked up speed, and was now close enough that he could clearly see that it was humanoid and of a tremendous stature.

It appeared to be running wildly toward them.

"Let's go," Mather ordered, shoving Galt's satchel into his arms.

Lady Fontaine had already started running toward the distorted shore of the isle. Galt quickly shouldered his satchel and, with Mather, raced after her.

A feeling of palpable grief rolled through him as he realized that he'd left his half-finished can of stew behind. He nearly turned to retrieve it, but the thundering footfalls echoing across the salt flat stopped him. They grew louder until they had dwarfed the sounds of the trio's desperate gasps and crunching steps. Each pounding stomp sounded like a massive boulder being dropped into deep water. The ground was beginning to shake.

Stumbling, Lady Fontaine faltered. Mather seized her by the collar and wrenched her back onto her feet before she could fall.

A wretched voice barked in mad laughter behind them, and Galt, unable to resist, turned to look. Closing in on them was a being that had clearly fallen from the highest echelons of grace. Opriseur's degeneration was obvious, but unlike Chortelak, she still exuded raw power, despite her diminishment. Easily the height of five men, she swung a cudgel as large as Galt back and forth with each of her colossal strides. Her footfalls punched rents in the ground from which swirling eddies of water burst forth, surging up and around her armor-clad legs. Her entire form was arrayed in the same bronze armor, which had clearly been ornate in the distant past, but was now tarnished, encrusted with barnacles, and missing pieces.

Above the armor's gorget, Opriseur's thin face rose, twisted in manic fury and streaked with blood. Her right eye had recently been gouged out and her left seemed impossibly wide. Like the rest of her, the pearl halo that hovered above her head was coated with barnacles and splashed with blood.

Beholding her now, Galt stumbled and fell, scraping his palms against the rough, salty ground before pushing himself back to his feet. She laughed again, a booming, terrible sound.

"Little ones! Oh, little ones!" she bellowed in a bizarre and chilling sing-song. "Come to gloat over Alminnian? Come to see what you've done to the World-Father? *I WON'T LET YOU TOUCH HIM!*"

Galt felt the earth shatter behind him where Opriseur smote the ground with her cudgel, sending up a plume of sand and salt that momentarily enveloped him. Emerging from the cloud, he saw Lady Fontaine and Mather reaching a toppled jumble of enormous boulders on the shoreline. As Galt's desperate steps took him closer to the shore, the air became almost electric, filled with the pulsating, otherworldly light of the isle.

Opriseur howled behind him and swung her cudgel again. It seemed close enough to brush across Galt's hair before it exploded into the ground. As he emerged from another cloud of debris, he watched Mather snake into a crevice in the rocks and disappear. Lunging forward with every last iota of strength he had, Galt scrambled after him. Once his top half cleared the opening, Mather grasped his arms and quickly dragged him in. Panting, both men stumbled to the rear of the small den, where Lady Fontaine was pressed against the wall, eyes wide with terror.

In another moment, Opriseur was upon them.

With a barbaric roar, she smashed the cudgel into the entrance of their haven, rattling the stone around them and sending dirt showering down from above. Again and again, she pounded the sides of the enormous tumble of rock, trying to dislodge one of the boulders, but to no avail.

Opriseur's shadow passed above them, blotting out the light that streamed in from a gap in the stones. Silently, they listened in horror as she stalked about the rocks, looking for a way to force their small refuge open.

"Come out. Face me. Show the honor your kind supposedly values so highly," Opriseur ordered, her previously erratic voice taking on a militaristic, clipped tone. "Your master has left you behind. He and the gutless deserter fled from our battle as soon as they had the chance. I expected to find them, to finish our war once and for all. Instead, I find his cowering underlings. Come forth. *NOW.*"

Galt looked at the others and saw his own fear reflected on their faces. The mad god could stand outside their alcove forever, not needing to eat or sleep. Unless her fractured mind somehow distracted her, he didn't see any way that they could ever leave. He pictured their bones half-buried in the sand, having succumbed to starvation long before Opriseur relented.

"*GET OUT! GET OUT! GET OUT!*" she shrieked suddenly when nobody answered her summons. The furious blows of the cudgel resumed. With every strike, she emitted a raging, incoherent scream.

"Either of you have any idea how we're going to get out of here?" Galt nearly shouted to the others over the din.

"I only see one way," Mather shouted back. "We'll have to fight our way out."

"Have you lost your mind?" Lady Fontaine asked. "How do you propose we do that?"

"We'll have to—" Mather winced and pressed a hand to his wounded throat. "We'll have to wait for some kind of opening."

As he shouted the last word, the assault abruptly ceased, and his voice filled the tight space. In the renewed silence, they froze.

A scratching sound was heard from the entrance. All three of them turned in unison to see a monstrous gray hand groping into the crevice. Broken, filthy fingernails as large as Galt's head scraped across the rock, seeking for them.

Slowly, Mather unsheathed his blade. As Opriseur's hand squeezed further into the space, he lifted it above his head. Sweat coursed down his face as he waited for the hand to be close enough. Sliding across the floor, the damp, reaching fingers finally passed before him, and in a swift, violent motion, Mather brought his sword down upon the base of the index finger. It cut through the flesh easily, wedging itself deeply into the bone beneath.

Opriseur's reaction was immediate. Screeching deafeningly, she ripped her hand backward, wrenching Mather's sword from his hands and yanking him off his feet. He landed on his stomach as Opriseur's arm withdrew through the crevice.

Her hand reached the threshold, and the sword jammed against the rock, trapping her. She screamed in pain as she tried to wriggle her arm free, twisting and bending the sword within the wound. Finally, the mangled blade tore free and clattered to the ground while her hand slithered out of view.

Mather rose and returned to the rear of the space, making no move to reclaim his sword. Galt observed with a small, detached satisfaction that the ruined sword wasn't Moore's old blade.

Outside, they could hear Opriseur angrily rambling to herself, the garbled nonsense occasionally rising to shouts. The light was suddenly blotted out again, and they looked up at the gap. Opriseur's large, wet eye now gazed back at them.

"You will suffer... *SUFFER*. Murderers ... you took Him ... I won't let you ... you ... Father of All ... King of All ... you *UNFAITH-FUL*, rebellious ... Father, I'm sorry ... I've failed, but I won't fail again ... I can still save you ..."

Her voice was a hideous, unrelenting whisper pouring forth from beneath the bulbous, unblinking eye. As she continued her hissing soliloquy, Galt turned his left side away and slowly lifted a dagger from his belt. His thoughts turned to his fight with Kovak, and the failure of this strategy then. He absolutely could not fail now.

He moved as quickly as his battered body would allow him to, dropping to one knee and transferring the dagger to his right hand. Before Opriseur could react, he flung the dagger toward her eye.

Galt was certain that his aim was true. It wasn't. The knife struck the rock to the left of the gap, missing its target. It wasn't a complete failure, however, as the impact shattered the edge of the gap, flinging dust and chunks of stone into Opriseur's eye. She reeled back, stunned and hurt, but not permanently maimed.

"*Fuck*," Galt hissed.

"Just like your master to the end!" Opriseur wailed. "I see no other course now, Father, no other course."

They heard her heavy steps receding from the rocks, and the trio exchanged cautious looks. Embarrassed by his poor aim, Galt opened his mouth, but not knowing what to say, closed it again and fetched his dagger from where it had landed in the sand. Turning back toward the others, he saw Lady Fontaine creep around the slick of blood left by Opriseur's hand and proceed toward the entrance.

"Get back," Mather whispered urgently.

She held up a dismissive hand and continued forward, peering through the opening. "She's wandered back onto the salt flat," she reported. "She's got her arms up over her head."

Galt and Mather joined her at the entrance, squeezing into the tight spot. They pressed their heads together so each could see.

"What's she doing?" Galt asked.

"Whatever it is, I'm sure it's not good," Lady Fontaine said. "Now's our chance to move up the shore."

Mather was shaking his head. "There's no other refuge; she'll catch up to us."

As they debated what to do, Galt watched Opriseur with growing dread, wishing terribly that he hadn't missed with the dagger. She was standing out where the sea had once filled the strait, chanting passionately. Beyond her, a black line grew on the western horizon. It swelled ominously with each passing moment.

"I agree with Lady Fontaine," Galt said blankly, hypnotized by what he was seeing. "We need to move."

They followed his gaze, and Lady Fontaine gasped.

"It's a wave," she said. "Opriseur's pulling the waters of the sea into a massive wave. She means to drown us in here."

"All right, we should definitely go," Mather said, grasping Lady Fontaine and thrusting her up through the crevice.

She scrambled through and turned to offer her hand to Mather. He followed quickly and then helped lift Galt out. The three of them gingerly hopped across the rocks until they reached the ground, where they ran inland as quickly as they could.

The ground was stony and uneven, hindering their every step. Ahead, the shoreline gave way to sharply rising walls of craggy rock, between which was the cleft—and the only way to go. As they grew closer to it, Galt could see that there was a winding path upward, choked with collapsed, petrified trees. From behind, a growing roar seemed to be pushing against them like a physical force. Once again, Galt was unable to stop himself from looking back.

He would have cried out in shocked panic if he'd had the breath to do so. Surging up the beach behind them was a wall of roiling, foaming water within which Opriseur strode unimpeded. The formerly placid sea raged about her, driving inland in a whirling torrent.

They reached the deadfall and started to clamber through the knot of collapsed trunks and branches. Petrified logs shifted uneasily under them, and wilted, long-dead branches snapped off as they grabbed them for purchase.

"We need to get to higher ground!" Mather shouted over the howl of the incoming wave. "Climb!"

He leapt onto a broad trunk that rested against the wall of the canyon, wedged into a notch. Huffing, he straddled the trunk and climbed upward. Lady Fontaine clawed her way up a similar trunk further up the path, leaving Galt seeking desperately for another way up. It had become clear that outrunning the wave would be impossible.

"Galt!" He looked up toward the source of the voice—Lady Fontaine, who was pointing manically toward something on the opposite wall.

"Climb!"

His gaze followed her wild gesticulating to a tangle of withered vines hanging from a lip of rock. Galt raced toward it with no time to consider whether it would hold his weight. He leapt onto the knotted tangle and started heaving himself upward. As he did so, the cacophony of shattering trunks rose as the wave funneled hungrily into the cleft.

Galt reached the lip of rock and clung to it desperately, squeezing his eyes shut, waiting for the wave to consume him. The noise became deafening, and Galt felt the brackish spray hitting his legs. He opened his eyes in time to see Opriseur wading through the raging water, which rushed by just under his feet. She was squinting with her remaining eye, searching for her prey, holding the cudgel above her head menacingly.

He had another shot. Galt slipped out a dagger, felt the weight of it in his hand, and took aim. He nearly whispered a quick prayer out of old habit, but it died on his lips.

With a controlled motion, he whipped the dagger toward Opriseur. At that exact moment, she looked to her right, spotting Mather clinging to the top of the leaning trunk, nearly at her eye level. With her head turned away, the dagger soared into her left ear, disappearing into the blackness of the ear canal.

She cried out in surprise and pain, clasping her ear and turning toward Galt, seeking the source of her suffering. Behind her, Galt watched as Mather pressed his boots against the rock wall and pushed the trunk he clung to outward with his legs. It tilted toward Opriseur, and the current did the rest, pulling the log forward until the jagged top slammed into Opriseur's back, buckling her brine-coated armor. She stumbled forward, her head crashing into the wall slightly above Galt. Desperately, he ripped his blade from its scabbard and drove it upward. The blade pierced the soft, gray flesh of the bottom of her jaw, and he plunged it in to the hilt.

Galt managed to hold onto his blade, which sucked free from the wound as Opriseur reared up and away from the wall, bellowing in pain and rage. She twisted to her right, and the trunk embedded in her back snapped loudly, firing splintered chunks of wood into the air. The half that had struck her fell away into the water, and the lower half now pointed crookedly, barely rising above the water line. Mather had vanished.

Opriseur's eye bulged as her obsidian pupil leveled on Galt. She whipped her cudgel into the air above her head, a shimmering spray of water flicking from it. The cudgel reached the apex of her swing, and Galt was preparing to leap from the wall and into the racing water when he heard the shrill voice of Lady Fontaine calling out. "*Stop*! *For Alminnian*! *Spare his children*!"

This invocation was enough to stay Opriseur's hand, at least for a moment. Her cudgel hovered above her head, and her features softened. "His children …" she repeated, blood staining her entire mouth crimson and oozing from the bottom of her jaw. Around her waist, the water continued to churn.

"We do not serve the usurper. We wish to stop him," Lady Fontaine shouted. She looked terrified to have gotten the god's attention, and her voice wavered as she spoke. "We want to avenge our creator—our father."

"He loved you more than anything. More than any of his firstborns," Opriseur said, her insanity ebbing for the moment, the cudgel lowering.

"Yes, he loved us." Lady Fontaine licked her lips and blinked several times. "He would not want you to hurt us."

This was the wrong thing to say.

Opriseur whipped around to face Lady Fontaine, and she cringed away. "You presume to speak for your *FATHER*?! You, who *CELEBRATE* the patricide?! He may have loved you, but you will *NEVER* understand the mind of the *CREATOR*! I am of Him, *I* remain to preserve Him, and you are only *DISOBEDIENT CHILDREN*!" Her voice thundered off of the rocks around them, and she hefted her cudgel again.

Galt watched helplessly as Lady Fontaine faced the brutal death she'd only just spared him from. He was opening his mouth to cry out something, anything that might distract Opriseur again, when he saw Mather. Hidden amidst the dark, wet curtains of Opriseur's hair, the captain had managed to cling to the back of her armor, scaling the buckled plate above where the tree had driven into her back. He now lunged upward, seized the edge of her gorget, and hoisted himself onto the crusted surface of her left pauldron.

Opriseur faltered, realizing that something was wrong. She turned her head to the left, and her remaining eye widened in shock. "*NO!*" she cried, and then Mather drove his sword—Moore's old blade—directly into the center of her eye.

She screamed raggedly as he plunged the blade into the gelatinous depths, the hilt, and then his arm, disappearing into the wrecked tissue. The great cudgel slipped from her grasp and splashed into the water, and she made one spasmodic, groping motion, her fingers bumping weakly against Mather. He wrenched his blade free, and the arm and sword emerged covered in a thick smear of bloody white ooze, more of which gushed down Opriseur's cheek.

Her body buckled, and Mather grabbed onto her hair to hold on as she stumbled backward and crashed into the wall above Galt again, banging her halo into the rocks and sending it spinning. A broken chunk of it was flung away, and hot, briny water spilled from the remainder, dousing Mather.

As Opriseur began to slide down into the water, Galt called to Mather to jump. He leapt from her shoulder and clung to the same lip that had saved Galt.

Together, they watched as Opriseur's bloodied head slipped silently beneath the waves.

CHAPTER 57

With a mournful burbling, the debris-clogged waters began to recede. Faye clung to the battered husk of the trunk that had been her salvation, resting her head against the ancient dead wood. With her adrenaline fading, her complete exhaustion threatened to engulf her. She forced herself to remain awake as she waited for the waters to drain back toward the sea.

Across the gap, Galt and Mather clung even more precariously to a small section of rock, their feet tangled in the dead vines below. Both men looked ready to drop from the wall at any moment. She couldn't imagine the depth of their exhaustion, having just endured the brunt of Opriseur's attack. She was extremely grateful that the two of them were still there.

Most of the deluge finally drained, leaving a muddy quagmire below them. Her limbs screaming for release, Faye skidded down the tree and plopped clumsily into the muddy water, sinking nearly to her knees. Plodding through the muck, she approached Mather and

Galt, who had just made it to the ground, and grabbed them both in a tight embrace.

"Thank you," she said. "I couldn't do this alone. I'm glad you two are here with me."

Mather nodded and smiled wearily. "I'm glad we're here too." His exertions had apparently reopened his wound; he was once again pressing a hand to the bloody cloth tied around his neck.

"I, uh…" Galt said haltingly, "I want to thank *you*, actually. For pointing out those vines. And for distracting her. You saved my life."

"Of course," Faye said, somewhat surprised. "You've probably saved mine a dozen times. It was the least I could do."

He nodded, then looked down toward the beach. Faye and Mather followed his gaze. Among the broken trees that had been washed out with the receding waters, Opriseur's sodden corpse lay sprawled across the dark sand.

Faye sought for something profound to say. Another god had been snuffed out. The last tenuous links to the living world of the distant past were being cut one by one.

"I say we eat everything we've got," Mather said, interrupting her thoughts. He crouched down with a small groan and began to splash some of the remaining water across his gore-soaked arm. "We need it."

"I left the rest of my can down there," Galt admitted, pointing toward the glistening flat.

"We'll split the last can," Faye said.

The three of them sat upon a log and devoured the very last of their food, dividing everything that was left evenly between them. They gave no thought to what might come after, completely depleted by their battle with Opriseur.

Faye tried not to think about the two gods awaiting them, finding it utterly demoralizing. She badly wanted to sleep, having completely lost track of how long she'd been awake, but knew that they could spare no time. Once the final cans had been scraped clean, they rose.

Leaving the empty cans behind, the three survivors began their arduous trudge inland toward the epicenter of the otherworldly distortion and the Gates of Paradise.

•   •   •

Opriseur's wave had crushed and torn away much of the collapsed woodland blocking the pathway, leaving a tract of sloppy muck leading up between the cliffs. Faye, Galt, and Mather scrambled up the muddy slope until, as it grew steeper, they passed the point where the wave had reached its apex.

At this height, the dead trees had naturally thinned out, and the path became much clearer. Within half a cycle, the canyon walls began to fall away to either side and, cautiously, they crested the slope. Below them, the interior of the island was laid bare.

Within the encircling cliff walls, uniformly steep and impassable aside from the path they'd ascended, was a vast bowl of open land. Filling the space was the skeletal wreck of a behemoth, a heap of bone that rivaled the size of Nordabor itself.

"The Father-God," Faye murmured. She fell to her knees.

The colossal remains stretched across the entire vista below. The skeleton was essentially intact, its limbs folded in on themselves around the mammoth ribcage. The skull of the overthrown god, easily as large as the Vinecrown Keep, was half-buried in the stony ground. What had looked like a tower from afar was actually Alminnian's halo, half of which stuck up vertically from the ground above the skull, rising beyond the height of the surrounding cliffs. The other half was deeply embedded in the earth. It appeared to be comprised of bone, and was as starkly white as the rest of the remains.

All around the immense skeleton, the bizarre, shimmering quality of the air seemed to intensify, appearing to pull inward toward the body. It leached the natural light from the sky, leaving only a pale violet phosphorescence that permeated the air.

Looking at the final remains of the creator of their world, Faye had the strange sensation that what she was seeing wasn't quite real.

It was as if the reality that she was occupying, this particular place, was *thin*. She felt a strong urge to flee back down the slope toward a more stable world.

"I don't like this place," Mather said, breaking the stunned silence.

"Neither do I," Faye agreed. "I think that what we're looking at is the decomposition of our reality."

"What do you mean?" Mather asked.

"She means," Galt cut in, "that the Father-God is dead and gone, and when his body decayed away, the world he made started to go next."

Faye nodded. "First it was the slow stagnation that we've seen everywhere outside of Nordabor. Now, I fear that each of the gods dying has only accelerated that decay."

"So, no matter what happens here, Nordabor's time is short," Mather concluded.

"Precisely. I think our only hope is if we can get into Paradise and stop the process. Even if it's just long enough to get everyone out of Nordabor and through the gates."

Faye considered the logistics of moving the entire populace of the city to the Isle of Creation. It seemed impossible. For one, they would never make it back to Nordabor to report their success before succumbing to starvation, so Phar-Mindorius would have to decide to start the exodus north before it was too late, based solely on a hope that they'd succeeded, while they sought refuge in the blessed realm.

And what would that look like? From what Faye knew of Paradise, it was where the worthy dead had been deposited by Ulesreto. There, it was said, they would enjoy eternal life with the Father-God. Were they aware that he had never returned from his last sojourn to this world? What would they make of the gates opening after so long? Were they cognizant of time or anything that was happening here?

The closer they came to their goal, the more surreal it all seemed. And what of the powers of creation that existed within, those confirmed to exist by Ulesreto when he'd revealed himself to Cyprian?

The idea of rejuvenating their world from inside Paradise had been bandied around before, and Faye had been certain that it was possible.

But now, seeing the unhinging effect of reality falling apart around her, Faye wondered if human minds could even comprehend such a thing. Ulesreto hadn't thought so, but he could be wrong. Perhaps, if she or either of her companions were to enter, they could restore their world single-handedly. It was a pleasant thought, but she understood that appealing hopes sometimes masked poisonous truths.

"Do you see any sign of them?" Galt asked, peering into the strange landscape below.

Mather scanned the area with his field glass. Faye attempted to join him, but the fragile, layered appearance of the air was magnified by the glass, and the kaleidoscopic colors and light briefly clipping in and out of view in geometric patterns nauseated her, and she had to lower the glass, a cool sweat beading on her clammy skin.

"There," Mather said, pointing down toward the halo, the base of which was blocked from their view by the gargantuan skull. "It looks like there's a bluish glow that's different from the … other light."

With a specific target, Faye looked again. As Mather had described, a blue light was coming from behind the skull. "Well, it stands out. I'd say it's the best lead we have," she decided.

There was no dissent. The three of them started down into the immense open grave.

· · ·

They descended the slope, which was as steep on the interior side as the exterior had been, though Faye was relieved to find that it was an easier trek, dry and clear of any vegetation, save some brittle, scrubby grass clinging to the otherwise-barren rocks. It did not take them long to reach the bottom of the basin.

Relying on the dimness of the light to offer them some concealment, the three rushed across the open land until they reached the cover of the titanic remains, then scuttled inside of the cathedral-like expanse of the ribcage and continued toward the head. Faye gazed up at the overhanging structure of bone, almost unable to comprehend the cosmic insanity of strolling within the frame of the creator's body.

The being who had formed everything from nothingness had taken on a physical raiment, bottling his own power and pouring it forth into his creations. It had eventually cost him everything. His corporeal form had become his prison and his downfall. It had left him subject to death, and now, these bones were all that remained of his once-immeasurable power.

It was difficult to fathom the proportions of the ancient war that had happened there. Neither the legends of the past that told of his fall nor the further truth revealed by Ulesreto properly illustrated what had occurred.

As they moved through the ribcage, the air took on a thick, almost-soupy quality at some points, while thin and tepid at others. The strange clipping of reality intensified, with small, perfect lines of visible blackness appearing and disappearing rapidly in the peripherals of Faye's vision. It made her want to squeeze her eyes shut. Though she was walking on solid ground, she couldn't help but feel that she was crossing a dangerously thin pane of glass, liable to shatter beneath her at any moment, plunging her into an abyss.

They walked along the bulk of the Father-God's spinal column and passed through the top of the sternum, arriving at the bottom of the gaping skull. Faye craned her neck to look at the bottom jaw, which reared up to an incredible height. Through its gap, Faye could see straight through into the inner cavity of the skull. Darkness reigned within, save for a jagged slit running down the top of the cranium, through which she once again saw the blue glow.

"If they're on the other side of the skull, we should pass through it," Mather advised. "Maybe we can get a view of them through that crack. Take them by surprise."

Faye nodded, though she didn't relish the thought of passing through the dank blackness of the skull.

"That's not just a crack," Galt said somberly. "It's a wound."

Faye reassessed what she was seeing. It made sense. "That's probably where Ulesreto landed the killing blow."

The long, ragged fissure in the skull spoke volumes about the power Ulesreto had once possessed. It occurred to Faye that as powerful as the gods they'd faced had been, their strength paled in comparison to what they once were.

"Yes, I suppose it is," Mather agreed. "It should work either way."

They continued on, passing within the shadows of the skull. Inside, the ground was littered with dried detritus, the last dusty remains of the organic tissues that once occupied the space. Briefly, Faye could see the purple light from above filtering in through the enormous orbital sockets.

As they neared the wound in the top of the skull, they slowed down, moving as silently as they could. The crack was much wider than it had seemed from afar, and they could have easily strolled through it three abreast. Approaching it diagonally so as to avoid the pool of blue light spilling into the darkness, they reached the edge and peered out cautiously.

Between their vantage point and the rising arch of the halo, they could see Ulesreto and Nuroh bathed in the luminous blue, the source of which soon became apparent.

Nuroh was hunched over the blade shards, all but one of which appeared to be newly fused together. His eyes were closed, and he was whispering to himself, moving his hands over the remaining piece, which exuded an intense glow as he worked. Ulesreto stood nearby, watching Nuroh's every move, his unblinking eyes waiting for the completion of the sword and the subsequent end of their fragile alliance. It was clear that Nuroh was nearly finished with his work.

Just beyond the halo, Faye could see the Gates of Paradise. A white marble arch twice the height of the gods rose from the broken shale, framing twin black doors. Filigreed across the surface of the doors were lines of gold etched in ornate designs of exquisite beauty. For all the time that had passed, the doors appeared to be untouched by decay. In their center, a keyhole stared out expectantly.

"It looks like they've almost reforged it," Mather whispered.

"Then we need to act now," Galt said, beginning to move.

"Wait," Faye said quietly, seizing Galt and pulling him back. "This might be our only chance to reforge the blade, remember? Ulesreto told Cyprian that only Nuroh could do it. We have to time our attack in a way that lets us gain control of the blade *after* he's finished it."

Galt blinked at her in frustration. She could tell that he was solely interested in revenge. All other concerns were secondary. "How do you suppose we do that?" he asked.

Before Faye could try to formulate an answer, Mather spoke. "You and I form a distraction," he said to Galt. "We draw Ulesreto away. If Nuroh's as eager to betray him and enter Paradise alone as we believe, he won't stop working on the blade. Faye, when he finishes the blade, you'll need to attack him. Keep him busy until we can help you. With any luck, we'll have taken care of Ulesreto by then."

Faye looked toward Nuroh, who appeared diminutive and weak. Of course, he was still a god, and certainly possessed powers far beyond her understanding. Either way, she saw no other option.

"Okay. That will have to do."

Faye and Mather both turned to Galt. He shrugged.

"Let's get on with it."

CHAPTER 58

The being who had masqueraded as a man called Duncan Starkad still tried to reckon time by the old ways. Even for his divine mind, it had grown difficult. The recounting of his long life, stretching back to the refounding of existence after the Great Culling, had grown muddled with the long ages of stagnation.

Of the hothouse blackness of his beginning, he could recall little. His explosive emergence, intertwined with Aedesda and born of Alminnian, was a mystery, colored only by the surging expansion of a strange new understanding and an unimpeachable purpose. The language of thought, passing freely between him and his new siblings, intermingled with the tongues of man, and he was given his name. He could recall the fear and reverence with which the ancient peoples held him, and the later devotion of his Vingallean followers.

Balanced against such an expanse of time, his most recent actions and the expedition he'd guided along the path of his choosing were such a miniscule sliver of his immeasurable experience that he already found it difficult to distinctly remember much of them. Of Cyprian Fontaine, very little remained save the memory of the dead lord's feverish desire to obtain the shards, an aftertaste of thought that mirrored Ulesreto's own aspirations.

Watching as the cowardly, slinking deserter finished his work, Ulesreto could feel all of reality, the heavy pressure of the ages, building behind him, pressing him toward his ultimate fate. He watched Nuroh's hands glide above the surface of the sword he'd carried for millennia, the sword that would soon grant him his ultimate wish.

When his part was finished, Nuroh would be incapable of stopping Ulesreto. The little fool, so smug in his boundless knowledge, had finally played out his options. Ulesreto would seize what was once his and pass through the gates that had once been his to command.

Still, Nuroh was wily, and Ulesreto had been taught caution by his long exile. Weakened, humiliated, cast down from the heights of power, he now appreciated the need to exercise vigilance.

He had been heedless before when he'd felt the same ineffable push of destiny. Aedesda's honeyed words had only fed that fire, drawing in not just Ulesreto, but many more of the gods, each eager to carve out a position of power within the new realm. All of them were willfully blind to Aedesda's plan to dominate, just as Ulesreto had been. Each had harbored their own delusions of rising to the pinnacle of creation, their own plots of betrayal. Even Naffabyin, one of the mighty firstborns, had been swayed by Aedesda's promised annihilation of the meddlesome humans whom Alminnian cherished, undoubtedly dreaming of a storm-scoured world in which only he remained.

Once they had openly declared themselves, the momentum only grew. Leading the Vingallean host to overtake the Isle of Creation, Ulesreto had been certain of victory, first over Alminnian, and then over his scheming brother.

From amidst the vast sea of time, certain memories of the doomed siege still shone clearly: the Vingallean dreadnoughts belching black smoke into the sky; Phar-Karrian, his most loyal and trusted captain, resplendent in his gleaming armor, crushed under the foot of Opriseur during the chaotic onslaught; the Scale of Judgment, awash in a crackling power beyond every limit he'd ever conceived of, piercing the skull of Alminnian, and the moment the creator's eyes had rolled up to white, as if he'd been trying to look inside of his own head to examine the damage within.

Yes, victory had been achieved, just as Aedesda had promised it would. But it was a victory that had cost him everything.

Later, gazing upon his nearly-powerless brother as he tried to escape, desperately clawing at the locked Gates of Punishment, Ulesreto had finally and truly understood the cost of his mistake.

But ultimately, it hadn't been Aedesda, or the cheering legions, or even his own thirst for power that had driven him to rise against the towering totem of which he had been but a splinter. The decision to murder his creator, to murder a part of himself, had been for her.

Alminnian had denied him Ellara, the eternal queen of Vingal-lea, shining paragon of righteous judgment and master of his heart and mind. For her, he would rend this reality to shreds, forsake all of existence, and topple the universe to its very foundations.

It seemed to him that everything that had ever occurred had merely been building toward this moment. Soon, if all went as planned, his reunion with his immortal warrior-queen, and the birth of their eternal dominion, would be within his grasp.

He just had to get through the door.

CHAPTER 59

Advancing across the threshold, Galt's heart thumped wildly in his chest. Though hatred filled him, fear threatened to swamp him if he didn't move now. Ulesreto's clear might, combined with the strange surroundings, nearly held him back, but he forced himself out into the open. Mather stood beside him.

The moment they stepped clear of the skull, Ulesreto's head snapped up. He looked momentarily stunned, but then a small smile creased his face.

"I underestimated the two of you. Verily, you are men of Vingallea." He looked at Galt and pursed his lips. "Though you appear to be of Faedalian stock. Either way, I'm impressed."

"Impressed?" Nuroh said, looking up from his work. "You should have been certain they were dead."

"Oh, wise one," Ulesreto said with mock reverence, never turning from them, "I believe *you* cut the captain's throat. You were sloppy. And, as I recall, we were moving in haste. I couldn't wait for every one of them to gasp their last."

"Kill them," Nuroh seethed, ignoring Ulesreto's words.

"I don't act on your command, but in this case, I do agree with you," he said, drawing the short sword he'd wielded as Starkad. "My blade is currently indisposed, so I'll have to make do with this primitive work."

"Enough talk, butcher," Galt snarled.

"I'm sorry," Ulesreto said. "I understand that I killed the woman you loved. I know what it's like to have someone you love taken from you. Truly, I do. I didn't relish it, just as I don't relish this, but bigger things are at work here—things you can't comprehend. You're good men, and I hold no ill will toward you, but you cannot interfere. You've both served honorably, and I will certainly grant you absolution in death."

Finished pontificating, Ulesreto stalked toward them, his sword held unpredictability low. Galt's stomach dropped as he recalled how easily Ulesreto had cut down Solgard. He braced himself, tightening his grip on his own blade.

Before he could plan his defense, Mather launched forward with a war cry. Galt followed directly after. He knew that the only way they could defeat Ulesreto was through unrelenting force.

Mather heaved his sword up over his right shoulder, coming in for a brutal strike. At the final moment, he revealed the feint. He pulled back and spun around, driving his blade toward Ulesreto's right side. With a punishing upward thrust, Ulesreto deflected the blow and tried to counter, but Mather had already leapt backward and out of range, skidding across the loose gravel.

Galt saw his opening. Ulesreto had swung wide, seeking Mather. Galt brought his blade down with everything he had, hoping to lop off Ulesreto's extended arm. Impossibly fast, the arm retracted back, leaving Galt's blade to plow uselessly into the ground. Ulesreto's left fist rushed toward him, plunging into his sternum with incredible force. Galt was flung backward, the breath crushed out of his body. He hit the ground and slid some distance across the stones, white lights dancing before his eyes.

Mather was suddenly at his side. "You still with me?"

Galt managed to nod, though he wasn't certain that he actually was. Something within his chest had cracked, and a wave of nausea rolled through him.

"He's coming this way—it's working. Get up," Mather whispered, dragging Galt to his feet.

With no urgency, Ulesreto was approaching them again. He was maddeningly calm.

"Submit, and I will make your deaths painless," he announced.

Ulesreto's casual bravado filled Galt's mind with fire. Every life spent unwittingly in service of his desires, every life he'd taken—they were utterly meaningless to him. He had traveled alongside them all; he'd broken bread with them and shared in toil and hardship, yet even then, Solgard, with her myriad of beautiful characteristics, had been nothing to him. He'd snuffed her out an instant, thinking nothing of it.

Ulesreto thought only of his own desires; he understood nothing of love or the human condition. His actions were not just, they were base. Quite simply, he sought power at any cost.

Galt felt the peculiar air make its way back into his lungs. He breathed deeply and coughed, which sent a sharp pang through the left side of his ribs. His mind swam briefly, and he took several small, shallow breaths. "There will be no submission," he said, channeling his hatred into a deadly focus.

"Then there will be no mercy."

With frightening speed, Ulesreto was suddenly before them. Galt raised his blade just in time to block a tremendous blow, his entire arm shuddering from the impact. Mather lunged forward, thrusting his sword directly into Ulesreto's side, but the god twisted away, and the sword bounced harmlessly across the side of his armor. Mather's attack earned him a backhand across the side of his head, which sent him stumbling away. Galt chopped at Ulesreto's exposed side, but his blade failed to cleave the heavy armor. In response, Ulesreto's sword whistled toward him, allowing him only the barest moment to duck.

Mather, who now had blood spilling down the side of his head, had regained his footing. He tried to hack at Ulesreto's neck from behind, instead bashing his sword into one of the god's pauldrons hard enough to make it buckle. Ulesreto shouted in indignation and whipped around. Clinging to his sword, which was now lodged in the damaged armor, Mather was hoisted off of his feet. Ulesreto grabbed him by his throat and squeezed. Mather's eyes bulged as the god's hand, clad in its iron gauntlet, crushed his windpipe.

Seizing the moment of distraction, Galt, ignoring the screaming protestation of his broken rib, drove his blade forward with all his might, targeting a small gap in Ulesreto's armor where the plates covering his side overlapped. He was turning, and Galt aimed for where his instincts told him the gap would be when the strike landed. His pulse thumping in his temples, his teeth bared in animalistic fury, his eyes fixed on the thin black gap, Galt felt time slow nearly to a stop. He could hardly believe it when the blade slipped between the plates and sank deeply into the body beneath.

Ulesreto jerked away violently, tearing the blade from Galt's hands, and bellowed thunderously, his formerly placid voice now shredded by pain and rage. Wasting no time, he ran Mather through with his sword, then hurled his body at Galt. The captain's head struck him directly in the face, sending a flash of white through his vision and instantly shattering his nose. The two men hit the ground in a tumbling heap, sending up a plume of dust as they skidded to a stop.

Galt tried to gain his bearings as he crawled out from under the crumpled body of Mather, blood gushing from his broken face. He could no longer breathe through his ruined nose, and his blood-choked throat made him gag.

His breath coming in furious gasps, Ulesreto pulled Galt's blade from his side. He looked at it in disgust. "I know you've had some success in killing my brethren," he said with oily admiration, "but you cannot best me."

He snapped the blade in two as simply as if it were a fragile twig.

"This," he said, waggling the pieces toward Galt in a scolding manner, "was a testament to your luck, *not* your skill."

He cast the pieces aside, reached toward his shoulder, and forced Mather's blade free, then snapped it as easily as he had the last one.

Galt tried to will himself to his feet, and searing pain emanated from his left knee. It had been contorted unnaturally by the weight of Mather crashing into him. He looked toward Mather; he wasn't moving. Beyond him, Galt could see nothing but Ulesreto's advancing shape. Though he sought some glimpse, he saw no sign of Lady Fontaine.

"Do you see now? You cannot win. Look there," Ulesreto said, gesturing toward the monumental skull, which was now directly behind Galt. "I did that. I overthrew Alminnian, the Tyrant. I slew the creator of the cosmos. You are but a man."

Faced with imminent death, Galt found all reservations had slipped away. He laughed wetly, coughed, and spat blood upon the ground. "You're little more than that now," he said, grinning manically. "Reduced to a husk of your former self. Left to skulk in the shadows, dependent on us to do your bidding. You've nearly been felled by two starving, dying men. Your survival is a testament to your ability to hide, not your skill."

Ulesreto's face contorted into a scowl, his puckering scar twisting downward with the curve of his mouth. A cerulean glow appeared to rise from him.

"This is only temporary. My true power will be restored. I will reign for eternity, and Ellara will—"

The rising glow suddenly exploded through him, bursting through his chest in a torrent of black blood. He shrieked in astonishment and stared downward, where a luminous blade jutted forth. He clasped it with both hands, but, slick with blood, it receded back through him and vanished, leaving him clutching at the air. His mouth moved wordlessly, and he fell to his knees.

Standing behind him, wielding the reforged Scale of Judgment, was Nuroh. With his other hand, he held a kneeling Lady Fontaine by a fistful of her hair.

"Finally, the usurper has received exactly what he deserves," Nuroh crowed. He looked down at Lady Fontaine. "Get over there with the rest of your dying kind."

He thrust her forward, and she staggered toward Galt and collapsed to the ground. She had her hands pressed to her stomach. Galt could see that she'd been stabbed. Her attempt to overpower Nuroh had failed.

"I'm sorry," she managed. He shrugged.

"The rebellion has finally been put down completely. Aedesda's long gone; Tariono, Naffabyin, and Chortelak followed, and now, Ulesreto has finally fallen. Brilliant."

Nuroh nudged Ulesreto with his foot and watched with mild interest as he fell to his side.

"Some of the loyalists had to die, true, but their loyalty was misguided, anyway. They refused to see which way the wind was blowing, and they refused to see the cause. You." He looked toward his vanquished foes with loathing. "Alminnian doted over mankind, his most precious creations, blindly ignoring every warning while you plotted to dethrone him. I was close among you; I saw you for what you were. I tried to convince him to take away your free will. I advised him time and again that his trust and affection were misplaced. You've consistently proven me right."

"I've listened to that one rant enough," Galt wheezed, pointing weakly toward Ulesreto. "I don't need to listen to you. Let us die in peace."

Nuroh looked at Galt as if he were shit the god had stepped in.

"I've had to listen to enough of your kind; please indulge me. Though you'd hardly be the first to ignore me. Thankfully, in Phar-Mindorius, I found someone who was eager to listen. Just the doddering old fool I needed, and at just the right time. I can only imagine how dumbstruck he was when he finally mustered the courage to come speak to me again and found only an empty chamber." He barked a high laugh. "And then Ulesreto came around, thinking he could outmaneuver me, just as Ganachim started to fail. I suppose she's dead by now. I must be the only god left."

Nuroh appeared pensive for a moment, then looked up with a bright smile. "There's going to be a new order now."

"Well, enjoy it," Galt said flippantly. He spat blood again. "We won't be there to see it. Shame."

Nuroh blinked in surprise. "Oh, but you will, my surly friend. Mankind will live on, and I'll make sure that you are there with the rest of them. You'll live forever within my realm, serving me for eternity. I'll mend this world and populate it with all of you, stripped of your free will. Like clockwork, you'll perform your tasks, ensuring that my world is harmonious, peaceful, and orderly. My counsel will be ignored no longer; all will obey my words. And I'll make sure that you know it, too. I'll see to it that some small part of you silently screams within to be freed from your endless enslavement."

"No, no…" Lady Fontaine said through gritted teeth, forcing herself to stand. "We won't let you. Galt, get up."

Nuroh tittered. "You are persistent. Ulesreto told me as much. He also told me how much you adored that old man I burned alive. A tragic loss," he said with mock sorrow.

"*Enough*," Galt said, rising beside the bristling Lady Fontaine. He drew two daggers and handed one to her. He'd been certain that Ulesreto could finish them, but perhaps against the weaker Nuroh, they stood a chance.

"I agree. I've heard enough of your petulance. I will thoroughly enjoy watching you dance upon my strings." Briskly, Nuroh turned from them and strode toward the Gates of Paradise, only a small limp betraying the wounds he'd received from Lowther.

Galt and Lady Fontaine looked at each other. "Stand and fight!" Galt shouted, stumbling after him.

The god turned and smiled apologetically. "No, I don't think I will. You're clearly a capable warrior, and even the lady might have a fortuitous opportunity to strike if I were to fight you both. My companion there may have let hubris get in the way, but I will not. Why fight you and risk everything when you're too hobbled to chase me down?" He laughed smugly and turned back toward the gates.

"Coward!" Lady Fontaine shouted, staggering only a few steps before falling to her knees.

Galt looked back toward her, then haltingly tottered after Nuroh as quickly as he could. He shouted impotently for the god to stop, but he knew that Nuroh wouldn't. It was over.

Nuroh reached the gates and, gathering his robes about him, levitated slowly to the height of the keyhole, breathing hard. Exercising the power seemed to take an extreme effort, and it was with some difficulty that he lifted the sword and slid it into place.

He looked back toward Galt, a wicked grin on his face, and with a dramatic flourish, turned the key and pulled backward. The ornate gates resisted for a moment before suddenly flinging wide open, blowing Nuroh backward and banging against the marble arch. A brilliant white light burst forth from within, freezing everyone in a moment of reverent silence. The Scale of Judgment remained sticking out of the gate on Nuroh's left, already forgotten.

After a brief moment, the white light quickly faded, leaving only a hollow, inky blackness behind. "This doesn't seem right," Nuroh said to himself, puzzled. He lowered back to the ground.

Galt stood riveted in place, no longer trying to catch up to Nuroh, no longer wanting to be anywhere near the gates. The blackness inside was a boundless nothing, the same emptiness that was seething just beneath the fraying seams of their world. He took a step back, and as he did, Galt felt the tickling of an unnatural wind across the back of his neck.

"Well, no matter," Nuroh announced, turning toward them. "Paradise must be formless now without Alminnian's influence. Ripe for its new master. You can choose to kneel now, by your own volition, or you can kneel later, as a slave. It makes no difference to me."

Without further hesitation, Nuroh stepped through the brink.

Almost immediately, he was racked by an intense spasm. Without choosing to, he floated into the blackness, no longer tethered to the ground. He rotated slowly and faced outward, his mouth frozen in a silent scream. His entire body shimmered and wavered, trembling strangely. Blood jetted from his nostrils, and his eyes crossed, his features pinching inward. Suddenly, his glass halo imploded into a shower of sand. Then, with abrupt and shocking violence, his entire body collapsed in on itself in a cloud of slowly diffusing blood.

There was no Paradise beyond the gates. There was only the Void.

As the haunting realization dawned on Galt, the chill wind suddenly increased, buffeting him from behind. Stones skittered across the ground, inexorably drawn toward the yawning chasm. The Void, now open to their world, had started to consume it hungrily.

"Get back! Get away!" he called frantically, waving toward Lady Fontaine as he struggled against the sucking vortex of air.

Braced on her palms, her hair whipping about her face, she struggled to rise. Galt limped back to her and snatched her by the back of her cloak just as she started to pitch forward with the wind. He pulled her to her feet, eliciting a scream of pain as her torn stomach was wrenched into movement. Crouching low against the riptide of whipping air, they struggled away from the open gates.

"*The skull!*" Galt screamed over the rushing wind. "*We need to get inside the skull!*"

As they plodded toward the fissure, Galt watched Ulesreto's body drag across the ground, ensconced in a blur of dirt and stones. It flopped clumsily past them and disappeared. Mather's body was already gone, lost in the rising plumes of dust. It had become difficult to see through the cloud of twisting earth, and Galt squinted against the whipping sand. The tiny granules were beginning to rush toward the gates with such ferocity that Galt could feel them shredding his boots and pant legs, where they blew the heaviest. Ominously, the ground beneath their feet began to shudder.

They were almost to the breach when Galt felt his feet begin to lift from the ground. Snatching wildly for some grip, his hand struck something that closed around his wrist. He held Lady Fontaine tightly as he was pulled through the swirling chaos and into the darkness of the skull. He toppled to the ground, entangled with Lady Fontaine and their savior.

In the darkness, he could just make out Mather's face.

"You're still alive," Lady Fontaine gasped.

"For a little while," Mather said with a rueful smile.

The three of them, only a few steps apart on the path to death, braced against the cranial wall to the side of the crevice, clinging to each other and watching in horrified awe as the world was torn asunder. The sucking air was still tremendously loud within the skull, and a stream of detritus poured forth through the crack, speeding toward the Void. The roar increased, as did the rumbling of the earth beneath them. Eventually, as the flow of dust and pebbles subsided, enormous chunks of bedrock were torn loose. Tumbling toward the gates, they exploded into fragments upon approaching the maelstrom's epicenter.

The clipping of their surroundings intensified; entire stretches of the ground vanished in rectangular patterns, only to be replaced with wildly colored fractals of quivering madness. The Father-God's halo wavered erratically, threatening to snap in two. The encircling mountains began to splinter, their peaks tearing free, pulverizing the sides of the surrounding cliffs on their way down. The toppling pinnacles were reduced to nothing as they were shredded by the savage winds. All the while, the black emptiness of the gateway remained clear, promising to devour all of existence with its insatiable hunger.

Their macabre sanctuary was not immune; the rushing wind and sand were eroding the edges of the crack, which was widening by the moment. Additional fissures now spread from the gap, and the walls of bone around them wavered. It was only a matter of time before the entire skull was either flattened or ripped from the ground in which it had been so deeply embedded.

The booming of the collapsing mountains was soon overshadowed by an earsplitting crack tearing through the air above them. Incomprehensibly, the sky itself seemed to be coming apart like a crumbling domed ceiling. Colossal pieces of the firmament splintered apart and sloughed downward, leaving behind impossible jumbles of black emptiness that flashed with an eerie light. As they approached the gateway, the pieces shattered into flurries of luminescent particles. The sun itself appeared to flicker with uncertainty, as if it would come roaring down upon the disintegrating earth.

Terrified beyond reason, Galt screamed into the convulsing insanity, unable to look away.

Then, watching a gargantuan piece of the sky shred before the unrelenting pull of the Void, Galt noticed a humanoid form climbing around the side of the gates. It was Ulesreto, skirting the edge of the boundless nothing. He was clawing his way around the gate to the right, apparently seeking safety behind it. His once-glorious raiment had been torn away, and his exposed flesh was lacerated deeply.

As he disappeared behind the gate, the Father-God's cranium finally buckled, and the top of the skull tore away, exposing them to the full brunt of the nightmare pull. Immediately, Galt and Lady Fontaine slid away, clinging to each other as they were lifted off of the ground.

Before they could be sucked away completely, Mather snagged the back of Galt's tunic. Twisting in the wind, Galt looked back toward the guardsman. He'd managed to wrap his arm around a jagged piece of the skull that remained intact and was holding on with everything he had left, teeth bared, eyes squeezed shut.

Presently, the force of the pull unexpectedly diminished, and the three of them fell jarringly back to the ground, causing Mather to lose his hold. They tumbled across the exposed bedrock, still pulled toward the gates, but with less force.

Grasping fruitlessly for any handhold, Galt couldn't help but look toward the maw that would soon annihilate him. Somehow, the gate to his right had been closed. The second gate was turning inward. Galt could see Ulesreto pressing against it. It passed the threshold of whatever blowback was forcing it open and snapped swiftly shut, slamming into place with a cacophonous bang.

Instantaneously, the pull ceased. As Galt slid to a stop, silence reigned.

Before the gates, Ulesreto collapsed. The Scale of Judgment, rattled loose by the slamming of the gate, slipped from the keyhole and fell harmlessly to the ground with a weak thud.

CHAPTER 60

Sprawled on the ground, Faye stared up at a broken sky. Though the swirling horror had ended, the damage had been done. The dawn that she'd known her entire life was now shot through sporadically with bizarre gaps of empty blackness, occasionally marred by silent flashes of enigmatic light.

She struggled to sit up, clutching her stomach. Like the world around her, the damage had been done.

Nuroh had seemed totally absorbed by his work on the blade. Faye hadn't anticipated how quickly he could strike.

She'd approached him as he'd risen, turning the completed sword over in his hands. Before she'd had a chance to do so much as raise her weapon, he'd whirled about and punched the Scale of Judgment through her gut, dropping her with ease.

She looked at her hands, which were stained crimson. Fresh blood pooled in the folds of her clothing where the sword had pierced her. Resuming the futile job of pressing against the wound, she looked toward the mutilated form of Ulesreto lying in front of the resealed gates. It was ironic that, after everything he'd done, he'd actually saved their lives. He'd also stopped the imminent collapse of the world he'd sought to destroy. Of course, to save himself, he'd had no other choice. Now she wondered if he'd survived the attempt.

"Lady Fontaine," a voice croaked from behind her. It was Galt. She didn't bother telling him to drop the formal title. He'd never listened before; she doubted he would now.

"I'm here," she said weakly. It felt like she'd used half of her remaining strength just to answer.

Galt reached down and helped her to her feet. Both of them were barely standing, but somehow, they managed to shamble several paces toward another crumpled form that Faye hadn't noticed before.

Though she'd believed her mind to be fried beyond any new shock or sorrow, the sight of Mather's sprawled corpse nearly broke her. The seemingly indomitable captain had finally succumbed to his injuries, but only after protecting them to the last.

"He saved us," Faye said thickly, unable to summon any other words.

"Aye, he did," Galt said as he knelt by the body. He closed his eyes and placed a hand on Mather's chest. "Rest now."

They remained like that for some time. Faye wondered if Galt was performing some ritual or just lost in private lamentation.

Wincing, he stood. "He would have gone shade by now," Galt announced flatly. "We're safe."

Faye looked back at the body and struggled to sort out her sluggish thoughts. She hadn't even considered the threat of a shade. They certainly wouldn't have survived another encounter. Even in death, Mather had somehow protected them.

With nothing further to do for the captain, Galt turned his attention to Ulesreto. He started haltingly toward the prone god, his bloodied face a stoic mask of resolve. Faye stumbled after him.

As they reached Ulesreto, he managed to raise his battered head. His scar was now joined by a patchwork of countless cuts and scrapes, and the intact section of his halo was equally tarnished. He bore a sucking chest wound that made Faye's injury look mild in comparison, yet he still clung tenaciously to life.

"I kept my word," he said wetly. "I judged him worthy."

In unison, Faye and Galt briefly looked toward Mather's body. Turning back toward Ulesreto, Galt seemed unmoved. He crouched down next to the dying god, his face unreadable.

Ulesreto was racked by a series of gurgling coughs, spewing blood down his chin. "It seems that I've failed. All I ever sought was a release from bondage. The freedom to be with Ellara. I would have seen her people delivered with me. I was their champion, their god-emperor. We were going to rule over a holy people, the masters of a peaceful dominion. For that, I followed Aedesda to damnation. This was my final chance at redemption, a chance to unite and heal this broken world. To see it reborn. A chance to see her again … why can't I just see her again? Why can't—"

Galt sank a dagger into Ulesreto's temple, silencing him forever. The god's body jerked spasmodically for a moment, then grew still. Galt stood, leaving the dagger buried in Ulesreto's head. "I've heard enough."

He shuffled a few steps away and sat heavily on the ground, letting out a long, rattling sigh. Faye stood, wavering on her feet, feeling only a vague acknowledgment of Ulesreto's death.

It would be too easy to heap the blame on him, to believe that Cyprian was corrupted by him as he assumed the role of Starkad, but the truth was, whatever his true motivations had been, they couldn't have been much worse than those held by the leaders of the expedition. Cyprian hadn't been led astray; he'd simply been put in a position that revealed the true darkness inside of him.

After everything, Faye could not hate Ulesreto. She was indifferent. He was just another ambitious, flawed being, seeking his own self-serving desires. They *all* had been, and they'd all received exactly what they deserved.

Faye flopped to the ground across from Galt. "So, that's it?" she asked.

"That's it."

Looking around at the shattered remains of reality, Faye tried to decide what to do next. After so much time spent planning and striving, it felt unnatural and foreign to have no next move in mind. She looked toward the dully glowing Scale of Judgment and considered retrieving the blade. Ultimately, it just didn't seem worth the effort.

"We never stood a chance," she observed with equal parts morbid humor and bitter resentment. "Even if everything had gone right, we would have opened the gates, only to find a howling abyss."

"The Void," Galt corrected.

"Yes, I suppose it was. Does that restore your faith at all?" she asked, the question coming off nastier than she'd intended.

"Not really."

She thought for a moment. "Paradise must have ceased to exist when the Father-God died," she observed. "It must have been some kind of extension of him, tied to his power. Nobody considered that. Not even the old ones."

"Aye."

"And so there's no hope." It wasn't a question so much as a statement of fact.

"Not anymore."

They lapsed into silence. Galt rested his elbows on his knees and steepled his fingers, staring at the ground. Faye found herself thinking of all those whom the death of their world would soon reach.

Ganachim would be dead shortly, if she wasn't already. The last divine ties would be severed. Phar-Mindorius would watch everything he'd sought to preserve slip through his fingers. With no food or water, the kingdom would quickly fall into anarchy, turning into another Vin-Sadavat. If it even lasted that long.

The opening of the gates had undoubtedly accelerated the disintegration of the natural order. Faye was certain that the same slippage of reality that had plagued the Isle of Creation would soon consume the rest of the world. Eventually, it would all collapse in on itself, leaving only a sterile black nothing.

Facing the end, Faye sought for something profound to say to Galt, something that would inject some meaning into the senseless devastation they'd both endured—perhaps some words of comfort regarding Solgard. Only empty platitudes swam to the surface of her mind, and, in the end, she settled on simply reaching out to him.

Galt looked at her extended hand for a moment, then took it and gave it a small squeeze. A single tear cut a path through the blood and dirt caked over his wounded face, and she nodded in acknowledgment of the indescribable grief they shared.

After some time, Faye realized that she felt very tired. Sleep had eluded her for so long, and now that their quest was finished, it seemed a proper time to rest. She released Galt's hand and slumped backward, staring up into the distorted, cracked sky. Her eyelids sagged.

Perhaps when reality finished its death spiral, and the last remnants winked out of existence, the way would be cleared for something new. After all, the Father-God was said to have sprung from nothingness; perhaps this new nothingness would serve as a cradle for the next creator. A new creator, free of the stains of their flawed world, who would not repeat the mistakes of the past.

Faye closed her eyes. She could feel darkness taking her, ripe with new beginning.

This time, she hoped, things would be different.

ACKNOWLEDGMENTS:

This story, from the first germ of an idea to the completed book, has been a labor of many years. In that time, there has been a lot of change in my life, but there have been two constants that helped to bring this book to fruition.

Britt, you have always given me your love and support, first as my friend and eventually as my wife. As our family grew with the addition of our two beautiful children, and life became busier and more complicated, you always encouraged me to keep at it. I cannot thank you enough.

Lucas, as my brother you were essentially obligated to be a test reader of my work. Thankfully, you did not shy away from honest criticism. Your insight and ideas helped to mold this story into its best form, and I am grateful for your help.

I would also like to thank my editor, Oren Eades. You were the first (non-family) reader of my work, and your enthusiasm, thoughtfulness, and expertise transformed my book into something greater. Any mistakes that fell through the cracks are mine alone.

Additionally, I want to thank Natalia Junqueira for the excellent artwork, map, and overall design of the book. Your vision was the last piece to bring the entire project together, and I feel that it couldn't have turned out better.

Many others, too numerous to list here, influenced or inspired me in some way as I wrote this story. I couldn't have done it without you, and I thank you all.

About the Author:

Tom Golden is a lifelong fan of fantasy, horror, and survival stories, and enjoys writing them as much as he enjoys reading them. By trade, he is a crime scene investigator and fingerprint examiner. When he's not working or writing, he enjoys painting, hiking, and traveling to distant and obscure lighthouses. He lives in Michigan with his wife and two children.

www.ingramcontent.com/pod-product-compliance
Lightning Source LLC
Chambersburg PA
CBHW031229310726
48971CB00004B/933